α

The Alph

Alpha Alpha

SiO_4

My'Rese A. Jackson

Imperfection is Beauty

— MRJ

First Edition

ISBN 978-0-9980482-0-8 (paperback)

Library of Congress Control Number: 2018913696

Disclaimer: This a work of fiction. This is a made-up story. This disclaimer was so annoying to write.

Cover credits: Damonza.com

Editing by My'Rese A. Jackson

Published by My'Rese A. Jackson

www.myreseajackson.xyz

Cosmic Inkling

To the baddie reading this:

You are amazing. Be your best self unapologetically. Pursue your passion, fulfill your purpose. I hope you'll be living your best life in 2019.

"We are all a part of the universe, and the universe has no limits."

My'Rese A. Jackson

"Keep up the fight. The Time is. They are the Light. We are the Knights in the Dark fight. Let there be Darkness."

Nonymous

Contents

Preface

I have always loved to read, but over the years I grew more and more unsatisfied. I wanted to see myself in such wonderful, beautifully written stories. I searched and searched, but I couldn't find anything that hit the spot. I started reading less and less. During my reading hiatus, I had more time to write. I've been writing things like poems and short stories ever since I could write, but I never really realized how writing is an essential part of who I am until then. Then, I got an idea!!! When I was 15, I decided to write a story called Oceanic Love (I know the title is lame) on Google Docs for my eyes only. Of course, it wasn't beautifully written, but I thought it was wonderful. I had an epiphany at 16: I can't live without writing. I created another story inspired by Oceanic Love. I did my best to mimic my favorite things about my favorite books. You see, all I had was passion, imagination, and creativity. I knew I had everything to learn, but I was like, "F*** it. Gotta start somewhere." Contrary to popular belief, I don't have a good attention span. I'm a huge daydreamer. When it comes to something I'm passionate about, my concentration stamina is out of this world. I would write for 15 hours straight (well, I took small breaks). I have no idea where all that energy was coming from. Yes, I do. Passion. Anyway, I watched a few pages turn into 240 pages. Then I graduated high school, got accepted to UCLA, and watched 240 pages turn into 668 pages. Now I'm here, independently publishing at 18. I still don't know what the hell I'm doing. In my defense, I finished English 4W freshman year, and I'm taking

English 10A now. I haven't even taken any creative writing classes yet. LOL. I did my research and figured out as much as I could on my own. I'm so nervous and excited to know what you all think. I know the formatting is unorthodox, and I probably shouldn't be breaking any rules as a beginner, but it was the only way. LOL. I'm sorry??? I know I'm not a professional, but I really did put my entire heart and soul into this. I don't mean that lightly or figuratively. This is more than just a book. These are more than just words. At least to me. I have so many more books planned! Eeeeeep! I promise you that I will work hard (and smart) to keep improving. Check out www.myreseajackson.xyz for more details and other cool stuff (like my blog and discussion forum)!!! I did the whole website thing by myself, so please go to it.

Oh and… Honestly, f*** commas. Like… Comman now. I did my best. LMAO. Sometimes it's on purpose. Well, with that said…

Enjoy!

Acknowledgments

To my mother, thank you for believing in me since day one. Thank you for assuring me that I can do anything.

To my brother, thank you for all the fun we've had over the years. Thank you for always having my back. Oh yeah and thanks for all the candy you got me.

To Grandma Shirley, thank you for being my best friend. Thank you for the National Geographic subscription. It's been so long, but lavender reminds me of you. I'll see you again one day.

To Papa, thank you for still being my grandpa despite the family drama. I'll never forget that. Sorry for being so distant.

To Sprite, thank you for being the best puppy ever. You'll always be my favorite. You're the cutest puppy in the universe.

To my peers, thank you for all the great times we shared. I miss all of you. I think about you all a lot. Thank you for your respect and friendship. HMU if y'all really serious about this future reunion because I'm so down. I got y'all.

To my teachers, thank you for all your care and support over the years. Thank you for helping me grow. Thank you for being there for me during my little breakdown that one time. Thank you for not forgetting about me even though I was MIA during my freshman year of college.

To myself, thank you for ALWAYS being there for me.

Thank you to every person, animal, plant, object, image, sound, smell, taste, and feeling I have ever experienced.

Thank you. I have learned so much from all of you. I'll never forget you. :)

Introduction

This story does not take place in your world or time period. Don't worry about where I'm from. This story takes place in 2015, but not your 2015. In terms of your time, think of this 2015 as the late 90s, early 2000s. This 2015 has hints of a soft retro-futuristic aesthetic in addition to aspects of modern pop culture. Why am I telling you this? Well, this is not just a made-up story. This is an account of true events. It's not like they're going to be describing everything around them. They aren't really going to say things like "I have Rugrats, Cyberchase, The Powerpuff Girls, and Sailor Moon on my television!", "Oh, look at that hyperspeed jet!", "Have you heard the new Drake?", "My ID card is completely digital!", "I have some TLC downloaded on my touch screen music player!", "Destiny's Child is on the radio!", and "Do you want to come to Blockbuster with me?" I don't mean to offend you when I say people from your world probably won't like them. You might not either at first, but you will learn to over time.

So, what are you reading? You are about to dive into a world no one in your position in space and time has any knowledge of unless they have read this book. A world where humans are taught hatred and have to learn to love. A world where people are labeled as less than because of their biological sex. A world where people are killed just because of the color of their skin. A world where few are rich while many don't have anything to eat. A world built on violence and oppression. A world full of heartache and pain. Think thrice before you call this world a dystopia.

I would never read this book out loud. You're probably wondering who I am. If you aren't, you will once you keep reading. As far as you're concerned, I'm your best daydream.

There are many things I could ask you to keep in mind, but I'll let my friends do the talking. I'll leave you with this question: How can we, in 2018, not be like these humans from the other 2015?

This story unravels over time. I strongly encourage you to pay close attention to every word written. I cannot express to you how essential it is to read this book a second time. If you don't want to do that, at least re-read the beginning. Even then, you still might miss some of the hidden elements.

I'm not one to ask for favors, but please, forget what you think you know. This is not your world. Open your mind. Allow your imagination to translate these words into images. Let it run wild.

DISCLAIMER: This is not the introduction to the story. This entire book is.

Prologue

Hi you all! Before I begin reading this aloud, there are some things you should know. Don't worry about my name. That will ruin the fun. Alright, listen up. This story takes place many, many years ago in 2015. During the Crystal Age, there were paramounts, Titans, goddesses, Olympians, and paragons. There was a sub prophecy about two paragons in particular. Scholars call them the Sisters of the Organic Outerworld Outcome Oath. That sounds terrible, right? An ameobiophysicist came up with the acronym SiO_4. O as in the letter O. I can't stand when people call zeros O's. Anyways, she along with everyone else realized how fitting that was. The chemical formula for silicon dioxide or silica is SiO_2. In nature, it's found in organisms, as quartz, and in other stuff. The most common crystalline forms of SiO_2 are made up of interconnected SiO_4-tetrahedrons or something like that. It's called SiO_2 instead of SiO_4 because this structure leads to the net chemical formula SiO_2. The sub prophecy revolves around the connection between the twin sisters, Iris and Amethyst.

Please remember to NEVER use the word n**** and l**** if you are not from the respective groups of people.

Ever since I was little, I have looked up to the paragons. I'm sure many of you do too. Without them, the world as we know it would not be the same. Actually, we wouldn't be here at all. Their personal stories are so tragic, but at the same time, they are heroes. Yes, they are all crazy. There's no argument there, but they are the most righteous people this universe has ever brought into existence.

You should also know that I'm going to be taking breaks. There is no way I can get through the whole story in one sitting. TRIGGER WARNING! I ease into heavy topics, so please don't hesitate to step away if you need to. I encourage you to take out your phones to look up names and terms. It will only make your experience better. I'll also probably be commentating, but once I get into it, I'll be quiet. Anyways, isn't it a beautiful morning? Everyone look around you. Look closely. What do you see? There's green grass and beautiful apple trees. See the pretty flowers? Don't they smell sweet? Oh, and the cute little animals. Notice how the sunlight is so soft and gentle. See how it caresses all the hedges and statues? I got lost in that maze once. It's so vast. Listen to the fountain. It's all so tranquil. It's like we're in a dream. It's so surreal, isn't it? It feels like we're in a garden from a children's literature book. It feels like a fantasy.

This story, however, doesn't just take place on the surface. In fact, most of it takes place in the ocean. Imagine living underwater, deep below the surface. Feel your gills and lungs inhaling and exhaling. Feel the extreme pressure on your body constricting you and dragging you down into the abyss. But no. This doesn't happen because you are strong. The ocean cradles you as you use your legs as one. You aren't scared anymore because you realize that you are home.

SiO₄

The beginning of our end...

SiO_4

The beginning of our end...

Doris Gives Birth

Circa Hella Long Ago

After giving birth in the privacy of her lair, Doris knew what had to be done. Her twin daughters were both identical and fraternal. They were indistinguishable except for the fact that her lastborn had a fluke instead of a pair of legs. Zeus declared all third generation sets of twins evil because he believed all of them carried the Titan gene. There was word of Zeus having scouts which meant her daughters would not be safe back home. Doris fled to the Aegean Sea where she planned to start a new queendom where those with legs and those with flukes would live amongst one another in harmony.

"Oh, my dear sister, how I wish you were here to see your beautiful nieces. In your honor, I will name the youngest after you, for she will always be wiser than the first because she will learn from the eldest's mistakes. Unfortunately, we will have to keep that between you and me. She will be called Thetis, after our mother, but she will always be Metis to us."

Metis and Doris were two of the eldest Oceanids, twins, born to Tethys and Okeanos. Metis was loved by Zeus, but then he learned of the prophecy that she was to have a child more powerful than their father. Zeus couldn't bring himself to murder the titaness, so he secretly imprisoned her on an island. He convinced the majority of everyone else that he murdered her. Zeus knew that simply imprisoning Metis would not be enough because she was clever. He shapeshifted into an enormous eagle and swallowed Metis whole. His plan failed. Metis was carrying poison she made from the toxic plants on the island. Somehow Metis was a step ahead of Zeus. He knew she was clever, but her actions implied there was more to it than that. Because Zeus was weakened by the poison, Metis was able to climb out his mouth. He perished shortly after. After being regenerated, Zeus returned to Olympus with his mixed emotions of anger, confusion, and most of all, fear. He dared not speak of what happened because Metis was supposed to be dead, so he suffered in silence. Years later, Hera greeted him with a child named Athena. When he asked who the mother and father were, Hera just laughed, so Zeus panicked and asked her about the gender of the child. Hera told him she did not know the child's gender, but she did know the child wasn't born biologically male. Zeus was relieved, due to his own folly. Metis knew that the prophecy wasn't about her but about her sister's child instead. Metis was the one who foresaw the prophecy. Surely, she could tell the difference between herself and Doris. She knew Doris well enough to realize that the womxn she saw in her vision was not Doris but her daughter. Therefore, although Metis wasn't present during the birth of her nieces, she presumed one of them must be named after her. Metis's actions were all part of the ultimate plan. After all, she was the one who forged the plan to free the Olympians from the belly of Kronos, so who would possibly think otherwise? Zeus would of course.

"And what of my eldest child?" Doris asked herself. "You are the first Nereid and you will be called..." She stopped herself. When the sea speaks, every ear must hear. She heard a voice calling out to her, telling her to name her child, "Amphitrite". She missed that voice so much. Doris liked the name and continued on her way to the Aegean Sea with her two daughters, Amphitrite and Thetis.

Doris knew the risks of traveling alone with young, especially on the path she was on, so she wasn't surprised when they swam into a shark. She was hoping she would run into another shark like *Prionace glauca*. Instead, she was face to face with *Isurus oxyrinchus*. Doris knew they were the fastest sharks in the ocean, so she wouldn't be able to flee. Her mate, Nereus, moved even slower than she did and was probably sleep in some cave. She didn't need him anyway. "Will you let us pass?" Doris asked. The shark circled around them, careful to never take her eye off them. Thetis accidentally moved a strand of seaweed that was covering Amphitrite's eyes. When Amphitrite saw the shark, she laughed. The shark charged towards them. Doris heard the sea's voice again, this time telling her not to worry. To her surprise, the shark gently rubbed against Amphitrite as if she were saying hello. Suddenly, there were more sharks coming up to her doing the same thing. "I presume you all cannot speak," said Doris to the sharks. "We apologize. We thought to protect our territory. We thought could you understand us, like your child. We are mute and don't talk with eyes very well, but somehow Amphitrite is speaking to we as we speak to Amphitrite. Let we guide them to our lair, a safe place we share if you allow it."

The sharks led them through a rocky passageway. Doris had never been so glad she was petite, unlike her other siblings. Then they made a sharp turn into a dead end and another sharp turn into the largest underwater lair she had ever seen. "We are happy to help you build your queendom, Doris. We can do what to help?"

"You all have done so much for us already. Thank you." But then Doris remembered what she was missing. Her mate, who was much more to her than just a mate and the reason for Thetis's fluke, needed to be located. Nereus would always go off on little adventures, but this time he didn't come back. At first, that had infuriated her because she didn't want to be alone but now… "Now you have we," said the sharks who soon realized that was not for them to hear. "We are sorry. We have an easier time eye talking when you feel emotions strongly. We will find him, so Doris will be glad." Some sharks swam out of the lair, but the largest shark emerged from beneath them. This shark was unlike any shark she had ever seen and had no problem eye talking. She asked Doris, "Which will lead? Huuuum?" "Can't they both lead the Nereid queendom?" "Nooooo." "Then I don't know. I cannot choose." "Ah, but you do, Doris. Who is the wisest?"

Hephaestus Is Cast Down

Starting Circa A Long Time Ago

"HERA! How dare you say such things! You would never do that to me!" yelled Zeus.

"You are right. I would never treat you how you treat me. I only stay with you because someone has to keep you in check."

"HOW DARE YOU SPEAK AS IF YOU ARE ABOVE ME!"

"I don't need to."

"HYPOCRITE! You too have cheated!"

"Liar. I have never. He is your child. My other children, I created alone. You know that. The test results make that clear."

Zeus used all his strength to punch her in the face. "I HAD NO PART IN THE CREATION OF THAT HIDEOUS CREATURE!"

Hera slapped him, breaking his jaw. "He is a beautiful, gifted child. Your pride causes you to feel threatened by him."

Hephaestus was only a child. He stopped playing with the gold toys he made by hand and came out of his room. It was almost his bedtime. Sleepily, he asked, "Mommy. Are you okay?" Thinking his son saw Hera slap him, Zeus was embarrassed. As if to reclaim his dominance, he threatened to strike her with a bolt. Hephaestus was wide awake now. With flames in his eyes, he said, "I can't hurt you, but if you hurt Mommy, I will build someone who will!"

"Don't worry, Sunflower. He can't hurt me any more than I can hurt him."

"You imbecile," said Zeus. "You side with the womxn who attempted to abandon you because of your physical appearance?"

"That wasn't Mommy. Another womxn took me while Mommy was sleeping. She was a shapeshifter disguised as Mommy. And Mommy always says I'm beautiful. You're the one who calls me ugly." Then

Hephaestus remembered something. "It was your fault. You were supposed to be watching me. Good thing Mommy rescued me."

Zeus's guilt led him into rage. Using his hyperspeed ability, he grabbed his son by the leg and cast him down from Olympus. Using teleportation, he disappeared to avoid Hera's wrath.

"Hephaestus!!!" She didn't have time to be enraged. Her first priority was the well-being of her child. "Oh, child," she cried. "My sweet child." She had to think fast. "Brother. Please find him and take him somewhere safe. He doesn't do well in the water."

Don't worry, my sister. I will make sure he's safe.

Hephaestus couldn't believe it. The last thing he remembered was almost drowning. He figured Poseidon rescued him. He was thankful he was actually alive and breathing on the shore. It was pitch black. The only light was a volcano erupting. Gaia's bright orange blood gushed onto the sand that resembled the ashes of the darkest coals. He didn't know how much more he could take. He had to get out of the heavy rain. He tried to get up and make his way to shelter, only to face excruciating pain in his left leg. Because of his body heat, the tears in his eyes turned to steam before they got a chance to run down his face. The same thing applied to the rain. Using his godly upper body strength, he pulled himself to the flowing lava tube. He changed the direction of the flow and had it carry him to the cave inside. Despite being in pain, he laughed. Zeus always punished him for playing with fire and molten metal. He recently confiscated his favorite hammer and anvil, but he forgot that he always slept with a separate pair in his belt. Now he was here. Poseidon delivered him to the perfect environment, but Zeus had sent him with his tools. He was in heaven.

Zeus was angry with himself the next day. He intended to cast Hephaestus to land, ensuring his death. He shouldn't have survived in the ocean, so he knew who was responsible for his survival. That cave wasn't just any cave. There was nothing Zeus could do to harm him. Persephone was born on that island, so it along with all its inhabitants were protected by law. Now his son could build whatever he wanted to, including a weapon stronger than him.

Now that the sun was out, Hephaestus decided to figure out where he was. He also needed to make sure he was safe. He used the lava tubes to exit the cave. Once he was outside, he carefully used his godly upper body strength to climb to the top of the erupting volcano. He located as many resources as he could before he climbed down. He dragged himself across the island in search for wood to make a cast. Now, he could at least limp. Like Zeus, he's stubborn. He fell from the same tree twice before he settled for the wood already on the ground. He found some ginger to help ease the pain. Back in the cave, he examined his leg. Zeus had cast him down with so much force, he morphed his bone structure permanently. There was no way he'd be able to walk without a cast.

"Oh, Sunflower. I'm so sorry." Hera wrapped her arms around him. "Where are you hurt, baby?"

"It's mainly my leg. I'll be okay, but I can't return to Olympus like this. Look at me. This is permanent. I can't even shapeshift anymore. What will the others think? I'm imperfect. No child of Hera should look like me."

Hera couldn't heal his leg, but she took his physical pain away. She also brought him his tools. "All that matters is that you're Hephaestus. You have a right to your seat on Olympus right next to your sister. I'm sorry I took so long. Your aunt killed Zeus for destroying a piece of art your uncle made for her, so I don't have to keep an eye on him today."

"Mommy," he cried. "I can't. I can't go back there."

"I know," she cried. "I'll come visit you every chance I get."

"Promise?"

"I promise."

She stayed and helped him organize his cave until the next day. By then, the volcano had stopped erupting. It was perfect timing. Before she left, she handed him a mirror with 'you are beautiful' engraved on it. "Take this, so we'll always be in touch. Always remember that you are beautiful inside and out."

Hephaestus knew his mother was just as heartbroken as he was. He had always been patient, and like Hera, he planned to keep his promise. Bored, he decided to take a dip in the magma chamber that was now a pool. He climbed to the top of the volcano and let himself fall all the way down. His black skin contrasted beautifully with the neon orange that slowly slid down his body as he pulled himself up. Then he explored the rest of cave. In a chamber, he found enough gold bars to satisfy even the greediest immortals. With the gold and magma, the very first thing he built was a miniature ladder to remind himself of his goals. Time passed, and he wanted a playmate, so he built one. He knew he would never be able to make a human nor did he want to. That was Chaos's creation. Their body was made of black glass. The eyes, teeth, and nails were made of gold. They were his most tedious project yet. A person was much more complicated than toy horses and chariots. He used his sister's drawings of the human anatomy for reference. He skipped the genitalia because he didn't think they would be needing that. After weeks of hard work, he finally finished with his masterpiece. He carried them outside and waited for the sunlight to give them life. To his disappointment, they didn't come alive. Eventually, he figured out the heart of the problem. He performed surgery on his masterpiece and created a chamber in their chest. He tried again. It frightened him when his playmate opened their eyes. "Ahhh! I mean hello," he giggled.

"Ahhh! I mean hello," they mimicked him.

"Huuummm… Let's see here. My name is Hephaestus. Your name is Cedalion. Don't repeat that."

"I like Cedalion."

Hephaestus continued finding new places deep within the cavern. There was a staircase that led to a gigantic door farther underground. The handle was far above his head, so he knocked.

"Bros! Did you hear that?!?!?" Brontes boomed. Arges rushed to the door next to his brother.

"Why you always gotta be so loud?" said Steropes.

"Only three gods know we're here! What if it's Zeus bros?!?!? What if he found us?!?!?" Brontes was worried.

"Oh, no no no no no!" Arges covered his face.

"You quit yellin' and you quit twitchin'," said Steropes. "I definitely smell a god. I ain't never met this one before. Open it, Brontes."

"I don't see anyone, bro."

Arges rolled his eyes. "Look down."

"Whoa. Bro. You're so little. You can't be a god."

"He must be the son of a god. He must still be growin'," said Steropes. "Who's your mom and dad?"

"I don't have a dad. My father is Zeus. My mommy is Hera."

"Oh, my goddess. You're Hera's child? He's too powerful bros," said Brontes. "What do you want? Just don't hurt us, bro."

"He does look like her," said Arges. "He really looks like her. Ahhh! The resemblance is striking."

Steropes chuckled. "You ain't goin' to hurt us, are you? You must be Hephaestus, the blacksmith. You're the Firestarter of the realms." Hephaestus was disappointed because he figured they also knew about his fire habits.

"Zeus says I'm just a tinkerer."

"Oh, come on. You can't possibly believe that. Look what you've built," said Arges.

"How do you know—"

"Ahhh! I mean hello," said Cedalion. Hephaestus could tell Cedalion was loyal.

"You three aren't angry? I used your gold. Isn't that your gold?"

"That gold belongs to Thetis," said Steropes.

"Look, bro... We'll try to cover for you, but she's going to find out."

"Who's Thetis?"

"The basilinna of the basileia. She's the wisest in Okeanos," said Steropes.

"Brains and beauty... Oh, how I would love to—" Arges stopped when he heard her walking up the staircase on the inside.

"What was that, Arges?" she laughed.

"Good day, Your Majesty," Hephaestus bowed.

"Ahhh! I mean hello. I'm Cedalion," they bowed.

"Hello, Hephaestus. Hello, Cedalion. There is no need to bow, for I am not your queen," she smiled.

"How do you know my name?"

"Hera talks about you a lot."

"Are you and Mommy close? Are you my aunt?"

"We are very good friends, so I think that is appropriate," she smiled.

Hephaestus ran into her arms sobbing. "Why is Zeus so cruel? I miss Mommy and my big sister."

"They miss you too."

"I'm sorry for using your gold. I didn't know anyone else was here."

"Oh, gemmie. I brought that gold for you. My sister told me you would be here."

"Really? Thank you!" he squeezed her.

"Have the cyclopes introduced themselves?"

"No. Why do they look 250? Aren't you guys thousands of years old?"

"What's up, bro? I'm Brontes!"

"I'm Arges. That's just how immortals age. We'll probably stop aging once we look like we're in our late 30s in terms of mortal years. Technically, I'm the youngest, but I'm far more mature than he is if you couldn't tell."

"And I'm the eldest, Steropes. Together we forged Hades's helmet, Poseidon's trident, and unfortunately Zeus's bolts. They were gifts since they released us. They were meant for good use. Because of Zeus's actions, we are forever indebted to you. We will help you build whatever it is you desire, even a weapon against the sky king. From now on, we cyclopes are at your service, Sky Prince."

Hephaestus was honored. "Th-Thank you so much but how did you know that—"

"Brontes heard you talking one day, but of course we didn't believe him," Arges laughed.

"So, what is our first task?" asked Steropes.

"We need to build a weapon powerful enough to keep Zeus in check just like Mommy." He noticed Thetis was gone. "Where'd she go?"

"I have no idea," said Arges. "She does that a lot. Oceanids don't say goodbye."

"How'd she even get in here?"

"That I know. There's a passageway that leads to Okeanos down those stairs."

"So, what will this weapon look like?" asked Brontes.

"I'm not sure yet, but I know how to get it."

"Do tell…" said Arges.

"So, you know how there's magma inside of here, right?"

"Yes," said Thetis. Everyone jumped.

"Man, how I wish I could teleport," said Arges.

"If I can get Zeus to throw a lightning bolt into the volcano then I think I'll be able to conceal some of its power inside a magma capsule. Then someone could absorb it."

"How is that going to be enough?" asked Brontes. "Zeus can make unlimited lightning bolts. A piece of one isn't going to do the trick."

"It's possible," said Steropes. "The power is relative to size."

"That's what I was thinking," said Hephaestus. "As long as the energy is in a small enough space it will have equal power. A fraction of the bolt's energy will be just as powerful in an amount of space reduced by the same ratio."

"Wait. The only other person who can use a lightning bolt is Hera. This power would be nothing to her. She'd gain nothing," said Arges.

"True but the wielder wouldn't have to use it," said Steropes. "They just need to be able to withstand absorbing a tiny piece of it. A person with an active Titan gene can do that. We just have to find someone. They HAVE to have an active Titan gene. That's important."

"So, what exactly will this do for this tiny Titan gene carrier?" asked Arges.

"It will allow them to shift much quicker than they'd be able to without it. When shifted, they will have the power to disable lightning bolts meaning they can prevent Zeus from making them if close enough. All the energy from Zeus's bolts will be attracted to them because they would be somewhat of a walking lightning bolt that can only absorb. We designed the bolts so that they have a natural inclination to connect. It might not sound like much, but that is one of Zeus's worst nightmares," said Steropes. "This is dangerous if the gene carrier hasn't mastered shifting beforehand. Plus, we can also only estimate a Titan's energy tolerance. Each one is different."

"Okay. It's kind of like reverse engineering a lightning bolt on a much smaller scale."

"When you capture the energy, how will anyone use it?" asked Brontes.

"The capsule would have to be opened by a lightning bolt or an influx of some other intense energy," said Steropes.

"Why can't they just crack it open?" asked Brontes.

"Hell... This is plasma we're talking here. We're kind of creating a tiny star. We need enough energy to break the connection between the outer layer without disturbing what's inside. The disconnection will only last for a fraction of a second, but that's enough time for the energy to find a new host."

"I don't get it," said Brontes. "We have to find a tiny person strong enough to handle a tiny piece of a bolt?"

"Yes. If the capsule is the size of a pearl, they have to be between 5ft 3 and 5ft 10," said Steropes. "Any shorter than 5ft 3 and it's risky business. It's a tight range, but the easy part is finding them."

"What's the hard part?" asked Arges.

"Finding a container for the capsule," said Hephastus. "It will be too hot for anyone except Mommy, Zeus, or myself to hold on its own."

"Yeah. I have no clue what we can do about that," said Steropes. "You can't use it because you'd need much more than you can capture and absorb."

"Even if I could... Look at my leg."

"We can enclose the capsule in a fraction of a stony-iron meteorite, but those are rare. Furthermore, a mesosiderite won't do. We must find a pallasite, and that's even rarer. My hypothesis is that pallasites are composed of core and mantle materials of celestial bodies which makes it perfect for the outer layer of the capsule."

"See. Told you she's wise," said Arges. "Where can we find a pallasite?"

"I will have to locate it," said Thetis. "I'll talk to Selene and the Asteriai. It's going to take time though. Also, pallasites feature olivine crystals inside an iron-nickel matrix. We'll know when we find one."

"Then we'll help you look," said Brontes. "Plus, it could be big. We're big. We can carry it."

"Thetis?" asked Hephaestus. "What's wrong?"

"Shhh. She's having a vision. It's probably important," said Arges. "Chaos only shows her prophecies."

She looked as if she had seen her own death. "I must go to Olympus."

"How's Heph—" asked Hera. "Oh, my goddess. What's wrong, hun? I haven't seen you this worried in centuries."

"In a forced marriage, I will have seven sons. Six will be stillborn, so I must give them to the fire. The last one is destined to die in battle."

They both cried in each other's arms. "What about daughters?"

"I won't have a single daughter. Not a single one."

"Zeus is going to force you to marry a mortal, isn't he?"

"Yes. I wasn't shown why."

"Don't marry him. I'll protect you."

"I have to or else he'll strike Hephaestus with a bolt."

"I doubt he'll attack Persephone's birthplace. If he does, you know a bolt has no effect on me. I'll deflect it."

"It's not a regular bolt. He's forging a weapon to combat the one Hephaestus is forging. It's not made of lightning. I think it was made of white light."

"Oh, no. He's practically going to sell himself to Leukos. It doesn't matter. I won't let him strike Hephaestus or you."

"I know that, but weapons made from complete light or total darkness can send gods back to Chaos. I'm not sure if white light counts as complete light yet. I can't let you die permanently. I can't risk that. Hephaestus needs you. You are also the only thing standing in between the love within the realms and Zeus's hatred. I've made up my mind. This is the only way. I'll outlive him anyway."

The years went by, but Hephaestus didn't have a reason to keep count. Nor did the cyclopes. Hephaestus had now matured to the equivalent of 16, by human standards. He grew up depressed because he hadn't learned to accept himself yet. One day, Thetis asked him to make her son, Achilles, a shield. He made the greatest shield anyone could ever make, but it wasn't enough to protect Achilles from death. Ever since then, Hephaestus felt guilty even though Thetis tried to explain that when she dipped Achilles in the river Styx, she didn't cover Achilles's heel.

"Who forced you to marry Peleus? Why won't you tell me?" asked Hephaestus. He was angry because he always had an idea who. He just needed confirmation. "I've watched you go through so many heartbreaks. I gotta know who's responsible, Aunt T."

"Zeus. Zeus is responsible."

"It's time." He cleared his workspace. "I'm strong enough now. It's time to forge the greatest weapon known to the gods."

"What's the plan?" asked Steropes. "How are we goin' to get him to strike?"

"That ain't the hard part. I just gotta piss him off. The hard part is fakin' my death. Sound travels through air. Zeus will be able to hear my heartbeat."

"There is a poison we can use. I will have my theia, Eury, bring it."

Eurynome didn't hesitate to get what she asked for. She brought it right on time. It was morning, and Hephaestus knew exactly what he was going to say to Zeus. "Make sure ya drink all of it, babe."

Balancing two large buckets on a sturdy staff, Cedalion returned with ocean water. Hephaestus stood on the edge of the opening of the volcano, spurting his suppressed anger in terms of lava. A large, gloomy cloud of volcanic ash hovered above. Then the sky became dark like a cigarette smoker's lungs.

"What exactly did you tell him?" asked Thetis as she watched from the sky in the form of an eagle.

"I just told him Poseidon is more powerful than him."

"Nice work," she laughed. "Incoming!" Hephaestus slid into the magma as if it was bath water. He waded there, at the top of the volcano, for the last ingredient.

"HEPHAESTUS!!!" Zeus boomed. "I am your father! Why do you say such things? What have I ever done to you?"

"Oh, I don't know... You only tried to kill me by casting me down from Olympus."

"I never did like you or Ares, but at least Ares isn't DEFORMED like you are!!!" Now the volcano was spitting lava erratically.

"Poseidon never wanted your crown, but you know he could take it if he wanted to. And you know what else? My momma is the most powerful god there is and ever will be. You know she will f*** you up. That's why you're too scared to strike me. She is queen of the cosmos, and you are nothing but a sky king." Just as planned, Thetis swooped down and gave Hephaestus the poison. Zeus struck a lightning bolt right through the volcanic ash, creating dirty lighting. Hephaestus used all his strength to compress the energy he could capture into a small magma capsule. He could feel his heart beating slower and slower as the eruptions began to die down. He closed his eyes. Then, in fetus position, he allowed the volcano to swallow him.

The sound of Thetis's voice brought him back to reality. "I must admit I was a bit frightened," she smiled.

Hephaestus got to his table as fast as he could and dumped his enclosed fist into the water, creating an igneous capsule. "There it is," he smiled.

"Hello, brother."

"Athena!!!" he wrapped his arms around her. "I haven't seen you in years."

"You've grown so much," they both said at the same time.

"I've been traveling. Zeus has done so many disgusting things. I tried to help them. Oh, brother… There's so much. It's like he becomes more and more evil by the minute," she said. "Woo. It's much too hot in here for me. I can't gradually adapt to temperature like Oceanids can," she laughed. "Anyways, I've learned a lot. There's good news and bad news, but it's the same news. I'll tell you later. Right now, I need you to come with me, Thetis. We'll explain everything."

"Hera always did have perfect timing," said Thetis.

"Oh, Thetis," Hera cried. "I would have done something, but even goddesses cannot change the cosmic code."

"I know, Hera. You've always been there for me."

"I assume you want to hear the bad news first, but I cannot say one without the other," said Athena. "Zeus will try to kill you because he can't change the fact that you will have a child more powerful than their father."

"Are you saying I'm going to have another child? Who will be the father?" She read their faces. "Oh, goddess no. Not him. I would never mate with him. Plus, he's your soulmate!"

"That's true, but we aren't in love in this life."

"Aw. Come on, T," said Athena. "We need a super titan-god, and it's the only way you can have a biological child since you and your soulmate can't have kids."

"We all know how evil Zeus is. He treats everyone horribly. Especially womxn. He's done the cruelest things. He even made Man. Poor humans," said Hera. "While it's true this possible child could be the solution to his bullshit, I don't want you to feel forced to do anything. The cosmic code will rewrite itself."

"Okay. We'll adopt a child."

"You've already adopted one, and your wound is still wide open," said Athena.

"What is the purpose of me having this child other than my own happiness and Zeus's dethronement?"

"This child is supposed to repair the universe when the gods fail to keep Leukos from disturbing the balance. A demi-god won't do this time. This is the beginning of the end. This child is literally the solution Chaos created in response to the future imbalance."

"Athena!"

"What? She asked… And we need this child. I'm also curious to see how they'll turn out. I hope they turn out to be female. I'm pretty sure they will. Life always comes full circle."

"I need to talk to my soulmate about this."

Thetis entered Olympus. "Where is he?" she asked Hera.

"Thetis, are you sure? You really don't have to do this. It's totally up to you. The cosmic code will—"

"I know what must be done."

"You're going to do it?" asked Aphrodite who was also in on the plan. "That's badass. You, Hera, and my mom are my idols."

"He's resting. I drugged him. He's still conscious, but he won't remember the prophecy for a while." Hera put her hand on her shoulder. "Thetis."

"Yes."

"I know you're Agathos, but make him suffer for all the people he's abused."

"You know I will." Hera sat on Zeus's seat and waited for Thetis to return. Meanwhile... "Hello, Zeus."

"Thetis? It's about time. I knew you'd come around. No one can resist my advances," he smiled.

They did not make love, they made darkness. Once it was done, Thetis shapeshifted into Zeus and teased to enter him from behind. "I forgot how strong you are. D-Don't do this."

"Why not? Don't you want to get an idea of how you made all those womxn, including children, feel?" She grabbed his throat and choked him, but that was the least of his pain. Violently, she entered him from behind and thrust until he cried her a river.

"Ahhh! No. Please, stop." Hera listened and smiled. He was only getting a fraction of what he deserved. "I'm sorry. Ahhh! I'm sorry. Please stop. I'm in so much pain."

"Swear by the river Styx that you won't commit any form of sexual assault on anyone regardless of gender or age ever again."

"I, Zeus, swear to never ever commit any form of sexual assault on anyone regardless of gender or age ever again."

"If you don't keep your promise, my sisters and I will take it personally."

"I'm going to keep my promise. Just please don't tell anyone about this."

Thetis changed back to her true form. "You're going to have to get on your knees for that." Zeus did as he was told. "Eye contact!" After Thetis was satisfied, she laughed, left him on the floor, and walked out the door. "It's done," she told Hera.

"Welcome to the dark side," she smiled.

"Oh, hush," she laughed. "We're both Agathos."

"Would you like to stay for dinner, Love?"

"I would love to," she smiled. "What did I tell you about calling me Love?"

"Everyone get in here! It's time for dinner!"

"I'm coming, Hera," said Zeus. Everyone gathered around the table and dined deliciously. Well… Except for Zeus. Hera was sitting at the end, Thetis was next to her, and Zeus was directly across from Thetis.

"Hera!"

"What the hell do you want?"

"That retched Nereid! Dammit!"

"Which one?"

"Thetis… The prophecy. It's happening."

"I always said your infidelity and crimes against life would backfire on you one day."

"Where is she?"

"The number one place to find a Nereid is in the sea," said Athena. "You dare enter Poseidon's realm?"

"Poseidon won't do anything unless I do something. He's usually too cool-headed to throw the first punch."

"True, but what of Amphitrite?" said Athena. Zeus and all the other Olympians fell silent. Except for Hera. She was laughing.

Airplanes

Starting A December Night in 2011

"Who are you?"

"Where am I is a better question."

"Is it really? Oh. Well, this is called a dream. We're in the dream plane. You're in my dream."

"How do you know this isn't my dream and you're in it? How am I communicating with someone I can't even see? Can you see me?"

"No. Well sort of. We have dream vision. I think this is our dream. We can see everything except each other's identity and ourselves. Reflections still exist, but our identity is blurred. I have no clue how we're communicating. We're speaking, but we aren't using English or a language like that. This is so cool."

"I feel like you're real. You're too real. This is a dream, but it's so real."

"We can't both be fake, so at least one of us must be real. We obviously feel like we're real, but we both have the same perspective that the other is fake."

"How about we try to prove to ourselves that the other is or isn't made up. Do you think I'm real?"

"Shit! IDK. My mind would totally make up some complex shit like this LOL."

"OMG mine too!"

"Okay, so we have to tell each other something we don't want to hear. Like... We have to give the right wrong answer to show we aren't subconsciously in control of one another. There are multiple right wrong answers, and we don't know exactly what they are. We will know it's not the so-called right answer though. You get what I'm trying to say?"

"Yeah. I like the way you think. Or I think... But then I would have never thought of that. OMG. First question. Do you think I'm beautiful?"

"No. What the f***? How am I supposed to know if you're beautiful or not?"

"Wow okay. Damn. That was so f***** rude. That's definitely not what my subconscious would have had you say. I'm insecure."

"What's your favorite transportation thingy?"

"Airplanes! The ones that go outside the atmosphere. Space planes!"

"What? LOL. A space shuttle?"

"No. The cool ones that are only good for one time."

"You think rockets are cooler than space shuttles?"

"Yeah. If I left, I wouldn't be planning on coming back."

"You're real."

"What? That was fast."

"I knew earlier, but I had to be sure. You don't know what today is, and you never asked for my name. You aren't my subconsciousness's creation or however the f*** you say that. Is it subconscious's?"

"Wait. Where are you going?"

"To my rocket."

"No. Don't. If you leave, take your space shuttle. I'm still not sure if you're real, but I want to see you again."

"This time I'm asking. What's your name?"

"Tell me yours first."

"S-Sapphire. Why are you laughing?"

"No reason. I'm Topaz."

"What's today?"

"My birthday."

"OMG really?!?!? Happy birthday."

"I'm just kidding."

"Oh. Speaking of birthday's... I don't like mine. My sister hates hers. Her sister is missing. Well, not really. Just absent. They're obviously connected. I can tell her subconscious misses her. My biological sister is missing for real though. She's probably dead," Sapphire cried. "I have two sisters. It's interesting because my sister's sister has been gone since the day after she was born. That day happens to be my birthday. I keep an eye on her sister because the surface is a cruel place. She can't come home yet."

"That's a lot of sisters. I'm sorry for bringing that up. I don't want you to be sad."

"I'm always sad."

"Can I hug you?"

"Yes. Huh! Flowers? How'd you do that? And how do you know I love flowers?"

"I don't know. I just did it. Also... You give me flower person vibes. I like flowers too. Ooooo! Let's build a world!"

"A world? We can do that? Okay."

"What should our world be like?"

"It's whatever you want, Princess."

"Princess?"

"You give me royal vibes."

"You look like you're fun to play tag with."

"Me? No," Topaz laughed. "I'll hide."

"You can't hide from me. I'll find you."

"BOO!"

"Ahhh! Where were you hiding?"

"I was right under your nose. Come on. Let's go get lost in the maze."

"You want to get lost? Oh yeah and tag, you're it."

"Why not? I can hear a fountain. It's either in the center or on the other side."

"You're hilarious. Didn't you build the fountain?"

"I also made the maze, silly."

"How can you still not be sure if I'm real? It's been months."

"Why do you think I'm not?"

"Because you never told me otherwise."

"Oh. I know you're real. I just wish I could find you in the physical."

"Why? So, we can keep up our game of tag?"

"Because I— Topaz."

"Yes. Why'd you get so serious?"

"Will you go out with me?"

"You don't even know my sex or gender. You don't care?"

"That doesn't matter to me. Does it matter to you?"

"Nope. I was just checking. F*** the physical. I'll go out with you."

"What's on your mind? You aren't good at hiding things from me, Sapphire."

"I-I… I think we should break up."

"Okay. LOL. Why?"

"Because we can only see each other when we go to sleep. I can't be in your life if I can't find you. I want you to have someone in your life."

"Alright."

"Are you cheating on me? I know you better than any of them."

"How can I cheat on you if you broke up with me?"

"You don't love me?"

"Define love."

"I can't."

"I love you."

"I love you more."

"I love you infinity."

"Me too. Please don't take off in your rocket."

"Tag. Come find me."

Submarines

January 31, 2013 – McWay Falls, Big Sur, CA

"Where's your sister?"

"I think she's at the cove."

"As long as she's not too close to that cliff. Remember last time?"

"What are you doing? No one's supposed to be down here. It's also early in the morning. Wait. Don't leave. What's your name?"

"I am Moon. Wh-What is your name?"

"Star. LOL. What a coincidence... Why are you hiding under the waves? It's too cold to be swimming."

"This is one of my secret places."

"Oh. Sorry. Bye."

"No goodbye."

"Yes stay?"

"Stay."

"Ooooo! Look! Dolphins! Eeeeep!"

"You sound like one."

"Oh, hush. Look at yo ears. Why they keep twitching?"

"You are fun," Moon smiled.

"Are you going to cover your face the whole time? There's nothing wrong with a little glitter."

"Yes. I do not want you to see me."

"You're so mysterious. You remind me of someone. Can I ask you something?"

"Sure, but I do not speak English that well."

"What's your least favorite machine?"

"The one I do not like? I do not like subskis."

Star knew what Moon meant but decided to say, "A jet ski?"

"They see through it. It has a periscope."

"Ohhh. Sort of like a third eye? It goes underwater right? A submarine?"

"Yes."

"How good is your memory?"

"I never forget."

"Never forgetting doesn't mean you always remember. Do you like origami?"

"Yes!"

"Here. What are you doing? It's not a hat, silly. It's an airplane. Throw it."

"Ooooo!"

"Don't let it get wet! I guess I didn't planet out too well. Whoa. You swim really well. Like… That was f****** spectacular."

"You make good jokes," Moon giggled. "Ah choo!"

"Ewww. Now it's all snotty," Star laughed. "How do you have that much snot?"

"I am sorry. I will clean it." Moon panicked and used the ocean water.

"I thought you never forget," Star giggled. "I said don't get it wet. Now it won't fly."

Moon started to cry. "I am sorry."

"Hey. Don't look so blue. Awww, don't cry. It's alright. I can make another one. I have lots of other cool things I can give you. Do you know where I live?"

"Uh. N-No? I should not know."

"You're funny." Star opened Google Maps. "We're here, and I'm going back here. You can swim there."

"Swim?"

"I'm not stupid. You're obviously aquatic or some shit. I think I met someone like you before when I was little. Are you a spy?"

"I am not a spy, and I am from an island. I cannot go to your place because of trouble, and I cannot go to the surface."

"Oh, okay. Is that the code for aquatic? Whatever. I'll play your little game. Anyways, I guess this is goodbye then. Bye, Moon. I know you're still there. Your third eye is closed as f*** by the way! I'll leave you a gift in the ocean every week."

My'Rese A. Jackson

Chapter 1: What the Hail?

Suddenly, there was a loud buzzing in her room. It startled her. She hated when this happened. It was like 6 AM. Who could it be? "Heeeey, Chance! What's up?" Amethyst giggled as she answered the phone. *HA. Y'all thought. I just needed somewhat of a hook.* She knew exactly why he was calling, and she was looking forward to telling him what he wanted to know. Only after having a little fun first.

"I saw you sneak out of the house again." He wanted Amethyst to know that she wasn't as sneaky as he thought she thought she was.

She was amused that it took him that long. "You did?"

"Yep. Sure did. You ain't slick. Where do you always go?"

"Just for a walk." She knew her little half answers were going to tick him off. She could picture him clenching his jaw underneath his red face.

"Oh, for Christ's sake. Where?"

"On the beach."

"With who?!?!? Spit it out!!!!!" At this point, he was already getting red.

Amethyst placed her hand over her mouth and did her best not to laugh. "No one."

"Amethyst! I swear to God! If you don't hurry up and say it!!!"

She thought about a tomato, and that triggered her. She couldn't hold back anymore. "Okay, okay. I'll tell you, but you have to promise me you won't say anything."

"I promise."

"Okay, so there's this—"

"A boy! I knew it. I need to meet this boy."

"OMG. Sure. We're just friends. I met him by accident. I was at the beach watching Jeremy surf, and he popped up out of the blue. He was about our age and wearing some grey sweats and a baby blue hoodie. When he saw me, he immediately tried to hide from me. He kept spying on me, so I decided to wave. He seemed surprised that he got caught, but he waved back. Then he stopped hiding and just stood where I could see him. I asked him what his name was. He told me it was October. I asked him where he lived, and he just smiled and shook his head. He just stood there far away and silent, so I didn't think he wanted to talk. I started looking for sand dollars, and I noticed he gradually kept getting closer. I told him that was rude and predatorial. Then he apologized and asked me what I was doing. After I told him, he offered to help."

"So, do you surf?" he asked nervously.

"No. I can't even swim. I haven't even touched the ocean. Do you?"

"I've never tried it."

He was completely frozen as Amethyst studied him. "That's funny because you hang around a lot of surfer dudes, don't you? You talk just like them."

"Yeah." He thought it was interesting how she waited for the ocean to get close to her before she ran away. "Here you go."

"Huh! Thanks. These are perfect. How'd you know I only like the purple ones?"

He thought of a quick save. "Ummm, you have mostly purple on." He quickly changed the subject. Sort of. "You like collecting things in the ocean too?"

"Yeah. I love the ocean. I've been drawn to it ever since I was little."

After she carefully put all her sand dollars into her cross purse, he accidentally blurted out, "Beautiful."

She assumed he was talking about the ocean. "Isn't it."

"I meant you." After he said that, he regretted not just going with it.

"Oh. Me?" Amethyst smiled. "Thank you."

"Sorry. I don't mean to come off as shallow. Sorry, that was weird."

"No, it wasn't." *She totally thought that was weird.* "It was sweet," she giggled. "I have to go. My dad is going to be looking for me. We're going to the diner right up there to get some breakfast." That was normal. *Notice how she pointed the diner out.*

"Will you come back?"

"I don't know. Maybe. Do you want me to come back? I won't hesitate to tase your ass if you try to pull some kind of stunt." He didn't know how to answer that, so he just kept moving his mouth. She thought he looked like a fish. "When?"

"Just come. I'll be here." He started to run away, but he must have tripped on the sand or something. *LOL.* She asked him if he was okay as she giggled. He was covering his face with both hands when he got up. Then he stood there for like 5 seconds before he took off again.

"We've been hanging out every morning since then."

"You've been sneaking out for two whole months?!?!? His name is October? Yeah right. You've gotta stop. What if he kidnaps you or something?" *Chance is such a dad.*

"He won't. I know him. Well... He seems familiar."

"Psychopaths have that effect on people!"

"Bye, Chance. I'll see you in an hour," she laughed.

"Daaaaaaad!" yelled Amethyst. He panicked and ran to her room. "Isn't she awesome? I love her."

"Woo. Ame, don't scare me like that. Let me see." She showed him a picture of Rihanna. "Wow. Okay. Yeah. I see why you screamed. How old are you again?"

"I'm 15. You know this."

"I know. It's just that you're turning 16 soon and…" Making silly faces, he jumped on Amethyst's bed as she laughed at his goofiness. "Am I a good father?"

"Of course you are. Well, you certainly aren't a bad one. You just worry too much, and you make everything awkward."

"You remind me so much of your mother. Alright Cupcake, time to get ready for school. Do you want me to drive you, or are you going to walk?"

"Uhhh. School," Amethyst sighed. "I'll walk."

"I packed you and Chance's lunches. Do you want to take something for later?"

"Thanks. I'm good. Riley is bringing me cookies today." People at school loved bringing her food, and she loved eating it. In her mind, it was a win-win situation.

"You're such a player. You get that from your mother."

"It's not like that. I use everyone for food." *Everyone.*

"Still a player," he told her as he pulled her two strand twists into a bun. Amethyst's mother taught him how to do her hair since she couldn't be there to do it.

"Alright, see you later."

"Ummm. Where do you think you're going with those chapped ass lips?" Jeremy was not about to allow his child to walk out the house looking crusty.

"I was going to put some on. It's in my pocket, see. You know what?" Amethyst applied her Chapstick. "There."

"Okay. TTYL." *He tried it. He really tried it.*

"Don't ever say that again," she laughed.

Amethyst met up with her best friends, Chance and Jasmine. As they dragged themselves onto the school campus, everyone greeted Amethyst, but no one said anything to Chance or Jasmine. That was normal. Then Amethyst looked over at Jasmine, but she wasn't smiling at her like she usually did. "Um. Are you okay?" she asked. *More like girl why tf is you looking at me like that?*

"No, Ms. Popularity. I'm far from okay."

"Whoa. Okay. Spill it. What's up?"

Caught off guard, Chance was speechless and eager to hear what Jasmine had to say. "Ever since I came to this school, I have tried so hard to fit in. I've tried so hard to get people to like me. But you… Everyone likes you and you don't do shit. I might not be pretty like you, have a curvy body like yours, have those eyes, that hair, and that skin, but I'm still a good person. Nobody sees that. Guess what? I was the one who started most of those rumors about you. Remember when you lost your phone? I took it. Then I realized I was doing all those mean things because I was jealous of you. I almost decided to clean my mess up, but then I read your journal while you were in the bathroom. I know all about you. That's a disorder you know. You're lucky psych wards aren't still a thing. I wonder what everyone would think about you if they knew. Don't worry. I won't tell. I don't want people to know I used to hang around a sinner. I don't want to see you ever again." Jasmine walked away before Amethyst could say anything.

"What the hell? I'm shook. I'm going to need a week to digest that shit. Did she just walk away from our friendship?" asked Chance.

"I think so." *Well, that didn't take long.* "Do you think she's going to tell?"

"Don't worry, Ame. She won't. Ugh. I never liked her ass anyway." He knew Amethyst was really hurt. "Well, you still have me. Correction. You will always have me."

She couldn't help but smile. "You're my only true friend. Come on. That's the bell."

Even though the school day just started, she and Chance couldn't wait until lunchtime. When lunchtime finally came, they weren't expecting to get harassed by a football player. *They were having quite the day.* They walked in the lunchroom and stopped by the cheerleader table to say hi and collect a few snacks. That was normal. The cheerleaders loved Amethyst, and they thought Chance was adorable. She had a thing for cheerleaders unlike Chance who said they were much too 'prissy'. They went to go sit down, but a few guys were sitting at the table they usually sat at, so they sat at the one next to it. One of the guys, Mason, approached Chance first and told him to give him his wallet. Amethyst shook her head no. "It's okay, Ame. You know I have much more where that came from."

"Don't give it to him," she said.

Mason turned his attention to Amethyst. "Oh yeah? What are you going to do, sweetie? Don't you worry. I'm willing to give it back in exchange for a little private time."

He made the mistake of caressing the side of her face. "Don't touch me!" she yelled. Then she socked him square in his jaw. That got everyone's attention. She made eye contact with Jasmine who had a guilty look on her face. Amethyst was about to throw a chair at him. Before she knew it, the whole football team was behind Mason, and they were pissed. Mason saw Amethyst's eyes widen and turned around only to receive the worst beating ever. The campus supervisors came and rescued Mason from the wrath of the football team. They only got an hour of extra practice because Amethyst told them everything that happened.

"If he ever bothers you again, let us know," said the team captain, James. "You're off the team, Mason. On this team, we respect womxn."

"I don't think he will. Thanks guys."

"No problem, sis. Besides, that guy's a predator. Us guys should support girls." *Probably not used to hearing that from a guy on a sports team, huh?*

She and Chance only had one more class after lunch. Then they were free to go. As soon as the bell rang, they grabbed their stuff and got the hell out of that government institution. While they were riding their Penny boards past Ocean Beach, Chance yelled, "Don't you love where we live?" at the top of his lungs.

"I do," she agreed. "The ocean washes all the negative energy away. The best place to be on the surface is as close to the ocean as possible."

They didn't have a care in the world as they were cruising down the boulevard, admiring the magnificent beauty of the ocean's waves and absorbing as much as they could of the sun's golden rays. Amethyst was completely captivated by the ocean. Meanwhile, Chance's ocean was Amethyst. He couldn't help but marvel over her curvy, petite, copper-toned body and her brown eyes that matched the color of her curly brown hair. Her hair. He remembered playing with a spiral before she swatted his hand away. Now that he thought about it, she kind of reminded him of a cinnamon roll. *Really bro? Are you serious? Take a picture, it will last longer. Also… Sun? Hum.*

"Chance. Are you checking me out?" she laughed.

"No. Ew. What the f***? Of course not. Not like that. You've just grown that's all. I want my future daughter to be just like you."

"So have you. You got taller. You might be 5ft 6, and you actually have an ab or two now," she joked. "Are you sure? I'm overweight."

"Hey, Cinnamon Roll."

"What?" she hoped he wasn't trying to nickname her.

"I'm going to start calling you that. It suits you."

"Only if I get to call you my Ninja Turtle."

"Which one am I?" Then he realized why she called him that. "Ha. Ha. Very funny. I do not live in a shell."

"You're definitely Mikey, and yes you do, boo boo."

"How come I can't be Leonardo?"

"Because Leonardo is bae."

"Ouch. Don't make me walk away from our friendship." She thought Chance's little stupid joke was funny.

"But for real though. I just don't get it. Why is Jas acting like—" Chance tackled her and started a tickle fight. *Awww, he was trying to get her mind off that.* "OMG. Stop. Stop it." She could barely get her words out because she was laughing so hard. "You suck."

"How'd you know?" *Huuum. Is that so? Do tell…*

"What? OMG. I been knew." She managed to free herself and ran towards the beach.

"That's not fair. You know I'm hydrophobic, short ass."

"Not even. You take showers, don't you?"

"Of course I do."

"Nah, I'm jk… I know what you mean. I wasn't going to get that close."

As Chance made his way over to her, he noticed someone sitting on a rock. "Ame. Ame!" He finally got her attention. "Who the hell was that?"

"I didn't see anyone. What were they wearing?"

"That's the thing. He was butterball naked except for some white spandex shorts. He was far out. Not even the surfers in wetsuits go out that far when the waves are like this. He must be suicidal." Chance realized what he said. "Well, maybe not suicidal. If he is, that's okay. I mean…" *And at this moment he knew that he f***** up.* "Sorry."

"It's okay, Chance. I know what you meant. Come on, let's go home."

"You don't believe me, do you?"

"I do believe you. I have a scope in my room. Let's spy on him."

"Wait, that scope in your room works? You never told me that. You can see me?" Amethyst nodded. "Like… You can see me in my room?" *Why so worried bro?*

"Yeah. See for yourself." When they arrived, Chance investigated the scope and immediately wished he could hide inside it.

"When do you look in here? What all have you seen?"

Amethyst started singing "Beat It" by Michael Jackson. "No way. You've seen me just-beating-it?" A red flag went up in Chance's head, and he started sweating. "Shit!"

"I was referring to the time when you were dancing in your underwear like the Great Value brand of a stripper."

"Oh." Chance tried to change the subject. "The Great Value brand isn't that bad though."

"You're right. You're not that attractive, and you have no booty, but you're packing. I'll give you that." Chance smirked. "I mean your abs dummy. Not your little friend you like so much." She laughed so hard she mustered up a tear. "Have you ever seen a chicken strip?"

"Don't start with those weak ass jokes. I do not have chicken legs. I am not that skinny witcho short ass. Hold up! So, you have seen me you-know-whatting! Uhhh. This is so embarrassing." He hid under her bed cover.

"I haven't." *Lying ass.* Amethyst almost threw up in her mouth thinking about how she's scarred for life. "It's okay. Everyone does it. I do it all the time. I've even done it right there. On my bed. Under those covers." *Petty.*

"Ewwwww." He freaked out. "You could have told me."

"What do you mean ew? I actually wash my sheets. Besides, you do it."

"Okay but that's different."

"How is it different? You act like womxn don't masturbate? Our society needs to clear the stigma attached to female masturbation. Masturbation can actually be quite healthy and have plenty of pros, especially for us gals. Female bodied people shouldn't be criticized for exploring and learning about their bodies. Males aren't..."

"Okay, true. I respect that. You specifically are just a freak though. I know about yo ass. Plus, we don't have the same situation down there. The clean-up could potentially be a lot more difficult."

Amidst laughing, Amethyst managed to say, "Let's call a girl and see." She could have used her cell phone, but she dialed the neon blue corded telephone on her desk. She loved how it glowed.

"What are you going to do? Call and say, 'Hey. Um. Do you masturbate?' Wait. Who are you calling?"

"Your girlfriend."

"She's not my—"

"Shhhhh!" Amethyst hushed him. "Hey, Eirian." She put her on speaker. "What's up?" "Can I ask you something?" "Sure. If you answer something for me." "Okay. Um. Do you masturbate?" "Yeah who doesn't? Alright, my turn. What does your best friend think of me? He keeps sending me mixed signals." Chance shook his head. "I'm not sure, but I think he definitely thinks you're cute. Who knows? He might ask you out. If he doesn't do it sometime this week then he's probably just not that into you." "Ok. Thanks. Bye, girl." "Bye."

"So, she does like me?"

"Yes, dumbass. I've been telling you that for the longest. Why don't you ask her out?"

"Because I'm not sure. You know how I feel about cheerleaders. Also, I'm still not over you know who, and I think I like someone else."

"It's not like you're getting married. You need a rebound date. I don't like the idea of rebound relationships, but ain't nothing wrong with a little date after you've had some time to get yourself together. Anyways, who are they?"

"It's a girl. Her name is... Uhhh. Am-eh-ly."

"Here you go finna pull one of yo little stunts." They were always making fun of people. "You mean Emily? Tell me about her," she played along.

"I could go on and on. She's short and has super curly hair. She's the perfect mix of sassy, smart, silly, and sexy, but my favorite thing about her is her smile." He was mocking this one boy who was crushing on Amethyst even though he could never get her name right. He puckered his lips and leaned in closer and closer.

"Take it easy before I throw you in the cold shower. I'm not Emily." Chance continued to be hilariously annoying and gave her a peck on the cheek. "Alright. That's it. You're going in." Amethyst dragged him into the bathroom and made him take his pants and shirt off. Then she shoved him into the shower, ran out, and locked the door from the outside.

"Did you lock me in here?"

"Yep and I'm not letting you out until I hear that you've been under the water for at least 7 minutes."

"C'mon. You know I wasn't really going to kiss you kiss you."

"The hell you weren't. That peck on the cheek was pretty darn close. You have terrible aim."

"Whatever. I'll get in. As soon as I get out, I'm telling Dad about this damn lock. Oh, and how do you have Eirian's phone number?"

"I have every cheerleader's number." *Ooooo. Savage.*

After he got out the shower, which lasted more than five minutes, she unlocked the door. "Watch out, Ame. I'm gonna have to go commando since you didn't give a brotha a towel."

"How are you a brotha?" she joked.

"I'm half Black remember. And who says white boys can't be brothas?" he laughed. He said that last part sarcastically.

"Sure, Chancellor Gregory Adamson, the third."

"I'm more African than you. My mom's from Libya. I'm Libyan. I came from a motherwomb. We don't know who the f*** you came from. You could be part divine for all we know. Hell, she might not even be Afro-anything."

"LOL. Now we bringing up ethnicity? What about nationality?" She paused. "So, you ain't gon claim Germany at all?"

"Bruh. My father was just living in Germany temporarily."

"I know he's English, but you were still born there. I think that's dope as hell. LOL. Black people are everywhere. You have a cool ass accent too. Huuuh! You know who you remind me of? You know Cameron Boyce? You're literally him with red hair and Reece King's accent. Ahhh!!! Daaamn. Witcho fancy ass."

"LMAO. Hella accurate. Aw, you couldn't get my clothes out for me?"

"Boy bye. Hurry up. We have some spying to do." Once he was done, Amethyst looked at him sideways. "Chance, what are you doing? We are going on the roof. Get a jacket." She rolled her eyes. "You be the main one always talking about you're cold."

"Right. Hold on a sec. How are we going to get on top of the Inn? Don't they have an alarm or something?"

"Yeah," she said sarcastically. "They have booby traps too."

From the top of the Inn, they didn't see much. Just Sutro Baths. Then Amethyst looked for a second time. "Look! There he is in the water. LOL. That wedgie though... Bruuuh. Yo but look at those legs. Zaaamn." She let Chance have a look.

"Too bad you can't zoom."

He gave her an idea. "Let's go to the diner!"

"I'm not hungry."

"With the scope numbnuts."

By the time they got to the diner, it was almost 4 o'clock in the afternoon. They both greeted Mrs. Jones before they asked her if they could sit by the window. That was normal. They were shook when she asked them if they were looking for the boy in the water. Mrs. Jones told them that she's seen unusual things over the years. She told them the mysterious boy started showing up occasionally ever since Amethyst and Jeremy moved there. Chance was looking through the scope when Amethyst blurted out, "I knew it! I knew I wasn't crazy! That is him! Oh, hell nah. Why his ass didn't open his mouth and speak?" She ran out of the diner and all the way back up the hill to their house. She never ran for anything. Her best friend followed her of course. He couldn't catch up. He called out to her, but soon enough, she was already in the driveway. The only reason she stopped was because she didn't have the key. Well, of course she had the key to the house. It's just that she pretty much always forgot to bring it with her. Chance, on the other hand, always had his. As soon as he opened the door, Amethyst ran all the way up the stairs to her room. After violently flipping through some of her old journals, she found the entry she was looking for:

July 7, 2007

I cannot believe what happened today. Well actually I do but anyways me, Dad, and Chance were at the beach and me and Chance saw Dad talking to someone in sign language. It was a boy that looked about three years older than me and Chance. Dad shooed him away and quickly came back by us but he didn't know that we saw him and the boy. While Dad was distracted by Chance talking to him I walked over to the boy waving at me. I was scared but he was funny and cute so I was less scared. He also wasn't that much bigger than me so I was sure I could take him if something went down. He gave me the piece of seaweed he was carrying and then disappeared. Chance is going to be mad since we're getting married next year. I can't wait to see the look on his face.

"Aye, I forgot about that shit," he laughed. "So, what are we on? Our 8th year?"

"Chance! You're missing the point! It's you know who!"

"If it is him then what does he want? If he wants you, he can't have you."

Amethyst rolled her eyes. Chance was so overprotective. That was normal. "Or maybe he just wants to say hello. And why not? Maybe he's a good guy."

"He's homeless and obviously crazy."

"You don't know that. He must live somewhere whether it be inside or outside."

"Homeless people live outside or in a shelter."

"Home is where you make it, but I do agree he might be houseless. Wait. You do believe me, right?"

"Honestly, no. I didn't even see him that day. I just saw you with that piece of seaweed." *LOL what is the truth?*

"That piece of seaweed was fresh, and it was *Saccharina japonica*."

"Ame, that would mean he most likely got it from somewhere by Japan or at least somewhere very far from this beach."

"Exactly. Maybe he's from somewhere else. Maybe he came here by boat, fell into the water, and got lost or something. Huh! Or maybe he's from the ocean or outer space. Both are equally cool!"

"You do realize how stupid that sounds, right?"

"I'm not stupid, Chance. Get the hell out."

"What? Why?"

"What do you mean why? Get the hell out!" She pushed him out of her room and slammed the door in his face.

Jeremy came home twenty minutes ago, but they were too preoccupied with their mystery to have noticed. "Hey, Chance. What's wrong with her?"

"Nothing. Something's wrong with me. I'll be right back. I'm going to ask Eugene if I can borrow his sleeping bag."

"Good luck with that. Why don't you just sleep in your room here?"

"I don't know. I'll be back in like 6 minutes and 24 seconds." He went across the street and a few houses down. He wasn't surprised to find his father drunk. That was normal.

"Oh, hey there, son."

"Hello, Eugene. May I borrow a sleeping bag?"

"What do you need that for? I thought you were staying over Jeremiah's house?"

"I am. I'm going to use it for extra cushioning."

"Extra cushioning? Sure, but that sounds a little feminine to me son. You a toggaf?"

"It's feminine for someone to want to be more comfortable? And being feminine doesn't determine a person's sexuality or gender. Also, there is nothing wrong with being queer, and femininity is awesome."

"You have a smart mouth just like your mother. You know what that got her? A slap on her pretty little face." Chance grabbed the sleeping bag and told himself to not get angry. "You know she left because of you, Chancellor. Y-You son of a b****. Now she's all the way in Libya probably thinking about how much she misses me." He thrust his hips, and Chance couldn't hold himself back. He forgot everything he learned from his anger management classes for a minute and beat his father so badly his knuckles were bruised the color of wine. That wine was all over his father's mouth. After he realized what he had done, he started hyperventilating. He breathed into his asthma pump and called the non-emergency number. He told them what happened. That was normal. This wasn't the first time they fought. It was definitely the most gruesome though. Yet all he could think about was Amethyst.

She ran down the stairs. "Dad. Dad! There's an ambulance!" Jeremy was an even deeper sleeper than Chance himself. "Dad! Sirens!"

"Sirens?!?!?" He was thinking about the actual creature, but at least he was wide awake now. "Where?"

"Th-They're at Eugene's house! Where's Chance?"

The last time her dad moved as fast as he did was when she was walking too close to the edge of an ocean cliff when she was seven. "What happened? Are you alright?" he asked Chance who was sitting on the edge of the sidewalk staring at his hands.

"This time I let things get far out of hand. I injured him pretty badly."

Amethyst did her best to quickly make her way through the crowd of neighbors and police officers. "Chance." She was frustrated because it was hard for her to push through all the neighbors.

"Dad, I can't let her see me like this. I hate having to leave."

"I know but you always come back."

"Yeah but this time I left on a bad note. Ame is mad at me. I pissed her off." He got up from the curb. Before he let himself into the police car, he asked Jeremy to give Amethyst a microscope slide. He didn't even look at her. He didn't want to. There is no way he could face her without crying.

"No. No. No. Chance! Chance!!! Don't let him take you. Ride in the other car. Chance!" Suddenly the sky became a hue of grey that was as close to gunpowder as grey could get. Then hail broke loose. That was unusual. Amethyst wasn't cooperating, so Jeremy carried her back inside their house.

"Shhh. Ame. Amethyst, listen to me. He'll be back. You know this. This happens all the time." Her father looked out the window. It looked like mothballs were being launched from the heavens. "Look. I need you to help me out here. I need you to calm down."

"I can't calm down. I don't like that Man that's driving the police car." The last three people she said she didn't like turned out to be murderers, so now he understood. "His eyes were white. Well, not white white. They were glowing white."

"What?" This was worse than he thought.

"White light."

"Stay here. I'm going to the station. I'll be back. Don't leave the house."

"How come no one else ever sees what I see?"

Jeremy didn't know how to answer that at the moment. "You're gifted."

Chapter 2: #FreeChance

While in the back of the police car, Chance thought about what was going to happen. He hated being locked up because he's claustrophobic. *Detained is much more accurate. *rolls eyes** He knew that they were going to have to hold him until his psychiatrist was convinced he was stable. What he didn't know is what Amethyst thought of him now. "Out," said Mitchell, the officer who was driving. "You know the drill." It wasn't long before he was in his dentention cell.

One of the younger officers, a rookie named Bailey, dialed the phone for him. "I'll pass," Chance told him. That was unusual. Every other time he requested to call the same person, Amethyst.

"Do you want to talk about it? I have to sit here all night so—"

"No, I don't want to talk about it. Earlier today I slipped up and used the word suicidal in place of a word like stupid. That was so stupid. She was suicidal or is suicidal. Whatever. Oh, speaking of stupid… I basically called her stupid. I know she's not stupid. She's far from stupid. I just said what I said because I didn't want to believe it was true. I did see the cute boy that one time at the beach. I went to get a sleeping bag from Eugene's house because I was going to lay by her room door so that I'd be right there when she woke up. My sleeping bag was in her room and she kicked me out, so I didn't want to bother her. I could have slept in my room, but I wanted to make sure I was able to catch her after she woke up from her post-pissed-off-nap, so I could apologize. Her birthday's tomorrow!!! I also got a microscope slide that I was going to give her. Not as a birthday gift. She should have it by now."

"Whoa. Dude. I'm so confused, but it sounds like you really messed up."

"Wow. Thanks, Bailey. You know… It's pretty funny how your name is Bail-ey, but you're working for the people who just lock people up if they don't murder them."

"Hey. Take it easy, Rich Boy. I'm not the one who is romantically frustrated."

"What did you just call me?"

"Romantically frustrated. You know…" Chance glared at him. "Oh, come on dude. It's like sexually frustrated but for romance."

Rubbing his temples, he said, "I get it 'dude'. I'm not romantically frustrated." His face turned tomato red. He watched an officer walk by the room. Then he and Bailey listened in on their conversation with another officer:

"Oh. Hey, Lenny."

" 'Sup. Have you seen Mitchell? He didn't look so good before he left."

"I haven't seen him. What do you mean he didn't look good?"

"When he came out of his office, he wasn't walking straight, and he kept rubbing his temples. He almost walked right into me. Maybe it was another one of those migraines."

"Maybe so."

"I'll go ask Clara. Maybe she knows. Be back in 5."

"Uh. Uhh. Uhhhhhhh," Bailey moaned.

"Would you shut up!" Chance hated when he did that.

"I'm bored. This sucks."

He rolled his eyes. "Welcome to the police station."

"Can you tell a joke?"

"Yes."

He waited patiently for about two minutes until he realized Chance was being a smart ass. "Uhhh. Just tell me a damn joke."

"Bailey."

He flicked him off. "You're such a dick."

"Your buddies put me in the cell with the broken toilet again. I have to pee." Bailey pretended to be asleep. "Like for real. I gotta go." He fake snored. "Bro, it's coming." Then he laughed and threw him an empty water bottle. "Really? You're cold, man. Cold."

"No. I'm a joke remember."

Chance chuckled. "Come on. You have to admit that was pretty funny. Now close your eyes."

"It was but not as funny as you peeing in a bottle. Wait what?"

"Yeah, yeah. Ha. Ha. Don't act brand new."

"Just turn the other way."

"We go through this every time. I cannot pee if you do not close your eyes, so close them."

"Make sure you hold it close, so you don't miss. Next time, I'll have a puppy pad for you."

When Chance finished, he threw the warm bottle of pee back to Bailey. *Ew.* "Lenny must be trying to holla at Clara. So much for 5 minutes. It's been 11.3 minutes."

"How do you know that?"

"Everyone knows Lenny likes Clara."

Another officer walked in. "How you doing, Bailey? What time is it?"

"It's 6:48 PM," Chance said.

"How do you know?" asked the officer. "There's no clock in here."

"Numbers are kinda my thing. I'm always counting."

"Interesting. Exactly how long have you been in here?"

"26 minutes and 46 seconds by the time I finish this sentence." Then they heard a loud bang from outside. The officer went to go check it out.

"Did you hear that?" Bailey said as he looked out the window.

"Yeah. I'm not deaf. Doesn't sound too good."

"Looks like someone crashed into a car. Oh man, look! There's a fight."

"N***** I can't f****** look!!!"

"Right. Well, there's a tall ass Black dude fighting Mitchell. I can't see his face because he has a hoodie on, and it's so dark out. I know he used to box, but I still got money on the other dude."

"Why?" Chance laughed. "Because he's Black?"

"Ummm, no."

"You're a horrible liar. You know I can tell when you're lying, silly. You never know. He could get whupped on."

"Not this dude."

"Do you think I'd win a fight with Mitchell?"

"Uh, there's a 50/50 chance."

"Wow. That was like your best joke ever."

"Surprisingly, no one has come to rescue Mitchell yet."

"What? Really? Go tell them. Isn't that your father?"

"Yeah but he's abusive."

"What? No way. Mitchell? To you? For real? Dude are you for real?" Chance started to get angry. He felt his temperature increasing as he was hyperventilating.

"Yep." Bailey wiped the makeup from his eye and took off his shirt to reveal his horribly bruised back.

"Damn. I'm sorry, bro. That's some bullshit!!! How come you never told anyone?!?!?"

It always scared him to see Chance like that. "Dude, chill. I'm afraid you might bust out of there. I never told because I don't want to end up in a foster home. You're the last person on earth I'd tell because I'm sure you'd do something that would get you sent to prison. I'm only telling you now because you're behind bars, and it looks like someone else got to him before you. Also, I could care less about what happens to him now that I'm emancipated and 17."

"I see." Chance took a series of deep breaths. "That makeup was pretty good."

"It's the contour." He paused. "You know, I think you're bipolar."

"I am Bailey. I already f****** told you that. If you're referring to my mood swings that's something else. Bipolar doesn't mean quick ass mood swings. We've been over this."

"Yeah, but I was distracted," he smirked. "Wait a second. Dude! Where'd they go? They're gone. I guess I wasn't paying attention."

"What are the rest of them doing?"

"I'll go check. Don't go anywhere." *Really? That's like being on the toilet taking a number 2 and then having to phone a friend because there's no toilet paper and then they say don't go anywhere. Same shit. Pun intended.* They were just sitting at their desks like nothing happened. "You all didn't hear the cars crash?"

"Yeah, we heard it," said one of them. "That was a drunk driver turning himself in."

"What about the fight?"

"What fight? I thought it comes on tomorrow night?"

"Oh yeah. That's right." He continued to play along to get more information. Now he knew exactly what happened, but he couldn't tell Chance. At least not yet. "Apparently, that wasn't him. They said Mitchell went home after he brought you in."

"Bro, you know your father when you see him."

"Exactly."

"Let's keep it on the low. You don't want them to think you're crazy like me."

"Okay. Dude, you're not crazy. You're just full of fiery passion that's all."

"You sound like Ame."

"No. I'm 98% sure that AJ would have agreed with you."

"How do you know that?"

"Girls are kinda my thing."

"Don't mock me." Once they finished laughing, Chance said, "What do you think is going on."

"I don't know. We'll find out sooner or later."

"You sound like Ame."

"Dude, if you mention her one more time I just might get jealous."

Chance blushed. "Sorry."

"Why don't you just tell her how you feel?"

"Huh? Who Ame? I don't like her. I mean—"

"Chance, buddy, it's obvious."

"How is it obvious?"

"So, you do like her?" Bailey felt like he outsmarted him.

"No. She is my SISTER. I mean what do I do that makes you think that?"

"You care so much about her. Like I can feel it when you talk about her."

"Okay, okay. Stop right there. Of course I care about her. I guess it's time that I tell you."

"Tell me what?"

"About me and Ame."

"I'm all ears, Romeo."

"It's not like that, Bailey. You can care about someone in a nonsexual or nonromantic way." He regretted it later, but he told Bailey everything because he trusted him. "When I first moved here, I was two and Amethyst wasn't born yet, so on top of being completely terrified, I was completely lonely. I've seen all my 'birthday party' pictures, and there was never a single kid at my so-called parties. I even asked my parents about it. They told me that I was just different and didn't speak English very well. Believe it or not, those weren't the worst of times. I started getting bullied in the third grade for various reasons, but I never told anyone about it. I was the oldest one in the class because I had to learn a decent amount of English first. Apparently, that wasn't enough to prevent me from being the laughing stock of the class. I eventually told my parents, but my father thought that I needed to 'man up'. Speaking of that, my ass is still traumatized from him forcing me to learn how to swim. I hate being in the water. Anyways, my mom contacted the school as soon as she found out, regardless of what my father said. That's my hitta. That stopped the physical beatings from happening at school, but sometimes they would follow me home after they ridiculed me at school. The right words hurt so much more than any beating. On my first day of fifth grade, I heard my teacher call a new name, Amethyst Jules, during the attendance. My first thought was damn that's a cool ass name. I looked around, but there was no new student. I looked out the window and there she was. She was running late. She didn't notice I was looking at her. I told my teacher not to mark her absent because she was here. It was no surprise she didn't believe me. I mean, how would I know? Honestly, I didn't even know what class she was in. I just really wanted it to be her. I got my wish. She walked right in, and everyone couldn't help but stare. Not because she was late, but because to us, she had the presence of a unicorn. Yes, as cringe as it sounds, a unicorn." He laughed at the memory. "There were two open seats left, so there was a 50/50 chance that she'd sit in the seat next to me. Once I realized what I had hoped for, I got so nervous. She asked if she could sit next to me. I didn't respond because I was so focused on trying not to pee my pants. I finally mustered up the courage to nod. She asked for my name, and instead of saying Chance, I said Chancellor Gregory Adamson, the third. I told her my whole ass government name. We didn't really talk much after that because of me being all awkward. Then when I was walking home after school, those bullies followed me again. I wasn't paying attention because I was thinking about Ame. They jumped me and nearly drowned me in the ocean. Then they laid me on the shore, and all three of them took turns beating my ass. I let them as usual. Then they threatened Amethyst. The leader had braces, and I beat him so badly that there was blood all over his face and my fists. You know how I have asthma. I lost my inhaler in the ocean. I was already hyperventilating, but I ran away as fast as I could anyway. I was hella scared. Then it happened. I had an asthma attack right there on the boulevard. Amethyst was walking the same route and she saw me. She was so small, but she calmed me down and dragged me all the way up that steep ass hill to her house. Jeremy called the ambulance. Amethyst saved my life, bro. Real talk."

"Dude, that was deep. I don't really know what to say, but I totally get it now. You could have told me."

"I guess I was just nervous because I didn't want you to think anything. Don't bring this up, and don't tell anyone anything about what I said. Don't tell Ame about that unicorn part. Now let's talk about something else."

"I promise I won't. Ummm, okay let's see. It's only fair that I tell you a little something about me."

"Go for it. I'm all ears."

"Remember that thing I changed my mind about telling you? You know how Mitchell isn't my biological father. I have no idea who my biological father is. My mom died when I was a baby, and I was left with him. Anyways, I always felt like I was never really his son. I don't think he thought of me that way. He never called me his son, and he never told me he loved me. Uhhhhh! I'm done. You can't say a word. Act like you didn't hear anything." Bailey's eyes started watering. "Anyways, let's get some sleep. Good night." He noticed Chance was fake sleeping. That made him crack a smile. "You're the same old Chance."

After Bailey finished reapplying his makeup, he made sure Chance was up. Chance turned around, yawned, and said, "Mornin', Officer."

Bailey didn't buy it. "First of all, it's like 1 PM, and I know you didn't sleep a wink. I'm going to notify Mrs. Sims about that."

"Why? That's normal."

"Exactly my point. Now move it. I'm bailing you out," he joked as he cuffed him and walked him to the police car. "Dad?" He was surprised to see his father with no visible injuries.

"Hey, son. Hello, Chance." His tone was friendly towards Bailey and stern towards Chance. That was unusual. Bailey couldn't believe he called him his son.

"Hi?" Chance was thinking about Bailey's back. He remembered what he told him and started to get angry.

"Have a safe trip," Bailey said sarcastically after he lowered Chance into the car.

In the car, there was nothing but silence for about 8 minutes. Then Chance said, "Now I don't mind when people treat me like shit, but I won't let a damn soul treat my friends like shit."

"Oh yeah? Shut up, boy. You can't touch me. If it was up to me, you'd be in prison where you belong, but your daddy's rich. I know about you, boy. You're a toggaf. You might as well be wearing a dress. You wanna be a girl? You probably fight like one."

"Let me out the car and I'll show your sexist, homophobic ass how girls fight."

"You know what? Let's settle this right now. I ought to teach you a lesson." Mitchell drove to somewhere where no one would be able to see them. He let him out, but he didn't uncuff him just as Chance expected. "C'mon, boy." At first, Chance purposely took a few hits, so he could figure out his timing. When he started fighting back, Mitchell asked who trained him. Chance told him his father was a Marine and is an alcoholic, so he learned the hard way. They continued to go at it until Chance choked

Mitchell with his handcuffs. "Finish it then. They'll catch you, and you'll go to real jail."

After giving it some thought, Chance said, "I'm not going to kill you. You won't say a word because I have a recording of you abusing Bailey. I also have a recording of our little conversation. Even if I didn't, what were you going to do? Say you got beat up by some toggaf?" He knew that if Mitchell didn't believe his bluff, he definitely wouldn't sacrifice his pride. He was more than safe. He grabbed the keys, freed his hands, and caught a Lyft to Mrs. Sim's office. When he looked back, Mitchell was gone somehow. He told the driver to let him out around the corner and walked the rest of the way. Where did Mitchell go that quickly? He just told himself he couldn't see from the angle he was at. "Good morning, Mrs. Sims. How are you?" He loved how her office smelled like citruses. She even had little candies in the sunflower bowl on her desk.

"I'm doing fine. So, is there anything I should know before we begin?"

"No, but I do have two things I would really like to talk about."

"Sure, but we need to talk about what happened between you and your father."

"Right. Can we knock that out first?"

"That's fine." Mrs. Sims tried not to sound disappointed. She wanted to hear about the two things Chance wanted to talk about. He never asked to talk about anything. "So, tell me what happened." She took note of everything Chance told her. "Although your father won't be pressing any charges, as usual, he will be in a rehab clinic full-time. He recommended that he'd be sent to a clinic if going part-time didn't work out. He wrote you this letter a while ago just in case." She handed it to him. "I haven't read it, but he told me it's short."

CHANCELLOR,

I AM GOING TO BE IN A REHABILITATION CLINIC FULL TIME UNTIL I AM FIT TO BE YOUR FATHER AGAIN. I HAVE ALREADY LOST THE LOVE OF MY LIFE, YOUR MOTHER,

AND I DON'T WANT TO LOSE YOU TOO. I HAVE TALKED TO YOUR MOTHER AND JEREMY ABOUT THIS. WE DECIDED TO GIVE YOU THE OPTION TO MOVE OVERSEAS OR STAY WITH AMETHYST AND HER FATHER. WE KNOW HOW WELL YOU'VE ADAPTED HERE. YOUR MOTHER WAS SURE YOU'D RATHER STAY HERE WITH AMETHYST. YOU HAVE PERMISSION TO USE MY CARD AND YOUR MONTHLY LIMIT IS THE SAME. JEREMY SAID HE DIDN'T NEED IT BUT I GAVE HIM SOME CASH ANYWAY. YOU CAN CALL ME OR WE CAN VIDEO CHAT ONCE I'VE MADE SOME PROGRESS.

EUGENE

When Chance finished reading the letter, he didn't say a word, but he was grateful. He at least had some respect for his father now. "So, what is it you would like to talk about?"

"Well first, I think Amethyst hates me. Second, do you know anything about the mysterious boy who loves to hang out at Sutro Baths?"

"Why do you think Amethyst hates you?"

"I messed up. I said some things I didn't mean, and I never got the chance to take them back. I also left without saying anything at all. Not even goodbye or sorry. She was right there. And today's her birthday!!!"

"I don't know nearly as much about Amethyst as you do, but from what you've told me, you two are best friends. I think you two can make up. I would suggest telling her how you feel."

"You know I'm not good at that."

"The effort counts."

"I hope so. Anyways, have you heard of the boy I mentioned?"

"You seem eager. Yes, I've heard of him. A lady I think you know by the name Mrs. Jones told me about him. I have never seen him."

"What did she tell you?"

"She said that she saw him grow up. I didn't ask any questions."

"How much time do I have?"

"It's only been ten minutes. We have a whole fifty minutes left."

"No. I know that. Actually, we have 49 minutes and 45 seconds left. I meant how much time do I have to make things right?"

"Right. You're always counting. There is no one answer to that question. It is all up to you and the other person."

Suddenly, Chance started crying. "I-I guess I'm just overreacting, but what if she doesn't forgive me? What if she didn't get the piece of seaweed I saved for her? What if she dies before I even get another chance to apologize?"

Mrs. Sims had been Chance's psychiatrist ever since he was 7, and she had never seen him cry the way he was crying then. "Would it help if we called her?"

"She won't pick up if she doesn't have the number saved. Use my phone."

"I think it would be better if you made the phone call."

"Yeah, you're probably right." After he wiped his tears and cleared his throat, he dialed Amethyst's number. "I'm going to put her on speaker." Amethyst picked up after three rings on purpose. She didn't say anything. She waited to hear what Chance had to say. He didn't know what to say. He managed to blurt out the words, "H-Hey, Ame. Happy Birthday! I'm uh… My bad." There was a moment of silence and she hung up. "Ahhhhhhh! God dammit!"

"What happened? I thought you were going to tell her how you feel?"

"I was. I just… I couldn't do it."

"Why not?"

"I don't know. I got suck."

"How about I help you write it down instead."

"You want me to write a letter?"

"Would that be better?"

"Yes. Now that I think about it, that would be great. Ame loves shit like that." She handed him some paper and a pen.

DEAR CINNAMON ROLL,

I APOLOGIZE FOR ~~WHAT HAPPENED~~ THE THINGS I SAID YESTERDAY AND FOR NOT EVEN APOLOGIZING OR SAYING GOODBYE. HOPEFULLY, YOU DON'T HATE ME.

~~SINCERELY~~ LOVE,

YOUR NINJA TURTLE

"All done? So, how's school?"

"Uhhhhh. School."

"I thought school was going well?"

"It was but yesterday, this f****** jerk was picking on me and Ame. He asked for my wallet. I was going to give it to him, but Ame always has to be so just and was like no. Then the f***** touched her face, so of course, she was heated. I was too, but she made me promise to not get into any more fights at school, so I don't get expelled. She let the whole entire school know that too, so I wouldn't look like a newfound pacifist. I wanted to beat his ass so badly, but I'm pretty sure I would have been expelled by now. Ame doesn't need me to protect her anyway. Jeremy taught us how to defend ourselves. She's also a natural. You should have seen her hit his ass. He doesn't even know she purposely pulled her punch, so she wouldn't break his jaw. Plus, some guys from the football team jumped him. Now that was a sight to see. Ame has goons."

"I'm glad you kept your promise." She tried to prevent him from getting angry again. "If he causes any more problems, let me know."

"Yeah, me too and he won't." He already had a plan of what he was going to do to him if he did. He was glad he didn't know Mason's address.

"Yesterday wasn't the best day, but today can be much better." Chance revealed a half smile. "How have you been sleeping?"

"Fine." Mrs. Sims just waited. "Huuuh. Sometimes I can't fall asleep. I keep having those nightmares, but can we please save that for next time?"

"Sure. Whenever you're ready. Have you had any anxiety attacks lately?"

"No, but I have been way more anxious than usual."

"Why is that?"

"It's because of... Umm..."

"A significant other?"

"No. I don't have a significant other anymore! Don't look at me like that! I'm not romantically frustrated!" *Yes, you are. It's okay. It gets better.* "I think it's because of the nightmares."

"I see. Next session is going to be heavy. I'll make cookies." He loved her snickerdoodles. "I have all of your school work for the week. I was thinking you could get it out of the way now. Lucky for you it's all math."

"Good. I thought you were going to say English." When he got through all his work, he heard a car horn. He looked out the window and saw Jeremy's truck outside. He made sure both letters were in his pocket, said goodbye to Mrs. Sims, and made his way outside.

"What's up, man? How'd it go? Feel any better?"

"Hey, Dad. Do you think... Is Ame still... Does she hate me?"

Jeremy pulled over right by the ocean and started laughing much harder than he probably should have. "Ame was over it by the time I got back to the house. She was so upset because she got another one of those feelings, and this time it was about Mitchell. She kept texting me all day. She was worried sick about you because you didn't call her at the station."

Chance wondered where he went, but then he remembered something more important, "Did you give her the slide?"

"Yep. You should have seen her face." He could tell Mrs. Sims delivered the message about his father going to rehab full time.

Chance couldn't stop smiling. "Thank you."

Jeremy acted like he didn't know, "For what?"

"For everything. For taking care of me all these years."

"Oh. You know you're welcome, son," he smiled. "Now let's go get some groceries, and then go get something to eat. We also have to go pick up her cake."

"Sounds good to me."

Chapter 3: An Alien & An Abduction

After putting up the groceries and Amethyst's galaxy themed cake, Jeremy and Chance ate three whole medium sized three-meat pizzas while watching as much of Creed as they could before they fell asleep on the couch. Jeremy's alarm went off, and they both jumped up. Looking down at his phone, Jeremy smiled and said, "It's time to go get the womxn of the house."

"I don't know what I'd do with two of her."

Jeremy almost choked on his last slice of pizza. He coughed it off, "Woo. Me neither. She alone is a hand full." Once they arrived at the school, it wasn't long before Amethyst spotted the car. "Hide." Chance did some acrobatic shit to hop in the back and lie flat across the seat.

"Hey, Dad. Where's Chance? I thought he'd prefer the front seat."

"You're too smart for us." Jeremy laughed. "You can come out now." *LOL.*

Amethyst and Chance were giggling about something. He emerged from the backseat. "Aw, how'd you know?"

"Chance, you are literally Darth Vader."

"Was that an asthma joke?" Jeremy laughed hysterically. "I'm sorry, but you were breathing pretty hard."

Usually he would have a good comeback, but he was just glad she wasn't upset with him anymore. All he said was, "Get back here, big head."

"I'm still not happy about that damn cheer squad. I don't understand why you can't be on the team even though you're qualified. They like practicing with you, don't they? Is this a racial thing or what?"

"It's not a racial thing, Dad. Don't worry about it. I don't want to be a cheerleader anyway. I'm just glad the school allowed me practicing with them to count as my performing arts credit because ballet was my only other option." Amethyst loved to dance. She would have gladly joined the cheer squad, but she wouldn't have felt comfortable with them. That's why she didn't really care. She did care how she was misidentified on her ID though.

"Alright Cupcake, but I'm still not happy about it. What do you have a taste for?" he asked.

"Well, I know you two didn't leave me any of that nasty three-meat pizza, so I'll eat the pasta in the refrigerator." Amethyst was dying to get home, so they could look at that slide.

"It smells like pizza in here?" Chance asked. "That was hella long ago."

"Yep. So what movie are we watching when we get home?"

"You two decide. I'm going surfing after I change," said Jeremy. "Then it's party time!"

"Do you always have to go when the waves are this rough? There's literally no one out there."

"Sure there is, Cupcake. Can you play that one song I like?" Amethyst always had the aux cord. He turned up the music. "Yeah, that's it. This is my song!!!" They sang along to "Teenage Fever" by Drake all the way home. Jeremy had the cheesiest dance moves. The three of them got out of the car, and Amethyst forgot to roll her window up as usual. As she went back to roll it up, she realized the guys were so caught up in the music they didn't complain about it being too cold to have the window down. By the time she got inside, Jeremy was already halfway in his wetsuit and on his way out the door.

"That was quick," Amethyst told him as he searched for his house keys. She handed them to him and let him walk out the door before she told him he forgot his surfboard. "You're going to see a womxn, aren't you?"

"Dad's got a girlfriend? I see you," Chance chimed in.

"I wish... She's technically a friend. I'll see you two later."

With his surfboard, Jeremy entered the water. He was no longer at Sutro Baths. He was in an entirely different realm. His realm. He used his strong legs to swim to where the waves crashed against the rocks as if they were trying to push the surface back. Then there she was. "Hello, my basilinna."

"Do not call me that. I am not your basilinna."

"It's good to know you haven't changed since we last saw each other."

"Oh, Jeremias. What happened to us?"

"You dumped me," he smiled. "You said it would be better for me."

"I know," she kissed him on the cheek. They both looked deep into each other's eyes for a moment. "How is Amethyst? I don't know if I can miss another one of her birthdays. I wish it didn't have to be like this."

"Me too. She's doing good. I can't wait for you two to meet."

"As I." They heard voices coming from the path behind them. "Why do you always choose to come to this particular spot? What if someone sees us? Next time, I choose the place."

"No one can see us from this angle. Would you like to move?" he joked.

"No. You know how hard it is for me to get down from this rock."

"I could carry you, you know."

"You mistake me for a seal pup."

"Oh, come on. I've carried you plenty of times."

"Everything is better underwater," she sighed. "I am leaving now."

"Was our kiss really that bad?"

"Yes." They couldn't help but laugh. "I almost forgot. Are she and Chance still only friends?"

"Yes, womxn. They have a sister-brother relationship."

"Good. I don't like him."

"Why not? You know what? That's fair. I don't like your son. Where is he anyway?"

"I have to go. Remember, next time I pick the location. Don't call me, I'll call you."

"Is this us getting back together?" She didn't respond. "I'll take that as a maybe." He continued to sit there for about thirty more minutes, thinking about how things used to be. He had no clue that she was watching him, thinking about the same things. Then he remembered he was supposed to be surfing. He managed to catch a few waves before he left, and she thought it was very entertaining to watch him use a board to ride a wave. By the time he got home, he could see his children were preoccupied with talking about something through Amethyst's bedroom window. He was sure it was about that piece of seaweed. Jeremy didn't understand why they were so fascinated by it. Before he went to sleep, he thought about Amethyst's mother. He wondered where she was, what she was doing, and when she was going to come back to him, but he had no way of knowing any of these things. He also thought about Bailey. No parent should treat their child like the way Mitchell treated him. Jeremy didn't even know Mitchell was abusing him until he saw him show Chance his bruises. If only he had known sooner. Amethyst proved her judgments to be true on multiple occasions. Jeremy wondered who Mitchell was going to murder. Bailey? Or even Chance? He also wondered why Amethyst always saw the eyes of people about to murder someone differently. Her mother didn't leave much information about that, and he had a feeling that shit was about to get real much sooner than he expected. Amethyst's mother did leave him a detailed survival guide on how to raise her. Plus, she was always within reach. They would be able to go home once she came of age, but what age is of age?

Amethyst and Chance were lowkey glad Jeremy went surfing. Now they had time to discuss seaweed and boys apparently. Once Jeremy got far enough, she yelled, "Chance, come on!"

"Okay, but why are you so loud? Damn! You know loud noises make me nervous. Especially your loud ass."

"I know, I know. Sorry. Anyways, thanks for the slide. I knew you remembered."

"Yeah. About that... This is for you." He handed her the letter he wrote.

"Awww, thank you. Wow. You are good with numbers but not with womxn." He was so confused. Amethyst laughed. "If I hated you, you would know it. Awww, you're so cute. OMG I caaan't. I frickin' love you. Next time don't scare me like that. Now fire up that expensive microscope of yours."

Chance examined the seaweed specimen carefully. "It still has that blue stuff on it."

"Well, what do you think it is now that you have more brain cells than you did when we first looked at it?"

"I'm not sure. I was thinking some type of bacteria, but I have no idea. Biology is your thing."

"I think it's some kind of magic alien substance!!!"

"Why you say that?"

"It glows in the dark a little bit."

"No way! Really? I've had it all this time and never noticed."

"You made the slide in the morning, and we looked at it during the day. I'm sure you put it in your drawer or something, so even if they were still glowing, you wouldn't have noticed. They only live so long... It's been years. If they're still glowing, they're probably immortal!"

"True. I'm going to open it up."

"Isn't that against science protocol?" she asked as she watched him make a new slide with some DNA dye. Then she got sidetracked and started playing with his hair.

"This shit just got even weirder. I think the bacteria is actually dude's cells. Come look. I don't know what kind of cells these are."

"What the deoxyribonucleic acid?!?!? How come his cells glow? How do they live so long? These cells must have something to do with why the seaweed is still in tip-top shape. He's definitely an alien!!!"

"I hate to say it, but right now, that is the only plausible explanation I can think of."

"How come you acted like you didn't believe me?" *Talk about out the blue.*

"What are you talking about? I literally just said I agree with— Oh, you mean yesterday. I was jealous."

"Of who? The alien?"

"Yes, Ame."

She found his reason more than amusing. "Well, aren't you going to say why?"

"You always talk about him like you have a crush on him or something."

She laughed so hard a tear rolled down her cheek. *She was just cackling away.* "Oh, wow. You cannot be serious. This is about attention? The last time I checked, you are the only person other than Jeremy that I see all day. Actually, I spend more time with you. Heck, now you live with me for real for real. Everyone at school thinks we're together. I mean how could they not? You sleep in my room sometimes!"

"I know but still. I thought you would have forgotten him by now. I wanted him to remain in your past because there's something about him that is very odd... Strange."

"You're the one who kept the piece of the seaweed he gave me." *True. I mean... She has a point.*

"Shut up, American."

"That's why we won the war." They both shared a little laugh. "Actually, no one won the war. When people talk about who wins a war, I often wonder what they mean because everyone lost simply because we went to war. Every time we go to war, we all lose."

"Damn, bro. That was deep."

"That's what he said."

"Well tell him that he better keep his damn hands to himself!"

"Chill, you know I was just kidding," she rolled her eyes. "You sound like Dad."

"I'm starting to notice that."

"And maybe I really was that deep," she laughed.

"Oh, hell no! There you go with that bullshit," he laughed. "Knowing yo ass, that definitely has a double meaning."

"Why do you think he won't introduce his wannabe girlfriend to us?"

"Maybe he wants you to meet your mother first."

"Yeah, but I want him to be happy."

"He has you. How couldn't he be?"

"You've been acting weird lately. Stop being weird."

"How?"

"You're hiding something."

"I am? What am I hiding?"

"I don't know because you're hiding it."

"I've been having those nightmares again."

"What are they about?"

"I want to tell you but nah. Not right now."

"Why won't you tell me? It must have something to do with a fear you have too much pride to admit." Chance just stayed quiet. Then Ame's phone rang. "Who the f*** is calling me at this hour?" *It's only like 7 though. LOL. This girl.* "Oh. It's Bailey Bail Bond. His aura is so green. He reminds me of a mermaid. Not a prissy one. A tough ass one. LOL that makes sense huh?"

"Bruh. Shut the f*** up," he laughed. "Why do you call him that again?"

"Because he's an officer and he's smooth AF." She put him on speaker after two rings. "Hey, Bailey Bail Bond. What's up, boo?"

"Happy birthday again!!! Chex Mix wasn't answering his phone. I was calling to check on him and make sure his hot-headed ass wasn't in an actual jail or dead." Chance blushed and Bailey heard Amethyst giggle. "I'm on speaker, aren't I?" he laughed. "How you gonna do me like that? What's up, Chex?"

"Thanks, Bailey. Umm, I kind of got into a fight with Mitchell."

"Who is Mitchell?"

"He's my father and a kop."

"A kop? Chaaaaaance! You could have gotten taken away for real for real!"

"It's the one you had the bad feeling about."

"He's missing. He was abusive though."

"Missing? As for the abuse... That's terrible. I'm so sorry. You didn't deserve any of that. I knew something was off about him. How come you never told anyone? Actually, never mind. I totally get it. I swear, Bailey. I know all officers aren't kops, but you're the only officer I know who isn't doing their job killing and imprisoning as many of my sisters and brothers as they can. You're so mellow, so good, so kind. You didn't deserve any of that shit." Her words really warmed his heart.

"Wait! Missing?!?!?" Chance's tone implied he wanted more information.

"You're hella late. They said all they found was his patrol car."

"After we fought, I left him right by his car. Someone else must have had some beef with him because I definitely didn't kidnap him. Ew. Hell no."

"I'm thinking it was the guy from last night," suggested Bailey.

"What guy?" asked Amethyst.

"There was this guy who fought that hateful ass n**** before I did."

"What was he wearing?"

"He had on all black. Why?" Chance wondered if she was thinking what he thought she was thinking.

"No reason. Are you sure you're okay, Bailey Bailey? Do you need anything?"

Chance silently mocked her and rolled his eyes. "Bailey Bailey." *So needy.*

"I'm all good, AJ. Alright. Bye you two. Oh, and turn that fancy phone of yours on, Chance."

"I will." As soon as Amethyst hung up the phone, he said "Okay two things. First, why does he call me Chex."

"Really? Do the math. Next."

"It was Dad wasn't it?"

"Yep. He drove off after I told him about that kop. I knew Mitchell was up to no good. I'm not a crybaby. I just thought you were going to die."

"He told me, and I know you aren't. You're quite the opposite actually."

"He's home!" They awkwardly waved from the window.

"Should we ask him if he has Mitchell?"

"Not right now. He's most likely going to go to sleep. Let's ask him when he wakes up."

"What if he has him in the basement or something?"

A chill ran down her spine. "Stop. That's creepy. As soon as we hear him wake up, we'll go downstairs." She couldn't stop pacing the floor, and he couldn't stop tapping his foot. "How long has it been?"

"Only 16 minutes and 29 seconds by the time I finish this sentence."

"Aw, man. Let's watch a movie or something."

"You pick."

"*Finding Nemo* or *Toy Story*?" Chance looked at her sideways because she knew he didn't want to watch *Finding Nemo*. "*Toy Story* it is. That movie also fits your aesthetic." Chance wondered if her comment was just a coincidence. How could she know about his nightmare? But then again... She is Amethyst. Jeremy woke up to cook dinner during the movie, but they didn't notice.

"Ame! Chance!" He called for them to come downstairs. "The food's ready."

"I guess we can just ask him at the table," she said.

"Ummm. Is that baked chicken I smell?"

"Yep. We also have broccoli, pasta, and mashed potatoes and gravy too. Don't worry, Ame. I didn't use any salt today."

When they were almost done eating, Amethyst couldn't hold it in anymore. "Dad, is Mitchell in our basement? It's totally cool if he is."

Jeremy almost spit out his drink. "What? No. Of course not. What made you think that?"

"Mitchell is missing. We fought. B-Bailey told us he's missing. He's glad about it. H-He was just making sure I was okay."

"That's odd. I don't know anyone who would just—" He actually did. "Where did you leave him?"

"We were at Fort Funston. We were hidden, and it was still kind of foggy. No one saw."

"Good. Um, you two are excused, or you can help yourself to some more." Jeremy's voiced trailed off as he went down to the basement. He had an idea who did it.

Chapter 4: Little Boy Blue(s)

"Xandra, the Aegean Sea is the most intense war zone. It is by far the most heavily guarded," Thetis reminded her. "What if you do not come back? What about Blinky?" Although Xandra was her best warrior, she was also a dear friend of hers. "I should be with you all on this mission."

"You have children now." Xandra was one of the few people who knew she had given birth to twins. "Everyone, including our children, will be killed or enslaved if we don't figure out what those retched Nereids are up to. Thetis, you are the wisest goddess in the ocean. You are our basilinna. The basileia needs you."

"When will my parents be back, Your Majesty? It's been a whole moon." Thetis was in such deep thought she didn't realize the boy had been tugging her gown.

She knew that the chance of his parents coming back was the same as if they'd be victorious, so she replied, "They will return when our side has won."

"Are we going to win?"

"I hope so."

"They why are you so sad and unhappy?"

"Me? Sad?" The boy couldn't have known where her lair was, so how did he know she was depressed? She smiled and asked, "Why do you say such things?"

"I can feel it." She knew a lie from the truth, and this boy surely wasn't telling a lie.

"Is that so?" She was impressed, but she didn't want to jump to any conclusions. "I can tell you are a very gifted child. I am just feeling a little down today that is all." The boy disappeared as soon as she blinked. She blinked again, and the boy was back with a few small pieces of kelp.

"Close your eyes, Your Majesty. It's a surprise." The boy weaved Thetis a bracelet. "Okay, you can open them now." It was beautiful. She was glad he made it for her wrist and not her ankle.

"Why thank you, young one. You have made my day. How did you make it shimmer this brilliant blue color?"

"That's a secret, Your Majesty."

"Fair enough."

"Do you remember my name?" he laughed.

"Yes. It is Xavier, is it not?" she joked.

He swam around in circles. "Noooo."

"It is Xerxes, yes?"

He continued spinning. "Noooo."

They shared a laugh. Thetis took him under her arm and said, "I am sorry. What is your name, little one?"

"I am Xenon, son of Xandra, Her Majesty's greatest warrior."

"Ah, how could I forget?"

"Look, look! They're back!" The sounds of excited young Oceanids filled the ocean except for her own daughter's." Thetis went to go check on Iris.

"Yes, Meter?"

"I think it is time you take a break from looking in that mirror of yours."

"The mirror already showed me. Why do they come back? It only fills our hearts with pain to watch them die."

"Oceanids always attempt to come back to show their loved ones they used every last bit of strength they had left to come back to them one last time. Now come help me greet our warriors."

"Meter, I said that because I saw them on the ocean floor. I could see the looks of heartbrokenness within everyone's eyes."

"Well then. Let us make haste." As the warriors approached, Thetis saw more dying Oceanids than she expected. The cries of children, relatives, friends, and soulmates echoed throughout the ocean as about 500 warriors performed the Katádysi. Even if you didn't lose anyone, your heart ached. There is no escape from the pain expelled by heartbroken Oceanids. Even the animals and plants mourned.

"We failed," said Xandra. "We weren't able to get their prime weapon, but we found it. In fact, it's not really a weapon. We rescued 35 hostages." She paused. "Thetis… It's a bolt. They seem to worship it. They were just worshiping it. This is deep."

"Oh, Xandra you have not failed." Thetis thought about what she told her. That's all the information she needed, and she knew exactly what it meant.

"I missed you!" Xenon came rushing toward Xandra. "Where's daddy? I made you this."

Xandra admired the pearl bracelet. "This is amazing work. I can only imagine how you got all these beautiful pearls. Ramses fought like a true warrior. He started breathing abnormally and died in my arms. I too am dying, Xenon." He knew better than to interrupt. She hugged him as tightly as she could. In Japanese, she said, "Give these pearls to someone who will love them just as much as I do. I can't take them when I go. You were named Xenon because on your mother's side, it's tradition for the second born child to have a name that starts with X. Twins count as 1. There's a Southern Oceanid saying that if someone doesn't like your mom's pearls, they're your soulmate." She opened her hand. "Give this to your soulmate as a ceremony gift. It's a family tradition on your father's side to give jade to your soulmate. It's for good fortune. Xenon, I always knew you were special. Remember to keep your head up and stay humble. You are so strong. We will meet again one day. I love you. Goodbye."

Xenon's heart sank. "I-I love you too." Xandra removed her armor and passed it down to Xenon. Then, like all the other warriors, she swam up to the surface and back down at her top speed. Xenon knew not to move even just a little because it was tradition to dive as close to your loved ones as possible. He knew Xandra would dive facing him, and he knew she would make the closest dive, only inches away from him. After everyone left, he just stayed there, by himself, in shock.

"Xenon." Thetis laid her hand on his shoulder. There was nothing to say.

"I want to become a warrior just like Xandra. I want to protect your daughter. She'll need a protector."

Thetis wrapped her arms around him. She could tell he was trying not to weep. "I am so sorry, Xenon. It's okay to weep. Warriors can weep." She knew which daughter he was referring to, but regardless, she said, "I'm sure you'd make the finest warrior, but Iris doesn't need any protecting. She has her own guards just like you do."

"I meant your other daughter."

"My other daughter? Who told you of such nonsense?"

"I don't remember seeing her, but Iris told me about her when she was born. She was sad because she knew she was being separated from her sister." Xenon could sense her worry. "I won't tell anyone. I haven't even told Iris, and she can't see the past."

"I know. I trust you, Blinky. Your training begins the next moon. Get some rest. You'll need it." Xenon thanked her. Then he started to swim away. "Where are you going? Your home is with us."

"Iris! Iris! Iris!" He swam like a little minnow into her lair. "I'm staying with you permanently now!" Thetis swam to her secret lair. She always wanted to take care of Xenon full-time, but she didn't want it to happen like this.

"I know, Blue. If you don't behave, your gills will be sleeping with the urchins. Got it?" *Way to talk to someone who just lost two parents.*

"Relax, Your Highness. I'll be a good boy," he rolled his eyes.

"You better be." Then she said, "We'll get through this, Little Brother. I know I'm not the touchy-feely type, but I will always be here for you. I'm so sorry this happened. I just want you to know that you aren't alone. If you want to talk, I'm here."

They cried, talked, cried, and talked some more. Then Xenon said, "You like pearls, right?"

"I looove pearls."

"Here. My mom told me the person who doesn't like these pearls is my soulmate. Well… She said it was a saying."

"How could anyone in their right mind not obsess over these pearls?" she smiled. "Thank you. I'll never take them off."

"Can you tell me who my soulmate is?"

"That was random. Sure." *How was that random?* Iris looked into her mirror. "That's odd. I don't see anyone. Maybe they aren't born or conceived yet. Or maybe the mirror is refusing to show me." She could tell how disappointed he was and did her best to lighten the mood. "Cheer up, Blue. We both have yet to find our soulmates. Honestly, I'm in no rush."

He sensed something. "You've seen yours. I want to see them."

"I haven't seen all of them. I have only seen their hair. I don't understand why I can't see them."

"Why are you so nervous? Tell me what you know."

"They definitely aren't an Oceanid. Not with that hair color. I think they're a Naiad, but what if they're a human." He freaked out. "Stop it. I haven't told Meter. I don't want her to know."

"Okay, okay. How come you aren't coming to training with me?"

"Me? You know I have to prepare to be basilissa one day. I have my own separate classes."

Xenon was more than excited to start his first day of training. "Not so fast. Come back here," Thetis said.

"I don't want to be late on my first day."

"There is no way you could be late." He looked up at her. He didn't understand. "I am the one who gives Leios the names of his new students, and you're with me."

"When do we leave?"

"As soon as you finish eating." She prepared some kelp strips because she knew Xenon wouldn't be able to resist them like all Haliai teknon. For some reason they were all obsessed with, dare I say addicted to, kelp.

"This. Is. The. Best. Meal. Ever," he said as he stuffed his mouth.

"You say that every meal."

"The next one always seems better than the last."

"Good morning," Iris said. She had just gotten up.

"You're up early," said Thetis who prepared a variety of raw fish for her. Iris hated everything about kelp. She was glad she couldn't smell it.

"I wanted to wish my best friend luck on his first day of training. Good luck, Blue." After she finished eating she went back into her lair to look at that mirror of hers. *There she go being nosy.*

"Alright. Are you ready?"

"Yes." He remembered something. "Uh, in just a minute." He jetted through the water to get Xandra's armor. He put it on, but it was much too big for him.

"Oh, Xenon. Her armor will fit you once you're done growing. For now, you don't need to wear it. We'll save it for when you're sworn in as a warrior. I'm impressed that you can even carry it for that long."

"When will I be sworn in?"

Thetis laughed. "You have a long way to go."

"What? But I'm ready now." She chased him throughout the kelp forest. When she caught him, she tickled him.

"Wow, you're pretty fast for a Haliai." *Petty. Just petty.*

"You still have a lot to learn. And besides, right now you are just a seal pup."

Xenon stayed close by Thetis's side as they swam through the open ocean to the training area. He asked her, "Do you ever feel like you can feel what the animals and plants feel? Like... Communicate with them how I'm talking to you right now."

"I don't, but I believe that you do."

"Why? Why do you always believe me?"

"I'll tell you one day."

"Today?"

"Some other day when you are more mature," she smiled. "You know that you can speak Tigrigna, Nihongo, or another language if you like, right? Iris and I are polyglots. Speak however you feel comfortable."

"Okay!" He became completely sidetracked by the high concentration of people. "Whoa! So, this is where all the action happens?" He hid behind Thetis.

"Are you scared?" she smiled.

Xenon nodded. Then he got a boost of confidence. "BUT I'm brave!" Then he hid back behind Thetis.

"Yes, you are. Come on. We are going this way," Thetis smiled. She thought it was cute how Xenon thought he could hide things from her. "You can't bring that nudibranch with you."

"Aw, come on. They're nice. And they're a pretty purple color! So kawaii!!!"

"Tell it to swim on home. It'll get smashed." *By who? She is lowkey a savage...* Thetis was not fond of those creatures at all.

"Okay but look. You've offended them."

"I mean they. Once we get there you must line up next to the teknon on your left. Remember what I told you. If you get confused between left and right, the left hand is the one that makes an 'L' when your palm is facing down."

"Hello, Your Highness. How are you?" an Oceanid passing by greeted them. "And you, Your Majesty?" He bent down to kiss her hand. That made her think about how much she missed her soulmate.

"I see the training area! I see it!"

"Are you ready?" Xenon nodded enthusiastically. "Go on."

"Ahhh, there she is. Our beautiful basilinna."

"Hello, Leios." She marveled over the great number of young Oceanids who wanted to become warriors. She was expecting thousands, and that's how many there were. "Unfortunately, this is the most we've ever had."

"Silence!" Everyone stopped talking immediately. "You all are not warriors. Yet. Soon you will be. First, you must learn. You will respect Leios and do as he says. You will behave. When I call the name of your parent, swim forward and state the name you would like to be called. This name will be different than your true name. Your true name will be used in this area and in the presence of other warriors only once you have become a warrior." She worked her way down the rows. She was almost done when she realized she never told Xenon he'd have to choose a new nickname. She looked over to him. He was not paying attention. Instead, he was waving at every fish that swam by. She hoped he'd be ready. "Xandra." It pained her to say her name.

"Blue." He sounded so certain. "Blue, son of Xandra." Thetis couldn't believe he picked that instead of something more noble. He could have picked Zen or something. She was thankful that he wasn't the one who picked Heracles. That was so cliché. "I will return occasionally to check in on your progress." Instead of swimming back to her lair, she swam to her secret cave.

"Alright. Let us begin," said Leios. "Here you will learn everything you need to know to become a scholar as well as a warrior. Once you graduate from here, you must choose the way in which you will serve the basileia." Of course, Xenon already knew what he wanted to do. He wouldn't dare say anything any time soon, because he vowed to keep Thetis's secret. "There are many of you, more than ever, so I will split each group into two." They were divided into the following main groups: feminine, masculine, neither, or both. This was only necessary because a high concentration of feminine and masculine energy mixed together attracts Nereids and sharks. They assume their prey is at their least focused and aggressive when they are caught in attraction. Any attraction that goes on within each group is fine because Nereids and sharks can't detect it. The choice of which group one goes to is made by the individual. If there are uneven numbers, a few people will be moved around. Leios secretly labeled each student who wasn't average as weak or strong. The groups were almost evenly numbered, but there turned out to be an extra person in the masculine group and one missing from the feminine group. He had to find someone that would be able to keep up with the feminine group. He swam far out and charged towards one of the larger Oceanids who jetted out of the way. Leios did the same thing to Xenon, and he didn't move an inch. In fact, he kept eye contact with him the whole time. Everyone just stared. Leios smiled. "Blue, you will go with the feminine group."

Xenon was terrified, but he refused to show it and swam over. "Hello, Blue." Xenon had chills when one of the tallest Oceanids in the feminine group spoke. "I'm Rei— Well, I'm just Ray now. Ray like sun ray. Welcome to the group."

"H-Hi. It's nice to meet you." Reign was so relieved that no one was filling her ears with comments about how beautiful her eyes are. Back where she's from, she's the only one with hazel eyes.

"Every warrior has a natural preference for fighting style and weaponry. Soon you will discover yours," Leios informed them. "As you can see, we have a variety of stations set up. Each group will visit each station, and you will be ranked by each master. All results are private. The stations are grouped by continent. Each day we will focus on a different country. Today we will begin in South America and make our way east." Xenon was so disappointed when he heard that. It would be days before they got to Japan. "Before that, we will go over a few basics." With a loss of interest, he started to zone out.

"It's time for our shift, Xenon. We'll be back in a few tides. If you need anything just ask Thetis." Xenon reviewed his master plan in his head. He was going to make a trip to Japan to get some of his favorite seaweed. He knew about the villages who grew it, and he knew a delphys who would be more than willing to give him a ride two-thirds of the way.

"I'm Xenon. What's your name?" he asked a seemingly friendly delphys who shook their head no. "You don't want to tell me. That's fine but would you mind giving me a ride to—" They cut him off and swam around in excitement. Xenon loved how delphys always knew what you were thinking. "Thank you." Just as he expected, the delphys took him two-thirds of the way. Then they pointed him in the right direction and swam back home. He had no idea where he was, but he kept swimming. Eventually, Xenon could smell the wonderful scent of kelp. He jetted to the farm. It was nighttime, so Xenon was practically invisible. After he ate as much seaweed as he could, he held onto the rope the strands were tied to and fell asleep.

He woke up to the sound of an adult yelling, "An animal has eaten our crops!" in Japanese.

A young boy noticed Xenon's hand, "Who's out there this early?" His mother looked to where he was pointing, but Xenon had already moved his hand. He explored the Japanese waters until the afternoon. He didn't see anyone at the farm, so he went back for some more. The same little boy who almost busted him earlier caught Xenon untying a strand of kelp. He called for his family to come outside, and they waited for Xenon to surface. He wanted to take some back home, but he had only stuffed one piece in his cloth so far. He surfaced one last time to get one more piece, and they saw him. They dove in after him, but Xenon was much too quick for them and ended up getting away. They didn't realize that jumping off the dock caused the little boy to lose his balance and fall into the water. Luckily, Xenon did. He stopped swimming when he heard the boy's heart rate beating faster than normal. He was drowning. Xenon raced back.

"Kainalu?" cried his mother. She knew something was wrong. Then she saw the cherry blossom she gave him floating in the water. "Kainalu!!!" She jumped in and searched for her son. Xenon swam up and sat Kainalu on the edge of the dock. "Thank you. Thank you!" The men came back and grabbed Xenon, but Kainalu's mother stopped them. "He might be a thief, but he saved my son from drowning. He gave much more than he took and took far less than what humans and Man take from the sea."

"I have never seen anyone as dark as you. Don't leave. I'm Kainalu. Thank you for saving me." He was curious to get to know the person that saved him.

"No problem. I'm glad you're okay. I'm Xenon."

"Mother, he's mute."

"Maybe he speaks English," she said. "If you help us with our crops, we will give you some in return."

He was speaking Japanese, so he didn't understand why they couldn't hear him. He didn't know English, but he was able to sense what was being said. He nodded. Xenon and Kainalu became good friends, and Xenon came back as often as he could. He learned how speaking on the surface was different than speaking underwater. Sound traveled differently. One day, he told them he wouldn't be able to come back as often because he would be training to become a warrior. They understood and told him they were sure he would bring his family honor.

"Blue," Leios called his name for the third time. He snapped out of it. "I asked you how you would feel if you were cornered by three sharks."

"I-I would feel scared." Some of the students laughed.

"And what would you do?"

"I would ask them to move." Now everyone was laughing.

Someone yelled out, "You can't talk to fish!"

Leios called on them since they wanted to talk. "What would you do?"

"I'd kill all three of them."

"Okay…" That was definitely not the Haliai way. "Ray, what would you do?"

"I would punch the biggest one in the snout and then swim away."

"Good answer. Does anyone know why Ray would punch the shark in their snout?" Xenon was the first and only one to raise his hand. "Blue."

"Punching the snout stuns the shark."

"Correct. Does anyone know why Ray would stun the biggest shark?" Xenon raised his hand again. "Anyone else? Alright. Go ahead, Blue."

"The biggest shark is always in command. If the biggest shark is stunned, the others won't move."

"Well said. Now go to your assigned stations."

Reign knew Xenon didn't know what station he was supposed to go to. "Don't worry. I know what to do. Just follow me."

Chapter 5: Cliff Jumper

"Come on, Chance!" Amethyst knew he was stalling.

He jumped. "Just one last piece of chicken. Where are we going?"

"To find out what Dad is hiding from us."

"He's probably not hiding a body. I was just kidding. We both know he isn't a killer."

"Fine. Maybe there isn't a body, but there is definitely something he's keeping from us. Now come on! We have to be as quiet as possible." He couldn't argue with that. He followed her down the stairs, but not without complaining the whole time. "Shut up. He'll hear us."

"What exactly is your plan?"

"Shhh. We don't need one. Chill. We're just going to listen at the door."

"Hello, Jeremias. Guess who it is?"

"The only person who calls me Jeremias is your mother. Is she there?"

"Maybe. What do you want, Germie?"

"Can I speak to your mother?"

"What happened to your face?"

"Oh, that's just barbeque sauce. Where is she?"

"You should wipe that off. Disgusting."

"Uhhh. Just let me talk to your mother."

"Why? Are you going to snitch?"

"You are the bossiest 16-year-old I know. Would you just do it? Hello? Finally."

"What's wrong, Jeremy?"

"I think that child of yours has been secretly visiting our beach."

"Really? Wait a moment. It wasn't him. He's been feeling really down. You know what tomorrow is."

"Right. Well, never mind. It must have been my assistant AKA mini Xandra."

"Tell Amethyst I love her with all my heart."

"What about me? And where did that child of yours learn the word 'snitch'?"

She laughed. "It is time you tell her. Try to stick to how we rehearsed it. Remember to take deep breaths. You are a wonderful dad. You can do this."

"Stop breathing so hard. We're supposed to be in ninja mode."

"You know I can't. This is my ninja mode."

"Asthmatic ass ninja."

"What do you hear, ugly? I just hear mumbling."

"Good to know I have a deaf sibling. Jeremy talks hella loud. He must be on the phone. I'm not entirely sure what he's speaking. It definitely isn't English. I think it was Greek. That shit sounded ancient though."

"I didn't know he's bilingual."

"The only word I caught was snitch and ah-meh-tis or something like that."
I think he hung up. It's time to gas up outta here."

"He was probably just saying your name. Let's search it up just in case.
Look! You came up," he laughed. Google suggested they meant amethyst,
and there were a lot of pictures of the crystal. "I mean I guess we could be
spelling it wrong. Or maybe we don't have the right alphabet."

"I know it's my name, but he wasn't the one who said it. I heard a voice.
It was a womxn's voice."

"So, his girlfriend is Greek too?"

"Well, I guess, but I recognize her voice, Chance. I know that voice. The
language feels familiar too. Maybe Dad taught me some when I was little.
Why didn't he keep teaching me? Oh yeah… I also heard meh-tair. I think
it's spelled m-e-t-e-r. Don't look it up. I think that's Attic Greek. I think I
know what that means, and I don't want to know if I'm right, right now.
I'll tell you later."

"Huuuuum. Can today get any more unusual? Why do you still have this
ugly ass shirt witcho ugly ass?"

"You're probably just mad because your skinny ass can actually fit it."

"Nooooo…"

"Oh yeah? Put it on." He did. "It's a little smug," she laughed. "I can't
believe you actually got it on." They heard footsteps.

"I don't want Jeremy to see me. He'll get ideas. I'm already a suspect."

"For trying on my top? Chill. You worry too much."

Jeremy knocked on the door. "Shit."

"Come in," said Amethyst. Chance flicked her off.

He caught Chance with Amethyst's shirt halfway off. *Awwwwwkward.*
"Almost ready? It's time to celebrate!!!"

"Where are we going? Do I have to wear a dress?"

"It's a surprise and no. You never have to wear a dress. Plus, I'd tell you if you had to get all fancy."

Amethyst loved car rides. She had the aux cord the whole ride there because Jeremy was always so focused on driving. Even though Chance was a DJ, he preferred to sleep in the back seat. She missed when Chance used to drive her around because although she had a volume limit, he'd let her play whatever she wanted. As they zipped past the other cars, the lights on the Golden Gate Bridge reminded her of stars. She wondered how many stars were on the bridge. That reminded her of how funny it was that humans tried to count the number of stars in the universe. She wondered where one gained the tendency to define things that couldn't be defined. Surely, it wasn't because of human curiosity. It was something else.

"Eeeeeep!!! Hana Japan!!! I love this place!!!" she hugged Jeremy. Amethyst ordered what she always ordered. She always got the chicken and rice plate. And of course, she asked for extra ginger sauce. The other people at the table thought it was adorable how she couldn't stop giggling as the chefs put on their cooking show. It was pretty awesome how they cooked your food right in front of you.

As soon as they got home, Jeremy handed her a gift bag. "Ahhhh! These are real crystals. OMG. It's a whole collection!!! The amethyst is especially beautiful! Dad! You got me gold jewelry too!!! Thank you! I love it!"

"And this is from me," Chance said softly.

"Car keys?!?!? No. Way." He led her to his garage and revealed her brand-new car to her. It was dark out and she almost tripped on the curb. Not because she couldn't see. She was just clumsy. Then the garage lights came on. "Eeeeeep!!! Chance! OMG! A Lamborghini! It's my favorite shade of purple! And look at the sparkles!!! How???"

"I had it customized," he said casually.

"Oh, Chance!!! You didn't have to spend that much money on me."

"I know but you're my little sister, and you're the kind of person who would be just as happy with a $20 gift card. Besides, I have all this money and only two people to spend it on."

"Awww, Choo Choo..." Amethyst hugged him. "You're the sweetest. You're the best big brother in the universe." *If you're wondering... No. She did not post anything on social media nor did she tell anyone.*

After that, they sang happy birthday and ate cake. They watched movies all the way past midnight even though they had school tomorrow. Amethyst was enjoying her night, but she couldn't stop thinking about how when she used to have birthday parties there was no one there except for Chance. She never really understood why her peers never came even though they went to other parties. Was it because they weren't really her friends? Was it because there wasn't any alcohol or drugs? Or maybe it was because she's Black... How was it that plenty of people liked her, but she didn't have any friends? She looked at Chance and smiled. She was okay with her one friend. That was enough for her. He was her right-hand man. *People always think Amethyst smiles for no reason, but that's not true. She's just always thinking. How do I know? You'll find out eventually. I know a pretty good source.* So many thoughts were going through her mind. She thought about why birthday cake tasted so much better than regular cake. She thought about who else was celebrating their birthday or not celebrating it for whatever reason. She wished she could share her cake with those people. Then she thought about the mysterious womxn who gave birth to her. "Dad. Can you—"

She didn't realize Jeremy was in deep thought. "It's time we have that talk."

"What talk?" she asked.

"Ummm. I gotta pee." Chance tried to get away. "I'll give you two some privacy."

"You too, Chance. It isn't that talk. We've already had that talk. Right?"

"Y-Yeah. We totally did." *Liiiiies.*

"What talk, Dad?"

"About your mother."

"You already told me she left me." She tested him to see how honest he was going to be.

"No. I told you she left you with me."

"Okay. I'm listening."

"Your mother and I met a long, long time ago. We crossed paths and she didn't even look at me. I turned around to follow her, but I lost her. Then she came from behind me and put me in a chokehold because she thought I was following her. Well, I was, but I wasn't going to hurt her. I was trying to catch up to her and say hello. Once she realized I wasn't a criminal, she let go of me and we started talking. She had a son from an unhealthy relationship."

"Wait. I have another brother? Is he hot?" Chance gave her a WTF look.

"Um... Sure, Ame. I guess he would have been considered hot. Anyways, we fell in love." Jeremy got a little carried away. "She told me she wasn't who I thought she was, but I didn't care. When we were free from our partners, we took it slow. She warned me that a relationship with her would be complicated, but I was willing to stay right by her side no matter what. Then she told me to tell me more about myself. I didn't really know what to say so I started off by saying: I am Jeremias, son of Jerica."

"Why did you say it like that? Not smooth, not smooth at all. You just lost like 20 cool points," said Chance. *LOL how many do you have?*

"What kind of ancient alien culture are you from?" Amethyst asked.

"I'm getting to that. Okay so after that—"

"I came along!"

"No. Ame, I'm not your real dad." That hit her hard. She started to get upset. Chance's jaw literally dropped. Of course, they knew Jeremy wasn't Amethyst's biological father. Chance knew how Jeremy phrased what he was trying to say was not going to sit well with Amethyst. "I know I should have told you that part sooner, but I didn't know how to tell you."

"Not only do I not know who my mother is, I don't know who you are either. My whole entire life is a lie." She was crying now. It started storming outside. The rain poured down more than it had all season. The wind and the waves were so rough, even the birds and the fish took cover. "I don't even know who I am." Then lightning struck, followed by the loudest thunderclap they had ever heard.

"Amethyst. Where are you going?" Jeremy blocked the door. "You can't go out there."

"Let. Me. Go. Leave me alone." For some reason, he moved. That's when Jeremy knew she had inherited another trait from one of her mother's aunts.

"You let her go! Ame! Wait! Come back!" Chance ran after her as fast as he could, but she was always much faster than him despite her being only 5 feet tall. Unlike Jeremy, he knew exactly where she was going. By the time Amethyst got too the cliff, he was desperately breathing into his asthma pump. She was fearlessly sitting on the edge singing the same hypnotic lullaby she always sang when she was daydreaming or upset. "Please get down from there. Stop being so dramatic."

"Dramatic? You know what? I'll show you dramatic." With her back to the ocean, Amethyst let herself fall off the cliff.

"Amethyst!" Chance's heart was beating out of his chest. He was afraid of heights, but he peered over the edge of the cliff to see if she landed on the rocks or in the water. He couldn't find her. He just laid there and cried his heart out. *What a concussion. I mean conclusion. Oops.*

Chapter 6: Royal Catch

"How was your first day of training?" asked Thetis.

"It was the worst. I almost got killed twice."

"Do not be so hard on yourself. Leios told me you did well once you got hold of a sword."

"Really? I don't like those swords."

"What kind of swords do you like?"

"Katana! I've never really held one, but I really like those."

"I presume you saw one in the village you used to travel to every week." *HA. He thought he was slick...*

Xenon froze. "H-Huh how'd you know?"

"You know I am the wisest Oceanid there is."

"They're really nice people and—"

Thetis cut him off. "It's alright. If you were in any sort of trouble, you would have received a consequence long ago."

"How come you never told on me?" He knew that if Xandra found out, she would have hired him a babysitter.

"Because I understand. Also, Aristide is a good friend of mine. He said you were very polite."

"Is Aristide the delphys? So that's his name?"

She smiled. "Yes, and yes."

"He didn't want to tell me his name." Xenon was still hurt.

"He is mute. He didn't want you to think he was any less of a delphys."

"Oooooh. Wait. So then how do you know his name?"

"My sister, Amphitrite, sent him to me. She knows both of his names. Aristide would have only told you the one you know how to pronounce. Amphitrite speaks Delphy, a language of no words.

"Huuuuuh. I want to be gifted too. How do you get gifted? Can Iris speak Delphy? Wait. I know! Hopefully my soulmate is gifted! That way they can translate, and I won't have to sting Iris about it! Can she speak Delphy?" Thetis giggled. He was too adorable.

"Iris! Come here!" Xenon yelled.

"What? Why are you so loud? Damn! I'm trying to sleep. I'm not going over there. You're peeing."

"I'm done now. Look, it's glowing."

"What's glowing?"

"Not that... Just come look."

"Huuuh." Iris decided to take a peek. "What did you drink? A f****** glow stick?"

"No. Stop laughing. This is serious. What's wrong with me? Is something going to happen to me? STOP! Iris, I'm scared!" he cried. "There's weird alien blue stuff coming out of my penis and you're laughing! I called you for support."

"Oh, my goddess. You're so f****** dramatic. How would I know?"

"Ask your mirror. Duh," he rolled his eyes.

"Just ask the wisest Oceanid in the morning," Iris mocked her mother. "Stop playing in it. That's weird. You're not 7 anymore, Blue. You are 16 and your birthday's coming up. You're about to f****** graduate. Take your blue ass back to sleep before I feed you to the hydra's last-born child."

"Good morning," Iris and Xenon said at the same time. He planted a kiss on Thetis's cheek and wrapped his arms around her.

"Can I ask you something?"

"Of course."

"Why does my urine glow in the dark now?"

Thetis had heard their conversation last night, so she was prepared to answer him. "Here." She handed them both some pre-caught skinned fish. "You might want to sit down for this." They both waited eagerly. "You are bioluminescent. All your DNA cells can potentially glow. As your body continues to develop, more and more of your cells will gain the same potential. During this time your body will go through a variety of changes you won't be able to prevent. Don't worry because after puberty, you'll be fine. Also, although you won't be able to prevent yourself from glowing or having a slight tint, it is possible for you to learn how to change the intensity of the luminosity."

"Cool! How?"

"It's something that rarely happens. For others, it eventually goes away. I believe your bioluminescence is permanent. I would have told you sooner, but I wasn't sure if you had that ability yet. There's more, but we'll save that for another time. Right now, just focus on your training."

"Wait. Urine doesn't have DNA in it," said Xenon. Iris still didn't understand why his urine glowed in the dark.

Thetis laughed. "You just need a significant other, that's all." Xenon had no idea what that meant. Iris did. "So, what do you want to do for your birthday? It's the same day as the ceremony. The delphys choose the date, not me. That doesn't mean we can't have two celebrations though."

"Um, yeah. That sounds fun. I'll see you two when I get back." He was never really happy. Especially during the first couple days of December.

"Meter, you know what he wants," Iris reminded her. "Why don't you let him go to the surface? He'll be a warrior by then."

"Can you see Xenon on the surface in your mirror?" Iris said no. "Exactly. Who knows what your father will do once he finds out. That's why we must stick to the plan."

"My father? You never talk about him and what plan?"

"At this rate, everything will be made clear soon. You and your brother are ready, but I need to make sure I'm ready."

They didn't realize it, but Xenon heard every word. He really hoped Thetis would come around. He went to his secret place on the beach sometimes, but that wasn't enough. He really wanted to see his old friend. On his way to training, he swam into a family friend that graduated 2 years ago because of her age and skill. If you ask Xenon, it's only because of her age. "Hey, Ray. I mean Reign."

"How are you, Xenon? I mean Blue," she giggled.

"Ha. Ha. Very funny. I'm graduating in a few days you know." He did his best to keep himself together.

"I know. You are aware that there must be a warrior within your family present, right?"

"Yep." He tried to hide how down he was feeling. Reign's bubbliness always made him crack a smile, but there was nothing that could make him smile on the inside.

"Even though Iris and Thetis will be there, neither of them can fill that role because they're also royalty. I told Thetis I wouldn't mind doing it. If you want me to, I will. She told me I have permission if you agree."

"You'd do that for me?" That meant so much to him because Reign was so much like Xandra. Everyone thought so.

"Uhhh yeah... You're like my little cousin," she gleamed.

"Thank you, Reign. I will never forget your act of kindness. Maybe one day I will be able to do you a favor in return."

"Ah, don't mention it. So, what are you going to do for your birthday?"

"Oh, you know. A party or two. I'll tell you what I'm not doing. Going to the surface."

"Why do you want to go to the surface so badly? Wait. You go to the surface all the time, don't you? Does Iris know?"

"Of course Iris knows... She knew since I first started sneaking up. Anyways, I need to go a little farther than that. I only stay within the beach area. I want to see the other people. What do you do up there anyway?"

"I see. I usually just get intel on the humans, but the other day I saw this Man fighting a young human. The human held his ground and defeated him with his hands tied. I know how the police work. The human didn't deserve to be punished, so I got rid of the evidence just in case." Xenon looked at her with a concerned look on his face. "I didn't break the law. I actually followed it. For some reason, the human smelled of Oceanid, Naiad, and something else. Anyways, why do you want to see humans? Humans are terrible!"

"Actually, I want to see a particular someone."

"No way. Are you in love or something? You're such a merboy. Awww... How romantic!" she twirled.

"No, I'm not. It isn't like that. She's just a friend of mine."

Reign studied him carefully. "Alright, I believe you. You know Thetis doesn't want you to go, so don't try anything. I don't even want you to go because there is so much more you need to learn about the humans. I still don't know half of everything that goes on up there."

"I don't want to know half of what goes on up there. I only want to know about one thing that goes on up there."

"Why do you always have to be so damn poetic? Go on, softie. Don't be late for ceremony practice."

"That wasn't even poetic! Anything you think is mushy gushy is poetic to you." They went their separate ways. Xenon couldn't stop thinking about his old friend even when he arrived.

"Blue." Leios tried to get his attention. "Blue." He looked up when he said it a little louder. "You haven't changed. During the ceremony, don't do that glowy thing you do. Try not to draw more attention to yourself."

"I will do my best. I haven't quite learned how to control it yet."

"That's fine I guess. Considering this just started tides ago."

"How do you do that?" asked some young Oceanids who were crushing on Xenon.

"I don't know. Sometimes I feel an electric pulse through my body."

"I have that feeling all the time except I know why."

"And why's that?" Xenon smiled.

"My soulmate." The whole class shared a good laugh and then it was back to ceremony practice. Xenon would be somewhere in the front because it was tradition to line up from shortest to tallest. The tallest person gets sworn in first, so Xenon would be one of the last ones. At least the ceremony was only about an hour long. Each student would swim forward after they are called by their true name. After Thetis swore them in, Leios would announce their credentials and hand them their certificates. Then, one of their older family members would give them their armor and weapons.

Thetis whispered one, two, three. After three, she and Iris said, "Happy Birthday, Xenon!" He didn't really move because he was so stunned.

"Wow, you two really got me. My heart is beating like crazy right now. Thank you."

"So how does it feel to be a 17-year-old warrior?" asked Iris.

"I'm not a warrior yet," he smiled. "The ceremony isn't until Selene's light shines on the ocean. Right now, the only light shining is Helios's," he laughed.

"I know, I know. You know that you will forever and always be Blue to me, right?"

"I know, I know," he mocked her. *I'm probably going to say this again but, he's really good at impersonating people. Insanely good.*

"Look what we have. You will get the rest of your gifts later," said Iris.

"No way. Are those surface candy?" He couldn't believe it.

"Yes, these are pieces of candy." Thetis giggled at his attempt to blend an unusual English word with ancient Greek.

"I love Watermelon Sour Patches!!! What are these called?"

"Skittles."

"Why did humans name a candy after schizophrenia?" he wondered.

"Even I don't know. They sound the same, but they are spelled differently. I don't think it was intentional."

"Oh, so they're kind of like homophones."

"Sure." Thetis could tell he had been doing his reading.

"You're such a nerd," Iris told him.

"I have a box of candies that have the word nerd on it, but I don't know what that means."

"A nerd is someone who is smart and/or sort of awkward or unusual."

"Oh, thank you."

"It's not supposed to be a compliment," Iris informed him.

"Wake up, kelp brain!" yelled Iris. "How are you taking a nap?"

Xenon sluggishly responded, "Huuuuuh." Then he remembered what today was. "Oh!" he perked up. "Is it time?"

"You're going to be late."

"Ahhh, what tide is it?!?!?"

"I'm just kidding. Don't worry, the tide is still high. Don't you feel it?"

"No, you know I'm not good at that, Iris. Why would you wake me up? That's mean. Don't be mean to me," he rolled his eyes.

"Huuuh. Relax. Don't start crying. We have to start getting ready. The ceremony is being held closer to Gaia this year. It's a pretty long swim. I was supposed to tell you earlier, but I forgot."

"You're always so organized though... Whatever. Why there?" Iris had been acting unusual lately.

"I don't know. The delphys choose. They have their ways."

"One day, I'm going to ask them how they know things."

"You'd have to ask in their language. Blue, no one can talk to delphys in their language except the Empress AKA Auntie Ame."

"I'll eye talk."

"Like the question, the answer you're looking for can only be said in their language."

"Then I guess I'll have to learn."

"Yeah, sure..." she laughed. "Come on. Meter wants you."

Xenon followed Iris into Thetis's lair where she presented him with Xandra's armor. "Whoa. Honestly, I can't believe I finally made it." He missed her very much, and his facial expressions made Iris and Thetis feel his heartache.

"It is yours to wear now." He swam over and hugged Thetis just as he always did. He gave the best hugs. "Now, go get dressed."

Looking in his mirror, Xenon remembered how this was all he ever wanted. It finally really happened, but something was still missing. He still felt incomplete. The kind of incompleteness he imagined the moons would feel without the stars. After he finished getting dressed, he swam out of his lair. He saw a platinum chariot led by delphys dressed in gold jewelry. Delphys are allergic to metals that aren't gold. Thetis and Iris swam out covered in the same platinum his armor was made of. Everyone else is supposed to wear silver. He could tell they were going to be the most decorated family at the ceremony, as usual. "You both look great!" he said. "But you know that."

"Why thank you," said Thetis.

"That armor looks good on you, Little Brother."

"It fits perfectly. Take good care of it." Thetis examined him. It seemed as if Xandra's armor was almost too small for him. She wondered if he would grow out of it.

"I will," he smiled.

"Shall we?" she signaled for Iris to get into the chariot.

Thetis waited for Xenon to get in, but he said, "After you."

Iris rolled her eyes and said, "Oh, no. You aren't turning into one of those guys, are you?" she smiled. She was just messing with him.

"Ewww. Do you really think that lowly of me?" he laughed. "I was being polite. Trust me, I know her strength. I am very well aware of the power of the feminine energy. That's why I'm so polite to those who possess it."

Iris was pleased with his response. They stopped along the way to pick up Reign. "Well aren't you a vision."

Xenon could sense that Thetis didn't care to pay much attention to what she looked like, and he was in complete agreement with her. Their image of her was centered around her skills as a warrior, and how headstrong she was, not her physical appearance. Xenon started to get squirmy. "How come we just can't go around?" Iris, on the other hand, was enjoying waving at everyone.

"Because it is tradition to stay on this path and greet our people," Thetis reminded him. "Now sit up and stop slouching."

"Okay well, how come we can't be in the front?"

"Because the basilinna must always file in last and I am the basilinna."

Xenon was playing with some fish the whole six hours it took them to get to the ceremony. There was so much traffic. "We're here," Iris said.

"Finally!" he shouted. They all got out and went to their proper positions. The ceremony began as soon as Thetis broke the surface. Down below, everyone turned off their lights and lanterns that only had ranges of a few meters. It became pitch black. Well, except for Xenon. *LOL, the struggle. Relatable. That was sarcastic. I was being sarcastic.* "Selene, my dear friend, we are here tonight as Oceanids partaking in a monumental ceremony to swear in our newest warriors. Will you be so kind as to bless your light upon us once again?"

"Why of course. Anything for you, Thetis." Like the goddess she is, Selene gracefully descended into the ocean as a pasty glowing light. Suddenly, the dark ocean around them glowed a gentle blue. All the silver and platinum began to glimmer which accounted for 70 percent of the luminosity. When everything was visible, Selene disappeared. The hundreds of soon to be warriors, their predecessors, and their families in the audience were all gleaming with excitement.

Right by her mother's side, Iris announced, "Now, a moment of silence for all of the warriors that have returned to Chaos." Each family of the deceased warriors released a small, unique sculpture handcrafted from marine clay, allowing it to sink to the ocean floor just as the warriors did. Xenon's sculpture was a replica of Ramses in Xandra's arms. It was a masterpiece. No one in any of the realms could sculpt like he could.

Soon it was his turn to be sworn in. "And now, Xenon, if you accept your role as protector, you may accept this weapon." He didn't like the term protector because he imagined Iris's sister would be just like her and therefore just like Thetis. He didn't think she needed his protection. He preferred the term defender because it implied people working together as a team. Defender would be more accurate because he simply wanted to be her left-hand man. Protectors are individuals assigned to the masculine, the feminine, the masculine and feminine, the neither, the all of the above… Literally anyone who is threatened physically or emotionally and in distress. The term defender is used for warriors who train in groups and go on missions to defend the outskirts of the queendom. Technically, defending the queendom was defending the princess. Xenon wondered why there was no term for being a defender of an individual. *Oh, there's a term for that.*

"Xenon, son of Xandra, I hereby present you with twin katana, the most noble of swords." Reign was so proud of him. He accepted the weapons. Then he swam all the way to the surface and back down at top speed, just inches away from her. Impressed, the audience roared.

After the few Oceanids shorter than Xenon were sworn in, the celebration began. Everyone was talking about how loud the thunderstorm was. He noticed Thetis distance herself and could sense her concernedness. "What's wrong? Why are you so anxious?"

"I know why the delphys chose this place."

"Is this where—"

"Yes." Then Aristide came rushing towards her with another delphys. "Oh, my goddess! Your eyes! You've been blinded. It was a Nereid wasn't it?" *You may be wondering how he was able to get back if he was blinded. Echolocation bish. He doesn't need his eyes to 'see'.*

Aristide nodded. He couldn't eye talk, so he had no choice but to speak to Xenon empathetically. "I will be fine, but her youngest daughter won't be if you don't go now. She's going to fall from the cliff you always hang around. Although she could never drown, the lone Nereid that attacked me will attempt to attack her."

"I have to go. It's your daughter," Xenon's heart was in his throat. Iris swam over as soon as she noticed something was wrong. She had her own theories about what was going on.

"Well, then make haste. And Xenon, teknon, be safe." This was technically his first mission, and everything was happening so quickly. It was storming, and he would have to break the surface. If Zeus did anything to another one of her children, she didn't know what she would do.

"I will." He swam as fast as he could to get to where she was. Once he got there, he didn't see anyone. He heard yelling in the distance and then someone running. That surface person did not sound like they were designed to breathe air or anything at all. There was no Nereid within sight, but regardless, Xenon stayed alert. Then he heard someone singing. A child? How could a surface child know Thetis's lullaby? That's when he realized who the singer actually was. In that same moment, the person with irregular breathing startled her and she slipped. She was going to hit the rocks. Filled with adrenaline, Xenon swam deeper and then leaped out of the water to catch her. He could tell she had been crying, but he wasn't sure if he should ask about that. "Are you okay? You can breathe, right?"

"I'm okay. Thank you. Your skin is kinda blue, that's kinda cool. It's pitch black out here, yet you're glowing. What are you doing out here? Who exactly are you? Tell me who you really are." Xenon descended into the water with her in her arms. "How are you talking underwater? How am I talking? Wait! Oh shit! I'm in the ocean. I-I can't swim." She began to panic, so he rose back up to the surface. That didn't help.

He was getting nervous because of how abnormally fast her heart was beating. "D-Don't worry. I'm a really good swimmer. You don't need to swim." Then he sensed that it was the waves that she was even more afraid of. He understood. He remembered his first time breaking the surface on a night like this. "It isn't as intimidating farther below the surface. I promise."

"Okay. Go fast." He did as she said. "Am I breathing? I shouldn't be able to breathe. Somehow, I'm breathing but not in a human way. How am I breathing?" She looked up at him and said, "So, you are the alien. I knew it all along." She felt safe. Wouldn't you feel safe with a glowy ocean goer who gave you a piece of kelp when you were younger? *Nope. Sorry. That's weird af. At this point, I knew that she is definitely on some other ish. He. Is. A. Stranger. Stranger danger.*

"You don't remember me?" He sounded disappointed. "I guess we're what surface people might call amphibious mammals. Your gills are in your lungs, esophagus, and nose. We are communicating with each other by eye talking, but you can also use your voice. I speak English proficiently. Don't try that right now though. You have to learn how to breathe while creating a constant water jet. Basically, exhale while you talk."

"Aren't you supposed to take me back to the surface?"

"I can't. You aren't safe there anymore. Wait. You did it! I'm impressed. I guess I have underestimated you. Just one thing. You don't have to talk so loudly. Sound travels differently down here."

"Why not?"

A monstrous lightning storm continued to rage across the ocean. "That's why. You'll be safer underwater with us."

"I can't swim though. Like, I can't swim at all. And it's dark! I'm glad you're glowy. You're like a glow in the dark chocolate bar. Who's us?"

"I'll carry you on my back, and you'll find out soon. It's not for me to explain. We're still too close to the surface. We have to go deeper. Hurry before we get bolted."

"Uh. I guess I don't really have a choice, do I? Alright." She climbed onto his back.

"Do you trust me?"

"Hell no I don't f****** trust you, but I remember you."

Xenon was hurt, but he smiled because the gem didn't shine too far from Gemini. *That means the clownfish didn't swim too far from the anemone. Or... The apple didn't fall too far from the tree.* "Hold on tight, Your Highness."

"What did you just—" Amethyst couldn't finish her sentence because he dove down super duper fast. She could tell he was anxious and eager.

It wasn't so bad underwater. She was enjoying it, and she was curious about this 'us'. Then she thought she saw a shark. "That's not a shark. That's a Nereid. It will attack us. I have to annihilate it. There is no way around." She didn't know what to say, but she held on tight. She was having way too much fun. He swam above the Nereid undetected and pulled out one of his katana. He was so quick she didn't even realize he had cut their head off. He slid his katana back into its saya. Xenon is a bit of a perfectionist, but his nerves were acting up. There was so much pressure on his first mission. "I apologize. Excuse me."

"What did you do?"

"My saya are right between your legs. It was inappropriate of me to insert my katana without asking for your permission."

"Oh. You're excused then," she giggled. She wondered how this alien was so polite and so damn fine at the same damn time. If only surface guys understood that it wasn't appropriate to insert anything without proper conscious permission. "There's another one. This one's definitely a shark."

"There's more than one. Don't say anything and don't move." The sharks circled around them. He planned to stun the largest one, but then he realized these sharks were different. These were karcharies. One Nereid? Fine. Two? Fine. But this? Xenon was officially terrified.

"Heeeeeeelllooooo. How are you?"

"Oh, I'm okay. Just surrounded by sharks!" she thought to herself. "I don't even eat shark, so why the hell y'all tryna eat me? Damn. Y'all bet not be tryna eat me."

"So, it is heeeeer." They all stopped swimming. She couldn't believe it. White sharks are obligate ram ventilators. They die if they stop swimming. They were also usually alone. She wanted to know more about these sharks. "She knows Thalassa's language."

"Will they let us pass?" she wondered.

"Yes, of course, child." The karcharies cleared a path for them.

"Oh, my goddess. You are truly amazing."

"What did I do?"

"You speak Thalassa's language."

"I only speak English and a little bit of Spanish. I thought you eye talked with them or something."

"Nope, that was all you."

"So, then how'd you know they were talking to me? I had no idea they were responding to my thoughts."

"I sensed it."

"Ummm… You did what? You got other powers? Do tell."

"I'll explain later."

"Whatchu mean you'll explain later? I want to know now. Tell me right now."

"I'm an empath. We're almost there," he smiled. He finally found someone that matched his level of sass.

"Where is there?"

"The basileia."

"Can you sense that I'm confused?"

"Sort of but not really. Usually, I can. I could earlier. I don't know what happened," he smiled. He loved outspoken people. They aren't afraid to showcase their thoughts.

"So, can you do any tricks?" *Tricks? She's hella funny. Get's me every time.*

"Tricks?" he laughed. "I can't do anything cool with all these clothes on."

"Huuum. I see you. You one of them. You're naughty. You better watch it before you get in trouble," she laughed. "I'm bored. The sharks are gone, and I'm getting sleepy. I usually play music when we go on trips." Xenon didn't say anything. "So, you aren't going to even talk to me?"

"Iris prefers silence, and you said you were sleepy."

"Who is Iris? Whatever. The reason I'm getting sleepy is because I'm bored. I don't want to be sleepy. I want to be entertained. By the way, you didn't even ask me my name. That's rude."

"Really?!?!?" He couldn't believe it. "Okay so during the last tide, I saw Mayli and his girlfriend at the sea shelter. They are totally soulmates. They were adopting a seal pup, but Mayli's ex told me that he didn't like seals. I have the screenshots. He was cuddling with the pup and everything. I knew his friends pressured him into being with his ex. He was trying to get out of that relationship for so long. Oh and I already know your name. It's Amethyst. Happy Belated Birthday!!!"

Screenshots? She wondered what kind of technology his people had. We're they going to Atlantis or something? Then she remembered Atlantis was supposedly off the western coast of Africa. The Atlantic. They were in the Pacific. Duh. "Awww, thanks. I would ask you how you know that, but I'm going to assume it has something to do with the thing that isn't for you to explain. I'm not tryna to jump to any conclusions, but I think I have an idea. Anyways, his friends pressured him? No way. They aren't his friends then. They're probably jealous because they want his soulmate. That's probably why they did that."

"Right! That's what I was trying to tell his real friends, but they still weren't sure."

"How? You're an empath."

"Exactly!!! You get me!"

"Look! They're back!" Iris let everyone know.

"Attention everyone. There is much that needs to be explained, but for now I present to you my youngest daughter, Amethyst." The Oceanids cheered.

"That's my mom? Damn! What the heck?"

"Our mom," he corrected her. She didn't quite understand. They couldn't be related. That would be disgusting.

"Hello, daughter. You probably do not remember me, but I am Thetis, the basilinna of the basileia. Xenon is the basi. You and your sister, Iris, are the basilissa. Welcome. Happy Belated Birthday. I have so much to tell you. I am so glad you are safe. All these years… I am so sorry. Can I hug you?"

"Sure. I love hugs, and you look extra snuggly." Thetis hadn't felt that much joy in a long time. She had fallen into the deepest depression when she sent her to the surface.

"Whoa. You are really tall. What are you? Like 7ft? How come you never came to see me, and what kind of aliens are you? Am I being abducted? Cool…"

"You are not being abducted, and we are not aliens. We are Oceanids and we come from below. I will tell you what you would like to know back at our lair. I am sure you've probably been through a lot already." Thetis didn't want to overwhelm her. Amethyst loved how Oceanids used sign language while they spoke.

"So, you're my sister?" Iris studied her. She ran a full report. Iris wasn't the touchy-feely type, but she was definitely the grabby-grabby type. She kept picking at her clothes and sniffing her hair. Amethyst couldn't stop laughing because she was ticklish, and Iris had very strong hands.

"Apparently. Huh! Are we twins?" Thetis nodded. "Happy Belated Birthday!"

Iris ignored her comment. She hated her birthday. "Wow. You look just like me, but then you don't. Your skin tone is warmer than mine because of your exposure to the sun. You're sun-kissed. You are so pretty."

"So are you." Amethyst thought Iris had such a magical, ethereal glow to her. She was literally glistening. "It's so cool how you're the basilissa. That's a princess, right?"

Iris was just staring at her. Xenon could tell she was having one of her mean moments. "Come on. Let me show you around. You sort of crashed the party," he joked.

"I did? Oops. Sorry. What's the occasion? OMG! Is it someone's birthday?!?!?" She really hoped it was someone's birthday.

"It's Blue's. I mean Xenon's," she rolled her eyes. "Xenon is Blue."

"Really?!?!? Oh, and I've noticed." She laughed and said, "Happy Birthday!" He wasn't expecting the hug she gave him. It was good to know she was at least somewhat of the touchy-feely type. Xenon wondered if she thought he was extra snuggly. "Birthdays are special! Why didn't you tell me? I'm sorry I crashed your party."

"You didn't. This celebration is for all the new warriors who were just sworn in. Myself included. My party is after this one."

"Liiiiiiit! Congratulations!"

"Thank you. Liiiiiiit!" He liked the word she used. Amethyst thought it was funny how he copied her so accurately. *Oceanid see, Oceanid do...*

"Are you hungry?" Thetis's parental instincts were already starting to kick in. "We have plenty of food. You can have whatever you like. You aren't cold, are you? I can get you some more clothing. Are you breathing okay?"

"I'm breathing fine, and I like the temperature. At least right now. As for the food, no thank you. I don't eat raw fish. I ain't 'bout that life."

She was officially the funniest person Xenon ever met. "We have other items on the menu. What do you desire?" He grabbed a menu and translated it for her. "We have octopus legs, tuna, squid, sea stars—"

She thought it was funny how he said 'desire'. "Okay, Ima stop you right there, buddy. Do you have crab, lobster, or shrimp?"

"Yes. We have all of those. I'll go order them for you." All of them? Amethyst was so juiced. *Yaaasssss.*

"Reign, this is Amethyst. Amethyst, this is Reign," Iris introduced them.

"Greetings, Your Highness."

"Hi. You don't have to call me that."

"If you ever need anything, just say the word."

"Look. That's Leios," Iris pointed out. "He teaches groups of young Oceanids and turns them into warriors. Isn't he handsome?"

"He's alright. A little too bulky for me. Too much yang and not enough yin."

"Iris, what did I tell you about older males?"

"I was only looking, Meter."

"I thought my brother, our brother, was dead."

"He is," said Iris.

"I did not give birth to Xenon, but I raised him. Nonetheless, I love you all the same," she smiled.

Xenon came back and said, "Your food is ready."

"We will go prepare you a room." Iris was never a people person, so Thetis said, "Xenon, would you mind sitting with her? We won't be long." *You're probably wondering how they got there since they were so far away. There's this portal thingy. I'll tell you later.*

"Will I see you two after I eat?"

"Of course," Thetis assured her.

"Right this way." Xenon showed her to the table.

The table was bigger than needed because Xenon thought the others were coming. He knew Iris liked her space, so he sat criss-cross applesauce on the other side of the table. Amethyst didn't know that was how you were supposed to sit. She always sat criss-cross applesauce. Sitting on the ocean floor was surprisingly comfortable. An Oceanid she identified as the waiter set her plate down on the table. She tried to move her plate closer, but it was much heavier than she imagined a plate would be. Xenon pushed it closer to her and then went back to his seat. "Ummm, this is really good. How did they cook it?"

"We can boil water, and we have hot surfaces to cook on," he laughed. "Our technology is very advanced."

"Really? That's cool." She couldn't take her eyes off Xenon's plate when it came. He noticed, but he didn't say anything. She wanted him to call her out. "What are you eating?"

"Octopus legs with a side of kelp."

"Sounds good," she said sarcastically. Then she burst out laughing. "Is secretly watching people eat an Oceanid thing. I can see you, you know. Stop acting like a little puppy. Where'd your octopus legs go? You must really like those huh? Yum. You still hungry or something, boo? Here," she handed him a piece of crab. "Oh zaaamn. You have a nice smile."

"Th-Thank you." Xenon was a bit surprised. Iris and Thetis would have just stared him down, but not Amethyst. "You're really funny," he laughed. "Always laughing."

"You're the one always pulling all these little stunts."

"What? I only did one thing. What else did I do?"

"On our way here, you did this quick ass head turn like this," she demonstrated. "I was weeeak. Then one time you were talking to yourself and you said 'f*** you' hella quiet. I got scared because I thought you were talking to me," she laughed. "You was trippin'. Then you said something in Japanese. I don't know what you said, but it sounded bad. I don't know what the hell was going on. Honestly, I thought the super sharks did something to you."

He was so embarrassed. "Oh, my goddess. I apologize. I had no idea."

"It's all good. You remind me of this one cartoon character."

"Let me crack that open for you."

"It's alright. I can do it." Amethyst had to use all her strength to crack one crab leg. "I'm not a weakling. This is much easier on the surface."

110

"I know. The pressure is much greater down here. You just aren't used to it yet. If you were a weakling, you'd be crushed by now. Although... I must admit I was expecting you to have a nosebleed or a cramp. Here, I'll crack the rest for you if you like."

Amethyst smiled, "Okay. You really want to bust it open for me huh? You gotta get closer to me first. Why don't you just sit next to me?" He was happy to move his seat. She watched how he pulled the crab meat out perfectly and organized them neatly on her plate. "Wow. Pull out game strong."

They both laughed. "I know what that means. I caught the first one too."

"So, what am I thinking?" she asked. "Use your powers." She was testing him. She remembered what he said earlier, and she knew why he could only sense her feelings sometimes.

"I can't tell what people are thinking. I can tell what they are feeling," he giggled.

"What am I feeling?"

"I can't tell what you're feeling for some reason."

"Well, that's unfortunate. So, what you're saying is that I'm immune to your powers?"

"Sure," he smiled. "Do you miss your mate? The one that can't breathe."

"My mate?" Amethyst knew he obviously wasn't Australian, so what mate was he talking about? "Are you talking about the boy with the red hair from earlier?"

"Yes. Well, I didn't know he had red hair. He isn't your mate?"

"Hell no!"

"Oh." He was glad, but now he was worried about the surface male being Iris's soulmate.

"Who's your mate? Is it Iris or Reign?"

He jerked his neck back in disgust. "Neither of them. They're family."

"Oh. Where do I put my plate?"

"I'll place it on the floor. They'll clean it up. Would you like something to drink?"

"Drink? Sure." She was curious to see how dense the liquid would be.

"They only have seaberry flavored drinks because the others aren't in season just yet. Would you like it hot, cold, thin, thick, icy? Would you care for a straw?"

"A nice cold, thick drink would be great. Seaberry sounds good. And yes, I'd like a straw please. I love a good straw," she mocked his royal voice.

"It is. My other favorite is oceanberry." *Yes, there is a difference between the sea and the ocean.* He could tell she was curious when he was going to order it. "I already made eye contact with him."

"What else can Oceanids do?"

"Ummm, I guess there's a lot. We sing."

"Can you sing something?"

"You want me to sing for you? I mean I would, but not here in front of all these people," he whispered.

"You're shy? Awww." His cheeks blushed blue. "It's cool how you can turn blue. Can you turn it on and off?"

"Not really. I've been working on it. Right now, it just does whatever it wants."

"Xenon is the name of a noble gas that glows blue when it's excited," she winked. "Hehehe. You know… By electiricity… Is that why you were named Xenon? You seem pretty noble. It fits your aesthetic. Xenon is also used for photographic flash lamps, deep-sea lights, as the propellant for ion thrusters in space shuttles, and other cool stuff. It's also very rare."

"I see you know about science. I g-guess that works too, but Xenon means foreigner or stranger. I don't understand how I'm a foreigner when I'm from the ocean."

"Well, you're pretty strange to me," she giggled. "It's a nice name. I don't know what my name means at all anymore. I've always pronounced it like the crystal, but everyone down here says Ah-meh-tis."

"For you," the waiter set her drink on the table.

"Thank you." He thought it was cute how she reacted to the flavor of the straw. "It's tasty and eco-friendly! Ummm humm. I love that eco-friendly shit. How come you didn't get one?"

"Oh, me? I'm not thirsty."

"You aren't?" she teased. Thetis and Iris came by to pick them up, but they saw they were enjoying themselves, so they decided to wait. "It's so thick! Ummm... It's an underwater milkshake!" She noticed he was shaking his head trying not to laugh. "What did I say?" she laughed.

Then his expression changed. "He likes you," he rolled his eyes. "How dare he? He's not even attractive. What a piece of plankton."

"He what?" she asked as she continued to slurp down her drink.

"He has kissy fish for you. Every single young Oceanid in here does."

"Ewww. Why would you tell me that?" she laughed. "Wait. Every young Oceanid?"

"I figured you find that amusing, and yes, every single one." He realized what he said. "Um, it's getting low. We should go."

While they were walking on the ocean floor, Amethyst saw a sea cucumber. "Ahhhhhh!" Bubbles flew out of her mouth in her attempt to scream.

"What's wrong? It's just what you call a sea cucumber. They're apart of the cleanup crew. It's okay. They're harmless." She made him way too nervous to understand. He panicked because his first thought was her being in danger. *When you both have anxiety. LOL.* She started having a panic attack when she saw more of them. Xenon finally realized she had a phobia of sea cucumbers. "It's alright." He picked her up and swam far above the ocean floor. "I'm sorry about that. I didn't know."

"I want to go home right now!"

He felt like he failed her. "I can assure you that I'd be pleased to take you anywhere you'd like to go, but it isn't safe up there. Judging his expression, Amethyst figured the reason she wasn't safe was because of more than just some storm. "I think you'll like your lair once it's finished." He tried to think of something, anything that would make her feel better. "I will make sure there are no sea cucumbers, or anything related, in your lair or anywhere near you. Would you prefer cleaning shrimp and fish in the bas instead?"

"Yes! You'd do that?"

"Of course. Climb on."

By the time they returned to the others, Amethyst was asleep, and it was time to head back to the bas. All five of them waited in the chariot until everyone else filed out. "Are you sure you don't want to ride with the other warriors?" asked Thetis as she held Amethyst in her arms. "You don't have to stay with us."

"I'm sure. I'd rather be here."

"With Amethyst?" Reign picked on him. Iris vortexed her. *Meaning she sent a swirly current towards her.*

"Yes." Xenon didn't understand why Reign was teasing him. He just wanted to be with his friend. "Why'd she fall asleep? Am I boring?"

"You must be. You are pretty lame," said Iris. He felt like crying.

"Oh hush," said Thetis. "Assuming she has a regular surface sleeping schedule, she would have been sleeping a while ago. It is hours after midnight. She just trusts you that's all."

"She does? She told me she didn't. I don't understand."

Halfway there, Amethyst woke up fully energized. It was almost dawn. "Chance, I had this weird dream. There were mermaids and ocean people. One of them is the mystery alien boy who is un-BLUE-lievably interesting. Oh, and I have a twin, a mom, and there's this warrior named Reign. You'd like her. They fed me. They're all bad as fu—"

"It wasn't a dream, sis." Iris stopped playing in her sister's hair.

"Ahhhhh! It was real? OMG. Yay? I think."

"That thing Xenon killed wasn't a mermaid. It was a Nereid," Reign reminded her.

Meanwhile, Xenon was still laughing about her pun. "That was a good joke about me being blue. You think I'm interesting?"

"Let her be you three," Thetis interjected.

"Why are there so many animals following us?" Iris asked.

"They're here to welcome Amethyst," he told her.

"Is that a whale?!?!?" Amethyst gasped with excitement.

"She's like a child." Iris shook her head.

"She is," her mother smiled.

Amethyst couldn't believe it. "Hello! I'm Amethyst!"

"You can't talk to animals that way," Iris was trying to prevent her from being disappointed.

"Yes, you can. All you do is talk to them. They respond. Dogs for example."

When they finally got back to the basileia, it was officially dawn. "What's everyone staring at? I want to see." She looked behind her and saw Iris waving to everyone. "Oh. Yaaasssss."

Amethyst reminded Thetis of her own sister. "They are staring at you. Wave."

"Oh. Me? LOL. Good thing they aren't too close." She spotted some delphys. "Look! Dolphins!" Everyone gasped, but the delphys didn't mind that she called them dolphins. In fact, one of them brought her a gift on their fin. "Thank you. I love sea stars, but I would never keep an echinoderm as a pet. More importantly, I think they would like to be with their family."

"You are so kind. I will always remember. We never forget."

"Who said that?"

"Me. Yoo-hoo."

"But how can you eye talk? You have eyespots. I thought you could only detect light and dark? What's your name?"

"Yet here we are," the sea star giggled. "I'm anonymous."

"Cool… Goodbye."

"This isn't goodbye. I'm going to tell everyone what you did for me. You can give me a name since you are who you are. Tell me what it is the next time we see each other."

Amethyst noticed the Oceanids trying not to make eye contact with her. "What are they saying?"

"They're talking about how you can speak to sea stars," Xenon answered.

"What's so special about that? Can't everyone do the eye talk thing?"

"Sea stars have eyespots like you said. They can't eye talk because they can only detect light and dark."

"I knew it! I knew something was fishy about that!" He laughed so hard at her little cheesy joke even Iris and Reign cracked a smile.

"Welcome, Amethyst," Thetis presented the bas to her. She was speechless at first. "I've been desperately waiting for this moment."

"Wow! The lights help, but it's still dark, so it's kinda creepy. Huh! They're powered by bioluminescent algae, aren't they! It's soooo blue! It's fantastic! The architecture is aesthetically pleasing. Who designed it? I like the contrast between the ocean and the squares. I wish I could see better down here. Everything's kind of blurry. Ooooo! Are my eyes going to adapt! Oh, and the technology. I love whoever hooked that up. They gotta be like the dopest person alive. To be honest, I'm tryna cuff them. I knew having night vision was unusual! Chance has it too. I wonder what he is. He's definitely not an Oceanid. Or maybe he's part Oceanid. I don't know."

"I heard you had Blue replace the cleanup crew or what you call sea cucumbers," Iris rolled her eyes. "She's already changing things."

"They make her uncomfortable. What Xenon did was very kind, Iris," Thetis told her. "I would have done the same as soon as I found out. I expect for you to have done the same thing. Plus, the shrimp take up less space and are much more discreet. Now, it's time we prepare for our ballroom guests coming later.

"Ballroom? You mean your home is even bigger than this?"

"We live in a palace. This is only a section of the bottom half," Iris explained. "I know it's a lot for you."

"Iris, sweetie. Help Amethyst find something to wear please. Remember the theme."

"I'd be glad to! Come on, sister. Let's go. We're going to drain the ballroom this year." She led her to her room. "You're so pretty, unlike me."

"Why do you say that? That's the second time. I think you're absolutely stunning. We're also twins." Amethyst examined her room. "Why do you have so many mirrors? I can't look around without seeing multiple reflections." Iris took her to the second floor of her room through a small opening.

"No reason. I just really, really love reflections. Especially mine." Amethyst wasn't sure if that last part was sarcastic or not. Somehow it seemed like it was both. "Oh, and I can see the f—"

"I'll see you there you two! Don't take forever. Haliai are always on time." *The prince of inside jokes everybody.* Amethyst noticed his voice cracked. It reminded her of when Chance was going through puberty. She wondered if his voice was just now changing. She was going to ask what the difference between Oceanids and Haliai was, but she got sidetracked.

"Don't worry about us. You're the one who takes forever to get ready." Iris took off her shells right in front of Amethyst without any warning. "Alright, I'm going to get dressed and then we'll get you ready. How's that sound? Feel free to look around. I've been planning my outfit for weeks."

"Okay." Amethyst thought about why Iris's shelves were so high but then she remembered she could just swim up. She was too scared to do that because she couldn't swim without an escort, and she couldn't imagine trying to swim back down. She found a handwritten note encased in a glass frame just before Iris finished. "Hey what does this say?" Amethyst thought she looked amazing. Iris's dress was mature, elegant, and covered in opalescent pearls that matched her shimmering dress. To Amethyst, she was the ultimate icon with the presence of a unicorn. Iris had this cold, ethereal glow to her that even the greatest Oxford lexicographer couldn't describe. Her soul was glass. "All these mirrors and you still can't see yourself." She could tell Iris didn't hear her question. When they made eye contact she said, "What does this say?"

"It's in English. Can't you read?"

"Oh, I see. You're a mirror writer. How ironic."

"How is it that surface people always use that word incorrectly. Me having a lot of mirrors and being a mirror writer is not an example of irony."

"I know that. I was referring to how you are able to read what you write, but you can't read what you see in the mirror. Writing is a way in which one analyzes themself. A mirror forged with pen and paper."

"Huuum. I never thought of it that way. I like how you think." All this time Iris was sure Amethyst was a simple-minded person. She's usually good at judging people's character within a few hours. Like all Oceanids, Xenon had optimal hearing and heard everything. So, did Thetis. "My mo— Our mother says I have a condition surface goers call dyslexia. Not because of my handwriting. Sorry. I forgot what I was going to say about that. Anyways, it's a letter to my future soulmate. No one has been able to read it. They don't even know it's mirror writing."

"I bet I can."

She was a bit disappointed that Amethyst could read the letter, but she was more fascinated. "How did you do that so quickly?"

"Your handwriting doesn't impact my ability to recognize each letter. I'm surprised no one has just put it up to the mirror."

"Is that what you did? Did you use my mirrors?"

"No. I can only read what's close to my face. My glasses don't work down here."

"So, you really are myopic? I wasn't sure. Some people wear spectacles for fashion on the surface. I'm myopic too. That's why I can't see as well on the surface. Speaking of fashion. Come on." She escorted Amethyst to her closet. *She's real familiar with that. *sips tea** "What do you like?"

"What fits the theme? You choose."

"I know you would look wonderful in a vibrant coral colored dress. Here, put this on." The more Iris thought about it, the more she didn't want her younger sister to outshine her. Iris knew Amethyst would look great in any dress, so she did the only thing she could do.

Amethyst thought the dress was much too girly, and don't get her started on the color. "How do I look?" She really didn't want to wear a dress at the moment.

"Eh, let's try a different dress. Here. Try this…" Iris handed her a long sleeve, classy, bright purple mermaid ballgown.

"I like this one." She was trying to be cooperative.

"Now, let me do your hair. I don't think we will have time to do your makeup, but you don't need it do you?"

"Makeup's cool, but that's totally fine." Iris used some special substance on her hair. Amethyst couldn't tell if it was gel, cream, or custard but it worked great. She liked her new weighted hairstyle, but she preferred her regular style."

"Now choose your lipstick."

"Huuuum. I don't know. You have so many."

"Do you like this one?"

"Ooooo! I love purple lipstick."

"I'm glad. Now all you need is shoes and a purse." She let her borrow her purple pumps and matching clutch. "Off we go. We're a little late, but that's okay. No one will notice."

"But aren't we Haliai?" Amethyst laughed.

"Come on. We have to hurry. Leave your glasses. Don't bring that human thing. You'll see better without them down here. It has to do with how the light refracts and something about the cones in your eyes." While they were rushing through the halls, Amethyst suddenly stopped. "Are you okay?"

"I'm fine. You go on ahead. I just need to take some deep breaths. I can make my way from here." She was having a minor anxiety attack. Meanwhile, Reign led Iris down the stairs.

"Iris, there you are," Thetis wasn't surprised she was late. "Where's Amethyst?"

"She stopped to take a breather. She's probably nervous. Where's Xenon?"

"He's at the top waiting for her. You could have at least made sure she was okay." Xenon was dressed in one of his favorite outfits. Xandra got it for him years ago. It was perfect because he wanted to show off his Eritrean heritage and honor her at the same time. He wore a bright, cerulean blue with hints of white. Iris waved, but he seemed to be preoccupied with something else. Someone else? She turned and found out that someone was Amethyst. Her skin bleed as she felt the sound of everyone gasping at the sight of Amethyst, who stood there frozen at the steps. Amethyst couldn't make out any faces. Everything was a blur. She was able to identify the three main colors everyone was wearing, but then she noticed she was a glitch in the pattern. Someone in blue was coming towards her, but she wasn't quite sure who it was. She hoped whoever it was would help her down the ballroom stairs and into a corner to hide.

"Amethyst." The blue blur spoke, and she knew exactly who it was.

"Xenon, is this a joke? Why am I the only one not matching the coral, grey, and white theme? Is that why they're all staring at me?" Her eyes began to water. Not because she was hurt. She was about to cry for the sake of the aesthetic.

"If it is another one of Iris's little pranks, I had nothing to do with it. Besides, you aren't the only one who isn't following the color scheme. They are all staring at you because you look like a goddess. I am admiring you because your aura is as alluring as the ocean and as mysterious as the cosmos."

"Sometimes you have a way with words, Prince Charming. I can't help but think you're flirting with me." Amethyst's smile revealed her dimples. She released a kaleidoscope of butterflies in his stomach and her warm, gentle gaze granted them immortality.

Xenon showed off his best ear to ear grin. "Now, Your Highness, would you allow me to assist you down these steps?" He bowed and stuck out his elbow. "You cannot see, can you?"

"Nope. Iris told me it would be best if I left my glasses."

"Your eyes need a few hours to adjust. Your other senses will need a few days. We were going to have you do that after the party, but I guess Iris had her own plans. No worries. I'll stay with you the whole time."

"You don't have to do that. It's your birthday. I'm sure you have friends that want to hang out with you."

"I was already hoping that I'd get to spend time with you."

"You were?"

"More than you know."

"If you don't mind me asking, Your Highness..." A guest walked up to her. "Who dressed you?"

"My twin sister, Iris."

"Well, she did a spectacular job. I'm not surprised."

"Attention everyone," said Thetis. The room fell completely silent. "It's time we dance."

"Dance? Well, why is no one dancing?"

"I have to dance with someone first. Will you accept?" He let out that dashing little smirk of his.

"Accept what?" she teased.

"Whom will you ask this year?" Thetis asked. The dance isn't a romantic gesture. It's more of a friendly honor. It's just that both Amethyst and Xenon are flirtatious little things. They literally flirt with everyone. *Everyone.*

He cleared his throat, looked Amethyst in the eyes and said, "Amethyst, daughter of Thetis, will you allow I, Xenon, basi of the basileia to have this dance?"

"No." He looked as if he shattered into a million pieces, Iris smiled, and Thetis laughed. Amethyst loved how Oceanids' eyes changed with their emotions. She wondered if she could do the same thing once her senses kicked in. "I'm just kidding. I will." Everyone cheered except for you know who. Iris was sure Xenon was going to ask her. Or at least that's what her mirror showed her a few tides ago. Amethyst and Xenon danced to the sounds of electric violins, a piano, and drums in complete bliss. "I don't know how to dance with a partner, but I seem to be doing fine. Why is that?"

"It's because it's tradition for you to lead first while I follow and..." He swung her around. "And then I lead while you follow. Once we switch 29 times, the dance is over. You begin and end the dance. Everyone is counting so they know when to stop. After we exit the dance floor, everyone may continue to dance but not to this song. Do you always dance alone?"

"Sometimes it's better when you're alone. You don't have to worry about your partner going to fast or too slow, being too tall or too short, being at the wrong angle or not having the right rhythm, being too traditional or too boring… I just haven't found a wavelength that can synchronize with mine."

"I couldn't have said it better. My previous partners couldn't keep up, but on the contrary, you seem completely at ease."

"That's because you're predictable."

"Interesting, everyone else says otherwise. You think I'm boring?"

"No, just predictable. To me at least."

Amethyst and Xenon had a fainted glow in the daylight due to the contrast between them and the crowd. Thetis watched from her table. "I can already tell she is what the basileia was missing. Iris and I are very organized and serious. She's so chaotic and fun," she told Reign.

"You're so gentle for such a strong, fearsome warrior," she laughed.

He panicked. "You think I'm to be feared?"

"When someone threatens something you care about."

"So fearsome is not a bad thing?"

"Not how I meant it. Not in your case."

"You like for me to be fearsome? You liked when I killed that Nereid? Why?"

"I like how you defended yourself. If there was a way for you to do that without killing the Nereid, I would have preferred that."

"I see. You know… Ummm." He was debating on whether he should tell her that he was defending her. Well, technically both of them.

"Know what?"

"You are so intelligent, kind, and pure of heart."

She laughed. "Me? Pure? No way. What made you say that? You don't know me. Do you?"

"I don't know. You're different. Never mind. That's cliché. I don't know what I'm saying." He felt embarrassed because he couldn't translate his thoughts into words.

"Enough about me. Tell me about you."

"You haven't told me anything about you yet. You start."

"My favorite candy is Watermelon Sour Patches, my birthday is December 1, my favorite color has always been purple, I suck at mental math, I'm slow to tell left from right, I'm 16, I have anxiety, I'm an outsider, I follow my intuition, and I'm depressed."

"I-I-I'm uh… The same is true about me except my birthday is today, my favorite color is blue, and I'm 17. That's crazy."

"You have anxiety too?"

"Yeah. Sometimes my heart pounds and pounds for what seems to be no reason at all. It isn't just that though. I feel like there's this feeling that can't be explained…"

"…because the only way to understand it is to have felt it yourself. Tell me something else about you. Something you haven't told me before."

"Exactly. Another thing is that sometimes I'm not too sure what is reality and what is fantasy…"

"…or if there is even a difference." *Here comes the drama. *rolls eyes*

Xenon couldn't believe it. Was it really them? Was she really there? Was she them? He thought he was daydreaming. They obviously didn't have dream vision so maybe… But then his dreams always felt real, and this possible reality was too good to be true. Amethyst giggled for some reason. "Why are you laughing at me?" he smiled. Did she…? Could she have…? Did he accidentally…?

"Oh, nothing. It was just a coincidence I guess."

"Just in case this is a dream and I wake up, I want you to know that I think you and I would have been great friends. I hope I get to see you again every time I close my eyes."

"If I am dreaming then I hope to see my mom, my sister, and you again. You all are what has made this dream so surreal." Neither of them was sure if this was real. Not because they have a few minor things in common but because both of them were always lonely. Although they had plenty of friends, none of them could ever really relate to them. Then, all of the sudden they come across someone who could potentially be that friend they always wanted. That friend that was always only imagined.

"Either way, would you like to stay with me after the dance? I feel like I'm stalking you."

"Don't be shy about that now."

Xenon wondered if she really knew or if he was making this all up. How could she know? "I still can't tell if I'm dreaming."

"Reality or fantasy, we're in the same one."

"True. You're scaring me. In a good way. Look! It's time to cut the cake!" Xenon pulled Amethyst, who was still practically blind by the way, over to the table.

"Y'all have cake down here? Yaaasssss. What kind is it?"

He was always aiming to please. "What kind would you like?"

"I'm sure whatever you have is fine. I just like cake."

"We have everything. It's no trouble."

"I've been craving chocolate lately." *Yo. Her mind is on a whole other level.*

"You heard the basilissa. A slice of chocolate cake for Her Highness," he smiled. The chefs went to go make a cake just for Amethyst.

"You didn't have to do that."

"I wanted to. Kind people deserve kind gestures. And you make me laugh inside and out."

"Thank you."

"You are the most welcome." Already, he could see how different she was from her twin. There was no singing, but there was what Amethyst considered a drumroll. Then everyone shouted, "Happy birthday!"

A man fell trying to make his way down the stairs. Some people started laughing, including Iris. Amethyst was the first one to help him. In her dress, she got down on the floor to help the man.

"Are you alright?"

"I'm fine, Your Highness. You shouldn't be down here with such a beautiful dress on."

She touched his ankle. "No, you're not. Your ankle is twisted. Don't y'all have doctors or something. Someone help him." Then she helped Xenon clean up the drink the man spilled."

"You don't have to clean it up, Amethyst. I got it."

"I want to help." When she was back on her feet, she was upset. "How could some of you laugh at that man. You didn't even ask if he was okay. You should be ashamed of yourselves but continue on. I don't want to see any of y'all moping. This is a birthday party for crying out loud. Excuse me while I go get this man another drink. Come on, Xenon." Thetis was very pleased. She was already winning over people's hearts.

Later on, a group of young Oceanids showed up and Xenon disappeared. He was hiding from them. He usually entertained them, but he didn't want to be bothered. Amethyst found Reign and asked her where he went. "He told me to meet him right here."

"I think he wants you to follow him, gemmie. He's on this floor." Reign pointed her in the right direction until she saw the blue blur. Reign wondered what those two weirdos were up to.

Every time Amethyst got within reach of Xenon, she had to find him again until she found him in a secluded room far away from everyone else. He was facing one of the transparent walls. There were various sea creatures on the other side of the wall, but she could tell he wasn't thinking about fish. She looked down and found that the floor was the same way. She gasped in awe. Then she remembered she was in a secluded room with a stranger. "Why did you lead me here?"

Xenon was confused by Amethyst's tone. "You think I would hurt you?"

"I don't know, but I'm pretty sure you definitely could if you wanted to, and no one would be able to see in here."

"I'd commit seppuku in advance before I ever hurt you. I was going to take you to one of my secret places. The place I go to when I want to escape."

Amethyst believed him, but that didn't mean she trusted him. "Xenon," she walked up to him. "You promise not to hurt me?"

He was lost in her eyes. "I promise."

While he was distracted, Amethyst took his tantō from his daishō. *That's right girl. Take notes ladies.* He didn't have his katana with him. He only brought his wakizashi and tantō. "I believe you." The two of them walked down a staircase that was also transparent. Once they reached the bottom, Amethyst realized that they were now in some kind of cavern with an opening that revealed the twilight sky. It was sort of like a planetarium. "Yo… This is like the coolest thing ever."

He admired how she just made herself comfortable and laid down. "You know… I-I've always searched for someone I could really connect with. Don't get me wrong. I have plenty of friends, but not someone I…" He had trouble organizing his words again. "Never mind."

"I totally get it. I think you know I feel the same way by now. Hell, I just met an alien, and now I'm in his dungeon." She laughed at herself. "I've been doing the same thing. I've never felt like me and another person looked up at the stars and… Never mind." Amethyst didn't expect him to understand.

"…and saw the same things? Me either. Not until now." They both looked up at the cosmos with the same eyes and then turned their heads at the same time. Since they were sitting shoulder to shoulder, their faces almost touched. "Sorry." Xenon's body lost all motion.

"What's wrong with you? Why are you so stiff?"

"It's just a bit cold." She could tell he was obviously lying. He was an even worse liar than she was. *LMAO. How TF are YOU cold. Come on now.* His cheeks blushed blue when she caught him checking her out. When she giggled, a wave of blue electricity rushed down his spine.

This was the perfect opportunity for Amethyst to put his tantō back. "Kiss me." *Ahhhhh. She that type. LMAO. Yaasssss.* That wasn't the only reason why she kissed him though. There was no denying that Xenon was a little baddie. They made out passionately, right under twilight's invisible stars, their stars, for about 11 seconds. *I ain't even mad though. She got hers in.* Afterward, they just sat there laughing every time they made eye contact. Amethyst was laughing for the same reason as Xenon, but she was also laughing because she purposely put his tantō back the wrong way. She was imagining the look on his face when he found out. "They're probably looking for us. Let's head back."

"Oh, there you two are." Thetis was judging them. *21st-century translation: She was judgin'.*

"What were you two up to?" asked Thetis number 2.

"Don't mind her," Reign giggled. "I'm sure Xenon was probably just showing her around." The kissy fish did their best to hide their grins.

"You'll love this next part," Thetis assured Amethyst. "Take a seat."

"Iris, I'm so nervous," Xenon blushed.

"Why? You're never nervous on stage."

"You two are participating?" Amethyst couldn't wait. "Good luck. I'm sure you'll both do great." Even Iris smiled. "So, what exactly is about to happen?"

"One of our traditional performances called *Ti Génnisi Eóns Tératos.* He always picks this one."

"The Birth of a Monster?"

"Yes. Good job. Iris and Xenon are both singing and dancing. It's of medium length, but you might want to gather any refreshments now."

"Fosho. Don't gotta tell me twice." They were sitting close to the snack table, so Amethyst was able to gather some seaberries. *Is it just me or do those sound hella good?*

Mayli walked across the stage and announced the start of the play. After that, the silence was so intense. It made Amethyst uncomfortable. Then there was the hypnotic metronome of a single African drum in sync with the pirouettes of an opalescent ballerina. She was impressed by Iris's dancing. The play is about two childhood friends who are separated in a war. Iris's character, Alyx, is mute. She is taken by the conquerors as a gift for The King. It is rumored The King's children became ill and died. His daughter used to dance which is why Alyx is forced to become a dancer. All day she has to practice, and every night she has to perform even if she is in pain. If The King isn't pleased, she is beaten and not given any food or water for 8 days. Alyx's childhood friend, Nala, is played by an Oceanid Amethyst saw by the cake table earlier. Nala thinks Alyx is dead and grows up without a care in the world. Years after Alyx is taken, her people form a rebel army. Nala enlists in the rebel army because she wants to die by someone else's hands rather than her own. She wants her death to mean something. One day, the rebels go on a mission to blow up the kingdom's weaponry. They succeed and Nala sees Alyx in her room, but she has no clue it is her. Not only is she under the impression that Alyx is dead, but Alyx has grown up to be exceptionally beautiful. That wasn't the Alyx she knew. Also, why would Alyx be living so luxuriously? Nala and the rebel squad always have their faces covered, so Alyx has no clue it is Nala. They kidnap her because they assume she is the princess. Nala and her crew see a door they think is an exit. Alyx tries to warn them that some beast lives in there. During the day, there is mysterious silence, but every night she hears a monstrous roar. Alyx always sees the servants bring it plates of meat, but they always bring forks, knives, and napkins, so she didn't understand. The creature secretly watches her whenever she walks by. The creature thinks someone is rescuing Alyx. He knows The King is cruel. Then he hears Alyx fighting against the rebel squad. When they burst through the door, Alyx sees a young man about her age. She figures he's the prince. He tries to fight, but it's useless. Alyx can tell he has some kind of disease. It is dark out, but The King's guards catch the rebels. When the nurses come to give The Prince the serum that is keeping him alive even though it causes him to become a maniac temporarily, The Prince is more temperamental than usual. He kills everyone in his path trying to get to Alyx. Once he reaches the fighting, Nala is about to shoot Alyx with a bow and arrow because she at least wants to avenge Alyx in some way before she dies. The beast takes the arrow for Alyx, and The King kills Nala. Nala's mask falls off, and Alyx sees that she is her old friend. She spells out her name on Nala's palm and tells her that she will avenge her. She lets them take her back to her dungeon. She steals one of the syringes filled with the serum they give The Prince. She takes it, kills The King, becomes The Queen, and frees her people. In order to keep living, she has to take the serum every night just as The Prince did.

Xenon's thoughts whirlpooled. Throughout the entire performance, he avoided making eye contact with Amethyst. He was worried that if he did, he would turn even bluer in front of everyone. Then he remembered no one would be able to tell because of the lights that went along with the performance. Amethyst was enthralled. It was by far the most captivating performance she had ever seen. "So, what do you think?" asked Thetis.

"I loved it! It was so dark and so beautiful." By the time Amethyst was almost finished with her sentence, she couldn't help but stare at all the performers kissing the people who complimented them on the lips. It was just a peck. She figured that was Oceanid culture.

"I'm glad you enjoyed it." Xenon lifted her hand and gently kissed it for about a second longer than the norm. "We should all get going before the mermies swarm around us."

"The what?"

"Mermies are... How do you say it?" Reign tried to explain.

"Fangirls," said Iris.

"Except the term mermies is more gender inclusive," added Reign. *LMAO.*

"Hey. We can't judge people like that," said Iris.

"What?" Amethyst laughed. "Why y'all judging? So where did that term come from?" She was curious to know if it had something to do with mermaids. She really wanted there to be actual mermaids somewhere.

"The Mer can be extremely clingy, and they tend to become obsessed with material things. They say that once you find a Mer's guilty pleasure, you have complete control over them." The way Iris said it gave Reign the chills.

"That's only somewhat true," Reign giggled. "You know, they say Mer always recognize their kin regardless of their fin." *Petty.*

"What's the difference between a Nereid and a Merperson?"

"Nereids have bold, smooth, sleek flukes," said Iris.

"And Mer have flashy, glittery, sparkling scales," Reign twirled.

"I want to meet a Merperson."

Reign laughed. "Why not a Nereid?" *Petty once again.*

"So far, Nereids don't seem to like me. I can't wait to meet a Nereid that won't try to hurt me. I want to meet a Merperson and a Nereid. Huuuh! Maybe even at the same time!!!" It was almost time to re-submerge and Amethyst was dying to get out of Iris's dress.

"Good morning, Amethyst," they all told her. She noticed that good morning and good night have double meanings for Oceanids. He told her good morning in place of good night because she was going to bed in the daytime.

"Good morning." That sounded so weird to say. It's good to know that you're a bit of a prankster, Iris."

"Ha. I guess I am. We have plenty of rooms, but you can stay in here if you like. Oceanids prefer to stay close together. If you need to surface just wake me up. Be gentle or else I'll smack you."

"Oh, okay." She took the offer because she didn't want to be alone. "Good morning." She tried to get some rest, but someone was making way too much noise. She crawled on the ocean floor and peeked into one of the thresholds. She thought it was cool how they were all connected.

"I thought I said good morning?"

Amethyst looked up and saw Xenon in the top corner. "Aw, man. This is your room?" she laughed.

"This is where we keep our scrolls. Scrolls are like books. How'd you know I was still awake?"

"I sensed it," she said sarcastically. "I freakin' saw you… Duh."

"I have to tell you something. You hit your head when you slipped off the cliff, so you probably don't remember what I'm about to tell you. You recovered much faster than I thought. Now that I think about it, I think you were just sleepy at first. The red-haired male was having trouble breathing, so I called Jeremy and told him your status and whereabouts. I sent a message saying that you were safe in the ocean but not on the surface anymore. I promised them I would take you back as long as it was safe. After I got off the phone, you woke up and… You remember the rest."

"Oh, okay. I was going to ask Thetis about them when she woke up. I'm going to need everything else explained to me in the morning or whenever your day starts. You can answer these two questions though. How do you know my dad, and why do you sleep in the top corner? Iris doesn't do that."

"He's an Oceanid. I've known him since before you were born. We talk every now and then. He doesn't like me," he smiled.

"Okay now answer my other question." She unconsciously did something silly.

Xenon thought it was cute. "Don't do that."

"Do what?" She stuck her tongue out at him. Her dimples almost killed him once again.

That was new to him. He wondered what kind of akanbe that was. He never saw anyone make that face before. "That. Uhhhh. Fine. I'm telling you this because I trust you, and I feel that I can be completely open with you."

"Is that an attitude I'm sensing?" she giggled. "Go on."

He rolled his eyes and tried not to smile. "I've slept up there ever since I watched Mom hand you to Jeremy. You didn't want to leave because you knew you would grow up without your sister. You thought I was funny, but I don't think you meant that as a compliment. Anyways, that spot was closer to the surface, closer to you. Now it's just habit."

"Okay, three more questions."

He rolled his eyes. "Sure."

"One, did you fart or something?"

He was highly disturbed by her accusation. "Ew. Goddess no. Of course not."

Amethyst was laughing so hard at his reaction that if she was on the surface, she would have definitely had tears. "Then what is that awful smell?"

Then he remembered. "Oh. I released excrement a moment before you came in." He was so embarrassed.

Amethyst laughed even harder. He was too cute. "Released excrement? What the shit?" He was taking this prince thing way too far. "It was probably those octopus legs you ate. You set yourself up for success by eating those. That's what I call an octoshit. Don't trip. Chance is just as terrible as you."

"You're quite the scallop, aren't you?"

"How can you remember communicating with me when I was just a baby and you were just a baby? What was the first thing you said to me?" She tested his memory.

"I still don't know yet. Mom hasn't told me everything because she's not sure about all the details just yet, but I can communicate with frequencies. I think it has something to do with why I have this blue tint. The first thing

I said to you was, 'If you aim right, you will never miss.' I was trying to make a joke. I was never good at those. No one thinks I'm funny. I guess that's fair. I don't really laugh at anyone else's jokes."

"That is the worst joke ever, but I like it. Actually, I don't even know if that's considered a joke. This time I'm laughing because I actually get it. Guess what? One of my nicknames is Ame. Ame like aim. On the surface, we pronounce my name like the crystal because no one wrote out the syllables."

"Would you prefer I say Amethyst the surface way or Amethyst the Oceanid way?"

"I like how you say it. A blend of both. Oh yeah. I don't think I thanked you for saving me. Or maybe I did. Thank you," she hugged him. "Alright, good morning for real this time." Then, Amethyst slipped into bed next to her long-lost twin.

Chapter 7: It's Getting Hot in Here

"Wake up, Amethyst! Wake up!"

"What, Chance?" Amethyst thought she was back home.

Iris forgot Chance was a name. "Come on. The chances of me waking you up were pretty high. You slept right next to me, and I'm always up first."

"What time is it?"

"The day is high."

"I don't know what that means."

Hey, Amethyst. Good morning. Mom said it's safe if you want to surface. She said I have to go with you though.

"Get up! Today we are going to have so much fun. We can go shopping, to the piercing pagoda, to get drinks, to the spa…"

"Where's Xenon? I just heard… Well, I didn't hear words, but he just said something to me."

"Oh, he does that to us a lot."

"Can we put our plans on hold? I really want to see my family. My surface family. I want to go home."

"But it isn't safe, and home is here."

"He just told me Thetis said so."

"Okay then. I'll wait for you."

"Where's the bathroom?"

"The what? You want to take a bath? Oh… I know what you mean," Iris helped her swim to where they relieve themselves.

The toilet was a circular energy disc with no back support. Amethyst was curious about where it went. She liked it because it glowed in the dark. "Hey, Iris!" she called from the top. "Can you hear me?" she tested her.

"Yes. I can hear you. You can be really loud."

"Cool. How do the people with penises pee from up here? They can't stand."

Now she saw why Xenon thought she was so funny. "Just ask Blue."

"He can hear me from here?"

"Yes. I stand on the disc. It adapts to your needs. To be honest, I usually just go by this one current. It's much more convenient." *Oceanids are just so comfortable about everything. LOL. That's probably where Amethyst gets it from.*

"Where's the toilet paper?"

"We use that stuff to your left. It's a special dried out plant. Just throw it in the hole. It's biodegradable," Iris told her. Amethyst tried to be brave and sink down to the bottom but then she panicked. "I got you." Iris looked her twin up and down. "We need to get you out of these human clothes."

It just dawned on her that she wasn't human. *I love how Amethyst is completely unphased.* "Maybe later. I'm going to land anyways. I can't wait to brush my teeth and cleanse my face. And shower."

"Fine," she rolled her eyes. Amethyst yawned and Iris noticed something. "Wait. Open your mouth again. Why is your tongue blue?"

Xenon was relieved it was daylight because if her tongue was glowing that would have been a dead giveaway. Amethyst looked at him and then she knew it was because of their kiss. "She drank one of those Seafoam Slipperies in the fridge. It should come off after a good brushing," said Xenon.

My mouth is like that every morning. Trust me, it works.

So, they do brush their teeth down here. Interesting. There's a fridge? I wonder how that works.

It's not your kind of fridge. It's more like a cooler. We keep stuff at the very bottom in what you might call an attic. No, a basement.

How did you hear me?

Because you can do the same thing I can do. That's how we were communicating when we were babies. All babies communicate with simple frequencies, but you and I are special.

"Did you hear what I just said?!?!?" They both looked at Iris. "Aristide is here."

"Hello, friend," said Xenon.

Amethyst's heart was doing somersaults because she had never been so close to a delphys before. "Thetis told me you two would be heading to the surface, so here I am at her service." Aristide loved picking fun at Xenon.

"Have you healed properly?" asked Thetis.

Aristide nodded. "Good as new! Absolutely optimal!"

"I'm sorry about what happened to you," said Amethyst.

"It's quite alright. We feel no physical pain. What would have pained me is if you were attacked by that Nereid. I told the little guppy as soon as I knew you were in danger."

"Thank you. You're my hero." Xenon was baffled. How was he her hero?

Iris sounded like Candace from Phineas and Ferb when she said, "Meter! Amethyst is speaking to Aristide in Delphys telepathically."

"I am?"

"Aristide is mute—" He smacked Xenon with his fluke for telling his business. "And you weren't eye talking or else Iris would have understood."

"You understood though."

"That's because I was picking up the frequencies. The only other person who can do what you just did is his mom, Amphitrite."

"Wait your mom is really Amphitrite? So, we're like cousins? Cool!"

Thetis emerged from her room. "What Xenon says is true. I'll tell you the rest when you return. There is so much." Amethyst was getting tired of the whole 'explain later' thing.

"Would you like a ride, Your Highness?" Aristide slightly leaned towards her.

"Yes. Thank you, but I'm not a princess. I mean a basilissa," Amethyst laughed. Thetis smiled because she sounded just like her.

"As you wish." Aristide shot Xenon a look as she got on his back.

Are you jealous, Guppy?

Is it that obvious?

To me. I know you. I will say you have a lot of work to do. You're still a stranger to her. How tragic.

Wow. That was pretty poetic. You sound like me.

You know I hate it when you use sarcasm. I bet she finds me more entertaining than you anyway.

"What are you two talking about?"

"Just nonsense. Have you eaten?" asked Aristide.

"No, I haven't. I could use a snack."

"Good. Hold on tight." Aristide did a series of loops at his top speed.

"Show off. I can do that too since I'm not carrying my katana," he rolled his eyes. Then he gathered some kelp and tightly wove it into the shape of a flower. "For you. It's my second favorite type of kelp. Taste it and see if you like it."

"Thank you," she giggled. "It's really salty, but it's actually pretty tasty. I hate salt. This would go great with rice and teriyaki sauce."

"The more time you spend down here the more salt you crave. What grade are you in at your school?"

"I'm in the 11th."

"Do you like surface school?"

"Not at all. I never felt like I belonged there, and it's really boring and stressful. Since you graduated, how old are you?" She saw a picture of Thetis and a young Xenon, but Iris wasn't in it. Aristide was mute, but she could tell he was laughing.

Xenon learned Amethyst was the type of person to ask the same question more than once. She was a detective. "Well ummm I-I'm…"

"Spit it out, kelp brain," Aristide teased him.

"When I was 27, I was hit with a time wave that reset my age. We don't know much about it. It's been 17 years since then. I guess I'm technically 31."

"You mean 44," Aristide laughed.

"B-But let me be clear. I am not that old… Like… I'm your age."

"A time wave? How long do Oceanids live?"

"I was lucky to have another chance. We're immortal. We live until we've been killed or have died from cancer or something. Sometimes it's a natural death. Basically, we go when it's time for us to return to Chaos."

"That makes all of what you said to me so much more meaningful."

"How so?" he gleamed.

"All that time has passed, you've met so many people… Yet you told me what you told me."

"Just between you and me, Amethyst… I thought he was asexual."

Xenon threw a shell at Aristide. "That's a very sensitive topic, and don't say that like there's something wrong with that."

"I know there isn't. I'm ace myself. You just get all moody every time I mention sexuality."

"How old are you?" Amethyst asked Aristide.

"You aren't supposed to—"

"It's fine. I'm 103 years old. I'm immortal too."

"But he acts like he's 12. That's probably why he's still single."

"Who knew there was so much shade in the epipelagic zone?" she laughed.

"I like you. Blue told me how funny you are. He also said you're adorable. What he said is true. He also told me how thrilled he is that you're home." Xenon smacked him after he blushed.

"So how old is Thetis?"

"All I know is that she's my meter's age, and I don't even know how old she is," said Aristide.

"We're here."

"How'd we get here so quickly?"

"The ocean is a sea of time, sea star," Aristide told her. She could tell he knew something. She always thought delphys had some kind of supreme knowledge.

"Welcome to my beach, girl."

"You thought that was cool?" Amethyst laughed. "I'm very familiar with this place. I come here every morning to see a friend. I guess I missed him today."

He acted like he didn't hear her. She didn't like being ignored. He didn't have much on, but he just started changing his clothes with no warning. Then he put on some short blue swim shorts and a smedium white tank. "If you take your clothes off, they'll dry faster." She socked him in the arm. "You're pretty strong for a little scallop."

"Turn your head. Is it difficult to switch from eye talking, talking, and sensing frequencies?"

"Not really. I prefer to communicate with frequencies though. Here." He tossed her one of his shirts over his back. "I think I have some shorts."

"It's alright. It's long on me. I can just wear it like this."

When she gave the okay for Xenon to turn around, he couldn't help but laugh. "You're such a sparkle." Then he realized what he said. "Uhhh. Give me your clothes. I'll put them in my hiding spot." It was about a 5-minute walk from Sutro Baths to her house. While they were walking up the hill, he asked her, "Where do you live?"

"Shut the f*** up. I'm not finna play with nobody kids. I know you know where I live witcho stalkin' ass." When they got there, Amethyst knocked. He smiled because he knew Amethyst never had her key. He stayed on the sidewalk near the edge of the curb, so they could have a family reunion. *Uh. As much as I hate to say it... Besides being a stalker, he's such a gentleman. He's so genuinely respectful. All people should be respectful so I'm not giving him any points for that. And he's still a stalker. Ew. So annoying.*

Jeremy answered the door. He hugged her so tight, she thought he was going to break her ribs. "Cupcake! I'm so happy you're okay. I'm sorry. I didn't mean it like that. You're my daughter. There's so much to explain so suddenly. I love you." He placed about a million kisses on her face even though he knew how she felt about kisses.

"Alright, alright. I love you too. We're good."

"IS that my Cinnamon Roll?!?!?" Chance had his signature Hello Kitty slippers on. "You're alive!!! You found your mom! I was so relieved when they told me what really happened. My little dream was a bit off. I'm so glad I didn't say what I thought I said. By the way, things are about to get a lot weirder. What's it like down there?"

"Hey, Ninja Turtle. It's sooooo awesome. Their technology is so advanced, and they have good food." Xenon was dying to know what a Ninja Turtle was.

"Come on in, stranger," said Jeremy. "You did good son, you did good. Thank you."

"The pleasure was mine." He was so happy Jeremy was being nice to him.

"Xenon, this is Chance. Chance, this is Xenon."

"Hello."

" 'Sup." Chance examined this 'other son' from head to toe.

Amethyst used her daddy's girl voice. "Daddy… Can Xenon spend the night?"

"Sure, Cupcake. I don't see why not. Chance will show you around." Jeremy and Chance had plans to keep an eye on those two.

"There's the bathroom. This is my room. You'll sleep in there, and I'll sleep in Ame's room. Do not go in Ame's room. All the food is downstairs. You need a shirt over that tank. Who do you think you are coming in here flaunting your body structure? N**** I got abs too. Here. Put this on." He handed him a shirt that said 'You Gotta Eat The Booty Like Groceries'. Xenon thought it was funny.

When Amethyst reached the top of the steps, she paused to look at the shirt he gave him. "Really, Chance? Come on, Xenon. I want to show you something."

They sat on her bed. "What is this? It looks like something we have at home. Can I open it?" He picked up some ocean blue nail polish that was on her dresser.

"Go ahead." Xenon jerked his head back at the smell.

Chance watched him as he painted two of his nails. "You aren't supposed to paint your nails. Why are you doing that?"

"Why are your jeans so tight?" *That comeback though.*

"Leave him alone, Chance."

"Girls paint their nails, not boys."

"What's the harm? This just shows that if it weren't for this society's norms, people would be able to choose what they want to do without having to worry about conforming to or violating a norm."

"So, are you saying boys would want to paint their nails?"

"I'm saying that some boys would paint their nails, and some boys wouldn't paint their nails. It would be their choice based off their own ideas. If it turned out that the majority of boys don't want to paint their nails, then that's perfectly okay too. The same thing applies for girls and everyone else. Plus, it's literally just color on your nails. How is that even masculine or feminine? Black is acceptable, and blue is supposedly a masculine color so... Also, I think it looks kinda cool on him."

"Ooooo she got on you. You just got served." Xenon tried to use some of the phrases he heard teenagers at the beach say.

"Alright, alright. That makes sense. I want to run some tests though."

"He's not one of your little experiments." She shook her head.

Chance ran into his room and brought back a bottle of his cologne. "Which one do you like better?" He gave him the option of his cologne or one of Amethyst's bottles of perfume.

"Your bottle looks better." Xenon smelled both of them. "But Amethyst's perfume smells the best."

"Which one of these would you rather wear?"

"Neither. I would choose this one." He held up her bottle of Moonlight Path from Bath and Body Works. "Or this one." He picked up Sea Island

Cotton. Then they start chatting about their favorite scents like they were best buds.

"GUYS!" Amethyst was so irritated. She was trying to show them something. "I still have the piece of seaweed you gave me when we were younger." She thought of another detail. "Remember when you sneezed? That was hilarious. Anyways, for some reason it's still perfectly healthy. We know it's because of this blue stuff, but what exactly is the blue stuff?"

"I remember. The blue stuff is my cells. I thought I washed it off better than that. Sorry."

"That's hella nasty! So unsanitary." Chance was second-guessing his whole existence. "Disgusting." Meanwhile, Amethyst and Xenon were ROTFL.

"I'm going to get in the shower." She couldn't wait to be reunited with her natural skin care products.

"What do you mean by a shower? Can I see it?"

"And this, drum roll please, is a shower!"

Chance smiled. "You and your theatrics."

"What do you do in there?"

"You get in, you wash your body, and you get out," he said. It was an inside joke.

"That's not the only thing you can do in the shower." *She can't help it. She is a dedicated innuendo opportunist in addition to being a punster.* Chance shot her a look. "What? You can sing in the shower." While she was in the shower, the guys just sat in awkward silence. When they heard someone knock they both looked out the window. "Who is it?" she asked.

"Was that the milkman or the paperboy?" Jeremy called out.

"It's that boy that likes you. I'll get the door, Jeremy!"

"Which one?"

"You know... Kevin from bio."

"Oh. I'm almost done putting my clothes on," she laughed. "Ew. That scrub." Then she started singing No Scrubs by TLC.

"It's time we set this straight. Can you just tell him you don't like him? He won't listen to me."

"Ahahaha. Kkzzzzz."

"I'm coming too." Xenon was right behind Chance. "I want to see this Kevin."

Chance opened the door. "What the f*** you want, Kevin?"

"What brings you here?"

"Ummm. I'm here to see Amethyst."

"You're here to see Amethyst? How?"

"Did she say she wanted to see you?"

"Ame, did you say you wanted to see him?" She shook her head as she came to the door. "I didn't think so."

"I got this."

"You got it? Oh. Okay," he backed away from the door.

"Look, Kevin. You seem like a decent guy, but I think we should just remain friends."

"Wh-Why?"

"Because I don't like you like that. I'm sorry."

"I understand." Kevin turned to walk away. Under his breath, he said, "You b****."

"What did you just call me?" Xenon was about to knock him out, but Chance told him Amethyst could handle it on her own.

"I said you bit—" The next thing he knew, Amethyst punched him square in his jaw.

"Think twice before you call a girl a b****. Now get off my porch and walk your little dusty dick ass home. Find some respect for womxn on your way there."

"Niiice." Xenon smiled. "Look how he's holding his face."

"You should have seen her when one of my exes came to the door and tried to fight me. She beat they asses. They were both at least 5ft 10. She's only like 5ft tall."

"Enough talk about fighting. Let's go watch a movie or something. What time is it?"

"It will be 24 minutes post meridiem after I finish this sentence. It's cold in here. I'll be back." He went to go turn the heater on.

"Don't turn it up too high, Chance. I know you like it jacuzzi high. Our buddy here is from the ocean, not earth's core." Xenon smiled because she called him her buddy again. *He's too precious.*

"What's a Ninja Turtle?" *Random AF.*

"I'll show you." She put on the 2003 series of TMNT.

"My favorite is Raphael, but she calls me Mikey."

Xenon danced and sang along to the whole theme song with them. "I have twin katana just like Leonardo, and my favorite color is blue!"

"That's Ame's favorite turtle." She acted like she didn't hear him. Amethyst and Xenon couldn't stop smiling. He was literally the real-life Leonardo. Then Chance did the math. "Wait a minute... Oh, hell no. Do you two like each other?"

"Nope. Not at all. He doesn't like me."

"She doesn't like me. We're just friends, buddies."

A few episodes into season one, she noticed Xenon looked like he was about to faint. "Are you alright?"

"Yeah. I'm just a little lightheaded." Then he dropped to the floor. Amethyst and Chance weren't surprised Jeremy slept through the loud noise.

She placed her hand on his forehead. "Chance, he's burning up. Turn the heater off. He's from the Pacific, not Atlantis. I mean the Atlantic. It was probably already warm in here before you turned on the heater. We're going to put you in some nice, cool water. Can you run the water?" She put him on a bed sheet and dragged him to the bathroom.

"I can carry him for you."

"It's fine. I need you to put him in the tub for me. Take his shirt off." Chance remembered when she saved him. "Put him under. He can breathe underwater."

"Right." After he pushed him down, they sat with their backs against the tub and waited for him to recover.

"I can't stay here."

"It is pretty uncomfortable on the tile."

"No, I mean I can't stay on the surface. I can only be here when it's safe. I don't even know why I'm in danger."

"I know that you don't know any more about this situation than I do, but do you have any idea when you'll be able to stay?"

"No. What if I don't get to see you for a while?"

"The ocean's right there. I'll come to you," he smiled. "How long do you think you'll be gone?"

"I don't know."

"There has to be another way. When are they going to explain the rest? I'm still in shock. Aren't you?"

"Yes, but everything feels so familiar down there. Like I'm supposed to be there. Maybe that's why I've always been drawn to the ocean."

"What about here?"

"I feel like I'm supposed to be here too, but the difference is that I have been here all my life."

"That makes sense. What's up with your little friend? How come he's so quiet?"

She giggled. "Just ask him."

Chance turned his head and found Xenon sitting up in the corner of the tub staring at them. "Ahhh! When did you move?"

"Uh. I've been here for like 3 minutes or maybe 9. No. Like 7." Then he put one of his legs up.

"Wow. Okay. You're pretty flexible. Nice." Chance remembered his question. "Why are you so quiet? That's hella creepy. You and Amethyst... I swear."

"I wasn't trying to be. I prefer to listen."

"To what? People's conversations?"

"No. Well that too, but I was referring to frequencies."

"Frequencies? More like freakquencies." Amethyst smacked Chance and Xenon giggled.

"Ame. Chance. Xenon. Autobots, roll out." Thetis wasn't the only one who needed to get their thoughts together. Jeremy's way of doing that was by sleeping apparently. "Ready for the facts?" He noticed Xenon looked nervous. "Don't worry. We aren't going to your little lair. Your mom told me." He said that last part by eye talking.

"So, you've still got it? You're pretty rusty but still... Hold on. Did you just smile at me?"

"Don't get used to it, little guy," he smiled.

"I could still grow you know," Xenon laughed.

Jeremy almost forgot. "I would put your watch in your pocket if I were you. Iris is heavily fond of shiny things."

"Who?"

"So maybe that's why she kept staring at my ears."

"Where are you going?" Chance asked Xenon.

"I'll catch up. I'm going to dive."

"Dive?" Amethyst and Chance said at the same time. "I'm coming too." Xenon and Amethyst ran for the cliff. He wasn't surprised that she wanted to do it, but he was surprised that she caught up with him with ease.

Meanwhile, Chance, and Jeremy speed walked to the bottom of the Sutro Bath ruins to try to get a better viewing point. "Hello you two." Thetis startled them. "I see you're looking for those two teknon. Look, there they are."

"I don't think she's going to do it. Didn't she just fall from that cliff?" said Iris who was out of sight. *That's what I'm saying.* "Oh, my goddess she is. Is she insane?"

Amethyst and Xenon both dove at the same time. He knew she didn't have enough mass or muscle to pull off the same dive he did from where they were. He had already suspected a bizarre yet reasonable truth. That's why he wasn't worried. She had to be aerodynamic, and that could only mean one thing. Once they were underwater, Xenon offered her a ride. *Lam-BLUE-ghini mercy, Xenon he so thirsty. I'm sorry. It had to be done.*

"There's one," said Jeremy. "Where's Ame?" Xenon and Thetis knew what she was doing.

"She's right there," said Chance.

Amethyst giggled and came from behind Xenon's back. "Nope. I'm right here."

"Wait." He looked at Jeremy. "There's two of you! She looks just like you. Sorry, I didn't see you before. What's your name? I'm Chance."

"I am Iris, daughter of Thetis, basilissa of the basileia."

"Hello, Thetis," he said. "It's great to meet you."

"Your mother is expecting you. We will cross paths with her eventually."

"You know my mom? Is she a sea person too?"

"She is a very good friend of mine and no, she is a land person."

"Whoa. I have officially lost my marbles."

Thetis smiled. "We haven't even started yet." Then her facial expression became serious. "We don't have much time, but we have enough." Everyone was eager to hear what she had to say. She told them everything they needed to know right now, starting at the very beginning. "And later on, I was given a glimpse of my future. All my sons were destined to die early. Six were stillborn, and the seventh was killed in battle despite my efforts to ensure that he wouldn't be harmed. Achilles was a great warrior. I was told that I wasn't going to have a single female child. Hera told me I was going to give birth to the child that would be the missing piece needed to restore balance back to the universe once the balance became disrupted by those in power. We and Athena agreed to follow through with the plan. As a result, I had not a single, but twin daughters. Jeremy and I knew you two would be in danger if we kept you together, so we separated you. One on the surface, one in the ocean. Your biological father was expecting the child to be male since the prophecy said I wasn't going to have a single daughter. He is also sexist. If he would have found out I had twins, he would have realized the loophole in the prophecy and commanded scouts to kill you both immediately."

"But why am I in danger now? I was fine on the surface. Well... Sort of."

"One of you is the one who will restore balance, and the other is the protector. When I gave birth to you, there was no way for me to tell. I figured we would find out soon enough. Amethyst, you're the child. He found you when you accidentally caused those thunderstorms. They were not caused by your father. I called and asked Hera."

Iris's eyes grew large. "HE is our father?"

"Who?!?!?"

"Zeus. Zeus is your biological father." Thetis hated to say it.

"So, she's the chosen one?" asked Iris. "Of course," she rolled her eyes.

"You both have essential roles, but it isn't safe for her to be in this realm. Zeus knows now."

"I wanna meet Hera!" Amethyst gleamed. Xenon was liking her more and more. Like… These are gods were talking about. Does she not understand what danger means?

"Ame is only safe in Poseidon's realm?" Chance needed some clarification.

"Correct."

"Isn't Zeus more powerful than Poseidon though?" Thetis, Jeremy, and Iris just laughed. Amethyst and Xenon were making sandcastles. "Oh, I see."

"I had humans write those books, so the corrupted ones wouldn't know the truth. Maybe I'll let you read the real records one day."

"This is so cool. I love Greek mythology. Well, history I guess. Wait, no. Ame told me those are two sides of the same coin." He looked at his sister. "Bro! You're Thetis's daughter. The one we used to read about. That makes you a demi-god, right?"

"Something like that," said Thetis.

Jeremy said, "I must say, I thought you'd react a lot differently, Chance."

"Memories never go away. We just have a hard time remembering some more than others. Just like how that nightmare you keep having is actually a memory. Your mother and I keep in touch. Generally, this isn't new to you," Thetis informed him. Chance felt so exposed. He just stood there, shooketh to the core. "Iris, you don't seem to be concerned. Any questions?"

"How could I be?" she rolled her eyes. "This should be fun."

"I have a question. Why do I... Why do we look so much different from the other Oceanids?"

Thetis smiled. "Now that is a question that will spark a series of events at the wrong time if I tell you the answer right now." *A series of books. Hehe.*

"What exactly is this chosen one supposed to do? How am I supposed to restore balance back to the universe? Chosen one sounds a bit cheesy by the way."

"The prophecy did not say anything about how, but you are going to be the one who is going to clean up the mess we get ourselves into."

You're a sea cucumber.

Amethyst threw some sand at Xenon. "Riiiiight. How am I the chosen one though? I don't have any superpowers. I really don't think I made those storms. How am I supposed to be some hero when I don't even have myself together? Are you sure it's me? Everything about me is chaotic. Iris seems like a better candidate."

"True. She has a point," said Iris.

"Amethyst, I have only been wrong once." She looked at Jeremy. "I have no doubts. I will answer all further questions unless the time isn't right. We must go."

"G-Goodbye, Amethyst." Chance was about to cry. Amethyst's heart broke when she looked at him. A wave almost reached Chance's feet, but he ran away before it did. "I want you to stay, but I want you to be safe more. Besides, we always talked about how dope it would be to be a hero."

"This isn't goodbye. I'll be back."

Her words reminded Thetis and Jeremy of a moment in their own relationship. "Awww. Look at him, Meter. Come on. I don't want her moping around the bas."

"There is a way he can come with us. It's risky, and you must conquer your fear."

"What do I have to do? I'll do it."

"Chance. Are you sure?" Jeremy asked. "We can—"

"I can do it. I go where she goes."

"All you have to do is walk into the ocean," said Thetis. "It is more difficult than it sounds. It will be somewhat painful at first. You will feel an internal burning."

"Oh, that's no problem. How will I breathe, and what are the risks? Wait. Lemme go put my watch back."

He already can't breathe.

Shhh. Stop talking shit before I beat yo ass. This is serious.

"It will be fine," said Xenon. "That's not a surface watch. The time won't be accurate because it's dependent on the sun."

"You must go alone. If the ocean accepts you, you'll live. The risks include death, drowning, having a panic attack, remembering your oldest memories, trouble breathing, etc."

"I'm ready."

"When you go under, clear your mind and inhale."

Out of the blue, Xenon said, "You aren't ready. I feel it."

"Yeah. I literally just saw you die," Iris giggled. She had a short vision a few seconds ago.

"Here. Hold still." Xenon tied a band of kelp around his eyes.

It's alright. I know why you did it. You didn't deserve to be treated that way. It isn't your fault, and I don't blame you.

"Are you staring at me? I feel your eyes staring at me."

"Trust me, I wasn't staring at you. I was talking."

"To me? How?"

"I was talking to your subconscious. Walk forward and don't stop."

Chance walked right into the ocean. It took him a while, but his will to go with Amethyst was so much stronger than his fear of the ocean. Once he let the ocean take him away, he got nervous because he thought about the deepness and the vastness of the ocean. He was a man of structure, and the ocean is so fluid. He couldn't hold his breath much longer. Xenon sensed that and told him, "There's something you keep denying. Accept it."

There are no tears underwater, but you didn't have to be an empath to know Chance was experiencing one of the most painful and emotional moments of his life. Amethyst felt relieved when she noticed Xenon wasn't tense anymore. Her relief was short lived though. Iris had another short vision and immediately went in after him. Meanwhile, Chance was excited because he was breathing underwater. Then he got caught in a rip current.

"Where is she going?" asked Jeremy.

"Chance got caught in a rip current." Xenon was unphased.

"This isn't good." Amethyst was worried sick.

"He'll be fine if he doesn't fight it. You think he'll try to fight it?" Now Jeremy was worried.

"He won't. He listened to me give a whole presentation about rip currents, but there is a huge rock up ahead. Something tells me he's headed straight for it."

"She's right," said Xenon. "That's why Iris went in after him."

"Iris is an elite swimmer. He'll be fine," Thetis assured them.

Once she was far enough, Iris shifted back into her natural form. She used her powerful fluke to catch up to Chance. Then she joined him in the current and propelled them both out just in time. She almost forgot to shift back on the way back. Iris tackled him on the shore. "Chance! Wake up. Did I swim too fast?"

He woke up saying, "A mermaid. She saved me."

"A mermaid?!?!?" Iris was not happy about that. Xenon laughed at her reaction.

"He doesn't know," said Thetis. "Give him time. He just woke up."

"I saved you. Not some mermaid."

"You did? Oh, yeah. Thank you. I owe you one."

"Eeeeeep!!! You can come with me now! You fought your fear for me. OMG. You're awesome. I know I say this all the time, but you're the best big brother in the whole universe." Iris was so annoyed by all their hugging and Amethyst's constant squealing.

Chance couldn't stop smiling. "Everything was fine before the current, so the ocean must have accepted me, right?"

"Yes," said Xenon. He was happy he was okay, but he wasn't exactly excited that he was coming along. Amethyst was glad, but what if he was Iris's soulmate?

"Why? Was it because I'm so courageous? Am I part god too, or was it simply because of my good looks?"

Xenon turned his nose up and jerked his neck back after that last comment. "You only survived because you're Amethyst's brother. There are tons of people that would accept the risk of death for Amethyst."

Iris rolled her eyes. "What a gem."

"Whatever. Where is she?" Chance asked. He was busy rubbing the saltwater out of his eyes and nose. He also still had a headache. In addition, Amethyst had a way of being dead silent. The ocean had a message for her.

Xenon's eyes grew. "Amethyst, what's wrong?" She was the only person he ever had to ask what they were feeling because he actually didn't know.

"This isn't right. So many people have died. They were slaughtered because…"

"What do you mean? Who died?" Chance encouraged her to say the rest.

"They died because of me. It can all be connected back to them believing this prophecy. I thought our worlds were different, but in both, people are killed by the thousands. For what? Whhhhhhy?!?!?"

The other Oceanids felt the tide going out more rapidly than it should have. Xenon was the closest to her and wrapped his arms around her as tightly as he could without hurting her. "That's why we need you. It's not your fault. You're the solution." The tide gradually returned to normal.

"'Okeanos is a friend to she who genuinely suffers the mourning of others even in her own white waters.' Amphitrite," Iris quoted her teachings. Thetis nodded. "I understand what that means now."

Just when they thought she was calm, Amethyst shouted, "Then who did this?!?!?" Xenon felt her muscles tense up and her body temperature rise exponentially. Everyone noticed the grey sky become darker. Once lightning struck dangerously close to them, they panicked. *If you're a simple person like me and are wondering where all the people are, they are all inside because they didn't want to take any chances going to Sutro Baths due to yesterday's weather. You're welcome.*

"I-Is she doing that? So, she really can cause storms." Iris didn't know what to think.

"Amethyst stop!" Jeremy called out to her. His tone only made her more nervous. "He'll be able to attack you much easier!"

"Amethyst calm down." Thetis tried, but now Amethyst was having an anxiety attack. 'Stop' and 'calm down' were the top two worst things to tell an upset Amethyst.

Chance was massaging her shoulders and going, "Shhhhh." He was also giving Xenon the eye for hugging her. He didn't care if that was Oceanid culture or not.

"Remember when you were falling from that cliff, and I caught you? What made you feel better?" *Look at these parents. LMAO.*

"The water. It felt like the ocean was cradling me."

"Why did it feel like that?"

"The temperature was just right. The ocean felt so welcoming, so surreal, so safe." Then she realized how much better she felt. "Woo. Thanks guys. Sorry. Sometimes I get like that. How was I doing that?"

"Zeus us your biofather. What did you expect?" Chance laughed.

"Xenon, what's that on your hand?"

Nothing gets by you does it?

"It's nothing."

"No, it's not. Nothing gets by me. You're hurt. Let me see." Amethyst grabbed his wrist and looked at his palm. "What happened? Did I burn you? I am so sorry." Chance was too busy being salty because he didn't have Amethyst's complete attention instead of thinking about why he didn't get burned.

"It's cool. It will be gone once I get in the water."

As they prepared to descend, Thetis said, "Be careful, Jeremy. You haven't been this deep in a while." *What a f****** queen…*

Amethyst and Xenon looked at each other like "Oh shiiiiizzzzz." Meanwhile, Iris and Chance were confused because they didn't pick up on that innuendo. In their defense, it was pretty slippery. You'd have to have a slippery mind to pick up on that.

Underwater, Chance was doing well for the same reason he feared the ocean. Of course, Xenon offered to carry Amethyst. "I'm not too heavy?" she joked.

"You're as light as a sea star."

"Then please do." She clamped onto his back. "Wait."

"What is it, Princess?" Iris and Chance cringed at the sound of that word.

I'm uh… You know… It's that time… LOLZZZZZ. I don't know how your senses or whatever are going to react to that.

I know. It's completely natural. Plus, you'll be more comfortable because of my body heat. Are surface guys weird about that?

"I don't feel like carrying you." Iris dove down for a long, sturdy piece of kelp. She tied one end around Chance's waist and the other around hers.

"What are you doing? I didn't ask for help. Ahhhh." Iris pulled him along. He was still trying to figure out the science of being able to speak underwater. He learned how to do it by accident when he almost died. *This queen just put him on a leash. I smell a kink, but that's none of my business.*

"Whoa, you just got hotter," said Amethyst. "Hotter as in your temperature increased."

"It changes automatically depending on my surroundings," said Xenon.

"Am I making you too warm? I don't want you to pass out again."

"No, it's not that. Oceanids' body temperatures adapt to make their friend or partner more comfortable. I'm not sure if it's a myth, but they say that soulmates become completely in sync with each other after…"

"After what? Why you holding back?"

He blushed and said, "After they mate."

"That's so cool!!! I knew soulmates were real. Everyone has one, right? Who's yours?"

"Shaaaaark!" Chance yelled.

"Aw, come on. It's a jumper or what the humans call a shortfin mako. It's the fastest shark there is." Iris was so annoyed. "And it's rogue. Great. This is absolutely fantastic."

"I'll handle the shark," said Jeremy. Chance needed to get used to Jeremy being an Oceanid.

"Wait, Dad. Don't."

"Hold on. Listen to her, Jeremias," Thetis said. He kept a hard eye on the shark as he let them swim by. The shark swam right up to Amethyst and opened their mouth. Everyone watched in amazement as she climbed in and pulled out a tooth. Xenon felt guilty about how attractive that was to him. He was thankful it was daylight, so no one could tell he was slightly glowing.

"He had a toothache?" Jeremy chuckled.

"They had a toothache. It was loose, so I think they were trying to slam it out or something." The shark followed Amethyst. It was cute until they swam above her. Xenon got so angry, she was scared for the shark. He swam up to the shark and made this terrifying sound that was a mixture of a groan and a series of clicks. She loved how large his pupils got.

The shark swam away at top speed. Amethyst realized what just happened and started laughing hysterically. "No way. If that was the case, they should have swum below me." *I'm weeeak. I cannot with her.*

"What is that supposed to mean, young lady?" Jeremy didn't think it was funny. *What a dad.*

"Oh relax, Jeremias. It was a joke," Thetis giggled. "If she was your son you'd cheer her on."

"Relax? How am I supposed to relax! That damn shark was all gilly. What about these Oceanids? I know she's her own person. Surface males made me this way. They're predators. All of them."

"I know. We already knew the charm of our daughters would be able to catch the attention of Narcissus," she smiled. "You mean one Oceanid in particular, don't you? Why don't you just ask?"

"Fine. I will."

"Why is Dad so upset?" Amethyst loved having her own personal empath.

"The possibility of us being more than friends shakes his shells."

"Did you say possibility?" *So, she just gon ignore that funny azz phrase that just came out of his mouth?*

"Xenon!" Jeremy used his so-called manly voice. "Explain how you feel about Amethyst. Be completely honest."

If I could I would.

"I'm glad she's back. I think we are going to be good friends."

"You haven't had any gilly thoughts about her?"

Jeremy, you have no idea.

"I've had gilly thoughts about all my friends." Jeremy lost it. Chance snapped out of being in shock and lost it too.

Iris found them amusing. "Men."

"Ignore those two," said Thetis.

"You aren't laughing at me? Jeremy just exposed me."

"I have respect for anyone who is honest. Plus, it's totally natural."

And I already hit it in my dreams.

You did? I did too.

How was I?

Goddess-like. How was I?

You were alright hehehe.

"What are you two talking about?" Iris knew they were flirting.

"Can we take a break?" Amethyst asked. Xenon stopped immediately.

"You're on Blue's back. How are you tired?" Iris asked.

"I feel sick."

"Oh, gemmie. That's because your clothes are too heavy. They're creating too much drag. You need to take them off," Iris explained.

"I'll make you some temporary clothing." Xenon dove down to get some kelp.

"Chat with me while we wait. When we get home, I'll help you decorate your room when it's ready. We have an actual room for you, but it needed to be cleaned up. We weren't expecting you this early," she giggled as she played with Amethyst's hair. "There is so much I want to show you. I can't believe I have a twin."

"What's our mother like?"

"She's not strict at all, but I know she has a crazy side. She's the chill parent."

"What happened between her and Dad?"

"She doesn't talk about it much. All I know is that they decided to put their relationship on hold. They met up all the time though. They can't stay away from each other."

"What do you think about all of the so-called mermaid sightings on the surface?"

"They're false. If humans saw anyone, they probably saw a Nereid or some other Oceanid. Mermaids don't ever leave the depths."

"Have you ever been caught?"

"Once. They kept yelling mermaid. Disgusting."

"Well, if they saw your legs then maybe they'd have thought otherwise." Iris put on her best poker face.

"Ready?" asked Xenon. "I hope you like it." He handed Iris a halter crop top.

"You made this from kelp? I'm impressed. I see you're good with your hands." Xenon didn't catch that innuendo at first. He wasn't expecting her to say something like that in front of them. He admired her boldness. That was something she and Iris had in common. Amethyst was like a nicer, wilder version of Iris.

"Here." Iris handed her a small strand of kelp she picked up. "Use this for... I don't know what humans call it. A pad?" Amethyst was a bit uncomfortable because Iris was watching her. *Oceanids bruuuh.*

"This actually feels a lot better." Iris took Amethyst's scrunchie off. "Hey. What are you doing?"

"Don't worry. We don't litter. I'm leaving it for the teknon that are going to pass through here soon. They collect everything."

"I need that for my hair. See… Bruuuh, now it's all in my face. Can you put it up for me? My curls don't hang down like yours."

"She doesn't know how to do hair that well. I do though. I'll braid it for you."

"Please do." Amethyst was curious to see how she looked, but she left her mirror. "How do I look?"

"Pretty of course. See for yourself." Iris handed her a small mirror. "I always have a mirror on me."

"That's crazy. Ame usually does too," said Chance.

"The look is missing something. What do you think, Blue?"

"I know just the thing." He brought her some reddish-purple kelp. He wrapped one strand around her arm and one around her ankle. "Wine kelp keeps invertebrates away and makes for good accessories." *Issa look?*

Once they arrived, all the Oceanids were shouting something about basilinna and basilissa. Then something about basi and horaios as Amethyst and Xenon went by. "What are they saying?"

"They're saying, 'Look they have returned with friends. The queen has returned, the princess has returned! The prince has returned! And the… I'm not sure how to translate that," Iris told her.

"They are calling you 'the blooming'," Xenon said.

"Yeah, that's it. How do you know how to translate that?"

"I'm an empath remember."

"I forgot." Iris giggled.

"What do I say back? How do I say thank you?"

He laughed and said, "No need. Just keep doing what you're doing. A smile is worth more than a thousand words."

Yours is worth all of them.

"Why hasn't the red one spoken?" Iris labeled him as unusual.

"He's counting. He does that a lot. Soak it in. He has a chatterbox phase." Xenon tried to see if he could throw him off.

"Are you hungry?" asked Thetis.

"OMG yaaasssss. I am staaarving."

"You are? I don't understand," Iris was confused.

"It's figurative language," Thetis explained. "It's a common surface phrase."

"Ohhh. Right. I remember. I guess I have been pretty off lately."

"First we're gonna take a nap," said Jeremy. "Then we'll get you dressed and show you around."

"A nap? Oh, hell yeah!" said Chance.

"The palace looks different during the day doesn't it?" said Jeremy.

"Yes, a lot less frightening."

"I'll carry her from here, Blue." Iris and Xenon swapped passengers.

"I know you said I'm light but thank you. Maybe you could give me swimming lessons later on."

"Y-You're welcome and sure, I'd love that. I mean... S-Sure." He scratched the back of his head in embarrassment. "W-Well, I'll leave you two alone. See you at breakfast. I-I mean dinner. No. Lunch. I'll see you at lunch."

"Wow. I've never seen him so off." Iris was judging. "Unlike you, I've been swimming for what you call hours. I'm going to sleep, but you can make yourself at home. If you're tired sleep. If not, play in my makeup or something." Before she could respond, Iris was knocked out.

"I guess Chance isn't the only one with the ability to fall asleep in under a minute." She wanted to know about underwater makeup, so she crawled over to Iris's dresser and did exactly what she suggested. Just as she was hoping, the makeup of this mysterious realm was able to be applied underwater. Amethyst climbed her way up to the second floor. She was too afraid to swim up there without a spotter. Although still technically underwater, the upper half had a dry, smooth surface. She still thought that was cool. The second floor extended in both directions. She didn't notice that last time. It sort of reminded her of a table aquarium. She went to the left. She didn't see anyone, so she lowered herself into the water to check it out. While she was holding onto the wall, she saw Xenon checking himself out in one of the mirrors.

"Oh, my goddess!!! What are you doing?" Xenon was so embarrassed.

"I'm exploring. Aren't you supposed to be sleeping? I thought the books were in the other room."

"This is the other book room."

"Impressive." *What a flirt.*

"What is?"

"I'm talking about the books. These ones are different. They're all digital. Why'd you blush, cutie?" *Petty.*

"W-We try to keep a balance of traditional scrolls and modern ones." He helped her the rest of the way down.

"What's that scroll about?"

"Ummm…" Xenon tried to swap the books.

Amethyst picked the book up herself. Now she really wanted to know. "An Analysis of Oceanid Romance and Sexual Attraction."

"How'd you read that?" He tried to change the subject. "What kind of books do you like to read?"

"I just sounded out what I could. I'm familiar with the Greek alphabet. I had to use context clues for the rest. So, tell me. How do Oceanids show affection?"

"F-For example, if their soulmate's life is in jeopardy, an Oceanid will never leave their s-soulmate's side. Instead, they will look deeply into their eyes to feel what they are feeling so they won't be alone. Their soulmate will force them to leave, but an Oceanid will forever be heartbroken if they obey and their soulmate dies."

"That's tragically beautiful. What else?"

"Oceanids shake when they're aroused," he laughed. "We call them bubbles. It's really funny."

"What does this say?"

Xenon stuck his ear stars on, so he could listen to the audio. "Oceanids make a purring sound when their ear is touched, especially when rubbed from behind."

"Whoa! Are those wireless earbuds? You just stick them on? They look just like little sea stars! Ooooo! And they're so squishy!"

"Yeah. I guess they are pretty cool. I um… I was the one who…"

"No. Way. You designed them? Shut. Up. That sounds like trouble. What's that one about," she distracted him. Then she rubbed behind his ear.

"Klllrrrrrrrrrrrrrrrr." He smiled and stretched his foot out while holding onto her thigh. "Oh yeah, d-don't stop." *Don't y'all go grabbing your boo thang's ear.*

Iris heard that and popped up on them, "What is going on in here?" Then she saw that Amethyst was just rubbing his ear. "I see you found out about the simeio," she giggled.

Amethyst let go of his ear. "Oh shit. Hey, Iris. You thought he was in trouble huh?"

"You are something else, Little Scallop." He gave her a little playful bump.

"Why did you have to listen to the audio? Are you dyslexic too?"

"Yeah. For me personally, I like having audio with the text."

"I knew it."

"You could tell?"

"You struggle with time and mental math, but that doesn't determine if someone has dyslexia. Dyslexia is so diverse. LOL. I was referring to the audio part. You did all that extra shit when you could have just read it. Plus, the book was upside down. I heard Aristide say something about you being the type of dyslexic person that doesn't like reading stuff. Anyways, why are you so interested in sex, love, and romance?"

"In my first half-life, I was missing something. I was incomplete. I searched and searched blindly. I would think I was in love because I was so desperate. Once I realized my mate wasn't filling that void, I would depart from them. For a while, I thought I was asexual. Then I realized that wasn't the case. I realized I was in love with a figment of my imagination but never the person I was with. I was horrible. Then during my second half-life, something felt different. I feel like I might find what I'm missing, but I don't know. Also, I know I'm demi now."

"You get more and more interesting each day."

"Mom is waking up. It's almost time to eat."

Iris mocked her Meter. "Xenon, put some clothes on."

"Mom always says that after nap time because I never have any clothes on. We usually have guests."

"Xenon! Put some clothes on," Thetis yelled from her room. "I don't want you scarring people for life."

"Don't worry, Mom. I'm dressed."

Amethyst loved how wearing shorts, somewhat of a top, and a few accessories was considered dressed. "Now let's get you some new clothes," said Iris. "You can keep the ones you have on for pajamas. If you don't wear pajamas, you can wear them as lounge clothes." She dragged her sister to her room. "You can choose from any of these. No pranks this time." Amethyst chose a short dress made from brown algae. She wore shorts underneath of course. She wished Iris owned some shorts she could wear on their own. "Nice choice. It compliments your curves. Now for makeup."

"Actually, I think I'll pass on that. I'd like some lip gloss though. Makeup has just never really been my thing. I just feel weird with it on. I'll probably mess it up anyway. Don't get me wrong, I love makeup. Makeup or no makeup, it doesn't matter to me. I think people should do whatever makes them feel good."

Iris was judging. She opened one of her boxes. "This is lip shimmer, this is lip glimmer, this is lip gleam, this is lip glass, this is lip glitter, and this is lip paint. If you want something less dark, you'll have to ask Blue. He also has eyeliner." Amethyst didn't know anything about makeup, but she was a lip gloss pro. She wasn't overwhelmed by the terms. She was about to choose her lip gloss when Iris asked, "Do you like my bracelet? Look. Aren't they beautiful? Be honest."

"Um. No. Why are you whispering? They're obviously some of the finest, but I just don't like them."

"Literally everyone else obsesses over them."

"Oh. I like this sand dollar purple lip glimmer."

Iris was so excited. "I call it that too! It's called poison purple, but that's totally inaccurate."

"Poison purple has a darker undertone with a hint of mauve."

"Exactly!!!" She hugged her twin.

"Can you ask Xenon if I can borrow his eyeliner?"

"You know how to do eyeliner! That's the only thing I can't get right."

"And I can't do foundation and stuff," they both laughed. "We sort of balance each other out. No. We're like inverses."

Xenon swam into Iris's room. "What color do you want?"

"What purples do you have?"

"I have lilac, midnight purple, lavender, and ink."

"Midnight purple. How do you open this?"

"I'll do it. What kind of line do you want?"

"Do you know about the cat-eye?" Amethyst hoped.

"Do I know? I'm the queen of the cat-eye."

"You did good."

"Good?" He was offended.

"Let me do yours."

He handed her the sea jelly blue which was a deep shade of pastel blue. Amethyst loved the sleek, creamy texture of Oceanid eyeliner much better. It was like a cross between ink and paint. Again, it could be applied underwater! That was so cool. "Huh!" he gasped.

"Looks like we have a new queen of the cat-eye," Iris teased him.

"I'm going to keep the pride I have left and go cry in my room," he laughed.

"Your hair still looks great but put this on it." Iris gave her a seashell with a glob of dense moisturizer gel. It made Amethyst's hair really sticky and heavy at first. She learned that the moisturizer was the secret to Iris's hair. "Ready? Follow me. Leave those glasses."

"Isn't this the way to the ballroom? I didn't know we were going to a luncheon?"

"Relax. You look fine."

The ballroom was drained again. This time it was completely filled with tables and chairs. Chance, Jeremy, and Thetis were already seated. Iris was escorted by Reign. "Shall we enter, Your Highness?" asked Xenon.

"You and your little princey-poo voice."

"I use it when I have to act 'royal'," he whispered.

"I can tell. Who are all of these people?"

"They're our guests. Every day we serve lunch to our people. We can't host everyone at once, so we have them sign up. I made a programmed system to make sure everyone has equal opportunities. They don't always see us though. Sometimes they only see one or two of us. Some people sign up as groups. Like there."

"That's awesome. Seems like you treat them well. On the surface... Well, all I'm gonna say is that they don't really care about us. Huh! There are so many people, and some of them got all dressed up. Ahhh. This is totally a formal event."

Xenon was disappointed because he didn't think she really heard what he said about the program he made. "It's not. The people who are dressed up are all trying to get me or Iris's attention. Or both. Now you're here, so they want your attention too. There are so many rumors and stories about you. Especially about why you were on the surface."

When Amethyst walked in, the room fell silent. "They're staring at me. Why are they staring at me?"

"Most of them have never seen you. The latest gossip is that Iris has an evil twin sister. They weren't sure if it was true. Say something. People can understand you even if they don't know English for some reason."

"Hello everyone," she giggled. "I see that I am a little underdressed compared to some of you. I apologize. I wasn't aware. I hope you all weren't waiting on me. Let's eat. I myself am starving. Not literally as you can see. I mean that figuratively." The room filled with laughter.

"Look at her. She's a gem just like her sister. Her name suits her," one womxn said to the people around her.

"Isn't she charming?" "Imagine a photoshoot of the twins!" "I have to get a picture with her at her coronation." "Oh, my goddess!!! Me too." "And she's foreign. Omega Mu Gamma!" The group of young fans Xenon pointed out were shelled.

"You're a natural," said Xenon.

"Naturally nervous," she told him as he pulled her chair out. He helped her read the menu. He knew it by heart. Amethyst was thankful she was able to find something edible. Xenon helped her put together a Greek phrase.

"What can I get for you, Your Highness?"

Xenon nudged her to let her know the waiter was talking to her. Everyone silenced themselves because they wanted to hear what she was going to order. "Um, I'll have the salmon plate with nori and extra rice." She did her best to say the phrase they came up with. "Do you have wasabi? Lots of that please."

"Wasabi?" asked the waiter.

"Kelp paste," Xenon told him.

"Of course."

"You eat kelp paste? That's spicy," said Iris. Everyone was listening to their conversation.

"I love spicy food." Then everyone started whispering. "What are they talking about?"

"Ocean goers don't like spicy food. You're the second one to like it. Only juveniles like that much kelp. Even then, it's eaten separately."

"So only you and I eat spicy food?"

"Yep."

"So why do you like it?"

"Because I'm not from around here."

They're talking about how extraordinary it is that the young princess is so similar to the prince."

"Shut up. That's what you're saying," she laughed. Amethyst was surprised at how fast the food came.

"I presume service is better down here than on the surface," said a man.

"From what I can tell, yes, by far."

Amethyst didn't notice everyone, including Thetis, watching her make sushi. *LMAO. This girl really made sushi.* "Did you learn that on the surface?" an Oceanid asked.

"Yes, we call it sushi."

"I'll have what she's having without the kelp paste."

"Me too." Soon almost everyone was imitating Amethyst.

"Do they not like sushi either?"

"I was the only one who did. I used to eat it in private because they thought it was weird. You just changed that," he giggled. "It will probably be trending now."

"Ayyye. They with the movement." *I'm deeead. What the sushi?* "What do I do with my plate?"

"Just leave it there, Little Scallop."

"You like calling me that don't you? Is that my nickname?"

"One of them. You remind me of something else, but I can't think of what that is."

"It bet not be something bad."

After the luncheon was over, the royal family helped the waitresses and waiters clean up. "About last night... You knew I wasn't telling you the whole story, but you never asked me about that. Why?"

"I didn't expect you to tell me more than what you said. We barely know each other here. What? Why are you looking at me like that? Don't smile at me like that. That's gon get you in trouble." *Please don't ask me what she means by trouble. What you're thinking is probably right.*

When they exited the ballroom and re-submerged, Xenon decided to show her another one of his secret places. "Can I show you something?" he whispered. "We have to be quick because we're about to leave."

"Sure. Let's go." Thetis saw them plotting something, but she didn't see any harm in a little fun, so she acted like she didn't see anything.

"Is it okay for me to carry you?" Xenon asked.

"Go ahead, princey-poo." She wrapped her arm around his neck, and he held onto her waist as he swam to the surface at his top speed. *I smell an innuendo coming.* "You like stroking in this position?" *There it is. What did I tell you? These two are huge flirts. I'll keep saying it until it's normalized.*

"Actually, I prefer a little more action." Once they broke the surface, Xenon sat Amethyst on the edge. Then he slowly pulled himself up. "Hi." He was trying to show off his muscles.

She just rolled her eyes. "I didn't know Haliai could swim that fast."

"They can't. Just me. I'm special."

Amethyst remembered how Iris was also a fast swimmer. He didn't mention her, so she added that to the pool of evidence she was gathering for her thesis. "I'm blind as f*** up here without my glasses."

"This path is flat. You won't fall. If you do, I'll catch you."

"So where are we going?"

"I'm going to show you something. It's kind of a secret. I'm not hiding it or anything, but no one else comes up here." He didn't ask her not to tell anyone because she seemed trustworthy. *Everyone says that about her.*

"You have a lot of secrets, don't you? I won't tell. I'm good at keeping— Whoa! What is this place?"

"I call it To Fengári Mou Kípo or My Moon Garden."

"This is breathtaking. I've never seen some of these plants before. When do you water them?"

"I don't need to. Check this out. This is my aquaculture irrigation system. I built it myself. I can control it from my phone. Feel free to look around. Just stay away from the— AMETHYST!"

"What?" she asked casually.

"Get out of there! What are you doing?!?!? Those flowers are toxic which is why the sign says do not enter," he rolled his eyes.

"I couldn't read it, and who told you that?"

"Selene. She's the one who gave them to me as a coronation gift. They help me keep my emotions under control. I can get really moody. I was already moody before the moon thing happened, but now I'm even moodier. She told me not to touch them without gloves. I carry some of the fallen petals with me in this locket. One time I accidentally touched them, and I almost died. Selene healed me. Thank goddess."

"Wait. Pause. Can you do me a favor? Can you put your gloves on and pull the wrist part, so it makes the sound? You know... Like the doctors do."

He did his little smirk. "Like that?"

"Ahhh! Boy you didn't have to add that little jaw clench," she laughed. "Ooo shit. I don't like alcohol, but I do have a sweet tooth, and you're a whole ass chocolate bar. Damn girl. Can I speak to the bartender? Ima have to get myself drink." Xenon couldn't stop giggling. "I don't throw money, but you're a whole ass chocolate fountain. I just might make a wish. Can I take a dip? I'm not the 9 to 5 type, but I'd love to work in your chocolate factory."

Xenon hid his face. "Oh, my goddess. I caaan't with you. You are too much."

"What happened when you touched them?"

"The what?"

"Your flowers."

"Oh, right. I got hives all over my body."

"You're allergic."

"What did you just call me?" *Lol. THE sass…*

"Allergic. It's not an insult. It's a diagnosis. Why do you need these again?"

"The smell soothes me, but I think it helps with these damn hormones that make me so moody."

"Even if you are extra moody, I don't think there's anything wrong with that."

"OMG you don't?" he smiled.

"Nope. Why'd you bring me here? I know it's not just because of these pretty flowers."

"I-I… It's just that… I know I just met you, but I really want to be friends, and I'm scared that once you learn the truth about me, you won't want to be my friend anymore, so I'm going to warn you, so you don't hate me, and I won't be sad." He started crying his eyes out.

Amethyst opened her arms and signaled for him to come to her. He didn't waste any time and plopped down right there on the floor next to her. "What do you mean?"

"I'm not innocent like everyone thinks I am." *No, no you aren't.* "I'm not some perfect prince."

"That's okay. I got issues too." *Yes, yes you do.* "If people knew what really went on in my head, I don't think everyone would think the same things about me. I'm not the good girl, straight A scholar with a perfect life some people think I am. I understand."

"Really?"

"Really."

"I'm sorry for crying on you."

"Don't worry about it. I love how you're not afraid to display your emotions. That's uncommon on the surface. Especially for males. We have a shit load of toxic masculinity up there. What's society like down here? Is that an Oceanid thing or a Xenon thing?"

"All Oceanids are really emotional compared to land goers, and ocean goers consider me moody. Humans would consider us 'touchy-feely' because we're more emotionally open and intelligent. Anyways, our society isn't built on heteropatriarchy. I'll never understand things like that. Don't get me wrong. We still have plenty of issues, and there are plenty of sharks swimming around. Just not like on the surface. Physical trash isn't the only thing that gets dumped down here."

"I see. When are you going to tell me about the programs you built?"

"So, you did hear that!" he gleamed. "I'll show you at some point. What perfume did you use?"

"I didn't wear any because I didn't want to bring those toxins down here. Many surface people do that already. And I didn't know y'all had perfume down here."

"Then it must be your pheromones that smell like that."

"Is it a bad smell?"

"Nope." He took an intense sniff. "It's the best smell ever."

"That tickles," Amethyst laughed. "Ummm, thanks. How come I can't smell yours?"

"You know how my hormones got screwed up thanks to that time wave that no one knows anything about? My scent hasn't developed yet."

"Awww, you're still going through puberty, aren't you?"

"Omega Mu Gamma! How can you tell?" Her comment made him blush.

"Your voice cracks all the time," she giggled. "Let's head back. I'm sure they're looking for us by now."

"Where were you two?" Iris, Reign, and Chance said at the same time. Iris's tone was suspicious, Reign's tone was calm, and Chance was just downright distraught.

"I had to go to the bathroom," said Amethyst.

"And you needed him to escort you?" Chance wasn't buying it.

"You didn't need to escort her," Iris said.

"I still can't see very well."

"You two are overreacting." Reign could tell what they were thinking.

"What were you two doing in the bathroom?" Iris asked.

"I was the only one in the bathroom, and I was taking a dump."

"How come you didn't come back after you showed her where the bathroom was?" Iris and Chance said at the same time.

"Because she doesn't have her glasses, and I'm her escort." *LOL. I swear...*

"Ummm hmmm. Whatever." Iris didn't believe them.

"What did you think they were doing?" Reign wanted to keep the fire going.

"It's obvious these two kissy fish have chemistry. I bet they've already made out."

"So, are you saying you thought they were doing it?" Reign added more coals.

"Oh, hell no. First of all, I'm PMSing, so don't mess with me. Also, if I was even thinking about having sex with anyone I would wait until I'm not bleeding anymore. There's nothing wrong with having sex on your period, but we weren't, so don't be making shit up."

"It's normal for Oceanids to start exploring that area of affection at a young age depending on their maturity," said Iris.

Help me make them uncomfortable, so they'll leave us alone.

"We would have taken much longer," Xenon said.

"And you would have heard us," she added. "Moaning like ummm ooo ah yes just like that. Right there. You like that, baby?"

"Okay, okay we get it." Chance didn't want to hear any more.

"Surface people turn their noses up at the thought of 16-year-olds doing it," said Amethyst.

"Why?" they asked.

"They claim it's because of teen pregnancy. No one really educates the youth on protection and safe sex. It's funny because adults have plenty of issues with raising a child and getting sexually transmitted diseases. I know teens who are better parents than some adults. Some people shame young people as if they forgot what they were doing when they were younger. If everyone was more educated about safe sex and protection, things would be so much better. Instead of making sex such a taboo for the youth, especially females, it's safe to say everyone would be a little bit happier. LOL. I'm not saying people should go all out like rabbits. By the way, statistics show teens aren't nearly as sexually active as people think they are. I'm just saying everyone should be able to explore their bodies safely. It's natural. People are going to do it anyway, so why not educate them properly in an inclusive and non-sexist way? Plus, often times uneducated youth grow up to be uneducated adults. They completely omitted sex ed from the curriculum, but it's not like it was done right in the first place. Sex ed is important! Everyone can't be a sexspert, but everyone should know the essentials."

"That's really unusual. It isn't like that down here. Also, males can't even produce sperm cells mature enough until they're at least 23," said Iris.

"Must be nice for some people. What do y'all use for protection?"

"There's this herbal paste. You put it in your vagina before or after and it disables all sperm cells. It's also pretty tasty," said Iris.

"Noted," she laughed. "How do you know it's tasty?" *sips tea*

Iris smiled, "I know a lot of things, little sister."

"Well damn," said Chance. "Can I know too?" Iris and Xenon rolled their eyes while Reign was just giggling away.

"There you are," said Jeremy. Now they were all giggling like scallops because their conversation ended right on time.

"Everyone ready? Here you are." Thetis handed Amethyst and Chance a little sack of small silver coins and other forms of currency. She gave them a little more than the others. "Spend it how you like."

"Whoa. Thank you! Your mom is dope."

"Not used to having that much money I see," Iris giggled.

"Chance is actually rich. Like hundreds of millions of dollars rich. He just doesn't flaunt it."

"Is that so? Never mind then."

"I don't need all of this. I have more than Iris." Her sister rolled her eyes at her comment.

"I'm sure you'll make good use of it," Thetis told her.

"And you literally don't have anything. I have a lot of nice things." Meanwhile, Chance was just now drooling over the chariot they were about to get in. He loved gold.

"Once we arrive in Aspasia, you may explore as long as one of you three is with one of those two," she instructed them. "And once we get close, you'll have to swim the rest of the way." The scallops were trying to hold themselves together because they were reminded of their little conversation when she said 'explore'.

"What's Aspasia? Is it a mall?" asked Amethyst.

"Aspasia is a city that is sort of like New York without the rats." She wondered how Thetis knew about the rats.

"Cool! How long do we have?"

"You all have until before the next tide."

"When is that?" Chance didn't understand what that meant. "Like… What time?"

"You're stuck with us. We'll know," Reign assured him.

"Ohhhh so it's one of those Oceanid things."

"Not all Oceanids can do it," Iris said.

"More like one…" Reign and Iris were teasing you know who.

"Classic." Xenon rolled his eyes with an upturned nose. His sass threw Chance off. *This was his first encounter.*

"Is it because of the time wave?" Amethyst asked.

"No. He was like that before that." Reign made herself laugh harder.

"Ame is the same way."

Really?

Yeah. I'm not good with time and stuff. Chance is though. It's like his ancestors invented the clock or something.

"Whaaaat… I see what you mean now, Iris," Reign said. "This should be good. Hehehe."

Thetis popped into their convo when they arrived. "Chance, I know you have a perfect sense of surface time, but ocean time is different. It changes. Low tide is in exactly 7 hours by the time I finish what I'm telling you. Just before always means about 1 hour and 30 minutes before."

"Got it. Thanks."

Reign was pumped. "Alright let's go!" she twirled.

"I'll take Amethyst," Iris volunteered.

"Looks like I'm with you, Freckles." Reign did what Amethyst assumed was the equivalent of skipping underwater. *Swimpping? Swimppickiking? IDK.* "I'll carry you, so we'll all get there faster." Amethyst wasn't surprised that Chance didn't complain.

"Where do the non-wealthy people live?" Amethyst asked.

"There are no poor or wealthy people here. Some are a bit richer, but none are poor. Oceanids share and live as one community," Thetis told her. "Our queendom is organized in somewhat of a circle. We can visit the homes afterward. Aspasia is in the main circle, and the bas is in the center. There are numerous cities all adjacent to each other."

"Look, Iris! The new face art shop is almost open!" Xenon was super excited. "At that one, we'll be able to customize our own lip shine!"

"Omega! Mu! Gamma! We have to take Amethyst when it opens! You can come too Reign and Chance. It'll be fun. You can even pick your own flavor!"

"I'll come, but I'm not buying any of that stuff," Reign laughed.

Chance was so confused. "I'm lost."

"Face paint is makeup, and lip shine is ummm… What did you call it again, sister? I forgot."

"Lip gloss. Eeeeep! I can't wait!"

"Isn't that a bit feminine?" Chance asked.

The Oceanids laughed. "You're one of those surface guys, aren't you?" Xenon smiled. "No color has a place on your scale of binary femininity and masculinity, but I guess red, orange, and green tend to be popular with those who consider themselves more masculine."

Jeremy asked, "How you two holding up?" Amethyst and Chance told him they were doing great. That made sense considering how things were on the surface.

"We'll meet back here," Thetis said. "Have fun." Then she and Jeremy took off. The rest of them followed Iris.

"So, you like my best friend?" Chance said with his big bro tone.

You have no idea. Wait. Does he mean like as in as a partner? Do I like her like that? She is them, right? Then of...

"Of course. Everyone does."

"You know what I mean man-child. I don't like you, but I can see Amethyst does, so I'm going to do my best to see a little bit of whatever the hell she sees."

I'm not a Man. Ohhhh. He means man as in male, not Man. Even then...

Xenon smiled. "So, does this mean we are friends?" He held out his arms for a hug.

"Hell nah." Xenon's expression sank. "You're more like my long-lost annoying little step-brother that I just met and don't trust yet." Xenon did his puppy eyes, so Chance was like, "F*** it. Bring it in."

"Awww!" Reign thought that was the cutest thing ever. "Anger Management has a sweet side."

"Is it that surprising? Girl, how you know about my anger issues anyway?" Chance loved how high-pitched Reign's voice was.

"Not at all, Freckles," she twirled. "Don't worry about it. I just know things."

That's when Xenon sensed something totally unexpected.

Guess what, Little Scallop. I think Chance and Reign just flirted with each other.

What? For real?

Yes. Actually, they definitely like each other.

JK. I know. I been peeped. He likes the bubbly athletic type.

Oh. We can't all have a thing for each other. Well, I mean like in pairs, not like a group thing.

I know what you mean. What's the problem? Something is telling me there's a problem.

Iris thinks Chance is her soulmate.

Why? They just met. How can she be sure? I'll tell you right now. They do not go together.

Exactly! You know how she can see the future in her mirror, right?

She can? I just thought she had visions.

Yes, but her mirror will also show her moments in the future depending on what she asks. She can't see everything though. The mirror only shows her some things. Anyways, one time I asked her who my soulmate is, and the mirror didn't show her anyone. Then she told me who the mirror told her who hers is. For some reason, she couldn't see their face, but what she did see fits Chance's description. Also, land people often have red hair. Especially his shade. Iris kind of has an unhealthy obsession about finding her soulmate.

I see.

She's got issues like us. She's self-abusive. Iris is obsessed with how she looks. She's obsessed with perfection because she never feels like she's good enough. One night, I caught her cutting herself with a piece of glass. That was the day of my birthday party last year. I was bringing her some cake because she hates celebrating her own birthday because she feels likes she doesn't deserve anything. To her it just means another year without being perfect. Anyways, I arrived with Reign and Iris and we were chatting with a group of other young Oceanids. One of them told Reign she was beautiful, but they didn't say anything about Iris. She was smiling, but I could tell she was thinking that something was wrong with her. I kept trying to tell her they didn't say anything because that was obvious. Everyone says that. She's literally considered the most beautiful in body and mind out of everyone in all the realms. She's always on the cover of a magazine.

OMG! I feel so sorry for her. I want to help her. It's not that she jealous or anything. She's just obsessed with the physical being perfect because she feels imperfect on the inside.

YES. Thank goddess. You get it.

I know I don't know her like you do, but to be honest I think Iris will figure out Chance isn't her soulmate soon. She's a smart girl. Right now, let's just lay low.

Lay low?

Play it cool.

??????

You know… Under the radar…

Ohhhhh. Okay. I'm good at that.

Ummm whatchu mean? What have you been doing to consider yourself good at it? Oh, snap. Incoming.

"So, you like my best friend?" said Iris.

"What can I say? He's a charming creature and so am I." Amethyst posed for her.

"Everyone thinks so. You, on the other hand, think he's more than that don't you?"

"What are you implying?"

"You looooove him."

Amethyst had to laugh. "Girl bye. Currently, I only love my dad, Chance, and my toys." *You know what? Never mind. Ima just keep reading. LMAO.*

Did Chance question you about me?

Yeah. I'm guessing that's what Iris just did.

Yep. Like dang. Why are they shipping us? Do you know what shipping is?

Yes. Both of our sibling besties are nosy ass seahorses.

Seahorses are nosy? Or is it just because of their snout? I love seahorses.

No, they're actually really nosy. They always have the best gossip.

"Reign, where should we stop first?" Iris knew what she was going to say.

"The jewelry shop of course!"

"Which one?"

"You know which one," they both giggled. At the shop, everyone kept trying on jewelry except Amethyst. She wasn't the metal accessory type. Almost everything broke her out.

"Here, Little Scallop. Try these on." He handed her some blue magnetic waist beads.

A customer said, "Are you getting those? You should. They look great on you."

Then another said, "Excuse me, Your Majesty. Do you mind if I take a refraction of you? My wife and I have a little girl at home. She wants to update her collage of the royal family."

"Sure. Hopefully, I turn out decent," Amethyst smiled. Then she asked, "What's your daughter's name?"

"Cleo."

"Tell Cleo I said heeeeey and give her these." She handed the womxn 11 silver coins. The womxn threw her arms around her and began to weep. "What's wrong?"

"Our daughter has cancer. This will pay for her treatment for 3 months."

"I'm glad I could help." When the womxn swam away, Amethyst asked them how much the insurance was.

"Lung cancer is rare down here," said Reign. "Zeus discovered the treatment, but he just wants to make money. He's a suspect. Not one sky nymph has ever had lung cancer. He's also the reason for all this pollution causing the cancer."

"Wait. I thought health care was free? Is cancer treatment an exception?"

"The sky realm is different," said Reign. "Our health care is completely free from physician appointments, to surgery, to medicine. The issue is that people have to go the sky kingdom to get treatment for lung cancer. All currency is converted by unit. Everyone has the same units except for the sky kingdom. Zeus made it so that sky currency is worth less per unit. That way Oceanids have to pay more. Treatment costs 1 skite a year. You have to pay by the year. 1 silver coin is equal to 100 coral chips. 1 coral chip is equal to 100 sandies. Zeus made it so 44 silver coins is equal to 100,000 sky bits. 100,000 sky bits is equal to a single skite. They use skites like sandies up there. Their currency is 100% digital. It's all credit. Down here we have a debit system. Card and cash are the same thing."

For some reason, Reign wrapped her arms around Amethyst. "Wow you really know your currency," Amethyst smiled. Then she looked at Chance who had his there-you-go-with-that-bullshit look on his face. "The numbers are confusing, but I get what you're saying. That's crazy."

"Royals aren't allowed to possess another realm's currency," said Iris. "Zeus did what he did on purpose. Meter would pay for everyone's treatment, but she can't. At least not directly. Citizens are allowed to convert their money to another currency. They have to pay the sky kingdom the money all at once. Thetis will replace all the money they spent after a year. That's when the contract expires. They have to renew it every year. Since you aren't coronated yet, you don't count as a royal."

"Holy shit. Socioeconomical politics," said Amethyst. "What other crap is Zeus responsible for aside from the medical industrial complex?"

"Sex trafficking, the prison industrial complex, corruption… Ugh. Don't get me started on the rest," said Iris.

"Oh. Damn. Okay." Reign was still hugging Amethyst. "Why are you still hugging me," Amethyst giggled. "You're squeezing me too hard now." Amethyst could hear Reign's heart beating out of her chest.

"Sorry," Reign smiled. "You're just such a gem."

Amethyst found Xenon in the woven bracelet section. "Try this on." She handed him a purple ankle bracelet.

"Where'd you find this? I've been looking for one of these for moons. This is antique, and this shade is hard to find. My meter had one just like this except it was for her wrist."

"She's one lucky pearl, isn't she?" said the clerk. "Someone sold it to me. They said it was from the southern waters."

"It is. How much?" he asked.

"The lucky pearl already paid for it."

Xenon gently kissed her hand and softly said, "Thank you. This means so much to me."

"How much for these waist beads?" She did a little belly roll.

"He bought them for you."

"Looks like we both had the same idea."

"Great minds think alike." Xenon tackled her in a playful way.

"Alright lovebirds. Iris, where we going next?" Chance was ready to leave.

"Iris…" Amethyst had a confession. "I think I just snapped your bra."

They all started dying laughing. "It's okay, sister. Come on. Let's go shell shopping!!!"

"Uhhhhhh." The guys absolutely did not want to go bra shopping. They both had their reasons.

"We'll be around. I'm going to go look for a refractor," Xenon said. "And we need to find you some clothes, Chance."

"Bye boys. Don't get into any trouble," Reign giggled. Once they were far enough away she said, "Hehehe. Blue must really like you, Amethyst. He stopped taking refractions after his cousin Xandra died."

"Hi, Despina. This is my twin sister, Amethyst. Twin sister say hi." Amethyst waved. "Do you think you can help us find her some shells? It's her first time."

"Follow me. I know you two are twins but let me just double check the measurements." So far, the process was similar to the process on the surface. "You have the same exact measurements except your shell size is gamma and hers is delta," she told Iris. "You can choose anything in this area here. You can also choose from this wall, but you won't be able to wear a covering over because from this size up all the shells are heavily decorated. Feel free to try anything on. There's a sale going on. If you buy 3, you get 1 free."

"Thank you," said Iris. Amethyst had no idea what they had said but she thanked Despina. "Which ones do you like?"

"I don't want anything pointy or completely circular. Where are the regular shells?"

"They're all regular."

"I think she means mermaid shells, Eye."

"Oh, okay. Here. This one's cute."

"Where do I change?"

"You don't have to go anywhere. Just change, sis."

"In front of everyone?"

"They don't do that on the surface? We'll cover you," said Iris.

"I like it! It's so sparkly. Do they have it in anything not yellow or orange?"

"They have a pastel pink, kelp green… Oh! Here's a deep teal."

"Good eye, Reign. I found this purple and blue ombre pattern!" Amethyst liked all of them. "You have to get these! You need to pick one more to get a free one. I really think this coral color will look nice on you."

"Eh, I don't know."

"Come on. Just try it, sister."

She looked at Reign. "Sorry, but I agree with Iris."

"Fine," she giggled. "What the hell… I'll get it."

After Amethyst paid, Reign reminded them, "Now we have to find the boys."

"Well, there's only one refractor shop around here."

They swam past about 11 shops before they found them waiting outside. "LMAO they look hella lost," Amethyst laughed.

"Look at these dumbasses," said Iris. "Can they not see us?"

"Guys! Over here," Reign waved. "Let's see your new refractor."

"Amethyst. What do you call a fish without fins?" asked Xenon.

"I don't know. What?"

"Sashimi." As soon as she started laughing he took her picture.

"That joke was horrible. I bet I'm the only one who laughs at them. It's so funny because you're not funny. Let me see the photo. Ooooo. That's a really good photo of me."

"It's just alright…" Xenon liked messing with her.

"Oh okay," she laughed. "But who gon put it on their wall?"

The rest of them went, "Ahhhh!" Xenon just smiled and shook his head in defeat. He didn't have a comeback. He was really going to put her picture on his wall.

"Your room is going to be finished soon, sister. We need to order your furniture. We'll have to go to a few different shops. We'll start with your dresser and then find you one of those things you pull out. What's it called in English again, Reign? I forgot."

She was determined to remember the word. "Drawers. It's hard to say."

The shop owner greeted them as soon as they swam through the doorway. "Everything is out on display today, but we have more options for the finish. What are you looking for? What color would you like?"

"We're here to by my sister some furniture. She doesn't speak any of the ancient languages yet. Do you know English?"

"Right. My apologies. Hello, Your Majesty. Are you looking for a specific color?"

"I'm not sure. I'll just choose something you already have out." Amethyst strolled around the shop.

"You want something brown? The one you're looking at is made from mangrove trees and designed to look like oak. It might remind you of the surface and make you feel less homesick."

"How thoughtful. I really like this one."

I was thinking that before he thought about that.

Well, you didn't say anything.

"Come this way. I have the following shades. The set comes with a large mirror dresser, two medium dressers for 3 silver coins, including delivery."

"I'll go with this honey oak color. Surely, this wasn't made down here. I noticed how Oceanids prefer things made from precious metals, and this doesn't seem to be carved in an Oceanid style from what I've seen. Who made this? Are there other basileia? Y'all just told me about the sky kingdom. I'm assuming that's sky as in clouds. Y'all have also mentioned land so…"

It's almost scary how observant you are. You never seem to be paying attention.

What you tryna say? Yo ass the one who don't pick up on shit.

"Good observation, Your Highness. I see you have an eye for the fine arts," Xenon told her. She knew what he was doing.

I said what I was thinking this time.

"Anything made from wood is manufactured by the land queendom," Iris informed her.

"There's a whole other queendom!!! I knew it! I saw someone surface yesterday, and they looked different than you all. They were also swimming with their legs apart like a surface person."

Xenon rolled his eyes. "That was Basil." For some reason, Iris and Reign were chuckling about something. *21st-century translation: They were talking head.*

"Who's that? Are they royalty?"

"Yes. All of our fellow princesses, prins, and princes came to wish me and Iris happy birthday."

"Enter your order here, sister."

Amethyst was becoming more and more amazed by their technology. To her, this piece looked like some completely digital futuristic tablet. "I can't read this."

When they left the shop, Chance said, "I'm freezing." They all froze. *There you have it. That's what happens when you catch an Oceanid off guard.* "Hey stop that. What's up with your eyes? Why y'all pupils get bigger? That's hella creepy."

"Why y'all freeze?" Amethyst laughed.

"He startled us. He hasn't said anything in a while," Reign giggled. "Here, take this." She took off a layer of her armor and put it around him.

"Th-Thank you." Chance's face flushed red. "I'm just now realizing how t-tall and mu-muscular you are." He couldn't help but admire her smooth, charcoal skin. *LMAO. When you run into your favorite Fortnite character IRL. Fornite is this game people used to obsess about. I never understood the hype. People like hopping on bandwagons.*

Xenon tried to get his attention for the third time. "CHANCE!" They all laughed. "We're going to what surface people call the bathroom. This way."

"Where do the men go?" asked Chance.

"What do you mean?" Iris asked. They had no clue what he was talking about.

"You know… There's a men's bathroom and a womxn's bathroom."

They were still confused, so Amethyst explained. "On the surface, we have this social construct regarding sex, gender, gender roles, and sexuality. Everything's so sexualized up there. It's violent. There's different types of violence. You gotta watch your back because of rape culture. Womxn get blamed for being assaulted and are told to do things to prevent being attacked as if we are at fault. They don't tell Men to not be predators. Men do as they please. I can't wait until the universe makes things right. I'll say more about that stuff some other time. Surface minds are binary and tend to like to put people in categories, so we have two different bathrooms. It works for a lot of people but… It excludes some people, so we have to fight for single non-gendered bathroom stalls. Did you know that they don't have a place for men to change their baby's diaper in the men's bathroom? Changing stations are only in the womxn's bathroom. I'm a germaphobe. There was this man about to change his baby on the floor, so I changed his baby's diaper for him."

"Ooooh! Right! We don't have that down here. We all use the same bathroom." Reign said. "Oh, Amethyst. You're such a sweetheart."

"Cool." Oceanids always go to the bathroom in groups unless they just happen to be alone. "I was just checking. Me and Ame always go together anyways."

Their bathroom was built over a small trench and their toilets were a series of turquoise colored energy discs. "Stand on the glowing circle and wait for the energy field to open up. Or you can sit on it. It will adapt to whatever you need to do. It makes a little current that sends it away, so we aren't breathing it in," Xenon told him. By the time he finished explaining he was done, but Chance was still struggling. "Don't aim there. Aim at the bright red dot."

"They both look red to me."

"The one on the left. I mean the right."

"Okay. Don't look at me."

"Why not?"

"I can't pee if you're looking at me."

"Trust me. I'm looking at you not your penis but fine," he rolled his eyes. "Surface goers are so private." Chance's nose started bleeding because he spazzed when Xenon said the word 'penis'. "Whoa. So, nosebleeds are real. Are you okay?"

"Awww. What happened, Freckles?"

"He's alright. He gets nose bleeds when he's really, really nervous or stressed." Amethyst pinched his nose and helped him take deep breaths. "It's probably easier for him to get them being down here with all this pressure even though the ocean accepted him."

"Speaking of that, I'm working on building him a breather. The one he has isn't going to last for more than a week, but I'll have a better one ready soon," said Xenon. "We have some already made for people from other queendoms, but I'm adding an inhaler in his."

"Really? Thanks, bro," Chance smiled.

Reign got excited. "Huuuh! See Iris. He does smile! Awww! OMG did you see him. He's not that mean."

"Would you like a bed, sister? I noticed how comfortable you were in mine."

"Yaaasssss! All Oceanids don't have beds?"

"Some prefer to sleep on the sand or float."

"Hello?" The young womxn sounded surprised she had customers.

"Hello. I'm looking for a bed for my sister. She's from the surface."

"I don't have any more beds. The next shipment comes two moons from now. One moment."

"Don't stare," said Iris. The young womxn revealed herself. She was missing her legs and thighs.

"I can make you an Aegean style bed, but it's going to take a few days."

"That's fine. How much?"

"No charge. Your Meter saved my life."

"And you have saved countless lives." Iris paid her anyway. Amethyst tried to join the Oceanids in what she called 'the salute'. Then Iris looked at Amethyst. "I told you not to stare."

"I'm sorry. She's just really attractive. I'm Amethyst by the way."

"Nice to meet you. I've never met anyone named Amethyst before. I'm Nadia."

"A pretty name for a pretty lady," Amethyst smiled. "I love a lady in uniform."

"Are you flirting with me, Your Highness?" she giggled.

"Would that be so surprising?" Amethyst winked.

"Come on, sister," Iris giggled. "Thanks, Nadia."

"You are such a cuttlefish!" Reign laughed.

"I guess there's two now. Blue is the same way, but he's lowkey."

"What is it with you two? Why everything gotta be so sexual?" Chance laughed.

"Flirting is more of a romantic thing," Xenon said.

"Yeah. That back there wasn't sexual," said Amethyst.

"This is what you might call a second-hand store," Iris showed her. "We can exchange your old shells for something. Coins and chips aren't accepted. I'll help you take them off. Sometimes they require a little extra strength because of the suction."

"Cool! I can't wait to see what they have."

"Oh, my goddess. Look, Reign. Doesn't she have nice breasts? They look just as great without the shells underneath." They were taking forever to decide which shells to give her.

"Yeah. OMG. I'm so jealous. A lot of people go shell-less, but it's much too uncomfortable for me. My breasts always make my back hurt if I don't wear a bra."

"Sometimes I just wear a netted, sheer, or translucent top. How come you look surprised? Is showing the chest area taboo on the surface?"

"Not for men."

"I've noticed that. Why is it taboo for everyone else?" said Reign. "It's the same thing. Surface people are weird."

"I know. LOL. The female body is hypersexualized and objectified. Men also love to 'control' womxn's bodies and sexuality. Can y'all hurry up? Y'all are making me feel awkward. Forget the shells. Just help me with my dress. My nipples are cold."

"Uhhhh. Okay, enough girl talk. Let's go inside," Xenon said.

"I agree," said Chance. "Ugh."

"What's wrong, Blue? You feel left out today?" Iris teased.

"Do you think I could find some shorts in here?" Amethyst asked. "I'm not really a big fan of dresses. I prefer skirts. Whoa! What are these clothes made from?"

"Kelp, other algae, hemp, cashmere wool, cotton, and linen. We work with the Naiads. Everything is eco-friendly," Xenon explained.

Reign had a feeling what Iris was about to say, so she covered Chance's ears just in case. Chance jumped because she was so strong. "Our pads and stuff are eco-friendly too. We don't make anything from harmful chemicals. Everything is all natural," said Iris. "And we make the best natural fabric dyes and pigments."

"Awesome!!! What else do they have in here? Is this edible?"

"Yes. That's our equivalent of candy except it doesn't rot your teeth." Iris was loving her reactions to everything. "Grab two pairs of shorts and 10 pieces of candy. After this, we have one more stop to make." Amethyst was loving this new world.

"What kind of candy did you get?" Amethyst asked Xenon.

"I got seaberry flavored kelp squishies. What did you get?"

"I got the river water strips. Wanna trade?"

"For sure." They both swapped a piece.

At the same time, they said, "We should combine them!"

"Look at those scallops." Iris shook her head. "They're worse than teknon. The best kind is sea milk squares. That's grown womxn candy."

"That sounds nasty," said Chance. "What is it kelp and milk?"

"No, no. We don't drink cow's milk. It's made from seagrass." She remembered a wrapper she saw in some ocean pollution. "It's probably like mint chocolate made with vanilla."

"What's your favorite, Reign?" asked Chance.

"I like the almond sea salt brittle."

Why don't you change into your new shells now that you have shorts? I thought you said you don't like dresses.

I just realized Iris and Reign both have a whole ass six-pack. They're so fit. No. Iris is fit. Reign is f****** ripped.

There only like that because they've had warrior training. Oceanids don't body shame anyone. Plus, most people don't have warrior training anyways.

In that case, I feel a lot better. Why do you want me to change weirdo? You ain't slick.

I want you to be comfortable, but I also want to know if you have stingray kisses. I think they're called back dimples on the surface.

LOL. Idk if I do. Thanks for the pep talk stranger.

"Hold on. I'm gonna change." Iris and Reign covered Amethyst as she put on her purple and blue ombre shells with her new purple shorts.

"Those colors look great on you," Xenon said.

"She knows that." Chance and Iris said at the same time.

He smiled and put his hands up. "I'm sure she does. I was just saying."

So, do I have them?

Oh yeah, you definitely have them.

What do they mean?

It's supposedly a mark of beauty given by Aphrodite.

You have them too. Awww. They're kinda cute. Bruuuh... Look how much bigger Reign is compared to them. Is that how I look next to her? Damn.

They both started laughing, so naturally, Chance asked, "What's so funny lovebirds?"

"Nothing." Amethyst kept laughing.

"This is our last stop. Choose your décor, sister."

"This is like a walk in Amazon!" Chance said.

"What?" Reign didn't understand.

"Amazon is an online store. They have everything from A to Z," Amethyst told them. "What is this made out of?" She pointed to a smooth white box.

"A mixture of ground up shells and sand. I can paint it for you if you like," Xenon offered.

"Really?!?!? Okay. I just need two more things. A shelf for stuff I find and a lamp."

"Here's a shelf," said Reign. "Why do you need a lamp? No one sells those."

Are you afraid of the dark?

"I'm afraid of the dark. I know we have lights, but it's still kind of scary."

"We all are," said Iris. "Even though we can use our senses and night vison, it's just not the same."

"No, I mean really afraid. Who knows what could be swimming over me while I'm sleeping?"

"You'll be fine," Iris assured her. "Blue glows brightly at night and your room is right across from his."

"Iris!" Xenon blushed.

"Why are you so embarrassed about glowing?" Chance asked. "That's weird." *I love how he's not tripping off of him turning blue.*

"Because I can't control it and— Never mind."

"Speaking of sleeping, where am I going to be?"

"In Jeremy's old room. We have lots of rooms, but Oceanids prefer to be close together. Jeremy doesn't need his room anymore because he's sleeping with Meter," Iris smiled. "Good for you because otherwise you would have to sleep with Blue, and he loves to cuddle."

"And you don't seem like the cuddly wuddly type," Reign giggled.

They met up with Thetis and Jeremy. "What do you think of this city?" he asked.

"It's great!" Amethyst smiled. "The people are really friendly, and the shops have cool stuff!"

"Plus, the bathroom is so high-tech," Chance added.

"You all didn't stop at the piercing pagoda?" Thetis asked.

"We didn't have time," said Iris.

"We'll stop there on our way to the communities." Thetis signaled for them to follow her.

"OMG! Come in! Are you all here for tattoos or piercings?" the womxn asked.

"Piercings!" Everyone responded except for Xenon. He just stayed quiet. Amethyst noticed him tense up, but she wasn't sure if she should ask.

"Do you all know what you want? Follow me to my lounge. I'm Victoria by the way. Thetis and I are good friends, so you can think of me as your play auntie. I know English, but you might still have to translate. So, who wants to go first?"

"I'm Reign. I want a nose ring, but I'm not sure what shape or which nostril."

"Wrinkle your nose sweetheart," said Victoria. "I recommend the left side because you scrunched your right nostril and a stud because a hoop or chain would distract people from your beautiful face."

"Okay, then I'll go with a ruby stud." Reign closed her eyes as Victoria pierced her nose.

"I'll go next," Iris volunteered. "I either want a belly ring or a septum ring. Something classy."

"Let's see your navel. Huuuum. You have a bit of a clam tongue, so I think you should go with a septum ring. Not many people can pull off a septum ring, but you definitely can."

"Let's do it. Can it have pearls?"

"Of course." After she was done with Iris she asked, "How about you? Don't be shy."

"What would you recommend for me?" asked Amethyst.

"Let me see your ears. Nice. You must have gotten these on the surface. Wow."

"Not a lot of people pierce their ears down here?"

"No one does. It's excruciatingly painful." Victoria began to weep. "I'm sorry it's just… I'm so happy I have another niece. I lost my own children many years ago. They were so young."

"Well, I'm told I'm pretty childish so…" That made her smile. "Why are ear piercings so painful?"

"All ocean goers have more neurons in their ears which allows us to hear better, but also makes our ears more sensitive," Xenon explained. "Earlobes are okay, but the upper ear is terrible."

"Blue is the only one who has a cartilage piercing. It's amazing that you have four cartilage piercings and four earlobe piercings."

"Amethyst sat there and got all four cartilage piercings at the same time. She didn't even flinch. I was there," said Chance.

"I just gave her the money to get her piercings. I had no idea she meant those," Jeremy laughed. "When she came back, I almost passed out. They looked great and we were on the surface so…"

"Why do you have one, Xe?"

"It's a long story."

When I was younger, in my first half-life, these older kids strapped me down and pierced my ear because I refused to give them the money I had on me. I had just earned it and it was all we had.

Oh, Xenon. I am so sorry that happened to you. You didn't deserve that.

Maybe not. They got what they deserved though.

"How come you all never said anything about my piercings?"

"It's considered taboo to have cartilage piercings in all of the realms. It's called To Sima Tou Kakou or The Mark of The Bad. We weren't sure if it was like that on the surface too," said Iris.

"I'm impressed with your daughter, Thetis. She has high pain tolerance just like Ame."

"Someone has the same nickname as me? Who?" Victoria, Thetis, and Jeremy just laughed.

"Ame is Amphitrite's nickname," Thetis giggled. "I sort of named you after her. It worked out because you are so much like her."

"Nooo way!!! That's so cool. Does she have kids? Do I have other cousins? Will I get to meet them?"

"Yes, and yes," she laughed.

"What piercings does she have then?"

"She has a lot, but let me see your navel," Victoria smiled. "Would you like a belly ring? It would look great, and your theia has one."

"I've always wanted one of those, but I'm allergic to everything."

"She isn't allergic to—"

"Pure gold," Victoria finished Jeremy's sentence. "I'm way ahead of you Jay," she laughed.

"How did you know?" Amethyst asked. "Am I really that similar to her?"

"Amphitrite and her daughter, Trinity, have the same condition. It's pretty rare in the ocean. Anyways, I have the perfect piece of jewelry for you." She returned with a golden bar with an amethyst star at one end and an amethyst crescent moon at the other. "Here it is. Gold goes great with your skin tone, and your name is Amethyst. Consider it a gift. I can't sell it to anyone else. Everyone wants platinum or silver. The moon goes at the bottom to fit the shape of your navel."

"Thank you! I love it!" she hugged her.

"Now, Xenon, honey. What did you have in mind? You already have your navel and earlobes pierced. Huuummm…"

"I don't want anything on my face. I have no idea, to be honest."

"You have a belly piercing!" Amethyst examined his belly button. "OMG you do! How come you aren't wearing it? You should wear it."

"In that case, I'll wear it more often."

"How do you feel about a nipple piercing?" Victoria asked.

"Umm, I don't know. What do you think, Little Scallop?"

I don't want you to get one if it reminds you of what happened.

I'm fine. I've gotten my others since then. Just tell me.

"Silver mini bar, left nipple, diagonal, lapis lazuli sphere on both ends."

You've thought about this before?

Yes.

I don't know. Will it look right one me? Are you sure? Why do you want me to get that?

It's a huge turn on.

"I'll get it exactly how she described it."

Victoria giggled. "Of course. I was going to recommend the silver mini bar, but I have to ask. Why the left nipple, diagonal, and lapis lazuli spheres?"

"Lapis lazuli because it's the cosmic shade of blue, water, esp, creativity, calmness, emotions, open-mindedness, etc. Lapis lazuli is ground up into powder to make the finest, most prized ultramarine pigment. The word ultramarine comes from ultramarinus which means beyond the sea. He is beyond the sea. He's of the ocean. Spheres represent more fluidity than shapes with hard edges and points. Diagonal because it's more spontaneous. Horizontal is far too basic and boring for him. The left nipple to balance out his ear piercings. Most people are right-handed and left brained. They tend to pay more attention to the right. When he's facing them, they can't miss it."

Also, you're always on my left side. If I happen to kiss you again, I'll be able to look at it without straining my eyes.

You know… You're the only who has ever given me sea jellies. OH! That's it. That's what you remind me of.

"That makes sense. I like how you think. You're next, redhead."

Chance cleared his throat. "The name's Chance."

"Aren't you adorable. What would you like, sweetie?"

"I've always wanted a lip piercing to go with my brow piercing."

"I recommend the right side since your brow piercing is on the left. Ring or stud? What do you think, Amethyst?"

"Definitely a black ring. It matches his aesthetic."

"Alright cool," Chance agreed. "I'm down."

"You know, Amethyst, I could use some help around here once you get situated. You give good advice, and you have a great eye. I'll pay you."

"I'd love too! Just don't pay me. No need for that. They're rich."

On the way to the communities, they all had a great conversation. Little did they know, Amethyst and Xenon were also having one of their own.

Why a sea jelly?

Well having sea jellies is our way of saying having butterflies. Also, you look just like a little sea jelly. You're so small, cute, secretive, friendly, and alluring. You also sting. Sort of like when you tried to kill me a couple tides ago.

So, you noticed what I did huh? Also, I did not try to kill you. I just didn't completely trust you. I've got trust issues.

I get it. You're very trusting which is why you have to be more than sure.

Exactly. People can be cruel.

You don't trust me yet, do you?

Of course not.

I'm trustworthy, but I don't think you'll like the real me. My past is full of storms. I think about them all the time, and I'm still able to sleep at night. Do you know why that is?

I understand. You're the storm. I feel the same way. Mine is full of embers and ashes. I'm the fire. Literally.

Looks like we're two peas in a pocket. What's so funny?

It's two peas in a pod, not a pocket.

Oh, that is kind of funny.

I like how you say it though.

"How are you doing Amethyst and Chance?" asked Thetis.

"I'm fine," she said.

"I'm surprisingly not in shock."

"Tell me about something interesting that happened today."

"When we were in the jewelry shop, this womxn asked if she could take a refraction of Amethyst for her daughter's collage of the royal family," said Iris.

"Then she gave the womxn 11 silver coins to give to her daughter as a gift," Reign added.

"And then the womxn started weeping because Amethyst unknowingly paid off 3 months' worth of her daughter's lung cancer treatment," said Xenon.

"She's a little rough around the edges, but she has the heart of a princess," Jeremy smiled.

"I could never be a princess. Too many responsibilities. Besides, isn't Iris already the basilissa? Why do you need two?"

"Nonsense. I know you can do it. Basilinna means queen, basilis means young queen, basilissa means princess, and basi means prince. There's a gap we need to fill."

"Let me guess." Iris rolled her eyes. "The chosen one is basilis?"

Thetis and Amethyst both started laughing. "Oh, Iris," said Thetis. "You're the eldest, and you know the queendom, the language, the culture…"

Reign had a question. "Wait. How do you know she's older?"

"Because I pushed her out first. You came at night, and Amethyst came at dawn. I could tell the difference between you two because you have different eye colors. Newborn Oceanids open their eyes soon after they are born. I named you Iris because your eyes are unique, unlike anyone in the realms. Your irises are actually black with scattered flecks of brown."

"I noticed." Amethyst stared into her sister's eyes. "Soooo pretty. Her eyes are like reverse chocolate chip cookies." Xenon was confused about the color of chocolate chip cookies, but he didn't say anything.

"So then what color are Amethyst's eyes?" asked Iris.

"Let's not talk about your sister's eye color because we don't want people to know about Zeus just yet. Also, try not to let the light shine on her eyes. They look black from a distance, but they're actually brown. Ocean goers don't have brown eyes."

"Hold on a minute. I have responsibilities?" said Amethyst.

Thetis smiled, "Yes, you have responsibilities."

"Aw, man… I don't want those."

"Calm down. Technically, you aren't even basilissa yet," said Iris with a snotty tone.

Thetis gave her the eye and sent a strong miniature vortex towards her. "What your sister means is that your coronation has not happened yet."

"Wait. Xenon isn't our cousin or anything right?"

"No, Amethyst. I would have told you," Jeremy laughed.

"We don't practice incest," Thetis giggled.

"Why does it matter? You two already kissed!" Iris exposed them.

"Iris!" Amethyst and Xenon said at the same time.

"You already knew, didn't you? That's why y'all said that," she said.

"Of course I knew. I'm the wisest Oceanid there is. Jeremy and I were talking about you two," she laughed. "We were young once. It's not a big deal. We won't sting you about it."

"Iris, can you swim Amethyst over by that coral," Xenon asked. "Smile." He took a refraction of her. "Look at your seahorse kisses. Your dimples are adorable, Princess." He was her favorite person to compliment just because. Thetis couldn't stop smiling because Xenon was so happy. Meanwhile, Jeremy joined the let's-complain-about-how-they-would-make-a-cute-couple-because-we-don't-want-to-admit-it-because-they-are-our-daughter/sister/brother club.

"You bought a refractor! Oh, Xenon. I'm so glad." Thetis wrapped her arms around him.

Jeremy just realized that. "Whoa! Nice. Blue's back."

Oh no...

What?

We're going to get physical exams. Usually, we get them back at the bas, but they're working on your room. Oceanids do the whole group thing. At least there's a curtain where we're going.

"Mom, are we going to get a physical?" Xenon asked.

"Yes. It's great because I have time to go with you. I want to observe and make sure everything goes smoothly. He's still fairly new."

Amethyst and Chance were oblivious to what was about to happen. "It's good to see you all again. I'm Balint, but you can call me Bal. Nice to meet you two. Xenon, my favorite patient, don't look so tense. Her Majesty just signed you all up for a basic check-up. Nothing special," he smiled.

I don't like him.

Neither do I, Little Scallop.

Well how come you didn't tell Thetis?

"I can examine myself." Xenon hated going to the doctor.

"I know. It's always good to double check though. Especially in your fascinating condition. Let's start with you, Iris." He closed the curtain after she laid on the table. "Everything's normal as usual. Just remember to do your foot exercises twice a day. Reign." After she walked in she almost forgot to close the curtain. Either way, Amethyst could see what was going on, and she was not feeling it. "All good. Just go easy on that leg."

"Do I have to go? I've already had my check-up," Amethyst said. "I just have hypertension."

"I'm sure your surface doctor is great, but I need to be sure you're alright," said Thetis.

"Why does he need to look in there though?"

"Just to make sure you don't have an infection. He's not looking inside. He's just going to take a glance at the outside. Does his gender make you uncomfortable?"

"No. I just don't want anyone looking at my vulva." *Chance didn't spaz because he was counting, and he didn't know what that was.*

Bal signaled for her to come in. "I'm going to check your temperature, bones, heart, lungs, gills, ears, and eyes first so just relax."

"Not their eyes," Thetis reminded him. She was starting not to like him. Something was a bit off.

"Right. She is very, very healthy. I will say that her heart rate and blood pressure are high for even for a surface person. You see Amethyst, ocean goers' hearts beat much slower. It's normal for those from the surface to have high blood pressure at first. Your heartbeat is extremely fast, but it seems to be working for you. I'm sure your surface doctor told you this, but they didn't tell you that you have an irregular heartbeat. A human ear wouldn't be able to tell. Even I'm not sure of the significance of that, but it doesn't seem to have any negative effects. You have a strong heart. Also, your temperature is about 3 degrees higher than it should be, but you aren't showing any signs of a fever." Bal washed his hands in the dense fluid Amethyst was still amazed by. "It will be quick, and you won't have to do it again for 3 months."

Xenon hissed and scared Chance. "What the hell's wrong with you, bro? You almost gave me a heart attack."

"Huuum. You and Amethyst are close, aren't you? I'm sorry. I didn't know you could imprint yet. I'll call Kaija in here. He's a gynecologist. Maybe both of you will feel better if he did this part."

You imprinted on me?

S-Sorry. Um… Imprinting isn't an Oceanid thing. That guy just has some wacky theories about me and my 'fascinating condition'… I just got a little defensive. Like… Because you're you. N-Not in a romantic way.

"Hi. I'm Kaija. He seems decent at first, but that man is kinda creepy once you get to know him," she smiled. "I totally understand. We don't get along at all."

"Are you his daughter?"

"Yes, how'd you know? People say we don't look alike. By the way, thanks for getting my pronouns right."

"You don't, but you have similar eyes and facial structure. And no problem. Don't thank me. That should be a given," she smiled.

"Ready? It'll be quick, and you won't have to—"

"Just get on with it womxn," Amethyst laughed.

"Congratulations!"

"What? Why?"

"You have a relaxed hymen."

"Okay, we're done here," Amethyst swam out.

"I knew it! I knew they did it," Iris thought she was right.

"WHAT?!?" Amethyst and Xenon both said at the same time.

"I wasn't referring to how sexually active she is or isn't. Remember, Iris? You know this." Jeremy and Chance were covering each other's ears. "Judging the appearance of the hymen is by no means able to determine who has had vaginal sex, who hasn't had vaginal sex, and who is or isn't having vaginal sex. People naturally have different types of hymens that vary between size, shape, and thickness. It also never really goes away, just stretches. Some people are even born without one. Also, the hymen can be stretched or broken from participating in things like gymnastics, dance, track and field, warrior training… Masturbating…"

"How much more awkward can this get?" Amethyst was so irritated.

"There's nothing wrong with masturbating. Did you learn that there was on the surface?" Thetis was worried about her. Amethyst looked as if she was doing her best to be invisible. "Masturbation can be healthy. Jeremy, does she masturbate?" Chance only spazzed a little this time. He was still scarred from a couple days ago.

"Why would I know? I don't have a clue."

"Don't worry, Thetis. Ame is very familiar with that department." *Poor Jeremy. LOL.*

"Chaaance!"

"What? She was worried. Also, I'm trying to get on her good side."

"Well here are some suppressants," Kaija handed her. "They're also antibiotic and more than safe for sensitive skin."

"I won't be needing these anytime soon," Amethyst said. "Do they expire?"

"Better to be prepared than unprepared and nope. I'll go get Bal."

"Ready, Chance? You know it's rumored that the sun god, Helios, has fiery red hair."

"Really? That's dope."

"You have asthma, correct?"

"Yee."

"Have you had any difficulties breathing?"

"I wouldn't say difficulties, but it is kind of uncomfortable. Feels like I'm drinking everything around me."

"While you're here, why don't we switch out your breather. This one is also temporary. I'm sure Xenon is building you a better one."

"He is. He said he's adding a built-in asthma pump. Thanks."

"No problem." Like Iris and Reign, Chance just took the suppressants. "It's time, Xenon. You know the drill."

"I can't, Bal. We've been through this."

"I have a good reason to believe you can." Amethyst saw Bal hand him a cup. Then he swam up to the second floor she wasn't aware of.

What are you doing?

He needs a sample of my reproductive cells for examination. He's never gotten any. He has gotten everything but those. I let him study them and then he gives them back to me, so I can study them myself.

Oh, I see... I'm rooting for you. Whoop whoop! Go, Xenon. You can do it.

Thanks, Little Scallop. I appreciate your support.

I'll let you do your thing. Go make that milkshake.

OMG! You are hilarious. I'll never be able to hear that word the same way.

Xenon tried thinking about something to help him out. He thought about all his past relationships but that didn't work. Then he got distracted. He accidentally thought about you know who and them bam. He was glad he got the sample, but he felt so queasy about it. He sealed the cup and did his best to not make eye contact with anyone as he handed the cup to Bal on the low. He was surprised how much was in there. There had to be at least 6 billion incomplete Oceanids in that cup. Everyone could tell Xenon was still irritated. "Alright. Here you are." Bal handed him some suppressants.

"I won't be needing these."

"Better safe than sorry."

For some reason that triggered him. "I wouldn't be sorry. I'd be overjoyed, and I'd comfort her and help her care for the twins." Then he realized that some of them might misinterpret what he said.

"Twins? I think you've got the incurable disease called love." Bal was totally off.

"No! STOP! I wasn't referring to how I feel about Amethyst. My biological mother practically raised us on her own. Sh-She had a miscarriage because my biofather was abusive." He began to weep. "They were twins."

"Also, how Xenon and I feel about each other or don't feel about each other is no one's business but ours. STOP sexualizing him. STOP sexualizing me. STOP sexualizing us just because you think we'd make a cute couple. It makes me uncomfortable, and it clearly makes him uncomfortable. Now, look what you've done. Sure, we can take a few jokes, but it's gone too far. Look. He's crying and now I'm crying. I'm starting to get very upset, and I do not want myself to get any more upset."

"See! Now she's upset and so am I! Uhhhhhh!"

"You don't want her/him to get any more upset." Iris and Chance were just now noticing how they often said the same thing at the same time. They both did their best to calm down their siblings. Reign didn't know what to do and swam around in circles.

Jeremy looked at Thetis with the look of any concerned dad. Thetis took a deep breath and said, "I'll handle this. Balint. It seems I've misjudged your true character. I should have observed you before. Then I would have known your true colors. You are disgustingly inappropriate. You are no longer the physician for my family. Kaija. If you accept, I will appoint you as the new physician. If you do not, I ask that you recommend me physicians you think are a good fit. Now, off we go children." They went to go eat at a place that served what would be considered street food on the surface. Chance and Iris managed to prevent their siblings from getting angry, but now they were both weeping out of control.

They sat at a stone booth. Thetis and Jeremy said, "Alright. Come here Cupcake/Blinky." That was all Amethyst and Xenon needed to hear. She sat on Jeremy's lap and wept while he sat on Thetis's lap and wept. Meanwhile, Iris and Chance were plotting something. Knowing them, probably revenge. Then Reign, the voice of reason, convinced them to surprise them with dessert after they ate because they owed them an apology. Bal wasn't the only one who made Amethyst and Xenon uncomfortable.

"Oh, my dear teknon. I'm so sorry. I would have gotten rid of him a while ago. I should have known. I would have never hired him."

"It's okay, Mom." Xenon said. "I should have told you I didn't like him."

"It's all good, Thetis. He's a jerk," Amethyst said. "That's why he's ugly!" Xenon nodded his head in agreement. Iris and Chance were talking smack about how clingy Amethyst and Xenon were to their parents. They sat on their laps the whole time.

"Oh, my goddess the food's here!" Xenon got excited.

"Huuuuh! So that's what a sandcake is! It's basically a small waffle pancake without the ridges. I bet the humans stole the idea from Oceanids. I love how they come in different shapes and colors! Did they do this by hand or with a cookie cutter? Look at the detail! Vegans would have trouble eating these."

"You're so cute, sister. How about you hand them out. Usually, I do it but go ahead. You're the youngest now."

"Hand them out?"

"Yes. It's tradition for the youngest to hand out everyone's first piece. You have to go in order from eldest to youngest regarding age not maturity. Maturity is different."

"I'm older than you three," said Reign.

"Okay. Thetis, you get the blue whale because you're the wise mommy. Dad, you get the blue shark because it fits your aesthetic. You moved a long way from home for me, and blue sharks travel long distances. Reign, you get the lionfish because you're headstrong, eye-catching, and aren't one to be messed with. Chance, you get the seagull because you remind me of the surface, and you're always high," she laughed.

"For medical reasons..." Chance added.

"Xenon, you get the orca because, in addition to being noble and sweet, you're also a mysterious, extremely dangerous trained assassin. Iris, you get the octopus or whatever kind of cephalopod this is because you're intelligent, you keep a lot of things hidden, and you give off bold vibes. I get the delphys because I'm silly, playful, and I like to have fun!"

"You're such a gem," Iris smiled. "You didn't have to do an in-depth analysis."

"Am I supposed to use utensils?" Chance asked.

"We don't use utensils to eat," said Iris.

"Look at those two go!" Reign pointed out how Amethyst and Xenon were playing with their food.

Do you play with everything before you eat it?

Always.

Me too.

Good to know.

Amethyst and Xenon were too busy caught up in their story they created with their edible characters that they didn't notice the desert that was placed in front of them. "Chance and I want to apologize…"

"Yeah. We're sorry we made you two feel uncomfortable."

"We got you sweet clay to show you we're sorry. Do you forgive us?"

They both laughed. "Duuuh."

Amethyst tasted hers and didn't like it. "I think he has mine." Xenon had the same reaction. They swapped bowls, and suddenly their desert tasted how it was supposed to taste.

"They're the same flavor," Iris said.

"We got you both seaberry."

"What is sweet clay made of? It's like Play-Doh plus ice cream." Amethyst loved the brilliant baby blue color and how it tasted like a cross between vanilla and blue raspberry. Imagine finding out blue raspberries actually exist. That's how Amethyst felt about seaberries. She wondered if they knew where to get the berry that inspired the blue raspberry flavor. Those had to be delicious.

"It's a mixture of a special type of seaweed milk, clay, seaberries, sugar, and salt all churned together. It's made just like ice cream," Thetis explained.

"Can you teach me how to do the vortex current thingy?" asked Amethyst.

"We need to teach you how to swim first," Jeremy laughed.

Chapter 8: How Low Can You Go?

This is how Amethyst learned how to swim in the open ocean. How fun. "Here's what we're going to do." Thetis had a plan. "Iris will teach you and Chance how to accelerate. Reign, you'll teach them how to start and stop. Xenon, you will help them with their form. Jeremy and I will be right back."

"First let me see you both swim towards me," Reign told them. Chance had no problem completing the task. He swam to her like any surface goer would swim. Amethyst, on the other hand, didn't move much although she was doing her best to kick.

"Why am I not moving?" When she turned around, she felt a sudden wave of terror because she was a staggering number of meters above the ocean floor and not holding onto anyone. It was bright where they were, but she knew there was darkness down below. Unaware, Iris and Reign started laughing. In their eyes, there was nothing to fear.

"Is it me or did the water just get warmer?" Iris joked. The water was getting warmer but not because Amethyst peed on herself. That's how much her body heat was increasing.

"HEY! Girls come on! Shhh!" Xenon finally got their attention. "Listen to her heart. She's having a panic attack."

I'm coming to get you.

I can't swim. I-I'm sinking. What if I drown? I'm going to drown.

Sinking yes. Drown? You could never. Open your eyes.

"This time we won't leave your side," Reign assured her.

Iris felt guilty for not noticing. "You should take a break. We'll work with Chance first. That way you have time to relax."

"Are you afraid of drowning? Heights? Sea-monsters?" Reign still didn't understand how serious it was.

Iris hissed at Reign. "This isn't funny. She's for real."

"I'm sorry. It's just that I can tell you're so strong. What could possibly make someone like you so afraid?"

"I've already told you. The dark! Being strong doesn't mean you aren't afraid of something."

"The dark?" Thetis asked. She and Jeremy were finally back.

"Yep. Is that not reasonable for 'someone like me'?"

"Quite the contrary. It was dark and stormy the night after you were born. It was like any December night except for the fact that Zeus and Poseidon were arguing about the birth of my rumored child. He threatened to enter Poseidon's realm and kill you. Poseidon protected you. If Zeus knew I had twins, he would have struck you both and caused a war all the realms would have participated in. When those two argue, no one can deny the terror. Especially those who happen to be being separated from their mother and twin sister. Newborn Oceanids are supposed to be kept submerged for a minimum of two weeks. Jeremy told me how your ears and nose would bleed, how loud you would cry, and how high your temperature would get. I think that's why you have those panic attacks. You are afraid of the dark because you are afraid of being separated. I'm so sorry." Thetis wrapped her arms around her. "I will never leave you again."

"I understand that you did it to protect us. I can only imagine how hard it must have been for you, especially since you've lost so many. Thank you. Now let's have fun. That's enough tears for today. Well... Weeps." Xenon admired Amethyst's ability to make everyone smile even when she was feeling down.

"Are you sure you're ready?" asked Iris.

"As long as Xenon doesn't let me drown."

"Sea jellies can't drown," he smiled. They all laughed. "First, let's work on your stroke. Try keeping your legs together. Watch Iris."

Amethyst watched closely and then mimicked her exact movements. Curious, Iris did a slightly difficult move. Again, Amethyst got it right on the first try. Then Iris did one of her signature moves. "That was sloppy, but I'm impressed. You're a fast learner." Amethyst smiled. Then she realized how far away from her spotter she was. She swam back to him as quickly as she could using the technique Iris showed her.

"You're both unusually flexible," said Reign. Amethyst practiced swimming in a straight line, how to turn, and how to stop until she knew enough to swim on her own.

"You're doing fantastic!" Iris gleamed.

"Yeah, but I'm still afraid to swim on my own. Especially when it's not this bright out."

"Do you trust me?" asked Xenon.

"I trust you if Dad trusts you."

"I trust him, Cupcake," he smiled. "I still don't like him though."

Amethyst was suspicious. She could tell he was up to something. "I trust you." Suddenly, Xenon dragged her down into the abyss. It all happened so fast. She fought and fought until she realized he wasn't dragging her down anymore. In fact, she didn't know where he was. She couldn't see anything. This was a different kind of dark. It was pitch black except for the mysterious glowing creatures that lived in the depths. She saw an unmoving bright blue spec in the distance. "Xenon?"

He swam towards her. "See. You're never alone. If Jeremy isn't there, Mom will be there. If she isn't there, Chance will be there. If Chance isn't there, Iris will be there. If Iris isn't there, I'll be there."

"Alright, Michael Jackson." Amethyst rolled her eyes and swam back up without any help.

"Well someone isn't afraid anymore," Iris said.

"Nope. Hehehe. Watch this!" She started swimming all over the place. "You know, when I first saw you, I was hoping for you to be a mermaid like in the movies, but then I saw that we're twins and everyone else has legs. I'm a little disappointed," she giggled.

"The only reason why I'm not losing it is because you all don't have a tail or anything. And because my heart rate is unusually slow. I'm counting 53 beats per minute, and I'm not an athlete. I'm also me."

"Iris, do you have any Nereid friends? Can I meet one?"

"You mean Mer? No, sister. I definitely don't have any Mer friends."

"Sure. Also, are they that different?" Amethyst asked a really good question.

"They are," Reign confirmed. "Mer are beautiful, and they don't sink ships."

"If I meet a merperson, I'm going to say: I would ask for the time, but I don't need a clock to tail that it's time for you and I to get to know each other." Chance tested out his pick-up line on Reign.

She started laughing. "That was terrible. Don't use that."

"Your room construction is finished. We'll move you in once your furniture comes. Would you like to see it?" asked Thetis.

"Yes! I wanna see." It was amazing. "Whooooa."

"It's much flatter and not as wide or as tall as Iris's. When I made the blueprint, I imagined you'd like something more surface like," Xenon explained.

"I love it! You made the blueprint? That matches your a—"

"Wow. It's so much smaller than mine," Iris laughed.

"I don't need a lot of space."

"Swim to the top. There's a little surprise for you up there," Jeremy encouraged her.

"Th-This is all amethyst! My favorite crystal! Is that a patio? I can see everything from here. OMG is that an amphitheater down there? This is like a dream come true. Wait. How is there an amethyst cave underwater? This is like the biggest geodude ever. I mean geode. I'm a Pokémon fan."

"I knew I picked the right name," she smiled. "A family member carved it long before you were born. I was going to make it a playroom just in case you had children. Amethyst is soothing and keeps teknon happy. The rest of the crystals are stored there. He even made a few statues and accessories. You'll meet each other soon."

"Why are they so purple?" said Chance. "They're the same shade you call cosmic purple."

"Probably just nature," said Amethyst. "Also, they aren't exposed to much light here."

"Keep swimming," said Jeremy. Chance cringed. He really didn't like *Finding Nemo*.

"There's more?"

"Of course, Cupcake. Go through there."

"But it's going to suck me up," she said as she went in. Xenon, Chance, and Iris caught that little comment. The upcurrent came to a stop after about 5 minutes. She looked around and found so much biodiversity. She was enthralled. Then Thetis came behind her and led her to a cave opening. "What is this place?"

"I used to live here many years ago."

"By a volcano? That's so cool! Did you see it erupt?"

"The one adjacent to here hasn't erupted for centuries but look at that island over there. That volcano is always erupting. You can't see this, but that island is covered in pitch black sand."

Amethyst gasped. "OMG! I see it erupting. Awesome."

"You should see this place at night."

"Ummm. Quick question. How do we get back?"

"Take the downcurrent."

"Right. I knew that. I'm supposed to just jump down there? Okay." Amethyst laid on her back and made her way to the hole head first.

"What are you doing? Amethyst don't…" She was already on her way down. Thetis sighed. "Jeremias wasn't kidding." Jeremy caught her on the other end. He had a feeling she was going to do something dangerous.

"So, what's up there?" asked Chance.

"It's an actual cave. Thetis said she used to stay there. It lowkey looks like a dragon's lair. Do you all want to see?"

"I'm sorry, Amethyst but we have to go." Thetis was a very good actor. "Your coronation is tomorrow."

"What? Tomorrow? I-I'm not ready for all that."

"I'm just kidding," she laughed. "It's 61 high tides from now."

"What does that mean? The middle of the 30th day from now?"

"Yes, which means preparations begin now," she smiled. "Iris, you are in charge of the invitations and the itineraries from tomorrow to the day of the coronation. Reign, you will take care of the décor, garments, and guest list. Xenon, you are responsible for the arrangements from entrees to entertainment. You all may gather any help you need. Make sure you work together and keep everything top secret. Do not let Amethyst find out about any details. If you have any questions, ask Jeremias. I will be teaching Amethyst as much of the royal customs as I can to the best of my ability."

"Hey! What is that supposed to mean?"

As the group split up, Xenon lightly bumped Amethyst as he swam by. "See you later, Little Scallop." She loved how he winked at her. She knew he was a Sagittarius like herself, but she imagined his moon sign was Gemini. How aesthetically pleasing... *Amethyst is far from being one of those die-hard astrologists so chill. I know some people are full-time astrology haters. She just finds it interesting.*

"OMG! Chance! Bruh! Finally... We're alone."

"Bro. What the actual f***?!?!? So, this where all the n***** at... This is so dope. Your mom's the queen! Damn. Your twin is a high ass femme, but she's a power femme like you. There's a whole ass world down here! We used to wonder about what was down here all the time! This is crazy. It's like the complete opposite of the surface. Bruuuh. I'm hella juiced. Did you notice how there's hella Q-tips?"

"IKR! And they all living they best life in 2015. Bruuuh! I'm still shook. I be trying to not make it hella obvious. Eeeeep! I love this place. We're breathing underwater! Underwater!"

"This is so f****** lit. And Xenon... Ame. My n****. You gotta put a ring on it. Fine ass n****. And he's richer than me! He got them legs too... Damn. What the hell? He straight out of Build-A-N**** Workshop."

"OMG I caaan't with you," she laughed. "But truuuuue."

"Wait. First you gotta see if he got good dick. You at least gotta hit it twice."

"You don't care about his personality?"

"Oh yeah... That too. Give me the signal so I know if you feeling him or not. Why the hell is everyone so damn fine down here? Shit. I gotta step my game up."

"Speaking of that... I know you crushing on my sister, but you know you lowkey like Reign for real for real."

"I do not."

"Whatever. She has a super bright personality, she's good with money, she's got broad shoulders and superhero muscles, she's hot ass f***, and not prissy at all even though she's girly as f***. Me and Iris thick, but she Serena Williams thick. She athle-thick. Don't forget to give me the signal."

Chapter 9: Garden

DAY 1

"The coronation of the basilissa is the most prestigious ceremony. Here are the basics. First, I will mark the beginning of the ceremony with my welcome speech. Then there will be various performances by Oceanids and other ocean creatures. Next…" Thetis gave Amethyst what Amethyst considered the full run down.

"Whoa. That was a lot. What is the basilissa supposed to do? I can't be a pretty pink princess. Well, I could but that's not my style."

Thetis laughed. "The role of basilissa has nothing to do with gender. You just happen to be you. The role of basilissa is essential. The basilissa, or princess, is the heart of the queendom. Your job is to spread cheer and hope throughout the basileia. You will go around and do daily check-ins. You will keep track of any complaints, concerns, and comments. You address them if you can. If not, you report the situation to whoever you must. Your duties are to keep the basileia safe and clean, feed the animals and plants, and make sure the basileia is attractive. You will also attend meetings and things like that. You have the least number of responsibilities, but you also have the greatest responsibility. You do what you can to keep everyone in the basileia happy, well, and filled with life."

"Oh, snap. I guess I should get a head start. I'll do my best. I'm a lucky cricket, but I'm also a danger magnet. I promise you I was listening, but do you think I could get all this in writing? I'm not going to remember any of this."

"Of course. You should also know that everyone except for the rest of the royal family is under your command, including the warriors. You may have whoever you see fit assist you. They will be waiting for their assignments once we transition."

"Does this mean I can't go back home?"

"I'm sorry we have to rush this, Amethyst. Technically, you can only be legally protected by Poseidon if you are sworn in as a part of his realm because you were raised on the surface. Not long after you were born, Zeus passed a law that anyone under the protection of a realm must be sworn in as royalty if they are not a part of that realm. Zeus couldn't track you until recently although he has been searching for you ever since. This law is beneficial to us now. By the way, Hera was part of the reason why it took him so long to track you. She was confident that your time would come before he found you. Anyway, you will be able to go back and forth as you please once you are coronated."

"Yes! This is so cool. Wait. I still don't get it. There are a few holes, but I'm sure you'll explain later. How am I supposed to act? Am I supposed to talk all proper like you?"

Thetis laughed. "Traditionally, yes, but I think everyone likes you just the way you are. You must learn about our customs and the various cultures. You must also learn ancient Greek."

"Which dialect? Also… Can you slow down? You're swimming too fast."

"Sorry. None in particular. Every city has different variations in dialect and some have a different language altogether, but everyone understands Attic Greek. All Oceanids have the same general traditions, but there are many subcultures. Oh! Everyone also knows Oceanid sign language. That is the only version of sign language throughout the realms. Your lessons start tomorrow. You'll be somewhat fluent in a few months. Sooner if I can get in contact with Hermes," she rolled her eyes. "The people are able to understand you even if you speak English, so you will be fine."

"Yeah. Why is that? How come you didn't have Dad teach me Greek?"

"Zeus has scouts everywhere. If they heard you speaking our surface dead language, they would have found you. The ocean translates for you when necessary. You inherited that trait from my aunt Klymene."

"Whhhaaaaaaat? Okay. Liiiiit! How did they not notice me and Iris are twins though?"

"I had Klymene make a special serum that prevented evil people from recognizing you. Jeremy would add it to your laundry.

"Whaaaaat? That's dope. So, what are we going to do today?"

"We are going to travel around the basileia after I give you a complete tour of the bas."

"Can't we do the tour later? Let's travel!"

"I suppose so. Follow me." They swam over to what Amethyst labeled the garage. "This is your chariot."

"Yes!!! Awesome!"

"Why are you so excited?" said a deep voice.

"Because you can do more with the average sized ones. You can also go faster!" *I'm judging.* Thetis just smiled. Now she was completely aware that she really had been making sexual innuendos all this time. "Who are you?"

"I'm Alexis and—" He was not expecting her to look so much like Iris. He was crushing hard on Iris. "I... Am... At... Your... Service... You can call me Lex."

"Watch yourself, Alexis." Xenon gave him a look. "Remember what I said." *What a cock block??? LOL.*

"Heeeey, Xenon. Can I have some?"

"How'd you know I have candies? You can smell them? I see your body is adapting." Xenon put his serious face on. "No, you can't have any." Amethyst made the face any daddy's girl would make when someone tells them no. "I'm just kidding. You are such a daddy's girl," he giggled.

"And you're such a momma's boy," she giggled. "I know about that little pouty face you do when you don't get enough attention."

"Alright, alright. Don't you have work to do, Your Highness?" Alex shooed him away. "We don't want to take up too much of your time. Besides, we also have things to do, places to see."

Xenon sensed Alexis was nervous, so before he left, he said, "Don't worry, Alexis. She's different than Iris is acting right now."

"What is he talking about?"

"Her Highness hired a new escort when she found out I'm transgender. She prefers to be around womxn. That was the first time I have ever heard of something like that happening. That's not how things are here. I know the surface is that way. Her Highness has been acting sort of unusual lately. Her Highness is rigid, but she's very nice. Anyways, it worked out because Her Majesty gave me a promotion!"

"My sister is something else…" Amethyst shook her head. "I don't mind at all. You're also kinda cute. Oh shit. Look at those shoulders. I bet you're really strong. I feel safe." She laid on his shoulder.

"Th-Thanks, Your Highness. Being a charioteer has been my dream job since I was a teknon." Once he was finished preparing Amethyst's chariot, he asked, "Where to first?"

"To Caris," Thetis told him. "I'm going to get some rest."

"So, tell me about Caris."

"Everyone there is a fashionista," said Lex.

"Most of our outerwear is designed there, and many of our celebrities live there. You could say it's like Hollywood," Thetis added. *I thought she was sleep.*

"Should I be prepared to ask for autographs? Oh… Never mind. HA."

"What's an autograph again? It's something someone writes about themselves, right?" He did his best to decipher the word by translating the Greek roots.

"Yeah, it's their name. They write it in their own unique way. Sort of like a signature."

"Do you have one?"

"I must say mine is pretty cute."

I bet it is sweetheart.

Amethyst was totally confused. "Did someone say something?"

"No one said anything after you." Thetis officially dozed off.

Can I read minds or something? I didn't hear words, but I heard something... Do all Oceanids do this? I thought I could only do it with Xenon.

It's complicated.

Ahhh. Xenon, how are you doing that? We're far away.

I'm not sure how far apart we can be.

Can you explain this whole underwater communication thing?

In the ocean, we communicate by sending sound waves through our mouths like humans. This is possible because we have multiple ways to breathe. I'm the only empath, but we all are very good at reading expressions and emotions even without words. That's basically what eye talking is. We also use sign language so...

Okay but what about you and me?

What about us?

Xenon.

Well, Oceanids and other people in the ocean already have a lot more neurons and neurotransmitters than humans. I have even more because I literally have moon energy in my DNA.

So, you weren't an empath before the bippidy bobbity boop?

I was somewhere in between. Bittity blogitty bloop? I've heard of that.

It's from a movie called Cinderella.

Right! You called me Prince Charming, but I feel like there's a joke there.

LOL. I was being a little sarcastic. We're a mixture of both of them, but you're more like Cinderella, and I'm more like Prince Charming. That piece of seaweed is your glass slipper. I can't stand that movie to be honest.

That's so true. I've always wanted to see a movie at a surface theater. Maybe we should go find one when we're allowed to surface.

Sure. You'll love it! Wait. So why can I do it?

I'm not sure. Zeus is your biofather, so maybe you have star energy in your DNA or something. HAHAHA.

So, we have the same powers?

Not exactly. Yours are a bit more complex. Aside from your Oceanid abilities kicking in now that you're down here, your unique abilities like causing storms and stuff are developing even further now that you're 16. You just need some practice. I think you're psychic. If you want to, you can know what people are thinking. Not telepathically. You can sense thoughts like I can sense feelings. It might come in handy one day because I feel like you're one of those people who likes to hide their feelings.

And I think you are one of those people who doesn't always say what's on their mind.

"This is Caris," Thetis presented. Amethyst didn't realize she had woken up.

"It's so bright here," Amethyst squinted. "The buildings are fantastic though."

"Apollo favors this city, so the sun shines brightest here."

"It really is like L.A. Just without the human infrastructure and pollution. What happens at night?"

"It becomes so dark that even the creatures with night vision can't see, and our senses are no use."

"So, what do y'all do?"

"We have lights of course," said Lex.

"Lights? What kind of lights?"

"Well, we don't have them yet. Her Highness thinks she may have found lights bright enough. They're being built."

"Artificial lights? I don't think those will work."

Iris was on her way out of a building. "And how do you know that?" she asked.

"Hey, Iris. I was just saying they won't work because if Apollo loves it that much, chances are Artemis doesn't. Her light is one of two types of light that can illuminate the dark."

"And those are what exactly?"

"Moonlight and starlight. The sun is a star, but it's hella dim."

"Star? Oh… Aster. Well, we will see what you come up with when you take my place if my idea doesn't work. It will work by the way. You don't know what you're talking about. I'll see you later."

"Wow." Lex had heart eyes for Iris.

"Don't mind her. Let me introduce you to someone you'll be working with often. He speaks English." Thetis led Amethyst to the same building Iris swam out of. Lex stayed with the chariot.

"You're back that quick? No way," he joked. "I'm just kidding, Your Highness. It is good to meet you. I am Bahadur. I'm my pater's assistant. He's always so busy. You can find a representative or any information regarding any of our services right here."

"Do business professionals shake hands?"

"No. We do this." Bahadur gave Amethyst a gentle hug and blew bubbles on her forehead. "It's the same as our greeting."

"Why didn't you greet us?"

"Her Highness requested for me not to greet her like that. I wasn't sure if you felt the same way. Here we greet everyone or no one at all."

"I see. You don't have to worry about that. I'm not Iris."

Bahadur smiled. "Good to know. I'll show you around." There were so many people working it looked like an organized Costco. "If you ever need me, my room is right there," he pointed. "I'm usually swimming around though. If I'm not here, just come to my home. I'm sure His Highness will program my contact information for you."

"Amethyst, darling, we have to go. Poseidon just called an emergency meeting at the next tide. We can come back later. Bahadur probably has much to do anyway." Amethyst was still stuck on how Thetis sounded like an American from the roaring 20s when she said 'darling'.

"It's no trouble. I can show her around the rest of the city. With your permission that is." Amethyst turned to her mother with hopeful eyes.

"He's talking to you," she laughed.

"In that case, let's go! Have fun at your meeting. Tell everyone I said heeeeey."

Thetis smiled at how adorable her daughter was. "I will tell them. Iris will pick you up. Next time, you'll have a phone."

"Okay. Bye… Oops. I mean see you later."

Xenon, Thetis just called me darling.

"So, are you enjoying the basileia so far?"

What is darling? Huh! It isn't bad, is it?

"So far so good, but I still miss the surface. You probably don't know what I mean, but it feels like I have more than one home."

No. It's just that I think she's trying to sound more surface like. I don't want her to feel like she has to do that. Plus, that word is from the wrong era.

"Can't you go back and forth?"

"Not at the moment. I'm wanted on the surface."

"Isn't that a good thing?"

"There are two types of wanted. I'm using the one that means wanted because someone has bad intentions."

"Interesting. Why are you wanted?"

"The someone thinks I'm someone I'm not."

"I see. Down here you are the good kind of wanted for someone you are."

But who am I?

"Did you hear my stomach?" Amethyst was hungry.

"I didn't hear anything."

He's lying.

I know. Wait. Was that empathy through me? Good to know I can use my powers through you. Why you being so nosy? Get out my head.

"What's good to eat around here?"

"What would you like?"

Macaroni and cheese... Chicken... Teriyaki chicken... Pineapple pizza... Snap peas... Oranges... Salmon...

"Salmon and rice would be great."

"Salmon? Oh, yes... The red-fleshed fish. Are you sure you wouldn't care for a more expensive fish?" Amethyst was beginning to get irritated. Why was everyone comparing her to Iris? *They look alike, but they are two very different people.*

Didn't he hear what the f*** I just said?

"I'm sure. Salmon is my favorite fish."

"As you wish. I know a place not too far from here. Afterward, I was thinking to show you our finest clothing store, but I think you would like another place better." *He must have read her expressions LOL.*

"What place is that?"

"Our… I'm not sure what you know it as… A botanical?"

"Yeah. A garden? I love gardens."

"Excuse me." Bahadur tried his best to get the waitress's undivided attention. "Excuse me."

"Hi." Everyone in the restaurant fell silent and turned their heads towards Amethyst.

"They don't speak English. Those who know it live closer to where I work."

"Another basilissa?" asked a child. "That's not Iris."

"Name is Amethyst? Yes?" a womxn asked.

"Yes," she smiled. As the people bowed to her, her heart broke. She just realized something.

Amethyst what's wrong?

These people…

Oh, you must have met the people Carisians call poor people even though we have no classes. They are the only people who live like that in the entire basileia. Iris told me she was going to take care of that. She should have taken care of that by now. She's been acting really unusual lately. I don't know what's going on with her.

WHY?

They have no money because they were charged. They were once prisoners. It's crazy because we barely have any cells. Honestly, it's not even a prison. We don't have one of those. It's a rehabilitation center. Everyone is supposed to get the help they need there, so they can live a better life. Their bank accounts are on hold because everything is provided for them at the rehabilitation center. The hold should have been removed. I asked Iris about it, but she was always so standoffish about it. I don't even know why she charged them in the first place. I heard that they've been marked but we don't do that so... That's all I know for sure. There has to be someone else behind this.

"Is it true that all of you were once prisoners? What is that on your back? Turn around." The man did as she said, and Amethyst began to weep. Crying is so much more painful underwater because there are no tears. "Bahadur, what does this say? What does it say!"

"I-It says Jabir, A Thief."

"And this one?"

"Maarit, A Prostitute." She pointed to another. "Octavian, A Murderer."

"Who did this to you? Who marked you? I know it wasn't my mother." She looked at Bahadur. "Translate!"

Bahadur was amazed at how they could understand her, but she couldn't understand them. "No, Your Highness. It was not Her Majesty. It was..." A father stopped his youngest daughter from speaking.

"Let her speak," said Amethyst.

"Leios. He was commanded to arrest them by the basilissa. He's the worst. He did this to us."

Amethyst was very upset. "Jabir, why were you branded a thief?"

"I would like to keep my pride, Your Highness. It is all I have left."

"Pride is not something you should hold onto so dearly. Tell me."

"I knew my partner was seeing someone else. They told me that they would leave me if I couldn't find a better job. I didn't want to lose them, so I bought a pearl necklace for them. When I came home, I saw them with the other person. I went on about how hard it was for me to get the necklace. Apparently, the pearls were stolen, and I bought them for far less than what they were worth. The person turned out to be a law enforcer and charged me with the crime."

"Maarit."

"I was raped by a group of males," she began to choke up. "Then I was beaten, stripped, and framed as a prostitute. I come from an honorable family. They disowned me. I never even got to train to be a warrior. I have nowhere to go."

"Octavian."

"I really am a murderer. I killed my family. I worked during the night. I forgot to turn down the temperature and take off the gradual increase setting before I left. When I came back home, they were dead. They died in their sleep. I was supposed to replace our outdated temperature system. My soulmate survived. Our 8 children didn't. She tried to tell the law enforcers what happened, but they just thought I threatened her to cover for me. She was assigned a protector, and I am forbidden to go back home."

"Jabir. You are not a criminal. You are someone who will do anything for the one you love. Your mate did not love you. They didn't deserve you. Octavian you made a mistake that cost you the lives of your children, but you are no murderer and you and your soulmate have lost enough. Maarit. It is not you who has lost their honor. Those Men never had any to begin with. They are weak-minded cowards who have no integrity. You are a strong-minded womxn with a strong, noble heart to match. Now stand up. Don't sulk. Keep your heads up. Of course, they all did as she asked. "Take this, Jabir," she handed him 8 silver coins. "Start a new life. This time find someone who loves you as much as you love them." She turned to Octavian. "Here. Soon Iris will become basilis, and I will become basilissa. Once that happens, I will make sure you are able to return home." Lastly, she turned to Maarit. "I invite you to train to become a warrior. All warriors are paid well and offered housing."

They all wept in speechlessness. Then someone said, "Thank you."

"You're very welcome. My mother told me what my responsibilities are, and I promised to do my best. As for the rest of you, take this and start a new, prosperous life. It baffles me to think that you were expected to change your life without the proper resources although on the surface there are much more than 30 who are forced to go through what you've been through. I can tell there are very few people who are corrupt. You all are obviously not of those few. I don't expect this to suffice, but I apologize on behalf of Iris. We just met, but something tells me she is going through something. I can tell the system is different down here, and this was just a fluke. I'm sure it will all be sorted out. She's going to be a wonderful basilis." They all cheered and blew bubbles on Amethyst's forehead. Then she felt a vibration travel down her spine. "Excuse me. Are you pregnant? You don't need to hide. I know it must be uncomfortable. Please, let us take you to the nearest hospital."

"There is no hospital in this city," Bahadur informed her.

"Please, no hospital. I'm afraid."

"Then just come with me back to the bas. I have a feeling the baby is coming sooner than you think. Thetis told me I'm responsible for the well-being of the basileia. Most Oceanid babies are born at night, and it's not safe to give birth here at nighttime."

The womxn gasped. "It would be an honor to have my child at the bas."

"Do you have any loved ones you want with you? I can ask Thetis about that."

"Yes, but they disowned me. The child is… Is…" She began to weep.

"Shhh. Everything will be okay," she said. "We'll come back with the chariot shortly. I figured you will need time to gather your belongings."

"Th-Thank you, Your Highness."

"The place I'm going to show you is not too far from here. We can go there and come back. That should give her enough time. I'll call Alexis to meet us there."

"I can't believe what you did back there."

"What did I do?"

"You helped those people."

"Oh, that. Why can't you? Thetis said that's what I'm supposed to do. It's my job."

"If Iris finds out, I don't think she'll be happy."

"Okay…" Amethyst really didn't care.

Xenon.

What? How was your little date with your boyfriend?

What are you talking about? It wasn't a date, and he is not my boyfriend. Ew. He's actually my least favorite person I've met so far.

Who's your favorite?

Thetis.

Second favorite?

Iris. OMG! Would you stop! I just helped like 31 or 44 people. Why would Iris do that? I don't really know her but…

Sorry. I know. I'm thinking the same thing. She's been having moments since a few moons ago.

I don't like Caris.

I don't either. Unfortunately, it's important for us to be in contact with that city.

Xenon.

Yes.

Who do you think I am?

So far all I know is that you are Amethyst, daughter of Thetis, intelligent, unique, strong-willed, and pure of heart.

Awww. Thank you, Prince Charming. Witcho Cinderella ass.

You know… I can only sense what you feel when you let me in your mind, but it kills me not having any idea what you're thinking. If you want to talk you know where to find me.

"This is The Garden of Caris."

She wasn't expecting to see what she saw. "It's hideous…"

Bahadur swam in after her. "Oh, no. My apologies. Her Highness had this garden made to add décor to the city not too long ago. It was beautiful once."

"What happened? Do tell."

"I don't know. Maybe Okeanos did not accept it. It was the sixth garden Iris had built."

On that note, they headed back to the meeting spot. Bahadur felt bad about everything. "Hello again," she greeted the womxn. "I'm sorry. I don't think I asked you for your name."

"I am Talisha."

"You'll ride with Alexis. Don't worry. I'll ask Xenon to talk to Iris. She's a good person. Is there anything else I should know?"

"Yes… One day I asked the basilissa for help. I told Her Highness I was pregnant, but not by my mate. I tried to explain to her how he was abusive. He was such a shark. I swam away from home. I live on the other side of the trench. There are escorts that help people cross. It was almost nightfall, so they weren't there. I was crazy and desperate. I swam across as fast as I could. Then someone grabbed me and dragged me down. He…" She tried not to cry. "He had a…"

Amethyst already knew why the womxn was so worried about the baby. "Shhh. You've said enough. Tell Thetis the rest when you're ready. She'll understand. Right now, just focus on your baby. You weren't crazy. You were courageous. There's a difference."

"I'm here, Your Highness!" Lex announced himself.

"This is Talisha. She needs our help. She's pregnant. She and her child are our responsibility, so take her back to the bas. If you can, please avoid Iris. Take her straight to Thetis. She needs to lay down, so I'll stay here. Iris is coming to pick me up anyway. I'll wait for her."

"I'll wait here with you." Bahadur didn't want to leave her alone. "But I have to be back soon. My pater is expecting me. We have an important meeting."

"That's sweet of you. Thank you. This might sound silly, but can you see the stars if you swim up closer?"

"No, not a single star. In this area, you would have to break the surface."

"That's what I thought."

"What are they like? The stars…"

"You've never seen a star?"

"I am afraid to break the surface."

"I understand. I was too. Now I love it down here."

"What are stars like?"

"I've never had to explain what stars look like to anyone before. Huuuuummmmm… Close your eyes. It's nighttime. Everything is pitch black all around you. In the distance, you see something that appears to be a tiny glowing plankton. Then thousands more appear. Imagine they're all spread out around you, and they all seem to glow neon white. You try to reach out and touch one, but then you realize they are much farther than they appear. That's what stars look like from the surface."

I wish I could explain things like you can.

How'd you…? Never mind. You were my inspiration for the scenario.

237

I was? Oh yeah.

It's funny how you saved me from falling, and then you dragged me down into the abyss a few tides later. What's next?

HAHAHA. That is kind of funny.

"You can open your eyes now. Bahadur. Baha, open your eyes."

"That was great. Is Baha a nickname? What does it mean?"

"I just shortened your name. On the surface, sometimes we use the word baja to describe something that is below or underneath."

So now you two have nicknames for each other? Is he aroused? He better not be aroused.

He didn't nickname me, and I don't think he's aroused. He doesn't have the bubbles.

Are you?

Hell no!

"I like English. It is complex. Hard to learn, but there's so much freedom. So much you can describe and so much you can't describe."

Okay, now he's flirting with me.

What did he say?

He said he likes English because it's complex. Hard to learn but…

…there's so much freedom. He stole that from me. I bet he said the rest wrong too! If he didn't, he doesn't even know what I meant by that. I like it because you can't describe much, and it reminds me of how cruel the surface is. English reminds me of freedom that isn't really freedom at all! It's one of the colonist languages! He is such a shell!!! Now I can't use that line! Uhhhh! What does he know about languages? I know lots of languages. He only knows one and a fraction of another! My favorite language is love. Uhhhhh!!! I can't stand him. He's so annoying.

I believe you. Trust me, I know a fraud when I see one. He's not making any sense. Honestly, you can't describe shit with words. I think it's funny how people think passion can be truly expressed by words alone. You've been in the library this whole time?

How do you know?

Same way you used empathy through me. I was bored, so I was reading along with you. It's cool because I don't even need to understand Greek. Why you always reading about sex? You one of them. Ummm hummm... You a freeky deeky alien.

Wait a wave. How come you aren't on your way back?

Because she's not here yet. What's wrong?

Nothing. She should be on her way.

"Your Highness?"

"Sorry, I was daydreaming."

"I have to start heading back. You can come back with me to my home if you like."

"I'm okay. Iris will be here. It was nice meeting you."

"The pleasure was mine."

"Iris, you should be halfway to Amethyst by now," Xenon was extremely concerned.

"Relax. I just stopped by to get something to drink. I'll be there."

"Iris! Amethyst is relying on you, and Mom is almost home. She always has guests with her. Iris, look. I think that's her chariot. She's here. I have to greet and serve!!! This isn't like you, Iris! What has gotten into you?!?!?"

"Okay! Stop yelling!!!" Iris said even though he wasn't yelling.

Xenon fixed his clothes and facial expression. "Greetings."

"I don't have any guests this time," Thetis laughed. "I'm going to take a nap."

"It's already drained, but can we drain the dining hall for dinner?" Xenon asked. "I was gonna ask you first, but you were sleeping."

"You know I don't mind." Thetis knew he was doing that to make Amethyst more comfortable. "Where's Amethyst?" she asked. She wasn't picking up her other child's scent.

"Iris went to pick her up."

"I know, but she should be back by now."

He dropped his glass. "She isn't back?!?!?" Immediately, he put on his armor and grabbed his katana.

The others arrived as he was leaving. "Where are you going, Blue?" asked Reign. He didn't answer.

"Iris, where were you supposed to meet Amethyst?" She looked as if her heart had burst. "Iris!"

"At this little restaurant. The one that serves red-fleshed fish. Meter knew she'd want to eat there. Not the new one. The one by the—" Iris froze when she came back to her senses. "Oh, my goddess. Xenon, she's by the trench. Tell her to swim away from that restaurant." Chance was so pissed, he didn't know what to say or do. He couldn't function. *That boy Chance be like: I don't compute. Error 404. Page not found.*

Xenon, it's getting dark. They've already locked everything up. Where is she? Am I in the wrong spot?

Amethyst, I need you to swim towards the garden Bahadur showed you.

To the center? There's nothing for me to hold onto. Tell me what's going on. Am I near the trench?

You're right by the trench.

Oh shit. Okay. I've been swimming as fast as I can.

I think it came out. Something's following me. Once I get to the garden, I'm going to hide behind that broken statue. I'm pretty sure anything that swims can catch up to me in the water.

Your heart rate. Do you remember when we were teaching you how to swim?

How could I forget you dragging me down?

Do you remember what I told you?

I remember. It's getting closer. I'm almost there.

Good. When I find you, get on my back. I'm going to swim as fast as I can, so make sure you hold on tight.

I can't see anything anymore. That whole senses-don't-work-anymore thing kicked in.

I'm here too. I just saw a purple light. Did you see it?

No. Um. Something is definitely in the garden with me.

I'm having trouble finding you. Focus. I'm searching for your frequency.

Xenon, you're glowing. Your powers… I mean your ability still works here.

Got you. You'll always be my favorite person to rescue.

Why is that?

Because somehow you remain efficient even when you're afraid. I wouldn't even be able to tell you were afraid if I couldn't hear your heart rate.

Thanks for coming to get me. Maybe I'll even the odds one day. It's kind of cool how we can track each other with this mind thing.

I hope you never have to rescue me.

Why? You one of those guys? Hehehe.

No. It's because I'm your defender and your friend.

Exactly. I need to protect my defender because if something happens to my defender then I don't have a defender. Friends support friends.

You're irreplaceable. You can always find another defender.

That may be true, but I doubt I can find another friend like you that was hit by a time wave, has the moon's energy in their DNA, and is as noble as you are. When a flower dies you can always plant another one, but you can't plant the same exact seed. You're also irreplaceable.

"That was the nicest thing anyone's ever said to me."

"Really?"

"Really."

They made it! "Oh, thank goddess you're back in one piece." Thetis wrapped her arms around both of them.

"Amethyst. I'm so sorry. I-I was so irresponsible," Iris cried. "I don't know what's wrong with me."

"Don't worry about it. I'm safe now." Amethyst felt abandoned, but she decided to not make it a big deal. She could tell how much Iris was already hurting. She was a complete wreck. Regardless, Xenon gave Iris the eye.

Chance said, "Well, I definitely don't trust this f****** twin of yours!" He looked at Iris. Jeremy held him back. "What the f***?!?!? You almost got my sister killed!!! My f****** sister!!! I have high blood pressure!" He started hyperventilating. "I need some air!"

"Woo," said Jeremy. "I can't tell you how terrified I was. I almost threw up."

Thetis took a deep breath. "Are you hungry?" she asked.

"No thank you. I kind of don't even want to be underwater right now."

"We're having dinner in the hall tonight. It's already drained."

"Sign. Me. Up."

"A word please, Iris." Thetis was very upset. Now she was almost 100% sure what was going on.

Amethyst sat down at the dinner table and Xenon said, "Actually, you're supposed to sit here. We sit in order of maturity not age."

"You just want me to sit by you."

"Are you in my head? Are you telepathic?"

"No. I don't need to be able to read your mind to tell when you're lying."

"Is that so?"

"Yep." She started shivering because she was freezing. She loved how confused Xenon looked.

"Mommy! Amethyst is shaking. What's wrong with her?"

"Nothing is wrong with me," she laughed.

"She's just cold," Thetis laughed. "Turn up the temperature." She and Iris didn't have a long talk. Now Thetis was doing her best to explain the situation to the others and calm Chance down.

"Okay!" he shouted. Amethyst liked this teenage boy side of Xenon much more than his Prince Charming façade. "Is that a surface thing or a you thing?"

"Surface people shiver when they're cold or turned on. I guess I'm just not used to the temperature down here."

"It's sort of like when we get the bubbles. Interesting. Are you cold or turned on?"

"I think you know."

Thetis and Iris joined them at the table. "Are we ready to eat?"

"Yes!!!" Iris added a note about Amethyst's enthusiastic reaction to food to the many observations she wrote down on her tablet. Amethyst was by far her favorite specimen so far. "Where's Dad and Chance?"

"He and Reign had an investigative assignment on the surface. Chance went with them."

"So, they're investigators? What other types of royal ambassadors are there?"

"Each royal ambassador has a main classification and a sub classification, but Iaomai usually focus on their rare, highly valuable healing abilities. In total, there are the following categories: Iaomai or healers, Phylasso or protectors, Anakrino or investigators, Amyntikos or defenders, and Sozo or rescuers. Jeremy is Anakrino and Sozo. Reign is Anakrino and Amyntikos."

"What about you, Xenon?"

"I'm all of them."

"There you go with that little smirk. How?"

"I'm qualified for all of them. Each master approved of me."

"So why aren't you a dedicated Iaomai?

"I-I really wanted to be y—" Iris took note of how Amethyst was able to make Xenon sway. "I really wanted to be your defender."

"Are you the only one who is all of them?"

"I don't know," he said humbly. *Oh, so now he wanna be shy... 2.2 seconds ago he was all confident.*

"He's the only one," Thetis smiled.

"Interesting… What about you, Iris?"

"Me?" She was almost sure her little sister wouldn't want to speak to her ever again. "Oh… I'm Sozo and Amyntikos. Well, not Sozo yet."

Makes sense.

"What's the difference between Phylasso and Amyntikos?"

"Amynikos are something like an army. Phylasso are basically guards."

"I don't get it. You're my army?"

You look very handsome right now.

"Y-Yes. Well no. I guess so." Amethyst giggled as Xenon finished his sentence. Iris continued writing down her Ame-servations.

"So, you're my left-hand? Are you going to eat that piece of shrimp?"

Xenon was surprised she used the same phrase he used to describe a personal defender. "N-No. You can have it."

"You're so funny." Amethyst gave him the octopus legs that were on her plate and didn't take the shrimp. "I love how big the shrimp are down here." Thetis was taking her own mental notes about how much her daughter reminded her of her sister. "Iris, can you crack my crab for me?"

"Yeah. I got it."

I don't understand. You asked for the shrimp, but gave me something instead...

I was just testing you.

Did I pass?

Yes.

Because I said you could have it?

Nope. Because you called me out.

I see...

"Thetis, what does your name mean?"

"Creation or nurse."

"Do you have another name?" *At this moment, Thetis was completely aware of her daughter's wisdom.*

"What do you mean?"

"You know… Like a middle name?"

"No, but you can call me whatever you feel comfortable calling me."

"I like Thetis. It makes my tongue tingle, and it sounds just like Thesis and Tethys. I read about you, but there's not much written about you. Tethys is your grandmother, right?"

"That's correct."

"And you, Xenon?"

"Stranger or foreigner."

You know this… What are you up to, Little Scallop?

"Why'd you name Iris, Iris?"

"When I first looked into her eyes, I had a vision of you looking into my eyes before you actually did. Teknon are born able to open their eyes. Iris is a prism-like messenger. I knew she was blessed from the moment she was born."

"Cool! I want to have powers like Iris. Why'd you name me Amethyst?" Iris was choking up. She couldn't believe Amethyst just said that. For a moment her mind wasn't cloudy.

"You kept crying and scratching yourself until Iris touched you. When I looked into your eyes, I had a moment of calm amidst the chaos. Then you laughed. You laughed, and took my pain away," she smiled.

"But amethyst is a crystal." *This girl is an expert on crystals, especially amethyst. She knew exactly why Thetis named her Amethyst.*

"Amethystos means antidote. Also, contrary to surface knowledge, the truest amethyst of the deepest hue is the rarest, most precious gemstone. Giving birth to you two was a miracle that surpassed finding the purest amethyst."

"I remember reading about how supposedly amethyst causes people to relax and prevents people from being intoxicated. Must have some truth to it. You did say amethyst is soothing and you are the wisest Oceanid so..."

"It also happens to sound like your grandmother's name, Metis."

"It kind of sounds like Amphitrite + Metis + Thetis + Tethys. Cool!"

"You're right. I never thought of it that way."

"Tell me about some of my family members. Who are they, and what are they like? Oh, and what do they look like. Tell me what they look like."

Xenon tried to hide his smile. "You ask really good questions."

"Well, Amphitrite has a heart of gold. She is so warm and sweet like honey. She's very spontaneous and bubbly whereas I'm more quiet and easy-going. She loves to eat," Thetis giggled. "Her eyes are like igneous rock, and her skin is mahogany colored like mine. She is more feared than Poseidon himself because of her temper. I think it takes a lot to enrage her, but her wrath is unmatched. She once drowned Zeus for destroying a sculpture Poseidon made her. When you kill a god, they just come back the next day. We were so glad to enjoy a day without that clasper. Poseidon has a heart as big as the ocean. I'm happy she chose the second most powerful god. He's often tranquil, but he's adventurous. He can snap within seconds like a rogue wave. His eyes are like sapphires, and his skin is of the deepest dark brown clay. He's a little peculiar. If you ask me, he's by far the most handsome of the three."

"Huuuuh!!! Awesome! I can't wait to meet them. What about Hades? On the surface, he's usually depicted as gruesome and cynical."

"Oh, quite the contrary," she laughed. "He is shy as an oyster, awkward as a clownfish, and gentle as a sea turtle. He's very soft spoken and not aggressive, but by no means is he passive. He just seems unapproachable at first glance. Some consider his appearance rather intimidating. He's often miserable because he knows what people think about him. His skin is the color of the freshest coals as are his eyes. He's the tallest and has a much more muscular build than the other two. When they were younger, Zeus used to bully him. Poseidon always had to protect him until Hades accidentally sent Zeus to Styx by throwing him a punch he couldn't handle."

"Awww, OMG. I love men who aren't afraid to show their vulnerability."

"Why are you blushing, Blue?" Iris teased him. She was also checking to see if he was still mad at her.

"Huh? Oh, I-I uh… I bit my tongue." *LMAO. Xenon and his terrible excuses…* Amethyst loved how he sucked at lying.

"What's Aphrodite like?"

"Oh, she's such a gem. From what I know, she's very different from how she is described on the surface. She is also far from the jealous type. She uplifts everyone around her."

"Okay, last one. Does Hephaestus really have a physical difference? I'm not sure if dis/ability is the term he prefers so slash dis/ability."

"Yes. He has a very prominent limp. He made a leg brace for himself, but he goes through so much because his leg is the only thing he can't 'fix'. He lives near the volcano I pointed out to you earlier."

"We should go visit him. Zeus hates both of us, so we would probably have a lot to talk about. We're also both his biochildren."

"I think so too, but he doesn't like company. He will only show himself if it's Hera, Athena, or myself. Hera has to keep a close eye on Zeus, so she hasn't been able to visit him that often."

"That's heartbreaking. When will I meet these Olympians, goddesses, gods, etc.?"

"On your coronation day."

"Yay! I have so many questions for them! I won't ask them as soon as I meet them though. They'll think I'm a mermie."

Why do you feel so awkward, Little Scallop?

Because even though I know they're my family, I don't feel like family yet. It's only been days... Tides... I know they feel like I'm family, but I still feel out of place.

Thetis could tell Amethyst and Xenon were having their own private conversation, so she smiled and said, "If you two are done, you're dismissed."

"I'm full. Thank you. The food was great." They planned to make it seem like they weren't going to go talk to each other. Iris and Thetis planned to have their own little conversation about them and some other important topics.

Xenon. You go to the left.

Okay, you go to the right.

Amethyst ended up going to the left, and Xenon ended up going to the right. It worked out though. When they got to the moon garden, he asked her, "So you're dyslexic too?"

"I don't know. I've never been tested. I always excelled in school so..."

"Huuum. Simple mistakes don't really count. I can have your official diagnosis by the end of the month. I love how we both have the same issues," he laughed.

"Jeez, Professor X... You don't have to go full physician on me," she laughed. "You know, you're the youngest, old physician I know."

"Ha. Ha. Ha."

"Are you crying? I'm sorry. That's a sensitive topic. I shouldn't have made that joke."

"No, no. I'm such a neem." Xenon walked to the other side of the garden to hide his face from her. "I-It's just my allergies." She did her best not to smile at how he was fanning himself. She thought that was adorable.

"Oh, hush. You didn't even know how to say that in English until I told you." They both let out a little chuckle. "Do you want to talk about it?"

Of course he did. Xenon walked over to her and laid his head down on her lap. "When I was younger... Like, younger in this half-life, the kids at school used to pick on me because they knew about me. Everyone knew about me. Anyways, they'd always say things like: 'Why don't you know the answer?', 'Haven't you done this before?', and 'Ew, he's a zombie.' Like, I know they were just jokes and they weren't trying to be mean, but they still hurt. Then on top of that, my memories of my first half-life came in small doses. I just remembered everything like last year. It all hit me. Last year was so rough." He paused and looked up. "Why'd you stop playing in my hair? Keep going."

"What kind of look was that? That's a new Oceanid expression. You actually literally looked like a little puppy." Amethyst loved his curly, black hair, so she kept playing in it. "Oceanids' eyes change a lot depending on the expression, don't they? I wonder if I can do any eye tricks."

"Do you want a seal pup?"

"Hell no, I don't want no damn seal," she laughed. "But I've always wanted a dog."

"A dog? Are those the ones that go meow or the ones I always see on the beach that go bark bark?"

"Wow, you are really good at impressions. Dogs are the ones that go bark bark."

"Oh, okay. I don't like the ones that go meow."

"Me neither. They seem to like me though."

"What kind of dog would you want?"

"I really want a black Labrador or a little cream Maltipoo but back to what you were saying..."

"You're a really good listener, but why don't you talk to me more? How come you don't talk about what you're thinking? You don't trust me, do you? I thought you trusted me? Didn't you say that when we were teaching you how to swim?" *Trust is a huge thing for Oceanids if you couldn't tell.*

"Xenon, I've always trusted you. I trust everyone too easily which is why I must act like I don't until I'm sure about them. That's no secret. You know this. Besides, it's still only been a few days or tides hasn't it?" she tested him.

"How can I get you to be sure you trust me?"

"Why is that so important to you?"

"Because I want to be your friend. Friends trust each other."

"Time is how."

"How much time?"

"All of it."

"Okay then."

"Why do you trust me? What if you're wrong?"

"I'm willing to take that risk."

"But why?"

"I don't know. I know what wrong feels like, and this doesn't feel wrong. You can trust us. I know how the surface is, but we're not surface minded. I don't know how to say it properly, but did someone close to you break trust with you? If someone did, we can talk about it."

"Don't worry about it. They're dead." Then there was a prolonged moment of silence. Xenon held back his tears. He was upset because he could tell she was heartbroken. But then that's partially why they understood each other. "Isn't Iris dyslexic too?" Amethyst broke the silence like she wasn't hurting. *RANDOM.*

"Yes, but she's really good at mathematics and literature unlike me."

"You should have seen her face when I read that little letter she wrote in English."

"I have. I read it too. She wrote like that, so no one would be able to decipher it but… She said I didn't count."

"LOL."

"I want to try something. When I give the signal, say the first word you think of that rhymes with ocean." After he gave the signal they both said, "Wind."

"Technically, I don't think that rhymes," Amethyst laughed. "Shit. Wait. The more you think about it the more it starts to rhyme."

He was laughing just as hard as she was. "Congratulations!" he mocked Kaija. "Aside from dyslexia and dyscalculia, your brain is just as confused as mine."

"Huh! The moonlight! The lotus flowers are out again! Can I—"

He loved her random bursts of excitement. "Sure."

Amethyst enjoyed twirling in the pool with the flowers. "Why didn't you correct me? These aren't lotus flowers. These are definitely water lilies," she giggled.

"I've been trying to figure out what type of flowers these are since Selene gave them to me. I know a lot about plants, but I couldn't find any information about these. How do you know what they are?"

"Lotus flowers rise above the water, water lilies float on the surface."

"I didn't know there was a difference. We use the words interchangeably here. Would you happen to know what kind of water lilies they are?"

"Of course! Nymphaea caerulea AKA the sacred blue Egyptian water lily. It contains the psychoactive alkaloid aporphine. It's used in aromatherapy. I know more about animals than plants. I know about this one because you can't do research on crystals and chakras without running into facts about lotus flowers and therefore water lilies. You know, it's interesting because they usually come out in the morning and go back under the water at noon. These come out at night. Also, this flower represents the continual renewal of life and was often used for funeral rites to feed body and spirit. Everything about this flower matches your aesthetic. Selene knows her water lilies." Xenon didn't know what to say. He just sat there and admired her. "Did you bring your camera? I mean your refractor. You should take pictures of the flowers. The lighting is perfect. Look how pretty they are."

"Here I come." She had no idea that he was actually taking photos of her with the flowers because she was too busy in her own world, obsessed with how they had a slight glow under the moonlight.

"Awww! Look, Xe. The ones in that pool over there are dying."

"I know. I don't know what's wrong."

"Well let's find out." She pulled herself out of the pool and peered into the other one. "Ew. It's too salty. I can smell it. You probably couldn't tell because of the smell of the flowers blocking the smell of the salt. Plus, you've never been in the pools."

"Wait. Are you saying the other pools aren't salty?"

"No. They just have very little salt. These flowers originate from along the Nile. The Nile is very low in salinity. Well, now it's getting saltier but still... I think this pool is so salty because of the tiny leak right above it. See how it drips?"

"Oh yeah. I've never noticed that. I'll fix it right now. I'm going to get my tools."

"Bring two buckets so we can change the water." After they finished the task they literally dropped down on the floor because they were tired somehow. *LOL they barely did anything though...* "How are you tired? Aren't you supposed to be in shape, Leonardo? Also, what's all that breathing and fanning yourself like a Southern church auntie?"

"I don't know what that is, but it sounds funny," he giggled. "It was just a lot of bending over."

"You're not used to bending over?"

"It's been a while," he smiled.

"What was that?"

"You heard me."

"Was that sass?" she smiled. "Damn. Okay."

"Maybe."

"Can you sing something?" He shook his head no. "Why not? You sang during the performance?"

"Yeah, but you could barely hear me."

"Exactly."

"Clever," he said with an English accent.

"Ahhh! Never mind the singing for now. You can do that accent too? What other ones can you do?"

"Any one. I'm good at mimicking all sounds. Not just animal sounds. I don't do tongue twisters well though."

"So, you can do impersonations too?"

"Of course I can."

"Do some other accents." He shook his head. "You like teasing me, don't you? I like your toenail polish. You have pretty feet."

"Thank you," Xenon blushed. "I did them myself." He examined his fingernails. "What is wrong with my nail? Our paint doesn't do this."

"It's chipped. Well, the polish is chipped."

He looked worried. "Can it be fixed?"

"Yes, I can fix it when we go back."

"How come yours aren't painted? You don't like to paint them?"

"Sometimes I do, sometimes I don't. I usually get some shade of purple. Chance and I plan on getting a mani-pedi when we go back."

"What is a mani-pedi?"

"So, you go into this place called a nail shop—"

"You have to buy new nails?!?!?"

"No, but some people get fake ones when they want longer nails or something. The proper term is acrylic. They usually glue them on."

"Oh okay. Continue."

"You go in and pick the colors you want. Then you sit in a comfy chair that gives you a massage, and let your feet sit in warm water with bubbles that tickle your feet. They pamper your hands and feet. Then they paint them how you want them."

His eyes got larger. "Bubbles that tickle your feet? I want to go to this nail shop. Wait, do I always have to get an opaque color? What if I don't want it that day?"

"You can get clear. You just have to tell them what you want."

"We have something like this substance, but the texture is different. We use it the same way though. It protects our nails from water damage and looks nice. Hold on. Clear isn't a color. How does that work? Why would you make clear nail paint when you could make color? If you're going to paint your nails, you need to have some type of pigment. Clear sounds like such a waste."

"Some people use it as a top coat or base coat."

"What? I understand if it was glitter or something but it's not. It's like… Just make better quality nail polish. Duh…"

"LOL. Oceanids are on a whole other level."

Xenon popped up. "Guess what?!?!?" Amethyst waited for him to tell her the 'what'. "I installed a drain system in your room."

"You did? OMG!"

"Want me to show you how to use it?" She was so excited. "This cube represents your room. To turn it on, hold your finger on one of the faces for five seconds. Then this line will show up. You can drag the water line where you want it to be or you can use the remote. You can also go to the menu for more options. There's full drain, complete fill, temperature, and other stuff. I set the default settings as what I thought you might like, but you can change all that."

"Eeeeeep!!!" she hugged him. "Thank you so much!"

"You're welcome, Princess."

"Did you call me princess or Princess? You've called me that before. Is that another nickname?"

"It doesn't have to be. I could—"

"I just want to know why you call me that? Is it because you keep saving me?"

"No. Princesses don't need saving. They're only protected because they are the most valuable royal heir since they are the strong heart and shield of their queendom. I can't wait for the others to meet you."

"That's dope. On the surface, princesses are depicted as damsels in distress because that's how girls are viewed on the surface."

"If only they knew," he laughed.

"I'm going to start making my way to Iris's room."

"Okay. By the way, you can use my skin care products if you like. Is that weird on the surface? Uh... Well, I'm sure Iris won't mind you using hers until you get your own. I don't mind if you swim in my room and grab them or anything else you need. Oh, and if you need anything else, just wake me up. I won't smack you. I'm warning you though. My room's kind of messy."

"Alright. Thanks, Xe. You're so thoughtful."

"Oh! Before you go, Mom told me to give these to you. I don't know what they are. They look weird."

"They're toothbrushes! Yes! I'll give one to Chance. Thank goodness. Those spongey rectangular prism thingies are weird."

"Do you like Iris's toothpaste?"

"Nope. It's hella nasty. Why'd she pick the plain one?"

"I know right. I'll give you one of my extra ones. Mine is also charcoal based, but it's flavored. Guess what flavor."

"Seaberry!!! It tastes just like blue raspberry."

"Blue raspberry? I'll have to try that. Anyways, good night. Sleep tight and don't let the bedbugs bite. Also, I like the nickname you gave me."

She thought it was cute how he tried to use a surface saying. "Good night, Xe." Iris was already sleeping when Amethyst got to her room. Amethyst almost froze to death. She expected the water to be cold, but she didn't think it would be that cold. Iris must have had the heater on last time. Amethyst didn't realize Iris had woken up to get her a kelp blanket. It startled Amethyst when she felt the long strands wrap around her. She wasn't sure if Iris brought her the kelp because she was disturbed by her shivering, because she cared, or both. Regardless, she thanked her.

Iris didn't sleep a wink. She couldn't stop thinking about what was happening to her. Not because she cared about what was going to happen to herself. She was worried about what would happen to Amethyst. What kind of protector could she be in her current situation? Now that she knew what was going on, she was determined to fight it. If not for herself, for her sister.

Chapter 10: Monster Go Bye Bye

DAY 2

"Jeremy." Thetis tried to wake up the lifeless lump beside her. "JEREMIAS."

"What womxn?" he said sleepily.

"Don't what womxn me. Go wake up the kids."

"Do why I gotta wake kids up?" Jeremy was still in the process of waking up and couldn't speak properly.

"I'm making breakfast, that's why."

"Fiiiiine."

"Chance. Time to get up, buddy. Womxn's orders."

"What time is it?"

"I don't know. Like 8. It's morning morning."

"Oh, okay." Sliding from underneath his kelp and sea moss blanket, Chance swam into the kitchen with just his underwear. When he saw Thetis, he said, "Mornin', Auntie."

Jeremy still couldn't get over how comfortable Chance was, but now he was really in shock because he and Thetis seemed to be best buds. "When did this happen?"

"I like Chance. He's my little fire coral," she giggled. "What would you like to eat? Are you allergic to anything, sweetheart?"

"I'm allergic to nuts, but I don't think that will be much of a problem down here."

Like any momma's boy, Xenon went to go reclaim the attention that was stolen from him. He said, "Good morning, Mommy." Then he wrapped his arms around her and laid his head on her shoulder. Jeremy was so annoyed.

"Good morning, baby." She gently rubbed her nose against his. She loved her little teknon. "Did you have that nightmare again?" With his signature puppy eyes, Xenon pouted and shook his head yes. "Oh, come here." She brushed her worried hand against his face. "You go sit down with those two. I can handle breakfast."

"No, no. I'm alright, Mommy. I can help." And to mark his momma's boy territory he added, "I love you, Mommy."

"I love you too, Non Non." Chance showed Jeremy his best barf face to let him know they were on the same page. When the food was ready, Xenon fixed Thetis's plate, then Chance's. He told Jeremy he had to get his own. "Xenon…" she said in her motherly tone.

"Really, Blue? What did I do?"

"You pushed me off the bed last night! I go into Mom's room about two-thirds into my slumber pretty much every night."

"JEREMIAS. There is enough room for both of you."

"Thetis. He's 44. He should stay in his own room." His comment made Xenon cry a little. Thetis facepalmed.

"You're 44?!?!?" Chance wasn't sure if he was more confused or disgusted.

"I'm 17. I was hit with the time wave no one knows anything about!!!" Xenon was about to throw a fit.

"Jeremy, honey, you know that's a sensitive topic."

He took a deep breath. "Look, Blue... I apologize. I won't push you off the bed anymore, but I would really appreciate it if you gave me and Thetis some personal space."

"I accept your apology." Xenon went over and hugged him.

"Alright, alright. Why do you have to be so clingy?"

"Clingy?" Xenon used context clues and his empathetic abilities to figure out what that meant.

"Good morning, Meter." Iris swooped up her plate on her way to the table.

"Hey," Amethyst said.

"Well hello ladies," Chance added to Thetis's and Jeremy's endearing greetings.

"Amethyst, do you think I'm clingy?"

"No." Everyone gawked at her. "You're just a very loving person. There's a difference." She turned to Chance and asked, "How you holding up, big brother?"

"I'm doing fine. Who would have thought that I'd like it down here? Besides, I'm like you. Neither of us belongs on land."

"But you're a Naiad..." Iris said.

Amethyst laughed. "I knew he wasn't human. He never smelled human to me."

"Wait. Is my scent a good scent?"

Xenon said, "No. You stink." Amethyst and Thetis couldn't hold back their laughter. His comment was so unexpected.

"WHAT?" Chance's accent became more prominent. "I like to think I'm well groomed."

"It has nothing to do with being 'well groomed'," Xenon mocked his accent. "Your testosterone level is a lot higher than it should be. Come by my lab, so I can run some tests."

"How come that doctor dude didn't say anything? And what about you, Jeremy?" Chance swam over to Iris. "What do you smell?"

"First off, Jeremy and that foamy shell are old men, so they can't smell the scent I'm referring to as well as a younger male could. Second, Iris has hyposmia." He sensed Chance had no idea what that was. "She can barely smell. She's also female. Females don't have the same reactions as males and others when it comes to an influx of testosterone in hypermales."

"Oh. Um, real quick... Did you say others? And what is a hypermale?"

"Yes. There's no way to translate the proper terminology in any surface language. Hypermale is as close as I can get. Don't think it correlates to hypermasculinity. A hypermale is literally just a male with too much estrogen or too much testosterone."

"So, then there's hyperfemales too?"

"No. That's the binary thinking for you," he joked. "I'm just kidding. Estrogen and testosterone imbalance can happen to anyone, but it usually isn't a hard problem to solve for females and others. Hypermales tend to struggle with self-care even after they are given advice."

"So, what kind of symptoms do hypermales have?"

"Too much testosterone can lead to poorer judgment, rash decision making, aggressiveness, impatience, mood swings, etc. Also, sometimes the body will convert extra testosterone into estrogen which can cause weight gain. In addition, the body could stop producing testosterone which causes the testicles to shrink and sperm count to decrease. A lot of unhealthy things can happen. Slide through, so I can give you a proper diagnosis."

"Where'd you learn that phrase?" Amethyst smiled.

"From some people by the beach. They had two bark barks." They all greeted Reign who had just arrived.

"Cupcake!" Jeremy could never handle Chance's nose bleeds. Reign was worried.

"I know. I got it," she giggled. Iris was fascinated. Thetis told her to stop staring.

"But I didn't say the p-word."

"You said the word that starts with alpha gamma gamma, the word that is the product of a synonym for exam combined with popsicle, and the word for the cell that looks like a tadpole."

"Ooooh. Sorry. I think I understand now. If it helps, I've been through a lot regarding stuff in those categories because of the time wave, so I can be your go-to person." *Ugh. Why is he so precious?*

Chance couldn't speak with Amethyst pinching his nose, so he smiled and gave him a thumbs up.

"I've got work to do at the bridge," Jeremy waved to them. "See you later my basilinna and my basilissa."

"Don't call me that." They all thought it was cute how Thetis and Amethyst said that at the same time.

"I'm going to give her a tour around the bas." Thetis wanted to keep her daughter close to her this time. "You all will have to continue your coronation planning elsewhere." The group minus Alpha and Theta went to a secluded tropical island. Meanwhile, Alpha followed Theta around like a little baby duckling.

Amethyst couldn't believe how large the bas was. There was a music room, an art studio, a bathing room, a lounging area, and so much more. She wasn't surprised to see how neat and organized Thetis's minimalist workspace was, but it was much too boring for Amethyst's taste. Iris's workspace was even neater except you could tell she was a fashionista from the moment you entered. Her theme was Rockstar Princess, but her workspace was much too orderly for Amethyst. Xenon's workspace, however, was colorful, chaotic, and had a clear aesthetic: Underwater Baby Blue Astronaut. "Wow. Did he paint all of this?" Amethyst admired all the artwork on his walls. *Keep this detail in the back of your head. There's a lot more I didn't point out. I just felt like pointing this out.*

You really like outer space, don't you?

"Yes. He did it all by himself in his first half-life when he first got here. He painted a reproduction of the print Kanagawa-oki nami-ura because it reminds him of his mother."

No, I looooove outer space. Especially the stars. I could stay with them all night. I wish I could see them all day too.

You know how everyone ships us?

Yeah. What's our ship name?

Huuummm… I don't know. How about Atoz?

Ahhh! I like it. Clever.

"What's through there?"

"That passageway leads to the grotto. Although it is on land and not on the surface, I do not want to take any chances. A lightning bolt could possibly strike you. You will see what's up there eventually."

"How's Talisha? Oh, and I have to pee." Then Amethyst got sidetracked. "WHOA. Were these people here the whole time? What is this place?"

"By surface definition, this is a cross between an orphanage, a nursery, an animal shelter, and an adoption center. We just call it a children's center."

"Whhhaaaat! Awesome. I can see you really care about the well-being of your people, including the animals and plants. People on the surface aren't nearly as fortunate. There isn't much support for parents who need help, especially young ones. Also, there are so many children and animals that need to be adopted, and the foster care system is terrible. Is this everyone or are there other centers?"

"This is everyone in the basileia. There is one center in each realm. I've been trying to figure out a way to help the people in the southern waters, but their leader is corrupt. It's all Zeus's doing."

"Xenon's from there, isn't he?"

"Yes. Zeus is the reason for all the terrible things that go on there. Our people used to mingle, but now we can't even swim there." Thetis didn't want Amethyst to feel down, so she said, "How do you feel about children?"

"I love kids! Will I be working in here?"

"Iris will be over all of the finances, records, filing, and what not. Soon you will be over the activities, conference check-ins, homework help, caretaking, etc. You have the same responsibilities regarding the school and after-school programs. We'll get to that later today. Again, you may hire whoever you need to."

"Eeeeeep! I'm like a super camp counselor!!! Can I meet them right now?!?!?"

Thetis loved her enthusiasm. "Sure." When they swam into the center, all the children fell silent because they thought she was Iris. "Good morning teknon. This is my other daughter, Amethyst. She is going to take Iris's place as director."

"Hi everyone! Why y'all look so tense," she giggled. "Is that a sandcastle? That's dope. Who made it?"

"I did, Your Highness," a little girl said.

"You have skills," Amethyst said. "Hold on. You all know English?"

"Our younger generations are taught English as a second language, so it is easier for them to learn about the surface world."

"Good to know, but I'll do my best to hurry up and learn Greek," she smiled. "I have to admit that I'm really bad at remembering names, but I never forget a face. Can we go around and say our name, favorite color, and why that's our favorite color? Let's start with the young sculptor over here."

"I'm Aisha and my favorite color is crimson because I love pomegranates. Persephone is strong-minded, and I'm going to be just like her."

"I'm Omari. I like green because green is the color of plants. Everyone knows plants are good for the environment, and we should take care of them because they take care of us."

"My name is Valentino, and I work out," he flexed his bicep. "Hot pink is my favorite color because it attracts flutterfish when I wear it. I know sky nymphs say it's a feminine color, but so what? What's wrong with that? I heard that guys on the surface are rigid. They don't understand that sometimes you have to embrace your feminine side. That's why the ladies love me."

"Alright," Thetis laughed. "That's enough, Valentino."

After the other children went, Amethyst said, "You all can call me Amethyst. My favorite color is cosmic purple because it's the aura color of my frequency."

"Whooooa!" They liked what she said just as she thought they would.

"Omega Mu Gamma! We have the same favorite color as Her Highness. I mean Amethyst," a young Oceanid pointed out to the others.

"It was nice meeting you all, but I have to continue my training right now. See you later." Their last stop was the nursery room. Amethyst gasped. Wide-eyed, she said, "Huuuuh. Look at all of these precious little angels."

"I gave the caretakers an extended break, so right now you and I will be feeding them. They're about to wake up soon."

While Thetis was showing her how to prepare a bottle she had one question, "Where does the baby formula come from?"

"They are fed Hera's breast milk. She sends just the right amount every day."

"Ooooh. That makes sense. She is the goddess of childbirth and stuff."

"Breast milk is better than baby formula which is why I had Jeremy come get mine for you."

"Thanks. It's kind of weird how humans stay drinking milk from other mammals huh?"

"It is. Naiads do that same thing. At least the Naiads care for the animals. Plus, they always ask." Thetis didn't think Amethyst was paying attention to how she was preparing the bottle, so she was surprised to see her prepare one so quickly on her own.

"Okay so today we are going to figure out the theme of the celebration, so we can make the proper arrangements," Iris informed them. "Give me some ideas."

"We should make it something that will remind her of the surface," Xenon suggested.

"It has to be exciting but still classy," Reign added. "Huuum…"

"I know the perfect theme!" Chance said. "Are you all familiar with *The Great Gatsby*? She loves Gatsby."

Xenon and Reign had no idea, but Iris did. "Huh! That's great. Oh, I can see it now. It will be absolutely fabulous." After they finished explaining to the others, Iris pulled up a series of pictures and videos up on her tablet, so they could get a feel for the aesthetic.

"We should all dress up as a character!!!" Reign squealed. "Who's going to be who? Amethyst should be Daisy."

"I'll be Nick," Chance volunteered.

"I'll be Gatsby," said Xenon.

"Why you can't be Tom or George?"

"Because Gatsby suits me."

"Why because you like Ame?"

"No…"

"So, you do like her?"

"What?" he blushed. "N-No."

"I'll be Myrtle or Tom then. Or maybe a combination. I'm not sure yet." Iris knew how she wanted to dress, but she was always so cautious about her appearance.

Reign looked at Chance and giggled. "Then I guess I'm Jordan."

"Amethyst is a very energetic person, so the music has to be dance-worthy. She seems to like contrast, so the music also has to be modern." Iris waited for them to spit out their ideas.

"Do y'all know about pop music?"

"Good thinking, Chance. I have a good playlist we can work from."

"You do? How?"

"Iris is an MC. She knows about music from all the realms and the surface world," said Reign. "She's pretty dope." She was already picking up on some of their slang.

"No way!!! I wasn't expecting that. Cool. I'm a DJ. I can help out."

"How are you going to send invitations to Olympus without Zeus finding out?" asked Reign.

"Zeus's messenger is Hermes," said Iris. "Hera's is Iris, the rainbow goddess. That's who I send the invitations to."

"We have to have surface food. What are all of Amethyst's favorite foods and desserts?" asked Xenon. "There has to be variation. I'm sure the Naiads can make them."

"Her favorite foods are macaroni and cheese, blueberry muffins, banana muffins with no nuts, pineapple pizza, shrimp fettuccini, cheese tortellini, pasta salad, cornbread dressing, cranberry sauce, red chicken enchiladas, black beans, corn cake, potato salad, potato soup, sweet potato pie, jambalaya, grilled shrimp, raw shrimp, lobster, crab, string beans, broccoli, salad, oranges, strawberries, blackberries, mashed potatoes, cornbread, beans and rice, or just plain jasmine rice. She also likes mango sticky rice. She loves dragonfruit and stuff like that. The list goes on. Her number one is macaroni and cheese though. She goes crazy for that shit."

"Okay. What kind of toppings for the salad?"

"She likes ranch or Italian dressing, olives, green bell peppers, banana peppers not peppercinis, cucumbers, and mild cheddar cheese. The bell peppers have to be green."

"And the desserts?"

"Cake. She loooooves cake. Her favorite is white cake with strawberry filling. Not the syrup kind, the real strawberries. Her other favorite is chocolate cake with chocolate cream filling or real strawberries. She has a pet peeve of vanilla or cream cheese frosting on or in chocolate cake and chocolate frosting on or in white cake. If you do marble cake, only use chocolate frosting. Oh, and German chocolate cake is different than chocolate cake. She hates German chocolate cake. Cupcakes are different but easier. She's less picky about those. She likes strawberry flavored cake, confetti, etc. She likes them unique flavors like green tea and ube too. You should see her eat one. She always licks the icing completely off first," he laughed.

"Aren't you supposed to eat surface cake with ice cream?" asked Xenon.

"Oh, yeah. She thinks vanilla is mediocre. Her favorite ice cream is Smurf ice cream, but no one f****** likes that one, so don't get that. That shit is f****** disgusting. Her favorite kind to eat with cake is Neapolitan. That was a lot. How are you going to remember this?" Chance asked. "I don't see you writing shit down. Are you recording or something?"

"I have a really good memory. We are going to have a lot of people to feed, so this is great. Is she allergic to anything?"

"Well, metals aren't edible so no. She hates everything about red meats though, and she barely eats chicken. She'll f*** up some teriyaki chicken wings even if they aren't boneless though. She like her shit well done as f***. She also likes the burnt pieces."

"Okay. We're going to need to video call the royals, so they have an idea what gifts to get Amethyst."

"Oh shit. Liiit!"

Reign remembered something. "Before we go, one last thing. What is the maximum number of people for the guest list? There are so many people that want to come to the celebration."

Iris was curious. "How many people have submitted requests?"

"About 3,000 and I just started accepting requests yesterday."

"3,000?!?!? Already? Huuum, let's see. Okay, we are going to have to combine the grand ballroom and the banquet hall for the after party. We're probably going to have approximately 150,000 people. We won't be using chairs, but the amphitheater is around 300,000 meters squared which is about 984,252 feet squared. Americans don't really use meters, right? According to my calculations, that should be plenty of room for our guests and performers. Most people will be streaming the coronation live." Chance was glad there was another mathematician in the midst. "Now we need to head back to the bas to gather some measurements. Everything must be perfect. The décor must be neat, the tablecloths must brush the floor the exact same way, the plates and what not must be evenly spaced... You get the idea. Then we can order what we need. Blue, I need you to be my second pair of eyes to make sure everything looks good. Chance, you are going to be working with me. I could use another brain. Reign, I'm going to need those pretty little hands of yours to help me do the heavy lifting."

"Yes, ma'am," said Chance.

"You got it, Eye," Reign smiled.

"Sounds good, sis. I'll get a head start to make sure Princess is preoccupied."

"Meter already knows we're—" It was too late. Xenon was already gone.

"Did he say princess like Princess or the princess?" asked Chance. "I heard Princess."

"Me too," Iris agreed. "Is that a nickname?"

"Yeah, he definitely said Princess." They were all judging.

"How are you, Talisha?" Amethyst asked.

"Thanks to you, I'm doing great. Thetis has been so kind to me."

"I'm glad! Do you have any ideas for baby names yet?"

"I'm going to name them Amory, after you. If you don't mind."

"Huuuh!" Amethyst gasped. "That's sooooo cute. I'm honored. I'll see you two later. The teknon are about to wake up."

It didn't take them as long as Amethyst had expected to feed all the teknon. "I'm going to take a nap," Thetis smiled. "These are the last two teknon left. They don't have names yet, so I'll leave that up to you. When I wake up, I'll show you the nearest school. Then it will be lunchtime." She handed them to her. "They're twins. They'll cry if they are too far apart." She placed her palm over her heart and just looked at her daughter. Amethyst didn't notice at first. "I love you." Amethyst gave her mother a contagious ear to ear grin with dimples that set her heart on fire.

"Hello you adorable little squishy poos. Today both of you are going to get a name." She studied the twins. Xenon swam to the doorway, but he waited there because he didn't want to intrude. He was also triggered by seeing her with teknon. Especially since they were twins! "Oooooooo. I know! Octavia and October. You like? I don't know which one of you is female, male, or whatever, but that doesn't imply gender, does it? Just in case, I think October is pretty gender neutral, and you can always add an 'n' to Octavia or change the 'a' to an 'o'. You could even go by Octa. Or you two could swap. I don't think that will be a problem though since you aren't born up there on the surface. Surface people would ridicule me for thinking about this. Everything is better underwater. Names are just names down here. Everyone's chill down here." The twins smiled. "That's what I thought. The number 8 fits your aesthetic."

Xenon snapped out of it when he saw Amethyst struggling. He rushed over to her. "D-Do you need help? Here, I'll take one."

"Oh. Hey, Xe. You're right on time. Thanks."

Octavia started crying, so Xenon looked at Amethyst with nervous eyes. "Wh-What do I do?"

Amethyst giggled. "They're hungry." Octavia started reaching for her. "I'm sorry, sweetie. I don't have any milk." She looked to her stash of pre-made bottles but, "Oh, looks like I miscounted. Give me one second."

"No, I-I can do it. Just tell me how." They had no idea Thetis was watching them. She had stopped by to check on Talisha again before she headed back to her room. On her way back, she just so happened to see two of her teknon helping each other take care of two smaller teknon.

Thetis wasn't the only one who saw. "Look!" Reign pointed.

"No way… That's Blue. Even Meter couldn't get him to help out in there. Babies make him seasick as a nautilus."

"So why is he in there right now?" asked Chance.

Reign laughed and did a squiggly motion as she said, "Because he's in looooove. Stop frowning, Freckles." Iris wasn't sure if it was a coincidence that Chance fixed his face.

"How the hell can he be in love? He just met her. He acts like he's known her for a while."

"Why don't you go ask him?" Iris called him out.

"Fine." When they swam into the nursery, Chance said, "Hey, Xenon. Whatchu doing in here with my little sister?"

He hissed at Chance. "Shhh! Lower your voice. Don't frighten the kids."

"Dude, relax. My bad. Jeez. I'm the one that's frightened. I hate when you do that scary ass noise."

"Xe's just helping me out with the kids. That's all."

"Xe? Iris, that's a nickname!" Reign giggled. Iris jotted something down on her tablet.

"Forget that. Can you stop saying 'the kids'? That's cringe as f***." Iris was thinking the same thing.

"How?" Atoz was so confused. *Atoz as in A to Z. Ame and Xe. You're welcome.*

"It just looks like y'all in here playing house or something."

They both thought that was hilarious and decided to play house. Xe put his arm around Ame. "Aren't they beautiful?" she said.

"They are. We did good. I'm so proud of you."

Reign was so into their performance. "They're so good at this. How romantic… I want to play house."

"Should we make another one?"

"It's whatever you want, Babygirl."

Babygirl?

You don't like that one? I heard someone say that on the beach.

No, no. I'm okay with that, Baby.

"Alright, alright. That's enough," Iris rolled her eyes. "There will be no third baby."

"How you gon call her babygirl when you're holding a baby? That's not how you play house."

"But she doesn't have any kids."

"Wait. Babygirl and not babygirl? You're calling her Babygirl for real for real? Absolutely not. Did she say she was okay with that?"

"She did, and she's literally right here."

"Whatever, I didn't hear her."

"Chance…" Amethyst laughed. "Chill."

"It's aight, sis. I got this. Come on, Xenon. We need to have a talk man to man." Xenon gave the baby to Reign because she was closest. She had no idea what to do with that thing, so she gave it to Iris.

"He's so protective of you, Amethyst," Reign said. "That's so sweet."

"How is that sweet?" Amethyst laughed.

"How is that sweet? Amethyst can speak for herself." Amethyst could tell Iris didn't know she repeated what she said.

"It's not like that, sister. He knows. One day you'll understand. The surface is a lot crueler than you know. He means well."

Meanwhile... "Aight so check this out. I know you like her. Ima need you to be honest with me. You like my little sister or nah?"

"Yeah. I like her."

"Thank you. I appreciate your honesty. Now, here are the guidelines I expect you to follow: There will be no hugging, kissing, touching, or anything like that without her consent. Do not go into her room without her consent. Do not scream at her or threaten to harm her verbally or physically. If you do anything inappropriate, I will have to prevent her from beating your ass, and I can't hold her back for very long."

"I promised her I will do no such thing."

"You did? Hum. Okay. Then we're good."

Sorry about him.

I totally get it. There's sharks swimming around.

"Hello, Jeremy. You're back early."

"I took an early lunch to bring you these," he showed her the sharks he caught. "Just like old times." *If you know many sharks are endangered and are wondering why Oceanids eat sharks, it's because sharks are not endangered in their society. They care for animals and do their best to keep them away from humans. Humans stfu because UGH!*

"Huh! Oh, you shouldn't have," she smiled. "Thank you. They look delicious."

"What did Cupcake think about the tour?"

"A lot of ooooo's and ahhhh's. The teknon love her already. Also, on my way back here I saw Blinky helping her out in the nursery. Isn't that amazing?"

"It is, but what the hell was he doing in the nursery with our daughter?"

Thetis laughed. "Relax. He was just helping her out." She slid into bed next to him. "How long do we have, Jeremy?"

"About 20 minutes."

"Perfect." He pulled her closer. "Ummm. We haven't done this in forever," she smiled. Then they both took a nap. *HA. Y'all thought. These two are such sleepy heads. LOL. Sleepy head.*

During her nap, Thetis continued to think about the conversation she had with her eldest daughter:

"What's going on child? You haven't been acting like yourself lately."

"I know. I'm sorry. I didn't mean for this to happen. I know how much she means to you."

"You know because she means just as much to me as you and Xenon do. I love you all the same. I'm here for you, Sunshine, but I need you to help me figure out what's wrong, so I can help you. I'm worried about you. So is Blinky."

"I'm trying to fight it."

"OH, MY GODDESS." Thetis jumped out of bed.

"What is it? What's wrong?"

"The emphasis on the 'it'... I was right. She's Agathos and Leukos is trying to possess her."

"Oh shit! Like Metis?"

"Tomorrow I must retrieve a scroll from Klymene. This is a new experience for me. I can't let her end up like Metis."

Chance put his foot next to Xenon's. "My feet are bigger than yours."

Xenon sensed what he was referring to. "Shoe size doesn't determine the size of what's down there. Besides, size is only part of it. It's all about the stroke," he did a short grinding motion.

"What are they doing?" asked Reign. The girls were laying on the ocean floor waiting for the boys to be done with their shenanigans.

"Probably comparing features they associate with their masculinity," Iris said.

"LOL. Reign has bigger biceps than both of them combined."

"Rigggght," Iris laughed.

"Oh look, now they're playfighting," Reign rolled her eyes.

"Chance, cut it out!" Amethyst yelled. She didn't want them to fight even if they were just playing.

"Hey!!! Quit acting like bull sharks before I come over there," said Iris.

"This is so annoyingly entertaining," said Reign. "I kind of like watching them. I love a good fight."

"I know right. We've never had another male in our group before."

Chance walked over to them with Xenon. "Y'all talking shit," he laughed.

"Something similar. We were talking about you." *Iris is the queen of throwing shade…*

"You're the best piece of shit," Amethyst laughed. "You never left me in danger." *But Amethyst is the princess of pettiness. LMAO.*

Thetis finally located the squad. "Who's ready to eat?"

"Meeee!" said Atoz.

"Childish," Iris and Chance said at the same time.

"Ew. Did we just do that again?" Iris said.

They jinxed each other again, "Disgusting."

"Awww, look at our siblings," Amethyst smiled.

"They're so cute," Reign added.

"Iris is cute. I don't know about the red one."

"OMG." Amethyst just realized something. "You're Blue and…"

"…he's Red. Ahhh hahaha. That's your new nickname." Xenon thought it was perfect.

"What was my old nickname?" he asked.

"Clasper."

"What is that? You know what? Whatever. Let's eat!"

"What do you all have a taste for?" Thetis asked.

"I need something fried." Chance was desperate.

"Why?" Iris asked.

"Because I'm Black. Y'all don't have that down here?"

"OMG, Chance. You and your little comments. You're starting already? Look, everyone. I am going to apologize for him in advance. This guy is a comedian. I promise you he's not prejudiced. He's educated. He just needs prayer and the Holy Ghost."

They all shared a laugh. Then Iris said, "We have fried food. We looooove fried food. It's a cultural thing."

"We out then." Amethyst was so down. She had no idea where they were going so naturally, she asked, "What's the place we're going to called?"

"Psarian Psaris AKA Psar Psar's! Duuuuuh!" Iris was so excited.

"What does that mean?"

"I guess you could say it means fisher's fish. It doesn't sound as cool in English though," Xenon smiled. "Mom, before we go can we stop by my room. I have something for them."

You do? What is it?

It's a surprise.

"Yo! Thanks, man. This is dope as hell."

"No problem. Someone I knew also had asthma." Xenon helped him swap breathers. "You can activate the asthma pump manually by pressing this button, but you won't need to do that because it's able to detect your heart rate and respiration. I know you have tendencies that can cause you to hyperventilate and your heart rate to increase, so this red light will flash three times beforehand. You can cancel it during that time by pressing the same button. And here's a phone for you. You can contact your mom. Her contact information is all in there. I also programmed an app that keeps track of moon phases and the tide. I use it too." Then he turned to Amethyst. "Here you go, Moon Jelly."

"Whoa!!!" Chance couldn't wait to see what his new phone was capable of.

"I love Oceanid technology!!!" Amethyst squealed. "You're so cool. Thanks."

You think I'm cool?

This time Iris, Chance, and Reign said, "You think he's cool?" at the same time but in different tones.

"The words are all in English except for the names of the apps. I programmed all the essentials, but you can download more. It's like a surface phone but better. You can even record with the front and back refractors simultaneously. I'll tell you about the apps as we swim to Psar Psar's."

"What's this one with the blue dolphin— I mean delphys on it," Amethyst asked.

"That's Voutia or Splash. We use it to post short thoughts."

"What about P-S-I?" Chance had to spell it out.

"Psi is short for psithurismos. It means gossip," Iris explained. "It's used for longer posts and videos. Pictures are posted if they have a good enough story behind it. You find a lot of stuff like fanfiction, rumors, and what not. Especially about us. Kairos is what we use for actual news. That doesn't mean some of the stuff on Psi isn't true though. Vinte-Oh! is like YouTube."

"Iros is where we post regular pictures and shorter videos. That's why it has the little refractor on it. It's the best app to be in people's business," Reign giggled. "The one with the bubble on it is Lalo. It's for calling, video calling and text messaging."

"Ooooo. Something smells good!" Amethyst said.

"That's the place," Thetis smiled.

"Wait. Chance. Pause. I smell fried chicken."

"Oh, my god. I smell it now."

"The fried chicken is everyone's favorite." Thetis handed out the menus.

"It looks like we all want chicken, so let's just get that in bulk and have everyone choose their own sides," Iris suggested. "I'll go put our order in. What do you all want?"

"I'll have a side of shark whites and clams," said Thetis.

"Swordfish and lionfish. The usual." *Reign, Reign, Reign… Just why…*

Xenon and Chance waited for Amethyst to say what she wanted. "I'll try the fish sticks and the shrimp."

"Go ahead, Blue."

"No, after you, Red."

"Xenon/Chance what do you want?!?!?" Reign was annoyed by Xenon, and Iris was irritated with Chance.

Chance almost flew out of his seat. "Oysters and crab." He never preferred to be called Freckles so much in his life.

"The last thing you need is some oysters," Xenon laughed. Iris gave him a death stare. "Sc-Scallops and f-fish sticks."

Iris's tone changed when she addressed her little sister. "What kind of shrimp do you want, gemmie?"

"Raw please," she grinned. They all looked like predators when the food came. "Ummmmm... What are all these delicious looking sauces?" Amethyst asked.

"I'm glad you asked," Thetis smiled. "You should taste them all. When this place was first built, I came here with Amphitrite, Jeremy, and Poseidon. I made them try all the spices because I knew Poseidon would hate the orange one. It's tangy. Unless you count Xenon's wasabi, it's as close as it gets to spicy down here. I told Poseidon it was sweet." They all loved her little story.

"Try this one first. It's my favorite." Reign gave her some of the dark brown one. "They're all made out of herbs, so don't worry."

"Ew! This one is disgusting! It tastes like musty barbeque sauce. Neeext."

"This is the tangy one," Thetis told her. Little did she know Amethyst was admiring how royal she and Iris looked even when they ate fried chicken.

"This is not spicy at all," she laughed. "It tastes just like Sweet Hawaiian. Ohhhh yeah! Me likey." Something about that phrase was cute to Xenon. "What about this black one? Yo! This one's actually decent."

Iris handed her another one. "Try this one."

"Oh snap. Chance. This is a cross between ketchup and cocktail sauce. Genius. Bruuuh." She picked up the last sauce. "What's this orange-yellow one? It smells nice."

"That's my favorite," said Xenon.

"OMG yaaasssss. It's like sweet ginger mustard or something. This one and the tangy one are the best ones. Huuuuuuh! What if I dipped my fish sticks—"

"Ewww. Blue does that," Reign turned her nose up. "Good thing you two are sitting next to each other."

"I see why." Atoz stuffed each other's faces with fish sticks. "It's delicious."

Xenon got an idea. "Let's mix them!"

"I'm down!" Soon she was down to her last few shrimps. "Where did the rest of your scallops go? You must really like scallops," she giggled.

"No, Little Scallop. I looooove scallops." Xenon felt a sudden wave of embarrassment. "I-I have to go. I think I ate too many sandcakes." Reign facepalmed.

"Terrible excuse, Little Brother." Iris shook her head. "We didn't even order those."

"Boiiiiii. I'm weeeak."

"Stop laughing at him, Chance. And wipe that dirty barbeque sauce off your face," Amethyst giggled.

When Xenon returned, he did his best not to make eye contact with Amethyst as he walked back to his seat. Of course, he looked at her and sunk into his shoulders. Amethyst thought it was cute how he grabbed his elbows like he was cold. "H-Hi."

"Hi," she smiled. "You're so silly."

"Dessert anyone???" Thetis asked. Psar Psar's only serves one dessert, and it comes with every meal.

"It looks good, but what is it?" Chance wondered.

"It's called a deep-sea mud square or just a sea square. It's just chocolate, marine clay, paste, and sugar. Paste is basically what we use as flour."

"Marine clay? I didn't know clay was edible." Chance was hesitant to try it.

"What are you talking about? You and Iris got some sweet clay for me and Xe. It's basically a brownie. Just taste it," Amethyst convinced him. "See. It's yummy." Amethyst loved how Oceanids didn't leave as soon as they were done eating. "Whose phone numbers do we have?"

"I only programmed Mom's and Jeremy's. You two also have each other's."

"What's your phone number?" Amethyst asked.

"M-My number? You want my phone number?"

"Don't worry. I won't call you," she smiled. *Prime example of one of Amethyst's little traps. We call them Alpha traps.*

"No, no. I-I want you to call me. You can call me as much as you like. Or text me. Or video call me. It's sigma' omega' upsilon' lambda' mu' alpha' tau' epsilon'."

"Interesting. Okay. Wait. What's my number?" She tried to find it on her phone.

Xenon knew hers by heart. "It's iota' lambda' omicron' beta' epsilon' upsilon' omicron' upsilon'." Iris did her best to hold her tongue while Reign was trying not to giggle so much.

"What did you all put me under?" Amethyst asked.

"I put you in as Thing 1," Chance laughed. "With the bear sticker and the honeypot."

"Little Sister with this sticker," Iris mocked Amethyst's smile. "And two pink hearts."

"Small Fry with the little fish sticker and a yellow heart." Reign couldn't stop giggling.

"I put you in as Moon Jelly with—"

"Let me guess. Lots of kissy faces," Reign teased.

"No! With a wave and a purple star."

"Oh, okay. You're in as Moon Beam with a wave and a dark moon."

"Iris is Sunshine, so I put Moonshine," Thetis smiled.

"Yo, that's clever AF. I see what you did there. Iris was born at night, and I was born in the morning," Amethyst laughed. "I love it. Moonshine like the alcohol and my name is Amethyst, the sobering stone. HAHAHA."

"Whoa. I didn't even catch that last part. I can tell you are going to be a perfect fit for our intellectual discussions," said Iris. Amethyst was really starting to grow on her.

"Before we go, let's make our social media accounts. I'm kinda curious," said Chance.

"You only choose one username and password. They're all connected," said Iris.

"Yeah, and all the realms share the same social media," Reign added.

"Cool. I'm going to be @SpicyBoiii98."

"Huuum. Iris, what's yours? Ours should match."

"OMG yes! Good idea! I'm @ImGoddessBlessed."

"Then I'll be @ImGodDamned," she laughed. "Hell yeah."

Everyone was laughing, but Reign didn't quite get it. "Wait. I feel like there's an inside joke."

"Zeus is their father," Chance whispered.

Reign was shooketh. "No. Freaking. Way. So... You two have powers?" She made sure to keep her voice low.

"Apparently I'm the so-called chosen one, but Iris is the one with the powers."

"What are you talking about? You can cause storms!" Iris said. "And you haven't even started your training yet. I have a feeling you can do a lot more than that."

"Zeus views her as a threat that needs to be eliminated, but he won't hesitate to kill them both," Thetis explained. "Didn't I tell you?"

"You did, but it just sank in. Ohhhh. I get it now. God damned..."

"Okay, what are your usernames?" asked Amethyst.

Xenon showed her a convenient feature. "If we all click here, it will link us."

"Wooow. @ThisFlutterfishStrong. Really, Reign? @Basilinna... Way to keep it simple."

"@ImSoBlue is lame," Chance told Xenon.

"Better than @SpicyBoiii98."

"Why do you and Ame have to have the most depressing usernames? Is the 'I'm' at the beginning a royal thing?"

"Yeah. Iris and I started that. The other princesses, princes, and prins copied us, but everyone knows we started it."

"Prin? I've heard you say that before. What's that? Is that for people who aren't a girl or boy?"

"No. It's just another junior royal title. The terms princess, prince, and prin have different roles, but they don't have anything to do with gender. They can be anyone, but I will say that there are gender trends within each category." Xenon and Iris clearly had an inside joke.

"Can you give me some examples?"

"Amethyst is the princess, Iris is technically the prin, and I'm the prince. Reign could be a prince. You could be a prince too, but I could definitely see you being a prin."

"But you have more sugar in your tank than I do."

"Prin doesn't have anything to do with any form of femininity or masculinity." They all laughed. "How much sugar do you have in your tank?" Xenon asked.

"I've got about a cup and a half. You have at least 5."

"Why do you say that?" Everyone couldn't stop laughing.

"First of all, all pretty boys have 2 cups of sugar at the very least. Second of all, can't no boy roll they eyes like that without at least 3."

"Where'd the last two cups come from?"

"There's never really a way to tell, but my radar is picking up some suspect vibes from you," he whispered.

Reign called him out. "How do you have a radar?"

He tried to hide his guilty smile. "That's besides the point." He leaned in closer to Xenon and whispered, "Look, all I'm saying is that I have a feeling you're fluid on two fronts, Mr. Where'd-The-Last-Two-Cups-Come-From." Xenon tried not to laugh as he made a guilty lol-no-comment-face and sipped his juice.

"Let's take a picture," said Amethyst. They had someone at the table next to them take it for them. Thetis and Iris posed like the queens they are. Chance showcased his dorky smile, and Reign did her signature peace sign. Xenon showed off his best smolder while Amethyst showed off her pearly whites. "Yaaasssss. We look hot. Iris, you post it. You have the most followers. Don't forget to tag us. Oh yeah, and I can't wait to lurk on y'all pages. That's what's finna happen as soon as me and Thetis get back."

Thetis took a selfie with Amethyst and Chance and captioned it, "Family…" with lots of hearts.

Xenon started recording a short video. "What's up everyone. Guess who I'm with! What's your username, Princess?"

"It's @ImGodDamned. I'm cute and funny so…" Amethyst stuck her tongue out and shot her finger guns.

"Add me too. @SpicyBoiii98. You already know wassup. Liiiiit."

"See you later!" Amethyst waved.

"This is the school??? It's so fancy looking."

"There are 5 schools in total. They are in a subring just outside of the bas."

"Who goes to what school, and how do the people who live farther out get to school?"

"Imagine each school has a line that extends from where it is in the basileia all the way to the outer ring. The sections are called pentarchs. Now imagine another line down the middle of each pentarch. Everyone swims to the left or right until they reach one of the main lines. The bisecting line isn't a border or anything. Some Oceanids choose to go with their friends even if they are closer to another main line. Sometimes they just like a certain theme better. Along the rings of homes in each quadrant, manta rays transport our teknon to and from school. The older youth are able to swim to school. If they are not, a manta ray will also transport them. Each of our schools offer the same quality education. No school or pentarch is inferior or superior to another." Thetis wondered if she was talking too much. Once again, she couldn't tell if Amethyst was paying attention.

"I see. Sounds like a pretty good system. I wish I could have went to school down here. By the looks of everything else down here, they probably would have been a better fit for me." Amethyst didn't want Thetis to feel like she failed her because she didn't. "Can you tell me about the themes?" *She was definitely paying attention. At some point, you'll learn that many things Amethyst says have complex purposes just like the question she just asked.*

"Sure. The Epsilon Zeta chapter is very preppy, the Epsilon Delta chapter is gothic, the Gamma Delta chapter is very technological, the Gamma Beta chapter is artsy, the Zeta Beta chapter is very traditional and cultural, and Beta Zeta is surface themed. I'll let the students tell you more."

"How is there Zeta Beta and Beta Zeta?"

"Technically, Zeta Beta is the name of the chapter, but a program grew to become a subchapter. They share a campus. They have their own separate teams and the most intense rivalry."

"Interesting. So, what about the warriors? Do they have a separate chapter or what?"

"All students have the option of enrolling in the warrior program. They all have to enroll in at least one extracurricular program each pentad. They may choose any program from any campus. They get a chance to join the warrior program each year and a chance to pick any other program every regular pentad. They can drop out anytime. There are different age groups of course."

"Isn't that a lot to balance with school?"

"Our students only go to school 3 days of the surface week or every other weekday. Class is not in session today, but people are always there studying, spending time with friends, and what not. Some programs are held on campus. Our programs are held on the days in between, and there is no school on the weekends. School takes place all year, but there is a break every pentad. Every break is five days, and the seasons are pentads. The fifth is during December 17th to December 22nd and is both a break and its own pentad."

"Whaaaat? Cool! How long is each school day?"

"From the first low tide to the first high tide."

"I see why surface time doesn't work. The tides change. Everything is fluid, including time. Surface people don't understand that. Everything is clockwork up there. Why is the fifth pentad so special? I feel like it's special. Winter solstice???"

"Partially. During those days, everyone takes part in paying their respects to Poseidon and Amphitrite. The official celebration is held on or near the winter solstice, but throughout the week there are many festivals, cultural performances, and more. The whole basileia is decorated during this time. December is our most festive month."

"So, what's it called?"

"Amphidromia. Amphitrite was born on the winter solstice. The date changes, so we just pick a day within the range. Poseidon insisted that be when we celebrate them if we must. He says an empire is nothing without the Empress, and the Emperor is nothing without his soulmate because without the Moon there are no waves, and an Ocean with no waves is no Ocean. He knows the wind causes waves, but he means it in a figurative way."

"Eeeeeep! That's so beautiful. Does he write poetry?"

Thetis laughed. "Yes, but he's just a whirlpooled romantic."

Are you a whirlpooled romantic?

Huh? Oh. Me? Is that a bad thing? I don't write poetry. N-No? Maybe. I'm not really good with words.

"So which chapter are we going to?"

"We're going to start at Epsilon Zeta and make our way around."

"Reign." Chance was surprised by how quickly she twirled around. "It's nice to not be the only one with a different accent than the others."

"What do you mean?" she giggled. "The only one of us who has a pure Greek accent is Iris."

"Blue does."

"No, he doesn't. It's an act."

Xenon broke character. "Why do you have to tell on me?"

"Dude! I'm not sure which East African accent that is but that's dope. I'm hearing something else too. My mom's from Libya, and my father's from England. I was born in Germany."

"Cool! My mother was Eritrean and Japanese. My father was Eritrean and Chinese."

"Reign, I'm not sure from what part but yours is Brazilian, right?" She nodded. "Do you know any Brazilian Portuguese?"

"Como vai, gatinha?"

"What does that mean?"

"She said, 'How's it going, baby?'" Xenon translated.

"She's flirting with you," Iris smiled. "Don't just sit there. Aren't you going to respond?"

"Uh... I-I don't know any Portuguese."

"She also speaks Arabic," said Iris.

" 'Ana 'aqwam bieamal rayie." *He was trying to say something like 'I'm doing great, beautiful.'* "Sorry. That was terrible. I'm not fluent in Arabic."

OMG. Moon Jelly! Guess what.

What?

Reign just flirted with Red and Iris totally encouraged him to flirt back. I'm picking up different emotions from her. I don't know how to describe them.

If they were a food how would it taste?

Bittersweet.

She must have realized he's definitely not her soulmate.

That was fast.

I think it was slow. I know how I feel about a person's aura within seconds.

You do? How do you feel about mine?

I like your aesthetic.

You always talk about my aesthetic, but what's my aesthetic?

Hehehe. I gotta go.

"Blue..." Chance tried to get his attention. "Blue! Do you know hella languages like Iris?"

"No. I don't know as many as she does. Iris is still adding more languages to her list."

"Speaking of languages, I don't like how you say my name when you try to say it the Greek way," said Iris. "Just say it the English way."

"Damn. Okay," he smiled. "How many do you know, Reign?"

"I only know 6."

"What are you thinking so hard about, Little Brother?"

"What's my aesthetic?"

"I don't know. Ask Amethyst. That's her thing. She told me I'm a pretty pink power femme version of Wednesday from the Addams family. That's so accurate."

"Oh shit. I'm f****** weeeak," Chance laughed. "Ame hella funny."

"Just tell me what you think. How would you describe me?"

"You like to show off," Reign giggled.

"You're very thoughtful," Iris said.

Chance added his two cents, "You're the typical prince who woos everyone with his perfect face, perfect bod, fancy looks, and all his fancy things."

"Okay, thanks!" he said as he swam to his room. He had plans for tomorrow. He would have done it today, but there was something else he needed to do.

"I am Epsilon Zeta Alpha: Alpha Alpha Angelica." Amethyst already didn't like her, but she continued to smile and be polite.

"And I'm Epsilon Zeta Omega: Alpha Alpha Ikatere. We are glad to meet you. Let us show you around. We will answer any questions you have."

"What do your titles mean?"

"We're a part of the student oligarchy," said Angelica. "I'm the Alpha of the Epsilon Zeta chapter."

"I'm the Omega. We're both Alpha Alpha. Two Alpha Alphas are always the co-leaders of a chapter's student oligarchy."

"Oh okay." Amethyst knew she was going to have to try hard to not zone out listening to all the titles. "Is Alpha Alpha your grade level?"

"Yes. We would be considered high school seniors on the surface," Ikatere responded. "In order, the elementary grade levels are Zeta, Epsilon, Delta, Gamma, Beta, and Alpha. The secondary grade levels are Alpha Zeta, Alpha Epsilon, and Alpha Delta. The tertiary grade levels are Alpha Gamma, Alpha Beta, and Alpha Alpha." *Huuuh this part is going to be a mouthful to read aloud. Just bear with me.*

"That makes sense."

"This is our library," Angelica showed her. "Ours is the largest of all of the chapters. Many students from other chapters like to study here." Some of the students inside quietly took pictures of Amethyst and Thetis and tried not to stare.

"Hello. We'll take it from here," said someone Amethyst figured was another Alpha or Omega.

"Epsilon Delta Alpha: Alpha Alpha Ariadne here."

"Epsilon Delta Omega: Alpha Alpha Nephthys here."

"And we are at your service," they both said at the same time.

"So, all of the campuses are connected? It's like a mega-campus."

"Exactly. Our campus isn't all that colorful, but we have the most plants," said Ariadne. "We even have a greenhouse filled with lots of land plants."

"Are these pomegranate trees? Is your aesthetic modeled after Persephone's? I haven't met her, but I'm getting earthy underworld vibes."

They both smiled. "It is." Nephthys was impressed. "I see you have quite the eye."

"Eh. What can I say? I know a brilliant theme when I see one."

"Whatever we grow is used as produce for the school lunch and for Amphidromia. Our pomegranates grow very fast because Persephone likes our campus."

It wasn't long before Amethyst noticed some other Alpha Alphas waving to them. "I'm Gamma Delta Alpha: Alpha Alpha Satet and…" Satet had a bit of a twitch. Amethyst thought it was kind of cute.

"…I'm Gamma Delta Omega: Alpha Alpha Psamantha. Do you love technology?"

"Um, technology's cool as long as it doesn't become unhealthy."

"I'll take that as a yes," Psamantha smiled. "As you can see, our campus is by far the most technologically inclined. We aren't stingy though. All students are welcome to utilize our equipment and are eligible for free repairs and upgrades on any of their own electronic devices."

"Before you go, what's Prince Xenon like?" Satet obviously had a crush on him.

"He seems like a nice guy. You probably know a lot more about him than I do," she laughed. She meant that sarcastically, but she said it like she didn't. *That's the difference between Iris and Amethyst's sarcasm.*

"What's up? I'm Gamma Beta Alpha: Alpha Alpha Icarus."

"How you doin'? I'm Gamma Beta Omega: Alpha Alpha Iapyx. We're cousins."

"Heeeeeey y'all." Amethyst loved their energy.

"This is the campus art gallery. Everything here was made by students. The as in THE art gallery is in the grotto. That's where the best pieces from all the realms are stored. Ours is tiny compared to that one," Icarus explained. "Only Hera, Apollo, Artemis, Athena, and Aphrodite's favorites go up there. All pieces come here first and are moved when they say so. It's not something that happens very often."

"There was this one artist that literally pleased the goddesses every single time. They want to give the artist their own section in Apollo's gallery, but they can't because the artist is an anonymous ghost. Then they suddenly stopped submitting pieces like 25 years ago. Their style is unique and very recognizable regardless of the piece even though they are all so different. We aren't able to categorize it. That's the only way we were able to be sure it's the same artist. We have refractions of their work in that room over there."

"Eeeeep! Can I see them?!?!?" They were more than willing to show her. "Th-This is… I-I… This is beautiful. I'm in love." Thetis loved what was beginning to bloom. *What exactly would that be? Well, you'll just have to find out and see.*

"This is the first piece. The artist seems to only use cool and neutral colors. See how they get darker and darker over the years?" Iapyx pointed out. *Not the hue…* "Whoever this person is has gone through heart-wrenching trauma, but the more you examine each piece the more you think that something else is there. Love is there."

"I don't know, Iapyx. I think they are just insane. By the looks of their art, it doesn't seem like love was a motive. Anyone who thinks their work is romantic is also insane."

"Whatever. That's why we call them Ble Skia AKA Blue Shadow."

"Wait why do we call them that again?"

"OMG, Icarus! Really? Don't you know everything about Ble Skia?!?!? A shadow is the soul of a person in the underworld, and this shadow has to be the most miserable shadow like… Ever."

"Isn't it amazing how they all go together somehow?" said Icarus.

"I know right. We know about the mood, but there doesn't seem to be any overarching theme."

Amethyst was so mesmerized, you would have thought she was looking at her soulmate. "Chaos."

"Huh?" said Icarus and Iapyx.

"Their aesthetic is chaos. Pure chaos. How romantic."

"But what exactly does that—" They both had an epiphany. OMG. That's it. That's why we can't categorize it! You're a genius like Iris! Your Majesty, your daughter is a genius! Do you mind if we publish that statement in your name?" Amethyst told them to go ahead.

"Now there's a much more controversial question," Iapyx wondered. "Who was Ble Skia's muse? Who fueled the faint traces of love that would have otherwise been non-existent amidst this chaos?"

"Oops, our times up. The others are probably waiting for us," Icarus laughed.

"What took you so long?" one of the other Alpha Alphas joked. "Khairete! Ti pratteis, Your Majesty. Se gignoskon kairo, Your Highness," he kissed both of their hands. "Zeta Beta Alpha: Alpha Alpha Alpha."

"Khairete! Zeta Beta Omega: Alpha Alpha Omega. We hope you are pleased with the campuses. Also, if there is anything we can do to make you feel more comfortable at any time, please do not hesitate to let us know," she kissed their hands.

"The Beta Zeta's couldn't be here today. They are currently hosting their general athlete preparation program."

"Thank you," Amethyst smiled. "What an introduction."

"This is the gymnasium. This area can be transformed into the official coliseum of the basileia. We host all of our athletic events here," Alpha explained.

"And this…" Omega threw her arms open. "This is our astronomy center. Our observatory is reached by taking that elevator over there. In the old days, it was used as a watchtower."

"Cooool!!! Is it true Saturn can float?"

"In enough water, yes," said Alpha.

"Is there really a metallic liquid hydrogen ocean on Jupiter?"

"Yes. That isn't the only thing on Jupiter," said Omega. "When you come back, I'd love to give you the whole presentation."

"How many major planets are in our solar system?"

"We don't have a static answer to that question yet. I know the surface only knows of 8."

"What's the 9th one called? Minerva?"

"Wow. Actually, yes," Omega smiled. "You know, humans weren't the ones who named the planets."

"Why'd y'all name my favorite planet after Zeus?"

"It's a joke," Omega laughed.

"Can you tell me about dark matter?"

"We know more than the humans, but dark matter remains a mystery."

"Aw. Well, what can you tell me?"

"About 18 years ago, we discovered the strongest GRB ever recorded. The afterglow was more like an afterflash, so we call it the Dark Burst. Some people thought the world was going to end because Hera told us it was a sign from Chaos. She said it was a warning. People like to joke and say a new god was born. The delphys say it was a newborn creation of Chaos. Nothing has really happened since then."

"She doesn't know what a GRB is, Omega," said Alpha.

"LOL. I love stars and stuff. Hypernovas are awesome. Gamma-ray bursts fit my aesthetic. Not the ones that leave behind those lame radio waves though."

"Well never mind then," he smiled.

"Is there life on other celestial bodies?"

"Yes. We do our best to keep the humans from finding out. You know how they are. Oh, yeah… The planets have different names on different planets and moons."

"They already found out there's water on Mars," said Amethyst. "I hope there's no life underground. All humans do is conquer, colonize, and corrupt."

"That's so true. They bring order wherever they go," said Omega. "I'm praying they don't find them. Chaos be with them."

"Aw, man!!! Nooooo! There's Martians? I'm praying for them too."

"We'd love to stay and talk with you, but we have to host our observation program. I'm sure you and Her Majesty have other plans."

"The tour was great! I'll see you around," she waved to them.

"XENON!" Iris always got irritated when he couldn't hear her because that meant she had to swim over to wherever he was. "It's been waves! What are you doing in your room? We need to figure out the decorations and their measurements while Amethyst is away."

"Okay, okay. I'm coming. There's something in my eye."

"Awww, come here, Blinky. I'll get it."

"Don't mess up my eyeliner."

"I won't." After all the theatrics, it was time to put in work. "The drapes should be a little lower."

"Right here?" asked Reign.

"Yes! That's perfect."

"What colors are we going to do?" asked Xenon.

"Amethyst's favorite color is purple right, Chance?" Iris asked for confirmation.

"Yeah. Cosmic purple. Ame prefers cool and neutral colors."

"She does?" Xenon's head popped up.

"Umm hmmm. I'm thinking purple, blue, and white."

"You have to be more specific than that," said Iris.

Reign had an idea. "She's going to want to wear a purple dress, and she has to stand out, so we have to use a different shade of purple and shades of other colors that will make her dress pop."

"What? How?" Chance was lost. "And by the way, Ame isn't the dress type. She likes skirts sometimes though."

"Think of this like a painting. The decorations are the background, but Amethyst is the focus. She is wearing a cosmic purple outfit. We don't want her to blend in with the background, we don't want the background to take attention away from her, and we still want to keep the cool, neutral aesthetic. A deep lavender, a soft teal, and a bold, shimmering silver should do the trick. We could add flecks of a gentle white to add some variation."

"Damn. You sound like an artist? You really paint, don't you?"

"I-I used to. Not very well though."

"We'll go with that. We have to have lights," Iris said.

"What kind of lights?" Reign asked. "Are we talking floodlights? Do we want them to move? What color?"

"Lights that move around trigger her anxiety. She's also sensitive to white light," Chance informed them.

"We can use cream light," Iris suggested.

"Okay, but what about the shape," Reign reminded them.

"Amethyst loves stars," said Chance. "Like, she's obsessed. She told me that she could watch the stars all night and all day. I asked her how she was going to do that in the day. You know what she told me? This womxn said the stars are always there, so whenever she looked up at the sky she

296

would be watching them. Then she said the stars are within everything and everyone, so all she had to do was open her eyes. I swear… Some of the things she says about the universe makes me think she was a star in a past life or something."

"That would explain a lot," Xenon said under his breath.

"So, we want star-shaped lights?" Reign asked.

"No, gemmie," said Iris. "We want lights that look like stars. Let's do tiny bulbs."

She was so excited. "String lights!!! Yay! Those are fun!"

As the Alpha negative squad gathered the measurements, Iris noticed something heavy was on Xenon's mind. "What's stinging you? Why is your ship sunk?"

He couldn't stop thinking about how that creature almost got Amethyst. Was he going to tell her that? No. "N-Nothing."

But of course, Iris had her ways of knowing things. "I know. I keep thinking about nothing too. I almost lost our sister, Chance. I almost lost her. 'A creature that would threaten such a precious gem is a horrid being. But what of a creature that somehow failed to be there for a gem that is so precious to them?' Tykhe." Iris began to weep, and Xenon held her in his arms. Reign was doing her best to hold it in.

"Look, Iris. I get it. I really do."

"How could you? She said you've never left her in danger. I caught what she said earlier."

"Ame wanted you to hear that. Not because she wanted you to feel guilty. She made that joke to show you she isn't upset anymore so that you wouldn't feel like this. Ame talks about you so much I get jealous. When y'all ain't around, it's always Iris this, Iris that. She admires the f*** out of you. She believes everything you say in your interviews and stuff… I don't know how or why she faithfully trusts you, but she does OPENLY for some reason. She didn't say that, but I can see it in her eyes. This is a f****** first. The point is... Ame doesn't hate you. You'd know if she did."

"Really?"

"I'm only going to tell you this because I trust you all for some reason, and I can see you all really care about her. I've known Ame since we were kids. Before we knew each other, all she had was Jeremy, and all I had was my mother. My father has always been abusive to me and my mother. My mom swears he's ill. She left me with Jeremy and Ame because she went to go find a cure for my father. She's a scientist, and she wants me to at least have a good relationship with him. I have Type 1 diabetes. That's partially why I'm so skinny. And I don't work out. I've also been diagnosed with bipolar disorder, BPD, major depression, and shit. They gave me all these damn drugs, and my dumbass started abusing them. I don't know how the f*** I'm alive. Must be because of Ame. I felt like I was a drug. I felt like I was toxic to Amethyst. My worst fear was corrupting her, so I tried to push her away. What the hell kind of logic is that? I don't know." Now Chance was weeping, and Reign couldn't hold back any longer. "I tried to get her to cut me off, but she's more stubborn than even me. She stayed by my side no matter what and never stopped trying to get me clean. Then she went through a depressive episode. Timing's a b**** ain't it? The episode had nothing to do with me, but I'm the person who is always at home with Amethyst when Jeremy's at work. She overdosed on a whole bottle of some strong ass pills she was prescribed. We still don't know how she's alive, but I just care that she's still here. I wasn't there, Iris. I wasn't there to stop her. It doesn't take long for Ame's thoughts to spiral downwards. I was the one who would always be there to talk it out and help her through it. But I wasn't there. Now I'm clean, but more importantly, I'm never leaving her side again. And you know what? Not once did Amethyst blame me, and not once was she angry with me. She was only worried sick. I laid in the hospital bed with her for days, and do you know what the first thing she told me when she woke up was? She said, 'Just say no.' It's a slogan of an anti-drugs commercial. She still had tubes in her airways, and she made a f****** joke. I had to get her to stop laughing, so they wouldn't take her to the psych ward. That place is terrible. Honestly, she scares me sometimes, but I love her. That's little sis. That's my little Cinnamon Roll." He went over to Iris. "You and

I think alike. I imagine you are having the same thoughts I had. Don't do it. That's what's going to hurt her."

"Thank you, Chance," Iris wrapped her arms around him. "For Amethyst, I'll keep fighting. I'll keep fighting for our sister. I'll never stop fighting for her." They all wondered what Iris meant. What was she fighting? They did their best to get themselves together before Amethyst showed up.

"Chaaaance! Iris! Xenon! Reiiign! I'm baaack." She froze when she swam in. "What happened in here? Why were y'all crying? I mean weeping. Same thing."

"We're good, Ame. We were just bonding," said Chance. *Good answer.*

"Iris! Iris! Iris!"

"What is it, Sister?" she smiled.

"Thetis told me all about you being a genius since you were little. Can you play "The Devil's Trill"?!?!? You play your violin underwater? That's so cool. Can you play some of it for me? Pleeeeease!!!"

"Sure. Anything for you, Sister."

"Is that that scary song?" asked Reign.

"Yeah but it's kind of catchy," said Chance.

"Lately, it's one of the songs I play when I'm feeling down," said Iris.

"Really? Oh, well maybe it will cheer you up," she smiled. Then she sat on Reign's lap.

"You don't want to sit on my lap?" Chance joked.

"You're too skinny, Choo Choo Train, and Iris is holding her violin." Amethyst used to call him that all the time when they were younger. The idea sprang from watching Thomas The Train.

"Choo Choo Train?" Reign laughed. "Why do you call him that?"

"Because a lot of steam comes out of choo choo trains when they get all fired up." They were all laughing so hard they forgot that they were weeping a few waves ago.

Why "The Devil's Trill"?

Seems fitting for what we're about to do. Doesn't it?

It does. Wait. What are we about to do? Were you in my head?

No. I have my ways. I notice more than you think.

What did you notice?

Two can play this game of secrets. I happen to be much better at it. You should know that by now. When are we leaving?

Why do you want to come?

I want to watch.

You're insane.

Are we really though?

Good point. We leave when they go shopping for decorations. I'm going to tell them I'm going to take a nap.

"That was wonderful, Iris!" Amethyst grinned.

"How about another? Any ideas?"

"Can you play "Danse Macabre" by Camille Saint-Saëns?" Amethyst asked. "Seems fitting for a child prodigy." Xenon tried to suppress his reaction to her clever little comment.

Chance laughed. "That's that Halloween turn up."

"I love that song and that poem," Xenon decided to say.

"Poem?" asked Chance

"The song is based off a poem," Iris explained.

"Will you dance with me?" Alpha asked Zeta.

"I will."

I think this one is more fitting. Don't you, Xe?

I do.

Xig, xig, xig…

I don't think I understand.

I think you do. It's a syzygy.

What do you hear?

Nothing.

What do you want to hear?

The rattling of bones.

I think I understand the riddle now, but I can't be sure.

Why do you have to be sure?

Because if I'm wrong, I'll lose what I have been missing.

If you're wrong then that's not what you have been missing, and you will have lost nothing.

But what if you're wrong?

Then I'll just keep on dancing alone.

Who do you think I am?

That means nothing if you don't know yourself.

Who do you want me to be?

Who I think you are.

"You two can stop staring into each other's souls now," Chance giggled.

"Yeah. I thought the dramatic pause was supposed to be short," Reign added. Then she changed her mind. "It was so romantic!" she twirled.

"What did you see?" Iris asked.

"Nothing," said Amethyst. *This part is scary to me because I myself am unsure if Amethyst was referring to the 'nothing' in the group's private conversation. If she was, it has a double, maybe even triple meaning. You'll see why... Huh! What if she was also referring to the 'nothing' at the beginning when she and Xenon were dancing at his birthday party.*

"We have to disguise ourselves," Zeta told Alpha.

"As what?"

"Flutterfish."

"What?"

"So-called girly girls. That's the closest term I can think of. We couldn't have dressed as shuttersharks because I'm much too masculine already."

"Ooooh okay. So that's what that means. I don't have clothes for that down here though."

"Don't worry," he laughed. "I have some things."

"Yay!!! I love playing dress-up."

They changed clothes and put on wigs. Xenon put on a long purple one with loose waves, and Amethyst put on a baby blue one with lots of curly ringlets. They looked in the mirror at the same time and said, "We should switch."

"Wear this so they can barely see your face." He handed her a headpiece with netting. "What color lip shimmer?" asked Xenon.

"Don't you already have some on?"

"It's faint compared to flutterfish. It needs to be more prominent."

"Use Pearl Sand." After he applied it she said, "Yeah that looks nice, but you're missing something."

"What? I have my... How do you say it in English? Oh, bag or purse."

"Come down some. You're so tall." He was happy because no one thought he was tall. He was short. Especially for an Oceanid. She added a braid in his hair. "There. That's cute. It adds a little umph."

They both laughed with each other when they looked in the mirror. "Wow, you look completely different."

"So do you," she giggled. "You aren't bringing your katana?"

"I don't want to alter the body." *So, she not gon question that? I cannnnn't with these two.* "Okay, try not to do anything cute. Whatever you do don't smile. We don't want to attract any attention."

"So, what's the plan?"

"We're going to sneak past the guards and swim down into the trench. Once the creature senses you, it'll come out of its lair. Then I'm going to sphyxis it."

Amethyst had a feeling that was a root word of asphyxia, and he did say he didn't want to alter the body. "You're going to choke him? You're going to overpower the trench creature? Do you even know what it is?"

"What is it, and how do you know?"

"It's a Nereid. I know what they smell like. Plus, no one in Caris can see at night. How did y'all not peep? I guess the survivors don't talk about it much. Anyways, I noticed how Nereids' noses twitch when they smell something potent like Oceanids. That's a sign of a highly sensitive nose. Then that reminded me of something. I was like ooooh they have thermal vision, not night vision. The animals, even those with thermal vision, aren't in the area because of the Nereid, not entirely because they all can't see. Xe, this one's hella big. At least bigger than the others I've seen so far." She took a mental note of how Xenon didn't correct her when she said others instead of other.

"Oh okay. Nereids can't breathe upside down, so I still got this. Hold up. Why wasn't he chasing after me then? I'm bigger."

"This Nereid wasn't hungry, Xe. He's not attracted to males as much or at all. Or maybe he just likes me better than you," she laughed.

"Of course. OMG duuuh. Male Nereids are known for doing that kind of thing, and the females are known for stealing teknon."

"Come on!"

"Why are you so eager?" he smiled.

"Because being the bait sounds fun!"

"Oh, shamberings. There's the squad. Iris will recognize me dressed like this."

"LOL. I love your slang. Chance will recognize me too."

"You do this often, Little Scallop?"

"The question is, do you?" she smiled. "I said I love playing dressing up." He did that little guilty smile thing he does. "Umm hmmm that's what I thought. You just played yo self."

"Whatever," he smiled. "It's just Reign now. The other two went inside. We can definitely get past her. We should walk, so we don't leave a scent trail."

"I forgot we can walk on the ocean floor." When they were past Reign, Amethyst saw something. "Ah!" She used one of her arms to grab her breasts and the other to grab Xenon's arm. *Amethyst is always grabbing her breasts. LMAO.*

"It's not a sea cucumber. It's a piece of kelp, see?"

"Oh. Woo. Shit. My bad."

"It's all good."

"Did you hear Chance say that like that?"

"Yeah. It doesn't sound as cool when I say it though."

"That's because you stay using that fake ass accent."

He was shooketh to the core. "You knew this whole time?"

"Uh, yeah... I can always hear tiny traces of your Greco-East African accent with hints of a Japanese flavor. I keep tryna tell you, you ain't slick. The person who told you that was 100% believable must be deaf huh, Xe? Alright, I'm going in."

"Wait! Let me go in front," he picked up his pace. "There he is. What is he doing?"

"It's still daylight. He's probably questioning the f*** out of his sexuality right now," she laughed.

"Oh yeah. So how do we want to do this? How do you want me to kill him? I can be sneaky, or do you want me to fight him? It's whatever you want."

"Huuum. Can you let him get close to me, and then sneak up on him from behind?"

"Yeah. I'll go up top. Nereids can't sense things right above them just like sharks can't. Hold my purse."

"Hello, pretty lady." The Nereid put on a polite act and was sure to move slowly. How creepy. Amethyst imagined this must have felt like a dream come true for him. A small female swam right into his lair. "I'm sorry I chased you last night. I just really, really wanted you to stay. Now that your friend's gone, we can have a good time."

"I forgot you could speak." Amethyst tricked him with a fake smile. He was surprised when she said, "F*** you."

The Nereid snarled, and his eyes rolled back. Then Xenon swam up from behind him and put him in a chokehold. The Nereid was obviously terrified as he tried to fight back. Xenon wrapped his legs around his fluke and rapidly turned them both upside down. Amethyst watched the Nereid twitch until he stopped moving entirely. Xenon felt the Nereid's neck. "Shit!" His surface profanity caught her off guard. She was able to hold back her laughter though. "I think I fractured his thyroid cartilage. Dammit!"

"An isolated thyroid cartilage fracture is hella rare. You versus a human sure, but Nereids are supposed to be strong as f***. You're that strong?"

"This fracture is associated with multiple trauma. Oceanids always fight back. But yes, I am that strong. I told you I'm special."

"I don't like evil Nereids. There are so many like him on the surface."

"I bet there are," he said. Amethyst took a mental note on how Xenon was unphased by her saying 'evil Nereids' instead of just 'Nereids'. She figured the others probably didn't notice what she noticed because they don't have that Nereid sense of smell.

"That. Was. So. Freaking. Cool." Her comment made him blush. "What are we gonna do with you, Frankenstein?"

"Frankenstein?"

"The cadaver…"

"Isn't Frankenstein the doctor?"

"The doctor is the true monster." She knew what he was thinking. "You thought I was referring to you? Awww, don't weep."

"I-I'm sorry. Ugh, I'm just so sensitive right now."

"Shhh. It's okay. That's how I feel about my flammables." Xenon was so worried that he exposed himself that he didn't really hear that last part. Amethyst knew he was preoccupied with his thoughts.

"I'll come back and get him later when the guards are gone. I'm not going to let them know the creature is gone. No need to take away their jobs, and they don't need to know it was me."

"I'm surprised we haven't been catcalled."

"What is catcalling?"

"On the surface, Men call out things to womxn they see if they find them attractive. They make little noises and say things that make people uncomfortable. They love to say they had to because of how a womxn was dressed or because of certain aspects of her body."

"Why can't they have self-control and be polite and respectful? They don't know how to give compliments respectfully? How about they just mind their own business."

"Womxn are viewed as objects Men are entitled to on the surface, and toxic masculinity causes Men to feel like they have to be macho and display their so-called masculine dominance in certain ways. They be showin' out for other guys. Or they simply just think it's okay because they see that behavior everywhere. Often times, womxn have to say they have a Man if they aren't with one. Sometimes, the only way they might back off is if they think they are 'owned' already. It violates bro code or something. Oh, and sometimes Men will even walk up to your car and shit... We have to be careful. It's dangerous to simply walk down the street. That's why Chance walks with me everywhere."

"Men are trash."

"Everyone is impacted by heteropatriarchy in some way. Men who feel guilty, threatened, or uncomfortable are always offended by that phrase. Men who are woke know that the phrase doesn't apply to them as an individual and recognize all the BS that comes with heteropatriarchy. Chance is definitely the best guy there is on the surface. I love him. HAHAHA you should see what happens when someone mentions feminism. Oh, and there's also hella toxic femininity."

"Thinking about the surface makes me very upset. I wish I could cleanse Gaia of all this hatred."

"Me too. Shiiiiit... They're lucky I don't have that kind of power. I'd f*** this whole shit up. I'm hungry."

"Saaaaame. OMG. Iris and Reign always give me a look. They don't have the same appetite as me. Iris just doesn't really eat much, and Reign eats a lot in one sitting. Me... Well, I'm always hungry."

"Chance and Jeremy always joke about how I always have to have snacks. I don't know what it is about food..."

"What do you want to get?"

"Ummm... I don't know. Give me some ideas."

"You love salmon, right?"

"Yaaasssss. I forgot about that place."

"Ew. Not that place. They can't cook. I'll prepare it for you myself. Bahadur is so irritating. You always ask a neari gynaika what kind of salmon she wants. Always. What kind do you want, Princess?"

"What kinds are there?"

"Oh yeah," he laughed. "You haven't been down here very long. It feels like it though. We can go buy some Atlantic salmon, or you can get king, sockeye, coho, pink, or chum."

"My favorite is the one that's really red."

"That's sockeye. That's my favorite too. I like it raw."

"Damn, okay. I see you, boo," she laughed. She caught his little naughty comment. "Which way is the store?"

"The store? Nonsense. I'm going to catch some for you. We can pick up some mochi too. What kind do you like?"

"Green tea is the best flavor."

"I agree. I'll get us each our own box."

"I don't know if I can eat raw fish."

He laughed. "I can cook you know. I know this one current we can ride so we can get there faster."

"Where are we going? Teach me how to catch one!"

"Sure," he smiled. "You know that little strip of islands just before you get to the Bering Sea? The best ones are on the east side. Wait, no. I mean west. Is it east? Whatever. The side closer to Japan."

"Let's go!!! Do we need bait?"

"Nope. It's still fall."

"Oh yeah... It's mating season. Huh! That means they'll be really red!

"There's gonna be lots of dead ones on the sea floor though."

"Trench mission part 2?" she joked.

"Hahaha. Hell yeah."

"Tell me more about these currents."

"Amphitrite and Poseidon made them for convenience. They're magic. Most people avoid this current because there are stories about where it leads if you ride it all the way through. People started making up stories when they heard about the Man village that was slaughtering delphys."

"What?!?!? That's terrible!!! We have to stop them! Thetis is working on that, right?"

"That was a long time ago. They were taken care of as soon as they were exposed. People found out about them afterwards. Before, people would only use the current in the summer. Now that they're dead, people don't want to take the current at all."

"Oh wow… Whoever stopped them is my hero. I love delphys." *I'm not sure about this sentence, but I think it also has a deeper meaning behind it.*

"What if the hero isn't a big, strong, aggressive person?"

"Who said they had to be big, strong, and aggressive. My ideal hero is thoughtful, caring, and sweet."

"What about the huuuuuge muscles?" he acted out.

"Ewww. No thank you," she laughed. "I'm not into that."

"Me neither. It's so cringe."

"What you know about cringe?"

"We know some things about the surface. Speaking of that, you wanna watch a surface movie or something while we're in the current? We only have Disney and Pixar stuff."

"What movies or somethings do you have?"

"I only downloaded *Princess Protection Program*, *Twitches*, *Twitches Too*, *Cowbells*, *Hannah Montana: The Movie*, *The Suite Life of Zack & Cody*, and *The Suite Life on Deck*."

"LOL they all fit part of your aesthetic. Let's watch *Hannah Montana*. Next time show me some Oceanid movies and somethings."

"How do you want it?" he smiled. *Here we go with the innuendos...*

"Ummm, you that type."

"And what type is that?"

"I think you know," she laughed. "Anyways... I like it pan grilled."

"Then Ima pan grill the f*** out of it. Do you like mango salsa on top?"

"Yaaasssss."

"Then I'll finish it off with that."

Amethyst has her own psychology she can't help but apply to interactions with living things. She loved how Xenon ate his food. "You really like salmon."

"Of course I do. Why you say that?"

"You just eat it so passionately and with so much care. Some people are sloppy and beastly, but not you. And you always finish your food."

"Ummm," he smiled. "I eat everything like this."

"Oh really? That's good to know. From what I can tell you're a really good cook."

"I like cooking for you."

"This is only the first time."

"I know, but you always do a cute little dance before your food comes." *Ahhhhhh... Atoz is too much. Hahaha.*

"Thank you," she giggled. "OMG! I can lift my plate! Look Xe! L—"

He caught it before she dropped it. "Your abilities are starting to come in. Soon you'll be ready for training."

"Training?"

"Well, it will be more like experimenting. You definitely have other powers. We just have to figure out what they are. In the meantime, you can come to my room if you like."

"Sure." They just awkwardly sat next to each other for about 2 minutes until she said, "Wanna listen to some Hannah Montana?"

"Yes! I have a teen pop playlist! It has all the essentials." For the next hour, Alpha and Zeta had their own karaoke dance party. Alpha had the idea to record themselves. Of course, Zeta was with it.

They had no idea Theta and Jay were home and heard them having a party. "Do they have to be so loud?" he asked.

"They don't know we're home."

The rest of the squad swam in laughing about something that happened on the way back. "Oh shit!" Xenon ended the recording, and they changed as quickly as they could. Iris's room was right next to his, so they didn't have much time before the group came in.

"Where are my shorts?" she asked.

"Here. Have you seen my waist beads?"

"They're on your dresser."

"We should act sleep."

"No. That will look wrong. Just act casual." They both took out their phones.

"Hey you two," Iris said as they swam through the connecting threshold.

"I already have 2,828 followers!" Chance was so juiced. "How many do you have?"

"Whoa! I have like 3,000 something."

"Everyone keeps screenshotting the video I posted," said Xenon.

"Have you seen the comments?" Reign asked. "Iris! Look at the pic Angelica just posted. The caption says, 'There's two of her, but there's only one me.' Who does she think she is? Why does she have to be so mean?"

"What the hell?" Xenon couldn't stand Angelica. "She better shut her mouth. Sandy ass shell."

"Who is Angelica?" Chance asked. "Do we need to roast somebody?"

"Remember how we were telling you about the schools?" Iris reminded him. "She's the Alpha of Epsilon Zeta."

"Her?!?!? I knew there was a reason why I didn't like her ass." Amethyst turned her nose up. "Why she tryna throw shade?"

"Her mother is Aphrodite, and her father is Ares. She's their youngest child. She's also Hera's granddaughter."

"What? Is the broad mad because you're more intelligent than she could ever be?" Amethyst laughed.

"A few years ago, Aphrodite sent her here to learn some respect. She has to go to school here until she actually learns some respect," said Iris.

"Okay, but why doesn't she like you?"

"She likes Ariadne. She thought Ariadne liked me. I tried to tell her that wasn't the case. Ariadne was only hanging around me so often to get closer to Nephthys. We were all in the same ballet program. Now Ari and Neph are the Alpha and Omega of Epsilon Delta. There also going out. I guess you could say she's the jealous type."

"Iris. I still don't get why she's mad at you."

"I'll tell you why," said Reign. "She wants to be Iris because she feels like she gets more attention from Aphrodite since she's one of the judges for what goes in the art gallery. Iris has written like 20 symphonies or something, and 5 of them were favored by the council. She only submitted 5."

"Iris is always the most popular topic because of her intellect, talent, and beauty," Xenon smiled. "Angelica's just mad because she could never be Iris."

"I don't understand why we just can't be friends. I let her know I didn't mean to make her feel like that. I even sent her flowers."

"You sent her fLowERs! You're hella sweet. She's just a jerk. Hell, the only person getting flowers from me is me TF. Don't stress over her. Forget her. It's simple. You're amazing and she's not," Amethyst said. "Show me some of the Olympians' Iros accounts."

"Okay, Sister," she laughed. "Amphitrite's is @IHaveAnAmplitude."

"Yooo. Your auntie is bad AF," Chance said. "But your mother though... That's Auntie T."

"Ew! GTFO! You can't like my mother," Amethyst laughed. "Wait. They're twins! I didn't know that."

"Where did you think the twin gene came from?" Iris laughed.

"It could have come from Zeus. Yo... Poseidon hella funny. Why is his username @PickASei? He's sooooo petty. That definitely has something to do with Zeus."

"I know right. He always has the best captions too," Xenon added. "Iris, show them the video."

"One time, Poseidon and Amphitrite visited Hera when she and Zeus used to live together. Zeus yelled at them from his room to stop being so loud. Then Poseidon was all fooling around on his throne, so Zeus was pissed. Amphitrite recorded it all. This video is super old, but he posts it as a throwback every now and then. Okay, look."

"Ahhh. I'm weeeak." Chance was dying laughing. "Ugly sleepyhead azz, rusty dusty looking azzzzz n****. I'm hella mad. Damn. Why he gotta be a lightskin n****? LMFAO."

"Look how he marched out in his robe. Look at his pajama pants," Amethyst added. "He really struck out with that one." The squad loved her little puns.

"That's a sandy ass robe too," said Xenon.

"And look at those dirty slippers," said Reign.

"Wuuuuud are dooooose!!!" they all said at the same time. Amethyst and Chance were surprised they knew about that, but they were slowly starting to realize Oceanids weren't completely cut off from the surface world.

"OMG! Thetis liked it. I caaaaan't." Amethyst was loving this underwater world. "Zeus commented, 'I hate you all' hahaha."

"But can we talk about Poseidon's actual pictures though. What is he doing?" Iris clicked on one of his photos. "What is this? He took a selfie with a sea star. And look at this one... He's posing with a shell on his head. How does he get so many likes?"

"Because Poseidon is fine as f***. No one can deny that. Not even the cishets," said Xenon. He caught Chance taking a screenshot. "And now he's Red's new screensaver."

"What?!?!? No... I don't know what you're talking about. It's for my body inspo."

"Whatever," Reign shoved him. "Go to @nobody."

"Who is that? Hades? Ahhhh. It's him. I'm deeeead. What the HELL. Literally..."

"I know right. All his pictures are terrifying."

"We don't roast him though," Iris said. "He's so reserved." The squad closed their eyes and shared a sacred moment of silence. *The drama.* "Let's go to Zeus's page. That's roast material."

Amethyst said, "LOL it's highly flammable? What's his username?"

"It's @AlmightyGod."

"Ewwwww! What is this?" She did not approve. "What do he have on???"

"Ame, look at this one. It says, 'You don't like me because we don't have the same dragon energy.' I caaaaannot with this man… You and Iris don't look nothing like him."

"Mom dropped the little lizard sticker under his pic," Xenon laughed.

"Go to the next one," said Reign.

"What a swirly sand shit," Xenon said. "He is proof that the uglier you are on the inside, the uglier you are on the outside."

"Hera commented, 'Looking good, babe' with a crying laughing skull sticker.

"Y'all! He posted a new video like 8 minutes ago," Amethyst said. "Is he trying to dance??? Where's Apollo???"

"He just commented, 'We need to talk.'" Iris laughed. "What kind of song is this? It's like classical trap music."

"It's lowkey fire though." Amethyst got up and mocked him. They were only just getting started but then…

Thetis walked in on the squad hyping Amethyst, Chance, and Xenon up. "I saw that video. Terrible," she laughed. "Jeremy and I need to talk to you all. Remember the emergency meeting Poseidon called? Well, it was about the possibility of a law similar to an old law called the Twin Titan Act being established. Long before the prophecy of you two being born, this act allowed any set of twins of any Titan bloodline to be killed. There is no genetic test that can prove anyone has an active Titan gene. Zeus convinced some of the gods that they carried active Titan genes and therefore posed a threat to Olympus. It wasn't hard for him to do so because the Olympians fear the Titans for good reason. Because of that, Amphitrite and I had to stay apart for a while. Zeus had scouts in every realm. I'm sure he blackmailed or threatened them or their loved ones. These scouts were very stealthy, and they reported a pair of twins as soon as they saw one. They would kidnap them and try to bring them to the surface so that Zeus could strike them down. Twins are already rare, especially down here. When I became basilinna, I did the best I could to protect twins. I taught Oceanids how to spot scouts and eventually people started acting like a twin was their own if they knew a scout was nearby. You see, Oceanids are peaceful people. We didn't learn to fight until the first war, but we are very intelligent. Anyway, the contract had an expiration date and needed to be renewed. After lots of arguing, Hera was able to prevent the act from being renewed, but Zeus is working on a new law. We aren't sure exactly what it is, but we know what the purpose is. The process for a law to be formed is lengthy. We're just telling you ahead of time. There's one more thing. As planned, Zeus knows that I gave birth to twins now. Everyone a part of the Olympic bloodline must have their DNA and refraction registered in the database. Before an Olympian is intimate with someone they get a blood check to prevent incest. The problem is that we know Zeus is also planning to put a drop of Amethyst's DNA in the sacred pool of knowledge to find out what her weakness is."

"It's okay, Meter. I can do it. I didn't need it, but I've had time to get myself together. Zeus won't even find out what my weakness is because he'll be unknowingly asking the wrong question about the wrong twin."

"Do what?" Amethyst asked. "I almost forgot you could see the future."

"Iris suffers from vasovagal needle phobia."

"What does the Vasoline part mean?" asked Chance.

"It just means I'm very likely to faint."

"I don't mind needles," said Amethyst. "They only need to get the white blood cells from one of us. I can pose as Iris. We're identical. Sort of."

"True," said Iris. "But we can't let Zeus find out what your weakness is."

"Why is that a big deal? I'll say it right now. My weakness is losing the people that I love, and I'm afraid of slugs."

"By weakness, we mean something that will combat your abilities," Jeremy explained. "We don't know what those are yet, so we can't figure out what your weaknesses are."

"He's coming this time next week, right? Can it not be on the day of the Last New Moon Festival please?"

"I know how much you love the festival, but the only other day is tomorrow."

"That's fine."

"Sunshine, are you sure? There's no rush."

"I'm sure. Plus, I won't be able to sleep if I keep thinking about him coming here. What's the plan?"

"We have to make him think he's getting Amethyst's refraction."

"Okay. Let me warm up. I haven't done this in a while."

"What are you doing?" Chance asked.

"I have to alter my body, specifically my face, to look like Amethyst." Chance's jaw dropped.

"Everyone knows about Iris's ability, but Zeus knows about Iris's needle phobia. He doesn't know how strong-minded she is, so her acting will be more than enough to fool him."

"Huh!!!" Amethyst smiled. "You can shapeshift? Cool!" She added that to her mental list of evidence. Not that she needed anymore at this point.

Iris morphed into a clownfish. "Can you do something bigger? Seeing you so much smaller is freaking me out. I also hate *Finding Nemo*."

She morphed into a seal. "Is it genetic? I know Thetis can shapeshift. Can I shapeshift too?" she asked.

"All gods can shapeshift. Meter isn't exactly a god, but she's gifted with that ability. It may have skipped you, Sister. We'll find out in the future."

"Ooo! Ooo! Can you camouflage and stuff? Do some skin tricks." Iris loved entertaining her. "Whoa! You're a cephalopod for real for real!"

"Why do you need to shapeshift if you two are identical?" asked Reign.

"They look completely different to me," Chi and Zeta said at the same time.

"They are mirror twins," Thetis said. "In addition, they have minute features that aren't exactly identical. Even if their DNA is a little different, Zeus will have no idea because he's under the impression they are regular identical twins."

"Standing in front of you is like standing in front of a mirror," Iris said. "Or at least that's how it's supposed to be. Physically? Sure. Psychologically? No. Anyways, how's this?" She morphed into Amethyst.

"Wow, that's pretty good," said Chance.

"I can't change my eyes, and I'm not the best actress, but I can give myself a tan. Plus, Zeus hasn't met Amethyst so we're good. I just have to be smiley and sassy. I'll make sure I use lots of facial expressions."

"Just to be safe, I need you to— I hate saying this, but I need you to go to the surface. Zeus's range is limited underwater, but who knows what he has up his sleeve. I feel much better having to only protect one of you front and center. I told him he could only see one of you at a time, so he requested there be no guards. There will just be him, myself, Iris, and Poseidon. Sei is going to be the one drawing your blood, Iris. He's actually a physician. Also, I could never allow Zeus to lay one of his filthy hands on you."

Amethyst didn't like the plan, but she knew it was the best plan. "I'm sorry, Iris."

"Don't worry about me, Sister. I'm a big girl," she smiled to convince Amethyst she wasn't terrified to the best of her ability. "Besides, I've always wanted to roll my eyes at Zeus."

Chapter 11: Skeletons

DAY 3

"What is that?!?!?! Where did it come from?!?!?" said Xneon.

"Dude, chill. This is my snake," said Chance. "You didn't see her because you didn't come in my room last time. You've never seen one before?" *Chance let Xenon use his sleeping bag that one time in case you were wondering. He felt bad that he almost killed him with the heater. He almost pulled an Octavian.*

"Not like this one. Why is she red, and why is she so small? I'm used to seeing yellow ones or white and black ones."

"I've always wanted a yellow one, but I never found one."

"Hello. I'm sorry I was rude. Come here, cutie."

"Right... You can read minds. I ain't gon lie. I thought you was talking to me," he laughed.

"First of all, no. I said cutie. Second, I'm an empath. Why would you name her Hot Tamale? That's something you cook."

"It's also the name of my favorite candy." Chance showed him a pack. "You know... I feel like I've met you before."

"You have. That time at the beach."

"Well yeah, but I mean like before before. Same thing with the others."

"Like in a past life? It's possible."

"Chaaaance!" Amethyst shouted from the shower. "Make sure you take your shot. Make sure you packed what you want to bring. Oh, and pack more insulin. Can you bring me my towel?" Xenon thought the word towel sounded funny, so he kept saying it to himself. *The more you think about it the more you agree with him.*

"Yeah. Hurry up! Quit looking at yo self. I'm starving, and Blue looks like he finna eat my snake." After all her singing and dancing, Amethyst finally finished her skin care routine that really wasn't a routine at all. "Would you put a shirt on?"

"Why you trippin'? I literally do this all the time. You walk around in your underwear all the time, and I have pants on. Also, you can't tell me what to do."

"Yeah but he's here."

"What's the difference between a bra, a swim top, and the shells I've been wearing? Do tell."

"Uhhhhhhh! Would you just come on!"

"You sound like Bailey with that 'uhhhhhhh'," she laughed.

"Who's Bailey?" asked Xenon.

"Really, Ame? Why did you have to bring him up?"

"Never mind. I get it, dude."

"Don't say dude!!! Don't f****** say that!!!"

"Can you stop yelling?" Xenon's eyes got a little watery.

"I'm not f****** yelling!!!!! N**** shut the f*** up!!!"

"STOP yelling at me." Now Xenon was upset.

Amethyst got in between Chance and Xenon. "Chance. Calm your ass down." He plopped himself down in his chair. "Breathe in. And out. Breathe in. And out. Now start counting by 1s until you get to 8 and then increase by the exponent of 8. Here." Amethyst handed him his Hello Kitty plush toy and rubbed some lavender balm under his nose. Once he cooled off she said, "Now what do you say?"

"Sorry," he mumbled under his breath. Amethyst gave him a look. "I said sorry!!! I mean… I apologize for yelling at you."

"I accept your apology."

"Now hug." Chance was not looking forward to hugging Xenon who opened his arms as soon as he got within reach. "Thank you. Chance don't forget your blood checker thingy. What do we want to eat?"

"You can pick, Blue."

"I've never had surface pizza."

Meter and Uncle Sei are going to be there, but I don't want to see this man. What if he tries to hurt me? What if he tries to hurt Meter? What if he figures out the plan? What if whatever is inside me decides to surface again? What if I mess up? What if I faint? What if I fail? NO. I have to be strong. I can do this. I can do this. I can do this. It's only twice and then it's over. Each one should only take about 8 seconds. Time passes. I can stay focused. I'll just think about something to keep me distracted. Yes! I'll think about Amethyst. I can do this for her. I'll do anything for her. She makes us happy. I've always wanted another sibling, especially a sister. I love Blue, but we can both get so emotional. I'm not saying Amethyst isn't emotional. She is *VERY* emotional. It's just… Uh. She and I are opposites. No. Not opposites. We're the inverse of each other. Holy f****** shit. She said that. Chance and Blue are opposites. Whatever. I'm just saying she's on a whole other level than us. She's hiding something. Something about her lets me know she is so much more than she appears to be. No. She isn't hiding. She's an open book. She just purposely wrote her words in a language unknown. She's so complex. My mind is brilliant, yet she puzzles me. I haven't figured her out yet. I'm usually good at this kind of thing. She's figured me out though. I know she has. Well, I think she has. I do know one thing for sure

though. **I'm a control freak. I'm obsessed with order. She's so spontaneous and so easy-going. I know I can't control everything and she seems to always be in control. Wait no. I figured it out. She knows she can't control ANYTHING and accepts... What does she accept? Huuum. Chaos!!! She accepts chaos. No. It's more than just that. How can I think like her? Can I think like her? Am I even afraid of needles or do I panic because I'm in a situation I can't control? Or both? SHIT! Never mind! I want to do this! I want to get my blood drawn. I want to protect Amethyst. I will protect my sister.**

After Iris got out of the mirror, she said, "I'm ready. Are they here yet?"

"They're approaching the bas." Thetis held her daughter in her arms. "You are so strong. If you feel yourself getting worried remember that this too, shall pass. They're here. Who do you want to do first?"

"Amethyst. That way I can gain some of her toughness. Even if it is just an act."

Thetis put her do-not-mess-with-me-or-my-kids face on and swam to the entrance. "Hello, Poseidon," she hugged him. "Zeus," she gave him a stone-cold look. "My youngest first."

Iris swam into the room how she imagined Amethyst would. Fierce, classy, and badass. "Oh! There she is. My beautiful babygirl," said Zeus.

"I'm not your babygirl. My name is Amethyst." She turned to Poseidon. "Hi," she giggled. "I'm Amethyst."

He smiled. "And I am Poseidon."

"Whoa. That's so cool! Do you have powers? Like, can you do stuff with water?"

"Yes," he laughed. "I can do a lot of things with water."

"I am the almighty Zeus and I can—"

"I didn't ask you. You came to get my blood and a picture, right? Right. Let's get this over with, so I don't have to look at you."

Zeus couldn't believe it. "That smart mouth of yours will get you in trouble in my realm little girl."

Iris kept a straight face when Poseidon drew her blood and smiled as hard as she could during the picture. "I'll go get Iris. Biiig siiister!!!"

"Greetings, Theios."

"Hello, Niecy."

Zeus was looking at her like he actually cared about her. "Look at here. You are beautiful. Hello, daughter." He reached out to touch her, so Thetis hissed at him and Poseidon clenched his jaw. "Relax. You people are so primitive. Would you like to come visit me, sweetheart?"

"No thank you."

"Oh. Well, at least you have manners and behave like a young lady should." Iris squirmed and flinched at the needle to make it more realistic. After the photo, Zeus said, "You should smile, little girl. How are you going to get a Man?"

Iris rolled her eyes. "I'm not looking for a Man. I also don't owe you a smile." She couldn't believe she actually said that out loud. "See you later, Theios. It was nice seeing you. I can't wait to come visit you again."

"You did great!" Thetis smiled. "I'm so proud of you. Let's go get mint chocolate sea squares. My treat."

"Okay!" Iris was so excited. "Did you see me? I rolled my eyes at him! And did you hear what I said??? I only feel this confident when I play my violin!" she laughed. "Theios is texting me."

Theios: You can't fool me, Niecy. Look at you conquering your fears. Is that how she really is?

Niecy: Yes. LOL. She would have said it with way more attitude though. She's so much like Theia.

Theios: Oh, no. That's a lot of personality in that household. Blue's already a hand full. LMAO. We should video call. You think that that's too much?

Nicey: I think so. Everything is moving so fast for her already.

Theios: You're right. I guess I'll just have to wait to see you two at the coronation. *sad face* *kissy face*

Nicey: TTYL. *kissy face*

"Why is everyone looking at us like that?" asked Xenon. "Oceanids have sticky eyes, but these people aren't looking at us in a friendly way. They are all feeling disgusted. If that's how they feel, they shouldn't look at us."

"Ex-f******-zactly," Chance agreed.

"They're just ignorant. They've fallen victim to the preconceived ideas that have been drilled into their heads by our society," said Amethyst.

"What kind of ideas were forced into their heads?" Xenon asked.

"The short answer is that… It's all bullshit. There are supposedly only two genders. Males are supposed to be dominant, superior, strong, aggressive, etc. and females and supposed to be submissive, inferior, weak, dainty… Females are objects defined by their physicality from physical appearance to reproductive organs. The two genders are the so-called definitions of male and female. They literally say the male gender and the female gender. Male and female aren't even genders! Up here, gender is defined by what genitalia you have or don't have. Anyways, patriarchy is damaging to everyone, but it favors some people. Also, the only normal sexuality is heterosexuality. All other identities are considered deviant and sinful. The many people who don't fit into this binary are either forced to conform and stay hidden, assuming they weren't successfully brainwashed completely, or they end up dead, in prison, or like us. We also have this social construct called race that only functions to divide and conquer. It can't be undone now. It's great to be proud of your nationality, ethnicity, and culture, but one specific group of people spread hatred based off their ideals across the world. We can't say who because we'll be punished if we get caught. Their acronym is WARMMACH, so we call them warmachines. It's obvious who though. They entitled themselves as superior and everyone else as inferior. These so-called inferior people are often slaughtered or thrown into prison. Especially people who look like us. People love to try and shut us up with shit like 'Slavery is over!', 'It's not like that anymore!', 'We have the same struggle!', and '#AllLivesMatter'. Guess what? I did a survey for a class assignment and the majority of my classmates voted #AllLivesMatter instead of #BlackLivesMatter. The majority of people in my class are people of color, and only a pinch of them are Black. These the same non-Black kids who love to use n****. Oh, and don't get me started on oppression Olympics. It's like I can't even open my mouth about my experiences without offending someone. I don't understand why people want to argue over who is 'the most oppressed'. Instead, we should be supporting each other with equity in mind instead of erasing people's realities. There's also hella racism within people of color. Then there's hella shit about religion too. There's so much. Intersectionality is important. Basically, we're all f***** up."

"Whoa. Okay. I knew about the basics, but just when I thought I knew how horrible it was… What can be done?!?!? By the way, I wrote a paper on that hashtag. I've always wanted the #BlackLivesMatter bracelet, but I can't go far enough on the surface."

"I'll get you one the next time I see one," Chance said.

"It's not a big deal, but you have to know this. We have people called police officers that go around and make sure the law is being followed. They are supposed to keep us safe, but they only keep certain people safe. Remember the group of people I told you about?"

"Yeah. We try to learn as much as we can about the surface."

"I've been detained hella times for fighting. The only reason why I'm not in prison or dead is because I look white until I take my hat off. That's why they accept the fact that I'm mentally ill. Black people can tell I'm Black though. Black people come in all shades. My father's a rich, white, marine so there's also that."

"Believe it or not, not every single police officer is evil. It's just that so many of them are corrupt that luck isn't even enough to run into a decent one. We have to assume they are all evil if we want to survive. It's not like the decent ones could protect us. We call evil officers kops. Anyways, there are also these Men called overseers. Police officers are just mini overseers, but these guys are the real deal. They do sweeps twice a month. You should see them ride through the city. It's f****** terrifying. If they don't approve you get taken. They can't take you just because of your race anymore, so they leave that to the kops. What they can do is take you because of your gender, gender expression, or sexuality. They'll be much more lenient if you're white or passing. Chance and I made a schedule. We tracked them. We learned that although they change the times, they keep the same pattern all year. Just to be safe, we monitor their every move just in case they switch up on us."

"Yeah. We don't hand out the agenda because you never know who's a snitch. We have this group chat with all the allies and people like us we can find. We send color-coded reminders."

"I'm impressed. How can you tell the difference between a kop and an overseer?"

"They're basically the same thing, BUT police officers wear copper buttons down the middle of their shirts. We call them kops because of that and because of this group called the KKK," said Chance. "I don't even want to talk about they asses right now."

"Trust me. You'll know. Also, all overseers are tall, white, male, and around 35. Sometimes police officers are people of color, and they aren't all male. Anyways, when overseers are on duty they wear all white and ride white horses. When they aren't on duty, they aren't in uniform and are just casually walking around."

"Can they take you while off duty?"

"No, but they'll grab you and stick a tiny tracker on your neck. It's practically invisible. They can make those, but they can't make skin tone inclusive band-aids and stuff. I swear... Anyways, it falls off in 8 days, but we know how to remove them," said Chance. "If you have a stinger during a sweep, you're fosho getting snatched. We call the trackers stingers because they sting at first. Oh yeah, and there are everyday people who get paid if someone they put a tracker on gets caught. We call them wasps. We call allies ants. People who could potentially be allies are called wannabees or just bees. If you ain't an ant or a bee, you're a wasp. Ame is hella good at spotting overseers and wasps. We also call overseers wasps by the way. Oh, and we call prison The Nest."

"What exactly are they tracking?"

"The trackers are audio recorders that have a built-in GPS. If it picks up one of the keywords, key locations, or you being too close to someone with a tracker, you get electrocuted. You get three strikes. The third time, the tracker injects poison into your system. It's like baseball," Amethyst said. "It's not just the things you say. It's also the things people around you say. The code to tell someone you've been bitten is to draw a shaded in circle or put a sticker on the side of one of your fingers. If you can't use fingers, you close your eyes for 3 seconds. We can't always point to our necks because if it picks up too much movement too close, you'll get electrocuted. The code word for a queer person is a Q-tip. When we want to be really specific and differentiate when we are talking about sexual orientation versus gender, we use teacup for gender. We use QT as the intersectional term. Q is for queer, and T is for the trans umbrella. Queer can be an umbrella term for sexuality and gender though. I made it up. Outside of that context, me and Chance use it for people that trigger our radars. We know you can't judge like that. It's not a serious thing."

"And there's censors on objects too… We're used to it, but this is some serious shit yo."

"How do you know what not to say or do?"

"You never really know, but we made a list. Every time we learn of another one we add it on there," said Chance.

"Basically, don't say or do anything that could suggest you don't fit the binary. There are two types of trackers. A so-called masculine one and a so-called feminine one. They give you the one they think you should have. Some people get lucky because they are either passing, judged inaccurately, or for another reason. Also, in the 10th grade everyone has to get an ID. They give you all these tests, so they can label you. You get hooked up to a polygraph during the test. Sometimes they're accurate, sometimes they kind of are, sometimes they aren't. Hell, someone who isn't queer could get labeled as deviant because they're just nervous. Most people who know they aren't considered deviant aren't nervous about the test, but you get the point. Some places like stores, restaurants, school clubs, and bathrooms ask to see your ID. If something is marked as deviant, they won't let you in. Since they can't discriminate against race openly, they will purposely ask people of color and let the majority of white people slide. One time, we went to this place we didn't know required you to swipe your ID to get into their bathrooms. Remember, Chance? We couldn't even pee. We made a map, but that place was new. We had no idea. This one guy from school saw us get denied and threatened to tell everyone unless I had sex with him. I would have just beat his ass, but he was fine as f***. I told him to get tested and bring me the results. You know I smashed. He was talking about he was in love with me and s***. HAHA. I was like sorry honey I don't date. After that, he bought me ice cream every Friday. Anyways, the three strikes before you get poisoned can be little things."

"For example, if I was bitten I would have been dead before I walked out the house. 1.) I'm wearing a soft pink pullover hoodie that says 'hey boys'. 2.) I'm wearing matching pink Converse. 3.) I'm carrying my Hello Kitty backpack. It's bullshit. Well... I will admit the backpack is pretty girly, but pink is just a color. Why does it matter if I like Hello Kitty?!?!? It doesn't even mean anything. It just means I like Hello Kitty... Like, come on... She's cute as f***."

"What about you?"

"LOL. I'd be dead too. I'm not supposed to be wearing these pants, and this is Chance's shirt. I also didn't feel like putting on makeup today. You have to apply at least two types of makeup before you walk out the house. It's so stupid. I don't get how this equates to gender or why it matters. Yes, there are sensors on the house too. They're basic sensors though. They can't do much."

"Speaking of that. How we feeling today, Ame?" Chance laughed.

"To be honest with you, I don't even know. I'm feeling bluish grey. How about you?" she joked.

"Do not start with that," he laughed.

"I'm lost," said Xenon.

"I'm like you," said Amethyst.

"In what way?"

"Both ways."

"Ooooh. This is great! I have so many memes to show you. I show the others, but they don't really get them."

"OMG! I have some too!!!" *I didn't know what they were talking about either.*

"What happens if you aren't there for a sweep?"

"I don't know, but all we have to do is lay low right now. We're missing so…"

"Oh, okay. Right… It doesn't apply to you two anymore." Chance didn't notice Xenon got his medicine out of his backpack. "Red, why are they telling you to put all of these chemicals in your body?"

"How the hell did you get that? You used to be a thief or something? F****** Robin Hood ass." *Chance bruuuh. This makes so much sense now.* Xenon just shrugged. "It's the best we can do up here on the surface. Or at least that's what they tell us." Then he snatched his medicine from Xenon.

"Swiper no swiping," said Amethyst.

"Ahhhhhh! I'm weeeak.," said Xenon. Alpha and Zeta were ROTFL.

"Shut the f*** up Dora and Boots."

"Oh snap!" Amethyst noticed something. "Wasps!" she whispered. "Xe, put your hood on."

"My hood?"

"The thing on the back of the hoodie Chance gave you. Try to hide your face."

"Ooooh. Duh. That's why you call them hoodies. Okay."

"By the way, I didn't give you that hoodie. I let you borrow it."

"Shhhh!" Once they left, she gave the signal. Then they went to pick up their pizzas. Of course, they got three larges. "Woo," she and Chance laughed.

"How was that funny?!?!? Something could have happened," he bawled.

"Oh my god. Suck it up," said Chance.

Amethyst punched Chance. "But we're okay though, Xe. See."

"I know. It just pisses me off. People shouldn't be treated like this. Everyone is so unhappy up here." Chance felt his own eyes getting watery. "I would annihilate every single last one of them for you."

"Here sit down on the curb. You'd do that? Xe, don't say that."

"I will slaughter every single evil being on this planet if I have to."

When she hugged him, she felt his heart beating like a drum even though he's 5ft 7, and his heart was far from her ear. "Your heart… Awww, Xe. Shhhh. It's okay. We're okay. I'm okay."

"Yeah, bro. You don't have to worry about us." Xenon was surprised Chance was rubbing his back. He was actually trying to comfort him.

When they were almost back at the house, he asked, "Where are the boards with wheels that you two ride?" Amethyst was secretly smiling about something.

"How do you know I have a skateboard, creep?!?!?" said Chance.

"Ummm, I saw it in your room?"

"It's not in my room."

"You two look like skaters."

"We can teach you after we eat!" Amethyst offered. He gladly accepted.

"What are the flavors we got again?" asked Xenon.

"This is the three-meat special with sausage, pepperoni, and ham. Yuck."

330

"This is a grown man pizza. That's why she don't like it." Amethyst just rolled her eyes. *She can't roll her eyes well lol... You should see her. It looks scary.*

"This is plain pepperoni," said Amethyst. "I could pick it all off, but it's just not the same as cheese. The meat juice still be on there and shit. And this... This is pineapple pizza with extra pineapples!"

"Blue, that one is disgusting. It's literally just hella pineapples. Pineapples don't belong on pizza. Exotic ass pizza."

Xenon tried the first two and liked them A LOT. Then he tried Amethyst's favorite. "Red. How come you don't like this one? It's delicious." She wanted to test one of her theories, so she threw a piece of pineapple at Xenon while he wasn't paying attention. He caught it between his fingers effortlessly. "You like testing me, don't you?" he laughed.

"Okay, one more thing." She fed him a slice of pizza while he was sitting on the floor. He looked up at her while he took a bite. Then he winked. "That was two tests in one. You passed."

"Have I told you that you have the best zygomatic bones I've ever seen?" said Xenon.

"No, you haven't. Thank you." She had another test regarding another theory, but he didn't need to know that. "Speaking of bones... Chance, you should show him your skeleton. He knows a lot about bones."

"Where did you get this from, Red?"

"I bought it."

"You bought a human skeleton?"

"Dude, it's fake."

"It's not. I can also tell you're lying. How did they get a basilar skull fracture?"

Chance shrugged. "I don't f****** know. I don't even know what the f*** that means."

"Look! It's a middle cranial fossa fracture. Look at the temporal bones and sphenoid bone. Wow! And look at the sternum and all these broken ribs. This person was young. My guess is about 17. Someone beat them to death. I don't think it was a human. How did you know them, Red?"

"Why would I know him, and how do you know he was 17?"

"Don't surface people keep the remainings of their loved ones? And I can guess their age because I can tell the xiphoid process is incomplete. Also, why would you keep a random skeleton? You don't know anything about bones. You also called them 'he'…"

"We'll save that story for another day. I don't know if you can handle it."

Xenon made his oh-really face. "Do you know about bones, Moon Jelly?"

"Not much." She felt like flirting. "I know there are 206 bones in the body, but I bet I could make you have one more."

He had to laugh. "They say I act like a bay b and I c why, but I'm good with my phalanges."

"Hahaha. That was sooooo bad. I cannnnn't. Your jokes suck. You're so silly, Senpai."

He smiled. "You like to read manga and watch anime, don't you? Do you know any Nihongo? I mean Japa—"

"I know what that is," she smiled. "I don't. I just know arigato, akanbe, manga terms, and how to pronounce my favorite things on the sushi menu. Maybe you could teach me after I'm at least somewhat fluid in Greek. Oh, and I heard you speaking Tigrigna, Habibi. Chance taught me a little Arabic, but I don't really know anything about Tigrigna, so you have to be even more patient with me with that one."

"Really?" he gleamed. "You want me to show you?"

"Yeah. I want you to teach me about your cultures and stuff too."

"I'd love to, Tsukizeri-chan."

"I see what you did there. Knowing your naughty ass, that could have so many different meanings. I know you made that up. I'll call you Tsukiko-chan," she laughed. "Do you want to ride mine or his?" She showed him their boards. "His is bigger, but mine can go faster and is easier to maneuver."

"I want to ride yours."

"Good choice," she winked. "You usually ride like this if you're right-handed and like this is your left-handed. This is called goofy foot."

"Are you leftie or a righty?"

"I'm riding goofy foot, aren't I?"

"Yeah but I noticed you use both hands for daily tasks. Can you ride the other way too?"

"I didn't know you paid that much attention to me. I can ride it however you want me to," she laughed. "It only feels comfortable this way. You try. I like lefties. You slow down by dragging your other foot."

"Yo, man. I just noticed those kicks. What the f*** are those?" *Ohhhhh. He on this boy head.*

"What do you mean? What's wrong with my sandals?"

"There's nothing wrong with your sandals, Xe. Chance is just talking shit."

"Ame. Bro. My n****. Come on. You can't stand sandals or feet."

"I know," she giggled. "I like his though." Chance's jaw dropped. He was amazed. At this moment he knew. That was the signal. "Don't try to do any tricks. Just go slow. You're supposed to have Converse or Vans on."

Chance caught up to Xenon who was doing pretty well. "Hey, bro. If you do a trick, it'll impress Ame." So of course, Xenon attempted to do a trick.

"Oh, no!" Amethyst knew Chance gave him the idea. She ran to where they were to go check on Xenon. "Are you okay, Moon Beam?" Xenon was so embarrassed. He buried his face in his arms. "Chance! Stop laughing. Let me see."

"I'm fine," he turned his body away.

"Chaaance! Look at his knee. Go get him some Band-Aids and some water."

"It's okay, Moon Jelly. The ocean's right there." Chance tried to help him up. Xenon wasn't having it. He pushed him off and said, "Don't touch me. Leave me alone. You don't have to be so mean."

"Can all Oceanids do the water healing thing?" she asked.

"Just me. Well, all ocean goers heal much faster than other people, especially in the water. I'm special though. I heal abnormally. It's quite fascinating. I think it has something to do with the energy Selene gave me, but I'm not sure. See. It's already healed." *So, he was just being dramatic? Lol.*

Amethyst and Chance laid on the beach while Xenon took a dip. Chance decided to take a nap on his Hello Kitty towel, but it didn't last long. Amethyst loved how Xenon came out the water. "Daaaamn, ma. Can I get yo number? What's your name? Where you from? Who you with? Where you been? Where you going?" she laughed. *I wish Chance would have been up. His reaction would have been priceless.* "That's an example of catcalling except they don't say it in a playful tone. They say it in the same tone a predator would use to say anything to its prey. They have the worst intentions, and it's creepy and hella sexualized. That wasn't a good example. I'm not good at being a predatory dickhead."

"Zaaaaamn, zaddy you fine as hell!" he told Amethyst. Then he stood over Chance. She knew what he was doing and couldn't stop laughing. "Wake up!" Xenon kicked him gently. "Can I have my hoodie back?"

Chance opened his eyes and was caught completely off guard. "Oh, f***. Hell nah you can't get yo f****** hoodie back. Damn. Wait. Blue? Move n****." Chance got up super-duper fast and threw his hoodie at him. "Get the f*** out my face!"

After they got the call to head back, Atoz told Chance to wait for them while they jumped off the cliff.

At the end of the day, Thetis went to go visit Klymene. Xenon finally gathered up the courage to go through with what he planned.

Moon Beam: Hey. Are you busy?

Moon Jelly: No. What's up?

Moon Beam: Can I talk to you?

Moon Jelly: Sure.

Moon Beam: Meet me in my room.

Moon Jelly: Kkzzzzz.

"Knock, knock."

"Follow me!" He took her to the fanciest room she had ever seen. The room was huge and covered in the shiniest silver, gold, and platinum. "This is where the greatest treasures from all the realms are kept. This room is only filled every once in a while. Otherwise, it's always completely drained."

"Whoa look at the designs on—"

"You know if these were for sale, I could buy all of them myself."

"Oh."

He could tell she wasn't the least bit impressed. Why did she stop making eye contact with him? "Check out this room. These are all the things people have given Mom as offerings. Offerings are different than gifts. She turned it into a museum, so everyone could benefit from it. She only keeps her favorites which are usually rubies. What do you like? Rubies? Emeralds? Diamonds? I know where the best ones are sold. I'll buy you whatever you want."

She felt sick to her stomach. She was slowly fading away into a numb callous. "No thanks." She was starting to choke up. "I'm not feeling too well. I want to head back. Good talk."

Xenon didn't understand what he was doing wrong. "Wait." Amethyst stopped hopefully. "I bought this for you."

Her heart collapsed like a neutron star, but she couldn't find the energy to move. Then he tried to place the gold 'A' necklace on her. She shook her head and gently pushed his hands away.

I don't want this. You don't even know what the 'A' stands for, do you? I just wanted to hear your Xylophone. I thought you were going to play your Xylophone. Why won't you just play your Xylophone? I can't hear you.

Xenon couldn't breathe as the echoes from Amethyst's heart caused his heart to ache to the point where it was secreting the fluid of heartbreak. Was this how it felt to drown? He had no idea, but he imagined drowning felt far better.

Amethyst swam through her room that was somewhat furnished and to her crystal cavern. She grabbed the Ziploc bag she put her journal and pens in and swam up to her cave. It was so dark up above. The only source of light was Hephaestus's volcano erupting. Or so she thought. Suddenly, various freckles of blue appeared across the ocean. Some of them swam towards her and entered her cave. They were baby leatherback sea turtles. "Ammmethyst. Why are you sad?"

"It was just a little dark that's all."

"What can we do to help?" one of them asked.

"You're helping me already."

"I am?"

"We have glow in the dark algae on our backs, dummy."

"What's this?" The turtles were curious about her odd objects.

"This is my journal, and these are my pens. I write in it. That's why I needed light. I can see in the dark, but it's just not the same without my night light."

"Huuuh! She's a writer." The baby turtles made themselves comfortable on her lap.

"Do you all have names?"

"Not yet. We were on our way to get them, but we heard you crying, so we came to check on you. Selene is going to give us names. What are you writing about?"

"Why I'm sad."

"Why are you sad?"

"Someone I know is acting like someone they aren't."

"Who?"

"I bet I can guess! Turtles are supposed to be wise." Their cuteness forced her to smile. "Activate turtle wisdom!"

"I'm getting something. Is their name Oxygen?"

"Is it Radon? I think it's Radon."

"Nooooo. I know!!!"

"Shut up, dummy."

"I do know! It's Xenon. She plays the xylophone or something. Selene just told me." *No. That's not a mistake. :)*

"Who's Xenon? How do you spell that?"

"He must be a musician. I think it's Z-N-O-N." *Neither is that.*

"Yeah, that makes sense. Look. I think she's done writing. Let's go find him after we get our names and knock some of that sense into him."

"See you later, Amethyst. Make sure you write about us in your book!"

"Who said she's writing a book, dummy?"

"Oh, I thought she was. See ya!"

"Here, let me help you," Amethyst grinned.

She picked them up, and they all said, "Weeeee!"

"Thank you. I'll be sure to write about you all in my book," she giggled. She wondered what else turtles knew. It wasn't long before she burst into tears again. She made the mistake of looking up at the stars. Their stars. The droplets from her ocean of pain provided enough minerals for an artist to sculpt a passionate reflection of the neutron stars collapsing inside of her.

Xenon tried to swim back to his room, but his body forgot how to do that. He thought he had everything under control. He thought he was doing the right things, but he was wrong. "What's wrong, son?" Jeremy asked. Xenon knew he must have looked as dead as he felt because Jeremy rarely called him that. He couldn't find anything to say. How could words answer his question? "Iris! Something's wrong with, Blue. He doesn't look good."

Iris stopped what she was saying to the group and swam as quickly as she could to where they were. "Oh, my goddess. Blue. BLUE. Xenon! Look at me." The others were so worried about him. They had no idea what to do. They felt useless. "What is it? What happened? Where's Amethyst?" He wept in her arms so passionately, the others had to revert their eyes. Everyone started choking up. Iris assumed the worst and grabbed her sword.

Xenon shook his head. Before she could slide it into her holster he caught her wrist and lowered the blade to his neck. "Not only did I break my promise, I lost my friend. I've been waiting for her for years and..."

"Xenon, you have to tell us what happened," Iris said.

"I was trying to impress her. I was showing her all the treasures and stuff. I don't know. I had this, but she didn't want it. I made her angry at me. I don't know what I did wrong. Was it something I said? I made sure the necklace was gold. She was so quiet. I felt all her emotions. It was too much, and she was holding back. She hates me."

Iris pieced everything together. "You were trying to have the aesthetic you thought she liked, weren't you?"

"Ame isn't materialistic at all," Chance said. "Why would you think that?"

"Because that's how you described me. She told me she liked my aesthetic, but I don't know what that is. That's why I asked you."

"Dammit, Blue. I didn't know you wanted to know how Ame sees you. I was just talking shit. I know you're not the flashy type."

"Yeah. I was just joking. You're nothing like that. I'm sorry. This is all our fault," Reign hugged him. Chance joined in on the group hug.

"I thought you couldn't sense her emotions," said Iris.

"I can't. I don't know how that happened."

"Dude. She must have done it on purpose," said Chance.

"Did she tell you anything?" asked Reign.

"Ummm… Oh, yeah. She said, 'I don't want this. You don't even know what the 'A' stands for, do you? I just wanted to hear your Xylophone. I thought you were going to play your Xylophone. Why won't you just play your Xylophone? I can't hear you.' I remember every word."

"The 'A' stands for Amethyst," Reign twirled. "Duuuh."

"I don't understand. Of course I know her name."

"Huuummm…" Chance was trying to help. "She's hella poetic or whatever you call that so…"

"We call Blue poetic as a joke," Reign giggled.

"Huh! I know." Iris figured it out. "She's saying you don't know her. She phrased it as a question because she wants you to think about it yourself and come to your own conclusion."

"Oh shit!" Xenon realized something. "The 'A' also stands for aesthetic!"

"But what is the Xylophone?" asked Reign.

"Has she mentioned it before?" asked Chance.

"No, but she told me a riddle I think has something to do with this."

"Why does she have to be so difficult?" asked Reign. "She's just like Blue."

"Because it takes a lot to earn her trust," said Chance. "It's her way of protecting herself so she doesn't self-destruct. That's also just the way she is."

"Self-destruct?" Reign asked. "Sounds like a bit much."

"Look, Ame is on some cosmic shit. With her, it's all or nothing. She's dramatic like Blue. In a good way. She's used to letting people in and them turning out to be toxic. That's why she prevents herself from getting attached. She's sensitive. She puts walls up because she's afraid of what she'll become if she keeps getting hurt. I can't tell you the whole story, but just know Ame was born with a pure heart that was broken by this world. Amethyst is the most generous person I know. She's the type of person who gives and gives just for the f*** of it. It's just her nature. She holds herself back until she's sure. I don't even know what that means. I know the structure of her mind, but I don't understand the blueprint. No one does. Xenon, she isn't angry. Trust me. I've seen her upset, but I've never seen her angry. I'm all too familiar with anger. She doesn't hate you either. She simply rebuilt some of her walls. Everything that she says and does is poetic, but she always leaves hints. She won't tell you a riddle if she doesn't want you to figure it out. She used to make me and Jeremy play hide & seek with her. It took me years to figure out why she liked that game so much. She likes being found. It was never about hiding. She never hid in a place I wouldn't be able to find her. One time she got upset because I didn't find her even though she was right under my nose. What's the riddle?"

"We were talking about Danse Macabre. We agreed that it was fitting. She said, 'Xig, xig, xig...' She said it was a syzygy. She said she didn't hear anything and wanted to hear the rattling of bones."

"The poem," Iris said. "Zig, zig, zig is the tempo. She was probably making the 'z' sound more like an 'x', so you would know it was about you. Maybe it has something to do with your tempo. A syzygy is when three celestial bodies align. Usually the sun, the moon, and the earth."

"What???" Reign was so lost. "She's like a confusing version of Iris!"

"Oh! The rattling of bones is supposed to be represented by the xylophone. You couldn't hear it because I was only playing the violin! She's so clever, but I'm still not sure exactly this means. Hell, the poem is about dancing skeletons."

"There's this surface saying about having skeletons in your closet. That probably has something to do with it," said Chance. "It's obviously about something she feels like you're hiding. You can't hide things from her."

"Oh, my goddess! I'm so f****** dumb. She does know. I get it now. It all makes sense. That is her!!! I see now. Everything is clear. She was literally screaming. I'm the one who couldn't hear. My third eye was closed shut. Not anymore. That's why she had you show me the skeleton! She knows. How does she know? She wants me to play my Xylophone. It's simple. Huh! That's why she let me in. She let me in. She let me sense her emotions. She knows. Eeeeep! I knew I wasn't crazy! This isn't a fantasy after all! That is her! I'm not dreaming. I have to make this right, but what do I do now?"

"Ummm. You're starting to sound like her. I'm glad you figured it out, but what in the actual hell is going on between you two weirdos?" said Reign. "Is it really this serious? My investigator senses are tingling. Somehow, you two have known each other for longer than we're aware of."

"Right now, you have to give her space. Just be yourself. Ame has a built-in BS detector. She picks up on even the smallest details. She was probably detecting your BS the whole time. Like Reign said, I can tell there's a lot we don't know about how you two know each other."

"She was! She even knew my accent was fake. How do I get my friend back? Truth is, after all this time, I really, really want to be more than friends. I've felt that way for the longest. Honestly, I think I'm in love. No. I know I'm in love. I'm not shy about that anymore. Well, I am but you get the point. We have to be friends first though. I just messed up, so what do I have to do?"

"You have to take things slow. Like really slow. She'll tell that ass bye if you're too pushy," said Chance.

Reign disagreed, "You should just ask her out already. You two obviously like each other."

"No. You should just wait until she comes to you," said Iris.

"Make sure you aren't all romantic." Then Chance realized something. "Guys! Now we're just saying what we'd want."

"She likes lip gloss, right? Yeah. I'll apologize tomorrow. I'll surprise her with that, but not in a materialistic way."

"That's actually a good idea. The main thing is getting her attention," said Chance. "She probably plotting on wiping you from existance right now."

After Xenon was gone, the older siblings spilled the tea on Amethyst and Xenon. They knew a lot, but there was much more they had no way of knowing. When Thetis came home, they told her about all the state-of-the-art drama that happened.

Chapter 12: Don't Mess with Her Sister

DAY 4

"Good morning, Amethyst!"

"Why are y'all so enthusiastic?" She wondered where Xenon was at. She was relieved breakfast wouldn't be awkward. Amethyst picked up her plate on the way to the table and everyone just stared. "WHAT?" she rolled her eyes. She hated when people stared at her when she just woke up. "Oh! Eeeeep! Does this mean I can start training today?"

"How about tomorrow?" Thetis suggested.

Amethyst could tell something was going on, but she didn't think too much of it. "Kkzzzzzzzz."

"Do you all want to come with me on my errands? I have to drop off a few things at the schools," Iris asked. They didn't hesitate to say yes.

After they were done eating, Chance said, "Oh yeah. I almost forgot. Blue said he wanted to talk to you. He's in his room."

Chance was never one to say he forgot anything, but Amethyst didn't feel like commenting on that. She was still a little tired, so she rolled her eyes and said, "Again…" Then she made her way to his room. She thought it was funny how he was waiting for her with an abnormally straight posture, but she had to hide that. "What?"

Xenon cleared his throat. It sounded so weird underwater. It was more like gargling. "Amethyst, I am so sorry. I was trying to be someone else because I was afraid to be myself. I didn't mean for this to happen. I'm just willing to do anything to impress you. I want to learn about what the 'A' means. Will you accept this?" He showed her the lip gloss he bought her. "I figured this could be the first one in your collection. It's not about the object. It's about the meaning behind them, right? Well, I find it fitting how you like glittery lip gloss because you're a star, and stars shine."

Atoz had no idea the others were being nosy. Thetis and Jeremy watched from a distance, and the other three were peering through the threshold that connected Iris's and Xenon's rooms. "Thank you. I'm sorry for being so dramatic. I know how I can get."

"We're both pretty dramatic," Xenon smiled.

Amethyst noticed a plate that still had food on it in his room. She knew he was giving her space, but she didn't want him to eat in his room. "I missed you at breakfast this morning. I guess I'm used to seeing you in the morning. You're coming with us, right?" There was no hug, but they were off to a good start.

"You seem happy," Chance smiled.

"Me? I'm always smiley," said Amethyst.

"Umm hmmm whatever."

"I'll tell you later."

"How did it go, Little Brother?" asked Iris.

"I'm still blocked from her emotions, but she's smiling. I think that's good. I think it's okay for me to be near her."

"That's good, Blue. We'll talk later." Iris turned to the group. "First stop, Epsilon Zeta."

"What school did you all go to?" Amethyst asked. She felt Xenon tense up because he wasn't sure if he should answer or not.

"Believe it or not, I went to Epsilon Zeta," Reign laughed.

"Really?" Chance said. "I can see that."

"What about you, sis?" asked Amethyst.

"I was homeschooled. I'm a functional antisocial," she laughed.

"What about you, Xenon?"

His face lit up. "In my first half-life, I went to Gamma Beta. In this half-life, I graduated from Zeta Beta."

"Cool." She left it at that even though she wanted to know more.

"So, you were an art kid? Ame loves art."

"She does? Y-You, do? What kinds?" Xenon gleamed.

"I love writing, music, movies, manga, or anything handmade. And paintings. OMG. I looooove paintings."

"What about sculptures?" He really hoped she was a fan of those.

"I think they're sooooo amazing. Like... Sooooo amazing. Someone has to be really gifted to be able to sculpt something. Especially a person. All I can do is make a chocolate bar. If I knew a sculptor, I'd obsess over their art."

"Are you an artist?" asked Xenon.

"LOL. I just know how to write emotional stuff. What do you do?"

"I haven't made anything in a while. It's been so long I don't know if I'm considered an artist anymore."

When they arrived at the school, the forcefield was still up. "Whoa. Why's that there?" asked Amethyst.

"We only put it up when it isn't active hours, so sharks and Nereids don't get in," Iris explained. "Also, in case of an emergency, we can use it for protection."

"Aren't we dropping something off, sis? Where the hell is Angelica?"

"I don't know. The forcefield should have been down a while ago. It's okay. We'll come here last. They won't be acting so professional since Meter isn't with us," she laughed.

Angelica was waiting for them with her mean girl posy. Amethyst looked at everyone in the squad. "Sis, what the f*** is this?"

"It's alright."

"Chance…" said Amethyst.

"I know right. Something ain't right."

"Would you hurry up? I don't have time," Angelica said. Amethyst was not feeling this AT all. She already wasn't in the best mood. Now they had an audience.

"Don't talk to me like that."

"What are you going to do, Ms. Perfect? Only my council can impeach me."

"Iris!" Amethyst didn't understand how she was so calm. "You are a f****** queen. Put this b**** in her place," she yelled.

"Thank you, Amethyst!" Xenon agreed with her.

"Shut up, princess. Oh. Wait. You haven't been coronated yet, have you?"

"Amethyst. I can handle myself." Angelica snatched the package from Iris. "How dare you?!?!?"

To everyone's surprise, Angelica slapped her. Now the whole squad was upset. "You ain't shit. I'm sorry. Did that hurt?" That was probably the worst decision Angelica had ever made in her entire life.

"OH, HELL NO!" Amethyst screamed.

Chance was doing his best to hold Amethyst back. Reign was about to help him, but he said, "Blue. Help me!!!" She didn't understand why he didn't want her help, but she helped him anyway.

"I'm not about to hold her back," Xenon said. "I'm with her. I say let her go."

"LET GO OF ME!" Amethyst was feeling something arise in her that she had learned to prevent. This time, she wasn't able to suppress it as much. "LET. ME. GO." They let her go, and she accidentally busted Reign's lip.

Angelica was ignorantly laughing away. "And what are you going to do? I am a daughter of Ares, the god of war. WAR. Who are you?" Amethyst swam up to Angelica and punched her. "Nice punch. Now how would you like it if I hit you back?"

Everyone was watching Angelica toss her around like a dead fish. Most of the squad was worried. "Okay, that's enough. I'm breaking this up," Xenon said. "I'm calling Mom."

"Nah. Why? She's doing that on purpose. Ame's weird. This is going to sound wrong, but she has a thing for pain. She's enjoying herself."

"Oh okay," Xenon said.

"WHAT?!?!?" Reign and Iris said.

"Look, she's smiling. You don't see her dimples? Oh shit! Now she's laughing. F***! Here we go. GO, SISTER!!! Beat her ass!!!"

"Chance. How are you not seeing what we're seeing?" asked Reign.

"SISTER!!!" Iris screamed as everyone watched Amethyst sink to the ocean floor. The people around them stared in horror. Then their expressions changed.

"Why are you all still here? It's over. I won. What did you expect from the sister of Iris."

Everyone except Angelica had noticed Amethyst swim from the depths like a sea monster from hell. Now she was literally right behind her, staring at her like an anemic vampire. "I'm glad she's okay, but why does she have to be so creepy?" said Reign. "She seems... Different. And since when could she swim that well? How does Angelica not know she's there? Ugh! I don't like horror movies, but I love fights! I have to watch."

Eventually, Angelica got the message. When she looked into her eyes, she saw something she didn't see before. The girl she was tossing around seemed to have become an entirely different person. Angelica wanted to weep, but she couldn't even do that. Now both of their true colors were showing. Amethyst wrapped her body around Angelica and turned her upside down.

"I've never seen that one before," Chance smiled. "What assassin did she learn that from?" Xenon was lowkey proud.

Suddenly, Amethyst grabbed onto her hair and dragged her down to the ocean floor. She threw Angelica against the rock wall by her ankles numerous times. She decided to continue to give the daughter of Ares a taste of what she was capable of. She slammed her on the ocean floor. Once Amethyst was on top of her, she gave her the non-stop combo she ordered with no f**** given and a side of sadism. When she decided she had given her enough, she said, "Get up! Get the hell up!"

"F***, Ame. She probably can't get up," Chance laughed.

Amethyst helped her to her feet. "We are not your enemy! The enemy is what is corrupting people throughout the realms. Especially, on the surface. Iris is not your enemy. What happened? You two were friends! And despite you bullying her, she has shown nothing but kindness to you. Do you know why that is? ANSWER ME!"

"N-No."

"Because Iris is good. She's such a good person. The world needs more people like her. ME though... Well, that's a long story. Stop promoting hatred. That's what the enemy wants you to do. Where is your fighting spirit, daughter of Ares? Iris was able to fight the thoughts she was having because of how you treated her. Don't underestimate her. I don't know her that well, but she acts the way she does to keep up her image on top of being so damn good. Iris is a QUEEN. How would it look if she fought back? You knew that. That's why you took advantage of her. Yes, we are twins, but I am NOT Iris. Yes, you're the daughter of the god of war, but I'm that nightmare you have while you're sleeping." She gently caressed her head. "I'm the rhythm you feel in your chest when you realize you weren't dreaming." She slowly placed her hand on her heart. "I am the darkness your mind, body, and soul dare not be consumed by." She ran her finger up the side of her arm. "If you cause her any more trouble… HELL. If you cause ANYONE any more trouble… I will become that sensation you feel when you're being burned alive from the inside. As entertaining as that sounds, I don't want to do that. Not to you. You're good at the core. Ask me what I want you to do."

"Wh-What do you want me to do?"

"I want you to spread love. I want you to encourage people to fight for what they love. To stand up for those who can't and stand with those who can. I want you to understand that the worst pain is not physical. It's not something you should wish on any good thing. It's alright. You didn't know what you were wishing for. You don't know what pain is. I want you to understand that spreading hatred only makes you feel worse. Cowards do that because they know it requires great strength to spread loving kindness when they're hurting. You're dead because of me. Start over now that you've learned some respect and remember what I said." She placed Angelica's arm on her shoulder. "Let's get you cleaned up." Amethyst turned to the people watching. "I better not catch any pictures or videos online!"

"Angelica," a deep voice boomed. After Amethyst swam her over to the huge man, she swam over to the squad.

"I think your Oceanid senses have officially kicked in," Xenon smiled. "Also, I think your powers are developing even further."

"You think so?" she laughed. "What about yours?" *Oh, damn. This little phrase has so much meaning.* As soon as she saw Iris, she stopped laughing. "Iris, you're okay right?"

"I'm okay, Sister. You know, it's funny… I'm supposed to be the one protecting you."

"I didn't protect you. I defended you." She looked at Xenon. He caught the meaning behind that and smiled. *So, we not gon talk about Reign's lip?* "Besides, I'm always in danger. I'm sure you'll get your chance. Speaking of chances… Choo Choo!!!"

Amethyst gave Chance a big hug just because. "Uh-uh. You're too strong for that now Small Fry," Reign joked.

She did her pouty toddler face. "My Choo Choo!" The crowd of Oceanids was still there, and they all thought that was cute. How? I don't know. She's their basilissa, and no one likes Angelica.

"Did you know you could take her?" asked Reign.

"No. I was planning on getting my ass beat, but I wasn't about to just let her treat Iris that way. She got me f***** up." Thetis and Jeremy came to pick up their badass kids from school. *Badass not bad ass.* "Am I in trouble?"

"No, no. Of course not," Jeremy said. "We know what happened."

"We want you to meet someone," said Thetis.

"I am Ares," he bowed. "My daughter has something she'd like to say to you Iris if that's okay."

"That's fine," Iris said.

Angelica looked at Amethyst for permission. Amethyst winked at her, and Angelica got a chill. Xenon tried not to laugh. *Y'all don't know this yet, but Xenon's lowkey mean.* "Iris. I-I… I am so sorry. I was so jealous. I got so caught up. I was so stupid. I don't know how I could treat you like I did. I thought my parents loved you more than they love me. Also, I knew you'd never like me back," she blushed. "Will you forgive me?"

"I accept your apology. I forgive you."

"Athena! Athena!"

"I heard you! What?"

"I think I found the group of kids."

"No shit, Ares. I've been trying to tell your dumbass. They're a squad."

"A squad?"

"You know… Like squad goals. Me, you, Aphrodite, Artemis, and Apollo are squad goals, but they are going to outdo us. Sparky is going to fry his own circuit when he finds out."

"Please tell me someone has the video," Thetis said. Jeremy shook his head laughing.

"You already know I got you, Auntie T."

"Good job my little fire coral," she ruffled his hair. "Why do you all look so surprised? We should review the video for educational purposes," she smiled.

"I was able to slow it down and zoom in," Xenon told them as he put his phone in HVM. *That stands for hologram video mode for those who don't know.*

"Whatchu girls doin'?" Amethyst walked in with an armful of snacks. "Oh snap! Y'all got footage. Fosho. I love being on camera, and I love watching my own videos." Xenon was the only one who picked up on that. They were both trying not to smile. Reign was sitting right next to Chance. "Ooo. That's perfect." She plopped herself on Reign's lap.

"Why do you like sitting on me, Tiny Mighty?"

"Because you're big and warm. And you smell like fresh Omega-3s." Her little comment went over everyone's head expect for you know whose and you know whose. *See why she scares me?*

"OMG, Sister. You continue to amaze me."

"Big? Ahhhh hahaha. She said you hefty," Chance was trying to start something.

"Shut up, Little Man."

"Ohhhh. She just got on you, Choo Choo."

"I taught her that body slam," said Jeremy.

"Watch what happens next," Xenon said.

"Dude. How many times have you seen this video?"

"Watch how Amethyst gets up."

"Why'd you pause it?" Reign asked. "Are you checking her out?" she teased.

"Huh? N-No. Well, yes. I mean no. Not like that. I was just admiring her hand structure. She has really pretty hands." Xenon kept his eyes low to prevent making eye contact with anyone.

"Thank you," she giggled. "You really like my hands, don't you?" Amethyst could feel the tension in the room. She could see they were all holding back their smiles. "Stop judging," she laughed.

"Now watch this," said Xenon.

"What kind of combo is that? That's not a regular combo," said Jeremy.

"Wait. Start it over." Chance counted her punches. "That's not a combo at all. There's no pattern. They're all random." Amethyst loved hearing them talk about her. She rubbed her feet together as she ate her snacks.

"Look how she throws her," said Iris. "Angelica is only a little smaller than Reign, yet not only did she pick her up. She threw her like it was nothing."

"Yeah, I don't know how I did that. Daddy's Little Angel is like 6 feet tall. I can barely lift Chance."

"Just try to lift someone," Jeremy said. "Try Iris."

Amethyst did her best, but Iris didn't get far off the ocean floor. "Woo. I'm tired."

"Iris how much can you lift?" Chance asked. She bench pressed Thetis effortlessly. His reaction was priceless. "Bloody hell!!!" He looked at Reign. "I bet yo ass can lift Thetis and Jeremy combined huh?"

"No," Iris said. "She's a lot stronger than that."

Chance was curious. "Who's the strongest one here?"

"Red, come on…" Xenon gawked at him. "Reign is by far the strongest. Not just out of us. We're talking all the realms. One time she pulled this injured whale all the way back to the bas. Not a calf. A full-grown ah-dult whale."

"Does that make you uncomfortable, Little Man?"

"Not at all. I love strong womxn. Especially ones with the physical advantage like yourself."

"Well isn't there a whole lot of love in the air?" Iris said. "Anyways, I think I figured it out. Amethyst can absorb energy. She doesn't really have any physical strength, but she doesn't need it because if she has enough energy she has enough power."

"That makes sense! The equation is simple," Chance and Iris had a moment, genius to genius. *What equation? Don't answer that. I don't care.* They continued to talk about a lot of numbers and concepts with Thetis. Meanwhile, Jeremy fell asleep and Reign zoned out. Nobody noticed that Amethyst and Xenon had somehow made their way to one another and were just being plain weird.

"Why are you playing in her hair?" Iris asked. She looked so disturbed.

"What the hell?" Chance laughed. "When did y'all move? Why are you playing with his feet?"

"Watch this." She put her fingers in between his toes. "Squeeze, Xe," she giggled. "See. That's amazing."

"Her hair smells really good and watch this." He sprung one of her curls. "They're so buoyant."

"But you can't stand when people's hair touches you," Iris said.

"I only like touching hers."

Iris and Chance looked at each other and said, "Ew."

"Thetis, you have a big ol' booty," Amethyst said. "Thiiiiick."

"You just now realizing that, Sister?" Iris laughed. "Meter is caking."

"That's all them sandcakes huh, Auntie T?"

"That's why Jeremy so sprung," Xenon laughed.

"Oh, hush your mouths," she laughed. "Cut that out."

Chapter 13: Sweet Then Sleepy

DAY 5

"I'm telling you. I don't know how to summon whatever energy I had yesterday. I don't even know where it came from. I know it had to come from somewhere. Energy can't be destroyed nor created." Reign punched her. Actually, it was more of a tap. "Ouch!!! Chill. This is my first day of training."

"Well, that didn't work," said Reign.

"Try making a storm," Iris suggested.

"I'm trying, but I don't know how."

Chance punched Xenon as hard as he could. "CHANCE! Why would you do that?" They heard a thunderclap. "Oh."

Iris took some notes. "I know what the problem is."

"Well…" Chance said. "Tell us, Genius."

"Like she said, the energy must come from somewhere. Amethyst absorbs energy in two ways. The normal way is eating. She can only extract energy from the outside when she's triggered by her emotions. She doesn't have enough energy inside of her to use because she isn't eating enough."

"What's wrong, darling? You don't like the food, or is something else going on?" Thetis looked at Jeremy to see if he knew anything.

"No, I like the food. It's just… It's nothing."

"Do you feel sick, Cupcake?"

"Maybe she only likes surface food," Reign suggested. *Sometimes I wonder how she's such a good investigator because she doesn't have the sharpest mind sometimes.*

"I'm not feeling too well. I want to head back."

"Aw. Come on, Sister. Just a little while longer."

Xenon recognized her tone from the other night. "We could all use a break. We've been out here for a while."

Chance was the first one to notice Amethyst had fainted. "Ame. Ame! Shit. She already doesn't eat enough, and she used a lot of energy yesterday. She's always been good at hiding when she's exhausted. She's drained. She'll be fine. She just needs some sleep. A lot of it." He tried waking her up. "Ame! Amethyst." That was usually enough. "AME! AME! Thumper!" Everyone was relieved when she woke up.

"You haven't called me that in a while," she smiled.

"Yeah, yeah. Don't scare me like that."

"I'm sleepy. I'm going to sleep."

"I'll swim her back," Xenon volunteered.

"When you get back, we can do some more coronation planning until she wakes up," said Iris.

"Ame is always very anxious when she wakes up. Someone should be there when she wakes up. But let her be for a little while because she's also hella cranky when she wakes up."

"How long do we have in hours?" Iris asked.

"She always sleeps for 11 hours after she faints."

"Stop f****** staring at me!" Chance told Xenon.

His freckles gave him a brilliant idea. "That's it! Hold up," Xenon told them. "I need to pick up some honey and cinnamon from land. I'll be really quick."

"The bridge is a portal? How did I miss that? And why the hell do you call it a bridge?"

"Because it's the passageway to the land queendom. Duh," Iris explained.

"Told you I'd be quick!"

"What are you going to do with that cinnamon?" asked Reign.

"It's not for me," he blushed. "Hurry up! We have to get back."

"We're two hours early," Thetis laughed.

"I hope that's not for Amethyst," Reign said. "Why would she want that?"

"She's gonna love it!" Iris smiled.

"Ame loves stuff like that. I don't know why."

Back at the bas, they were all entertaining each other as they waited for Amethyst to wake up. "Shhhh!" said Xenon. "Keep it down."

"Hey everybody. What's—"

Chance knew what Amethyst was going to ask. "Just come see."

"OMG. What is that smell? Is it? No... I didn't know you had that down here."

"She has a good nose," said Iris.

"It's nice to see that you're okay." Xenon was stalling because he just realized he had an audience. "I got these for you. I was looking at Chance's freckles, and they reminded me of the cinnamon I always smell in your hair. I got you the honey because you are what you eat, and you remind me of honey."

"Eeeeeep! Thank you so much! It smells so amazing. I've never had a honeycomb before. Let's split it."

"You want to share?"

"Yes. Don't worry. I'm keeping the cinnamon for myself. Here," she smiled. "Ummm. You're so thoughtful. I looooove honey."

"How come you aren't eating, gemmie?" Iris asked.

"I just ate a honeycomb."

"You know what I mean."

"Fine. Sometimes I feel so down that I just don't feel like eating anymore. Also, sometimes I'm uncomfortable eating around people. You and Thetis don't eat as much as I can and you're so fit. I'm so fat. I really need to lose weight, but I can't. I eat too much."

Jeremy was in full dad mode. "Come here, Cupcake. What can we do to help you not feel like that? Or at least how can we make you more comfortable?"

"I don't know. Time, I guess. You all are great."

"Ame, you aren't fat, and you don't need to lose weight. Your appetite is your appetite. That's what works for you. That's what your body needs. And even if you were considered 'fat' there's nothing wrong with having more weight on you as long as you're healthy. And by healthy, I mean living your best life. Not how the surface defines health."

"You say that all the time."

"Because it's true."

"Where are you going?" Iris asked.

"I'm going back to sleep." Amethyst swam up to her crystal cavern where it was warmer.

"I thought she only slept for 11 hours," said Reign.

"She's not going to sleep. She's going to cry," said Chance.

"Uhhhhh! Why do you guys have to ask her so many questions at once?" Xenon swam to his room to go cry too.

"Did he just storm out?" asked Chance. "He did that shit— I mean he did that stuff masculine AF."

"What? Surface people are interesting..." said Iris. "He does that a lot."

"Ame storms out too except sometimes she does it quietly."

"Why is she sad?" Reign really didn't like when anyone was sad. "I wish I could help."

"Because she doesn't like when that crazy side of her comes out. She's got a lot of things building up inside her. She's been trying to keep it tucked away. She got good at it, but it gets harder every day. Now you're asking her to open up. She doesn't want to hurt anyone."

"It isn't good to suppress her feelings like that," said Iris. "She needs to let it out."

"Wait. Wasn't she excited to watch the video?" asked Reign.

Chance shook his head. "Yes. You all have a lot to learn." He felt himself was beginning to weep.

"Aw, Freckles... We'll get through this together," she opened her arms.

"I'm not crying!!! Don't touch me! Leave me alone!"

"And he was talking about Blue..." said Iris. "So much personality. So many emotions."

"What do we do?" asked Reign.

"We wait."

"For..."

"I don't know. I haven't had much social experience."

Chapter 14: Food for Thought

DAY 6

"Did Ame come down?" asked Chance.

"Nope," Iris said with tired eyes.

"Were you waiting for them?"

"Yes."

"We only have to be strong for our siblings."

"You don't need to be strong for me."

"We don't have to be strong for each other." He put her arm around her. They rested their heads on each other's shoulders and talked about their feelings.

Xenon couldn't wait for Amethyst to wake up any longer. He couldn't just waltz into her room, so he waded in the doorway. Her room was still incomplete, and he didn't see her anywhere. He figured she was in one of the extensions of her room. He took the long way to her cave. "Good morning, Amethyst! Can I come in?" He looked around at the tropical flora as he waited for a response. "Amethyst. Are you awake? It's time to wake up. Wake up, Amethyst," he sang.

Finally, she emerged from the back of her cave. "BOO! Stop looking at me. What the f***? Who the hell you think you are coming to wake me up and shit??? I was sleeping!!! What the hell do you want?!?!? Damn…"

Now he saw what Chance meant by cranky. "I just want to know if I can come in."

"Yes, you can come in. Damn…"

"Where can I sit?"

"There. Wait." Amethyst noticed something on him. "OMG. Get the hell out! Hurry up." Xenon didn't know what happened, but he hurried the hell up. "Get them off!"

"What are you talking about?"

"The nudibranch! They're on your leg. Get them off!"

"Oh. I'm sorry. I didn't know. I had to make my way through some anemones to get here. How'd you see them? They're like an inch long. Look. I'm moving them. They said they're sorry."

"No. I'm sorry. You're harmless. I'm just scared," she told the nudibranch.

"Can I come back in?"

"No. Wash your leg. Like, wash it really good."

"Now?"

"Wash it some more. A lot more!"

"Now?"

"Yes. Wait." He went back in the water. "Some more. Okay. Now you can come in."

Amethyst scanned his body and her cave. "What are you doing?" Xenon asked.

"I'm checking for others."

"There are no others. I'll help you check again."

"Thanks."

"I'm worried about your health."

"Don't give me that shit. You have eating problems too."

"How did you know that? OMG. Can you tell? Do I look fat? Or do you think I'm too skinny? No… You can't. I know I'm too fat. Shit! How much do I weigh now?"

"I notice more than you think. You're not fat or skinny. We're both f*****."

"I'll tell you about me if you tell me about you."

"Really? Wow. Now that's an offer I can't pass up. Deal." *Signals. LOL.*

"My appetite is way too big. I am terrified of gaining weight, but I can't hold back. I can't stop. Idk… My weight… I make myself throw it all up or something. Anything to get rid of it. I have these sessions… I just… I'm already short compared to other Oceanids, and I'm not as big and buff as the other warriors. I don't know how to explain it."

"You want to get bigger, but you don't want to get fat."

"Yeah but I am fat. Your turn."

"Sometimes my depression causes me to lose my appetite. Aside from that… I'm overweight according to surface doctors. I just feel so uncomfortable. I feel fat, and I feel like other people think I'm fat. I feel like I can't express myself how I want to. I feel like I can't wear the clothes I want to wear because I need to lose weight. Other people have bodies that are accepted and put on a pedestal on the surface. My fit friends look at me like they're disgusted. Uh, whatever this probably doesn't make any sense."

"It does. I always feel like they're thinking I shouldn't be eating that much. Then they always comment on what you're eating and the fact that you got more."

"Right! And then they act like I'm holding them up because they're done with their salad and I'm not f****** finished."

"OMG duh! The others want to help, but they don't understand how this isn't a choice. I can't just not worry about it. Like… It's not something I'm choosing. I don't know how to help myself."

"I know… I don't know why people think this is something that can be helped by simple words in the first place. I get that they want to help, but this is an eating disorder not a f****** diet."

"I feel the most comfortable around Mom, Iris, and you."

"I feel the most comfortable around Dad, Chance, and you."

"Do you want to get lunch today? Just us." Then he blushed and said, "N-Not in a romantic way. In a let's-eat-hella-shit-and-rant-about-our-feelings way."

Her face lit up. "I'd love that, Rich Boy."

"Rich Boy? That's funny. I like it. Wait. It is a joke, right? That means you aren't mad anymore?"

"Yes, Moon Beam. It's a joke."

"I like that nickname too."

"Isn't it cute? I'm Moon Jelly and your Moon Beam."

"Because I'm cute huh?"

"Um, you're alright," she laughed. "Let's go get ready."

"What do you have a taste for?"

"Eh. I don't know. Take me somewhere cultural. Oh f***. I'm so hungry."

"Is Amethyst still asleep?" Thetis asked the group. "Where's Blinky?"

"Amethyst is still sleep," said Iris. "I don't know where Blue's at."

"He disappeared a while ago," said Chance.

Reign gasped. "You think that they're—"

"OMG. No, hun," said Iris. "You are obsessed with sex and romance. I don't get it."

"How do you know?" asked Reign.

"It's before 5PM," Iris and Chance said at the same time.

"How the hell do you know that?" Chance asked.

"Yesterday I texted her to see if she was ready, and she said, 'Sorry my hours are from 5 to 1' and sent lots of purple laughing devil stickers with some sexual ones."

"Oh. That sounds like a typical Amethyst."

"Hours for what?" Jeremy was being nosy as usual.

Iris rolled her eyes. "None of your business, Germie. Move. Your breath stinks." *LMAO. You know it's bad if Iris says that.*

Chapter 15: Eye Contact

DAY 7

"Ahhhh!" Chance screamed. He was up a lot earlier than he had anticipated, but he wasn't expecting to see HIM.

"Ahhhh!" Xenon screamed back. "Why are you screaming?" He remembered what Amethyst did when Chance's nose bled and tilted his head back.

"Why are you naked?!?"

"Why are you awake?!?"

"I'm hungry."

Xenon knew how to get rid of him. "You want some of my meat?"

"Hell nah. N**** GTFO."

"Why are you leaving?" Xenon laughed.

"Ahhhh! Don't chase me," he said. Xenon wasn't even chasing him.

"Let's do this!!!" said Amethyst.

"Well someone's hyped up," said Jeremy.

"You have no problem with thunder, but try to cause lighting," said Iris.

"Whoa! That was dope," said Chance. "Now it has a double meaning when I call you Thunder Thighs."

"Try making the most powerful storm you can," said Thetis.

"What kind of storm?" Chance asked.

"A cyclone."

"What kind of cyclone?" Reign asked. "Aren't there different ones?"

"No. They're all the same storm," Amethyst informed her. "It's called a hurricane, typhoon, or cyclone depending on the location. Where we are at it could be considered any one of those, but I like hurricane. It sounds the most dramatic. But that could be just because I'm from California. Ayyye. Shout out to Oakland."

"Good to know you know some things about science," Iris smiled. "Let's see the hurricane. Keep it going for as long as you can. Everyone's far below the surface, so feel free to let it rip." On her 13th try, Amethyst conjured up a massive hurricane. "Nice! Chance keep time. I'm going to the surface."

"Yo! It's been 15 whole minutes."

Xenon got a text from Iris. "She said the storm surge is already 4 feet and that that's really impressive."

Amethyst was beginning to like it more and more. After 11 more minutes, Iris swam down as fast as she could. "Okay, okay. That's enough. Tell her to stop."

When Amethyst opened her eyes, Thetis said, "Xenon, take a refraction." He was already on it.

"Ame, guess what! Your eyes can turn purple, bro. Like... Not just your pupils. Your whole eye!"

"That's the light I saw when I came and got you from Caris!" said Xenon.

"Heeeeeeeello... Iris?" Amethyst tried to get her attention.

"Oh, my goddess," she smiled. "The storm surge was at least 8 feet. How did you form a category 2 hurricane in 30 minutes? It takes days for one to form naturally. With special abilities, you never know what to expect, but this is your first time."

"I made a lot of thunderstorms first. I'm good at that."

"Still…"

"Why did my eyes turn purple?"

"I'm not sure," Thetis said. "Did you feel anything that felt abnormal other than the sensation of conjuring up the storm?"

"Yeah. Once I was really getting into it, I felt this change in my body. I felt less heavy. It was like someone gave me an energy boost."

"An energy boost?" Thetis was even more intrigued. "Say more."

"There was a lot of pressure and then suddenly something about me changed, and I was able to move freely."

"Everyone get ready for an important lesson," Thetis said. "The Protogenoi or primordial gods are Okeanos, Tethys, Thalassa, Gaia, Ouranos, etc. We call them paramounts sometimes. There's a lot of overlap, but then you have the Titanes and Titanides. Those are the children of Ouranos and Gaia that the Olympians overthrew. We call them all Titans. There are others who are of Titan blood that aren't Titans with a capital T. Those who are carrying the Titan gene can't produce children who can use their Titan power."

"And you're a titan, right? I read about that somewhere," Amethyst said. "Why are you telling us this?"

"Athena, Hera, and I are still developing our theories about this topic, but we think it's possible certain titans and gods can produce a child that can use their Titan power if that child is created with a certain titan or god. I'm leaving out all the talk about genetics out, so I apologize if this sounds under-explained."

"So, are they gods or titans?" asked Reign.

"They're titan-gods, and I think Amethyst can learn to use her Titan power."

"What is Titan power?" asked Xenon.

"I was just about to ask that," Amethyst said. "That sounds lit AF."

"Every Titan has their own unique abilities, but they are all the same if you strip away the details. All Titans can increase their energy levels exponentially, giving them more power. Some Titans are also able to increase in size. We call them shifters."

"So, that's different from shapeshifting?" asked Chance.

"Yes. Shifters cannot change their shape. Although shapeshifters can change size, they gain no power in doing so. Shapeshifters also can't make themselves much bigger than they already are compared to shifters."

"So, shapeshifting is like using the same amount of clay to make different shapes, and shifting is like making the same shape with more clay?" Amethyst asked.

"Exactly. Well put. Iris and I are going to do our best to develop some solid information, so we can figure out your abilities and ensure your safety."

"Yo! I can't wait to go Titan! I want to be able to shapeshift, but that's Iris's thing and besides, we can already shapeshift huh, Xenon?" she smiled. They loved how some of them didn't know what that meant.

"Oh, absolutely not. You will not be shifting anytime soon. All the Titans are already humongous, and you're so small. I don't know if I can handle losing any more children. Plus, there's still so much research to be done, Amethyst. If you can access your Titan power, you will be the first and the last because that would imply— Never mind."

"Imply what?" asked Iris.

"It would imply that the current prophecy I told you about is in fact connected to the ancient prophecy."

"Aw, come on!" said Amethyst. "I can't stand when this happens in books. I want to know about the other prophecy!"

"It's nothing to dwell on now. There are already so many things that need to be explained and things that need to be figured out. Let's focus on one thing at a time. That's enough for today. Let's head back," she smiled. "I'm sure you all have things to do."

"Iris, come on!" Xenon was ready to go. "I'm hungry!"

"Hold on." She was doing her best to suppress what was trying to control her, but it seemed to be getting stronger.

"There she is," said Chance.

"Look at my wife," Reign smiled. Chance was a little jealous. He didn't know why.

"OMG. What a queen," Xenon added.

"Yaaasssss, sister. You betta weeerk. Spin around. Let me see you."

"Just a quick change," she smiled.

"Oh, she one of them. Over here talking about a 'quick change'. You knew what you was doing," said Amethyst.

"Who is the 'them'?" Reign asked.

"You know… Them."

"Meanwhile, Ame looking hella bummy."

"Shut up, Chancellor."

They were so entertained by his full name. "Did you have to say my government name?" he laughed.

"I like Chancellor," Reign said. "It's a nice name."

"You think so? Thanks."

Xe, did you peep?

Yeah. He's starting to have a thing for Iris and Reign. He hella likes Reign though.

"Sunshine, one more thing before you leave." Thetis rubbed some of the special herb cream she made on Iris's forehead. "This should help with the headache." That was code for her little secret.

"Now I'm going to help Meter figure out Amethyst's abilities."

"What are you about to do, Reign?" Amethyst asked.

"I'm going to head back with Iris. A new season of my favorite show just dropped. Ahhh! I'm so excited!" she twirled.

"Oh, okay." Amethyst wanted to go do something fun, but she and Chance followed Reign and Iris.

Xenon noticed how disappointed she looked. "I-I'm going to the land queendom to run some errands. Do you want to come with me?"

"I thought I couldn't go to land?"

A chill ran down his spine when she flashed those starry, brown eyes at him. "You can't go to the land on the surface. The land queendom is in the land realm, not on the surface."

"In that case, let's go!" Xenon couldn't wait to see her reaction to the portal. "Whaaaaat? No way. This is dope. It's spring over here!"

"Technically, Naiads are Oceanids."

"LOL. They're the ones that can't swim."

"Basically," he laughed. "Watch out for that—" Amethyst tripped on a large tree root, but Xenon caught her. "You can't see, can you?"

"Nope. I don't think my senses fixed my aerial sight," she laughed. "My glasses are in Iris's room. HA. That's interesting. She can see the future, and I can't see what's in front of me." *Gasp.*

"Just hold onto my arm then."

"They're going to think we're dating," she giggled.

"Is that not a good thing?" He was obviously nervous. "Is that something that shouldn't happen? Like… Ever?"

"Whatever happens happens, Funny Girl," she giggled.

"Okay, Funny Boy," he smiled.

Amethyst loved how there were so many different shops and booths. "O. M. G. Is that blue corn cake???"

"Ohhh, that's what you call corn cake. We call it tanaashgiizh."

"Say it again slowly."

"Tanaashgiizh."

"Is that a Navajo word?"

"Yeah. How'd you know?"

"I knew the word. I just didn't want to butcher it. I figured you'd correct me," she smiled. "Hi, beautiful! I'd like to buy some tanaashgiizh, please. I'm sorry, I'm just starting to learn Greek."

"It's okay. I know English. I'm Citlali."

"I'm Amethyst. You have a pretty name. I love stars."

"Thank you! No need to pay. Her Highness already paid for it a couple days ago. She said you'd want it. Here you go!"

"I thought Iris couldn't see me?"

"She must have seen me and assumed you'd be with me. Do you want something to drink to go with that?"

"No thank you. I don't drink milk. Do they have orange juice?"

"Oranges aren't in season until next month, but they have other juices and milks made from nuts."

"Huh! Okay." Xenon was going to pay for it, but she said, "It's alright, Moon Beam. I got it. Do you want some?"

"N-No thank you."

"I'll have two cups of almond milk please."

"I said I didn't want any."

"I knew you just didn't want me to buy it."

"Thank you," he smiled. "I guess we're both stubborn."

"Bruuuh. I need a scrunchie. My hair's all over the place. Jeremy would say I look a hot mess."

"I think it works for you. Plus, everyone that walks by keeps admiring your hair. I think it fits your aesthetic."

"Don't try to use my word," she laughed. "You don't even know what my aesthetic is."

"I know about aesthetics too. I just never use the word like you do, and I have no idea what mine is. I'm in the process of figuring yours out. Why are you laughing, Little Scallop? You're always laughing at me."

"You're funny." *She uses the words funny and weird in various ways.*

"A scrunchie is that thing Iris pulled off of your hair, right?"

"Yeah. I forgot to bring the ones I have in my room at home. Actually, I don't even remember where I put them."

"Oh, you just reminded me! Your room is ready, and your furniture should be there when we get back. I noticed you like to touch all the plants we walk by. What kind of flowers do you—"

"Eeeeeep! Baby blue eyes!!! These are so pretty. What's the scientific name?"

"Nemophila menziesii. Are those your favorite?"

"LOL nope. I do love blue eyes though."

"Blue eyes? Like... Only blue eyes? You only find blue eyes attractive?" Xenon was already thinking about how he could get contacts.

"Why do you sound so anxious? You have blue eyes."

"What? My eyes are black. Wait. Is this another riddle? This time I'm asking. What do you mean?"

"I'm not talking about the color. The darker the eyes the better. Eyes are the reflection of the soul of whoever they belong to. They follow a soul from life to life. I know people just by their eyes. It's not entirely about the color. Your eyes are soft, safe, passionate, cool, comforting, and abyssal. Blue like the ocean. Your eyes are blue. You have ocean eyes." She looked up at him. "Are you crying?" she smiled.

"No," he turned his head. "It's just my allergies. Also... You're right under my nose." Amethyst continued to smile at him. "I could never fool you could I, Moon Jelly. Turtles are wise, but they say sea jellies are the wisest creatures."

"You are what you eat," she laughed.

"I know you know this, but you have an amazing mind. I admire the way you think."

"You know how I think?"

"I'm beginning to. Do you like when I weep?"

"Of course not, Moon Beam. I just like how emotional you are. I like how vulnerable you are. Remember how I said I like people who aren't afraid to express their emotions?"

"You don't think I'm weak?"

"The more emotional you are, the more strength and courage it takes to be vulnerable. Passion and vulnerability go hand in hand."

"You think I'm passionate?"

"Unfathomably."

"Princess! Princess!" A little boy ran up to her. "For you." He handed her a single stalk of lavender.

Xenon noticed how her face lit up like when he gave her the honey, cinnamon, and lip gloss. "They're delightful! Thank you," she hugged him. "What's your name?"

"People call me Twiddler, but I don't really like that. My real name's Twilight."

"Well, you tell them to call you by your name. Have a good day, Twilight." Amethyst reminded Xenon of twilight. Both twilights. Simultaneously, she is the one between day and night and the one between night and day.

Amethyst dropped the stalk of lavender, so Xenon picked it up and placed it in her hair. "There." When they made eye contact, the tension left Xenon's hand, and his fingers gently traced the back of her ear.

"I heard you," she smiled.

"I didn't say any— Oh. You did?!? What did you hear?"

"A seashell," she giggled.

"I know what that one means," he smiled.

"That means you're making progress."

Xenon stopped walking and stood in front of her. "Amethyst."

"What?" She knew he had been wanting to ask her something.

"December 11th which is Friday I think, is the day of the Last New Moon Festival this year. It's here in the land realm. I know it's soon but... There's going to be food, music, dancing, games, jewelry making, face painting, and lots of other things. It's really fun! Everyone's going. Would you like to come with me?"

"That sounds fun! I'd love to go with you. Is it a date?"

Xenon panicked. "Ummm. Uh. Do you want it to be? Uh... No?"

"Okay."

"Alright, Blue!" Chance called out. "You can come out of your room now. Ame went to her cave."

"What did you want to talk to us about?" Iris asked.

"You already know, don't you?" said Xenon with his signature sass.

"I saw you coming to us, but there's never any audio. I only know what is said if I can see faces. I can see the future not hear the future. You know this," she laughed.

"I asked her out."

"Out like girlfriend out or like date out," Reign asked.

"Like date out. I asked her to come with me to the Last New Moon Festival."

"Well, what did she say?" Chance waited.

"She said yes, but then she was like, 'Is it a date?'"

"And what did you say?" Iris asked.

"I got so nervous. I wasn't prepared. I was like, 'Do you want it to be?' Then I was like, 'No.'"

"Brooo! Come on!" They all laughed. "She was asking you that to make sure it was a date. All you had to do was say yes. Too late now. Not smooth. Not smooth at all."

"Now you two are stuck with us," Reign added.

"She was probably just being nice. She didn't even ask what tide!" said Xenon.

"Trust me, dude. Ame would have clearly and politely said no if she didn't want to go. If it helps, you're the only person she hasn't rejected."

"She didn't ask what tide because you're supposed to tell her, dummy," Reign said. "You're the one who asked her."

"Since you didn't tell her what time, she's expecting we'll let her know later," said Chance.

"Whatever you do, don't act like it's a date," said Iris. "Just be a little flirty."

"I agree with Iris. Ame is a huge flirt."

A guard swam in and told them someone's here to see Amethyst. "What's their name?" Iris asked.

"Zeta Beta Alpha: Alpha Alpha Alpha, Your Highness."

Iris told the guard to let him in and swam up to get her sister. "Hey, Sister. Alpha's here to see you. I don't know why."

"Can't you see the future?"

"I don't see everything," she smiled.

"Hey. What's up, Alpha?"

"How are you, Your Highness?" Xenon sensed why he was here.

"I'm doing good. How are you?"

"Great but I would be even better if you'd be my date for the Last New Moon Festival. Would you like to go with me?" The squad started picking on Xenon.

"Awww, Alpha... That's so sweet of you, but I'm already going with my friends. Sorry to make you swim all the way here."

"It's no trouble. I'll see you around?"

She gave him a hug and said, "See you around." She turned to the squad. "OMG!" she smiled. "How cute is he? He's such a gentleman."

"You think he's cute?!?!?" Xenon was so jealous. "Ughhhh! I can't stand him! Sandy ass lassa. I hope he steps on an urchin on his way back to where ever the f*** he came from. Have you seen his Iros page? All his refractions are wack. As a matter of fact, all his shit wack. Omega told me he has a micropenis with his clammy ass. What a f****** shwirly ass shipwreck."

"Chill. Why you salty, Blue?" Chance laughed. "I know you live in the ocean but damn. Let the man live. Why you gotta expose him like that? And what's up with you and those funny ass words?"

"That's because he went to Zeta Beta," Iris laughed.

"That's where all the so-called cool nerds go," said Reign.

"What does that 'l' word mean? Is it like n****?" asked Amethyst.

"Yeah," said Xenon. "It's a Southern Oceanid term."

"No one else can say it," said Iris. "It comes from a history of ongoing trauma unique to Southern Oceanids. Everyone respects that."

"Wow," Amethyst was shocked. "It's not like that on the surface. N**** also comes from a history of ongoing trauma unique to Black people. People who aren't Black love to say n****. When you ask them to not say it, they act like they entitled to say it because they aren't white. Hell, even white people say it. They love to say it because it 'sounds cool'. On the surface, people love Black culture, but not Black people. I'm proud to be Black, but it's not a choice to be Black, and it comes with a shit load of hatred. Ain't no type of respect. Even my classmates... My non-Black peers say n**** more than I do every single day, word after word. I asked them to not say it, but they don't give a f***. And they know where the word comes from!!! I heard hella macro- and microaggressions come out of they mouth all the time. I always wondered if they were really my peers. Then I remembered ignorance is a heavy weight to lift."

"OMG you get me! Sky nymphs love to say lassa! It's so easy to not say lassa. I don't know how people think it's okay for them to say it in the first place. It's not complicated. Then if someone not a part of their culture says a reclaimed hate word that belongs to their culture, they get all upset. There is no equivalent to the word lassa in any f****** culture in all the realms. The n-word is the only equivalent because the histories overlap. They're directly intertwined."

"Riiiiight!!! Say more about directly intertwined," said Amethyst.

"Let's save that for another day. I don't want to darken the water," he smiled.

"LOL. OMG. That's a whole ass mood," said Amethyst. "I lowkey feel like training."

Thetis and Jeremy swam into the room. "Then let's go."

"I'm your coach! Wait. How do you say it in English? There's a better term," Reign said. "Oh! Fitness trainer."

"We think we know why your eyes glow purple when you intensify your power," Thetis smiled.

Jeremy said, "I don't understand anything they've been talking about, but it sounds awesome."

"Argon!" Iris was so excited.

"That's my favorite element!!!" Now Xenon was excited.

"That's my second favorite," Amethyst smiled.

"What's your first?" Xenon asked.

"Xenon." He couldn't help but gleam. "I already told you that. You just wanted me to say it again. Keep going, Iris."

"This is bizarre makeshift science, but it's the best we could do, and it's the only science that can be done regarding Amethyst. We think Amethyst has lots of argon inside of her. There's so much more we have to figure out but listen up. She has to close her eyes when she's about to change energy levels because of the pressure. The energy causing all the pressure comes from cosmic rays. The cosmic ray spallation going on in Amethyst's body allows her body to adapt to where she can utilize the incoming energy. Somewhere along those lines, some silicon-32 is produced, and you get some argon-36. Amethyst is able to create intense, amplified electric currents inside her body whether she does so voluntary or not, just like how she can cause storms on the outside. If you put argon in an electric field, it emits purple, well technically violet, light. Depending on how many energy levels she has, her whole body could potentially emit violet light. Oh, and Amethyst is also aerodynamic if you haven't noticed already. She could possibly be Zeus aerodynamic like the sky nymphs. HOW? COOL. IS. THAT. What kind of zygote did I split from?!?!?"

"Hold up." Xenon realized something. "Argon-36?!?!? That isotope is made in stars. Argon-40 is the majority of the argon on earth. Cosmic ray spallation! Nucleosynthesis! Silicon-32! We're talking stars here! I mean… We're all made of star stuff, but this is a whole other thing."

"I'm so lost." Poor Reign had no idea what anyone was saying.

"Holy f****** shit," said Chance. "Are you saying Ame is a STAR?!?!?"

"She might as well be. Let's just say she's a highly energetic body for now though," Thetis smiled.

"So, I have other abilities besides causing storms? YES! It's lit! LOL. Literally."

"What on earth is about to happen? Whatever it is is going to be big and I mean big," Jeremy smiled. "Oh, my little girl is growing up."

"You've had one hell of a month so far," Chance said.

"Come on y'all," Amethyst smiled. "I have to train. I have a feeling that what happened with Daddy's Little Angel is nothing compared to what's coming."

"Speaking of that," Reign said. "Did you mean everything you said? Like… Literally?"

"Every word."

"It's official. You scare me. It's always the small ones. I know a savage when I see one. Hey, Blue. Hey, Freckles," she smiled.

"I'm not a savage!" Xenon started weeping. "I'm fine. Continue with training. I'll just be a moment."

"You're so cute," said Amethyst.

"Small Fry! Are you ready? Give me 30!"

"30 what?"

"Right… Um. Push-ups."

Amethyst was only able to do 5 in a row. "Awww. Come on, Ame," Chance laughed.

"Shut up, Little Man. How many can you do?"

"15." They all thought it was hilarious how he was proud of that.

"Now do 20 pull-ups."

"Where?" Reign held out her arm. "Oh."

"Okay now WTF." Chance liked what he saw. "Do me next!"

"Now throw these rocks as far as you can. Like this," she demonstrated. She tossed one as if it were a pebble.

After Amethyst completed the various tasks Reign gave her, she sunk to the ocean floor and watched the others do their workouts while she caught her breath. "I'm… Hun… Gry…"

"Hungry and… Tired… Mean the same thing… For Ame."

"Psar Psar's?" Amethyst suggested.

"Psar Psar's," they all agreed.

"Do you still want me to paint your box?" asked Xenon.

"Yaaasssss!" Amethyst was surprised at how he immediately went to go get his things. "You don't have to do it right now, Xe. I'm sure you're probably busy."

"I'm never too busy for you, Princess." He realized how that came out. "Uh… B-Because you're the basilissa and I'm the basi." Xenon tripped on his way up the stairs. He must have thought he was still swimming even though the bas was completely drained. When he returned, he asked, "Can I come in?"

"Yes, you can come in," she smiled.

"How would you like me to paint it?"

"Paint it however you like."

"What colors would you like?"

"What colors do you have?"

"I can make any color," he smiled. "Amethyst. Just tell me what you want."

"Okay. Eventually, my room is going to be decorated with lots of purple. I want the box to stand out, so can you do a deep lavender, a soft teal not turquoise, and a bold shimmering silver? Oh, and a little bit of white to add a little umph?" *Did someone say freaky mind connection?*

"You got it. Would you like glitter?"

"Eeeeeep! You have glitter?!?!? Can I see? Can I see? Can I see?"

"Sure, Little Scallop." He showed her his collection. "You really like glitter, don't you?" he laughed.

"OMG! Look at all these colors!!! Huuuuh! You have so many different grades. Sparkles, shimmers, glitters, glimmers... Ahhh! They're so sparkly! They make surface glitter look so dull. Duller than a dead Man's eyes. What is this made from?"

"Depending on the color... Fish scales, insects, ground up crystals, sand, and stuff. It's all good for the environment. We also make edible glitter."

"I frickin' love it! I love it! Use this one." She picked the medium grade multicolored glitter with the cool aesthetic.

"What's all that noise in there?" Iris yelled. The rest of the squad was working on planning the coronation.

"Sorry," he yelled back. "I just showed her my—"

"What is he saying? I can't hear," said Iris.

Chance could barely hear himself. "He said he showed her his— HEY! What you show her??? Don't make me come in there." Chance and Iris looked at each other. They were already judging.

"Why is your brother upset?"

"He's always jumping to conclusions."

"So is Iris. I said I'm showing you my glitter. Why did that trigger him?"

"I don't think he heard the glitter part. He probably thinks you're showing me your penis. You know how it is... If the surface was a food, it would have tons of sexual a-SALT. He just thinks your swinging it around like this," Amethyst demonstrated.

"Oh, I see... Why would he think that? I wouldn't show you my penis. Well... Unless you asked me to," he smiled.

"OMG. Shut up," she laughed. "If it ain't got glitter on it, then I'm cool."

"Don't play... I can make that happen," he smiled. Then he reached for some glitter. *So that's what that inside joke is about.*

"Shhh. You're too loud," she giggled. "Here he comes."

"You ain't finna make shit happen." Chance burst into her room. "What's going on in here?"

"I was just about to show her how much glitter I have." They could not stop being silly. That's just how they are.

Chance looked at all the art supplies. "Oh shit. My bad y'all." He still wasn't satisfied. "So ain't no little thing going on in here?"

"I hope not," Amethyst joked. Xenon held his tongue. "Nah. I'm just kidding. Chance, come on..." She felt like being petty. "Now go away so he can finish whipping out his—"

"His WHAT?!?"

"His glitter," she laughed. "Chill. You're such a dad. Always cock blocking. You never know. He might have a nice looking— Set of glitter..."

"Ohhh wow. HA. HA. You got me. I just wanted to make sure you were safe that's all."

"I know, Choo Choo but something tells me there was a little curiosity in there too. Round two maybe?"

"HEY!" he laughed. "Don't f****** start that. Wait. How do you know about what happened? You told her?"

"Of course," Xenon laughed. "What is it with you and p-e-n-i-s-e-s? It's literally just a p-e-n-i-s. What's the big deal?"

"Uhhhhhh." Chance got mad at himself for making that noise because now he was feeling some type of way.

"Let me know if you get hungry!" Xenon said as Chance walked out. Atoz was crying laughing.

"What do I do? Should I just give them to her or…?"

"Blue. There you go making things more complicated than they need to be," said Chance.

"All you have to do is ask her a question about how she's doing, give her the glasses, and then we'll tell her what tide to be ready," said Iris.

"Watch him strike out once again," Reign laughed. "Here she comes."

"Is that my Moon Jelly?!?!?" Xenon welcomed her in.

"Is that my Moon Beam?!?!?" Amethyst sat down next to him on what she called the stone couch.

"Do you know what you're going to wear to the festival yet?"

"Yeah but it's a surprise. Iris and I have something planned. How about you?"

"All I'm gonna say is that it's going to be hot so…"

"Ooooo okay. You finna have yo ass out?" she smiled. She loved making Xenon blush.

"Oh, my goddess," he blushed. "No. You are too much." They couldn't stop laughing. Iris couldn't believe she said that out loud. Iris loved how her little sister didn't give a f***. "I'm just going to have my arms and legs out. Maybe a little stomach."

"Ayyye. I see you, boo."

"And so you can see me better…" He pulled out her glasses. "I repaired these for you. I removed the scratches. It's a shame that people on the surface have to pay for glasses, (feminine) hygiene products, inhalers, contraception… Things for your well-being. I'm so happy you're here now."

"Huuuh! Thank you," she hugged him. "Wait. You did it yourself? So, you have other talents other than those in art, medicine, and technology?"

"I don't know about talented, but I'm also an engineer. I'm good at building and fixing things."

"Why are you smiling at me so much?"

"Because you're still holding onto me."

"Oh," she giggled. "Sorry."

"No, no. You don't have to let go if you don't want to. Keep holding onto me."

"In that case…" Amethyst made herself comfortable. "You're warmer than other Oceanids. Not too hot. Not too cold. Hold up." She lifted his arm. Xenon just let her. Then she proceeded to snuggle under him.

"Sister, you're the cutest."

"What did you just do?" Xenon laughed. "You're like a little seal pup. You have the eyes and everything."

"I had to check your armpits to make sure they look like mine."

"You'll never have to worry about that. I prefer to be delphys smooth," he smiled.

"I don't know why... It makes him look premature," said Reign.

"I agree," said Chance. "Real men have a decent amount of body hair like me."

"Yeah. Chance has a good amount and so do I," said Reign.

Chance examined her body hair. "Niiiiice. See. This is a grown ass womxn," he smiled.

"Look. There's nothing wrong with body hair. It's natural. I just prefer to only keep a little on my arms. That's it, that's all."

"You sound like Ame."

"Well, they are always around each other," said Reign.

"Nah, that's all that sugar in his tank. That's what's wrong."

"There's nothing wrong with him, Chance. He's just different. Leave him alone."

"He's just different," Chance mocked her. Then he got up and sat by Iris. "You wanna cuddle?"

"Get the f*** out," Iris turned her nose up. She wasn't really the cuddly type, and she really didn't like Chance.

"Was that profanity?" he asked.

"Oh, you didn't know?" Xenon laughed. "Iris is a potty mouth just like you. She just feels like she has to be in queen mode all the time."

"You don't have to be in queen mode around us, Iris," Amethyst smiled. "Just be Iris."

"Awww, Sister... That means so much to me." Then she turned to Chance. "Quit playing. Take your skinny, irrelevant ass over there and cuddle with Reign."

"Do she look like she wanna cuddle with me? How is that going to work? She needs a big, strong man."

Listen to Toxic Masculinity… That's what the problem is.

I know right. Toxic Femininity is nothing like what he thinks she is.

"You don't know what she wants. Besides, you could snuggle under her arm. Now move before I beat your ass."

At this rate, it's only a matter of time for that to happen.

I can't wait. Red vs Eye.

"Alright, alright. I'm just tryna get to know you, beautiful."

Iris was tired of looking at him, so like a lady, she picked him up, threw him over her shoulder, and placed him back in the seat next to Reign. "Sit." Chance blushed because of her strength.

LMAO. She told him to sit. I know what she's into.

Deeply into…

AHHHH. I'm weeeak. Good one.

"Reign, come cuddle with me," Iris smiled. Reign gladly went over to her.

Damn. Hella bossy. What's up with these two? What's the tea?

Duuuh. I'll tell you later.

"Can I at least sit in the middle?"

Iris shook her head. "Stay."

"Hey, Reign. Have you ever tried Goldfish?" said Amethyst. "Chance loves those, but I think Cheez-Its are better." *I swear.*

Chapter 16: Cursed Phoenix

(This title has a double meaning you'll understand later. Hint: twins)

DAY 8

"If y'all girls don't hurry up!" Chance yelled.

Iris was too focused to respond so Xenon did. "Shut the f*** up before I come in there and beat your ass."

"Blue, what are you doing with those short ass shorts? Man... Take those off," he laughed. "How do y'all even have denim?"

"Lassa, what the f*** did I say? You got one more chance, Chance. I will f*** you up."

"Even I'm growing impatient," said Reign.

"Well, there's three of us now," said Iris. "I have to do my makeup and Sister's makeup so deal with it."

"Blue, what's taking you so long?" asked Chance. "I thought you were done with your face and just had to put on lip glimmer or whatever it's called."

"Lip SHIMMER and I decided to do my eyeliner."

"Oh my god," Chance complained. "That takes like 30 minutes. And why can't you do your own makeup, Ame?"

"Are you kidding me? You know damn well I don't know how to do that. I just know how to do eyeliner and simple eyeshadow. I like having a big sister. She said we're doing a natural beat."

"You're replacing me already?"

"How could I? You're irreplaceable, Choo Choo."

"Hey, Moon Jelly. Do I look manly without a wig? Like... My face."

"What are you going for?"

"Just tell me."

"You're handsome but you're pretty-handsome. Like... You have a more feminine face. Why you smiling, cutie?"

"No reason. Thanks."

"Ummm hummm. We have a lot in common," she smiled. "Girls! Are we doing mascara?" Of course they were.

"I already did mine," said Reign. "I'm going to get a snack."

"Okay," said Amethyst. "After Iris does mine, I can do yours, Xe."

"Huh?" he asked.

"Oh. You don't want any? Sorry. I just thought—"

"No, no. I do. I just wasn't sure if you... Never mind. What color should I do?"

"Me and Iris are doing a rockstar purple, so let's do an electric blue for you."

"You really don't mind?" asked Xenon as she prepared to apply his mascara.

"No... We'll be done quicker this way."

"You're a really cool person to be around. And you have really pretty eyes. The dark ring around them... And your lashes. And your Eros bow. Sorry," he blushed.

"Thank you but stop moving!" Amethyst sat on his lap and held his face."

"OMG, Sister," Iris laughed. "You're so small."

Xenon also thought it was funny. He acted like Amethyst was strong enough to hurt him. "Cut that out, Silly," she laughed.

"You're heavy handed, but not strong. How is that?" he smiled. "Should I cut my hair?"

"No! It's already short! I like your short curly hair! Leave it like this!" Amethyst remembered something. "Oh! I saw these glittery hair clips, and I had to buy them for us." She gave Iris the purple star clip and Xenon the blue crescent moon clip. She kept the clip with the black star inside the crescent moon for herself.

As soon as Xenon walked out of Iris's room, Chance had something to say. "Perfume too? Look at this fruity ass n****." Then he walked up to him and tried to smudge his eyeliner.

Xenon was ready to through hands. It wasn't long before he and Chance were fighting. They weren't trying to injure each other though. "I don't know what fruity means, but whatever it means you're saying it in a weird way. I told you to shut the f*** up. Don't talk down on my face art. Xenon pinned him to the ground. DON'T touch my face. If you do, I'll pull my punches a lot less."

Although it was highly entertaining, the last thing Reign wanted was for Chance to get hurt. "Oh, my goddess. Blue, that's enough. Relax. Don't hurt him."

"He got himself into that. Oh well," said Iris. She couldn't care less. "He'll be alright. Blue won't hurt him."

Iris finally finished the finishing touches of Amethyst's makeup. "Chancellor Gregory Adamson, the third! You know how I feel about you fighting!" said Amethyst. "Cut that shit out right the f*** now!!!" They both stopped. "You can't be making those jokes when they only know you as the supremely ignorant cishet you've been acting like."

"Look, Blue... I was just messing with you. I couldn't pull it off, but I think your cultural face art is dope."

"No, I think you could pull it off," said Reign.

"Not like Blue's but I can see you with Kohl eyeliner. That's what they wear in the time province and the fire dominion."

"The timekeepers stay beating their faces," Xenon smiled. "They look damn good though. No one is on their level."

"I know right!!!" said Iris. "They are GOALS."

"Can you tell me more about all the realms?" asked Amethyst.

"Let's start with the sky kingdom," said Iris. "There's the Nephelai who live in the clouds. They live the closest to Olympus, and some of them have been brainwashed to believe they are superior and everyone else is inferior, especially Oceanids. Well, I should say Haliai. Nowadays, people use Oceanids to refer to ocean goers. Anyways, there are flyers and floaters. Flyers have wings and are smaller than floaters. Floaters don't have wings and can fade into their surroundings. They are Zeus's favorite people to recruit as his scouts because they are so silent and discreet. Then there's the Aurai who live far away from Olympus. The can't fly, but they can jump, so they call themselves jumpers. They love to run around. You'll rarely meet an Aurai, and they travel alone. No one knows where they go. They don't talk much, but they always come from the north, with the wind."

"So, everyone's an Oceanid?" asked Amethyst.

"Almost," Xenon said. "The Hesperides are of the starlight. Basically, they're daughters of Nyx. They are made of light, and they love gold. They're nicknamed lightwalkers. The Asteriai are known as stargliders. We know where their palace is, and we can see it, but no one else can go there except for Hera. Sometimes they descend on the darkest nights, but other than that we don't know much about them. We think they know the secrets of the cosmos. It's rumored that there's a prophecy about a being who can hear the—"

"Alright, Blue," Iris stopped him. "Let's not fill her head with stories."

"Tell me about the story. I love stories!"

"Basically, there's this idea that someone can hear the cosmic code. No one said anything about the purpose of that, but that's pretty much it," Iris explained.

"What's the cosmic code?" asked Chance.

"That's just what we call it, but it's described as being able to comprehend the writing on the stars," said Iris.

"Cool! So like reading frequencies, right?" asked Amethyst.

"Yes. Exactly like that."

"Ame loves talking about auras, chakras, crystals, and shit like that," Chance laughed.

"You should analyze the squad," Reign smiled. "Tell us our aura colors."

"Usually people have a mixture of aura colors or some variation of a color but not Chance. Chance's aura is red. Pure red. I knew that from the first time I saw him. You're yellow, Reign. Xenon, you're blue. That's why I find it funny how your nickname is Blue, and you glow blue," she laughed. "And how Chance is a redhead... Iris, you're purple. Wait no. Violet. You're pure violet. Oh, my goddess! All of you are pure. This is f****** crazy. I love it. Each of you is a pure wavelength. By the way, purple is not the same as violet. There is no purple wavelength. It only exists as a combination of blue and red, unlike violet which has its own wavelength. OMG. This aesthetic gives me butterflies. Ahhhh! Now I'm anxious!!!"

"Why? What's wrong?" Reign asked.

"She hates when an aesthetic is ruined or incomplete," Chance explained. "Some more than others. It all depends. For example, do not mess up her confetti cupcake pancakes from IHOP. LOL. I don't know why she likes that boysenberry syrup so much. I get that it's purple, but it can't be that good. Certain textures and patterns make her get like this too. Anyways, she'll hide most of her feelings, but she's internally losing her shit. Like now. Well, this is definitely getting external."

Iris was curious. "What ruined the aesthetic?"

"Nothing ruined it. It's incomplete. Ahhh! Where are the others?"

"What do you mean the others?" asked Iris.

"We're missing people. Uhhhhh! So many gaps!"

"I'm not sure I follow."

"Don't you see? You're all a pure wavelength. There are only 4 of you. There are supposed to be 7. There are 7 pure wavelengths. Oh, and that number!!! 4… Ahhh! Where are the other 3? You don't have any other friends? It's killing me!!!" She began to hyperventilate, and her eyes started to water.

"Um, is she shifting? I think she's shifting," said Reign.

"Go get Meter." Now they were all nervous because Iris didn't know what to do and Amethyst's eyes were glowing.

"Amethyst, darling," Thetis said softly. "Shhh. It's alright. It'll be okay." She had learned from the mistake she made the first time she attempted to calm an upset Amethyst. "Look at me. Talk to me. Tell me what's wrong."

"Th-There's supposed to be 7," Amethyst started to cry. "Th-There's supposed to be 7."

"I see. This group might be incomplete but look around you. In a group of 14 waves, which is the biggest wave?"

"The 7th."

"Do you remember how many main sections the basileia has?"

"S-Seven."

"And about how many major oceanic plates are there?"

"Seven." Amethyst was beginning to cool off.

"And how many parts of the ocean?"

"Seven."

Iris wanted to help. "Can you guess how many sisters Meter has?"

"Seven?"

"Seven."

"How many words are in this sentence?" said Chance.

"Seven," she smiled.

And finally, Xenon asked her, "How many questions have we asked you, including this one?"

"Seven!"

"Amethyst?" Reign was worried about her and a bit frightened.

"Sorry. I don't know what happened."

"Your emotions caused you to absorb energy," Thetis explained. "Listen up you all. Whenever that happens, and I'm not around, just be patient and do your best to soothe her. She's adorable… But in theory, she's a ticking time bomb. We don't know exactly what the bomb is, and we don't want it to go off, so act quickly."

"I ain't gonna lie," said Chance. "I was a tad bit scared. It's the eyes."

"Do you feel tired?" Iris asked.

"Nope! I feel very energized though. Iris this makeup is awesome! I was crying, and everything stayed the same!"

"That's because it's waterproof, Sister," she laughed.

"Finish telling me about the realms while we head to the festival!"

"The Lampades are the nymphs of the Underworld. No one knows who their parents are, or parent is, but we think they are children of Nyx just like the Hesperides. The only time you might see a Lampad outside of the Underworld is by a pomegranate tree. They are extremely shy though," Iris told her. "Then there are various Naiads. There's a lot of overlap, but they're split up into the following main groups. Dryads of trees, oreads of mountains, epimelids of pastures, the limonids of water meadows, and the Potamoi of rivers."

"So what kind of Naiad am I?" asked Chance.

"Your mother is from the time province, and your father is from the fire dominion. I'll let her tell you the rest."

"So, if mostly everyone is an Oceanid, what's the technical term for you all? Well… Us I guess," asked Amethyst. "Oh, wait. Is it Haliai? It's Haliai, right?"

"Yes. We're Haliai, the first Oceanids," Thetis smiled.

"Oceanids includes Nereids and Mer, right?" Amethyst asked.

"That's correct."

"How are we going to get to the land realm without getting wet?" Amethyst asked. "And where's Dad?"

"Oh, you can make a portal to the land realm by using this," Thetis showed her the crystal she was holding. "Anyone can get one. The Naiads and Haliai have always been close. We're the only two realms that agreed to partner like this. This same crystal can open other portals, but there are only so many. Sometimes it's better to swim, travel by chariot, or teleport. I can only teleport myself unless the person I'm trying to teleport also has the ability to teleport. Jeremy is asleep. I'm just dropping you all off. Ready?"

Once they were in the land realm, Amethyst noticed Chance checking out her mother. "Stop looking at her booty," she laughed.

"Damn. Is that a sundress Auntie T? I see you."

"Hush your mouth, child."

Xenon blocked his view and stood right behind his mom. Of course, he also flicked Chance off.

Iris and Amethyst were both wearing baby blue denim jeans and purple halter tank tops. Chance felt the need to comment. "I didn't know y'all had denim down here. It's crazy how much you two look alike with makeup on. I'm still getting used to that."

"Yes, Chance." Iris rolled her eyes. "We have denim. The Naiads make denim."

"Hehehe. Your hair is so different though," Reign smiled.

"Y'all are like those twins from that show Johnny Test," Chance laughed.

"Blue is Bling-Bling Boy," Reign joined him.

"OMG! That's genius. Ame is Mary and Iris is Susan."

"That's why you're Dukey, Reign," said Xenon.

"That Alpha dude is Gil huh, Blue?"

"Shut up, Johnny," Amethyst clapped back.

The twins noticed Xenon trying to get Amethyst's attention by calling attention to himself. "Look at him. He looks stupid. Why is he moving like that? I guess this is how some males attract a mate. Ew," said Iris.

"Hey, Xe. Can you do tricks?" Amethyst encouraged him.

"Not in front of Mom," he smiled.

"Not those kinds of tricks, Silly. Tricks like flips." Xenon did a series of cartwheels, somersaults, front flips, and backflips. "Ayyyye! Nice! I can do a better backflip though. I used to tumble. I'm not an Olympian, but I can do a little something. I'd show you, but not with what I'm wearing. Maybe I'll show you what I can do on the balance beam sometime."

"Oh, yeah? Then maybe I'll show you what I can do on the pommel horse. Neeeeeigh." His horse noise was only second to an actual whinny.

Amethyst caught him with her imaginary lasso and reeled in her noble steed. She tried to use some type of country accent. "Come on, girl."

"Howdy, Cowboy," Xenon laughed.

Iris thought their little act was cute, but Reign and Chance were so annoyed. After Thetis left, Chance asked, "So, what are we doing first?"

"Eating. Duh," said Iris. "They have the best deep fried panchuques. They're huge. "Americans would call them corn dogs."

"Wait. What kind of meat is it?" Amethyst hoped they weren't made with red meat. "It's not beef, is it?"

"They have turkey," she smiled. "Most Haliai don't eat red meat."

"Yeah but I love it!" Reign twirled.

"I want some real meat," Chance added.

"I'm so hungry I could eat a horse," Amethyst grinned.

"You wouldn't eat me. Would you?"

"I don't know. You look kind of delicious. Something tells me you'll melt in my mouth." She flicked her tongue, but only Xenon saw. Iris saw his reaction and figured Amethyst must have said something slippery.

"How many do you all want?" Iris asked.

"I just want 1," said Chance.

"I want 4," said Reign. "I ate something a little while ago."

"Sister. Blue. I'm waiting… Don't be shy. I'm eating 2. How many do you want."

"1's fine," they both said at the same time.

"Sauces?"

"A little ketchup," Reign and Chance said.

"Sister?"

"Mustard. LOTS of mustard."

"Yuck! You and Blue. I swear…" Reign giggled.

"I know right. Who the hell puts mustard on corn dogs. I mean panchuqes," said Chance.

They don't know what they're missing.

I know right…

"Looks like I'm bringing a whole bowl then," she smiled. "I know you two are going to want more than just one. I like mine plain, so it's all yours."

Atoz turned their noses up at how Reign and Chance bit the tops of their panchuques. "Why are you looking at me like that, Small Fry?" Reign said with her mouth full.

"Why do you and Chance do that?" said Amethyst.

"Why don't you eat the outer part off first," Xenon added. "That's the best part."

"Yeah. And why do you have to eat so rough? So violent…"

"I'll go order you two some more," Iris said once Atoz finished round one.

Soon they had an audience of young Naiads cheering them on as they drowned panchuque after panchuque in their sea of mustard. Atoz was much too into eating to care. The panchuqes were that good. "Whoa. Is that Iris?"

"Come on… Really? That's her twin, Amethyst."

"Look at those two go!"

"Blue's going to eat 7," Reign said.

"Ame's going to eat 9!" said Chance.

"Actually, they're both going to eat 11. I saw myself buy 29 panchuques."

After their panchuques session, they got their faces painted. Then Amethyst asked a good question. "What exactly is our location?"

"The realms exist in hidden pockets of space, but surface wise… We're in the Congo. There are all types of fauna and flora from surface continents though. We'll see the animals later. Don't freak out if you see something you consider unusual."

"Wakanda shit is this!!!" Chance laughed.

"That's what I'm saying!" Amethyst noticed Naiads and Haliai taking pictures of them. "OMG my hair. I like it messy, but who knows what they're going to do with those pictures."

"I made this for you." Xenon handed her a purple scrunchie.

"No way! Thank you! Yaaasssss!" The ocean goers in the squad watched in amazement at how she put her hair in a bun. "What?" she smiled.

"Are y'all serious?" Chance said. "Well, I guess you don't know. That's that same old bun she stay wearing at the house."

"Wow. That style really makes your eyes pop," Xenon said.

"Now I see why Meter was so sure to not draw any attention to your eyes, Sister."

"Why? They're nothing special. Yours look a lot cooler."

"Haliai don't have any shade of brown eyes. Meter and Jeremy weren't shy about their situation. They told everyone they were thinking about getting a sperm donor or asking Hera to bless them with an element child. They wanted Xenon to have a playmate. That was before the prophecy," Iris told her. "The only Olympian with brown eyes is Zeus, and Haliai are smart enough to figure out the connection. Honestly, it isn't that difficult."

"Awww, seriously. What the f***? How come I couldn't have Thetis's eyes? What kind of twins are we?" she laughed.

"Your eye color is really noticeable in this lighting. I'm sure even the Naiads noticed by now. Hehehe," said Reign.

"I swear," Iris giggled. "I love Naiads. They're so intelligent, but they are terrible detectives. Your brown hair color is also not a natural Haliai color. Well, some have brown hair, but your shade is so warm. Also, ocean goers don't dye their hair this brown. You're the only one in the family with brown hair."

Reign checked her phone. "Oh, look. Now everyone's talking about it. They finally figured it out. Thetis made a post confirming it."

Xenon froze. "IRIS."

"I know. What is a floater doing here, and why are they hiding?"

"What's that noise? Do you hear that?" Amethyst said.

"I can't hear anything," said Iris.

"I can feel them," said Xenon. They're running."

"So that floater must have been leaving. What did he do? There's never only one floater," said Reign.

"I smell fire," Amethyst said.

"Look!" Chance pointed to the smoke. By then the Naiads had notified their emergency response team.

Amethyst did her best to try and make a rain cloud, but she had no idea if she could do that. With the animals, the Naiads came running out of the forest. They were preparing for their performances before the floaters set a part of the forest on fire. It was so sad. Xenon and Amethyst were doing their best to hold back their tears. They had their own emotions and thoughts to deal with as well as the emotions and thoughts of each other and other people, including the plants and animals. *I don't expect anyone to know what that's like, but you can try to imagine how overwhelming that was for them.* "Xenon, why is that child so upset? I know most of them are crying but…"

"I know what you mean. They're too young to speak well enough to tell their mother what's wrong, and they are having trouble signing it. I think they left something. Their favorite toy maybe?"

The squad saw Amethyst's head twitch. "What do you hear now?" Iris asked.

"Someone's in there!!!" Amethyst yelled as she snatched off the scrunchie Xenon made for her. She ran towards the fire. A few people started recording.

"AME! STOP! What are you doing?!?!?" Chance turned to Iris. "Is she fireproof? Please tell me she's fireproof."

"We're about to find out." Iris was so nervous. Xenon was holding onto Iris because he was scared to death. He couldn't stop shaking.

"Why would she run into a fire if she doesn't know if she's fireproof?" asked Reign. *Like I said. Reign, the voice of reason.*

"Because she's naturally caring and impulsive." Chance was starting to hyperventilate. "F***!!!! Why does she have to be so god damn kind?"

"Oh, my goddess! The sprouts!" a Naiad shouted. The young plants were considered teknon.

"Her Highness is running into the fire! Where is the response team?" said a news reporter. Everyone was horrified and heartbroken. "Was this violence towards Gaia? Who would do such a thing? She is already suffering."

"OH NO!" yelled a Naiad. "How is she going to get out?" The response team had finally arrived and was working on putting the fire out.

Amethyst ran out directly through the flames as black as an igneous coal. Then she collapsed. The squad ran as fast as they could to her side. "AME! Oh, my god." Tears ran down Chance's cheeks. He wasn't sure if he could touch her because she was covered in burns. They had no words. Reign hid her face in her arms, Iris looked as if someone sucked the life out of her, and Xenon was bawling his eyes out. A paramedic rushed to her side. "Why? Why dammit?!?!? I can't lose you!" She opened her hands to reveal the three baby birds she rescued. "You're too damn good for this world you know that?"

"I-I'm reawly nawt." She could barely speak with all her burns.

"Is she going to live?" Iris asked desperately. "Please tell me she's going to live."

"I don't know. I don't even understand how she's alive and so calm. Maybe the fire caused so much damage to her nerves that she can't feel anything, but that's only a theory, and I don't think she was in there that long. They're almost here to come get you."

"I am inw pwain, bwut I'll bwe fwine. I cwan handwle itw. Awre the bwaby bwirds owkay?"

"They both survived."

"Bwoth? Thwere awre thwree!!!" Amethyst's heart rate began to increase exponentially. Everyone watched as she rose to her feet. The burnt skin peeled off into flakes that vanished into the air like ashes. She was good as new, and everyone cheered. "They work for Zeus, right? This is Zeus's doing, right?" Amethyst was very upset.

"Yes," Iris answered her. "Sister, what are you going—"

She gave herself some space. She didn't need everyone breathing on her. Especially since she just got out of the fire. "ZEUS! You want to kill me? Fine. But you don't have to murder other people! You're going around massacring innocent lives because of me? You gain nothing unless it is my broken heart you desire. Even then, you could never have that. And getting people to do your dirty work... That's sick. For the record, people who comply because you threaten their loved ones are not loyal to you, 'Sky King'. Plants may not experience any physical pain, but they are connected to the life energy around them. They have feelings too you know." Amethyst began to tear up. "They FEEL. They are the reason why we can breathe, yet there are so many who murder them. Irony or tragedy... Call it what you want, but all I'm saying is that you have a problem with me. ME! Not any of these good people. Is air not important to your realm, 'Sky King'? Do birds have no place in your realm, 'Sky King'? You also murdered a... You also murdered a little baby bird today." She held the baby bird in her hands and looked at all the Naiads and Haliai. "You all were so happy. I'm so sorry. Everywhere I go I bring destruction, and I can never fix anything."

"What you say is not entirely true, Niece." Demeter emerged from the burn site as a body of ashes. "You also bring restoration. Zeus knows nothing about Gaia, child. Fire gives more than it takes." Demeter helped the flora grow back more abundantly than before, and her body changed to flower petals. "Evil is never victorious. The sprouts have died, but the roots live. The leaves weren't healthy. It happens. Sometimes plants get sick. The fire grazed the soil, so that the plants could have another chance at life. You need not fix anything. You have already done so."

"R-Really?"

"The plants are thanking you."

"B-But the baby bird."

"Life is energy. We cannot create nor destroy energy." Demeter walked over to her and touched her hands. "Open your hands, child."

"You're alive?!?!? How are they alive?" Everyone was so happy to see the baby birds be reunited with the child who thought they lost them.

"Chaos determines when a soul shall return to her, no one else." She wiped Amethyst's tears. "And don't worry about the festival. It's not over. It's just begun." Everyone cheered as Demeter upgraded the festival costumes and decorations. "Goodbye, all. Enjoy the festival. Enjoy life."

"Naiads don't stare like Oceanids," Amethyst giggled. "I mean Haliai. Well… Oceanids."

"Yeah but as soon as they get the chance they'll join everyone else in the gossip," Iris smiled. "Oh, Sister."

"What's up?"

"Don't f****** 'what's up' us," said Chance. "You almost f****** died and shit and you're talking about some f****** 'what's up'. We were all scared as hell. Especially me. Oh my god! What the f***?!?!? You're my sister. MY LITTLE SISTER! What was I going to do without you? You and I do everything together. You're always right here with me. That's what I'm used to. You keep me as sane as I can be. You're why I'm still here. I can't even imagine life without you, Ame. You're my sister!" Chance wrapped his arms around her as tightly as he could as if that would be enough to ensure she would never leave him.

"I can't imagine life without you either, Choo Choo." Amethyst looked at the squad. "He rarely hugs me, so take notes y'all." She did her best to lighten the mood as usual.

"Group hug!!!" yelled Xenon. He was still bawling.

Are you really alright, Moon Jelly?

I'm fine.

I'm getting better at understanding you every wave.

Good.

"HUH! Are those flower crowns?!?!?" Amethyst squealed. "Let's all get one!!!"

"Oh, hell yeah. I'm so down," said Chance.

"Each one is made on the spot," said Reign.

"Well hello," said one of the Naiads running a flower crown booth. "You made quite a scene back there, young lady. We admire your character. And your hair. It says: I am fierce, I am mystery. What can I get for you all?"

"We need 5 flower crowns. I'll go first so you can see how it's done, Sister. I'll have both cream flowers with an alpha omega alternating pattern."

After the Naiad measured her head, Iris encouraged Amethyst to go next. "I feel so bad because I don't know any Greek. What's your name?"

"I am Chiamaka! You can call me Chia."

"Is that an Igbo name?" Chia nodded. "It means god is beautiful, right?"

"God as in Chaos? Then yes," she laughed. "When you say it, it means the same thing."

"Sorry. I mean Chaos. I've been on the surface for more than a decade," she smiled. "Uhhhhh. Can I get this shade of purple, this shade of blue, this shade of green, and the cream please? And for the pattern... Do whatever you want as long as it alternates."

"Lemme get all pink and red. Can you do alpha alpha omega omega? That's how you say alternate by twos right?" Chia showed Chance a sample to see if that's what he met by pink. "Nah, not that bright ass one. The soft pink."

"Can you alternate the 3 shades of blue alpha beta omega?" said Xenon.

"As long as you stick to earthy tones, I'm happy." Reign wasn't picky at all.

As soon as they got their crowns, they went straight to the henna booth. "Xe, make sure you get the right foot!" Amethyst giggled.

"Okay. You should get the other foot then."

Chance looked at Iris. "I'm hurt."

"Honestly, same," she said.

"We always get matching fake tattoos/hennas," Chance and Iris said at the same time.

Once they got their hennas, Reign noticed something. "I thought you were getting it on the right foot."

"That is the right foot." Atoz was confused. "Ohhh. I see what you mean, but that's the foot I meant," said Amethyst. "He's my left foot."

"And she's my right foot." Atoz linked their legs with the non-hennaed foot and walked as one.

"I swear," Chance smiled. "Their chemistry makes me think they knew each other in a past life or some shit. Just look at them."

"If it's possible for people to fuse into one body, I could totally see them doing that," said Iris.

"Hey, Iris!" Amethyst rode over to her on Xenon's back.

"Ugh. I'd never want someone to carry me like that. I can walk myself," said Reign. She noticed Chance look back and smile at her, but she didn't think much of it.

"Aw. Come on, gemmie. It's cute," said Iris.

"Are you an Oracle? How can you see the future? How far can you see? How come you can't see me? What exactly can you see? Do you have to be in front of your mirror?"

Iris loved how she was so interested. "Oracles can see any future moment by will as long as Chaos allows it. They don't need a mirror at all. Meter and her aunt Metis see prophecies, but that's different. I can only see the basics of whatever events I'm allowed access to. Oracles can use all their senses psychically while looking into the future. I can't hear psychically, but I can read lips depending on how the scene is set. Meter says I inherited a gift from one of her aunts. No one else can see what I see in the mirror unless I show them. It's not about how far I can see, it's about what I can see. The what is whatever Chaos allows me to see. Sometimes I ask questions. Sometimes the mirror calls me. If Chaos doesn't give me a vision, I have to be in front of the mirror. It can be any mirror."

"The name Iris fits your aesthetic. How about any reflection? Like... Does water count?"

"That's a good question. I don't know. All these years and I've never thought about that." She noticed a poisonous plant she could see Amethyst wanting to touch. "Sister, don't touch that."

"Eye eye, Captain!"

"Do you want to go see the animals?" asked Iris. "The performance is about to start."

"What kind of animals are these? I have never seen any animals like them, and I know a lot about animals. Wow. The realms are so much cooler than the surface. I'm so glad you kidnapped me, Xe."

"Anytime, Moon Jelly."

"Do you see the colorful cubs over there?" Iris pointed out. "Those are blinks. I guess you could say they're like hyperactive koala bears. I don't know if blinks are marsupials though. I forgot."

"OMG, Chance! Don't they remind you of Care Bears? They are sooooo cute. Look how they keep hugging everyone. Is that why you call Xenon Blinky?"

"Yes," Iris giggled. "And because he's fast for a Haliai. He is just like a blink except blinks don't glow in the dark. We call them blinks because they flutter their eyelids when they want attention. If they don't get what they want, they start crying lots of tears."

"We call Ame Pooh because she looks and acts just like Winne-the-Pooh. He's this funny ass bear on this one cartoon."

"Oh look!" said Reign. "That's a wishbird," she twirled. "They have wings, but they can't fly. They run fast though. Aren't they beautiful?"

"Ahhh! Oh, hell nah. That's one huge ass bird! Prehistoric lookin' ass!"

"Are you scared of birds, Little Man?"

"I'm not scared!!!"

Reign threw a leaf on Chance to scare him. "Watch out!" she yelled. "Yep. He's definitely scared," she giggled. "Awww…"

"Is that *Paraceratherium transouralicum*?!?!?!? Those are long extinct on the surface. I love how the elephants, zebras, and giraffes are just chilling right next to them."

"Yes," Iris confirmed. "And these are similar to the elephants. I think they are called mastodons. I forgot."

"They're definitely wooly mammoths," Amethyst smiled. "Mastodons are very different from their teeth to their physical appearance. Mastodons have cone-shaped teeth. See how mammoths have flat, ridged teeth like elephants? And mammoths have humps for nutrients. It's necessary for their freezing cold environment. Which brings me to my next point… Why are they here? Some of these animals are just visiting, aren't they?"

"Great. Now we have a botanist and a zoologist," Reign rolled her eyes.

"Yes. Many of the animals came from other parts of this realm just to perform with the local animals or mingle," said Iris. "Come on they're about to start."

After the performance, they all couldn't stop talking about it. "Yo! That shit was actually dope as hell," said Chance.

"Did you see the chimpanzees and the Naiads doing acrobatics!!! Together! That was insane!!!" Amethyst said. "On the surface, humans abuse animals and force them to do what they want them to do. Even if they aren't abused, it's still a cruel act. We have shit like the circus and SeaWorld. It makes me so happy to see mutual communication. What was your favorite part, Xe?"

"When the slender apes all did synchronized backflips on top of the mammoths," he said. "I was not expecting that." They all laughed in agreement.

"The concert is even better!" Reign was clearly excited. "This year Amphithemis is performing!!!"

"He's one of Apollo's sons," said Iris. "He named him after Meter and Theia Amphitrite. He's a Potamoi."

"The Potamoi look like centaurs, but they aren't evil and they're much smaller," Xenon explained. "They're all fine as hell. You should see when the herd comes around. F***!"

"Especially Amphithemis's chocolate ass," Reign said. He has a major crush on Iris," she giggled. "He has no idea he's sooooo swimming up the wrong river."

"The family pervert is also performing," said Iris. "AKA Hermes."

"I'm weeeak. Who else is performing? Are they all Naiads?" Amethyst asked. "And what genre or genres?"

"Nope. It's a little bit of everyone," said Reign. "As for genres, there's going to be indie, rock, rhythm and blues, pop, country, reggaetón, bachata, hip-hop, rap… And a few romantic duets."

"Each act gets to perform two numbers." Iris read the list from her phone. "There's Mint and his siblings. There's Sayen, Xochitl, Maya, Apricot and her brother Gingerbread, The Rose Petals, Lilac Lush, Cloud 9, The Water Babies, Charm, Ash Wednesday, Wave Goodbye, The Spell Casters, The Dream Catchers, Diamond Heart, Glass Paint, Metallurgy, Glitter, Domino, and Persephone's Cult." Iris rolled her eyes. "And this one girl named Atalanta and her fraudulent ass squad. They call themselves the Gemralds."

"Who are the Gemralds?" Amethyst asked.

"They're the most popular group of friends in all the realms. Zeus says they're perfect. They all act like goodie two shoes and people think they are."

"So what's the tea, sis?"

"Behind the scenes, they are really disrespectful to Hera. I wouldn't be surprised if they turned out to be working for Zeus. They're all the same.

Not because they all have green eyes, but because none of them act like their own person. I think they're under a curse. No. I know they are under a curse." Amethyst picked up on something. Iris emphasized her last two sentences in a way that implied she was trying to tell her something. "That's the only way anyone could be forced to act like someone other than themselves. Plus, Atalanta is the only Naiad. The others are all sky nymphs. Anyways, Atalanta is the general of the island of Lesbos and she has plant powers or some shit. I feel sorry for her, but I totally despise their leader, Zark. He's such a f****** shark. I also can't stand how Atalanta calls herself a queen." Iris laughed. "B**** where?"

Xe. Has Iris been trying to tell you something lately?

Yeah but I'm confused about what. I hope it's not what I think it is. Did she tell you something?

I think she's trying to say she's under a curse. Is she the poetic type or...?

She's definitely not the poetic type. Shit! Mom is probably already figuring out how to lift the curse. That's probably why she was so eager to visit her aunt Klymene! That's who keeps the ancient scrolls now.

Oh shit. Alright. We'll continue this talk later. I'm gonna send her a message back.

"I'm weeeak," Amethyst laughed. "I'm sure someone will figure out how to free them eventually. How come you all never performed? Or have you?"

"I have a great voice, but much to operatic for a band. Much too professional, plain, trained, classical, and boring. Plus, it doesn't go well with Xenon's voice. We just don't go together musically." Amethyst had an interesting feeling about the word operatic. She couldn't help but think of The Phantom of the Opera. She felt like that fit Iris's aesthetic.

"She's always putting herself down," said Xenon. "She's talented."

"What about She-Hulk over here?" Chance asked. Reign shoved him.

"She can't sing. At. All," Xenon laughed.

"But I can play the bass," said Reign.

"Do you play any instruments, Xe?"

"What do you think I can play?"

"The drums or the piano."

"I can play the classic piano and any drum. I can play any percussion instrument."

"Interesting…" she smiled. "The piano is one of my favorites, and I have a thing for drummer boys."

"You do? Wait. How'd you know?"

"I didn't know. It just fits your aesthetic. Oh, and your hands. Plus, you're always tapping your foot, nodding your head, or twiddling your fingers when you aren't staring off into space," she laughed. "Chance can't sing that well, but he can play the guitar."

"Hmmm…" Iris had an idea. "How well can you sing, Sister?"

"HA! Me? Tell her, Chance."

"She's trash as f***."

"Nonsense. It runs in the family," said Iris. "With some vocal training, I'm sure you'd be alright."

"I heard you singing in the shower," Xenon giggled.

"Why are you smiling so hard?" Now she was smiling because he was being way too cute for her to not. "What's this little dance you're doing?"

"Nothing."

"It's clearly something."

"You make me feel like singing."

"Then sing, boo."

He shook his head. "Nope."

"Why not?"

"If I sing my heart out, I don't know if I'll get another in exchange. I'll be a dead man."

"Dead men still have hearts, but don't worry. I'll never let your song die."

"I understood that one. The water becomes clearer every day."

"It's not the water that's cloudy."

"Why can't you two just speak without all the theatrics?" Reign sighed. "What does all that even mean?"

"Exactly womxn!" said Chance. "Thank you! Oh my god!"

"I bought you all your wristbands. You're welcome," Iris smiled. "Oops. Blue must still have yours, Sister."

"IRIIIIIS!!!" Xenon hid behind a tree.

"Oh, my goddess. Relax. Come from behind the tree. Now she's going to ask you about it."

"You bought my ticket, didn't you?"

"Yes. I got it for our date, but don't think this is a date or anything." He realized how that came out. "AH! I mean…"

"It's okay. You changed your mind. I do it all the time." *The squad noticed her little Alpha trap.*

"No, Moon Jelly. I wanted this to be a date, but then I got so nervous when you asked me if it would be a date."

"LOL. I know. Next time don't hesitate." Then she caught up to Iris.

"Wait! Next time? Did you say next time? You said next time!" Xenon ran up behind her. "Boo!"

"Ahhh! OMG. Watch out," she laughed. Then he jumped in front of her and continued with his silly dancing. "Did you fall? I'm weeeak. Are you okay?" He picked her up and tossed her in the air. "Whoa! I forgot how strong you are. Do it again!"

Reign rolled her eyes. "He's not that strong!"

"I'm starting to think you like when I catch you."

"You like catching me. I think it's fun when you throw me. Wooooo! Look, guys! I can fly!"

"Good point, but I like dancing with you better."

"Now we have an audience."

"Oh, what the hell!" Reign smiled. "Iris, dance with me."

"So y'all just gon leave a brotha hanging?" Chance noticed a group of people arrive. "Holy shit. Um… Guys! ALERT! I think that herd of Potamoi just showed up. Y'all didn't tell me they're all ripped as f***!"

"Daaaamn. Who put oil on them?" Amethyst laughed. "How far do we have to walk?"

"See that stage all the way over there?" Iris pointed out.

Amethyst didn't feel like walking. She decided to wave at them. "Heeeeey boys!" she giggled.

"Ame! What are you doing?"

Xenon was thinking the same thing as Chance. "Now they're going to come over here!"

"Yeeeeesssss! Nice going, Small Fry."

"Well hello, Your Highnesses," Amphithemis bowed. "You must be Amethyst. It's a pleasure to meet you. I'm very fond of your sister so excuse me if I'm a bit off." Iris was unphased.

"I understand why. She's lovely, isn't she? She's been talking about how her feet have been hurting since a few days ago, and she still took me to this beautiful festival. Isn't that sweet? What a kind gesture."

"Oh, Your Highness. You should have told me. I'll give you a ride. My friends can take your friends. It's no trouble."

Reign didn't waste any time, but the other three were hesitant. "You heard him," said Amethyst. "Come on girls."

"I'll take the red one," said one of Amphithemis's friends. "I'm Twinkle. Hop on handsome. I didn't bring my saddle today, but I'll go nice and slow."

When they arrived Chance said, "Thank you, pretty girl."

"I'm a boy, but if you think of me as a girl, I guess that's okay too."

The squad held in their laughter until they left. "All Potamoi are born male Chance," Iris said as Amethyst tended to his nose bleed.

"B-But the flowers in her— I mean his hair. And the arm and leg bands… Then the eyeshadow and mascara… I had no idea."

"How much sugar does he have in his tank?" Xenon asked.

"Oh, he definitely got you beat. That n**** got a whole ass gallon," he smiled. "F****** pretty ass boy. Wow," he smiled.

"Sister, you are something else."

"What? I was just using my resources. These ones just happened to have rock hard abs and hooves."

"Can't argue with that," Xenon gave her a thumbs up. "I've always wanted to ride a Potamoi." Atoz clearly had their own little joke going on.

"I f****** caught that," said Chance. "That's bestiality. Nasty ass."

"Potamoi also have a bipedal form, dumbass," Xenon laughed. "Trust me. I don't want no horse p-e-n-i-s. Hell no. I would never pull a stunt like that." *LOL did he really just use Amethyst's word? Soon she'll have the whole squad using stunt like that.*

Amethyst called Chance out. "Hold up, bruh. You would have sex with a mermaid, wouldn't you? So what's the tea, sis?"

"The tea is that that's different," Chance laughed. "There you go with yo bullshit."

After the concert, it was time for the squad to eat again. "Yo! Y'all got tacos!" said Amethyst.

"They also have jollof rice, fufu… Oh, shit is that bazeen?!?!? And kusksu?!?!?" Chance knew what he was ordering. "My mom used to make this all the time! I'm telling you, Ame. This is hella delicious. You don't know what you're missing. Go on ahead and enjoy your lettuce tacos," he laughed.

"What's wrong with lettuce tacos?" she giggled.

"You're supposed to have some meat!" said Reign. "Uhhh! You and Blue are annoyingly alike."

"LOL. He got chicken."

"I'm talking about real meals like barbacoa or something," said Reign.

"What did you get?" Chance admired Reign's meal.

"Feijoada. One day I'm going to take you to a churrascaria. I don't think the others could handle it."

"I wanna come too! I love barbeque. I'll get chicken and some sides," Amethyst said. "I'll get some feijão com arroz." Back at the bas, they posted the best photos and videos from the concert! They couldn't stop talking about how much they enjoyed it. "I've never been to Coachella, but it was like Coachella without the cultural appropriation!"

"The only way Coachella could be on their level is if Beyoncé performs," said Chance.

"Then it would be Beychella," said Iris. "I know she'd have a culturally iconic performance. I f****** love Beyoncé. She's my fav."

"Fitting for a queen," Amethyst smiled.

"What about you, Small Fry?"

"I have way too many favorites."

"Out of your favorites who do you vibe with the most?"

"Rihanna. Yaaasssss Bad Gal RiRi!!!"

"OMFG! I looooove her," Xenon gleamed. "She's a Naiad. I vibe with Frank Ocean the most though. That's my lassa. He's also a Haliai if you couldn't tell."

"Shut! Up! What?!?!? I could listen to him all day," said Amethyst.

"What about your favorite rapper?" asked Reign.

"Nicki Minaj!!!" Atoz said at the same time. "She's from the fire dominion," said Xenon. "Oh, and Beyoncé is a Hesperid."

"Oh, my goddess!!!" Reign covered her ears. "What is different about you two?!?!? I swear!!!"

"Lots of things…" said Amethyst. "I asked him what kind of magical creature he would want as a companion and this shaky ass shell said a sprite. What the hell you gon do with a little ass sprite?"

"Sprites are good listeners," Xenon laughed. "And they're really silly."

"LOL Sprite is my favorite soda," Amethyst said. "I only drink it every once in a while, so I don't get hella bumps on my face."

"What magical creature would you want?" Iris asked.

"I'd want a huge dragon! What are dragons like? Do y'all have those?"

"Once they get to know you they talk a lot. They aren't dangerous unless you piss them off," said Xenon.

"What do they keep in their lairs?" asked Amethyst.

"No one really knows because no one gets that close to one and lives," said Iris. "I would think it depends on the dragon. They all have unique personalities."

"I'm feeling a bit tired," said Xenon. "I'm going to get some sleep."

"Still thinking about that song?" said Amethyst.

"Yeah. I don't think you're going to like it. Good night."

"Good night, Shy Guy." At this moment, Xenon was done arguing with himself. Well… Sort of.

I know she knows about the other thing, but this is a different thing. But what exactly does she know? Or maybe I'm just paranoid. How much does she know? She can't know everything. Can she? I've never told a soul. Not even Mom knows. I've already established the fact that I can't fool her. I guess I still think I'm slick or however she says it. She even sent me signals on purpose. Everything was on purpose. Clever. No. Iris is clever. MJ is psychic. Not just with the whole mind communication thing. I mean psychic as in knowing things. Wait that's not the right word. Iris knows things. Moon Jelly says sometimes she doesn't know and just thinks. This is crazy. Nothing gets past those two. I bet the whole squad knows now. I'm sure Moon Jelly said something about our little rendezvous in the physical. What's the plural of rendezvous? Is that also the plural? WAIT! If Moon Jelly knows about me that means she won't hate me if I tell her because she already knows! So that's what she meant when she said, 'It's not the water that's cloudy.' Huh. Just when I thought I figured this out. I'm so blind, but I do understand now. At least I think so.

Amethyst called out to him from across the hall. "Shhh. I'm trying to sleep!"

"You heard me?!?!? Wait. I thought you were still in there with the others?"

"You've been in deep thought for a long time. All the others went to sleep. I didn't hear you. I wouldn't hack into your mind especially when it's something like this. Your thoughts were jamming themselves into my mind. I kept seeing images… I was having a violent dream. I kept seeing flashes of all our little rendezvous, so yes, I think I know what you were thinking about, Moon Beam. Our minds are connected remember."

"I broke my promise."

"No, you didn't. You promised to never hurt me. I wasn't hurt. I was passionately patient. Now can you stop moping, and turn up that light of yours? It's still pretty dark in my room."

Xenon responded from his doorway. "It must be because of the angle. I'll buy you a night light to increase the brightness."

"I can buy it. Just take me tomorrow. Where are you going? It's still dark."

"You want me to come in?"

"Yes, Moon Beam. You'll be my night light for the night. Make sure you turn the heater down, so I don't end up as a dead man like Octavian." She already had an idea, but she asked, "What's your favorite signal that I sent you?"

He let her know he was aware. "Aside from all the ones you just sent me in this conversation... I'd have to say the airplane. That was a multi-metaphor or some shit. You and your metaphors. You're a professional metaphoress. You make metaphors like you're from the metaphysical plane, but your mind works like you're from the psychic plane."

"I'm deeead. Shut the f*** up. Was that supposed to be a pick-up line? Stop trying to be like me."

"Oh yeah... And the one where you named the twins teknon Octavia and October. That was so petty."

"I figured that would get your attention," she laughed. "And it really does fit their aesthetic. The number 8 is the number of order and good fortune. That's a contradiction, but 8 also has to do with duality. 8 also looks like an infinity symbol. I don't like even numbers, but 8 and 2 are cool."

"How come you haven't told me what my aesthetic is?"

"I have. You're the one who never opens their f****** mouth. Remember when you asked me about your eyes, and I told you they are a reflection of your soul? Your aesthetic is the pure essence of the ocean."

"So that's how you determine everyone's aesthetic. You read souls. When did you know mine?"

"I've always known yours."

"Something about Chance and the others feels familiar too."

"I heard you two talking about that while I was in the shower. I agree. Me and Chance already talked about that. We wanted to talk to you all about it, but I wanted to wait for you," she giggled. "Chance likes to do everything at the right time, but I like to do things when the time is right. What is time?"

"Really? Usually, I'm the one that's waiting for other people to catch up. The tables have turned. Is that why you call him your right hand? I feel like there's a clock pun there. Wait!" Xenon realized something. "That question wasn't rhetorical. In the garden, you told me that trust is time. Time is trust!!! Chance is your clock! Also, I noticed how Chance is actually his nickname. It fits his aesthetic. You gave it to him, didn't you?"

"I did. At first, I just thought it sounded cool. Then over time, I realized it was more than that. The universe has a way of weaving things together. Sort of like how a storybook unfolds."

"Oh shit. You can read the cosmic code. I wish I could read it with you."

"You don't need to. You understand me. I'll tell you all about it. Plus, you can read me. You're just out of practice. Sometimes I do psychic things by accident and don't even notice." Amethyst was fed up. "Why are you still on the floor?!?!? Look, I love the whole empath thing you got going on, but sometimes you gotta tell me what the f*** you want. I like figuring things out, but I also love communicating, so start speaking up, and stop being so damn distant. Also, start calling me out more. You know I do shit on purpose."

"Yes, ma'am," he smiled. "Can we snuggle? I want to be the big spoon."

"Hell yeah," Amethyst rolled her eyes. "I've only been freezing cold... I like being the little spoon."

Xenon held her tight and said, "You know your sister would have let me down easy. Mom too. But not you."

"Is that a bad thing?"

"Yes, I f****** love it. Now kiss me." *There is so much encrypted into this conversation, but those last two lines will make sense in a minute. Hold on.*

417

Chapter 17: Exorkismos

DAY 9

"Reign, where do you live?" Amethyst was curious where she always swam off to.

"I live in the outskirts of the epsilon pentarch."

"You swim all the way here every day?!?!?" Chance asked.

"She doesn't want to live with us," said Xenon.

"No, I just prefer to be independent. There's also a lot more open space for me to swim around in."

Iris looked at the Alpha Zeta Chi trio. "What do you want to talk to us about?"

Chance blurted out, "We think we know each other from past lives!"

"Oh, my goddess! Iris and I were thinking the exact same thing, but we thought it was crazy!!!"

They could tell Iris had thought long and hard about this. "I just don't understand how…"

"Who cares about how? What matters is why," Amethyst giggled.

"Good point," said Iris. "Anyone got any ideas?" Everyone except for Amethyst shook their head.

"Well, if the prophecy is about you and I and they are connected to us then they're connected to the prophecy!"

"They don't have any powers though."

"Xe's an empath, Reign's super-duper strong, and Chance is good at remembering things."

"How is that going to be useful in a fight against whatever causes the universe to become imbalanced?"

"I don't know. Maybe it's our friendship!"

"Friendship? Really? I don't understand."

"Are you familiar with rock, paper, scissors?"

"We call it kelp, sword, rock."

"Love beats hate."

"Light drives out the darkness," said Chance.

"That's not the same thing. You said it backwards," Amethyst giggled. "Darkness absorbs the light."

"Sunshine, are you ready to go?" Thetis swam to where they were.

"Wait! Iris. I wanted to ask you about something. It's important."

Iris hissed at Amethyst viciously. "Well, WHAT is it!!! You better hurry up and f***** say it b****. I dare you. I f***** dare you." Now her eyes were completely black.

Thetis shook her head, so Amethyst would know not to say anything. Thetis held Iris back from attacking her. The others were so confused and frightened. "Iris. IRIS!" Thetis called for Jeremy. He had already jumped out the bed and was bringing the sacred oil.

Thetis anointed Iris with some of the oil as Jeremy did his best to comfort her. "We're here. It's alright, Sunshine. We'll get through this." He realized that the oil wasn't working as well as it was before. "Thetis."

"Reign, come help me hold her down, so she doesn't hurt herself. We can only wait for it to pass. Jeremy, can you call Klymene?"

"Wait. I see." As Amethyst swam up to Iris, her hyperactive body became more and more still until she was a frozen block of fear. Amethyst stared into her eyes. Suddenly the black was transferred to her own eyes, and Iris's returned to normal. Then she leaned into one of her sister's ears and said, "Iris."

Iris took a long, desperate, ghastly gasp before she fainted. Then she woke up. "Th-Thank you. I am so sorry," she cried.

"It's alright, sister." Amethyst held back her tears. Seeing Iris in so much pain hurt her heart. "It's not your fault. I think something evil is trying to take over your body to get to me, but I won't let it."

"She speaks the truth," said Thetis. "I must ask what you did, Amethyst. How were you so calm?"

"Well, yesterday Iris sent me a signal about a curse. When whatever is inside of her lashed out at me, I realized this was no curse, and she is fighting against being possessed. Iris is deaf, so I figured that's where the evil thing entered her. I commanded it to let Iris come out."

"She's been dealing with my anger issues for years now. I lash out a lot. We also watch a lot of paranormal videos on YouTube. We're lowkey obsessed with exorcisms and shit. My bad. I mean stuff."

"How'd you clear her eyes?" asked Jeremy.

"I don't know. I didn't do it on purpose. I just wanted to know if she could see me. Sort of like knocking I guess."

"Hold on! You're deaf?"

"Yes, Chance."

"Don't get any ideas, Little Man."

"How'd you know I'm deaf, Sister?"

"You always have to make eye contact when you're talking or if someone's talking to you. The others are always so sure to make eye contact with you too. You read lips and your eyesight cancels out your hearing difference. It helps that Oceanids often use hand gestures and sign language. Other times you sense vibrations in the water and make inferences from a combination of pitch and intuition. You're amazing. Why don't you wear your hearing aid though? I know you have one. Sound is different up there. I know it must be annoying for you. Oh yeah, and I remember how uncomfortable you looked when you broke the surface at the beach that one time."

"She's very observant," Jeremy smiled.

"Speaking of that. I caught when you said 'of course there is' in response to me asking you why you have to go surfing when no one's out there. I peeped."

"Meter we should tell them now. I understand that it's better to have a support group than fight on your own."

"That's what friends are for!" Amethyst smiled.

"I'll go with Jeremy. See you all later."

"We can't say much about Leukos in front of her because then he will come out entirely," said Thetis.

"But don't we want him to come out? We have to get rid of it. I mean him," said Amethyst.

"And who is this Leukos dude?" asked Chance.

"Why does he want Iris and Amethyst?" Xenon cried.

"He's coming back?" Reign added. "What do we have to do to get rid of him?"

"Leukos is of the white energy. The light that comes from Helios is good, but the light that comes from the white energy is pure evil. Humans have been influenced to associate white with good and dark with evil, but that is not true. He wants to take over Iris's mind because he wants to disrupt the prophecy. The herbs I gave her should have taken care of the situation by now. We didn't think he would be this desperate. What we just saw was Leukos fighting back harder because Iris was winning."

"Why not possess me?" asked Amethyst.

"He can't. Every being has a nature that is either Agathos, Skotos, or Kakos. In English, they translate to good, bad, and evil, but like I said before, they can't be properly translated in English, so keep that in mind as I explain. Think of two coins. One coin is good and the other is evil. The good coin has Agathos on one side and Skotos on the other. The evil coin is Kakos on both sides. Does that make sense?"

"Basically, 'good' and 'bad' are two sides of the same coin," said Amethyst.

"So, then what's the difference?" asked Chance.

"Agathos are of the good light, and Skotos are of the darkness. Skotos cannot be possessed by Leukos because darkness absorbs the light."

"So, Skotos are stronger than Agathos?" asked Reign.

"Not necessarily. They are both equal. It depends on the individual. They both combat evil. You can think of Skotos as those who will do bad things for the right reasons. There's much more to it than that though. I think it's better if I tell you your natures. That way you can learn what they mean as you get to know each other. Reign, you are Agathos."

"Aw, man! I wanted to be Skotos! If Leukos comes for me, I'll beat the crap out of him!"

"Leukos cannot be beaten in the physical. Also, Skotos is not something you want to be. You'll change your mind. It comes with certain... Issues. Everyone is who they are for a reason. We need both Agathos and Skotos. Soon you'll see why there are far less Skotos. You three are Skotos."

"Oh." That's what Chance expected for himself and Amethyst. "Blue is Skotos? Wow. You'd think Reign and Blue would be swapped."

"Right... I've done some very bad things in the past," said Reign.

"Did they feel natural? Do you have an inner feeling of satisfaction? Would you do them again?"

"No. Wait. Are you saying doing bad things is natural AND pleasurable to Skotos? So Skotos are insane?"

"Sanity, insanity… I used to think the same thing, but over time I learned that those words are their own paradox. Just trust me. You'll see why. Sometimes it's better to experience than explain."

Amethyst was worried. "What are you and Dad?"

"We're both Agathos, but don't worry. I know what to do. Now I just have to figure out how to find them."

"Do what? Find who?" They were all eager to help.

"On this scale, Endymion is the only person who can conduct the ritual that will free Iris from Leukos."

"Who is Endymion?" asked Xenon.

"They are the prince of an ancient society we shouldn't bring up at the moment."

"What kind of ritual?" Chance asked.

"They specialize in crystal healing. They aren't the only person, but they are the only one with the pure selenite wand. That is why I must find them."

"Selenite as in Selene, right?" asked Amethyst. "Why can't you just ask Selene where they are then?"

"Selene's first love and soulmate is Endymion. Hera and Zeus are soulmates, but they are not in love in this life. Zeus has been jealous of me. He still is. Hera and I used to date when we were younger."

"Oh shit! I see you, Auntie T."

"Oh, hush. Anyway, Zeus was also jealous of the love between Amphitrite and Poseidon. He wouldn't dare mess with them, so he tried to break the bond between Selene and Endymion. He knows nothing about love, and it only ended up backfiring on him. Zeus cast a spell on Endymion so that they be in eternal slumber. He knew love can break any spell, so he made it so if Selene wakes Endymion up, Endymion will commit suicide. Zeus made himself even more miserable because he realized that they would still love each other no matter what he did, and they still do after eons."

"OMG. I feel so sorry for them," said Amethyst. "They're both so strong. I'm sure it was for the greater good but, if someone did anything to my soulmate, we fosho boxin'. I'm sarry." *Yes, sarry not sorry.*

"N**** are you crying?"

"Oh, my goddess…" Reign rolled her eyes.

Amethyst held Xenon in her arms. "Shhh. Ignore them. Let it out." She turned to her mother. "So where do you think they are?"

"I have a few locations. I sent some warriors to go check them out because I'm stubborn. My aunts Tykhe and Telesto told me that everything would work itself out. Peitho had to persuade me to believe that, but I had to do something. I don't know how they expect me to rely on chance."

"I do it all the time," Amethyst giggled. "When we find Endymion, how will we wake them up?"

"We have to find a way to make a sound. Oh, how do I say this. Not just any sound. It must be of a specific frequency. That's what I'm currently trying to figure out. Zeus doesn't know. The only person that would know is Metis, but she's been missing since before Zeus cast the spell on Endymion. She's been missing since before I was born."

"I know that's my grandmother, but who's Metis?"

"She was the keeper of ancient scrolls, but Klymene had to take over when she disappeared because my mother, Doris, also disappeared. We believe Leukos has something to do with their disappearances." Thetis needed to go lay down. "That's all I have for you all. Don't sulk around Iris, that will make her feel worse. I'll see you all at dinner. I have a lot of work to do."

"Talk about family drama," said Reign. "We have to fix this. Poor Iris."

"I think she also used to date Selene or something," Amethyst smiled.

"I know right. Iris and I talk about that all the time," said Xenon. "You can totally tell."

"Y'all mom is pullin' em'," said Chance. "I ain't even mad though. That must be where Ame gets it from."

"What do you think about the new software update?" Xenon asked one of his employees at work. "I took your advice and made a few changes."

"I think it's great, Your Highness. Wow. I'll make sure it's available in a few tides. I just received a message. Someone has a delivery for you."

"Interesting. Tell them to let them in." The delivery person presented Xenon with a diverse bouquet of various types of green, red, and purple kelp. "Wow. Oh, my goddess. These are beautiful! Who are they from?"

"Her Highness, basilissa Amethyst, Your Highness. They came with this message." The Oceanid played the audio: Heeeey, Moon Beam. I hope you like the flowers. Well, the kelp. Even though the whole fire thing happened, I really enjoyed myself on our non-date yesterday. On the surface they say, pretty girls deserve pretty flowers. I like to say pretty people deserve pretty flowers. Besides, yah never really know do you? LOL. Anyways, have fun at work! Muah."

Xenon was blushing so hard he didn't know what to do. He couldn't stop smiling. He placed his flowers in the vase on his desk and told his social media followers all about it.

As soon as Amethyst got the notification she was tagged in a photo, the squad asked, "What did he say! Tell us."

"He posted a photo and captioned it 'she knows the way to my heart.'"

"Awww!" Reign twirled. "Look at all the stickers he put!"

"Whatever. It isn't that cute," Chance said.

"Have you seen the video?" said Iris.

"Huuuuh!" Reign gasped. "Look how he's smiling! And look at his eyes! Adorable!"

"It's literally just him smiling, but I ain't gon lie. That was hella cute," said Chance.

"He just sent me a text," Amethyst smiled. The squad hovered over her trying to be nosy. "Move," she laughed. "This is a private message." She did her signature eh-heh noise with her tongue out and couldn't stop grinning at her phone screen. Chance and Iris were still determined to see what was on her screen, so they sat next to her on the stone couch. "Mooove. It's nothing."

"Ummm hmmm. I know what that's about, Sister."

"He said he's cumming." *SMH.*

"Told you!" Xenon swam up to Amethyst and threw himself on her lap. They started making out right in front of the squad.

"Oh, hell no! Ewww," Chance said. "What the f***?"

"How romantic!" Reign held her heart.

"Well damn," Iris laughed as she took notes.

"So, I guess it's not a secret anymore," Chance laughed.

"What are you talking about? You already knew I liked her."

"You two already knew each other," Iris said. "I figured you were visiting someone on the surface. Mom knew too. When I saw how determined you were to go save Amethyst from crashing into the rocks, I knew that whoever you were going to get was important to both you and Meter. Plus, why would I be the chosen one?" she giggled. "I always thought there had to be someone else. Also, why else would there be another bedroom in the family quarters? Reign was never moving in. And why would Meter and Jeremy be apart? Duh."

"Everything happened so fast, but Amethyst told me you were the same guy that she was talking to on the beach. Honestly, dude... Come on. How could you not expect us to put two and two together?" he laughed. "Also, something tells me you two have known each other for much longer than two months."

"LOL don't worry about that part yet. Anyways, you picked some funny ass names, Xe. I love how you told me your name was October in October," Amethyst smiled. "Why do you think I didn't ask you where

426

you were going trick or treating? That necklace you wore doesn't work on me boo. Also, why'd you pick October? I feel like it has meaning."

"It does, Moon Jelly. I'll tell you later. When were you 100% sure I was the person at the beach?" he smiled.

"Well I was always sure, but I can be very doubtful when it comes to myself, so I'll say as soon as you caught me."

"No way! How? I could have been another 'aquatic'," he smiled. "We never made eye contact on the beach."

"True but I can sense you. I know you. And that wasn't the first time you caught me. Remember when I tripped that one time? I know you don't have a pheromone scent yet, but you still have a smell. Also, you have a funny walk. Watch." Amethyst couldn't stop laughing as she copied his walk. "You have a cute little walk to go witcho yo cute little butt." Xenon covered his face.

"Oh f***, Sister," Iris laughed. "He does walk like that."

"Duuuh. Then he got those long as legs," Chance added.

"You've been checking me out lassa?"

"N**** shut the f*** up. That's Ame who has a thing for long legs."

"Is that so?" Xenon put his leg up.

"Ooooo. Not only are you leggy… You're a stretchy boy."

"Can you put your leg down? Damn." Chance was so irritated. "Why the hell are you so damn flexible anyway?"

"Iris and I used to take ballet classes together. I took other types of dance lessons too."

"Oh, heeeeeeell nah. Ima have hella jokes," said Chance.

"Yaaasssss!!! You go boy."

"Show him some of your moves, Blue." Reign loved to instigate. She was starting to like messing with Chance more than she liked messing with Xenon.

"Iris, play my song." She hooked up her phone to the speaker and played "Skin" by Rihanna. Xenon danced for Amethyst.

You like that?

No, I love it. F***.

Chance was so uncomfortable. "Shit! Why the f*** you gotta do stripper moves? *Magic Mike* ass n****. You were definitely a stripper in a past life or something." He looked at Reign. "And what the f*** you laughing for, Miss Brazil?"

"Don't be mad just because you're romantically frustrated," said Reign.

He smiled. "You sound just like Bailey."

"Remember your birthday party? This is how I felt," Amethyst said. "Sister, can you play "Don't Stop the Music" by Rihanna? Turn it up! Come on! Dance with me!"

"You always did love to dance. And you're the wild-type... That night this goddess managed to get my tantō 'for safety precautions'," he smiled. "She was going to kill me."

"That sounds like her," Chance laughed.

"How did you feel last night?" He knew what song she was going to pick, and she was fully aware of that.

"Can you play "Say It" by Rihanna."

"Aye!" said Chance. "No grinding. Cut that shit out. Damn."

"How did this turn into karaoke?" Reign smiled. "She actually doesn't sound that terrible. You either, Chance."

"I know right! You sound like a teknon, Sister. It's cute."

"What are you talking about witcho deaf ass? You can't even hear. How you even know you like songs?"

"And you can't f****** breathe. Shut the f*** up before my deaf ass swim over there and beat your diabetic ass up."

"Alright, alright. Chill bro, chill."

"Sisssssster," Amethyst whined. "I want to meet a mermaid!"

"Why? What do you think they're like?"

"Just like Reign except with a tail!!! Strong and fierce. Maybe even a little magical!"

"What do you think, Reign? Is she on point?" *Oof.*

"Uhhhh… Um. Yeah. I-I guess that sounds about right."

DAY 10

Amethyst summoned the squad. "Girls come check out my room!!! Come see my decorations!!! Xenon helped me paint!"

"Niiiiice, sis." Chance was impressed. "When'd you do all this?"

"After we finished our Greek lessons for the day! I'm getting better. Can y'all speak Greek around me more often?"

"Sure, Sister. What's your room like on the surface, Red?"

"Alright, so my shit dope as f***. My walls are soft pink. Like… Baby soft. Damn near everything is Hello Kitty. My curtains are black, and my bedding is mostly red. Everything is red, black, white, and pink. Pink is my favorite color."

Iris and Reign looked up Hello Kitty on their phones. "OMG! I love your room," said Iris.

"I know right. Isn't she kawaii AF?" said Amethyst.

"Traaaash. Way too soft," Reign giggled. "My room is sports themed to go with all my trophies."

"Trophies?" Chance asked.

"Reign was a jock in school," said Iris.

"Come check out my lip gloss and eyeliner collection! Thetis took me to the store on her lunch break for some bonding time." She found a surprise when she looked in her makeup bin. "Eeeeeep! Hair products!!! I love it! Thank you!"

"I had Chance sneak it in there for me. Now me or Mom can do your hair if you want. I can do braids, twists, spirals… I can do whatever you want. Iris's hair products are too heavy," he laughed. "She likes that weighed down look."

DAY 11

"Alright y'all, look," Chance pulled up a video. "This is Winnie-the-Pooh. This n**** hella funny."

"See," Jeremy laughed. "Cupcake acts just like him."

"LOL she does… He's so cute. OMG she did react like that when I gave her the honeycomb."

"Watch how she reacts when she realizes what's in the oven," Chance laughed. "Hungry ass."

"What's that yummy smell?" Amethyst asked as she walked into the kitchen. "Oh snap! I'm not swimming. I just noticed the bas is drained."

"Blinky made breakfast today," said Thetis.

"I don't like him, but he can cook," Jeremy joked.

"Oh hush, Jeremias," Xenon mimicked Thetis.

"Whoa. You do impressions crazy good, bro."

"NO. WAY. Are those blueberry muffins?!?!? Eeeeeep! Yaaasssss! I looooove blueberry muffins! Huuuh! Banana with no nuts too?!?!? How did you make these?"

"We have an oven, Little Scallop. See."

"Whooooa! That was the oven the whole time? I'm shook. I would say I'm overwhelmed, but it's more than that. I'm underwater."

"And we have turkey bacon and oranges," said Xenon. "It's good to have a balanced diet."

"I knew I smelled oranges! I thought they weren't in season?"

"I had them imported," he smiled. "They usually taste sour to Oceanids."

"Awww, Xe. Thank you," she hugged him. "I love oranges. So, oranges taste like lemons, and pomegranates and grapefruits are sweet? I agree except oranges are still sweet to me."

I see your eye art... It looks nice. I love the glitter.

Thank you, Moon Jelly. I was hoping you'd notice.

Iris noticed something. "How are we feeling today, Blue?"

"4 out of 5."

"I know what that means. I say the exact same thing," Chance said. "Me and Ame have our own system for that too. How about you, Ame? How we feelin'?"

"Purple."

"Pink and purple go well together," Xenon smiled.

"We always go well together, Moon Beam. Like blueberries and muffins," she laughed. "You're the blueberries to my muffin."

"Isn't my night light cool!" She pointed to the large figure attached to her wall. I wanted a sea dragon, but they didn't have that, so I got a seahorse!!!"

"Damn. That's a big ass night light," said Chance.

"It has to be, so it can light up her room," said Iris.

"Come closer, Chance! It's an aquarium of *Noctiluca scintillans* or sea sparkle algae. Then there's some little tiny fishes eating them. I have to take care of them and stuff. They can reproduce asexually or sexually. Isn't that cool! You don't need men do you, cuties?"

"How you know they female?" Chance laughed.

"Algae are just algae. They prefer feminine words," said Xenon.

"Xe, what did they say?"

"They said, 'Hell no, cutie.' Algae pick up words from people around them."

"Eeeeeep! So, you can talk to plants too!!!" Amethyst noticed they said something else. "What did they say? Why are you blushing?"

"They asked if I'm your boyfriend."

"That's funny for reasons you might or might not know," she laughed. "He didn't ask me out yet. He hasn't even taken me on a date. I'd ask him, but I want Shy Guy here to practice speaking up."

DAY 12

"What did you buy from the market, Sister?" Iris asked.

"I got a Megaminx. I got it for you, Night Light."

"Oh, my goddess I love it!" They all watched as Xenon solved it quickly. "Do you like the pattern?"

"WHOA!" Amethyst was impressed. "That was awesome. Next time, I'll buy you a Zettaminx. Shit. I might have to get you a Yottaminx."

"Damn dude. I thought your ass was a little dumb."

"Well, I'm NOT!" he rolled his eyes. Then he turned to Amethyst, "How'd you know I love puzzles?"

"Because you like figuring me out."

"You're like a minx that keeps changing randomly," he laughed.

"LOL. That was a good pun, Moon Beam."

"You're the most challenging puzzle I'll ever face."

"Or maybe I'm not a puzzle."

"Okay. Even I don't know what that means, Ame."

"She's saying she's not something that needs to be figured out. She's saying I already figured her out. Wait a wave! Why do you say that? How do you know?"

"Our minds are connected remember… You know how we used to go to the dream plane?" she whispered. "We did that, but we were definitely in another plane. I think it was the psychic plane. We haven't been there in a while. Didn't it look different?"

"It did. Wait. So, you mean everything that happened was real? Our conversation and everything? Woo. I was going to ask you just to make sure. You know how that plane is."

"What you mean 'and everything'?" Chance was judging.

LOL. He has no idea we've done what he's implying many times before in multiple planes.

Duuuh. Let's try doing it in the metaphysical.

Ooo. Are you going to record? Let's make an ASMR video. Hehehe.

AH! OMG. You are so naughty but sure. You love to be on camera.

Don't try to do that. I know about you, Mr. Cameraman.

"Be quiet, Darth Vader," Iris laughed. *How she gon talk about his breather like that? Oof.*

Xenon kept smiling at Amethyst. "What's this? Is your confidence level increasing?" she laughed.

"Meet me at the grotto once we get back."

"Hey! Meter said she couldn't go up there yet because Zeus might strike her."

"Relax, sis. Mom knows I've been working on a forcefield. It's built from the same technology as the forcefields around the schools except stronger."

"Good because I have a feeling you're also on Zeus's hit list," said Amethyst.

"F*** Zeus," said Xenon.

"Period," Iris and Chance said simultaneously.

"I hate that I'm used to us jinxing each other," said Iris.

"Same."

"You're going to love the grotto, Sister. Plus, there is never anyone swimming underneath that area because it's considered a private part of the bas."

"Do you like the purple? I just thought I'd add a little something. You can turn the color off and on here. I programmed it so that if it isn't on before you come up here, it will turn on as soon as it senses you."

"How'd you know I was up here?"

"I sensed you."

"Are you turned on then?"

"Am I your forcefield?"

"We're each other's forcefield."

"Amethyst. Can I take you on a date?"

"Sure. That wasn't so hard was it?" she giggled. "Where?"

"It's a surprise. Are you free on Thursday?"

"I'm not doing anything after my training and lessons."

"Okay. I'll come get you after that."

"See you later, Shy Guy."

"Wait. You dropped your audio stars," he laughed. "You're always leaving things."

"Thanks. Chance is always there to pick up after me."

Clever.

Chapter 18: Bells & Whistles

DAY 13

"Hey, freak! What's wrong with your tail?"

"He's a mutt remember. Help me out... There's a better word for something like him."

"An abomination."

"Can you guys just leave me alone? I really don't want any trouble."

"Shut up, smooth tail. Come on boys! Let's get him!" He was terrified of what they'd do to him, so he swam as fast as he could wherever he could.

Amethyst was in her crystal cavern when she noticed a door she hadn't seen before. She wondered where it went. It turned out that it led to another part of the grotto up above. "Cool!" Amethyst strolled through the new part of the garden. The grotto was much bigger than she expected. It was actually an archipelago, but she decided to stay on the island. She loved how everything was so tropical but so Greek at the same time. "Welp... I'm officially f****** lost." She decided to sit down on the edge of what she thought was a rectangular pond and cracked open her snacks. She had brought some Tubberware from the surface with her just so she could transport her snacks. Amethyst was so stressed out because of everything that was going on, so naturally, she started singing to herself. The same song she always sang. Thetis's lullaby:

If I was a star, I would shine so bright.

Doesn't even matter if I'm big or small.

If I was a star, I would shine so bright.

It doesn't even matter if I'm big or not.

"You can't out swim us, mutt!"

They left him no choice. He swam upwards with all his might. "Look! He's swimming towards the surface! How far is he planning to go?!?!?"

"Come on! We have to catch him before he leaves the depths!"

"SHIT! We lost him. I hope the Nereids get him. Or even better… The humans."

The light was too intense for him at first. Once he got used to it, he realized it wasn't bad. It actually felt great. Now, he had another problem to worry about. He was now at risk. He sensed something coming towards him and panicked. He had no idea where to go. He wasn't familiar with his surroundings. Then heard someone singing. They sounded friendly. "Wait. Nereids don't sing. At least not like that. How is a Haliai singing an ancient Nereid lullaby? Speaking of that… I don't know why the Mer sing it. Anyway, maybe they're mixed like me!" He followed the sound hopefully until…

"Ahhh!!!" Amethyst screamed. "Who the hell are you?!?!?" He continued to gasp for oxygen through his gills. "Oh shit. You can't breathe." Then she noticed what he was doing. "Stop using your gills! You broke the surface. Use your nose or your mouth or both."

He did as she said and was a combination of in shock and amazed. "Thank you. Somehow, I can understand you, but I don't speak your language. Can you understand me? Can you understand Greek?"

"I'm sorry, I don't know what you're saying. I'm sorry. I'm still learning Greek, and I barely know sign language." She tried her best to say something in Greek. "What is your name?"

"Bellerophon but I go by Bella. You can call me Bella."

"Hi, Bella! I love your name. I'm Amethyst. What are you doing here? I thought this was a pond."

Bella did his best to explain using hand gestures. "[I] [Up] [Swim] [Scared] [3]"

"You swam up here because you were scared of the three things that were chasing you?" Bella nodded and clapped his hands with excitement. He wasn't expecting her to get it so quickly. "Well, don't worry. I won't hurt you," she smiled. Amethyst loved how he was sniffing the air like a little puppy. "Do you want some?" She offered him some of her Skittles. "Are you hungry? I'll ask my sister to bring some food for you." Bella shook his head. Amethyst kept walking. "It's no trouble."

He swam to the edge of the pond and crawled out of the water, onto the grass. "Ne pas! Ne pas!" he grabbed her leg. "S'il vous plaît ne pas. Ne pas!" he cried.

"Stop! That hurts! Let go of me. I'll stay. You speak French too? That's cool, but I don't know French either. You gave break a leg a whole new meaning." *I love her psychic ass. Look up the phrase. She actually knows what it means.* Amethyst turned around and understood why he grabbed her. "Ohhh. I see… Here, I'll help you get back in the water. You're really heavy." Bella had the saddest look on his face. Then he hid his face halfway under. "Oh, come here you."

"[You] [Two fingers] [Tips of fingers] [Yes] [No]"

"You want to see my feet? Sure," she laughed. "Eeeeeep!" Bella jerked back. "Sorry… I'm ticklish. Can I see your tail?" Bella dove and waved his tail at her. "Oh, okay. So you're a smart ass," she laughed. "Can I touch your tail?" He smiled and pulled himself onto the ledge. "Whoa! Your tail is beautiful. I like how it has a faint green shimmer over the grey. Are you a mermaid?" He shook his hand. "Part mermaid?" He nodded. "Mermaid and Nereid?" He nodded again and protected himself as if she were going to hit him. She could tell he had suffered physical abuse. "Yay!!! I've always wanted to meet a mermaid! And I'm glad that I finally met another Nereid! One that isn't trying to kill me!" She hugged him, and Bella planted a friendly kiss on her cheek. He was so happy that he did a series of jumps, leaps, and twirls. "Wow. You're huge."

"[You] [Tiny]," he laughed.

"Ha. Ha. Ha. I guess I am," she smiled. He swam up to her and grabbed her leg again. This time to examine it. "Ouch! I get that you have a lot of extra strength since you live in the depths but check this out... Be gentle with me. I'm not one of your little abnormally strong friends."

"[Me] [No] [You and me]"

"You don't have any friends? I used to have one friend, but now I have more. They can be your friends too. They're awesome."

"Amethyst really likes being up there," Iris told the squad. "I want to be nosy." She pulled up the live bas security camera footage. "Who the f*** is that?!?!? Why is he grabbing her leg?!?!?" Now they were all looking at her screen.

"So, what's the next move?" Chance asked.

"Let's f****** go," Iris said.

"He's probably a Nereid. Time to go kick some ass!" Reign cheered. "We should swim right under him!"

"I'm coming, Moon Jelly."

"N**** you mean we..."

"Bella, what's wrong? Why do you look scared?" asked Amethyst.

"[Me] [Cut] [Tail]"

"Someone's going to cut your tail off? Is that what people do to mermaid Nereids?" He nodded.

Iris swam up first. The squad followed behind her. She put Bella in a choke hold and said, "Were you trying to take her? I won't f****** let you."

"Ahhhh! STOP!" Amethyst cried. "He's my friend! He's not trying to hurt me. Let him go!!! He's not evil. Let him go!!!"

"Alright. What's your name?" Iris asked. "And don't move."

"Bellerophon."

"You're a Nereid. What are you doing here?" Iris asked.

"I-I was swimming away from some bullies. I came from the depths. I'm also Mer."

"You're a mutt?!?!?" Reign shouted.

"Don't call him that!" Amethyst yelled. "What's wrong with being ethnically diverse?"

"Yeah. What's wrong with that?" Her comment really cut Chance deep. Iris and Xenon didn't like her comment either.

"I didn't mean you, Freckles."

"It's the same thing. If he's a mutt, I'm a mutt."

"I-I'm sorry. I was told it was wrong. I shouldn't think like that."

Amethyst got in the water and swam next to Bella. "I'm sorry. I promise you they're nice. They just thought I was in danger."

"Amethyst was kind to me. We are friends. She's my only friend," he began to cry. "What's happening to me?" This was his first time experiencing tears.

"Great. Now we have another crier in the group," Chance said.

"Chance!" Amethyst shouted.

Xenon smacked him upside the head. "Ahhh. N**** did you just POP me? What the f*** was that for?" He looked at Amethyst. "Oh, okay… So, you didn't just see that?" Xenon thought it was funny how Chance flinched at him.

After they finished introducing themselves, Iris said, "You can stay here. No one comes over here but us. I have to tell Thetis though."

"Yes!" he clapped. "Thank you, Your Highness. Please, take me to her! I heard she accepts people like me." Bella recognized Iris's voice.

"She does. She accepts everyone that isn't evil. Follow us."

"Hello, Your Majesty. I am Bellerophon, son of Bima," he bowed. "It is an honor to be in your presence."

"Welcome, Bellerophon. I will show you your room while we chat. Come." When they came back, Thetis said, "Oh, one more thing. You are free to go out. Don't feel like you have to stay inside."

"How? He has a tail…" said Reign.

"There are plenty of Haliai-Nereids in the basileia, but they often do whatever they can to stay hidden. Everyone is welcome, but you know how Oceanids have sticky eyes. Some of them may have inappropriate thoughts, but most people have none at all."

"I knew it!!!" Amethyst was proud. "Is there a program or something? Like for self-love and education and stuff? They go to school, right?"

"There is but they all choose to be homeschooled."

"I bet Sister could convince them to go to school," Iris smiled. "I'm confident she could have convinced me."

"I agree. She inherited the gift of persuasion from Peitho, but she doesn't even use it. She doesn't need to. You and I are more of the data and evidence type aren't we, Sunshine?"

"That we are," she laughed. "Let us know if there is anything we can do to make you feel more comfortable, Bellerophon. Also, call me Iris. No need to be so formal."

"Thank you. [Question] [Counting] [Iris] [Amethyst], Amethyst?"

"I don't know. That's a tiny decimal. Chance, it's alright you don't have to calculate that. Aren't we like less than 5 hours apart?"

"Yes. Huuum. Let's see. I think you two are three hours apart. Jeremy, honey! When were the kids born?"

"Iris was born on Wednesday, December 1, 1999 at 3:39 AM and Amethyst was born on Wednesday, December 1, 1999 at 6:39 AM. Well... In ocean time. I don't know what time zone we were in though. Somewhere in between here and Japan." Jeremy swam in from his room and said, "Oh. Hey. I'm Jeremy. I went grocery shopping earlier so help yourselves."

"Um... Okay, so two things... How the hell did y'all understand those hand gestures? Oh, never mind. That's an Oceanid thing. Anyways, how the hell can you not see that they're twins?"

"I was thinking the same thing," Reign said.

"Bella's blind, Chance," said Amethyst.

He nodded. "[Question] [You] [Mind]"

"How'd I know? Well... You obviously couldn't see that you had broken the surface. You were still trying to use your gills! You also didn't think I was Iris. She's the basilissa! Everyone knows who she is. You didn't recognize Xenon until he spoke so... Oh yeah... And I stuck my tongue out at you and you didn't react," she giggled. "I did it three times just to be sure."

Bella smiled and stuck his tongue out at her. "You are of the most profound beauty."

"She knows," said Xenon. "He said you're beautiful."

"Thank you," she smiled. "You're so sweet."

"N**** you can't even see her."

Iris translated for them. "He said, 'Beauty comes from deep down, but I know her smile is on the surface.'"

"HOW?" Chance smiled.

"He said, 'Because she laughs at everything.' That she does," Iris agreed.

"That's why I call her Little Scallop," said Xenon.

"He said, 'She is just like a scallop… Tiny and giggly…' Now he asks, 'Do you think we can be friends?'"

They all said yes, of course! Then Amethyst said, "Chance has asthma, Iris is deaf, Reign has ADHD, Xenon's dyslexic, and we're all labeled mentally ill! Welcome to the club!" Amethyst laughed. Thetis thought it was funny too, but Jeremy didn't agree. *LMAO. F****** Jeremy.*

"Look, Bella. I'm sorry but you have to come out," said Xenon. "Hey! Don't mess up my eyeliner! The bas is going to be completely drained soon. We have to clean it. Also, we need to go to the store and get you a phone." *Yes, a phone. Their society isn't exclusive. Note: The Mer aren't very techy.*

"No way!" Bella was terrified. "I would very much prefer to stay in here."

"Your tail is going to dry out, and you won't be able to move," Iris said.

"Where's Amethyst? Can't I go with her?" said Bella.

"She's with Thetis taking cultural lessons on how to be basilissa or some shit," said Chance.

"You won't hurt me? What if someone tries to hurt me?"

"Are you going to try to rape anyone?" Iris asked.

"No. I would never commit such a horrid crime."

"Okay then," said Iris. "We won't hurt you, and we'll take care of whoever tries to hurt you, but no one will try to hurt you up here."

"But I'm part Nereid."

"That's not the problem," Xenon said. "We only don't like Nereids who try to hurt people. We don't like anyone who tries to hurt people... Nereid or not."

"If it helps, we didn't even know you had a tail. We just saw a stranger grabbing Amethyst's leg," Iris added. "Come on. You can help us plan her coronation."

"Thetis." Amethyst was very uncomfortable. "Something isn't right."

"What's not right? Do you feel sick?" Thetis checked her forehead.

"No. I don't know... Can we go back to the others? I'm worried about them."

Thetis read her expressions, and now she was worried. "Climb onto my back."

"This little island is our secret meeting spot," Iris said. "We need to choose who is going to perform from the finalists. After that, we'll use the rest of the days for rehearsals and set up. Then we have to prepare ourselves. We are almost there people!"

"I just have to finish helping the squid with their choreography," said Xenon.

Bella was surprised. "You're going to the depths? How? I should go with you."

"It's alright. I glow just like my friends. Plus, I don't want to have to hurt anyone. I don't like bullies." Bella wasn't sure how Xenon meant that.

"Does everyone know what they're performing? It needs to be on the itinerary."

They all nodded except for Xenon. "I'm not sure if I should dance."

"Why not? Ame is going to f****** love that. You said that you were going to sing to her later this week. She would rather have you sing to her privately. She likes to have some things all to herself. Plus, she thinks dancing is more attractive than singing."

"You're right. I'm going to do a cultural dance. Wait until you see! Uh!" He got a chill. "I'm just so nervous."

"Blue, you're the best dancer in all the realms," Iris smiled.

"You all are performing also? That's really cool," said Bella.

"Yep. At least 5 of the basilissa's friends must perform after the others. We're literally each other's only friends." Iris realized something. "SHIT! We need one more. There's only 4 of us. We could ask Alpha. He'd be more than willing."

"Absolutely the f*** not. That lassa will not be performing at my Moon Jelly's coronation. Especially as one of the main 5. He can sink to the bottom of the sea floor for all I care."

"Then who!" Iris asked.

"Bella's our new friend. He can perform if he wants to. Please tell me you can do something," Xenon said.

"Oh, my goddess!!! I'd be honored!!!" Bella did a series of leaps in the water. Reign was jealous. "I can sing and play the keyboard!" He gave them a little taste of his singing skills.

"Whoa! Okay, that's perfect. She'll love you. Hell, everyone will love you!" Xenon cried. He was so moved by his singing. They all were.

"Dude, that was amazing. I thought you didn't know English."

"Thanks you all. No one has ever told me that except my mom. I usually just sing in my lair. I don't know English. I just know a lot of songs in English. I only know what I'm saying because I had one of my exes translate some of them for me," he smiled.

"That was exceptional even for a Mer." Iris was impressed. "I have a feeling we are all going to impress the panel! Now that you're here we could probably start a band," she joked. "You can't tell her about any of this."

"I won't. What song should I sing?"

"Maybe a surface song… What are some of your favorites?" asked Xenon.

"I love anything by Mariah Carey, Prince… OH! I love the song "Chandelier" by Sia."

Xenon and Iris squealed with excitement as they slapped their hands together. "I hate it when they do that," Reign rolled her eyes.

"Shhh. Can y'all f****** girls be quiet," Chance laughed. "Ame loves that song too."

"Shut up," said Iris. "This. Is. Going. To. Be. Epic."

"Moon Jelly has no idea what's coming for her," Xenon smiled.

"METER?" They were all shook because Thetis showed up. "What's wrong? What are you doing here? Is something wrong?"

"Hide anything about the coronation. Amethyst is with me. She said she is worried about you all."

"Shit guys. Now we have to get a new island. But more importantly what the hell is going on?" Iris asked herself.

Bella swam around Amethyst playfully as she rose to the surface. Then he hugged her because she was his first and is his favorite friend. They all waited there in silence for something to happen, but nothing happened. "Dude, can you stop hiding under the water like that? I can only see your eyes. That's creepy as hell," said Chance.

"I guess I was wrong." Amethyst was so embarrassed. She and Thetis went for a walk. As soon as they were a good distance away from the squad, she heard something. So did Bella. It didn't take long for her to realize what it was, and she knew exactly who it was aimed at. She ran as fast as she could back to the squad. Xenon was laying down on the sand. When she stood over him ready to handle whatever was coming their way, he sat up. At this moment everyone knew what was headed towards them. In fact, it was headed straight for Xenon's face. Amethyst did a one-armed back bend over his body and caught the lightning bolt just in time. For a short moment, Atoz made eye contact with each other and couldn't help but smile. Then, Amethyst slung herself forward Slinky style and threw the lightning bolt right back where it came from. It was an amazing sight. 11 out of 10. "Oh, hell no!" she yelled at the sky. "Now you want to attack my friends? Did you really just attack my Moon Beam? You better leave him the f*** alone before I show you how I really feel b****!" Then she turned to the squad. "Let me calm my little ass down. I can't fight no damn god."

"Holy shit, Ame. Where the f*** did those godly reflexes come from?" Chance laughed. "How did you move so fast? I mean... I know but still... Damn."

"HOW?" Reign couldn't believe what she saw.

"OMG yaaasssss, Sister. OMG you're such a bad b****!"

"That was spectacular!" Bella clapped. "I don't know the entirety of what's going on, but I adore it. I absolutely adore it. I know it has something to do with Zeus."

Thetis squeezed Xenon and Amethyst as tightly as she could. "I'm so glad you two are okay. I can't lose another child," she cried. She checked Xenon's face and Amethyst's hand. "You're all okay right? Okay. From now on, you are not allowed to go on land during the day. You may go at twilight or if AND only if Selene is completely visible." She looked at her phone. "Hera said that the lightning bolt went right back into his hand. She's proud of you, and she said she's sorry. She went to the bathroom, and he decided to make his next move. Speaking of bolts... Now, you and Hera are the only two people who can touch Zeus's lightning bolts. Bella, we have a lot to talk about." She could tell Atoz was holding back because she was there. "Gather your things. We'll talk over dinner at Shelly's," she smiled.

As soon as she left, Amethyst jumped on top of Xenon. They started making out on the edge of the ocean. Bella swam up next to them and just watched. "You're my hero," Xenon told her. "My psychic hero."

"I won't let you die on me. You can't die on me. Hella nah. F*** that."

"Bella! Dude! Stop that," Chance got up and shooed him like someone's auntie shooing kids off her lawn. All he was missing were the rollers, and his pink slippers were in his room on the surface. "Weird ass. You can't even see them." He turned to Iris. "How the f*** can they turn a near-death experience into this? What the f***?"

"Because they care about each other duh. And they obviously find danger erotic." Iris's response made Chance's nose bleed. Bella could smell the blood. He was so fascinated. This time Reign took care of his nose bleed.

Amethyst grabbed Xenon's arms and pinned them to the sand. That made his cheeks turn blue. She acted like she was going to give him another kiss and then got up. "Really?" he laughed. "How you gonna do me like that? I can't even breathe. I feel like Chance. I almost died, you saved me, and then you left me with a heart attack. I love it. This is proof that lightning really can strike twice."

"Ooooo! I know. We should all order each other's food," Iris suggested. "It's sort of like a bonding exercise! It'll be fun!" she giggled. "Don't worry, Bella. I know what you want. I can see the future. This will be entertaining for you. We have a lot to explain, so let's hurry up and order the food."

Iris, Reign, and Bella were mature about the activity, but the other three…

"Chance will have the tuna bowl without the yogurt, but can you add extra flaxseeds," Amethyst laughed. She could barely tell the waiter the order. "Like… A lot of them. Go crazy."

"The basilissa will have the salmon symphony plate with a whole stack of moon patties," Xenon smiled. "Just plain moon patties."

"His Highness will have the queen's rack of octopus legs with an extra-large side of kelp." When the waiter was gone, Chance turned to Xenon and whispered, "Oh yeah! Yo ass finna be shiiiiitin'!'"

"LOL. All three of us are. I knew you were going to order me moon patties. That's cold."

"No, what's cold is you ordering me tuna with EXTRA flaxseeds. Then you told the lil n**** to go crazy with it."

"Whatever. You know how bad of a combo octopus legs and kelp is. That's vicious."

"This is why I'm not having children," said Iris.

"What are you doing?" Reign asked.

"We're purposely trying to set each other up for success," Amethyst explained.

"Success?" Reign asked.

Atoz burst into laughter so Chance had to tell her. He mouthed the words, "That's code for shitting."

"Why would you order something you don't want?" Iris didn't understand.

"We do want that." Amethyst could barely get the words out. "That's why we call it success."

Thetis and Bella were quietly chuckling. "One time your mother slipped some laxative into my drink as one of her little pranks," Jeremy shook his head. He was obviously still salty.

"We've been over this, Jeremy," Thetis laughed. "It was a placebo. I told you it was a laxative to see what would happen."

"KABOOM!" said Amethyst.

"The mind is a powerful thing huh, Germie?" Iris laughed.

After they caught Bella up on all the details he smiled and said, "I'm intrigued. I'm always getting myself into trouble."

Once again, Iris's children she doesn't want started laughing. They were triggered by the word 'trouble'. Amethyst had recently informed them what 'trouble' meant when she said it. Bella just smiled and shook his head. "Meter, is Bella Agathos or Skotos?"

"Let's ask the scallops what they think."

"LOL. He's definitely Agathos," said Amethyst. "But I can see him doing a few things." They all agreed. Thetis told them they were right.

"Phew! I don't know much about natures, but I remember something about Skotos being of the darkness. I don't think I could handle the darkness," said Bella. "I don't even wanna know."

"Would you like to see Nadia today?" Thetis asked Bella.

"My aunt?!?!? She's here? How?"

"His theia is Nadia from the store?" Xenon asked.

"What happened to her?" Amethyst was concerned.

"Moonshine, that's private information."

"It's alright. Go ahead. I don't know myself. My mom won't talk about it. I trust them even though most of them tried to assassinate me at first," he smiled.

"Nadia was there when your mother was attacked. She tried to protect your mother, but the Nereid ended up damaging her tail to the point where she could barely swim. There was no way she could survive in the depths without her tail. Your mother is so strong. So is Nadia. After the attack, Bima swam Nadia all the way here. She was in so much pain, and she was losing so much blood. Nadia told Bima that she would rather not have a tail than leave her. At the time, our surgeons weren't familiar with operating on Mer, so I performed the operation myself. It was so hard for me to do because I know what some people do to Mer. We made her a prosthetic. I used her scales to make it as realistic as I could. We are much more advanced now, but she says she likes the prosthetic she has. Nadia is also one of our lead warriors. Your mother and I keep in touch. Oh, and I had a sperm whale send a message to her to let her know you're okay."

"Why didn't she stay? I truly hate it down there."

"She wanted you to grow up with your culture."

"So... My mom's job... She sends people here?"

"Yes. She must keep her work classified because people talk. If the wrong Nereid finds out, they will tell Zeus, and who knows what he'd do. All Oceanids lived in harmony until Zeus interfered."

"Why would Nadia want to see me and be reminded of the attack? Won't I remind her of the grotesque creature I am?"

"Nonsense. You look just like your mother and Nadia always wanted a child."

"Bella, guess what? I was flirting with your aunt," Amethyst giggled. "She looks so young. I know this doesn't correlate to maturity or life stage or whatever, but how old is everyone in time years and not life stage years? Xe, you don't have to answer that."

"I'm 23," said Bella.

"I'm 49," said Reign.

Jeremy said, "I just know I'm like half your mother's age."

"Woo. Ooo, child," Thetis smiled. "I lost track a while ago. I'm thousands of years old."

"Damn y'all hella old. Except for you, Auntie. You're like wine that only gets better with time."

"Aye!" Jeremy said. "Cut that out. What did I tell you about that?"

"Chill, Dad," Chance laughed. "It was just a compliment."

"Just a compliment my ass."

As soon as they left Shelly's, the least mature members of the squad did what they do best. "I call Xenon's bathroom!" Amethyst yelled.

"I call Chance's!" Xenon shouted.

"I see what you did there, Ame. You just want him to shit in my room. That's okay because I call your bathroom. No one's worse than me."

"We'll see… It's so worth it," she smiled. "This is payback for all the times you farted on me."

They couldn't stop laughing and talking shit on the way to each other's bathrooms. Once they were finished planting bombs in each other's rooms, they reunited with the squad and told everyone all about it. "It's good you're comfortable with pooping. That means you're healthy," said Iris.

"Shit… Does it?" Amethyst giggled.

"I don't know about that," Chance laughed. "And we weren't pooping. We were shitting. There's a difference."

"Shitting takes about an hour at the very least," Amethyst said.

"Yeah," Xenon agreed. "And you can't go in until about 30 to 45 minutes after."

"Why do you all like to shit so much?" Reign asked.

"Because you get a special shitsation!" Amethyst said.

"The adrenaline!" Xenon smiled.

"The shitisfaction!" Chance added.

"It's hilarious how you guys are actually serious," Iris laughed.

"They're dedicated shitologists," Bella laughed with them.

"Red, what time is it?" Xenon smiled.

"Alright, where the hell is my phone? You took it didn't you? SHIT! It's in my room, isn't it? Now I got to go in there. Well planned."

"Holy shit! Wait!" Amethyst said. "We must pray for him. Lord, watch over Chancellor Gregory Adamson, the third as he embarks on this special journey to shit creek to retrieve his cellular device. Amen."

"Sister, you are terrible." They were all dying laughing.

"He could have just asked one of us and waited," said Reign. "He wanted to go in there."

"Awh! F*** Blue!" Chance was not expecting that. "That's foul. You're one nasty ass n****. I must say. We are definitely tied."

"Hey, Bella. You don't talk much do you?" Amethyst asked. He shook his head. "I heard you humming earlier. Is it true Mer love to sing?"

"Only some of us. There are some Mer who can't sing at all," he laughed. "We also love to dance. I'm not an excellent dancer though."

"So then why do people say that?"

"Because Triton is the father of some of the first Mer, and he's known for having a remarkable voice. All Mer used to be called Tritones, but then we learned that most of the original Mer were sculpted by Thalassa or Pontos themselves."

"Who's Pontos? That's the primordial sea god, right? Wait. Never mind. That's Thalassa, right?" Chance asked.

"Thalassa is Pontos. Their pronouns are she or he. They have a female and male form and are fluid between the two."

"Oh, okay. Do you know about the term mermies?" Amethyst asked.

"Sister!"

"What?"

"Yes. That's a fair term," he smiled. "We call Haliai crybabies."

"How do you get around?" asked Amethyst.

"I know my surroundings, and there isn't much to swim into in the depths. Plus, I can hear and detect motion very well. I have to hold onto Reign because I'm not familiar with this place. There is also a lot more motion, noises, and objects up here."

"Don't you want to know what we look like?" Amethyst asked.

"I was scared to ask. I didn't want to be creepy."

"That's not creepy. Besides, we're all weird." Amethyst let Bella touch her face, and the others followed. "Chance has spicy dots on his face!" she laughed.

"Your face matches your beauty," Bella told Amethyst. "Your mate is devilishly handsome. All of you are good looking. I like the mean one. Also, I love your accent, Amethyst. I've never heard one like yours before. It's so warm and has so much power."

"I'm not mean!!!" said Chance.

"He just needs to be tamed," Reign smiled.

Chance liked her little comment. "Oh yeah? You talkin' shit? Are you my ringleader?"

"I can be."

"So, what do you see?" asked Chance. "Do you see blackness or what?"

"I don't understand what you mean. I've been blind since birth."

"Blind people seeing blackness is a common misconception on the surface," Amethyst explained. "There are different types of blindnesses. Is that a word?"

"Yes. That's a word," he smiled. "I see nothing."

"Cover one of your eyes and try to see through that eye," Amethyst told Chance.

"I wish I could see myself and my mom."

"I have lots of mirrors, but Amethyst says I still can't see myself. I'm sorry. I know that's not the same thing."

"Don't apologize. You're only trying to comfort me."

"I have an idea!" Amethyst gleamed. "Bella. Do you know what chocolate tastes like?" He nodded. "Now imagine it too hot to put in your mouth. Then ice cold. Now imagine what it tastes like when it's just right. Now add some copper. Then add a spicy flavor. That's the color of your skin. It's a deep brownish black with a red undertone."

"Bella, what's your ethnic background? My mom's from Libya, and my father's from Germany. I was born in England and raised in America."

"Let's zoom out. Generally, I'm Melanesian, Polynesian, Southeast Asian, and West Indian," he smiled. "What about the birthmark on my back? My mom describes it as onyx black." *BTW it's not a big ass mole looking thing. It's flat and smooth. It's a section of darker skin.*

"It is. Ummm... Xe, help me out. What's something that tastes black? I was going to say bones or crystals, but I don't think he's tried that. Have you? What's something in the ocean?"

"Oh, I know! Marine clay!"

"Good one! That's what black tastes like."

"And my hair? Mom says it's blond."

"It is. You know how bananas smell and taste?" asked Amethyst. "It's like that. It's a warm banana bread color."

Bella was loving this game. "And my eyes? Mom says they're sea green."

"You know what kelp smells like right?" said Xenon. "That's the color."

"You're very handsome," Amethyst said. "Right, Xe? And look at those muscles. Damn. What are you eating? OMG! Babe. Look at his f****** jaw. WTF."

"OMG! IKR! Yaaasssss," Xenon snapped. "Daaamn."

Bella said thank you, but he didn't believe her. "Trust me. Ame wouldn't have told you that if you weren't," said Chance.

"So, my tail is like kelp?"

"Not quite," said Xenon. "Mix sand and clay together."

"Then add a little piece of kelp," said Amethyst.

"That one's difficult. I've never tasted sand." Atoz prepared him a mixture of the three and placed some on his tongue. "Interesting."

"And it glitters a little," said Xenon. "Imagine the feeling you had when you left the depths except in teeny tiny dots."

"You can't eat this but imagine this." Amethyst put some glitter in his hand and on his tongue. "Did that sort of add some detail?"

"It's much better than having no description I can understand. I'll use my imagination. I read a lot. Do you think you could do the same thing for some other words?"

"Sure!" said Atoz.

Thetis swam in and said, "Bella, your mother said you may spend the night. She said you can come back as often as you like."

"She isn't mad at me?"

"She's glad you're safe and that you met friends and Nadia."

"We became friends quickly," Bella smiled. "It usually takes longer in books. I feel like I know all of you from a past life maybe."

"That's what we said about each other! That's because you're the green wavelength," Amethyst gleamed. "There's supposed to be two or three more, but this is great! Our group still has gaps, but we aren't necessarily incomplete."

"So, I'm officially in the squad?"

"You're in the squad!!!" They all tackled each other.

"So, let's see… Who do we have here?" Chance said. "We got Super Vision and Mega Ear. LOL. Y'all make a good team. We are one handicapped ass squad," he laughed. "Blue sticker ass squad."

He always talking shit.

Watch this.

"Chance has a thing for mermaids," said Amethyst. "He has a mermaid fantasy."

"AME! What the f***?!?!?"

"What's your little fantasy about?" Reign was disgusted. "The prissy, helpless mermaid that needs to be rescued?"

"No. It's about the overpowering mermaid that drags me down into her world."

"Oh," she smiled. "I stand corrected, Freckles."

Bella started swimming around him. "Uhhh. What are you doing, dude?" Chance asked. He wrapped his tail around him and just looked at him. "Um… You gotta stop that. Why you pointing to your cheek? N**** I ain't finna kiss you."

"You didn't have to push him Chance!" Amethyst yelled.

"It was not that big of a deal, Toxic Masculinity," said Xenon.

"Next time I'm smacking the shit out of you, little boy," Bella told him. "You're exceedingly rude."

"It's not that kind of kiss, Chance. Mer kiss each other's cheeks as a friendly gesture. It's just like how Haliai gently rub their lips and noses together. Think of it like a hug."

"That's weird."

"How is pressing your body against someone less weird?" Reign asked.

"Good point," said Chance. "My bad." He made his way over to Bella. Iris had a plan. As soon as they got close, she called Bella, so he'd look towards her. "Ah! What the hell, Iris?"

The squad couldn't stop laughing. "Relax, Little Man. It was just a peck."

"Judging your reaction, it didn't seem like something all that new for you," Iris laughed.

"You and your little pranks… You're such a bully," said Chance.

"Look who's talking."

"I hate you."

"I hate you more."

"Shut up. You know y'all love each other," Amethyst smiled.

"He's my long-lost younger step-brother."

"No! You're my long-lost little step-sister!"

"Rigggght," Iris said sarcastically. "Anyways, I was thinking we should all have a group circle tomorrow."

"Like to talk about our feelings and stuff?" asked Reign.

"I'm down," said Chance.

"I'm in!" Bella clapped.

"It sounds lame but sure," said Reign.

"Blue? Sister?"

"LOL," said Amethyst.

Xenon laughed too. "I don't know."

"I don't think y'all want to hear about our shit, but f*** it," said Amethyst.

"Yay! Blue?"

"I guess."

"Can y'all whistle underwater?" asked Amethyst. "What does that sound like? What about yelling?"

Chapter 19: Tea Party

DAY 14

"Hello everyone. Let's have our circle in the plant room," said Iris.

"This is beautiful!" said Amethyst. "Looks like a Disneyworld land."

"They smell heavenly," Bella added. Something about what he said made her psychic senses tingle.

"Look how Wonder Womxn and Stevie Wonder sit the same," Chance laughed. This time Bella really did smack him with his tail, and Reign punched him in the arm.

"Who wants to go first?" asked Iris.

"Here. This can be our talking piece." Chance tossed Iris one of his Hello Kitty plush toys.

No one volunteered. "Okay... So, we need an icebreaker," Iris smiled. "Let's go around and say our sexuality, gender, and pronouns. We'll just go in order. Whoever starts chooses the direction."

"That's one hell of an icebreaker," Amethyst laughed. "Watch us all be queer."

"For real," Xenon smiled. "I have a feeling no one is straight."

"That's why we're in a circle." They all laughed at Amethyst's little comment.

Ima just drop hints for that second part.

Me too. They can figure it out.

Right. Hell, they were going to find out eventually.

Haha. True…

"Oh, my goddess," Reign rolled her eyes. "I'll start the icebreaker. I'm attracted to men, but I guess you could say I'm a little queer. I'm a girl, and my pronouns are she/her. There."

"I'm very gay," Bella smiled. "I'm a boy and my pronouns are he/him, but I won't kill you if you use feminine words."

"Alright so…" Chance was ready.

"Here we go," said Amethyst.

"You don't have the talking piece, do you? No. So shut the f*** up. Okay so here's the deal. I'm heterosexual, but my romantic orientation is different. I'm biromantic. Like… I love dudes too. I'll be with dude but we ain't f******. Hell no. There will be absolutely none of that if I'm supposed to be bottoming the whole time. I don't f*** with dicks. Sure don't. Well… Oral's fine. No anal though. I do not like that shit. My ex, Bailey, was my one and done. Might have been twice," he smiled. "Anyone with a non-penis can slide through. Oral included." Chance flicked his tongue. "Yummy. You'd have to be the finest n**** ever, and I mean ever AND have hella money if you wanna get me to do that shit again. Oh yeah, and I'm a boy and my pronouns are he/him."

I'm sensing some denial.

LOL.

Iris was next. "Wow. Thanks for that, Chance. I appreciate your honesty," she smiled. "I'm asexual and biromantic. I'm a girl and my pronouns are she/her."

"Welp. I'm bisexual," Amethyst shot her finger guns. "I make good puns. My pronouns are she/her, but they/them is cool too. It's whatever," she blushed. "Sometimes I feel purple, sometimes I feel grey. Less often, I feel pink. Every now and then, I feel blue. The grey can be mixed in, but I'm always of the overall feminine energy. If you know, you know."

"Ooo! Ooo! I know a good pun!" Reign twirled. "If someone on the surface asked me 'rain or shine' I would say this: Rain or shine? Both. Hehehe… Get it? Because my name's Reign and I shine!" she giggled.

"I'm deeead," Amethyst laughed. She saw Chance try to hide his smile. Xenon had an attitude because it was his turn and Reign interjected.

"No, gemmie. Just no," Iris shook her head. "Sorry, Blue. Go ahead, hun."

"We're basically the same except flipped," said Xenon. "I'm bisexual. I'm also demisexual," he blushed. "My pronouns are he/him, but sometimes I prefer they/them. I could be a 1, 2, 3, 4, or 5. I'm rarely a 1, and I'm of the masculine energy. That's it, that's all."

"Why do you two have to be so cryptic? You two are too cute," Iris smiled. "They're saying they're fluid," she explained to Reign and Bella. "Now that we've established that, we should all go to Agapi together. It's not this month, but it's coming up."

"LOL. All we're missing is a lesbian, a transgender person, a… Wait! What's that? Is it a festival?" asked Amethyst.

"Yep. It's a festival celebrating love. The second day celebrates self-love in particular. We added it to remind ourselves how fortunate we are to be able to be who we are and still be safe and happy."

"Oh shit. Liiiiit," said Chance.

"What exactly is it like on the surface?" asked Reign.

"If you don't fit their standards you're f*****," said Amethyst. "It's obvious that we all don't fit sexuality wise, but none of us would fit according to gender rules either. They'd say y'all are gender non-conforming, so you can only imagine what they'd do to me and Xe. Plus, none of us are white."

"Iris could probably pass with gender," said Chance.

"She ain't safe either. I've been in her closet. No pun intended," said Amethyst. "She's got more than just dresses." Then, she and Chance gave them the full rundown on the surface.

"Wow. That's is like a thousand times worse than the sky realm," Bella said.

"The topic for today is secrets," said Iris. "Your deepest, darkest secrets. I'll start. Like Amethyst mentioned, I have more than dresses in my closet. In addition to my obsessive love for dresses, I love dressing dapper. I don't because I feel like our people have a certain idea of what they want their basilissa, or basilis, to be like regarding clothing even though I doubt that's the case. Of course, it has nothing to do with gender or anything. It's about image. It's all in my head. I'm the pretty pink type, and I looove dresses OMG yaaasssss, but I don't always feel like wearing a f****** dress. Then you showed up, Sister. Now I'm slowly gaining the courage to wear what the f*** I want to wear whether it is a dress or not. Now, for the dark stuff. I have an on-going history of self-abuse. I know that I can never be f****** perfect, and even though I try, I always f****** fail. That's why I often think about how much I f****** hate myself. I have scars from cutting myself. See." Iris shapeshifted to show them what her legs and arms really looks like. "Meter doesn't know that I still do it. I really think I deserve it. Everything about me is ugly," she cried.

The squad did their best to comfort her. "Oh, sister. You know I wish there was something I could do to make you not feel that way," said Xenon.

Iris passed the talking piece to Chance. "Well, I already told you all about the drugs, my abusive father, and shit. I was f***** up. The reason why I was held at the psych ward was because they said I was too feminine to be a boy. Like… What the f*** does that even mean? I don't consider myself feminine. I'm obviously pretty f****** masculine. It was probably about my clothes. It's not my fault all the pink shit in the girls' section. But other than that, I dress like your average skater dude. Anyways, the law changed. By the way, you'd think I'd be in there for my anger issues but no… Blue, you remember that skeleton in my closet? It is real. People get married super young on the surface. One day I saw this young Man beating his wife through the window while I was driving home. I was so angry, but Ame was in the car with me, so I was in dad mode. Ame called the police. We waited for them to come. By that time, the young womxn had managed to free herself and she drove away. I was still so angry. I got Ame home and neither of us could sleep. Then something came over me. Honestly, I barely remember anything. It was dark out. I remember speeding in my car. I drove somewhere and came back with a Man in my passenger seat. We were listening to hip-hop or rap or something. Then we were on some beach. I was clean then. There were no drugs involved. I felt so..." Chance began to hyperventilate. "So... Liberated. It was amazing." Ame snapped him out of his trance. "I woke up at home. Then me and Ame found this skeleton on the shore and brought it back to the house. It keep it in tip-top shape. Ame, can you fill in the gaps?"

"All I know is that you seemed to be starting your hypomanic phase. Actually... Scratch that. You were starting your manic phase. Honestly, that shit wasn't bipolar disorder. Your body temperature was warmer than usual. It was still increasing when you left. Same thing with your skin. You looked like you were going to burst or something, but you seemed okay. You said you were going on a joyride. Honestly, you were giving me major Joker vibes. I tried to stop you but then you said that you had to do it. Like... You really meant it, so I let you go. It sounded like a life or death situation. When you came back, you had blood all over you, so I cleaned it up. It's a good thing we were home alone. You've done the same thing before multiple times, but this time it was different. Now that I think about it... It seemed like it was getting worse and worse as you got older."

"That's why I don't drive anymore. I think I killed the guy who was beating his wife. I don't know how only his skeleton was left. It had to be me. They said he was missing but... Everything felt like a dream."

"Damn," said Reign. "I don't really know what to say, but justice was served. Besides, in order to be that angry, you have to have a caring heart. I'll go next. Speaking of justice, I sort of killed that Man that was fighting you. Remember the kop? Anyways, my mom was a great person, but my dad was abusive. Physically and mentally. I was much younger. I was always physically strong, but I was always weak mentally. I couldn't even protect her," she began to cry. "She got cancer, and she was one of those people who didn't like going to a physician. She had lung cancer. We didn't have much money because my dad had bad spending habits. He didn't love her. I'm sure he was seeing someone else. He didn't even care about her. I got a job as a hitwomxn. I'd kill people I didn't know anything about for money for my mom's treatment. I'd shoot poison darts at them.

I wasn't thinking. I was also under a contract. After the contract was up, I never went back. The cancer progressed so quickly. It was terrible. She was miserable. I told her she didn't have to keep fighting for me, but she insisted. She's just like me. Right before she died, she told me about where she found me as a baby and about a place I should go, but I don't know how I could ever go back home. My dad tried to take her necklace and sell it, but I refused to let him. We fought, and I accidentally killed him. The whole thing makes me sick to this day. I still feel guilty. I'll always feel guilty. I wish I could undo it somehow. I'm a murderer. If I would have had the confidence to stand up to my dad, this wouldn't have happened. Also, Thalassa created me. Like… Thalassa Thalassa. The goddess. Apparently, she left me a gift. I don't know why she created such a criminal."

"You did it to save your mom," said Bella. "I'd do anything to have been able to even attempt to save my mom even if it meant I would never exist. Also, no one who is as brave as you are is weak-minded." The squad nodded in agreement. "I'm next right? You know how I've been bullied my whole life? Well, I was convinced that the only good person in the world was my mother. Everyone was always so cruel to me except for her, and I believed I was an abomination. I still do. I would sit in this place far away from people and just slaughter anything that swam by. You aren't supposed to kill animals like that. I would only eat some of them, and I was killing for the wrong reasons. I convinced myself that by killing them, I was freeing them. Why not people? Why not myself? Well, I didn't think any of them deserved to be freed. Every day, I felt myself becoming more and more emotionless. Then one day, I decided to stop killing animals. I even became vegan. Sounds great, right? Well… No. Instead of killing, I began torturing people who bullied other people. I ended up becoming the monster everyone said I was. I've been bullied all my life. I didn't care about myself, so I didn't feel the need to fight for myself. I came to my senses for a moment and was going to commit suicide yesterday but then I was chased by some bullies. I heard Amethyst singing and followed her voice. She was the first person I met that was friendly to me, and she changed my mind about the world. Then she told me about you all, and you actually turned out to be nice. Now, I'm obsessed with the fact that I can't change the past. Now I know that I was just selfish. I wanted others to feel what I felt. I was addicted to torture. I couldn't stop. Ever since I stopped, I've been addicted to masturbating. I don't know what the f*** is wrong with me. I guess it works as a substitute because I get off from thinking about torturing people. But then they say that once you're addicted, you can never become un-addicted."

"I don't think anything is wrong with you," said Amethyst. "I get why you did it. People don't understand what pain can do to someone. It isn't your fault. People fed you hatred every single day. That's what happens sometimes. I'm glad we changed your mind."

"Come on… One of you has to go first," said Iris.

"I'll go but we're only going to tell you our least dark secret," said Xenon.

"Yeah. We'll tell you our darkest secret in a future circle. We don't want to darken the water," Amethyst added. "Y'all still have to wake up tomorrow."

"You kept a secret from me!" Iris and Chance said at the same time to their original siblings.

"Oh okay. So, we keeping secrets now." Chance was hurt. "F*** you too."

"Relax, Choo Choo. We haven't even told each other yet."

"Oh. Well, okay then. Never mind," said Chance. "Proceed."

"This is pretty light, but you know how I'm from the south right? Okay so in my first half-life I was poor, and my mother was ill. There aren't good physicians in the south. It's not really a queendom or anything. It's every person for themselves. It's so dangerous to live there. Only the smartest and strongest survive, but no one is safe. I wasn't strong, but my sister Radon was. We had to steal because we didn't have any food or money. That was the only way we could survive. Plus, our father was never home because he was always out gang banging or something. It was an if-you-need-it-take-it world. I got so used to it. Radon and I were good at it. When I got older, I didn't want to steal anymore. I decided to get a job as a dancer. Not how you think. It was an extremely sexualized job. It wasn't like stripping. It was more like prostitution without sexual intercourse. They often wanted oral and make-out sessions. Sometimes they wanted more than that, but I always denied. That didn't always work though. Sometimes they threatened me with weapons. I was only 15 when I started. My sister had no idea what I was doing. I kept my earnings secret and showed them to her little by little, so she wouldn't figure it out. It wasn't much, but it was a lot compared to what we had. One day, I was swimming back home, and some older males attacked me. It was personal. I refused one of them sex, so I guess that's why they were so angry. I was never a fighter. They grabbed me and tried to take my money. They told me they'd pierce my ear if I didn't give them my earnings. I refused to give up my earnings because how else were we going to eat? It was so painful. Then they tried to rape me because they thought I was female. That's interesting because they should have been able to pick up on my scent. Once they found out I was male, they changed their minds and beat the hell out of me instead. They attempted to rape a female dancer that was walking by, so I killed them. I'm not sure how. I didn't have any weapons or anything on me. I felt so... So at ease." Xenon wiggled his jaw as his gums began to tingle. "It was so satisfying. Anyways, the girl thanked me and then asked me if I was a changer. I didn't know what she was talking about. She was known for being mystical or something. She loved myths. I had blood all over my mouth, so maybe I bit them or something, but it still doesn't make sense. Later on, I found out they were missing. Anyways, when I got home that day, my father was there. Perfect timing, right? He was yelling at my mother. She always told us to stay out of it, but that time it was the worst I had ever seen it. Then he saw me, and I triggered him even more. He hated me because he said I was weak and small. He also hated how I'm queer. Plus, I was dressed in clothes people there consider feminine because I just got back from my job. You see... The only people who go there are heteronormative patriarchs who just want to have their way with you. Anyways, he started beating me up and then Radon protected me. Then I bit him the same way I bit the guys from earlier. It was all a blur, but Radon and I killed his ass. My mother didn't look surprised. She told us to leave her because if they found out, we would go to prison. I heard that that place is horrifying. It's governed by Man, and once you go, you don't come back. No one knows what goes on there. Well... People talked about someone who came back and talked about the horrors they faced. That person ended up committing suicide. Anyways, I broke down because I didn't want to leave her. There was no way I could leave her on my own. She told us how she was dying, and she didn't want to die without knowing her children were anywhere but the Icebox. Radon knew she was right. Radon was always the strong one. It was hurting her just as much as it was hurting me, but she dragged me away because she had to. Radon would have stayed, but she didn't to save me." Xenon threw himself on Amethyst and continued to weep. "We were swimming away. We had no idea where we were going. We were both exhausted, but Radon carried me. Then we swam into some Nereids. We were terrified, but of course, Radon didn't show it. There were 8 of them, and they were all female. The females are usually much larger than the males. There was no way we were going to get away from them. They didn't see us yet. Radon covered me in kelp to repel them from me. Everyone always said she was the fastest swimmer. She knew I wouldn't leave her, so she tied me up and swam away from me. By the time I was somewhat free, she was far away. Even though she told me not to look back, I watched. She wounded herself, so they'd follow her. By the time I broke free from the kelp, there was nothing left but a faint trace of blood. Oh yeah... Before she left, we swapped bracelets. That's why I have the red one and she has the blue one. Also, the reason why the purple bracelet Amethyst bought me is so important to me is because it's the same bracelet my mom always wore. My mom was just like you Amethyst. Small, sassy, and silly. She used to do that little thing you do when you laugh out of nowhere." He managed to crack a smile. "Anyways, I was just drifting. I fell asleep, and when I woke up, I was under the fin of a blue whale. N'ayaini had a calf and still took care of me. She brought me here. Everyone was staring because she literally swam right up to the bas. I got here when I was almost 16. That's all." He started weeping even harder. "I don't know if I'll ever see my big sister again. She's probably dead. If she isn't, how will we find each other?"

"We'll find her, Blue," said Iris. "If she's alive, we'll find her."

"But she's dead," he cried. "It's been years."

"You don't know that, Moon Beam." Amethyst caressed his head. "If Chance was dead, I would feel it. Siblings know. From what you just said, Radon sounds kinda like Chance. He picks on me a lot, but he is always there looking out for me because I'm his little sister. Look, I can't tell you if she's still alive, but you all told me Oceanids always say goodbye."

467

"Oh, my goddess! She's right," said Iris. "Blue. She never said goodbye, did she?"

"No. She just said, 'I love you, Moon Beam.'"

"Xe, I had no idea she called you that. I'm so sorry. I'll find a new nickname."

"No, no. Don't. That's why I like the nickname so much," he smiled. "You two would have gotten along very well."

"Well, then I can't wait to meet her and thank her for saving you." She knew the squad was waiting for her to go next. "What y'all looking at me for?"

"N**** because it's your turn."

"Alright so check this out…"

"Don't be sugar coating shit either," said Chance.

"Fine. Shhh! Do you have the talking piece? Okay, this isn't dark but, when I was like 10 or 11, I went to go visit the first family we stayed with when we came to the surface. We lived in Oakland. Dad was working in construction, so he couldn't be home all day. I asked him about that a couple days ago. He said that working was the only way to get surface currency. He told me about Man. He also told me my non-Oceanid powers slash abilities started to kick in at 7. The Man's eyes didn't look all glowy and white to me because that didn't start happening until I was like 15. LOL. Anyways, the dad of their particular household was a Man. That's probably why I never liked him. He didn't cause much trouble when I was staying there. He wasn't their biofather by the way. My friend Jessie was older than me but the youngest child in the family. When their parents finally allowed them to have a phone, they told me all about everything that happened over the years. I couldn't believe it. He was doing all types of shit from abusing animals to rape. He even picked up a smoking habit. They had gotten a divorce, and the mother had full custody of the kids. Dad let me visit their new house since the dad wouldn't be there. But guess what? His ass came to their house crying and shit. He was talking about how he was sorry and wanted to at least see the kids. Of course, she didn't let his ass in. She called the kops, but he ended up killing them. Jessie's mom had us go hide upstairs, and he used their weapons to break into the house. They have hella land and their house was huge, so they didn't have any neighbors. Good thing I had called Dad. He was coming from San Francisco. There was hella traffic because he just got off work. If you're wondering why Jessie's dad wasn't in jail, it's because of our justice system. He was a wealthy, white, male, able-bodied cishet. Anyways, their mother did her best to convince him the kids weren't home. I didn't see this part, but it sounded like he raped her and then shot her. The eldest child knew where her mother's gun was and shot him multiple times. We thought he was for sure dead but no... We heard the eldest screaming and then another gunshot. Jessie kept apologizing to me. I kept trying to tell them I was the one that was sorry. We were hiding under the bed but then I heard him say, 'I know you're under the bed, Jessie. I was the one who told you to hide there when a bad guy comes, remember?' We were sitting ducks. My little ass was hella scared. There were so many loud noises. Certain noises drive me crazy. Jessie got into their wheelchair and told me to sit on their lap. I'm glad they had carpet in their house. Originally, Jessie formulated a good ass plan, but there was still the risk of something happening to Jessie, so I was like nah. They were always protecting me. Jessie was always saving my ass. I'll tell y'all later. I knew they would sacrifice themself for me. Jessie was pissed because they wanted to stay with me, so they could protect me. Naturally, my stubborn ass was like hell no. Anyways, I wheeled them to the escalator thingy and told them to get as far away from the house as possible. I was so sad about pushing Jessie in their wheelchair like that for weeks because I used our physicalities to my advantage, but I had to. By the way, there's this machine that goes on the staircase, so it can transport the wheelchair. Anyways, I could have snuck out the house, but I had a better idea," Amethyst smiled. "As soon as Jessie made it to the bottom, I wheeled them as fast as I could out the door because their dad had seen us. He said I was a fool to leave myself with him, and I just smiled. I let him beat my ass, so I could get his lighter. Once I got it, I started a fire and made it so that the detectives would think he started it after he killed them. I couldn't have them thinking about who killed the dad because then they'd blame Dad. While the fire was burning, I literally pulled his ass apart. I started with his ring finger and then worked my way around the body. I took his heart out and then I returned it. I was gentle. I didn't break it. It was still beating. I placed the flowers that were in the vase on Jessie's mom and sister. I prayed for them to go to heaven. Awww, I was so cute. Don't ask me how I pulled his ass apart because I don't f****** know. Hell, I don't even know how their bodies ended up vaporizing or whatever because I don't think fire works that fast. Speaking of fast, I must have done what I did hella fast because I was able to run out before I got burned. If I would have known I could have survived, I would have stayed longer. If you want to know why I did what I did, it was because he had me f***** up. The thing is though… I was having way too much fun causing him pain for causing others so much pain. My ass was dying laughing. LOL," she laughed. "Zzzt! Operation in this b****! SHIT! I'm sorry. You see what I mean… I'm just glad I was able to hold back this time. Dad was like, "Are you okay.' I was like, 'I'm cold.' Jessie's good though. We still talk. They live with their aunt now. Oh yeah… I was the one who called the firefighters. They were all hot as f***." Amethyst noticed how everyone except for Chance and Xenon were staring at her. "See. This is why I didn't want to tell y'all. If you don't want to be my friends anymore, I don't blame you."

"I know I keep saying this, but you're a hero!" Xenon hugged her. "Why would anyone not want to be your friend? You feel for everyone so deeply."

"I'm more of a tragedy," she smiled.

"I know. You're a tragic hero."

"I tried to f****** tell y'all," said Chance. "That's my little angel."

Bella was speechless and just started clapping. Iris said, "Sister… Do you think you could f*** Zeus up like that?"

"Girl he is a god. Hell no I can't."

"I don't know, Sister… You are the chosen one."

"Ew. I can't stand how that sounds."

"Wow," said Reign. "Now I see what Thetis was saying. All of you are insane!!! I really don't understand how Bella and Iris are Agathos. Especially Bella."

Chance said, "Shut up, Assassin's Creed. Your ass is crazy too. Y'all three are Agathos because y'all didn't like what y'all did. We all did some crazy shit, and y'all right here with us."

"Okay so now we need nicknames," said Iris.

"I like Assassin's Creed," said Reign.

"Iris is Cookie Cutter," said Chance.

"You're the Joker," Iris laughed. "Like Sister said."

"Bella is CIA," Amethyst said. They explained to him what that was, and he loved it.

"Xenon is Rhythm and Blues," Bella smiled.

"Ame, I don't know what the f*** to call you. We just gon call you Giggle Bot."

"I love how we're all so chill about this," said Iris.

"We're all so f***** up," Xenon laughed.

"Why did the universe bring all of us together," said Amethyst. "This should be fun."

Moon Beam: Hey, Hero. Are you done with your lessons?

Moon Jelly: Yeah :)

Moon Beam: I'll pick you up at twilight. Bring your Converse.

Moon Jelly: Ooooo! Okay. I'll be waiting.

Moon Beam: <3 <3 <3

Xenon was there at twilight just like he said. "You know Aristide, but this is Silvercrest. They're going to give us a ride."

"Oh, my goddess!" said Amethyst. "Purple sand! Is this Pfeiffer Beach? Eeeeeep! I've always wanted to come here. Did Chance tell you?"

"No. I don't know what Pfeiffer is. I just know you like purple. Come on. I want to show you something." He took her to the spot where he made a huge heart out of purple sand dollars. "Most people don't care much for shells. Actually, they are the equivalent of surface twigs. But not to you," he laughed. "Why do you like them so much?"

"Look how beautiful they are! They aren't shells. These are skeletons. I love what I find on the beach. My favorite things are the ones that come from the ocean. Kind of like you, Shy Guy."

"That one almost went over my head. I guess that's another thing we have in common. See the sky? Twilight helps me imagine complete bliss. You're my twilight, Twilight."

"You're Night Light and I'm Twilight," she giggled. "Do you come up here often?"

"I haven't been up here in years. You're the only reason why I ever surfaced."

"Did you sing on this beach too?" she giggled. "Yeah, that's right. I heard you singing "Una Furtiva Lagrima" from *L'elisir D'amore*. You must have really been in love to sing your heart out like that."

"You know what the lyrics mean?"

"Yep. I used to listen to that song but then you started singing it every night, so there was no need. I love how you still have your rasp when you sing. Uh! I love it when you talk. I also love tenors. Do you want to lay down?"

"I forgot to bring a towel. I know how you had a towel last time."

"A what?" she giggled. He fell for it and said 'towel' again. "You're so cute. I don't need one."

When Xenon laid down on the sand, Amethyst sat right on top of him like a little puppy. "You're so small. Just like a teknon," he laughed. "Why don't you just lay next to me?" He had an idea why. "Don't say because I'm warm."

"Because you smell good."

"You know what I mean."

"I know Thetis said Zeus won't strike during this time, but who knows. If he hurts you, I will find a way to tear down Olympus, and I don't want to have to do that."

"Why Olympus? What about the other gods?" he smiled.

"I don't want to hurt the people in the sky kingdom. Plus, the other gods failed to protect you so oh f****** well. I don't give a heavenly f***."

"You learned that stuff about me earlier, yet you don't look at me differently. You aren't disgusted by me?"

"Why would I be?"

"You know what I'm talking about. I'm such a beast."

"And I'm a savage."

"Why'd you pick a xylophone?"

"Because it starts with an 'x' and because of the zzz sound. It's one of my favorite words. Plus, if you translate the Greek roots it means wooden sound or voice. That's what your voice is like. It's like wood because it floats on water. It can also be made of bone. There's also an instrument called bones, and it's a concussion instrument. See what I did there? To show you we aren't dreaming this time. Oh yeah! Have you seen that one video with the dancing skeletons? I think it's called "The Skeleton Dance". You're such a silly symphony. Now that I know you play the drums and piano it is even more fitting. That's what you get when the drums and the piano have a baby."

"I can play my Xylophone now that I have been reunited with my Muse."

"But can you catch her though?" Amethyst ran along the beach. Xenon got on all fours and howled at the moon just like a werewolf. "Whoa," she laughed. "I know you're good at impressions, but how can you run on all fours like that? Ahhh!"

He tackled her and asked, "Are you hungry?" After Amethyst collected as many sand dollars as they could carry, they headed back to the bas. Xenon cooked her favorite salmon for her. They were eating the same thing, but Amethyst popped a piece combined with some rice in his mouth. "You like feeding me, don't you?"

"Yeah. You always make eye contact with me when you eat it. You also do this cross-eyed look when something gets close to your face."

"Everyone doesn't do that?"

"No. Only you," she laughed. "How come you aren't wearing your lip shimmer today?"

"Well... Chance doesn't wear it, and I looked up photos of surface boys just in case you wanted more of a surface date. You know... To remind you of the surface."

"He'd wear a little if it was red tinted, and I don't like surface people. I like people from the abyss. Don't feel like you have to be someone other than you around me. Just be you."

"What if I wear more than that and it's not all exaggerated for acting. What if it's not drag? What if I feel girly?" he blushed.

"Oh, Moon Beam. However you feel and present is fine with me as long as you're comfortable."

He displayed that rare ear to ear grin Amethyst loved to see. "I'll be right back." Xenon was shy to come out.

"Come on. Let me see you."

"Don't make fun of me. What if you think I'm ugly this way?"

"I won't. Just come out." When she saw him she casually said, "You look pretty. I don't see how you thought I'd think you'd be ugly as a girl when you're not ugly otherwise."

"Reign literally said I look better as a boy."

"She probably meant to say she feels uncomfortable when you dress this way. Plus, how would she know? You could be a boy and still dress this way. Clothing doesn't equal gender. It's just clothing, and it can mean whatever you want it to. Gender can mean whatever you want it to too."

"True. I don't make you uncomfortable?"

"Dress how you want regardless of people being uncomfortable or not, but no... You're still the same person. You're still the same Xenon. I've lived on the surface for years, but I've never had a surface mind. By the way, look at those legs. That's all me."

He squeezed her nose. "I love how when I do that you stick your tongue out," he smiled. "Guess what? We also have dessert! I'll go get it."

"Where did you find Smurf ice cream?!?!? I can't believe it! I've never been able to find this anywhere after me, Dad, and Chance went to Florida."

"If it's on the surface, the Naiads know about it. I had them find some for me. There's more tubs in the fridge."

"This. Is. The. Way. To. My. F******. Heart." She shoved a spoonful into his mouth.

While she was posting pictures of her ice cream, Xenon reacted to the flavor. "Ummm! It's actually really good. Chance said it was nasty but then I guess he says a lot of things."

"Help me eat it. Let's go watch a movie in your room. My first date is awesome."

"Mine too."

"How has your fine ass never been on a date?" Amethyst laughed.

"I could ask your fine ass the same question," he smiled. "I guess I'm just too much for everyone else."

"LOL THAT'S A MOOD!"

When *The Cheetah Girls 2* was almost over, Iris, Chance, and Bella joined them on the bed. "Wassup. How y'all gon watch this without the squad??? This is a squad film," said Chance.

"What are we watching next?" Iris asked.

"*Twitches*?" Xenon suggested.

"I love that movie!" said Bella.

"Oh, hell yeah. I haven't watched that in a while." They all ate candy as they enjoyed the movie. Amethyst and Chance were used to having English subtitles because they stay watching anime. "Yo! They are Amethyst and Iris AF," Chance laughed. *If you're wondering... Iris doesn't even need the subtitles because she can read lips.*

They heard Reign arrive. "Where you going, Xe?" said Amethyst with a concerned look on her face. "You know you shouldn't have to change if you don't want to."

Do you want to change?

I don't.

"Hi!!!" said Reign. "*Twitches*? OMG, that's so Iris and Amethyst." Her expression changed when she saw Xenon. They could all feel the tension.

"Reign, fix your f****** face," Iris hissed at her. "Stop f****** frowning at him." Bella had an oh-shit-oh-shit-oh-shit look on his face.

"Why are you looking at him like that?" asked Chance.

"She feels uncomfortable when Blue dresses like that for some reason," Iris responded.

"Why? What's wrong with what he's wearing?" asked Chance. "He looks nice."

"It's just weird."

"How is it weird?!?!?" said Xenon. He was doing his best not to weep.

"A warrior shouldn't be wearing that."

Amethyst couldn't hold back anymore. "Who the hell are you to say who should and should not wear what?!?!?" Reign spilled her drink on Xenon's dress and Amethyst hissed and snapped her teeth at her. She was officially pissed. "Okay so now you finna catch these f****** hands." Reign used her wrestling moves on Amethyst, but Amethyst managed to slip free because she was so small, so Reign gently tossed her against the wall.

"SHIT REIGN! Don't f****** kill her!" yelled Iris.

"HOLY SHIT! I heard her bones crack!" yelled Bella.

"OMFG! If you killed her, I'm going to f****** kill you," yelled Chance. "I don't know how! I'll poison you or some shit!"

Amethyst popped her arm back together. Her bones healed so quickly she barely noticed how many were broken. She said, "B**** I watch WWE too," and hit her with a spear and then an RKO. Reign is by far much stronger than anyone could ever be, but she has terrible balance, agility, and flexibility.

The squad broke up the fight, and Reign said, "Look, I'm sorry okay!!! Damn!"

"Well, I'm not. Don't apologize to us. Apologize to Xe."

"Xenon, I'm sorry. I'm not transphobic. It's just that I wish I could wear that kind of clothing too. At work, they don't treat me how I want to be treated. I don't want to be treated as one of the guys. I guess I'm just jealous of how you express yourself. Sometimes I feel like the other warriors, including the girls, can't see my femininity because I'm so muscular and rough. Actually... The other girls probably don't think that way. My boyfriend told me I don't fit in with them. I know that's not true but... Ugh! He's a leech sucking my confidence. I'm so sorry. Do you forgive me?"

"Yes, I forgive you. Forget that jerk. We see your femininity. You should make friends with the girls."

"Yeah. You're definitely the 'girliest' one here," Amethyst laughed. "You and Iris are not masculine at all. Like... At all."

"OMG! Sister! That was your first hiss!"

"Awww," Chance mocked her. "At least we know Ame can do that bone thing now."

"Wait a wave. GIRLS!" said Iris. "Do you know what this means?"

"SHOPPING!!!" Amethyst, Xenon, and Iris screamed. Reign was wondering why they had to scream, but she was happy.

"Ummm… We'll stay here," said Chance.

"Yeah. We'll wait for you ladies to come back," Bella agreed.

Amethyst and Iris told Reign and Xenon not to say anything, so they wouldn't interfere with the plan. "But we need two big, strong men to help us with our bags," said Iris.

Chance said, "Reign and Xenon are with y'all. What the f*** y'all need us for? Y'all ain't even ready to go yet."

"We're aware of what you're trying to do," Bella smiled.

"Come on boys," Amethyst used her daddy's girl voice. "Pleeeeease." It worked of course. Iris and Amethyst gave each other a victorious nod. They had won.

"Why'd you do that?" Reign asked. "I can carry my own bags."

"We all can," Iris laughed.

"But why when you don't have to," Amethyst smiled.

"You two are terrible," she giggled. "Is that how I should act with my new clothes? I don't want people to do things like that for me or anything. I just want them to… I don't know how to explain it."

"We get it. You want to be treated like the queen you are," said Iris. "You don't have to change who you are."

"What we just did didn't really have shit to do with anything. We're just hella extra," said Amethyst. "Also, always remember that you can be feminine in your own way. There aren't any rules or anything. Femininity can be whatever it means to you."

"Just for the record, we're going to buy the boys food and stuff," Iris smiled. "And we aren't going to make them carry everything."

"Yeah," Amethyst giggled. "It's not like that. We take care of our boys. We love them!" Amethyst hugged Chance and Bella. "They take care of us, and we take care of them!"

"Blue, what the f***. It doesn't take this long to put a dress on."

"Lassa say something else. I will f*** you up!" Then his tone changed. "Girls! I need help. I don't know what to wear."

"See how he isn't referring to me! I know about that kind of stuff too!" said Reign. "What's wrong with me?"

"Womxn, there ain't nothing wrong with you," Chance smiled. "Plus, Blue probably just wants to give you some space."

"Girls!" Iris shouted to Chi, Beta, and Rho. "Go get dressed up. Let's go out tonight! Reign, you can change later. Can one of you come get this outfit for Bella?"

"Iris! Don't let HIM in here," Xenon whispered. "Have Reign come get it."

Xenon told Reign to close her eyes. "Why? You swim around in your underwear all the time."

"I know, but this is different," he blushed.

They were about to enter the store when Reign said, "I don't know... Are you sure? I'm so muscular and..."

Amethyst said, "Well duh, Toxic Femininity. So are the other warriors. You've seen the other girls. Girl, stop acting like you live on the surface. You live in the ocean. That's toxic femininity talking. How the hell did it get all the way down here?"

"Oh, my goddess! That's the term! I was with that big, buff guy and acting all submissive trying to make myself feel more feminine as if that's what femininity is. I really have to stop reading those sky nymph articles! Uhhh! I'm so stupid. I was doing so many things... I was practicing toxic femininity and enforcing toxic masculinity all this time! Uhhh! Thanks girls. I don't need Marc Anthony. He is such a shark! I deserve better! I'm going to find me a man who isn't trash! But first I need me! From now on, I'm going to be me! I'm gonna do me!"

Reign dialed her phone, and the boys asked what was going on. The girls hissed at them, so they'd be quiet. Chance said, "Wow, man… Girls are so beautiful, but damn. They will f****** kill you." Then he used his phone to play the translation.

"I can't believe I just did that. I broke up with him! I'm free!"

Amethyst said, "Yaaasssss, Cleopatra yaaasssss."

"Yaaasssss b****!!!" said Iris.

The boys were mocking them in a supportive way. "Ummm hmmm, girl. That's right. F*** him. Men are trash," said Chance.

"Who needs men anyway?" Bella added. "Emphasis on needs."

"I agree," said Chance. "We have food."

"Exactly," Amethyst agreed. "And we have each other."

"Sister came and made everything better," Iris smiled.

"What? LOL. Y'all all literally in danger because of me."

"True but f*** it," they all agreed.

"F*** Zeus after three," Iris laughed. "1, 2, 3…"

"F*** ZEUS!"

They stopped by Reign's apartment, so she could drop off her new clothes and change into her new plunging, yellow dress. They all agreed it looked great on her. "Join the goddess club, warrior goddess," Amethyst smiled. "You look hot! It's so cool how your bio-parent is literally the sea."

"The restaurant we are going to is called Stone Edge. They also serve land food," Iris told them. "A lot of Naiads come here. They aren't open during the day. When it's this late, they usually drain it. When you walk in, you get dried off by the air system. All our clothes are waterproof, and water doesn't stick to us like sky nymphs. Chance, you're a Naiad, so you'll be fine."

"A small number of Naiads have become a bit too engulfed in Zeus's ideals as if they are zymphs, and don't really know much about identities. They in particular aren't hateful. They just don't know how to ask to be freed from their ignorance. Oh. A zymph is what we call sky nymphs that have been brainwashed by Zeus," said Xenon. "Can you all do me a favor and address me as she," he blushed. "I don't want to feel their confusion when you all use my proper pronouns. Let's eat without the BS. People ask questions. We usually educate them but, I don't feel like giving people lessons tonight."

"Sure. Won't they recognize you?" asked Bella.

"Klymene sent me this necklace for my birthday last year. No one will recognize me unless I want them to. No one knows that I dress like this sometimes. Most people in the realms haven't been brainwashed to think anything bad about non-binary people. I just want to keep it a secret until I'm sure no one has any evidence of my past. That's the only reason why I wear this."

"What name should we use for you this time?" Reign smiled.

"I don't know. Give me some suggestions," he smiled. "What do I look like?"

"Sapphire?" said Chance.

"Hell no. That was my stage name. Oh. You just gave me an idea. Call me Topaz," he laughed. "Remember that, Moon Jelly? I'm going to steal that one from you. Now you and I match. Let's stick with that one from now on. Amethyst and Topaz. LOL."

"Y'all are truly gifted regarding fluidity," Chance joked. "Like damn… How the f***… Speaking of that, y'all should see what happens when Ame is near a femme or surrounded by femmes. Ratios really do something to her LMAO. Anyways, in addition to ignorance, I think the people at school are so confused and uncomfortable because they find Ame attractive."

481

They all couldn't help but laugh. "I know you're all probably going to swirl me for this, but you three don't feel embarrassed by me?" asked Xenon.

Of course, they swirled him. "I can't even see," Bella laughed. "And no, I'm not embarrassed by you. Plus, I'm the one who has a tail."

"I know you mean me," said Reign. "If anyone has a problem with you or Small Fry's gender they can fight me."

"Yeah. She'll do the fighting. I'll do the shit talking," Chance smiled. "Wait until y'all see Amethyst in girly mode. Now that is something else."

"OMG. I'm weeeak," Amethyst laughed. "It's so funny how he finds that more interesting than when I'm feeling boyish."

"How are you feeling right now?" asked Iris.

"Purple. That's the usual."

"Ayyye. As for me... I don't know. I'm just me," he laughed.

"Hello. I'm Isaac and I'll be your waiter for the night. What can I get you all to drink?"

Dark blue hair looks nice on you. I'm also loving the bangs and loose waves. You looking like a full course meal.

OMG. Thank you! I was trying something different. Iris said it goes well with my skin tone.

After they ordered their drinks, Iris said, "We're ready to order. Go ahead, Sister."

When Xenon and Chance were the last two left, Chance said, "After you. Ladies first."

As soon as the waiter left, Xenon got up, reached across the table and smacked him. He knew Chance was messing with him. Amethyst pulled Xenon's dress down, so his underwear wouldn't show. "Thanks," he blushed.

"No worries. I got your back. Chance, why you lookin' at me like that?" Amethyst tried to hide her smile.

"I f****** saw that. You did a little more than just pull her dress down. Why else would she be smiling so damn hard? Knowing you, it wasn't no damn accident."

"Even I saw it," Bella laughed.

Well, keep going…

Xenon placed her hand on his thigh. Reign and Chance didn't notice for a while until Xenon got a chill.

Shit, Moon Jelly. We got to stop. They totally saw that.

Yeah, before you get yourself in trouble.

I'll swim into your trap any day.

Who said anything about a trap? The table's right there.

"Amethyst! Can you move your hand?" Chance laughed. Damn… Can't take y'all asses nowhere."

Iris said, "Oh, relax. They're cute."

Amethyst put her arm on Xenon's chair. Chance knew exactly what she was going to do. She waited for Xenon to look at her. Then she said, "Come here. You've got something on your face." First, she tucked some of his hair behind his ear and then she planted a slow kiss on his cheek.

"Not on the lips?" he smiled.

"I didn't want to mess up your lip glimmer."

"That was lowkey smooth as f***," said Iris.

"Bro! What the f***! At school, I'd try to do some simple shit like that to the cheerleaders and get called basic, but when she does it to them it's smooth. Now this. How? That's not f****** fair."

When they were back at the bas, they all changed into their lounge clothes. I would say pajamas but Alpha, Zeta, and Beta prefer not to wear pajamas.

Of course, Chance was decked out in Hello Kitty literally from head to toe. He thought they were looking at him funny, so he said, "Oh, bloody hell!!! I just really love Hello Kitty. If you have a problem with that f*** you!!!"

"Chill, Red," said Iris. "We don't have a problem. What's wrong with Hello Kitty? They don't like Hello Kitty on the surface or something?"

Xenon came out with his favorite baby blue shorts and tie-dye crop top. "I have my belly ring in today," he said. "See it?"

"Oh, I see it," Amethyst smiled. She patted her lap, so he'd come sit on her.

"You and Iris…" Reign giggled. "I swear."

"Bro. Where's the rest of your pajama shorts?" Chance laughed.

"Shut up," said Amethyst. "Leave my Moon Baby alone. There's nothing wrong with his shorts. You just think he's cute. Why you looking at his booty anyway?" Xenon's hair brushed Chance's face. Of course, Chance took the opportunity to pull Xenon's hair, so Xenon pushed Chance off the couch and rolled his eyes. Amethyst said, "What the hell, Chance! You want someone to pull your hair like that? That's what the f*** I thought." She rolled her eyes and made a stank face.

"Wow," Chance laughed. "There is way too much sass in the middle of this couch. Damn. Attitude on 10." Chance made fun of them by doing a sassy snap.

"I f****** love them," said Bella. "They're so fierce. Chance is such an asshole."

"Hey! Just because I have a thing for mermaids doesn't mean you get to call me an asshole, Asshole," he flinched at him.

Bella was picking up on something. "Is that your way of flirting with me, Little Boy?" he laughed.

"Ooooo. Little Man has a crush," said Reign.

"I wasn't flirting with you."

"Chance… Bruh. Come on. It's okay," Amethyst laughed. "Bella's so big, strong, and muscular just like Reign except he's a mermaid Nereid. Did I mention he's a mermaid?"

"Why are y'all focusing on me? Reign's obviously crushing on Iris."

"Well, yeah… She's my WCW. Duuuh," said Reign.

"Oh, that's what you mean by crush… Not like an I want to get with you crush… More like a damn, you're fine crush, right? Then yeah…"

"Yeah what?" Bella smiled. "Finish your sentence."

"Never mind."

"Awww. What's wrong, Freckles?"

"Nothing. Only girls can do that whole WCW thing. Dudes can't be talking about they got an MCM."

"Why not?" Reign asked. "Everyone does it."

"Same reason why they can't comment heart eyes and shit under their guy friends pics."

"Again, why not? Everyone does that down here," said Reign.

"It's because of toxic masculinity," Amethyst explained. "We have hella that on the surface. Toxic masculinity and toxic femininity work together. They come from patriarchy."

"That's why we call you two that," Xenon added.

"I totally get how you feel. Remember how I was practicing toxic femininity. Don't be like me. You're in the ocean now," Reign smiled. "You shouldn't have to worry about that like you do on the surface. Of course, there are still sharks swimming around, but our society isn't built around heteropatriarchy. Amethyst taught me that word," she giggled.

"Don't worry, Chance. I won't think you want to be my boyfriend or anything. Also, you're cute, but I don't f****** like your rude ass," Bella smiled.

"Shut up, cutie. Give me a kiss. Naaah. Jk, jk," Chance laughed.

"Another one?" Bella asked. They all couldn't stop laughing.

"Supposedly Chance has a sugar-o-meter," Reign said. "He says it's only for non-females. It's not about being flamboyant or anything. It's about how feminine you are," she giggled.

"He said he has like 1 cup of sugar," said Iris.

Bella was curious. "How many do you have, Xenon?" he asked.

"Apparently I have 5. I'm not denying it," he smiled.

"Yeah. That sounds about right," Bella laughed. "So how many do I have?"

"N**** you got like 3."

"Waaait. Hold on," Iris laughed. "No f****** way. Come on, sis."

"Iris. You know it's true," said Chance.

"I think your sugar-o-meter is broken," Reign giggled. "Or maybe you just want to be the most masculine."

Atoz just sipped their tea and kept laughing. Iris said, "Chance. Sis, come on now. Bella obviously has the least sugar in his tank."

"Alright fine! Damn," he laughed. "I guess I'm more like a 2 maybe 2¼. Bella only has less than a cup. Masculine ass mermaid. Where the f*** the feminine ones at? I'm trying to make one of them my wife."

"They're around," Bella smiled. Reign and Iris gave him a look and tried to hide their smiles. "But in the meantime you'll be my trophy husband," he smiled. "Don't worry. I'm versatile."

"Well damn. Iris and Reign are married. Now Bella and Chance… I guess we should get married too," Atoz laughed.

"I'll be your wife okay, husband?" Xenon smiled.

"Alright, wife."

"The surface is so weird," said Iris. "We have a ceremony and celebration for soulmates who want to have one. In the realms, marriage is a contract used to bind two people who don't want to be together. Zeus does that shit all the time. He manipulates people or threatens them into signing the contract."

"Thank you!!! The concept of marriage is such an interesting topic. There's so much to talk about," said Amethyst. "Surface adults get heated about stuff like that," she giggled.

"Ex-f******-xactly," Chance added.

"I'm adding that topic to my list of group conversation topics," said Iris. "We also need to have a conversation about sexual assault, but we'll save that for later. I can tell we need to get closer first." Amethyst knew she was talking about her. "I hate how they teach Men that that's acceptable. Aside from the few sharks we have swimming around, consent is not even a question down here. I'm really mind blown. Why to surface people hate their womxn consciously and subconsciously? I couldn't last a day up there. You are so strong, Sister. If I had to get an army together, I would want womxn of color from the surface."

"I know right. The surface is fueled by hate. Sometimes I want to cleanse the world from all this hatred, but that would mean wiping out everyone in the physical. I'm not saying I could, but I'm pretty f****** sure I would. Look. I'm an optimist, but all I'm saying is that I have another one of those psychic feelings, and this one makes me sick with pleasure."

"Oh, Sister." Iris threw her arms around her in tears. "I wish I could have traded places with you." Chance and Bella we're trying not to cry, but Xenon and Reign were in tears.

"Don't say that, sis. It should have been me." Now Chance and Bella were also wiping tears. "You and I are twins, and we're both strong, but you and I are cut from a different fabric. You're what people want. I'm what the world deserves. People don't deserve you."

Chapter 20: Psychic Soulmates

DAY 15

Nothing that important happened. *The squad was just doing what they do. Don't worry. Dead or alive, they're all still crazy AF. No one's dead. No one's going to die. I don't know why I said that. LOL. Spoiler alert.* Amethyst and Chance continued their Greek lessons, training, and what not. Bella was learning English with them. I guess you could say they were helping each other. Iris convinced Amethyst to be ahead of the children's choir. Xenon was gaining confidence, and Amethyst was patiently waiting.

DAY 16

"Amethyst. I-I…"

She was so eager to hear what he had to say. "Yes?" she gleamed.

"Can I talk to you?" In his garden, they talked about flowers. *Yep. Flowers. Way to stall…* "You know how I can communicate with animals? I can do the same thing with plants."

"I know that, Xenon. I pointed that out already."

"A-And fungi too."

"Okay…"

Just tell her already… She's going to leave. You're irritating her. You two obviously like each other… Even we know that…

Shhh. I'm just nervous.

"The flowers communicate well," said Xenon.

"Really? Can you hook me up with one of them then?" Amethyst was so annoyed. "Is that all you brought me in here for? I don't want to engage with you in this dry ass conversation. I'm leaving."

Told you... You better act fast. Maybe you should sing to her since you can't talk. It's a good time to sing your heart out... Like this. La la la la la. La la la la laaaaa.

Xenon went after her and said, "Amethyst. Wait." *I absolutely love how he didn't grab her.* Now he had her full attention. She could tell he was serious. "Let me show you the music room." When they got there, he pulled over a couch stool and said, "Sit here."

Amethyst was liking this newfound confidence. She knew he had it in him. Everyone does, and everyone should embrace it. "Someone's feeling some type of way," she smiled.

"You damn right. I'm not losing you this time. I know it's my fault, but we gotta stop doing this." As soon as Xenon started playing the piano, Amethyst got butterflies. The way he was looking at her was so intense. Then he started singing Mood by dvsn. He didn't want to be predictable and sing a Frank Ocean song. Amethyst got chills when he switched to the drums while he was singing to her. Xenon came up to her and gently lifted her chin, so she'd be looking directly at him. She smiled at him and made him hit a high note.

"Oh, my goddess. Reign!" said Iris. "He's singing. He's actually f****** singing. Sister got him to f****** sing. I didn't think he was really going to do it."

Reign squealed. "This is so romantic!"

"Damn," Bella smiled. "His voice is so damn sexy."

Thetis and Jeremy went to go find the squad as soon as they heard the first note. "Oh, my goddess. That's Blinky!" Thetis was so moved she wiped a tear from her eye. "I'm sorry. Xenon hasn't sung a note in years. He was the lead singer in the central choir. Then he stopped coming to basilica. We only have it once a month. It's just not the same without him."

"Honestly, it's been so long I forgot he sang. Hell, I forgot he could play the piano and drums. Amethyst has that effect on people," Jeremy smiled. "This is great. No one say a word about what we just told you. Maybe he'll come back to basilica. That would be a miracle."

"Why'd he stop singing?" asked Bella.

"He never said why, but he felt like no one understood him," Jeremy said. "The thing is that no one could possibly understand him. He's literally the only empath there is."

"He thought Amethyst could for some reason," Thetis smiled. "I guess he was right."

"Wow. That sounds just like Ame," said Chance. "Okay, Reign... Now I totally agree with you. This connection thing they got going on is pretty freaky."

"He made himself look happy for the basileia, but everyone could tell something was wrong," said Thetis. "He was miserable. He would cry every night after he came back from his secret trips to the surface."

"He would sing up there," Chance said. "I ain't gon lie... It was heartbreaking. I see why he stopped singing. He was probably so sad that he couldn't sing anything happy. Shit. I'm tearing up."

"Oh, my goddess that's so sad. Sort of like when orcas sing their Lachtara," said Bella. "They sing the saddest Lachtara of all whales. Humpbacks are the best singers and dancers, but orcas are in their own lane when it comes to pouring out emotions."

"I know it's a song, but what's that?" asked Chance.

"A yearning song," Thetis explained. "Not any kind of yearning though. Whales sing it when they've been separated from their loved ones.

Especially their soulmates. They believe the song will bring them back to each other. In a way, it's infallible because if they aren't reunited in the physical, orcas will sing their Lachtara until death. Literally, the only reason they don't commit suicide is because of the possibility of being reunited."

"Bro... That's some *Free Willy* shit." Chance's nose was running now. Reign was rubbing his back to comfort him. "Dammit, I need some tissue or whatever it's called."

DAY 17

The Zeta negative squad was about to watch a movie, but of course, Alpha insisted they wait for Zeta. "Where is he? Can we just play the movie?" Beta was patient, but Rho was tired of waiting. Chi was frustrated.

"Amethyst!" Xenon called out to her. "Where are you?"

"I've been in here waiting for you."

"Well, I won't make you wait any longer." When he ran in, everyone could tell what was on his mind. Iris started recording. He stopped Amethyst from pressing play and said, "Amethyst. I've been searching for the right words but... Uhhh. This is going to sound weird..."

"It's alright, just say it. I'm here for you, baby."

"Amethyst, I'm drawn to you. Not just my heart. My soul. We've met in every life. You remember me, and I remember you too. Remember that time when we were younger, and I gave you that piece of seaweed? Ever since then... I don't know what it is about you, but I couldn't stop thinking about you. Wait. Well... I do know. Our dreams... Then our little rendezvous on the beach in the morning... That's when I realized why I can't get you out of my head. Honestly, I don't even want you out of my head. You're the person I talked to pretty much every day all these years. My third eye was so closed. You're helping me open it. And that song I would sing... Uhhh! Sorry. See what I mean. Amethyst. I-I love you dammit! I'm so happy I found you. I can't explain how I feel, but I can show you. Even if you don't love me back, I want you to know that I will always love you and only you. After all these years, I'm sure. I want to be your lover, your partner, your defender, your best friend, your Night Light for eternity. Yes, eternity. When I say eternity, I mean eternity. The love I have for you is unfathomable. You said your trust requires all time, but I'll give you more than that. I'll give you all of me. I will love you unconditionally forever. You're what I've been missing. You understand me. You have my heart. You have my soul. I know you've told me this before but… Will you be my mate?"

"Yes! I've been so anxious waiting for you. I've been sending you signals in the other planes for years. I had to be sure," she smiled. "Our souls can't be apart, can they? Even when we weren't physically together we were together. We go together. I love you too. The connection we have is so surreal. Something about it is unique isn't it? We're like two neutron stars. The love I have for you is cosmic, infinite, eternal. I've been missing you even though I didn't know exactly who I was missing. You know how doubtful I can be. If I would have known you were really my soulmate, I would have fallen off the cliff a long time ago. Like you couldn't stay away from the surface, I was drawn to the ocean. I love you so much. I never expected you to have the words. I don't either. There are no words. I just wanted you to try. That's all we can do. Eeeeeep! I love you so much!"

"I love you more."

"I love you infinity."

"Me too, Moon Jelly." *Huh. Finally… That's over with. I'm not jealous or anything. I'm just anxious to get to the action, the OMGs, and the sister bonding. Today's Friday, so we won't be able to get to those parts. I'll finish up this section of the story and save the rest for next week. How's that sound? Hint: Soon you'll get to see their true colors. Remember this is just the introduction. We're going to end with the beginning. Your queries will be answered next week. LOL. See what I did there? I'm warning you. Once we get through this lighthearted intro, the story gets exponentially darker and darker and darker, so soak this in.*

"Isn't the proper word infinitely?" Reign whispered.

"I think it's an Atoz thing," said Iris. "But who cares. We are in the midst of two soulmates. This is amazing."

"Wow. They're hella dramatic. So passionate. So raw," said Chance. "You can feel how much they mean it too. Damn."

Bella pulled himself up on the edge of the pool they had installed for him. "Huh," he sighed. "I want that! I adore them. I absolutely adore them."

"Right!" Reign twirled. "So romantic."

"Now we'll get to see their true colors," Iris and Chance said at the same time. "This is going to be entertaining."

"Who's home?" Amethyst asked Xenon.

"Just the squad. Mom and Dad went out to eat."

"You wanna have sex?"

"Oral and hand jobs?"

"Exactly what I had in mind. I'm glad the bas is drained. This should be good."

"They really don't care that we're right here do they?" Reign asked.

"Nope," Chance and Iris said.

"Why are you stressing, Chance?" Iris teased. "For them, it's just child's play."

"They don't take it seriously?" Reign asked.

"I think they're more of a psychic couple rather than a physical one," Iris said. "Stop being such a dad, Chance," she laughed. He was still recovering from his nose bleed.

"So innocent, but so hot…" said Bella.

WARNING!

I'm just kidding.

Amethyst gently pushed him on her bed and climbed on top of him. Xenon said, "To be honest, I'm a little nervous."

"Why? You're the one that bites," she smiled. "I'm just kidding. Do you want to go watch a movie instead? That's cool too."

"No, that's not what I meant. It's a good nervous. Just go slow."

"Xe. Come on. I can tell. Let's go do something else fun."

"Okay. I'm sorry. There's just so much on my mind right now."

"You don't have to apologize, and there's no need for an explanation. If you want to talk about it, I'm here, but I don't want you to feel like you have to."

"You aren't irritated with me or anything?"

"No," she smiled. "Of course not, babe. Awww, don't cry. What's wrong?"

"I... I-I just love you so much. I don't really know why I'm so emotional. I've always been blue. I've got the blues. You're the first person to react that way. I'm just so overwhelmed. You're here. You're really here. I can't believe I finally did it. You make me feel so confident and secure. OMG. I'm so overwhelmed. I found you. Well... Maybe you found me. Whatever. Remember when we used to play hide and seek? You were right under my nose. You told me that! I was never good at hide and seek. I always took a long time to find you even when you came out of hiding."

"You still found me though. I'm patient," she smiled.

"What if I mess up? What if I'm not good enough for you? The physical plane is different. What if I'm not the same? I'm not the wild type. What if I'm not masculine enough for you? What if you think I'm too feminine or something? It's hard because I can't read your emotions. I'm also not the type of intimate partner from the other realms you think I am. I'm not all wild, and according to surface standards, I'm as unorthodox as they come."

"I'm sorry I made you feel that way, Moon Beam."

"It's me. I just keep needing you to remind me that you're different from those jerks I've had to deal with."

"You want me to be blunt?"

"Yeah," he smiled.

"If I can see through your bullshit in the physical plane, what makes you think that I can't see through it in the other ones? I knew it was all an act, Moon Beam. That's why I kept trying to get you to talk about it. My soulmate is a tranquil, quiet yet loud, mysterious, shy, reserved, abyssal, fluid, chill, cool, soothing, moody, emotional storm. I'm the wild one, and I love your true self. Sexually, you know you and I are a perfect match. Did you forget what happened that one time by our fountain? Xe. You know me."

"How could I forget?" he smiled. "Huh," he sighed. "I know, Moon Jelly. I'm just so needy. Why am I like this?"

"You just need lots of upfront, in your face love," she giggled. "And I'm willing to give it. As for the whole masculine feminine thing, you'll always be the yang to my yin unless you say that's changed. If it does, that's fine. You'll always be my Blue Moon Baby. Plus, who gives a f*** about that anyway. My soulmate is Xenon. Not masculine, feminine, girl, boy, sex, no sex, man, womxn, gender, biological sex... Just Xenon. Whoever Xenon is, is who I'm in love with."

"Uhhh! I'm so annoying."

"No. I have to start talking about how I feel more. Don't say I'm annoying when I remind you every day. Hell. Multiple times a day. Under one condition... You have to promise to tell me what's on your mind."

"I promise."

"And I thought you like talking in frequencies better... We can do that more often."

"Really?" he smiled. "Okay. I also really like the sound of your voice."

"Awww. I love my little moon alien," she smiled. "What? Why are you doing your puppy eyes? What do you want witcho cute ass?"

"I want you to stop blocking me from your emotions," he blushed. "Babe, I'm serious. Stop laughing at me."

"We really have to work on that third eye of yours, don't we? Closed ass chakra…" she laughed. "And stop sucking your stomach in."

"Okay. Wait. Babe. What are you saying?"

"I'm saying I was never f****** blocking you. Your third eye is a lot more open than it was before, but you have so much more potential."

"I'm so f****** shook. What the actual f***?" he laughed. "I could have sworn you let me in that one time though."

"Your third eye must have blinked or something," she laughed.

"I don't get how you're the only person this happens with. How are you both me and Iris's blind spots?"

"Because you can't see the present or the future without analyzing the past." Her palm glowed purple, and she gently touched his forehead.

"Wow. What was that? That was cool. Oh, my goddess that was insane."

"I asked Chaos to show you when our souls were born as a pair."

"So, when you said we're like two neutron stars you meant that literally? Whoa. Does anyone else know that? What else do you know?"

"I know a lot of things that no one else knows," she giggled. "I've been dying to tell you about them. Eeeeeep! There's so much."

"You know I'm going to be doing a deep analysis of everything that you say, don't say, do, and don't do right? Wait. So, you knew you had powers all this time?"

"I just knew I knew things. It's funny because there's a lot I don't know. Anyways, I had no idea about everything else I can do, including that glowy palm thing I just did. That's new."

"Babe. I know you're a titan-goddess, but of what?"

"I don't know."

"You know what I'm asking."

"You tell me about you first. Then I'll tell you."

"After that, let's tell the others. Let's make them wait though."

"Okay. Their reactions are going to be hilarious. Anyways, I'll tell you later. We've had enough for today. Oh, and I won our cosmic game of tag. Let's not play that game anymore."

"Okay," Xenon smiled. "What should we do now, partner?"

"Wanna watch some anime?"

"That's f****** racist, Amethyst," he joked.

"Shut yo fine ass up," she laughed. "Ooooo! You know what we should do?"

"Play one of our sex tapes, so they think we're having sex?" he smiled.

"Wow. Yeah. How'd you know? And you sound confident."

"That's because all of our sex tapes are from our rendezvous in the metaphysical plane. I was thinking the same thing," he said as he connected his other phone to his speakers. "Let's put it in HVM."

"LOL. Bluetooth…" she laughed. "Aw. I just realized I don't have them on this phone."

"We can share this one, but I'll get you another one. The password is— LOL. You know what it is. Naturally, both of my phones also recognize your face and your voice," he smiled.

"This is the time I was talking about earlier, right? What did we name it again?"

"Waterworks," he laughed. "Wanna cuddle?"

"Sure. Hold on then."

"Where are you going?"

"To put my clothes on."

"I don't have mine on. Just come over here like that."

She examined his belly. "Is this a tiny scale? What the hell?" she laughed.

"No. It's just skin. You're hella observant. I just call it a tiny glitter rash. Must have something to do with this whole moon energy thing. Mom doesn't know about them. I scratch them off as soon as I see one. That one must be new. It could also be eczema."

"You're a physician, and we both have eczema. You know damn well this ain't no damn eczema. Sparkly ass eczema," she laughed.

Bella turned down the movie. "Girls listen. Is that Xenon?"

"What?!?!?" said Chance. "Shhh!"

"Now I hear Amethyst…" Reign said. "What the hell are they doing to each other? Are they laughing?"

"Oh hell no. N**** turn that back up," Chance said.

"Awww, I'm happy for them," said Iris. "That's good. That's healthy."

"I agree. Sounds like fun," said Bella. "That's an interesting dynamic."

"Aye n****… Don't be getting all excited by me," Chance laughed. "We know about you. F****** perv."

"I. AM. NOT," Bella splashed water on him. Chance responded like a little lion cub and shook the water off.

Reign asked, "How are the youngest members of the squad the sexsperts?"

"Because they aren't f****** normal," said Chance. "Nothing about them is normal. They're both on some cosmic shit. How the f*** are their minds connected? I still don't get that! Also, what do they mean my other planes? How long have they known each other? Iris, bro… You know you wanna ask."

"I'm sure they'll tell us eventually," Iris said. "Besides, it's obvious they've been f****** in the other planes. That was made clear by his reaction to those flowers," she laughed.

"That's one thing, but my thing is that they know we're right here!!!" Reign said.

"He's/she's an exhibitionist," Iris and Chance said at the same time.

"Both of them?" Chance knew what needed to be done. "Oh shit! I'm ordering everyone earplugs and a memory wiper right the f*** now. Do y'all have those?" After Atoz woke up from their nap, they were hungry, so naturally, they went to go see if the squad was also hungry. Chance said, "Y'all nasty as hell. How can y'all wanna eat?" Reign secretly gave them a thumbs up behind Chance's back.

"What are you talking about?" Xenon laughed.

"We already peed and took a bath and stuff," said Amethyst.

"Nah. I'm judging," said Chance.

"Relax," said Amethyst. "I just needed a tune-up."

"And I just needed my oil changed," said Xenon.

"You two are mechanics now?" Bella laughed.

"Yeah. I'm her gynecologist, and she's my 'colonoscopist'. Vroom vroom."

"Ahhh! You are both hilarious," Reign laughed. "Don't give Chance another nose bleed."

"You two are too much," Iris giggled.

"What's my diagnosis, doctor?" asked Amethyst.

"Goddess as usual. You know that. So where are we eating? I've got a taste for scallops."

"Still?" Amethyst smiled.

"I always have a taste for scallops."

Chance was so uncomfortable. "F***! I know y'all glad y'all finally found each other in the physical plane and all, but can y'all please just stop talking!!! Damn!!! Can y'all stop flirting with each other for 2 minutes?"

After they ate, Amethyst said, "Y'all! Come up to the grotto! Xe got me some lavender bundles to go with my oil! I guess that's what happens when you put it on him," she laughed.

I'm deeead.

They actually think we were having sex.

LOL ikr. We've never even done it in the physical.

"What are you going to do with those?" Reign asked.

"You'll see," Chance smiled.

"Alright so check this out…" Amethyst was excited. "Five days ago, when me and Xe were up here, I found some lavender, sage, hibiscus, and roses. I made some incense, but y'all can help me make smudge sticks. And Thetis bought me a diffuser, so there's that too."

"What are those?" Bella asked.

"Things you burn," Amethyst smiled. "Natural herbs and stuff are good for cleansing and aromatherapy. Come on. We can go under that tree with the big ass leaves."

"Different plants have different effects, but Moon Jelly and I are professionals."

"Ame put me on. This is partially how I got off drugs and shit," said Chance. "I'm telling y'all… I don't know what the f*** she do, but this shit is mesmerizing."

"What do they do?" asked Reign. "I think the Naiads know about this kind of thing."

"That's who I ordered the rest of my supplies from. They just make you feel relaxed. Really relaxed."

"They make you high as f*** if you do it right," said Chance.

"I guess but it's not like that. Let me be blunt. I don't smoke. LOL. There is no smoking involved. That's not good for your body no matter what you smoke." They were all down to try it. "First we have to make a sage smudge stick to cleanse the negative energy."

"Oh, hell yeah. Look at how she wrap that shit. That's my f****** sister."

"Oh, my goddess," Amethyst laughed. "Can you not? You over here acting like it's weed. It's not. It's better. I don't like the way that shit smells. Speaking of weed… I'll get hemp oil for us next time. I love hemp! We could take lavender baths and then rub hemp oil on our bodies. What we're doing today is just a preview. Anyways, y'all ready?" Amethyst took out her purple Zippo lighter and burned the smudge stick.

"You really like fire don't you, Moon Jelly?"

"Yes, yes I do," she laughed.

"Ame is a pyromaniac or some shit."

"No, I'm not. That's something else. I have pyrophilia. I'm not an arsonist. I just get a little excited that's all."

"A little?" Chance laughed. "This kid literally be chilling at the house looking at a flame y'all."

"Now we just wait for the smoke to diffuse and then we can get started. We can make tea with the hibiscus, lavender, and roses. I wouldn't mix the lavender and rose though." After they all got their tea, Amethyst burned a little bit of the incense and turned on the diffuser. "Now we wait. The lavender oil is highly concentrated. Shout out to the Naiads. Here. We can massage some of this oil mixture on our bodies. It's good for sensitive skin and safe for your tail, Bella."

Some time passed, and Iris said, "Wow. This is something else. Who knew?"

"I can totally feel my heartbeat," Xenon added. "Damn. It's like surround sound."

"Here. Pass this vial around. It's a peppermint and tea tree mixture. Just take one quick whiff at a time. It helps open up your airways."

"Even my muscles feel relaxed," Bella added.

"This Naiad shit strong as f***," Chance said. "They really plugged it."

"That's because it's all natural," Amethyst laughed. "They don't use hella chemicals like surface people. Oh yeah, I forgot to tell you the amethyst cluster helps rid the body of stress, anxiety, depression, and stuff. It's good for clarity of mind. We'll still be f***** up, but you get the point... This is a good time to just let things out. Can someone put some music on?"

"What do y'all wanna hear?" Chance asked.

"How about some Frank Ocean?" Xenon suggested.

Amethyst said, "Yaaaassss. That's perfect. How about we start with *Channel ORANGE*?" They all agreed.

When "Super Rich Kids" came on, Iris said, "We need a squad playlist. This will be the first song on it. You can add to it, Red. Only some of the lyrics apply to us, but it fits our aesthetic. Right, Sister?"

"Hell yeah, it does." After she finished her hibiscus tea, she took out a shot glass and filled it with juice. Xenon watched her and smiled.

"What did you just do?" Iris asked. "I didn't see. I know that wasn't alcohol."

"I took communion," she laughed. "I hate alcohol like a Nereid hates kelp. It smells terrible. Ew. This is grape juice. I got this from the Naiads too. They hooked it up." She handed out the other shot glasses and passed around the juice. "What about y'all? Do y'all drink?"

"I have a drink every now and then. Don't tell Meter," said Iris. "Ah. Who am I kidding? I f****** love alcohol."

"Oh shit, Iris," said Chance. "I see you. What you like to drink? Red wine? Beer?"

"I like my liquor crystal clear."

"Oh okay, so you're a vodka girl? I'm sober right now, but I'm a whiskey guy."

"Something like that," she laughed.

"Iris has a problem. She can handle 8 shots of rectified spirit. 8 shots! I sat there and watched her. I don't know how the hell that's even possible," Reign said. Amethyst was getting another one of her psychic feelings for some reason. "It's not an Oceanid thing. That's an Iris thing."

"LOL. That fits your aesthetic. Now Thetis's nicknames for us are even funnier. You can really hold yo shit huh, sis? She's so classy... I love it."

"No way. Shut the f*** up," Chance laughed. "Rectified spirit? That's 95% ABV!!! Bloody hell!!! Why would you drink that?!?!?"

"It's 96%. I get mine imported from Europe. I don't know. Nothing else really does it for me. Must have something to do with my powers or something."

"Look at the alcoholics getting along. Awww," Amethyst laughed.

"What about you, Miss Brazil?" said Chance. "I like your afro by the way."

"Awww! Thanks, Freckles," Reign smiled. "I might have a beer or something, but after one, I'm done."

"I'm with you, Reign," said Bella. "My limit is one."

"What about you, Blue?" asked Chance. "You real quiet over there."

"I mean I guess some drinks taste alright, but I prefer smoothies. Plus, alcohol is a depressant, so I'm the last person that should have a drink if we're talking sadness. Sometimes I wish I was dead."

"Same," said Amethyst. "That's a whole ass mood."

"Damn, Eeyore. Don't kill the vibe," said Chance. "Wait... Now we got Winne-the-Pooh and Eeyore. I'm weak as f***."

"Shut up, Piglet," Xenon laughed. The squad was rolling because they never expect Xenon to cap on someone so suddenly.

"Can we stop talking about alcohol?" said Amethyst. "Dang... Here. I brought snacks, but we gotta start talking about real shit."

"You know that Mark Anthony guy I broke up with?" said Reign. "I'm going to tell you something, but promise me you crazy people won't do anything crazy."

"B**** we ain't promising you shit. What the f*** did he do?" said Iris.

"He was such a shark. I would only have sex with him because I felt like I had too. I'd tell him no sometimes, and he couldn't accept that. Come to think of it I never told him yes." Iris threw her arms around her, and Bella rubbed her back.

"Reign, that's rape," said Amethyst. "Oh hell no. Sounds like a squad mission."

"Now we got to go f*** this n**** up," said Chance. It's a good thing he was under the influence of lavender or else who knows what would have happened.

"I knew he was a jerk, but I would have never thought he'd do something like that. This is who we were sitting next to in class?" Xenon wiped a tear. "I haven't killed anyone in a while. Where does he live?"

"Let me torture him first," Bella said calmly. "My urges have been building up."

"No! Don't kill anyone!" Reign cried. "What if you get caught?"

They all looked at each other. "B**** by who?" Iris cried. "Look who the f*** you're talking to."

"Should we tell them, Xe?" Amethyst giggled.

"Yeah," he laughed. "MJ and I killed the Nereid that was attacking people. You know the trench monster? He's been gone for days."

"Days is a while?!?!?" Reign said. "Oh, my goddess! I was thinking a month maybe! How'd you get past the guards?"

"In drag. I didn't want to wear my necklace because I didn't want to lose it or anything," said Xenon.

"That's how I learned that move where you turn someone upside down," said Amethyst.

After the squad had a long, much needed talk of the utmost importance that is often non-existent in a particular otherworldly society about what happened to Reign, Iris said, "I'm starting to think I don't have a soulmate because I'm asexual."

"Sex has nothing to do with soulmates," said Amethyst. "Sex ain't love, love ain't sex. You'll find them, Iris. Have you checked your mirror lately?"

"No, I haven't. There's probably no one there. Speaking of that... Guess what, Whiskey. I thought it was you when I first saw you because I only saw red hair, and Oceanids don't really have that shade of red hair. Soon I realized that was f****** impossible," she laughed. "Hell no."

"Well I'm sorry, Ugly," he laughed. "I was hella crushing on you, but then I came to my senses. I can't f****** stand you."

"Awww, f*** you too. Reign, hook me up with your firstborn child when they turn 29 okay?"

"Ahhh!" Amethyst laughed. "You're a cougar? I ain't even mad."

"I want a man older than me," said Bella. "Preferably a Naiad. Like Chance has a mermaid fantasy, I have a Naiad fantasy. I want to be spoiled. I like that honey-I'm-home type."

"And you're a sugar baby," Amethyst laughed. "I'm sure you'll find a sugar daddy."

"I know the perfect Naiad," said Xenon.

"Basil would be perfect for you," Iris smiled. "He used to be obsessed with Xenon."

"We were barely even friends, and he was talking about I'm his boyfriend. Like lassa what the f***? He was always sliding in my DMs. He literally does that to all the young royals. Ew. I blocked him. I hope you two fall in love, so he'll stop acting like that. He's just desperate for attention. He'll definitely spoil you."

"You two will meet soon enough," said Iris.

"Ooo! I have something juicy," said Xenon. "People don't really have to come out in the realms, but I'm not out yet. Mom doesn't know, and I haven't told anyone or dated anyone. Basically, no one knows but you all."

"LOL saaame," Amethyst said.

"Yeah. Dad doesn't know about us either," said Chance.

Reign was curious. "Sexuality or gender?"

"Both," Atoz said at the same time.

"But I know she's seen you dressed as a flutterfish," said Reign.

"Yeah but since I haven't said anything she's under the impression that it's just for dress up," he smiled.

"But is she really though?" Iris smiled. "Anyways, I've always used his face to practice my makeup skills. I also design my own clothes so... Meter knows about me though."

"How come you're hiding it from them?" Bella asked.

"I don't want to be treated differently or anything," said Chance.

"Yeah," Amethyst agreed. "For me, it's mainly about the gender part."

"That's a whole other thing," Atoz laughed. "Shit."

"Have you noticed how each of us has a role?" Iris giggled. "Chance is the hot-headed maniac, Reign is the hard-headed muscle, Bella is the sociopath, Xenon is the cool guy, I'm the good girl, and Amethyst is the badass."

"LOL truuuuue," Amethyst laughed. "At least we know we're mentally ill. Wait. Never mind. We aren't mentally ill. We're the bad guys."

DAY 18

"You love to write right, Moon Jelly?"

"I looooove to write. That's my thing."

"They also sell paper, pens, and ink here."

"You have paper down here? Cool! What's it made from? And what is your energy made from?"

"Our paper is made from mainly algae and cotton. Most of our energy comes from algae. Everything we make is eco-friendly and waterproof. Well... The paper is dense enough to survive absorbing water. Think of it as a thin piece of fabric. When you write on it, you can rinse the ink out before you dry it. Nowadays, we all use holographic tablets. The other realms still use paper and ink for some things though. We've always been the most technologically advanced."

"You're a writer, Your Highness?" said a man. "What kind?"

"Creative, not academic. I just write what I feel." *I felt that.*

"What do you mean? Say more."

"My writing is a reflection of my soul and therefore cannot be expressed academically. I'm not that good at academic writing anyway. My writing isn't about skill, it's about passion. I don't have much skill. I'm not a scholar. I'm just someone with their body on earth and their psyche in the stars that likes how ink feels on paper."

"What is ink?"

"Blood."

"I like you," he smiled. The man yelled to his crew, "Get Her Highness the finest paper, pens, and ink!!! It's on us."

"Oh, you don't have to do that."

"No. I insist. No one buys it anyway. Just make sure you come back every now and then."

"What is your name?"

"I'm Hussain."

"Thank you, Hussain," she giggled. "Please, take these." She handed him some silver coins.

On their way back to the bas, Xenon noticed Amethyst was in deep thought. He could also hear her heart palpitating. "What's wrong?"

"Huh? Oh. Iris, did you have a vision of ink? Like a lot of ink. Gallons and gallons of it."

"No. Why?"

"I don't know. I was admiring the ink, and I got a bad feeling. It's not about the ink itself. There's just something about it. I feel like something is trying to tell me something. Feels like the ink is trying to warn me."

"Sister, you're scaring me. The last time you thought something was wrong, Xenon almost died. I'll check right now." She pulled out her pocket mirror. "I didn't see anything. But then I didn't see the bolt either."

Amethyst couldn't help but worry and did a full body analysis of Xenon. "How's your vision? Can you breathe okay?"

"I'm fine, Moon Jelly. See."

She checked the others and then Thetis and Jeremy. "So, everyone's okay? Okay then."

"We'll be back," said Jeremy.

"Don't worry, Amethyst. I'll make sure he's safe," she smiled.

"And make sure she's safe too, Dad." Her comment warmed Thetis's heart. She didn't think she cared about her yet.

"Yes, ma'am," he smiled.

Once their parents left, Iris said, "After our circle, I'm meeting with a few Alphas and omegas to inform them about the coronation plan and work out a schedule for set up. We'll be in the same room if you want to say hello."

"Okay. What's today's topic?" asked Amethyst.

"We all ask one person a couple questions, they'll answer them, and then we'll keep going around. You know… A hot seat."

LMAO. Girl… I already know what the f*** they gon ask us.

Ezzzzzactly. HAHAHA. Mooooooon Jeeeeellllly. Hi, Moon Jelly. You're my little squishy wishy ishy fish.

I'm f****** weeeak. You're the cutest. You're my little fluffy wuffy snuggle puppy.

We're hella weird.

"Ooooo!" Bella clapped. "Start with me!"

"What happened to your exes?" Chance asked.

"They all double-crossed me when I broke up with them, so I gave them what they asked for. We were dating in secret because they didn't want to be seen with a mermaid Nereid, so I was safe. Plus, I'm blind and people get eaten all the time. I'm not saying I ate them. I'm vegan."

"What do you torture people with?" Reign asked.

"I have a whole set of supplies."

"What's your item? All Mer have one, right?" Iris asked.

"Knives," he laughed. "I'm just kidding. It's scrolls."

What the f*** is wrong with us, Moon Jelly?

Nothing. Well… Not regarding that. LOL. We're just on some other shit. I like it though.

Me too.

Reign was up next. "Where's your treasure?" asked Amethyst.

"I never looked at the map. I just assumed it's back where I'm from."

"Why compete if you already know you're the strongest?" asked Xenon.

"I really, really like trophies. They're made of pure gold. I could care less about the title."

"Did you ever have to kill a child?" Chance asked.

"No. 19 years old was the youngest."

Aside from what they're about to ask us, we're so bad. They have no idea.

True but f*** it.

OMG. Ammmeeethhhyst. I love your energy. What the hell are we?

Bad b******.

Ahhh. Yaaasssss. Hell yeah.

It was now Iris's turn. Amethyst asked her, "How often do you cut yourself and what do you use?"

"All the time. I usually use broken glass."

Chance asked, "Why'd you pull that prank on Ame? The one where you had her wear that dress that didn't match the theme?"

"I didn't want her to take any attention away from me at his party. I was only used to sharing the spotlight with Blue, but there's plenty of room for one more," she smiled.

Xenon asked Chance, "How come you were so focused on my eyeliner and lip shimmer when Jeremy wears eyeliner and lip gleam now that he's living down here again. Most people wear it."

"Jeremy's eyeliner is like a dark olive green and not that noticeable. His lip gleam is a dark ass navy and also barely noticeable. Your shit pop. Bright ass blue eyeliner. Then your lip shimmer got sparkles in it. I also just like messing with you because you got a lot of sugar in your tank," he laughed.

"Five cups is not that much! What's the max?" he smiled.

"I don't know. It's all relative."

"Did you ever have a crush on Small Fry?" asked Reign.

"No. What the f***? That's like asking Blue if he ever had a crush on Iris. Ame is my sister."

Atoz watched as the squad discussed something without them. "What?" Amethyst giggled.

Chance said, "Basically, we have the same question for both of y'all and it's kind of heavy so…"

"We decided that we'd only ask you each the same one. It has multiple parts to it though. We figured you'd help each other answer anyway," Iris said. "If you don't want to answer, don't feel like you have to. Let us know if we're overstepping."

Iris is such a mom. I love it. Grown ass.

"Well… Go ahead…" Xenon smiled. "It's not a big deal."

I'm nervous. LOL. Iris knows about me though.

Duuuh. Same. Chance knows about me. I'm just worried about Reign and Bella.

"Please, don't take it the wrong way," said Reign.

"Yeah. We just want to listen," Bella added.

"Just spit it out," Amethyst said. "We already know you want to know more about our gender and stuff," she giggled.

"LOL. You all have no idea what you're asking for. It's complex. You're going to be like what the f***?"

"We already think that about y'all," Chance laughed.

"Can you like summon a gender whenever you want?" asked Reign.

"Summon?" they laughed. Xenon said, "It's not something you control, but I guess I could channel a different gender for acting or something."

"What genders are you fluid between? Also, we know your pronouns, but how should we address you regarding gender?" asked Bella. "Can you give us the long answer with the context and everything?"

They really wanna know. They want complete honesty.

What are you gonna do? You go first.

I'm gonna give the gays everything they want.

*Giiiiirl. You are such a f****** meme.*

"First off, I want you to know that it's different for everyone. For me, I'm female. I'm biologically a girl, and I f****** love that. That's the physical. If we're talking about gender though… That's where shit can get a little complicated depending on who you're talking to. I'm not completely a girl or a boy. Sometimes I'm neither. Sometimes I'm a combination. It's cool that the binary works for some people, but why can't I just be me? I can't stand all these man-made rules and shit. Like… Why make such strict categories knowing everyone won't fit and then be mad when they don't? Don't get me started on my theories about that. The rules don't determine my gender or anything. Regardless of the binary existing or whatever, my gender has to do with how I feel. I'd still be me if the binary didn't exist. This world is all about defining things, and I can't be defined. I swear… Why can't I just be Amethyst? I only use labels, so I can understand myself better and connect with people easier and stuff. Labels also say I EXIST. I just make them my own. To be honest, they've kind of grown on me. Anyways, I wonder who the hell said people could people could make that shit up anyway. LOL. Who started this? Eh. I don't be tripping that hard though," she laughed. "If someone asks if I'm a girl, I'll just say yeah sometimes because I know what they mean. Some people think the physical body and gender are the same thing. I know people won't get it. I understand that there are some people who just don't know in addition to people who are just full of hatred, so I don't hate anyone for what they think about me. If someone asks, you can say I'm female, Amethyst, or fluid. Sometimes I'll just be like LOL and say something clever. Despite the BS, it can actually be pretty fun once you stop giving a f***. Plus, they don't need to know anything, and I'm not finna walk around with a megaphone. It's not that serious. You might be wondering why I don't just say I'm a non-conforming girl. Well, I'm always non-conforming, but my shit changes. It's not about clothing. It's about how I feel. Does that make sense? I was born in the right body, but I should have been born with shapeshifting powers too. I still feel weird, awkward, sick, invalid, and uncomfortable sometimes. I have my moments. Sometimes I cry at night, but I always pick myself up like 'f*** them' and tell my fine ass to go be me unapologetically. It's a cycle. Honestly, they can all suck my clit. Okay. It's all you, boo."

"I love hearing you talk," said Xenon. "Let's say there are two worlds. In one world, there's no rules or categories about who has to act a certain way, wear certain clothing, etc. People just are who they are, and their identity and self-expression mean whatever they want them to mean. In world two, there are two strict categories everyone has to fit into depending on what's between their legs. If you take some people from world one and place them in world two, some people will fit in, some people will sort of fit in, and others might not fit in at all."

"What did you mean when you said, 'of the masculine energy?'" asked Reign.

"Uh… Moon Jelly, can you take this one? I have no idea how to explain that."

"Are y'all familiar with a yin-yang? Before I say this, I want you to know that I'm not saying this is THE definition of a yin-yang. I'm just using applying it to the way my mind operates. You feel me? OMG I love yin-yangs. They represent the universe and shit. And I like to think of a yin-yang as a soulmate pair. A pair doesn't have to be yin and yang. It can be yin and yin, yang and yang, yin/yang and yin/yang… It doesn't matter. It's my favorite because it represents the universe, and I like to see it as that and as a soulmate pair. The bond between soulmates is cosmic anyway… LOL. Uhhh. My bad. I got sidetracked. Just know that this is what it means to me. I made it up. Alright so check this out… Think of me and Xe as a yin-yang. I'm yin and he's yang. Notice how yin and yang are also within each other. Notice how a yin-yang is fluid. It's infinite. If you wanna know more about all my little theories, I'd love to tell you some other time," she smiled.

I love how they're so intrigued. They're so cute. OMG. I caaan't.

Duuuh. Oh, my goddess. I love them. I'm trying not to cry.

"Wait. Can you give me one more example?" said Reign.

"OMG, gemmie. Really?" said Iris. "You're literally the only one…"

"It's alright, sis," Amethyst giggled. "I know this shit can sound bizzare if you just know about existing in the physical. Fun fact: You don't even have your earth body in the other planes. I appreciate you asking for clarification and stuff. On the surface, people aren't the least bit accepting. I wouldn't dare tell the majority of people up there. They'd be like, 'No no no! Shut the f*** up!', 'What's wrong with you?', 'You're lying. You just want attention!' even though attention is the last thing I want LOL. Honestly, I just want them to leave me the f*** alone if they're going to be hella rude and disrespectful. I get that some people don't get it or whatever, but people really gotta chill. I don't get why they care so much. They get so damn angry, and they don't even know why," she laughed.

"OMG that's a mood! It's the same way in the S.O. It's difficult as f*** trying to explain the cosmic in the physical," Xenon laughed. "That's why we keep some stuff to ourselves. Ooooo! I know the perfect example to help Reign out! Tell her the flashlight example. Me and MJ were f****** around, and it actually turned out to be a fantastic ass example."

They have no idea how literal you meant that last part.

For reeeal. I thought they would have caught on by now.

"LOL. Okay look… There's layers to this shit. My gender is the actual flashlight. I have multiple flashlights. My overall encompassing energy AKA yin is the light that never changes regardless of anything. My sub energies are the different filters that change. The colors of the filters make the light appear that color. I can't really make a list of all the flashlights, but the colors of the filters can be narrowed down. Pink is for mostly girl. Blue is for mostly boy. Purple is for anything closer to 50 girl/50 boy. Grey is for agender. The grey can be with the purple, pink, or blue indicating bigender + agender. I count bigender as one gender. Think about shaking something up or blending it. Woo. Okay. There you go, Raphael."

"Ohhh!" said Reign. "Okay. Thanks. Sorry. Who's Raphael?"

"He's a Ninja Turtle," said Chance. "Ame just say that because she likes how that shit sound. It was in this funny ass parody video we watched online."

"For me, it's just like that except the intensity doesn't really change that much. I'm either a 1 which means completely a boy, 2 a demiboy, 3 evenly split bigender, 4 a demigirl, or a 5 which is completely a girl. For 2, 3, and 4, a part could be boy, girl, or agender."

"Do you experience dysphoria?" Chance asked. "I know you kind of already told me, Ame. I just want more information, so I can try to understand better."

"Moon Jelly and I talked about this the other day. I would much rather exist as my soul body and not my physical body. That way nothing is permanent, and I can go back and forth. That's how we're all going to end up anyway, so I'm okay with waiting I guess. Uhhhh! No, I'm not. Sometimes I wish I could change, but dysphoria doesn't impact me in the ways it impacts some people, so I'm grateful for that. It could be worse, but still… Sometimes I'm so f****** sick."

"Yaaasssss preach, baby. I love my situation," she gestured. "But I do think about having a different body sometimes. And my height. I like being small but… Uhhh! I wouldn't want to change them permanently, so I'm okay with using my imagination since I can't f****** shapeshift. I know some people have it worse but damn. Sometimes I be f***** up y'all. Oh, and just so you all know, not all people under the trans umbrella experience dysphoria."

"And some trans* people have binary identities and that's totally okay. On the other hand, Amethyst and I are always non-conforming no matter what gender we are."

Shit. This got hella deep, hella fast babe.

Iris asked a follow-up question. "So, if you had the ability to shapeshift like you can in the nonphysical that would make it better because then your bodies would match your souls, right?"

"Yeah because that way we could change and…" Xenon left his sentence incomplete, so Amethyst could finish it. *They do that a lot.*

"…always be able to go back to how we originally were."

"You're so lucky, Iris," he said.

"Isn't it interesting how people can accept Iris's gender regardless of her having the potential to change her body, yet some people can't accept our gender. Hell, she could change at home, and they wouldn't f****** know. They accept her as a girl. It's crazy because our situations are simply swapped. You don't see them labeling her as fluid, yet we're accepted as anything but fluid. I swear… Like what the f***? The physical plane doesn't make any damn sense to me."

"Sure f****** doesn't. This world makes my head hurt," Xenon added.

"Uhhh!!! OMG! I wish I could shapeshift so f****** bad even if it's limited! Forget the animals and shit… I don't even want to change my face, voice, and hair. People accepting me is great, but it's just something extra. Even if they didn't, I would care a lot less if I could shapeshift because I'd be so much more comfortable with myself! Iris, I'm so f****** jealous."

"OMG yaaasssss! Say it queen! Ugh! I need to vent. Can I vent to you all? Don't respond to it though."

Ugh! I'm gonna cry. I can feel it. Dammit. How did we get here?

"Sure, Blue. You too, Sister."

"Life in the Southern Ocean is so f****** terrible. Like… I had to watch for all these things. Not getting caught stealing, not getting caught in the wrong place at the wrong time, not getting caught as a sex worker, not getting caught with somebody rumored to be queer, making sure no one found out I'm queer… Hella shit. Ugh! It's like… I don't really care if you don't agree with my queerness or whatever the case might be. I just want to be treated with respect. That's all," he cried. "I don't get how people can think the physical body is equal to the soul. Me being male doesn't have shit to do with my gender. Like… The difference is simple. How would you describe yourself if you didn't have your physical body? I'm not saying everyone is fluid like me. Some people's gender would still align with the physical how some people say it's supposed to, and that's perfectly fine and valid. I don't get how they don't think I'm valid. Like… I'm not just plain masculine. So what? What's wrong with that? So what my gender has layers and you can't always point your finger on it? So what I don't fit the categories you said were the only two that exist as if that's true? Who the f*** told you, you could make up categories anyway? Why the hell do you care about who or how I'm f******? Why does it matter? Oh, my goddess I really don't understand. Why do they have to make me feel like this? Then their emotions. It's overwhelming sometimes. My father was so cruel. When he would catch me and Radon playing dress up he'd get so angry. He'd yell at me for doing anything he considered feminine even if it was subtle. The things he would say were horrible. Then he'd keep going because of course I would weep, and he said males can't weep because that's a sign of weakness. I never even knew about terms and things until I got here. Ugh! I hated how my father kept saying, 'You're male!!!' Oh, my goddess. That would make me so mad because I— Never mind," he blushed. "The Southern Ocean f***** me up. Now I'm scarred. I have all this internalized trauma. It's still problematic even though I can identify it and try to fight it. Damn. F*** the S.O. on some real shit. I hate that place. Alright I'm done. I don't want to talk anymore. It's all you, MJ."

"I hate the f****** surface. The surface literally hates me because I'm female, black, and queer as f***. LOL. I'm a good ass example of the importance of intersectionality. The kids at school like parts of me or hate all of me. Like… All I really miss is the animals and nature that hasn't gone extinct yet, but I know about land now so… Surface logic is so f****** stupid. School is a safe zone. They can't sting you or take you when you're at school, but the bullies will call me all these things and say I'm not a girl or a boy. If I were to say that about myself, they'd ridicule the f*** out of me and say I don't exist. I'd get treated like shit either way. They're basically right about my gender, but they don't understand that the physical body doesn't always reflect the soul according to their dumb ass laws. They say I'm too open about my sexuality and gender even though I'm hella quiet about it! I try to hide it and keep it from attracting too much attention even though I should be free to express myself. They're the ones who bring the shit up, and even then, I try to talk around it. It doesn't really matter what I say or don't say. They'll believe whatever they want to believe. Even if I try to conform or ignore that I don't fit the binary, it's a problem. I even tried claiming tomboy, but they saw past that shit. In P.E. the girls don't want me on their side because of my gender and sexuality. I can't go to the boys' side either. I don't f****** want to anyway. Also, they treated me worse than the girls. Usually, I'd just sit out or do the activities by myself. I was so happy when they put me and Chance in the same class. Then the showers… OMG. I hated that. I'd go to the girls' showers, but they were always looking at me to see 'what I am'. Sometimes they'd make me wear a blindfold. I get why they were so uncomfortable but damn. Plus, I wasn't looking at them. I'd always go to the shower farthest away from them. They the ones who be doing shit. Stupid ass public showers. I can't tell you how many videos and pictures of me there were. Sometimes they tried to molest me. I guess they were trying to tease me or something. One time they pushed me into the boys' showers and wouldn't let me out. I don't even want to talk about what happened in there. The girls were usually pretty chill about the bathroom once they realized I was just coming to pee. If I happened to be feeling more masculine and wearing so-called boys' clothes, I'd have to change before I could go in. That's why my backpack's so big. That's crazy because they have no problem with the tomboys. No one really does. There's only 3 of them, but they say 2 of them are still girly. They say I give off different vibes. But the other one is yang as f***, so I really don't get how that works. I asked them about it, and they said she's still a girl and I give off grunge pretty boy skater vibes. LOL accurate. I was lowkey juiced, but I acted like I wasn't because I still gotta pee. People love to spread rumors, but they know I'm female. They hella know I'm female. I guess I just confuse them and make them uncomfortable because I change. It's funny because my clothing doesn't always imply my gender. There's so many scenarios. Then some people love flirting with me and love when I flirt with them. Other people are pervs. One time someone put their hand under my skirt. People stare at me and shit. Sometimes I think they're curious. I tried to wear a full face of makeup one time, but they laughed at me. I mean… It was terrible I guess. No one f****** taught me. I didn't know what the f*** I was doing. They could have at least helped me. Now I feel weird about makeup sometimes only because I'm reminded of what happened. I can still hear them laughing at me. If it's more than lip gloss, eyeliner, and mascara, I won't wear it unless Iris does it for me. Then I couldn't even be on the cheer squad because of my stupid ass, inaccurate ass ID. I hated that test. I knew what results I was going to get. Our school is better than the others though. Ugh! There's a girl on the football team, but they won't let me on the f****** cheer squad. WTF. Anyways, I get called an abomination, a sinner, and other stuff because I don't fit the binary. Hell, some cis people don't fit the binary! I don't get it. There's nothing violent, threatening, or hateful about my identity. Uhhh! Sorry, I'm talking too much. I'm done venting."

Atoz surveyed their faces. "Uhhhh. We shouldn't have said anything. Now it's just awkward."

What if we said too much? MJ, maybe we said too much. They're in deep thought. They feel sorry for us. I don't want them to feel sorry for us. I'm fine… I just had to let that out.

Shit. I was trying to be all confident and bold but… Let's try to play it cool. We only have to last for a few more waves. Never mind. Tell my boy Benny to watch out. I'm about to snuggle under you.

They were so embarrassed. Amethyst tucked herself into Xenon, and he hid his face behind her. "We know what you're thinking," she said.

"Awww," said Reign. "They're both shy. It's alright."

"When we try to explain it, everything sounds complicated, but it's simple to us," Xenon said. "We know it probably doesn't make any sense to you. We know it was a lot. Sorry."

"They're probably disgusted and weirded out by us too."

"No, we aren't," Iris comforted them. "We're just doing our best to try to understand, so we can support you."

"I don't know if this is going to come out wrong, but I think it's kind of cool how you two don't fit into categories. You're different and that's awesome," Reign smiled. "I admire the courage you have to be you. I know it's not always easy. Plus, we're in the Pacific Ocean! Not the

Southern Ocean or the surface!" she twirled. "If we do happen to swim into a shark, I'll take care of them!"

"Not that it equates, but speaking of categories, if you zoom out, none of us really fit into a single category," said Bella.

"We're all here for you. We don't want you two to feel like you can't talk to us. I love you, Ame. Hell, I love your ass too, Blue."

Iris announced, "Group hug!" Then they all tackled and tickled Amethyst and Xenon until they both couldn't help but laugh. "We love our cosmic genderfluid bisexual and our cosmic genderfluid demi-bisexual."

"So, we have three shy bis?" Reign smiled.

"They're shy. I'm insecure," Chance laughed.

None of them knew Jeremy came home a while ago and had heard the last few comments in their conversation. Naturally, he thought about what he should do as a parent. He cared about them too. He deciphered the codes the squad often used and weaved together the details. He completely forgot that Iris was having a meeting, and by the time the Alphas and Omegas arrived, he was already in another part of the bas gathering his thoughts. The Iota negative squad was chilling in Amethyst's room waiting for her to get out of her meeting. When Jeremy found them, Amethyst smiled and said, "Hey, Dad."

Then he said, "Ame. Chance. Blue... You could have told me you're bi. You could have talked to me about your boy problems if you needed to, Chance." Alpha, Chi, and Zeta were completely frozen. They felt sick. The rest of the squad tried to quiet Jeremy, but he wasn't paying attention. "It's totally okay for you two to let me know your correct pronouns, so I don't misgender you. I didn't know I made you feel like you couldn't tell me. I know you didn't know I'm from the ocean. Don't worry, I'm open-minded and—" They finally got his attention. "What's wrong?"

"Iris is having a meeting with some of the Alphas and Omegas in the other room," Reign whispered. "And you have a very loud voice."

Iris acted like she didn't hear anything, so she could wrap up the meeting and get everyone out as soon as possible. Then she went to Amethyst's room and said, "Jeremy! Why would you do that? Just because you overheard our private conversation doesn't mean you get to bring things up. If they wanted you to know they would have told you. You should have just kept it to yourself instead of calling them out. Where'd they go? And where's Meter? She'll know what to do."

Chance went up to the grotto while Amethyst comforted Xenon who was throwing up. After that, Atoz met him outside. "UHHHHH! WHAT THE F***!!!" Chance kept punching the force field.

"I know, Choo Choo, but please don't hurt yourself." Amethyst was numb, but she was doing her best to calm them down.

Xenon couldn't stop shaking. He was having a panic attack. "Soon someone is going to expose me. They'll find me and take me to the IB. I'm so dead. My life is over. Again."

"That was years ago, and we're so far away from the Southern Ocean. I don't think anyone will blackmail you or try to take you, Moon Beam. You're here with us. We got you, baby." Amethyst held him in her arms. "Try taking deep breaths."

Thetis rushed home. She asked Jeremy, "Do you know where the kids are?"

"They probably went to the grotto," said Iris. "I don't think they swam too far."

"I was trying to be a good parent."

"I know that honey, but you just outed them. You are an awesome parent. Absolutely fantastic. Oh, I could go on and on. We all make mistakes. We know it was an accident, but they didn't want anyone to know about those aspects of their identity. When children keep secrets from you, it isn't always because they don't love and trust you. In their case, they were keeping those things secret because the last thing they want is for anything to change. They've seen and experienced people and parents who aren't accepting, so you can't blame them for being cautious. Often times things do change after people come out. Honey, you know the surface better than anyone down here."

"But we're down here now."

"Yes, but they only know the surface."

"What about Blue?"

"You never know if they're in a safe space or not. You know where Blinky's from. He probably doesn't feel secure. He's traumatized too. Plus, they are supposed to choose when and who they want to know. People don't really come out down here, but coming out is a personal decision. The Alphas and Omegas talk, Jeremias. It's not a part of our culture to keep things hidden because there's no need. Plus, that was private information they were discussing with their friends. It can be embarrassing in general and sometimes more discomfort is added when it comes to parents knowing. You can never really know for sure, but of course I had an idea they were queer. I never approached them about it directly because I figured that if they decided they wanted me to know, I'd find out. This is something they probably feared would happen, and now it happened. Right now, we need to go to them and apologize before we say or do anything else."

"Are you sure they even want to see me right now? Maybe I should give them some space."

"Chance is like you, Jeremias. He is probably angry but still wants to talk. Blinky is like Poseidon. He's probably bawling out of control right now. Which leaves Amethyst trying to comfort them when she herself needs comforting. She's like me, but she's also like Amphitrite which means we're going to have to go above and beyond to get her to even look at us. You were the one who told me how rapidly her thoughts can spiral, so we must go now. Teknon stay here for a moment."

"I am so sorry. I can't tell you how sorry I am. I didn't mean to out you. I forgot they were here. Even if they weren't here I shouldn't have brought that up. Especially like that. It was impulsive, and I didn't mean for this to happen. Do you forgive me?"

Chance calmed down after he apologized. "Yeah, Dad. I'll get over it. I don't really have a choice. Amethyst's the one you should be asking for forgiveness. If I were you, I'd try calming down Blue first."

"Xenon. I know I can't undo what happened, but I'll do anything and everything I can to support you moving forward."

"Whatever," he cried.

"I'm serious. I mean it. You're my son too." That was enough to get Xenon to begin to calm down, and he threw himself into Thetis's arms. "About Amethyst..." Jeremy whispered. "What should I do? What do I say?" Amethyst was sitting criss-cross applesauce off to the side.

"I don't know. She's complex. You know her better than I do."

"Amethyst. Look, Cupcake... I am so sorry. Please don't shut me out. Let me try to—" Suddenly, they all felt an earthquake. "Oh, my goddess. Is she doing that? The last time she did that it wasn't this strong."

"If she is, it means you already missed her willing-to-listen phase," Chance said. "She is now upset which is perfectly reasonable." The rest of the squad came to where they were.

"Why is the sky getting darker? Is she doing that too?" asked Jeremy. "That would be a new thing. She's never made the sky this dark before."

"No. Amethyst made the earthquake, but this is Hera. She's trying to calm her down, so she doesn't destroy the place. Now Sei is trying to cheer her up." Poseidon formed some cute little horses from the pond water, but Amethyst was not pleased and swatted them away. Amphitrite told him to try something more entertaining, so he made a dragon. That got her attention.

"Amethyst." Jeremy's voice triggered her, and she was upset again. Hades sent a lighter. A huge flame appeared and immediately got Amethyst's attention. *Or did it?* "Cupcake, I wish I could take it back. I really do. I understand why you're upset. I didn't mean to hurt any of you."

"You got what you wanted. Now you know. What do you want now? Forgiveness? Fine. I don't care. There. You can have it. But you still ruined everything. I don't have control over anything. Not even myself. I don't want to see you right now. Just leave me alone. Oh, and FYI… Hera, that little thing you did didn't help. Poseidon, I happen to like dragons, but that was a mere lizard. Hades, that flame was cute, but I'm used to fire. The only reason why I came to my senses is because I accidentally weakened the force field by absorbing energy, and there's a lightning bolt coming this way." Amethyst turned off the force field so that it wouldn't shatter, caught the lightning bolt, and threw it back. "Zeus! I just got outed. You think my queer ass gives a f*** about a lightning bolt?" Amethyst was twitching because she was so upset. Every time she twitched, her thunderstorms got louder. "I can't fight a god, but I have a feeling I'm going to do something stupid eventually. Please don't f*** with my family. Especially during a family crisis. That's just plain rude. Why not just attack me? Are you trying to cause me pain?" she laughed. "Neither of us wants that. I am very unstable and very mentally ill."

They were all just staring at her. She was full of surprises. "What are y'all looking at?" she smiled. "I'm hungry. Oh, you want to talk huh? Can we dinner over talk? I mean talk over dinner."

Xenon smiled and rolled on the grass. "This is one of the reasons why I'm in love with her."

"What? N**** you're f****** insane."

While they were dinnering over talking, they were able to make up and have a conversation. "So, you two don't care?" asked Xenon.

"We care because we want to support you," said Thetis. "But this new information doesn't change how much we love you."

Chance asked, "Y'all probably were suspecting something anyway huh?"

"There's no real way to know without you telling me but… Chance, I had a feeling you and Bailey were more than just friends. You were always so happy to talk about him, and then one time I saw you two kissing through the window. You two were really going at it, so I went surfing."

Chance smiled and folded his lips in. "Wow. Okay, so I guess I ain't slick either. Continue."

"Yeah," Amethyst agreed. "This is cringe but interesting."

"Your faces would always get red when I brought up anything queer related. I could hear your heartbeats during particular scenes in movies and TV shows. Cupcake, you were always different from the surface kids ever since you were little. When you got older, I started noticing that there was possibly more to it than being from here. I noticed you were hiding things sometimes. I always had the idea that gender was involved in the back of my head. Then the whole thing with the trackers and your IDs. I noticed the neck marks and how you would avoid certain objects and places sometimes. You two never wanted to show me your ID's. Your teachers always talked to me about how you never participated in certain activities. I figured it was because of the categories. Oh yeah… One time, I was putting your clothes up I found your boxer drawer. I assumed they were just comfort. Then I start making connections because I kept in touch with your teachers, and they told me about things they noticed at school. The main thing was when that cheerleader from one of the other schools came to the door and asked you to be her boyfriend. You said you would have accepted if you were into relationships. Then you opened the door all the way and told her you're female."

"What about me?" Xenon asked.

"Blinky, it's pretty much the same thing. You and Iris would play dress up all the time. You never grew out of it, so I thought maybe you just really liked to dress up. Then I began to notice differences and things, sweetie. Even when you were trying to hide it. One day, you asked me if you could learn how to shapeshift like me and Iris, so you could look like us. At first, I thought it was about being blood related. When you got older, your changes were more noticeable. If you were in more feminine clothing, you would always change before we went out. Once you got the necklace from Klymene, you started going outside. I was the one who had her make that necklace for you, so you'd feel at least somewhat safe. I heard you and Iris talking about your crushes before. When you were younger, you would tell me when you were a boy or not. You were sooooo cute. Sometimes

I'd ask if I had two girls today. Sometimes you'd say yes. Sometimes you'd shrug. You started keeping secrets when you got older."

"Sometimes I would say 'there's my little girl' and Ame would just stare me down like she did a little while ago in the grotto. She wouldn't say anything and then she'd just walk away. It was creepy as hell," he laughed. "I tried calling her 'he' one day and she did the same thing."

"They always had minds far beyond their years," Thetis smiled. "Sometimes your gender expression would change more than once in one day."

"Same with Cupcake."

"It's more noticeable when you're a girl, Blinky."

"Which gender is the most noticeable for me?" asked Amethyst.

"When you're a girl," Jeremy smiled.

"I'm weeeak," she laughed. "That is so funny to me."

"How do you feel right now?" Thetis asked.

"I'm cool I guess," said Chance. "It's whatever. I'm just glad y'all chill about this."

"Honestly, I'm still a little shy about it," Xenon blushed. "And worried."

"Yeah. I know I'm in the ocean now, but I'm still uncomfortable. I still feel exposed," said Amethyst.

"What gender are you right now?" asked Jeremy. "I figured out your cryptic systems so…"

"I'm purple," Amethyst laughed.

Xenon covered his face. "I'm a 2 right now."

"Sometimes we forget to think, sometimes we just have no idea, sometimes we can't think, and sometimes it's a little bit of all of those," Amethyst laughed.

"And what about pronouns?" asked Thetis.

"My pronouns are he or they. I won't get upset if you accidentally use the wrong one. I'll just shake my head or something."

"Mine are she or they. I usually don't have a strong preference, but if I do, I'll let you know. Just don't make it awkward. Just be chill."

"This isn't about us being queer, but Jeremy why do you work?" Chance asked.

"Yeah. I feel like I don't see you anymore, Dad."

"You see me more than you did on the surface," he smiled. "I just want to give you and your mother some time. I don't work for money. I just like being a coach."

"A coach?!?!? That's lame. You just lost all your cool points," Chance laughed.

"OMG, you are such a dad," Amethyst laughed. "Good thing because you have more kids now."

Thetis laughed with them. "You did say you wanted six."

"You two should do your Jeremy impression," Iris laughed. Thetis shapeshifted to look like Jeremy, and Xenon did his voice.

"Alright, alright," he smiled. "Very funny. What's everyone going to do right now?"

"Anyone in the mood for a girls' night?" Xenon suggested. "I'm stressed out."

Iota, Alpha, and Zeta squealed in agreement. Beta, Chi, and Rho discussed it with each other before they agreed to join them.

Chapter 21: Oil Painting

DAY 19

"Moon Beam!" Amethyst squealed.

"Uh oh, bro. Yo girl calling you." As soon as she came into the living room he said, "Never mind. Your soulmate's calling you."

"Can I have some? What are you eating?"

"How'd you know he had food?" Reign laughed.

"I love how she asked for some before she asked what it was," said Bella.

"Ahhh. Watch out. Mooove. I thought you didn't want anything." Xenon laughed. "Alright here. But you gotta give me a kiss."

"Ewww! PDA!" Chance made barfing noises.

"You came right on time, Moon Jelly."

"Don't I always?"

Iris giggled. "I caught that, Sister."

"I made this painting a long time ago," said Xenon. "It's you."

"Oh, my goddess! Did you do this all from memory?"

"He probably just used Iris," said Chance.

"He's painted me before, but he did that from memory also."

"I love it! This looks just like our foggy morning rendezvous on the beach. I love how you painted the same beach in my eyes. We were seeing the same thing. I was seeing you, and you were seeing what I was seeing. You are hella talented," she gleamed. "You know why I call you Shy Guy, right? It's not just because you're shy."

"I know, Moon Jelly. That's part of the reason why I showed you this."

"What's your favorite stuff to paint with?"

"Watercolors and oil pastels."

"Ooooo! Can I see them?!?!?"

"Sure, Little Scallop." Xenon came back with some of his art supplies and loved how Amethyst was so intrigued. "Would you like to see my art room?"

"Huuuuh!!! YES! I can feel the aesthetic." Xenon took her up to the sunroom that was his art studio. "Wow! It's so bright in here. A good bright. It's soft, clear, and comfy."

When Xenon started changing into his art clothes, Amethyst covered her eyes. "What are you doing?" he laughed. "You see me naked all the time. Why are you so damn cute?"

"Eeeeeep!!! You even have the light blue denim overalls with the paint marks!!! Ahhh! And they're cuffed!!! OMG, I love you. What are you about to paint? I'll leave so I don't distract you."

"I want you to stay. You're helping me figure out what to paint next."

"Don't planes fly over here? How come no one knows we're here?"

"We're surrounded by a field that creates a hidden space pocket just like the one the land queendom is in."

"What about the basileia?"

"Okeanos is sort of like one huge interportal. Okeanos only allows humans to see and discover certain things. Even if they swam through our coordinates, there'd be nothing there. You could think of the ocean as a sub plane. LOL. That's so fitting. Airplane + submarine. Remember?" he smiled. Xenon noticed how the light was hitting her perfectly. "Stay right there. Don't move. Okay, you can move. How is it that both the moon's light and the sun's light compliment you? You're a star. My favorite star."

Amethyst was gleaming. "What did you do?"

"I memorized that image. Now I'm going to paint you. This will begin my new wave of art."

"When's your debut? It's only been decades."

"We'll see what happens by the end of the month."

"Cool! What kind of medium are you going to use?"

"Oil pastels. What's wrong?"

"I don't know. I'm having that weird feeling again. The same one I had with the ink."

"Would you like to come with me to Gamma Beta?" Thetis asked Amethyst.

"Are Icarus and Iapyx going to be there? I know they were at the meeting so…"

"No, Moonshine. I just have to make sure everything is ready for the celebration later today. We'll be gone before they return."

When they got there, they swam into Xenon. He was preparing one of her coronation gifts. "What are you doing here, Moon Beam?"

"Uhhh. Nothing. I was just—"

"Did you feel that? What's that noise? Something's going on," Amethyst panicked.

"Amethyst, darling, I don't see or hear anything," said Thetis.

"XENON! WATCH OUT!" Suddenly, there was a burst of oil. Then there were more bursts throughout the area. The noise caused unbearable pain to the Oceanids' ears. Amethyst rushed into the oil to rescue Xenon who couldn't breathe. So many people were being suffocated by the oil. Amethyst had no idea what to do. She couldn't possibly get to all of them in time, and even if she could, the oil was in their systems. She knew it would spread, killing all the ocean life in its path. "I'm the chosen one dammit! Why can't I do anything?!?!?" When Amethyst moved her hands, she noticed the oil follow. She did her best to keep the oil bursts contained. Once she was focused, she tried drawing the oil from out of people's bodies. It worked. She shaped the oil into a huge snake and made it slither all the way to the surface. She had no idea what to do with the oil. There was nowhere she could put it that wouldn't be harmful, so she made a large black oil cloud and just held it in the sky. She wasn't experienced with her abilities, so she was struggling to keep the cloud up.

Thetis had already called Poseidon, and he was on his way. He appeared as a gigantic body made of water. "I've got it, Amethyst. Thank you. You can let it go."

She did as he said. "Where were you at this whole time? Can't all gods teleport?"

"Yes. I teleported to the bas, but I didn't know exactly where you were," he smiled. "It's easier to find you when you make storms. You make better storms than my son did at your age by the way."

"Whoa. Really? Wait. Triton? Hold up! What the hell did you just do? Was that alchemy?"

Before Poseidon disappeared, he said, "See you later, niece."

When Amethyst swam back down to the surface, they all cheered, but she swam straight to Xenon. "Are you okay? Did I get all the oil out? Can you breathe? Are you okay?"

"I'm fine now," he smiled. "You know... I'm starting to get used to you saving me."

"What's that on your leg? Moon Beam, is that a cut? ZEUS!!!" Amethyst swam back up to the surface and said, "I know you did this b****!!! You sent your little goons to drop oil bombs down here. Nice move making them invisible, but you can't win! I can barely do anything, but your little plans always fail when I'm around. I told you to leave my family the f*** alone yet here we are. Stop f****** testing me. Honestly, I don't know what the f*** your problem is. I don't want your fake ass throne, I'm like 5ft tall, and all I can do is make baby storms. Shit. I'm already f****** depressed! You trigger my anxiety! You are so lucky I can't fight you!" Amethyst was so upset she didn't even notice she had made seven separate hurricanes, oceans apart, in a circle around her. Just like the old days. "You want to suffocate people??? Now I know I can move shit, so choke on this." Amethyst forged a large aqua bolt and threw it just like she threw the other bolts except this time she didn't need to touch it. How'd I do, Hera? Did he choke? Just in case I missed, let's try this since you wanna make peoples' ears bleed." Amethyst forged a thunderbolt. Yes, a thunderbolt. Not a lightning bolt. "How'd that sound? Did it make your ears bleed?" she laughed. "Oh yeah! I just invented some new shit!"

Xenon hugged her and said, "You're so little, but so dangerous."

Thetis held her heart and said, "Soon you'll be coronated, and he will be able to be held accountable for personal attacks such as this one."

"Thetis, no one cares about the law. What is law?"

"I know, but I just don't know what else to do. I want to avoid a war."

"A war? You think Zeus would start a war because of me? Wait. Am I going to start a war? Oh no."

As soon as Icarus and Iapyx arrived, Atoz took off. "Why'd they leave?" asked Iapyx.

"I think they're just exhausted."

"Oh. Well, can you like, tell Amethyst she's like... The most awesome person ever!" said Icarus.

"And maybe you should warn them about social media," Iapyx added.

"Yeah. I don't know if you saw already, but word is out now, and it's spreading quickly. I know she's from the surface, and you know how the Internet trolls are."

Amphidromia was beautiful! The festival was so colorful and lively. There were so many flowers! Amethyst and Chance were in awe because ocean flowers were so unique. They seemed extraterrestrial. If Amethyst would have known, she would have ordered Xenon a different bouquet. She wondered if they were edible. Everyone was dressed in their best cultural attire and face art. They all looked so happy singing and dancing, but Amethyst, Xenon, and Chance were just sitting inside hiding from everyone. Iris had to be there while Thetis delivered a speech celebrating Poseidon and Amphitrite, but after that, she joined them. "Where are the other two?" Iris asked.

"They went to go pick up some food," said Amethyst.

"I wonder how many people know already," said Xenon.

"Oh shit!" said Chance. "We haven't checked social media!"

"Don't do that. Let's just watch a movie or something." Iris tried to steer them away.

"Look what people are posting!" Amethyst said. "This is terrible!"

"Why do they have to be so mean?" Xenon cried.

Chance wiped a few tears. "Wow. These posts actually cut really deep."

"F*** them. They're just ignorant ass trolls who have nothing better to do than cyberbully people," Iris said. "They're always the ones who respond first. How about we just stay off social media for a couple days?"

"I figured out how we can wake Endymion up," Thetis explained. "I had Hephaestus build me this frequency detector. It's not just a regular detector. This device is designed to show us how close we are to reaching the chaotic frequency. There's not really a name for the frequency, but I decided to call it that. Anyway, all we have to do is measure one frequency at a time. This device will then add them together to see if we reach the chaotic frequency."

"Okay, so what do we use to make the sound?" Chance asked.

"Well we all play instruments, and Bella is the best singer," Xenon said. "How about we just see what happens?"

"Let's get started," Thetis said. Chance played the guitar. "Maybe try electric. Where's Amethyst?"

"Sweet! That's my favorite! I have no idea where she is. She'll probably pop up in a minute." He played the electric guitar, and a line showed up on the detector.

"Hey! I know that song," Reign smiled. "That's "We Are the Champions" by Queen. Now it's my turn." She played her bass, and another bar showed up.

Bella decided to stick with the same song and played his keyboard from his pool as he sang. "That was wonderful!" said Thetis. "We're making progress."

Xenon played the drums, and a bar showed up on top of Bella's. Then he went to Iris's room and said, "Hey, Iris. Have you tried out that new electric violin you just got? Do you think you could play it for a wave? We're all playing "We Are the Champions". Join us."

Her bar got them closer to their goal, but they were still only halfway there. "At least the device can tell us what frequency we need. Here's what it sounds like."

"It's so soft but so high. What kind of instrument is that?" Chance asked.

"How about you all try playing all together in a different key? Let me just change the settings. Okay. Go ahead." They did just that, and she said, "It's getting there. Try singing with Bella."

Amethyst walked in. "No invite? I was all the way on the other side of the bas. I'm glad I walked by. I mean swam by. Whatever. Liiiiit." Then she started singing along.

"We did it!" Thetis smiled. "It worked!" They all explained to Amethyst what Thetis was talking about.

"Oh, okay so we're a rock band now? That fits our aesthetic. Cool!!! Wait. What's my role?"

"You're the main singer," said Thetis.

"What? No way. How come Bella can't do it? Plus, I sound horrible."

"We'll all be singing, Ame," Chance laughed. "It's just that you don't play any instruments, and you have to sing with us anyway. We need your voice."

Bella smiled and said, "You do sing terribly, but it's a rockstar terrible."

"And you have the theatrics to go with it," Reign twirled.

"We need your energy!" said Xenon. "Personally, I think you sing beautifully. Your voice is so soothing and charming."

"Wait. What are we forming a band for?" Iris asked.

"Ummm…"

"We were thinking about trying out for the Last New Moon Festival next year," said Amethyst.

"So where is Endymion?" asked Amethyst.

"These are the coordinates. Selene said she has no idea where Endymion is located which means they are in a cave that the moonlight doesn't touch. There aren't many caves like that. I visited each spot. Here's where I found them." She pulled up a holographic map. "There's plenty of rocks for you all to stand on."

"How are we going to get the speakers and stuff there?" Xenon asked.

"The whales will help. Also, Endymion's body is being preserved in the pool inside the cave. We want the sound to travel through the air and ocean. The first songs you play should be loud enough to wake them up. The last songs should be smooth enough to remind Endymion of their love for Selene because we cannot tell them anything."

"Chance, can you make a playlist?" Amethyst asked.

"I'm on it."

"I think it's helpful to know that they were going through a rocky time in their relationship," said Thetis.

"Did you just make a pun?" Amethyst laughed.

"Let's tell Iris we're just practicing," said Xenon.

"Go in three days. There will be a full moon out."

DAY 20

The squad rehearsed all the songs in the playlist Chance made. "We're pretty good," Iris smiled. "And pretty damn talented to have learned them this quickly. We kind of already knew the songs, but still…"

"We're awesome!!!" Reign twirled.

DAY 21

"What should we do about what's happening on social media?" Iris asked. "I got them to take a break from it, but there's no way we can avoid this forever."

"Maybe we should make a video about what happened," Reign suggested.

"Yeah," Bella agreed. "That way people will understand better, and it's a fantastic way to shut down rumors."

The squad filmed an honest, emotional video and posted it online. After that, they decided they'd wait a couple days before they engaged with social media again.

"AHHH!" Iris screamed, and everyone swam as quickly as they could to her room. "I just saw myself lose. I'm going to lose. He's going to take complete control of me. Oh, no. I-I..." She tried to grab her sword, so she could kill herself, but Xenon stopped her. "I saw myself kill Amethyst."

"The future is never static, remember?" Thetis said.

"We have a plan that you don't know about," Xenon added.

Amethyst didn't want anything to happen to Iris. "It'll be alright. We won't let him get you."

"I don't know if I can keep fighting much longer. Isn't today what some surface goers call Christmas Eve? Let's go watch the Naiads decorate the tree. I need to get my mind off this." They all headed to the Naiad queendom. "They do this because trees give oxygen to the world. Tomorrow there's going to be a huge candle lighting festival. Kwanzaa starts on December 26th. Families are going to have feasts, and people are going to give each other gifts. There's going to be one huge feast on January 1st after basilica. The royal families eat together and exchange gifts on that day, but we're not attending this year due to the crisis we're in. The humans used to live side by side with us, so we celebrate various holidays from various cultures. The second biggest holiday in December is Kwanzaa. I think you know what the first is," Iris smiled.

Chapter 22: Soul Sisters

DAY 22

"We should wear all black!" Amethyst suggested.

"Hell yeah," they all agreed. Chance, Reign, and Xenon put on the same black skinny jeans except Xenon's weren't ripped. Chance wore a large black shirt. Reign chose a ripped top, and Xenon wore a crop top. Iris decided to wear a bralette halter top with a jean skirt and fishnets. Bella wore a dark, translucent top, and Amethyst wore black shorts and a smedium black shirt. Naturally, all the bi members of the squad had leather jackets on.

"Come on, Reign! You too, Chance. Let us put makeup on you," Iris said. "It's just eyeliner, mascara, and a little lip shimmer. We did ours to match our wavelengths. Sister just went with black."

"Really!" Chance yelled. "Y'all already got me to paint my nails black!"

"Come on you two!" said Amethyst. "Do you want to be rockstars or not?"

"Fine! Damn!" Chance agreed. "Just make sure I look hot."

"Reign…"

"Uhhh! Whatever. Don't do too much."

"Thanks for your help!" Amethyst told the whales. "Are you sure we won't hurt any animals with all this noise we're about to make?" she asked Thetis. "I don't want to do them like the Navy."

"Yes, I'm sure," Thetis smiled. "We've cleared the area. I'll see you back at the bas. Call me if anything doesn't go as planned."

As soon as they finished setting up their equipment, Iris started to lose control of her shapeshifting abilities. "Oh shit! Dammit," Chance said. "We're losing her."

"Try shapeshifting into something easy for you to maintain," Xenon said. "As long as you can still play the violin."

Iris shapeshifted into a Nereid and her fluke scared the shit out of Bella. Not only did she grow a whole foot but, "Wow. That lowkey looks natural as hell," said Chance. "Don't shift back. Your skirt's long gone."

The squad got into formation. Bella was on the far left, wading in the water with his keyboard carefully placed on the rock in front of him. Iris was on the far right sitting on a rock with her violin. In between them, the other four were on a large, somewhat flat rock. Reign was on the left, Chance was on the right, and Xenon had the center of the back all to himself. Amethyst was in the last place she wanted to be in, "Why do I have to be in the front? Can't y'all scoot closer?"

"We have to be connected to the amps, Ame," Chance laughed.

"I feel so out there."

"Don't worry, Moon Jelly. We've got your back. Especially me," he smiled. "I won't take my eyes off you." Amethyst did a little twerk move.

"What's wrong with Iris's eyes?!?!?" said Amethyst. "Oh shit! Hold on, sis… She can still play the violin for some reason. LOL… The devil's trill. Whatever. We better start playing. Let's get our sister back! HIT IT!"

"They actually sound really good," said Aphrodite. "I love how strong their friendship is already. It warms my heart."

Apollo had something to say about that. "What the f*** are you talking about? Reign and the little boy are good. Iris, Xenon, and the mermaid have beautiful voices. Especially that mermaid. Iris and Xenon were always gifted, yet Amethyst is just flat out f****** terrible."

"Oh, shut up," Artemis said. "You're just mad because you like her voice even though it's unconventional."

"You know what? I know what it is…" said Ares. "He's jealous because they're probably going to be iconic as f***."

"Shut the f*** up. That's why Amethyst beat your daughter's ass."

"Why'd you have to bring that up? Can we not make Ares upset?" said Aphrodite.

"Aw… Come on, Pollo Loco," said Artemis. "Do you hear her? Sure, she could use a lot of training. She didn't grow up in the ocean. But you have to admit her voice is so sweet and soothing yet dark and passionate."

"Iris sings like Thetis with Amphitrite's loudness, and Amethyst sings like Amphitrite with Thetis's softness," said Aphrodite. "Uh! My heart! They're working together for love! I'm gonna cry!"

"He knows you're right," said Athena. "He's just in denial. More importantly, we should be discussing what we're going to do about Sparky."

"You know… At first, I thought she was a weakling," said Ares. "Then I thought I saw what she was capable of when she fought Angelica. Now I just don't know… Mom told me about her…"

"That's why! If they succeed in waking Endymion, Zeus is going to want so-called revenge," Athena explained. "I think she can take him. Zeus has no idea what's coming for him."

"What exactly are her abilities?" Apollo asked.

"I thought she was a stormcaster like Triton," said Athena. "Then she caught a lightning bolt and threw it right back into Zeus's hands. That's when I knew. She's an energetic. She's also aerodynamic. Otherwise she wouldn't be able to move like that. I knew that part as soon as she jumped off that cliff."

"Wait. Hera is the only energetic there is," said Apollo.

"Not anymore," Athena said. "But wait. There's more. Mom is Agathos."

"SHIT! She's Skotos?" Apollo almost choked. "What are the f****** odds that the chosen one would be Skotos? Especially regarding this prophecy!"

"We also think this prophecy is linked to that ancient prophecy they're always talking about," said Aphrodite.

"This should be good," Artemis laughed.

"Wait what's Skotos again?" asked Ares.

"It means she doesn't give a f***," Athena told him. "I have a feeling she's even more savage than Amphitrite. Look at her f****** bloodline. That's two times the insanity. She was also raised on the surface."

"Say more," said Artemis. "I like her already."

"Remember when Zeus drugged Poseidon and Amphitrite killed him? Well, something tells me Amethyst is the type to tear down Olympus if you f*** with her soulmate."

Apollo asked, "Who's her soulmate?"

"Really, dumbass? We've only been keeping watch over them for years… That's a whole other topic."

"Have you noticed how queer this new squad is? I'm jealous," Apollo smiled. "Awww, they're baby gays. I'll set Amethyst's terrible singing aside for that."

"What the hell are you talking about?" Artemis laughed. "We're all queer too. Are you high?"

"Oh yeah… Wait. Who's what again? I'm gay as f***. I mean high as f***. Eh, both statements are true."

Athena smacked him. "I'm the ace, Aph and Ares are the bisexuals, and Artemis is the lesbian. Speaking of that, I'm so glad Amethyst is female, Black, genderfluid, and bisexual. These evil f****** are going to be furious. Sparky is probably going to bust a circuit when he finds out they're queer. I bet he'll try to connect their queerness and dis/abilities to their 'craziness' in addition to them being Oceanids. SMH. Now get off me before I beat your ass. I advise you all to scram before Mom finds out we're using her skeye. I'm going to bed."

"Oh my god! Look!" Chance yelled. "Endymion is floating in mid-air now or some shit. How'd we do that?"

"I don't know, but I think it worked!" Amethyst said.

"I think Selene is doing that! She found them!" said Xenon.

"Um… You do know the Naiads have been recording everything right?" Reign asked. "I wasn't expecting Naiads to be there. They're going crazy. I think we have fans," she twirled.

"What portal is that?" asked Amethyst. "That's definitely not the Congo."

"They're Northern Naiads. That portal leads to the Northern queendom and the Western kingdom. Basil's perverted ass might be in the crowd," said Xenon. "How'd they find us? Never mind. Look! There's Selene. The spell is definitely broken."

"Damn, Selene's fine as f***," said Amethyst. "Moms fosho tapped that. Look how she walk across the water. I love how she made everything look all glowy. It looks like that one scene from the *Life of Pi*."

"Yaaasssss queen!!! Go get your soulmate!" Xenon cheered.

"Oh shit," Bella laughed. "We're supposed to be playing "We Belong Together" by Mariah Carey. Come on!"

"You six are such blessings. Thank you so much," said Selene. "I thought I'd never see you again," she cried. "You were in a psychic deep sleep."

"Oh, Selene," said Endymion. "Not a night went by where I didn't dream of you." They turned to the squad. "I don't know how to thank you for this miracle. Is there anything I can do for you?"

"Actually yes. M-My sister, Iris," Xenon pointed.

"Can you save her?" Amethyst asked.

"AH! We must hurry," said Endymion. "I just need to get my—"

"I'm one step ahead of ya, Endy," Selene smiled. Suddenly, all of Endymion's crystals were levitating in the air. One for each chakra.

After Endymion cleansed the crystals, they cleansed Iris's body with the selenite wand. "What did you just do? Why'd she stop moving?" asked Xenon.

"I used the wand to absorb her energy and Leukos's energy. Now I'm going to reactivate her energy with these crystals."

"Um. That crystal just cracked," said Xenon. "Was that supposed to happen? And why are our instruments glowing? Those are our colors."

"Your instruments must be fluorescent. They must have absorbed some of your energy. The wavelength of the crown chakra is ultraviolet. The crystal being destroyed released UV light. And no. This wasn't supposed to happen. Leukos is trying to enter her body again through her crown chakra. This is the most desperate I've ever seen him. I need a much bigger amethyst crystal, but amethyst is rare. It's the last crystal needed."

"WHAT?!?!? What happens without the last crystal?" asked Xenon.

"She's going to stay in the astral plane until I get it."

"Well, that's not that bad is it?" asked Reign.

"She's safe there right?" asked Bella.

"Yes, but it's more complicated than that. Her physical body is not completely reactivated yet. She doesn't have a reference point in the physical world. Her psyche is with her soul in the astral plane and not in her physical body, so her soul is inclined to return to Chaos."

"Then I'll go," Amethyst volunteered.

"You'll go as in go get another crystal?" Reign asked.

"No. I am going to the astral plane to get our sister back."

"I got it, Moon Jelly. You know it's way too risky to follow someone's path to the astral plane. What if you get stuck up there too?"

"I know the astral plane much better than you do, Moon Beam."

"You know that doesn't matter. Stay here. I'm going."

"No, you're not. I am her twin which means if anyone has the best chance of making it to where she is and back it's me. We're mirror twins, so we should have inverse sequences. We were delivered from the cosmos together. We shared the same sac. Plus, Thetis can't lose another child. There's no time to argue about this." Amethyst slid into the water and held both of Iris's hands. "I'm coming, sister."

"Wait! How are you going to transport two souls?!?!?" he asked. He ran over to them, but it was too late. Amethyst was already gone. "Dammit!!! Uhhhh!!!" Xenon was bawling his eyes out. Chance comforted him while he was throwing up. Reign and Bella had no idea what to say.

"Look, man. I don't know anything about the astral plane, but I do know they both have to come back. How else will the prophecy be fulfilled?"

Meanwhile... "Iris! Iris! Where are you? Iris!"

"I'm right here. I was waiting for you. Are you ready to go?"

"What? No. Iris stop! It's not time for us to return to Chaos, remember? The prophecy! Xenon! Thetis! We still didn't get to do all the girly things you wanted to do!!! It's not time, Iris. We still have to f*** shit up!"

"How? My body's dead. I failed you. Your body's dead now too. Leukos won, didn't he?"

"He didn't! What do you mean you failed me? Girl, I ain't dead! Iris! Come on! Your body is on standby because Leukos broke the last crystal.

It was too small. Leukos is out of your body now, but if you don't come back soon he might be able to get in, and you won't be able to come back."

"How will both of us get back?"

"The same way we got here. In each other's arms."

"But what if the forces pull us apart?"

"They can try, but I'll never let you go."

Thetis and Jeremy arrived, but they weren't worried. Unlike Xenon, the others were patiently waiting for a much-needed explanation. "Mom! How are you so calm?!?!?"

"Some are only twins in the physical, but they are more than that. I was doing some reading. If soulmates are an even graph, soul twins are an odd graph. Soulmates are one, and soul twins cancel each other out. Therefore, a soulmate has the additional option of bringing the other back from the astral plane without leaving the physical, and soul twins are limited to moving back and forth together."

They descended as purple twin phantoms in fetal position. "Sister!" Iris gasped when she returned to her body. "Oh, no. Sister! Where is she? Sister! Sister!"

"Hey, Iris," Amethyst laughed. "That's payback for having me ruin Xe's party aesthetic."

"Oh, my goddess," Iris smiled. "You gave me a heart attack. This is why I'm the older twin." Sobbing, Xenon tackled them.

They all wrapped their arms around them and enjoyed a miniature family reunion. "I have a secret island in the South Pacific. It's yours now," said Selene. "I'll send you the coordinates. Oh, I can't thank you all enough."

"Well, you did bring back Xenon," Amethyst smiled.

"I'll never forget any of you," Endymion said. "I know all of their names. What's yours?"

"Amethyst."

"Wow. How fitting," Endymion smiled. "What a gem."

"We should celebrate!" Selene gleamed. She created a shimmering, translucent dance floor on the moonlit ocean. Some Oceanids underneath swam by and said hello while others recorded everything with the Naiads. Atoz preferred to play in the ocean. Xenon kept tossing Amethyst in the air. He did it so much that she started to change energy levels.

"Xe, I think I'm shifting. I think if you use all your strength, I'll shift."

"We're going to get in trouble. Mom's going to be pissed."

"Just throw me as hard as you can."

"You are so bad," he laughed. They climbed onto the dance floor, and he swung her around and around. Then she went flying towards the stars.

"Blue, what the f*** did you just do!" Chance yelled. "Holy shit. That's dope as hell! Ame learned how to shift!"

Thetis closed her eyes and took a deep breath. "Why would he throw her?" Didn't I tell her not to shift?"

"I know honey, I know…" Jeremy sighed. "That's Amethyst. She definitely told him to do it."

There were a lot of ooooo's and ahhhhh's from the crowds of Naiads and Oceanids. "Yay! She did it! I knew her body could become violet energy!" Iris cheered.

"Bella, what's wrong?" asked Reign.

"I'm seeing something." Bella's heart was beating out of his chest. "I-I doubt it's the same thing you're seeing, but it's something. I see two dots moving around. I-I think it's them." *You are probably wondering why he couldn't see their energies before. We'll get to that next week. Chill. Stop trying to look for mistakes. The Storyteller did their task exactly right. Trust them.*

"That's because in addition to visible light, they are emitting other wavelengths," said Thetis. "Your eyes must be detecting traces of higher frequencies. Each one of you is gifted. I believe you're all connected to the prophecy."

"What's happening with Blue?" asked Jeremy. "He keeps flashing or something."

"He looks like a strobe light," Reign laughed.

"Every time he catches her, she sends an electric current through his body, and he responds by sending a wave pulse into the ocean. He keeps going from dim to bright because of Amethyst, but the water around him glows because of the algae reacting to the wave pulse.

"Huuuh!" Iris got an idea. "Chance, play "Neon Lights" by Demi Lovato!!!" When they heard the song, Atoz decided to put on a light show. *If the cheer squad could see her now... Actually, no. Forget them.* The squad joined them by showcasing their best dance moves. Well... Bella was doing a series of jumps and twirls. He even jumped over the entire dance floor! They were calling Amethyst and Xenon show offs, but they themselves ended up showing off too. And it was all on camera.

"Sire! They have lifted the spell."

"Ganymede, that's impossible you imbecile! No one can break the spell!"

"They did it together, sire. They tapped into an unknown frequency once thought to be a myth."

"Dammit! Why does Thetis have to be so much like Metis? Why?!?!? Why did they do this?!?!? Why now?!?!?"

"Iris was possessed by Leukos, sire. Endymion is the only one experienced enough to perform krystallikí therapeía on someone suffering a direct possession on that scale."

"Why are none of my plans working?!?!?"

"I-Isn't Iris your daughter? A-Aren't they your daughters, sire?"

"They leave me no choice!!!!!"

"I know you know Amethyst is an energetic, sire, but she shifted. She's a T-Titan sire. How are…"

"WHAT?!?!? No matter. She has no experience. I only must kill one of them. I just must make sure I strike the right one. I guess we're going to have to do this the hard way. I only have one option left. I must go."

"That's going to start a war. You're going to start a war?"

"She's already done that!!!!! War has already begun!!!!!"

"I'm sorry, Sunshine," Thetis wiped a tear. "I can't tell you how happy I am that you're free now. It's just…"

"Zeus is definitely going to declare war on the basileia," said Jeremy. "It's inevitable now. He just announced a lockdown on the sky kingdom."

"He knows you're an energetic Titan or else he wouldn't have put his kingdom on lockdown. Now, I'm sure being coronated is not enough to protect you. According to the law, you're still safe, but Zeus is enraged now. I knew he'd be upset about the spell being broken, but now he knows you're a Titan. Now he knows this prophecy is directly linked to the ancient prophecy."

"I-I started a war?" A tear ran down Amethyst's face. "I-I didn't know. I-I just thought it was dangerous to shift because I'm so small. This is all my fault."

"It's not your fault, Moonshine. I should have just told you the rest of the reason why. I just… The ancient prophecy is so vague…"

Amethyst wasn't listening. "How's he going to know which twin to kill? What if he gets Iris instead of me?" she cried.

"Don't worry about me, Sister."

"Can't they get each other from the astral plane if they die?" asked Chance.

"Not if the physical body is destroyed. Zeus has two types of bolts," said Jeremy.

"A hyperbolt is basically a supercharged bolt. It takes 6 days to forge," said Thetis. "Your coronation is in five days. At this point, the law means nothing. He will strike the day after, and the war will begin the following day."

"You can't catch a hyperbolt because it moves so fast you can't see it. Especially during daylight. You can't hear it either. It's also much too powerful to stop. Hera and Zeus can't even catch those. That's the whole point."

"The only person to have survived a hyperbolt is Triton. Zeus struck him when he was only a teknon. This was before the protection laws existed. In fact, he's the reason for them. Zeus thought Amphitrite was me. He thought he was striking the chosen one. Triton only survived because Zeus threw it through a cloud. Poseidon was able to track it. Even then, it was extremely unlikely that he'd be able to save Triton. The bolt only scarred him. Zeus always aims for the head. His scar begins from the inner corner of his eye, goes through his eyebrow, and then stops just above his ear. That's why he has a white streak of hair and a partially grey eye. A hyperbolt is of the white energy. Think of it as bleach that causes people to disappear. It's a silent, discreet, villainous weapon."

"So why didn't he throw a hyperbolt before?" asked Iris.

"After he forges a hyperbolt, he's not as powerful because it drains his energy," said Thetis.

"So then why would he start a war?" asked Xenon.

"He must have a plan," said Thetis. "Zeus and Hera cannot go to war with each other because they are married, so the only god he has to worry about is Poseidon. Who knows how far he's willing to go to prevent Poseidon from attacking him…"

"A hyperbolt can strike anywhere, but there's no need to take precaution until the 31st," said Jeremy.

"I must deliver a speech and hold a meeting. Guards! Jeremy and I have these bracelets on just in case anyone tries to pose as us. If anyone else and I mean ANYONE else approaches this location, you slit their throat without hesitation. Understood?"

"Understood!"

After Thetis and Jeremy left, the squad just looked at each other. They were all worried. Iris broke the silence. "Let's stream Meter's speech. I'll pull it up on my phone."

"Oh, my goddess!" Reign twirled. "Look at all the support people are showing in regard to the you know what happening!"

"Look! They even made hashtag. There's #Agapi2k16GonBeLit, #WeLoveOurBasi, #WeLoveOurBasilissa, and #WeLoveChance. You three inspired hella people. Everyone's sharing their stories. Did you see Meter's post? Look at all the goddesses and gods that reached out. Even the other princes, prins, and princesses responded. And some Alphas and Omegas. OMG!"

"Lots of people clapped back at the trolls!" Reign added. "There's some funny stuff too. They're even talking about us waking Endymion up. They weren't close enough to know about the whole Leukos thing, but there's #WeWantABand," she smiled.

"OMG. Look. Now people are responding to Meter's speech. There's #ProtectThePrincess, #ProtectThePrin, #LongLiveThePrincess, and #LongLiveThePrin!"

"Awww," said Xenon. "Check your DMs too!

Their smiles didn't last long though. "We need to have a circle," said Iris. "There's no topic."

"What's Zeus's army like?" asked Chance.

"It's terrible. Every single male floater has to be in the army," said Iris. "They are trained since birth. Sometimes, other sky nymphs enlist by choice, but it's mostly floaters. Then, Nereids obey Zeus... We have to fight on two fronts."

"Can't the other realms assist us?" asked Bella.

"If they do, the other gods have to get involved," said Iris. "The war would be amplified. Some gods will side with Zeus, so it's best to keep this small scale."

"Thetis said we're all gifted. But how? What powers?" Chance asked.

"I have no idea."

"Have you had a vision? Have you seen anything?" asked Reign.

"I haven't. I've been trying, but I still haven't seen anything."

"What did he mean when he said a hyperbolt can strike anywhere?" Bella asked.

"Zeus can only use his spyglass when he's forged a hyperbolt. Hyperbolts aren't thrown like regular bolts," said Iris. "They have to be thrown through his spyglass. This allows him to be able to strike anywhere. He just has to know where his target is. Sometimes it takes a while for him to find his target, but you can't hide. Hyperbolts are made of white light. We can't stop light."

"So, then what the f***!" said Chance.

"I know. Even if he does manage to find us, it's a death wish. Option one was to strike us with a regular bolt before coronation. That didn't work. Option two is to strike us with a regular bolt once coronated. Even if we died, he'd come back the next day after Poseidon kills his ass. Hera would then be legally permitted to add the sky kingdom to her realm. Zeus would have lost all his authority, and we probably wouldn't be dead. Option three is to use a hyperbolt to ensure one of our deaths. Zeus is in a weakened state, he dies because Theios, Theia, or Hera beats his ass, he comes back the next day and still has his authority on Olympus, but at the expense of his whole kingdom."

So… After this hyperbolt thing, what do you want to do, Moon Jelly?

"So, he was never going to go with option two and because Amethyst can throw his lightning bolts back, he has to go with option three now," said Chance.

You can show me something sparkly if you want.

"Do the sky nymphs know? Does the army know what they're fighting for?" asked Reign. "I've always wondered why they fight for him."

I was thinking about going for a walk, but this is perfect. I got a new toy for you. Only you can turn it on.

"The soldiers don't, but some of the other sky nymphs do. They are probably moving out as we speak. They are going to live in Hera's realm. I'm sure she's spreading word about a safe haven now."

Oh yeah? What is it? Does it make noise?

"Wait. Who's going to destroy the sky kingdom?" Bella asked.

Lots.

"Poseidon. The sky kingdom is literally on the clouds. So is Olympus by the way. He knows Hera is moving the non-corrupt sky nymphs out," said Iris. "Plus, Hera is going to want to rebuild it anyway."

Is it cute? Can I eat it?

"On the surface, they act like clouds are a part of Zeus's realm. They also say he's a stormcaster," said Chance.

That's up to you. It's melt-in-your-mouth chocolate with the creamiest vanilla filling and has glitter all over it. Your name is on it. What do you think?

"That's so funny to me," said Iris. "Small clouds are literally about 1 million pounds of water droplets. Honestly, all Zeus can do is cause lightning and winds, electrocute people, move fast as f***, make stuff invisible, and make stuff levitate. The rest of his power is political. Also, all stormcasters are ocean goers."

I think it's time to blow the candle out.

"Atoz why y'all so quiet?" asked Chance.

"What was it like…"

"…being possessed by Leukos."

"I'm still not used to that," said Reign.

"I felt like I was a ghost inside my own body. I keep thinking about how I treated people. I'm nothing like that. I tried so hard to keep everything under control. I can do my best to fix things, but I wish I could take back my mistakes."

"Thetis said the fight against Leukos isn't physical. You have a strong mind," said Reign. "I admire that."

Iris got a feeling to check her mirror. "I saw something. Hella goddessess and gods are going to stand with us, so they can try to protect us. As of now, the future looks bright."

"I'm sorry," Xenon cried. "I can't hold it in any longer."

"Y'all were fine before I got here," said Amethyst.

"Sister, that's not true. Zeus has been plotting on this realm for the longest. This isn't the first war. Plus, you're the reason why we're all together now. We all need each other."

"I don't understand how I'm the chosen one that's supposed to restore the universe's balance when I can't even do anything to stop this."

"That's what you said about the oil," Xenon said.

"Yeah, and Hera and Zeus were the only ones who could touch lightning bolts," said Reign.

"Hell, you can go to the astral plane and back," Chance added. "You've done so much already."

"I don't know what's going to happen, but I wouldn't be surprised if you made another miracle happen," said Bella.

"Look, Ame. After all these years, you taught me that things always work themselves out. This situation isn't any different."

DAY 23

"You didn't tell Xenon did you, Miss I'm-not-a-good-actor?" Amethyst asked.

"Tell him what?" Iris smiled.

"That we were meeting in the dream plane every now and then."

"Oh. No," she laughed. "You know how he is. I'll tell him later. HA. We're familiar strangers."

"You were hella mean to me in the dream plane. Usually you just walked by or pushed me out the way. Remember when we fought?!?!?"

"Sorry. I didn't know it was you!" she laughed.

"I didn't know who you were either! Also… You can drop the sunshine persona. I like your sarcastic Wednesday ass."

"Okay," she laughed. "I didn't think there were other planes. Why was I in the dream plane anyway? How did I keep running into you?"

"Everyone goes there when they have a dream. Sometimes people run into each other when their dreams overlap and stuff. What were you dreaming about?"

"I was dreaming about you I guess. I just didn't know you actually existed."

"That's why. Believe it or not, the dream plane isn't the trippiest plane. The psychic plane is on some tipsy-turvy shit. Your favorite would probably be the meta plane."

"Wow. I want to learn more about these other planes. Make sure you tell me about them some time."

"I have a feeling we're going to be iconic as f***. Like…"

"I can see that. This whole thing is so under explained, but so intriguing. Honestly, I'm just like f*** it. Plus, well probably make people cry themselves to sleep, so that's a pro. Do you have any outfit ideas yet?"

"Honestly, no."

"That's okay, Sister. We're just here for inspo. I'll draw whatever it is you want to wear and get it custom made." Iris noticed she was feeling down. "Hey. Don't worry. Our clothes are grouped by style, not surface categories."

"I don't have to wear anything in particular?"

"Of course not. If it helps, I'm wearing a shimmering silver pantsuit with a lilac bralette and matching heels. You don't have to wear heels. There are other options." Amethyst wondered what Iris needed shoes for. And why didn't she choose something more cultural? She had her theories.

"Yaaasssss! Now I'm excited to go to this mall!"

"I'm really sorry about putting you in that dress when we first met."

"It's alright, Iris. It was just a prank. Plus, I was looking A1 thanks to you."

"No. I mean… I noticed how you were uncomfortable, but I didn't ask you about it. I'm also sorry for leaving you by the trench. I'm usually so organized and responsible. I don't want anything to happen to you."

"Iris, it's all good. We're good."

"How is it that you forgave me before you knew I was possessed?"

"I don't know. It's not hard to see the good in people like you. Plus, Xe told me you weren't acting like yourself."

"I'm sorry about the Nereids. I should have seen the first one coming. I should have been there to catch you. I should have been there to get you from Caris. I should have been there."

"Iris. Don't dwell on that. Stop apologizing."

"I just want you to know that I will do everything I can to prevent something bad from happening to you."

"Why do you care about me so much? I've only known you for a month in this life."

"Because you make me feel alive. Plus, you're what Blue's and Meter's heart was missing. You're the piece we were all missing."

"Whatever."

"I'm serious, Sister. I was so rigid. Meter was heartbroken. Xenon was miserable. We didn't smile or laugh much off camera. It was rare. We couldn't really make each other feel better. Then you showed up. Your laugh is contagious, and now we smile unconsciously. What's the surface game with the rectangular wood pieces called?"

"Jenga?"

"Yes. You're the piece that will cause the whole tower to fall if pulled."

"You really think so?" she blushed. "Thanks. Honestly, I was always nervous you wouldn't like me that much. We're so different, and I thought you would want a fluttery sister."

"I did at first, but I like you the way you are much better," she smiled. "Plus, I already have a fluttery sibling, and you're so interesting."

"Well, then how come you don't hang out with me?"

"I didn't want to be too clingy, and I'm not good at the whole social thing."

"Too clingy? Look at your sibling. Hell, his weird ass was highkey stalking me, and my ass finds that shit romantic," she laughed. "Iris, I know we have a deep ass connection, but we need bonding time. You and I have a lot of catching up to do."

"How about we start tomorrow? Where should we go?"

"I don't care as long as it's not by a trench," she laughed.

"OMG! Siiiiister. That's not funny."

"Just so you know, I know all Nereids aren't evil. Some of them are sweet and caring like you."

"So, you do know?"

"Of course I know. I been knew. LOL. Then that whole shapeshift glitch shit... You ain't slick either."

DAY 24

"Our siblings are going to be so jealous," said Iris. "This place is called Chymos Paradeisos. Everyone calls it Chymopara. They have the best drinks ever from smoothies to milkshakes. They just got remodeled."

"Yo! This is sooooo cool! This place is huge! OMG! Are the tables holographic?"

"Yep. You can play games and watch videos on them. Are we ready to order?"

"Ummm," Amethyst scanned the menu. "Ooo! They have banana! Oh, hell yeah! Yaaasssss! I want a banana milkshake. I want almond milk instead of that other shit though. Ooo! Can I try the glitter sprinkles and purple whipped cream too! Can you order mine? I'm still scared to use my broken Greek."

"I'll have a chocolate milkshake with chocolate whipped cream and dark chocolate sand. They'll have a banana milkshake with purple whipped cream and glitter sprinkles. And a straw please. Blue told me how much you like straws."

"So, you like dark chocolate? That's mature. LOL. You hella grown."

"You don't like it?" Iris gasped.

"Only when I'm on my period. Let's take a picture of our shakes!"

"Do you want to be in my vlog?"

"Yes! Heeeeeey y'all. See this milkshake? It's banana. Ummm. It's so thick."

"OMG, Sister! Did you just deepthroat the straw? You and your innuendos," she laughed. "That's going to go viral. I can see it now. I think

I know why you like straws. I read something about people who have oral fixations."

"Do not start," she laughed.

"But am I right?"

Amethyst stuck her tongue out. "Eh-heh. Why do you always wear that necklace? I feel like it's for a reason other than fashion. What does the pearl do?"

"It's the source of my visions when I'm away from a mirror. Meter gave it to me, but an Oracle blessed it at my coronation. It can't be destroyed, and I can never lose it."

"That's dope. Can you move it with your mind?"

"No. Think of it like a crystal ball except I don't ask for it to show me things."

"I know about you."

"What do you mean?"

"I know about your sex dungeon."

"You do?"

"Ahhh!!! So you do have one!!! I knew it! You give me sex dungeon vibes. Go ahead and change the subject."

"What's your surface room like?" she smiled.

"All my walls are my favorite shade of purple, and I have this bluish light. I don't really care for much furniture and stuff, but my dressers are black. I have hella posters and neon signs on my walls. My bedding is purple too! I have a star projector! That's pretty much it. It's not all elegant like yours. It's also semi-messy. You'd probably freak the f*** out."

"Sounds pretty cosmic. What's up with Meter and Jeremy?"

"I was going to ask you that. What do you know?"

"Not much. Same as you. They share the same bed and seem to be getting along, but I haven't seen them kiss or anything."

"I want them to be officially together. I feel like they're doing the whole co-parent thing."

"I agree. We should hook them up!"

"You know I gotta admit… You're way bubblier than I expected now that we got rid of Leukos. Not like Reign bubbly. Like… Sweet and sour b**** crazy."

"OMG I cannnnn't," Iris laughed. "I wish there was a cure of RBF. I come off as mean at first."

"Well, the people you don't fight in the dream plane also shouldn't be so judgmental. LOL. It's okay. Chance has RBF too. Do you watch porn?"

"Yeah. Every now and then. How about you?"

"Same, but I haven't been able to since I've been here because I don't know the website."

"I'll show you later. Have you ever been to a sleepover?"

"Nope. I was never invited to one. What about you?"

"I always declined. I was thinking we should have a sleepover!"

"With all girls?"

"With the squad!"

"Oh shit! In that case, hell yeah! Liiiiit!"

"So, you're down?"

"I'm so down."

"Where the f*** they at?" asked Chance.

"Out sister bonding…" Xenon rolled his eyes.

"Our siblings are cheating on us with each other. What the hell?"

"I know right."

"Now I'm stuck here with a moody ass grown man."

"What?!?!? Oh, hell no. Square the f*** up right now."

"I don't fight girls," he laughed.

"You do today. Get up lassa."

"Where's Blue and Freckles?"

"They've been watching TV."

"Oh. They've probably fought like twice by now. Hehehe."

"True. I'm bored."

"Wanna go hunt squid?"

"Yeah. This is perfect! You can eat mine."

"Whoa. What's with all the romantic stuff," Reign asked. "Are you proposing to me?" she giggled.

"Awww, babe. Are the flowers for me?" Xenon joked.

"Nope," said Amethyst. "I've got something else for you. I know they say to give your loved ones flowers before they go, but you'll be cumming later."

"Ahhh! OMG," he laughed. "Okay. When you get here, there's no need to knock. The door's wide open. Wide open. Just cum inside."

"Ew! Can y'all stop!" said Chance. "I didn't order raunch with my salad."

LOL. I think he tryna toss yo salad, boo.

OMG stop it! Ew. Get the f*** out.

"Y'all talkin' shit?" said Chance.

"Xenon said you look like you put raisins in yo potato salad," Amethyst laughed.

"That's f****** racist, hoe!" said Chance.

"Calm down," Amethyst laughed. "I said that. He wouldn't know about the raisin thing, dumbass. And yo ass know you wanna laugh. You be getting fake mad."

"Whatever. He still a hoe," Chance laughed.

"Me?" Xenon laughed. "You're rich, and you will still f*** for money! You literally said that! My life depended on it. What's your excuse, hoe? If I'm a hoe, you're definitely a hoe. I prefer the term sex worker by the way. Don't get it twisted. F*** wrong with you?"

"Bro. Alright fine. I'm a hoe," he laughed. "Damn. We got three hoes and three pimps in the squad. Liiit."

"Who's the third hoe?" asked Reign. They all gave her a look. "Whaaat?" she laughed. "I have needs. I get what I want. Amethyst, you have hoes?"

"I might," she laughed as she sipped her tea.

"Bro, lemme tell you… Ame has hella hoes. She probably got some I don't know about."

"This is so funny," Iris giggled. "I guess it's official. Red is the lowkey hoe, Blue is the sophisticated hoe, and Reign is the shadow hoe. I'm the lowkey pimp, Bella is the sophisticated pimp, and Sister is the shadow pimp."

"Why are we like this?" Bella laughed.

"Anyways, we're trying to get Meter and Jeremy to officially get back together," said Iris.

"F****** Parent Trap genius ass twins," Chance smiled. "This is going to work. Damn. *The Parent Trap* in real life."

"Hooray love!" Bella twirled.

"N**** did you just say hooray? Scratch that English word from your vocabulary right the f*** now."

"Hey. Girls. I got a question," said Amethyst.

"What is it?" said Chance.

"Was Mary raped in the European version of the story?"

DAY 25

"Oh, Jeremias. Was I selfish to go through with this whole thing? Was I greedy? I had a miracle child delivered straight to me. Now we have daughters and they're all in danger. Did I only do this because I want someone to put Zeus in his place? I can't lose any more children, Jeremias. I just can't."

"You did this because we wanted another child. It was a win-win situation. There's hope for the universe, and we get another child. Actually, it turned out to be better than that because we got two more. Plus, this was the only way we could have children aside from adopting."

"But will they be safe, Jeremias? Whenever I try to protect them, things always seem to go wrong. Hera, Athena, and I came up with three possible scenarios. The last scenario was least likely to happen, and it happened. This is the worst scenario. How are we going to protect them from the hyperbolt? There's a future plan, but a hyperbolt is infallible. Zeus has had practice. The prophecies... Zeus's hatred is personal. It was always personal."

"Look, I'm scared too. I have no idea how, but we are going to get through this. We have to. I doubt it's time for any of them to return to Chaos. Plus, who knows... Maybe they can't be killed or something. I know it doesn't work like that for demi-gods, but they aren't demi-gods. Also, Amethyst has the best luck ever. It's blind luck too. Hell, I don't even think luck is the right word. I think it's Chaos's doing. Honestly, it feels like favoritism."

"Hyperbolts were designed for Titans, Jeremias. That doesn't matter though. You're right. We'll get through this. Each one of them is special. They're all miracles. Everything will be alright. Also, Leios has been doing things behind my back. Iris did many things when she was possessed, but Leios was in on many of Leukos's plans. As soon as I get rid of him, I'm going to appoint Reign as supreme general."

"She's perfect for the job. Come on. Let's go get something to eat. You need to relax."

"This is why I love you, Jeremias. We balance each other out. You're so cool-headed."

"I love you too."

"Did you send me these pearls?" asked Thetis.

"No. Did you send me this new tablet?" asked Jeremy.

"I think the kids are trying to 'hook us up'," she laughed. "Look at all of this. They decorated everything. They want this to be a date."

"They want more than just a date. Look at our room," he laughed.

"Oh, my goddess! They are too much. There's even wine and music."

"This was definitely Cupcake and Iris."

Thetis wrapped her arms around him. "I guess they don't know we're officially back together."

"I guess not," Jeremy tackled her. "Told you I could pick your ass up."

"Do you think it worked?" asked Reign.

"I don't know. I hope so," said Iris.

"We should have put a camera," said Bella. "With audio."

"Ew. No. That's hella nasty," said Chance. "You filthy perv."

"Whaaat? Jeremy's hot. Oh, and his voice! That's so much man. Ooo. And he's such a good dad…"

"I'm bored," Amethyst sighed. "I want to be entertained."

"Do you want to go find Marc Anthony?" Xenon suggested. The squad thought that was a great idea.

"No! Don't do that," said Reign. "You people are crazy!"

"Well, b**** we're going, so do you want to stay here or come with us?" Iris asked.

"I'm coming."

"Wow. I heard that, girl. I'm surprised," Iris smiled.

"Come on, Eye. Even I saw that one coming. Can I call you that too?"

"Sure," she laughed.

"You gon snitch, Bella?" asked Chance.

"Of course not. If anyone asks, I didn't see anything," he smiled.

"Huh?" said Iris.

"Sei. He's going to throw a hyperbolt," said Amphitrite.

"Not at our f****** nieces!"

"So, what's the next move, babe?"

"I think hyperbolts can be slowed down."

"Let's tell Sister. I'll call Athena and Hera too."

Chapter 23: The Day Before

DAY 26

"Wake up! Wake up! Amethyst! Wake up!" yelled Iris.

"WHAT?!?!? Do you know how loud you are?"

"Today is rehearsal day!"

After breakfast, everyone met in the amphitheater. The run through was more of a lecture for Amethyst and a refresher for everyone else. They went over everything in English and then Greek. "Um, quick question."

"What's up, Cupcake?" said Jeremy.

"Who's going to translate my speech?"

"I'll do it," Iris volunteered.

"Shouldn't Blue do it?" asked Reign. "You'll have just finished your speech, and you'll be sitting all the way over there."

"Good point. Plus, we won't be making eye contact."

"Lastly, you are going to be the first one escorted out. People are going to want to interact with you, so that part will take a while," said Thetis.

"Okay. Eeeeeep! I'm so excited!"

"It's time I introduce you to Hania. She will be with you until the start of the ceremony."

"Why? Starting now?"

"No. Starting after we have dinner in Raisa. You and Iris can't be seen until you swim down this path."

"So what kind of restaurant is this?" Amethyst asked.

"It's like Hana Japan or Benihana," said Jeremy.

"Whaaat? Underwater? I can't wait."

"After you," Chance signaled for Reign to get in the chariot.

Xenon was holding the door open for Amethyst, but she decided to climb over from the other side. "That's my, Moon Jelly," he laughed.

"Real ladylike huh?" Chance laughed.

"Shut up, Choo Choo."

During the entire ride there, the squad had a roast session. Their ability to make and take jokes reminded Thetis and Jeremy of their younger days. "These fish want to meet you, but they're acting shy," said Xenon.

"Sounds familiar," she smiled. "Hey cuties!"

"Friendly! She's friendly!"

"I told you."

"I like your scales. My favorite color is purple."

"Huh! Let's go to her coronation. We should tell the others."

"Incoming!" said Bella. "Cetus alert."

"AKA a really big whale," Iris giggled.

"Excuse me, Your Highness. Would you mind if some friends and I come to your coronation?" *If you're thinking about doing that dumb whale voice, don't. Whales aren't dumb. They are very intelligent and regal.*

"Thetis, can they come to me and Iris's coronation?"

"All friendly living things are welcome."

"See you there," the whale sang.

"Animals really like you," said Bella.

"If they knew about you, I don't think they'd be approaching the chariot," Chance laughed.

"There he is!!!" Three young turtles swam at top speed towards them. "Let's get him!"

They took turns smacking Xenon with their flippers. "You made Amethyst cry you big meanie pants."

"Stop smacking him. He's not mean," Amethyst laughed. "We're good now. See," she planted a kiss on his cheek.

"Oh. Okay. Sorry," they snuggled against him. "AHHH! She has a clone!"

"Yep. This is my sister, Iris. We're twins."

"Wait a minute. This is the royal family!!! They freed Selene's soulmate!"

"So, did you get your names? I see you three have grown a little bit."

"I'm Loyalty! That's Honesty, and the dumb one's Hope! See ya at your coronation!"

"Did you see how they jumped him?" Reign laughed.

"I know right. They some hood ass turtles," Chance laughed. "They some real n*****. Like on some real shit though. They can come to the cookout."

"I was so astonished," Bella chuckled. "They came out of nowhere."

"I didn't know you had goons down here too," Xenon smiled.

"Whoa! Is this the place? It's freakin' spectacular!" Their waiter seated them at a square stone table with a cooking surface made from igneous rock. "Dad, what are you getting?"

"A platter with three types of shark, octopus legs, and rice."

"What kind of shark?"

"Blue shark, bull shark, and white shark."

"LOL. I'll call it the Shark Week Special. No wonder you like that one show so much. I'm still not over how y'all catch white sharks. How do you catch them? And aren't they endangered because of humans?"

"That's easy," said Jeremy. "Also, we have multiple shark nurseries, and we try to keep them away from humans. We teach them safety tips. How about we all go together later next week or something?"

"Kkzzzzz. Iris, what are you getting?"

"Oysters and shrimp over rice."

"I'll call it the Madame Shrimpette. How about you, Reign?" she laughed. "Actually, never mind. Thetis?"

You don't want to name Reign's meal?

I don't want to be rude.

"Oysters, a variety of shark, and crabs."

"The Royal Catch! Chance I already know you're getting a Crab Attack. Bella?"

"Seagrass and lots of Caulerpa."

"LOL. I'll call it the Animal Lover."

You should do it. It'll be funny. What do you think she's getting?

A whole ass kraken...

"What are you two laughing about?" Reign asked.

"Oh, nothing. What are you getting?"

"White shark, octopus, lionfish, and leopard seal."

"Wow okay... Everything that might kill you AKA the Sea Monster Meal!"

"Are you calling me a sea monster, Small Fry?" she laughed. Even the people at the table next to them laughed.

"What are you getting, Xe?"

"Squid, shrimp, eel, and scallops of course," he licked his lips. Iris and Chance gave each other an are-they-really-doing-this-in-front-of-mom-and-dad look. Mom and Dad didn't notice though.

"LOL. You're getting an Electric Slider. I think I know what I want now. I'll have the shrimp, salmon, and rice AKA a Moon Jelly Meal."

That womxn has to pee.

Amethyst noticed how she was all alone, so she used her broken Greek to say, "I'll hold your baby."

"You will? Thank you, Your Highness."

"Hello, little one. Aren't you adorable..." Atoz made silly noises and funny faces as they tickled her baby.

"Aren't they..." Thetis said quietly. Jeremy knew what was on her mind, so he did his best to comfort her.

"I love babies, but I don't like children," Iris smiled.

"Babies are just alright..." said Reign. "They're so fragile and weak."

"How's she going to eat her food and hold her baby?" asked Amethyst. "She seems stressed out about something."

"You can invite her to the table if you like," said Thetis. She did just that. Reign went to go have her order transferred to their bill.

"I'm Mara. It's nice to meet you. You're very kind."

"Pretty name!" said Amethyst. "It suits you. You are very beautiful."

"You're young. If you don't mind me asking... Where's your mate?" asked Iris.

"He died protecting me and Mori from a Nereid. I don't have any family out here, but his family is wonderful. I'm so grateful for them." They all did the warrior salute, so Amethyst and Bella did their best to copy them.

Please do that thing you always do.

What? Ohhh. Kk.

"OMG! We got the same thing, Mara!"

"I'm trying to introduce Mori to teknon food," she smiled. After Mara finished eating, Amethyst handed her baby back. "It's time for you to eat." Mori only ate a little piece of kelp before they requested milk.

What's wrong with Chance?

Breastfeeding makes him uncomfortable. A lot of people on the surface turn their noses up at the thought of public breastfeeding. Chance isn't like them. He's just awkward. Anything having to do with mothers makes him think about how much he misses his. Did you know the stigma around breastfeeding in public is greater than the disgust for men peeing in public? It's like damn. There shouldn't be a stigma for breastfeeding in the first place.

That's sad. I'm going to cry. Breastfeeding is natural and good for the baby and mother. Why are people so cruel? They just hate womxn.

"I know this is random, but when's your birthday?" asked Amethyst.

"It's today actually."

"Really? In that case..." She crawled over Xenon's lap to exit the booth.

What are you...

Don't worry. I won't hurt Benny. How do you say, 'Excuse me everyone today is Mara's birthday!'

After she made the announcement, everyone blew bubbles. A few people shouted happy birthday. "Oh, my goddess," said Iris. "Sister, you are such a wild child. I love it."

When she, Chance, and Jeremy started singing the R&B version of the happy birthday song, some people joined in. Xenon started making beats and soon everyone in the restaurant was participating by dancing, singing, or making additional beats with their mouths or objects. Mara was so happy she couldn't stop smiling. Once everyone settled down, the chefs brought a dessert to their table. "What is it?" asked Amethyst. She examined the shimmering, multicolored jelly cube and admired the star-shaped sprinkles inside of it.

"It's kosmiko zele." Xenon showed her the corresponding hand gesture. "It's our version of cake. It doesn't work when the bas is drained." She watched Iris smash a piece in Mara's face, Thetis smash a piece in Jeremy's face, and Reign smash some in Chance's face. As soon as she looked at Xenon, he smiled and smashed some in her face. Then they all fed each other the floating pieces. "It's tradition. Mom started it."

"Many years ago, when I was far less mature, I played a joke on Poseidon with Amphitrite. We were celebrating his birthday at their palace. We blindfolded him with kelp and led him into the dining hall. As soon as Amphitrite moved the kelp, I smashed the entire cake in his face."

"You were a prankster?!?!?" said Bella.

"Saaaaavage... My mother smashed a whole cake in Poseidon's face!!! Awesome!"

"She sure did," said Jeremy. "That's where Iris gets it from."

"Okay. It's official. Being badass is totally genetic," Chance laughed.

Once they got back in the chariot, Thetis said, "Later on, Iris and Amethyst won't be seen until tomorrow, so chat it up now."

That was totally directed at us.

Why would it be directed at us?

Amethyst punched him in the arm. "You sandy shell!" she giggled. Xenon blew so many bubbles on her face she couldn't see.

"Quit flirting with my daughter," Jeremy said playfully.

"Do you know how to make chocolate chip cookies?" Xenon asked. "Jeremy told me you make really good melt-in-your-mouth ones."

"Of course I do! Those are my favorite! I'll bake you some one day."

"Are they really blue? Jeremy told me they're blue."

"I've never seen blue ones, but I can make them blue," she laughed.

Xenon sent a small vortex towards Jeremy. "What was that for, Blue?"

"Chocolate chip cookies aren't blue!!!!! Why'd you lie to me?!?!? I knew you were lying to me!!!!!"

Thetis punched Jeremy in the arm. "Hahaha. Did I say that?"

"I'll tell you what is blue…" Iris laughed.

"Come on, sis. That's private information."

"Xenon's urine!"

"Not anymore!"

"Thanks to Amethyst," she teased.

"Really, Iris! I'm sure the last thing she wants to hear is that she's the reason why my urine doesn't glow in the dark anymore! We've only known each other in the physical for about 60 tides, and now she probably thinks I'm a total weirdo!!!"

"You are. LOL. I like weird. Weird is good. And I already know about the glowy thing. I love that ish."

"See! Wait… You do?"

"Amethyst is just as weird as you," said Chance. "She's just lowkey, but you know that."

"This is Hania. She's about your age, and she speaks English. She'll be your caretaker."

"Hello! Nice to meet you!"

"Are you ready to be pampered?"

"Yes!!!" She loved Hania's bubbly personality.

"First we are going to the spa to get you fresh and clean. It's been closed off for you and the others. It isn't far." When they arrived, Amethyst was amazed at how exotically beautiful it was. There were multiple levels connected by a milky underwater waterfall. It met with a creamy river at the bottom and led to a series of pools. *You all probably haven't seen an underwater river. Look it up.* "We'll start with a full body cleaning. Do you prefer sea stars, fish, or shrimp?"

"Um, I'll definitely go with the shrimp."

"I'm aware that it's common for people on the surface to prefer to undress themselves, so after you get undressed, enter the third room on the right. The shrimp will move away from you once they're done. After that, you may put on the body wrap and meet me by the waterfall. I think we arrived last."

"Oceanids don't wear body wraps?"

"No. The only reason why we wear clothing at all is for fashion or protection purposes."

Amethyst couldn't stop laughing because the shrimp kept tickling her. Once the job was done, she couldn't believe how amazing her skin looked and felt. The shrimp even managed to cure her skin of any clogged pores. She still had her scars and stretch marks though. She giggled because she could hear Xenon saying, 'It's natural.' The body wrap was tiny compared to the pieces of kelp she had seen in the kelp forests, but it fit her just right. "All done!"

"Fabulous. Would you like to have any body hair removed?"

"Everywhere except my arms, please. Wait. Removed as in wax removed?"

"Wax? Oh no. Removed as in mask removed."

"Oh okay, so it's like Veet."

They entered a different room and Hania gestured for her to lay down on a spa bed. "Alright. Once it dries, you can go down to the baths with your friends."

"But they'll see me... In the bath... Naked! I thought they weren't supposed to see me!"

"They won't. They have sea stars covering their eyes. Don't worry. I have jelly circles for you, gemmie."

"Phew!"

"I have twin brothers. They really admire you and Iris."

"Are they close?"

"Yes. Like the ocean and the sea."

"I wish me and Iris were closer. I never had a friend that's a girl before. We haven't had much time to get to know each other yet. There's so much going on and she's been so busy."

"December has been quite busy. I'm sure once things settle down you two will have time to hang out."

"Ready?" Hania led her to her bath.

"Someone's coming! Who do you think it is?" Reign asked.

"The only person left is Ame, womxn," said Chance. "Wassup, sis! Welcome to paradise. I love it down here! Thank you for being the daughter of the basilinna."

"Wow. You sound incredibly happy for a grouch," said Bella.

"You had Hailey as your caretaker, didn't you?" asked Hania.

"I sure did. She is wonderful. Woo! I wasn't expecting our caretakers to be close to our age. I kind of want to ask her for her number."

"I know. She's my sister. She's also not into males," Hania laughed.

"Y-Your sister. Oh shit. My bad."

"Ooooo! HA! Got em!" Amethyst laughed.

"Here's your sponge. Your wrap is next to you. I'll be back to pick you up."

"Who am I next to? Chance?" asked Amethyst.

"Yep," said Chance. "Reign's next to me, so I'm assuming we're in order from slowest to fastest."

"I guess you're at the other end then huh, Iris?" said Amethyst.

"Really? Very funny," Xenon let out a dry chuckle.

"What are you talking about? I can beat you!"

"When we were teknon!"

"I still can. Why do you think Meter had me rescue Red?"

"For training…"

"What? I was a training dummy?!?!?"

"Girl, stop playing. You'll never be fast enough. Not with those legs." Iris vortexed him. "Ouch! Did you have to hit my neck!"

"Oops. Did I do that?" she said sarcastically.

"I thought we can't see…" said Chance.

"We can't. We can sense everyone," said Iris. "You can't because you're a Naiad."

"These sea stars are so fun!" said Bella.

"Why the hell do you need those?" Chance laughed.

"Shut up you discourteous fowl. I like how they feel." Bella vortexed him.

"OUCH! That vortex shit is no joke!"

"Chance, do the air trick Naiads and surface people do!" Reign said.

"The air trick?"

"The fart trick. Surface and land people do it so loud. I'm not sure if it sounds different because they don't live underwater. I want to see what happens when a Naiad farts underwater."

"Oh, hell no!" said Xenon. "DON'T."

"You want me to fart?" Chance smiled. "Hold on. I got you."

"Noooo!" Amethyst covered her nose with her sponge.

"Did you really get out of your bath?" Iris laughed.

"I'm not going to fart in my own bath water," he laughed. "Errrrrrrrrrrrp!" Chance farted.

"Cool!" Reign giggled. "I love farting too."

"It smells like dead whales," said Xenon.

"HAHAHA! I'm weeeak," said Amethyst. "Daaaaamn. That's plural too."

"Shut up, Team Rocket," Chance laughed. "Don't hate." *Some of y'all don't get the joke. Jessie and James from Team Rocket were always 'cross-dressing'. Notice how Chance always seems to accidentally hint at the past. Crap. Maybe I've said to much.*

"You know what, Shrek?" said Xenon.

"You and Fiona can take that shit somewhere else," said Amethyst. "Literally."

The squad was dying laughing. "Alright, alright that was pretty good." Chance decided to throw a piece of candy at Bella.

"You are such an asshole!" Bella threw his sponge at him.

"Ahhh! Was that your sponge! That's foul! It's been in your butt crack!"

"He doesn't have one," Amethyst laughed. "Why you throwing candy anyway? These are hecka good. What are these called?"

"Seabursts," said Iris. "Chance is about to say some more sharkshit."

"What?" he said. "Did any of you have a male caretaker?"

"Some of us," said Reign. "Why?"

"It's not weird?" asked Chance.

"No... Everything isn't sexual," said Reign.

"So, I could work here?" asked Chance.

"I'm sure they do background checks," Amethyst giggled.

Their caretakers came to transport them to the next room. "You all can continue your conversation. We're all going to the same place." Hania replaced Amethyst's jelly circles with two shells. The first facial was a mixture of sand, salt, and something else. It was definitely for exfoliation. The second one was smooth and creamy. She never smelled anything like it. She had no idea what it did to her skin. After it dried, it was really tight and sticky. The final mask was a cold, thick, sweet-smelling gel solely for moisturization.

"Chance, did you wear a kelp wrap?" asked Amethyst.

"Nope. I was free as a bird."

"LOL. I didn't want to risk it," said Amethyst. "These goodies aren't for everyone."

"You don't feel comfortable around us?" Iris sounded disappointed.

"How come you don't want to be naked around us?" asked Bella.

"I don't feel comfortable being butterball naked around anyone!"

"You sure?" Xenon laughed.

"Shut your fine ass up!" she smiled.

"I love how Oceanids are so free. I support that shit. Reign, you in here? I'm still hurt about you calling me a mutt."

"I'm sorry, Little Man. There's nothing wrong with being white too. I was just thinking wrong. I know better now."

"Amethyst, you should instruct us on how to be so effortlessly charming," said Bella.

"Yeah. I wish I was like you," said Reign.

"I don't know. I don't think it's something you teach. Everyone has their own unique personality and characteristics that make them charming in their own way. I will say some are more charming than others though."

"Well, what do you do?" asked Reign.

"I just be myself. Flaws and all."

"But that's hard. Plus, what flaws do you have?" Reign asked.

"What do you mean what flaws?!?!? I have scars, I have anxiety, I'm not fit like y'all, I started a war, the list goes on…"

"Okay, but how do you make them work for you?" asked Reign.

"To be honest, I just be like f*** it."

"She's telling the truth," Chance said. "I swear that could be one of her mottos."

"What's your beauty routine?" asked Reign.

"I just play with skin care products. I love making masks and scrubs! I'm lowkey a skin care expert."

"I just want to know how you make everyone fall in love with you."

"Look, Reign… When I first met you, Thetis, and Iris I was like wow they are beautiful. What on earth are they going to think of me? You're all so proper, neat, and extremely fit which is intimidating. I'm none of those things. Trust me. You do not want to be like me. Anyways, the best advice I can give you is to embrace everything that makes you, you. If you're worried about what people might think, that's okay. We all do. Just know you're supported by a group of five tough guys and one small fry."

"What if I'm a liar? What if I'm not who people think I am?"

"Then show us who you really are. We'll accept you even if you're a sea monster. I'll even feed you lots of kelp. Wait. I'd feed Xenon lots of kelp if he was a sea monster. I'd feed you lots and lots of flesh!"

"Thanks, Small Fry."

"What's a butterball?" asked Xenon.

"Where'd that come from?" asked Bella.

"Out of the blue," Amethyst giggled.

"OMG! Sister!"

"You and your damn puns," Bella smiled.

"We have to lead Iris and Amethyst home separately," said Hania.

"Tomorrow's the big day, sis!" said Iris. "I can't wait to see you looking all royal and shit!"

"See you tomorrow!"

After Alpha and Iota were gone, Chi said, "Guys I'm still terrified."

"Me too! This is crazy!" said Rho. "I'm trying to stay positive but…"

"Imagine how they feel. This is so bad," said Beta.

"Who knows what's going to happen the day after tomorrow?" Zeta added.

"Iris."

"Yes."

"Usually Chance is here to calm me down."

"It's alright. Let it out."

"The basilissa is supposed to make people feel safe. How can I be coronated as basilissa when I started a war? How can I make people feel safe when I'm literally a walking danger magnet! I don't want to hurt anyone."

"You aren't the one hurting people. That's all Zeus's doing."

"If only I could bring the danger to him…"

Chapter 24: Coronation Day

DAY 27

The very first thing Amethyst got done was her hair. "Did you have any style in mind?" asked Hania.

"Do what you think is best. I just want to look bomb AF."

"What about makeup? Yes? No?"

Amethyst looked at Iris as she swam by. Iris approved, so Amethyst said, "Yes!!!"

"I was hoping you'd say that. Mira and I also want to do the same henna designs on you and Iris but in different colors. Silver for Iris and gold for you. We're going to do Iris's face, hands, and feet. For you, we want to do that and your arms, torso, and legs. We also really want to highlight the fact that you're mirror twins, so we're going to give you the same hairstyle aligned on the opposite sides." She looked at Amethyst's ears. "We need to show your piercings off. Your look has to say, 'Bow down I'm the badass basilissa.' Your favorite color is cosmic purple right?"

"Yeah. Can I go to the bathroom? I have to pee."

"Sure. It's right to the left." Of course, Amethyst went the wrong direction.

Whatcha doin', Moon Jelly?

I'm finna pee.

No way. Me too. Do you want to race?

Hell yeah. Ready. Set. Go!

Done!

Crap. LOL. Now we're tied.

After Hania was done with her hair and makeup, she helped her get into her outfit. "This. Is. Amazing! I love it!!!"

"When Iris was coronated as basilissa, she wore silver. That's tradition, but silver breaks you out. Gold goes much better with your skin tone anyways."

"Iris, you're awesome!!!" she yelled.

"Thanks, sis!"

"Thank you so much, Hania."

"It was my pleasure. Now. Are you ready? You and Iris are going to walk in from opposite ends."

"I'm ready." So were the Oceanids in the amphitheater and the other people watching on screen. Even people from the other realms were watching and waiting.

Xenon. I'm coming.

I've heard that phrase before.

HAHA. OMG. Is everyone there?

Yeah. We're all waiting for you two.

How many people are there?

The most there's ever been. I'd say it's about the number of people that were at Iris's coronation and my coronation combined.

Is Poseidon there? I hella want to meet him for real this time.

Pretty much everyone's here except for Hephaestus. Come on. Everyone's so anxious to see you.

Mira escorted Iris to Reign's position, and Hania escorted Amethyst to Xenon's position. Then both of their escorts gave Thetis the cue. "Well don't you look handsome. I like your crown too. Zamn, zaddy. Sexy ass prince. How do I look?"

Xenon took a deep breath. "W-Wow."

Thetis wore a combination of platinum, silver, and gold. This was the first time Amethyst saw her wear her crown. As soon as everyone saw Amethyst, they started cheering. Xenon translated for Amethyst, and Chance had a tablet that did all the translating for him. "Welcome everyone. I am so glad to see so many of you here today. You might be wondering why this year we have decided to begin the coronation ceremony just before dawn, between night and day. My daughters, Iris and Amethyst, are mirror twins like Artemis and Apollo. As most of you now know, I had no choice but to send Amethyst to the surface only a day after they were born. Even then, their safety was only temporary. I am proud to stand here today with my daughters. Not only is Iris of genius intellect, she is responsible, elegant, ambitious, and headstrong all at the same time. I've only known Amethyst for a month. She's quite the handful, but it only takes a wave to feel the warmth that radiates from her heart of gold. Now, enjoy the performance as the sun comes up." Various multicolored bioluminescent creatures from sea jellies to squid appeared all around. It was a beautiful sight. On the stage, the teknon choir sang the sweetest melody Amethyst had ever heard. Then pairs of delphys dressed in platinum did a series of synchronized tricks, some of which seemed extremely dangerous. The performance ended as soon as the sun's rays illuminated the ocean. "Weren't they amazing? Unfortunately, our bioluminescent friends must return to the depths where it is dark. Now, please welcome a group of our royal ambassadors."

What's a royal ambassador again?

It's just a fancy term for a warrior.

In unison, the royal ambassadors recited the oath all royal ambassadors live by. "Long ago, all realms and queendoms lived in harmony. As Oceanids, we are not from a culture of hate and violence. We are from a culture of love and kindness. As Oceanids, we swear by the river Styx to serve and protect all Oceanids regardless of sex, gender, sexuality, dis/abilities, origin, or skin tone."

Then Leios stepped forward and said, "Our beloved basilinna, Thetis, Her Majesty, we do not know what is to come, but we want you to know the basileia is in good hands. Your daughters are in good hands."

"Thank you. Thank all of you for all your support. Shall we begin the ceremony?" The crowd roared. "You all know her as the basilissa, but today she will become basilis. Welcome my eldest daughter, Iris."

Reign escorted Iris to the podium. Iris was wearing a shimmering silver pantsuit just as she told Amethyst she would. It went well with her silver septum ring and henna. Her curls were pinned to the left side and decorated in matching glitter. Her cape was draped from her shoulders so elegantly. "Thank you. First, I want to start by saying Amethyst, you have no idea how much I can't wait for us to really get to know each other. I know I haven't made the greatest first impression, but I'm the kind of sister that will do anything for her siblings. I'll do anything for Xenon. And now, I'd do anything for you too. I want to apologize to anyone I have shown any disrespect to these past moons. Leukos was trying to take over my body, but I defeated him thanks to my friends and family. I promise to work alongside my mother to help her make our home an even better place. I was proud to be your basilissa, and now I'm proud to be your basilis. A goodbye to the past, and a blessing to new beginnings." Amethyst loved how Iris was always so serious, but so easy-going at the same time. So did the crowd. As they cheered, Thetis, Jeremy, Leios, and Reign prepared to coronate her.

LMAO. Look at Chance sitting on the stage. I love how his legs are crossed. And look at Bella smiling and waving at everyone.

He looks like a proud mom. Look how he's taking pictures.

They're going to make him a meme. Bella too. LMFAO. Tag yourself.

Jeremy held Iris's crown while Reign and Leios stood next to Iris as Thetis said, "Being basilis is a responsibility that requires great maturity, diplomacy, and regality. Iris, do you swear by the river Styx to serve and protect the basileia?"

"I, Iris, daughter of Thetis, swear by the river Styx to serve and protect the basileia."

"I, Thetis, daughter of Doris, herby pronounce Iris, daughter of Thetis as the basilis of the basileia." Thetis gently placed Iris's crown on her head. Everyone cheered as Reign escorted her to her patio. Her silver crown was an upgraded version of her previous crown and covered in opalescent pearls.

Ready, Cinderella?

When you are, Charming.

Xe. I'm so nervous. I'm so numb.

Me too. Just be yourself.

"This next gem is the most dynamic person I know. Her aura enchants you, and her laugh can brighten anyone's day. She brings the fun, playful, chaotic energy the basileia was missing. She is wearing gold today because she is allergic to silver. Reminds me of someone…" Thetis coughed, "Amphitrite." They all laughed. "Please, give a warm welcome to my youngest daughter, Amethyst." Amethyst was surprised at how much everyone cheered for her because they barely knew her. While Xenon was escorting her to the stage, a teknon dropped their toy, so Amethyst got down and picked it up for them. The crowd thought that was adorable.

She was dressed in shimmering purple shorts and a matching crop top with a cape trailing from her shoulders. Like Iris, her curls were pulled to the side. Instead of being on the left, they were on the right and coated in gold glitter. Her gold bands and henna complemented her look. "Wow. There are more of you here than I expected. I must admit that I'm a little nervous. On the surface, I only had one true friend, my big brother, Chance. He has always been there for me. For those of you who don't know, he's the short red-headed Naiad sitting behind me with the breather," she smiled. "Jeremy is the best dad anyone could ask for. He was at every parent meeting and always made sure I had everything I needed. He's sacrificed so much for me. At one point, we lived far from the ocean. He hated driving across the bridge we had to cross. I would always ask to go to the beach. He'd joke and ask if I wanted to go to the bay. I would always say,

'No, Dad. I want to go to the ocean!' and he'd take me every time. No wonder I was drawn to the ocean... I found my mother, my sister, awesome friends, and my soulmate. Honestly, when my mother told me I was going to be basilissa I was like ahhh! Responsibilities?!?!? Then she told me that my responsibilities are spreading hope and cheer throughout the basileia. When I heard that, I was like eeeeep! I'm so excited! Then I realized I don't know Greek!" she laughed. "My family has been so supportive. Bella always makes me smile. Have you seen him? Isn't he precious? You should hear his voice. Reign is literally the best fitness trainer ever. She has all these goals for me. I'll probably get there in a few years maybe," she giggled. "I can tell my mother is awesome. She doesn't know this, but I fell in love with her as soon as she wrapped her arms around me when I arrived. Well, I guess she knows now. I really look up to Iris. She is goals. I know that we have a cosmic connection that runs deep, and I can't wait for us to have more bonding time! Then there's Xenon. I don't even know where to start with this one. He's my loyal left hand. He's my defender. He's my Moon Beam, my Night Light, the blueberries to my muffin. Ladies, fellas, everybody... Get you a mate that can glow in the dark. It's only been a month, and although I do miss somethings about the surface, I feel at home here. I'm new to this whole royalty thing. I'm still learning, so please be patient with me. As basilissa, I promise to do everything I can to keep those wonderful smiles on your faces. I'm so proud to be your basilissa! It's liiiiit!" Some teknon started chanting, 'Do the thing! Do the thing!' Their parent quieted them as quickly as possible. "Hehehe. Sure. I'll do it." Amethyst blew a stream of bubbles out of her nose and mouth at the same time. She thought it was just Oceanids that found that hilarious, but the goddesses and gods were laughing too.

"The role of basilissa requires great spontaneity, creativity, and kindness. Do you swear by the river Styx to serve and protect the basileia?"

"I, Amethyst, daughter of Thetis, swear by the river Styx to serve and protect the basileia."

"I, Thetis, daughter of Doris, hereby pronounce Amethyst, daughter of Thetis as basilissa of the basileia." *Yaaasssss.* Once again, the crowd cheered. Her crown was made of gold and decorated with twinkling amethyst crystals. She was so excited.

Iris was escorted off the stage first. After she got through the crowd of people wanting refractions, it was Amethyst's turn. She even gave out hugs. Then Thetis, Jeremy, and the whole squad took group pictures. Amethyst thought it was over, but when she got back to the main part of the bas, Hania told her she needed to get ready for her first meeting as basilissa. She was glad because she wanted to show off her outfit. "Where are we going? Where's everyone else? Who's going to be at the meeting? How long is it?"

"They told me you'd ask a lot of questions. Right this way." Hania dropped her off at the large, closed ballroom doors. As soon as Xenon sensed her, he gave everyone the signal and got into character. Some guards opened the enormous doors, and Amethyst couldn't believe her eyes. She stood at the top of the ballroom steps in complete awe. Then the squad yelled, "SURPRISE!"

She ran down the steps and into her friends' arms. "Thank you all so much! This is so f****** amazing! Huh! You're all dressed as characters! I love the modern Great Gatsby theme! So fitting! Eeeeeep! I love you all so much!!! Where's Xenon?"

As soon as she said that, the lights went out. The squad disappeared before her eyes could adjust. There was an electric blue light covered by the crowd. Then everyone created a path that led to the squad. They acted out one of her favorite scenes, the party scene. She couldn't stop smiling when Xenon said her favorite line, "I'm Gatsby." Then he said, "Welcome to Amethyst's first annual welcome home party!" After he got the party started, they all made their way over to the goddesses and gods."

"You look amazing," said Jeremy.

"Doesn't she…" Thetis agreed.

Amphitrite and Poseidon met them halfway. "Oh, Amethyst! We finally get to meet you!" said Amphitrite. "Eeeeeep! We have sooooo much to catch up on. Your whole life really… I'm your Theia!"

"Hello, niece. Before today, this moment only existed in our dreams." The squad was trying so hard to keep it together because they were both so charming, and they were all lowkey (or maybe highkey) crushing on Poseidon. *Zeus and Poseidon aren't related so calm down. All will be explained at some point.*

"Can we have a hug?" Amethyst smiled.

"Of course!" Poseidon grinned. Thetis and Amphitrite were quietly giggling while Jeremy was in dad mode. "This is our son, Triton. Our daughter is currently on her honeymoon. She and her soulmate had their ceremony last year. You two will meet eventually. Something tells me you and her will get along wonderfully."

"What's up? I'm Triton. Sea King to you," he frowned. The squad noticed that he was obviously using his shapeshifting abilities to hide his markings.

"Triton! That's no way to talk to your cousin!" said Amphitrite. "Fix your attitude."

"It's all good. You know what, Sea King... I get why you don't like us, but it isn't our fault our biofather is a jerk. You were struck by one of his hyperbolts before we were even born. Oh, and just for the record he wasn't even trying to kill you. He thought you were me. Me. I'm the one being hunted, and I would really appreciate it if I had more support from my newfound family member. I am a very fragile package right now. I mean... I'm only about to be struck with a hyperbolt for real, for real. This could be the only time you ever see me, and this is how you acting? Why are you so frumpy witcho Disney ass?" *If only you could see the height difference.*

"You're right," Triton sighed. "I'm sorry. I'm just insecure about how I look. The markings are permanent."

"Congratulations, Thetis," Poseidon smiled. "You've cloned yourself, and it turns out you've also cloned your sister."

"You should come visit us sometime. You and your friends. If you want to," said Triton. "Can we start over? Hi, little cousin. I'm Triton, the Sea King. It's a pleasure to meet you, Your Highness."

"Awww. You're like a big, friendly sea bear! I knew it! Hi, big cousin. I'm Amethyst." They both laughed.

"I'm confident she could turn a rogue wave calm," said Amphitrite. "We also have another child, Aphrodite. She was born from the sea, so of course we took her in."

"You two talking about me?" Aphrodite analyzed Amethyst. "You're beautiful. Absolutely divine. Spin. Huuuum. You did amazing, Thetis. Nice job. I wasn't sure how you'd turn out. Not all twins are identical, and not everyone is a gem in body and psyche. But you, Amethyst, have the divine beauty to match your beautiful psyche. Also, I'm proud of you," she winked. Amethyst had an idea what she was referring to.

"OMG! No way," Amethyst blushed. "Aphrodite just said I'm beautiful! I'm shook. Oh, my goddess I can't breathe."

"Ares! Get over here!" said Aphrodite.

"Yes, honey... Oh. Hello again! Athena!"

"What, Ugly? Oh. Hello, Amethyst!" Then everyone else joined the meetup.

"It's so great to meet you all! You look so young," said Amethyst.

"You sound surprised," said Ares.

"She is," said Athena. "The surface people always depict us as old people. I find that funny because why would we look 55 instead of 25? The surface really has something against their youth. I don't understand it."

"Where's Hephaestus?" Amethyst asked. "However he looks is fine with me. We won't make fun of him." They could hear the disappointment in her voice.

"I haven't seen him in years," said Aphrodite. "We were really good friends. I don't know what happened."

"I know how much you want to meet your brother, but at this point, it will take a miracle for him to show himself," Athena added.

"Ares and I have six kids. Eros, also known as Cupid, has terrible aim. He doesn't really do that bow and arrow thing. He writes poems and stuff. Like Eros, our daughter Harmonia is incredibly sweet. We have two sons named Deimos and Phobos. They're twins. They aren't the brightest, and Phobos is no warrior," she giggled. "Deimos, on the other hand, is just like his father. Then there's Hermaphroditus. You probably heard about them, but they go by Maph. You're familiar with our sixth child."

"You're probably wondering if Hades had any kids," said Athena. "The answer is no.

"That's good news because he's going to spoil the hell out of you," Aphrodite laughed. "Hades is here. He's just very, very shy. He also doesn't like crowds. He probably made himself invisible and is hanging out by the staircase."

"I'm Hestia and this is Dionysus. They're drunk," she giggled. "They're your brother too."

"They're always drunk right, sis?" Apollo laughed.

"All day, every day. They have the alcohol tolerance of a cotton ball," said Artemis.

"Dionysus is really sweet," said Hestia. "You'll have to meet them when they're sober."

"Demeter, who's this?" asked Dionysus.

"I'm not Demeter," said Hestia. "We don't even look alike. This is Amethyst, your sister."

"Sister? Oh, my goddess. I've always wanted a sister. Wait, Amethyst? I'm sorry. I'm so sorry," he cried.

"Not Amethystos, silly. Amethyst," said Demeter. "Hi, niece. Remember me? I want you to meet my daughter. Persephone…"

"LOL. She's your offSPRING," Amethyst laughed. She loved how Demeter snorted when she laughed.

Dionysus was just now responding. "Hello, Amphitrite. Did I tell you, you look just like Amphitrite? I'm mean Amethyst. I mean… Hi. It's nice to meet you."

"Yes, mother. Huh! Hi! Hi! Hi! We're sisters! Just so you know, I'm not Hades's wife nor did he kidnap me. Long story short, I died because Hermes tricked me into swearing something I couldn't live up to on the river Styx. Hades explained to her what happened and brought me back. I just like visiting him. He's my favorite uncle."

"Oh okay. I was wondering what was up with that because Thetis told me how nice he is."

"You want to know a secret about Hades?"

"Yeah sure. What's the tea, sis?"

She leaned into her ear and whispered, "Hades is crushing on Styx. There's more tea where that came from. You wanna know how many people I've killed?"

"How many?"

"You really want to know? 666. I'm serious."

"Oh."

"You don't sound impressed. How many people have you killed?"

"I haven't killed anyone."

"Oh. That's okay," she hugged her. "Iris is my favorite sibling! You're cute like Iris. I like you. I have two favorites now! Hermes!"

Hermes was busy spiking one of the punch bowls. Amethyst figured that's how Dionysus got drunk. "What can I do for you my lovely sister?"

I really don't like him. He gets on my nerves.

"Bring me something to drink. Please." Then she said, "Hermes, say hi. This is our sister."

"I don't want to meet her." He threw himself on to a table. "She's probably just going to treat me like the rest of you do. Don't tell me. I know it's tragic."

"Suck it up, brat," said Athena. "We shower you with tough love because you look just like Zeus with that olive ass skin and that brown ass hair. You also molest everyone."

"So, do I have any other—"

"Shhh." Hermes put his finger to Amethyst's lips.

Amethyst swatted his hand away. "N**** I will beat your ass. Don't ever touch me like that again."

"I'll do anything you want me to." He gently put his hands around his own throat in an erotic way. "Anything."

"Let's start with 11 feet of personal space."

"As you wish. Oh, how I love you. You magnificent creature. You will never love me, will you? I see you belong to someone else. At least I know he'll take good care of you. Sometimes you have to let go of the ones you love."

"I don't belong to anyone."

"I love you. You're a poem. What a goddess…"

"Xe, where are the drinks?" Atoz dismissed themselves from the meet and greet.

"You're filthy," they all said to Hermes.

"Oh, what a beautiful tragedy," he moped.

When they sat down at the bar, Xenon asked her what she wanted to drink. "A Purple Sand Crawler sounds nice."

"We'll have two of those." Then he realized there was no one there. "Ummm hello?"

"Ah, what a coincidence that I run into the two most beautiful creatures ever created," said Hermes. "The bartender had to take a little break, but that's no problem. I'll fill in for him."

"Make it three," Xenon rolled his eyes.

Red will want to taste mine.

"Do you want a shot of nectar?" asked Hermes.

"No. That's inappropriate." Xenon was doing his best to calm himself down.

"Amethyst, you're welcome to come to my house anytime. I think you'll find me very… Pleasing."

"Hermes," Xenon clenched his jaw. "You're making me upset."

"P-Please don't get upset," said Hermes.

"Didn't you say you'll do anything I ask? I asked for 11 feet of space."

"Oh, it seems I have forgotten. I was distracted by the insults I received after you left. I'll be leaving now. Enjoy your drinks," he moped.

"Damn, babe," Amethyst smiled. "I thought you were going to grab his ass."

"Look who's talking," Xenon smiled. "What did you do? I know you did something. You kept smiling."

"Well duh… He invaded my space, so I invaded his. I planted a stinger. One time I got hit with a defective one. It didn't sting when they shot me with it. All it does is record audio. I still had it in one of my pockets. I figured it would come in handy."

"I feel like there's more to it."

"There is. I want to know more about this mysterious hyperbolt and Hermes is Zeus's messenger."

"How are you going to listen to the audio?"

"All stingers use Bluetooth technology. They hook up to certain checkpoints and objects. They also automatically get locked onto your phone. This one is defective, but all I have to do is hook it up to my phone."

"In that case, I can make a holographic map."

"I love having a techy soulmate witcho aquatic, glow-in-the-dark ass."

"This is perfect because now I can add parts of the sky kingdom to my secret map of all the realms. This next part is going to be so awkward. The princesses, prins, and princes keep trying to marry Iris. Now they'll be onto you too," he sighed. "Your magnetic aura and electrifying personality... Everyone wants to marry into the basileia," he rolled his eyes. "They won't bring it up, but I'm going to feel all those emotions."

"Don't they all want to marry you too?"

"Not really. I'm too mysterious."

"Aren't I mysterious?"

"It's a different kind of mysteriousness. If people found out about your past, it wouldn't matter in the sense that you aren't hiding who you are. They have already fallen in love with a true image, not a false one. As for me, the image they fell in love with is false."

"So, they know I'm Skotos and love me as Skotos, but they see you as Agathos and suspect that you're Skotos and are hiding that for the wrong reasons?"

"OMG! Exactly! They don't want to take the risk of me turning out to be the beast that I am."

"You keep calling yourself that. This is connected to the one thing we you haven't told anyone isn't it?"

"Yes. I worry about what you're going to think. I don't want to sound cheesy, but it's so bad the others would change their minds about me."

"Good. Then maybe you'll be able to handle my one thing. Plus, I don't want to feel like I'm a bad influence on the others. Especially on you."

"Why won't you just tell me already?"

"Because I want to know what you did first."

"Why?"

"So I can prepare myself for possible rejection."

"Amethyst. There is nothing that can come between us. Hell, if you told me you were going to set the whole world on fire, I'd release the chlorine trifluoride without hesitation. I mean that."

"You're so bad," she smiled.

"Yes, we are."

Alpha and Zeta followed the rest of the squad up to the grotto. There were people from all the realms waiting to see her. When she entered, everyone gasped. There was quiet chatter as she walked to a stone bench surrounded by an arch of branches and flowers. She noticed there were pairs of young people giving her royal vibes lined up. Pair by pair, they introduced themselves. "Greetings, Amethyst," said one of them. "I am Basil, the Naiad prince."

"And I am Althea, the Naiad princess." Then at the same time, they bowed and kissed her hands. "Welcome home, Amethyst."

"Hello! I'm Juniper!" she threw her arms around Amethyst. "It's so great to meet you!"

"I'm Sage. Sorry about her," she smiled. "We're the epimelid princesses."

The next two were really quiet. They both looked Amethyst in the eyes for about 6 seconds and then at each other for about 3. The dark one said, "Ebony. Limonid princess." Then the pale one said, "Ivory. Limonid prince."

The next pair was arguing about something before they came up to her. They didn't realize it was their turn. "I'm princess Estuary, and he's prince River."

"We're Potamoi. We are delighted to be in your presence, ma'am. See my hooves? Nice, aren't they?"

"They are pretty shiny."

The next pair was so bold. "I am Tzari Chauncey of the fire dominion, and you are quite the flame."

"I am Sharun, pharaoh of the time province." Then they both bowed.

"Hello, brightness," said a soft voice. "I am Anemone, prince of the Nephelai. This is Naseem, prince of the Nephelai." Nassem waved. "He is mute." When they hugged her, she was surprised how light they were.

"Well, hello there, sunshine. I'm Dawn, the princess of the Hesperids. Isn't she adorable?"

"That she is. I'm Eden, the prince of the Hesperids. Good day, madam." Amethyst loved their warm personalities. There was something really parental about those two.

"We are the princesses of the Asteriai," the next pair said in unison.

"To find Celestia, you must look to the stars," said one of them.

"But all you have to do is look in here," she pointed to Amethyst's heart, "to find Aster. Do you know who's who?"

"Yeah. LOL. Aster means star. You said look to the stars to find Celestia. The stars are within us, and you said to look into my heart to find a star. You're Celestia because when I looked down at my heart, your finger was there. Plus, Celestia means sky. To find the sky, look to the stars? That's not right. If you swap Celestia and Aster, it fits. You could also do it like that."

"You're clever. I like you," Aster giggled.

Then it was time for everyone to move to the amphitheater and present the new princess with gifts. Amethyst had no idea there was also an amphitheater in the grotto. She wondered what else was up there. "I can't stand this glow worm," said River. "I know he talks shit about the rest of us. He's so mean."

"I bet you won't say it to his face though," Sage laughed. "All you do is run your mouth. Whoever named you was spot on."

"Hell no, I won't. There's no telling what his moody ass will do to me." River paused. "And why are you always trying to burn me? You're the one who's supposed to get burned. SAGE."

"That was terrible but nice try, Ponyboy."

"May I have everyone's attention please?" said Xenon. "As your host, I am honored to say we are gathered here today to celebrate the return of our beloved basilissa. Many of you know Amethyst was raised on the surface due to the intentions of a tyrant." Everyone shouted in agreement. "You all don't know her that well, so I'd like to point something out. I'm sure many of you are aware of how materialistic and callous some royal figures are, but Amethyst is nothing at all like them. Look at the smile on her face. She's been put through so much on the surface and ever since she got here, yet she still has the ability to uplift our spirits in a time like this. Isn't she inspiring? Do your favorite prince a favor. Let's show her that we're here for her." The crowd cheered for her for so long, she had to hide her face. The standing ovation they gave her was so overwhelming her cheeks turned red.

The amphitheater seemed to have been sculpted from the ground itself, for the relationship it had with the tropical flora was exquisite. Suddenly, pairs of the native animals emerged from the forest. Tamarins, capybaras, glass frogs, cassowaries, sun bears, toucans, anacondas, and others all came to welcome her. "Holy f****** shit," said Chance.

"What's wrong?" Xenon teased. "I thought you liked snakes."

"That's not a f****** snake. That's a serpent."

"Where's Bella? He should have made have made it to this side of the pond by now," said Reign.

"Hey! I'm right here."

"What were you doing?" asked Chance. Bella smiled with a guilty sense of pride. "Actually. Never mind. Nasty ass. Make sure you wash yo hands."

"Oh, my goddess!" Xenon turned to Iris, Thetis, and Jeremy. "That's a jaguar! I wonder… Is that Ailuros?"

"Dude. What are you talking about? That's a black panther."

"How about we just ask Amethyst later," Iris laughed. "More importantly we should pay attention."

"Iris is right," said Thetis. "Bastet is a goddess. She only shows herself when she has an important message regarding danger. Amethyst will be fine as long as she doesn't try to touch her."

Everyone stared in absolute silence as Bastet approached Amethyst. At first she was frightened, but something about Bastet's eyes made her realize there was nothing to fear, so she decided to pet her. She didn't know you weren't supposed to do that. Everyone gasped, and Thetis was on the edge of her seat, ready to teleport. Then the goddess purred. "Do not worry, Thetis. I would never harm such a pure thing. Amethyst. Always remember laws are definitions, and you cannot be defined."

"Mom!!! Did you see that?!?!? That was sooooo cool!"

"Yes, I did see that," she smiled. "Jeremias. She just called me mom."

Amethyst was so caught up in the flower canopy she was sitting under, she forgot people were about to bring her gifts. Of course, she was sitting criss-cross applesauce on the stone bench. Aster and Celestia started it off. "You can't always see them…"

"…but the stars are always there."

Celestia opened her palm and revealed a small floating ball of light. "This is Little Spark. Through Little Spark, you can contact our realm and allow us to guide you if you ever get lost. Little Spark will disappear when you close your palm and will reappear if you do this," she showed her the hand movement.

"Whoa! Hi, Little Spark! Thank you. They will definitely come in handy one day."

Hahaha. I'm the host but you have better jokes than me. You're such a dork.

Dork as in whale penis?

I hope not. I don't know if I can handle all that.

Eden was carrying a large woven basket, and Dawn was carrying something Amethyst assumed was the source of the delicious scent she was picking up. "For you, we have a basket of the sweetest golden apples and a jar of applesauce," said Dawn.

"And apple pie," Eden blushed.

"It's his very own recipe! He's insecure about his baking even though it's absolutely wonderful."

"Yuuum! This looks so good. I'll let you know how delicious the pie was."

Anemone and Naseem were next. "I made you a blanket from spun clouds. It's completely waterproof, and yes, it floats. Naseem got you— He knows you don't know sign language yet, but he wants to know if he can try to tell you himself with hand gestures."

"Of course. I'm all eyes," she smiled. "I'll do my best to hurry up and learn OSL."

"[I] [Give] [You] [Butterflies]"

She gasped with excitement as she mimicked the gesture for butterflies. Then he signaled for a kaleidoscope of monarch butterflies to descend from the sky. "OMG! This is amazing!" She made a heart shape with her hands and placed it over her heart. Then she threw it towards him. He caught it and gave her a gentle hug.

"The fire dominion gives you rice, candles, and these gold beads," said Chauncey.

"I give you this hourglass and this water clock on behalf of the time province," said Sharun.

"Dope! I love it!"

"I heard about how much you love skincare products!" said Estuary. "First, use the Congolese silt scrub. Then, use the açai clay mask. After that, follow up with the freshwater spritzer. I made the Amazonian cacao lip balm myself. There's some other stuff in there too."

"And we know you love animals. This is Snow Brownie. We found him injured not too long ago. He's a river otter. It doesn't snow where we live, so he's extremely vulnerable to predators because of his rare naturally white fur. He also doesn't know how to hunt. I know it doesn't snow here, but the grotto is a much better home for him. He's super sweet and loves to cuddle." Snow Brownie rubbed against her leg. "We were going to take him up to The North, but he didn't want to go. He got excited when he saw you on screen so..."

"Hey, little guy! I'll take good care of you. Awww, he's so adorable. He must get it from you two."

"Two swans. Two Koi. Two turtles," said Ebony.

"One ebony. One Ivory. They'll have lots of babies."

"And lily perfume."

"How thoughtful! Thank you so much!"

"Here are some of our finest butters, jams, beans, veggies, milks, and custards!" said Juniper.

"All of our animals and plants are handled with the utmost love and care. Here are some seeds for your garden."

"Y'all tryna fatten me up huh? I'm overweight, not underfed," she smiled. "This looks so yummy!"

"On behalf of all Naiads, I present to you the rarest flowers and the sweetest berries," said Althea.

"And lastly, this orange tree and some of the finest lavender," said Basil. "Now you have it in your very own backyard."

"Eeeeeep! Thank you all so much! You're so kind!"

From Aphrodite, she received a beauty kit with the best lip glosses, eyeliners, and mascaras she thought only existed in the psychic plane.

Featherweight body armor from Ares, a matching shield and helmet from Athena, a music box from Apollo, a bow and arrows from Artemis, bread and a honeybee farm from Demeter, and grape juice and ciders from Dionysus because he knows how much she dislikes alcohol. Hermes gave her a telescope and thoroughly explained how he would give her all the stars in the sky if he could. Then he uploaded Greek and OSL to Amethyst and Chance's brains. He also taught Bella English. *The family perv came through.* Persephone gave her a crown and armbands made of flowers that will never die. Hestia gave her multiple gold body chains, and on behalf of Hera, shimmering body lotion made from actual gold and a key to her house that she can't lose. Hades gave her a lamp for her cave and a treasure chest filled with crystals. Triton gave her a miniature sea in a magical rectangular aquarium. She could command it to make storms, sink ships, and do whatever else she wanted. Poseidon gave her two unicorn pegasi foals that were technically his grandchildren. He introduced her to her other cousin, Christos, son of Pegasus's twin brother, Chrysaor. Christos was dressed in worn down overalls shorts with no shirt underneath and a floral bucket hat. Amethyst loved how he was leaning against a palm tree chewing on sugarcane. The squad already had so much to talk about. Lastly, Amphitrite gave her a delphys calf named Kynthia and a high-tech whistle made from silver and pearl. She told her that it could only be used underwater, but its listener can hear it from anywhere. "Blow it during the worst hour, when you need a god strong army, and the cavalry will come." *So mysterious. Oh and no. A god strong army is not* needed *in this war. LOL.*

"We know how much you love to read," said Thetis.

"And we know how much you love secrets," Jeremy added.

"We give you complete access to the Isle of Scrolls. Before you were born, we had Hephaestus make Iris an omipearl, and we had this star-shaped charm made for you. It contains energy that we think you'll be able to use once you master shifting."

Hephaestus was watching the ceremony from his island. Eventually, he convinced himself to show himself. He put on his favorite gold jewelry, gold lip shimmer, and gold eyeliner. When he got to the grotto, everyone created a path for him. Persephone offered to help him walk, but he didn't need any help. "I got it. I'm gon do it. I'm gon get there," he smiled. He made his way down the path wearing a golden leg brace. It was the most intricate leg brace Amethyst had ever seen. Most of the crowd was surprised that he was far from the ugly beast Zeus described him to be. He mainly resembled Hera. His perfectly smooth skin was the color of aged brass, his eyes like cinnamon, and his hair like cashmere. He was 6 and a half feet of heavenly beauty.

"He has the exact same eyes as Ame," said Chance. "They have the same hair too!"

"How we doin' family? Thanks for bein' so supportive when my father threw me out the sky. Oh, wait. Never mind. Just Thetis, Athena, Amphitrite, Poseidon and of course my mother. But don't y'all worry. I won't be in your presence for very long. I just came to introduce myself to my other little sister. Why you smilin' at me?"

He was surprised when Amethyst threw her arms around him. "Because you came!!! Look! That's Chance. He's my brother. Those are my friends! We're all misfits! I can see your island from my cave!!!"

"Is that so? It's a pleasure to meet you all. I brought you a little something."

"A lava lamp?!?!? OMG. Is this real lava? I love it!"

"Here's my number. You can visit me if you like. Your friends are welcome too. I could use some friends," he smiled. "I better get goin' now. Our father is gon lose it when he finds out I came to land. Speaking of that… I was supposed to be dead. I shouldn't have survived that fall, yet here I am. I know about your current situation, but his plans don't always work the way he intends them to. I'll see you soon."

"They told me I didn't have to get you anything, but how could I not?" Bella smiled. He handed her a bejeweled comb. "I know you like hair products, so I figured you'd like this. I made it myself."

"Awww, Bella. I love it! You're the sweetest."

"I wasn't sure what to get you, but then I remembered you like glowy things, so I got you these." Reign handed her some wall decals and posters. "They're all neon cool colors."

"Yo!!! These are dope! I'll put them up tonight!"

"What kind of sister would I be if I didn't expand your lingerie collection?" Iris giggled. When she gave the signal, 8 royal ambassadors brought out 4 bags each. One of them said Victoria's Secret. The company is quaking because she's short, overweight, and trans*. "I might have gone to the surface without permission." Thetis smiled and shook her head. "There's also some comfy stuff made by the Naiads and sky nymphs as well as some comfy masculine stuff."

"OMG! Iris, you did all this for me? Thank you! Something tells me you're trying to get a niece. Sorry but that's years down the road, sis. Xenon won't be getting pregnant anytime soon." Everyone was amused by her little comment. "LOL. We might not even want kids."

"Alright, alright. It's my turn," said Chance. "I got you the newest speaker system, the new writing tablet that just came out, and a few gowns to go over all that lingerie."

"Thank you, Choo Choo! You're the best big brother ever!"

Xenon had zoned out for a minute. "Oh, right. I got you two pairs of Converse, fireflies for your garden, and bioluminescent flora. I also got you a cross purse for all the little things you like to carry and an outdoor movie projector. I also installed an outdoor shower for you. Here's some soap made by the epimelids. It won't break you out. They're all earthy and floral scents. I told them they could make whatever they wanted as long as half of the batch was lavender. Here's an album of some of the refractions I took of you. And this is a little something I put together." He clicked something on his phone, and a video was projected from another device so everyone could see. He had been secretly recording moments since the night Amethyst arrived.

"What?!?!? No way!!! Xenon you didn't have to do all this for me. Thank you so much." Chance started recording was about to happen next. "Wow.

I only knew you recorded some of those. Are you trying to make me cry?" she blushed.

"There's one more thing. Well, two…" He turned off the force field that was hiding his last two gifts and everyone gasped. Even Apollo. "I had been working on this sculpture for a while. It's made from the finest Zambian amethyst." Amethyst got up from her bench and ran over to the sculpture in awe. "When I started it, I didn't even know your name. You just reminded me of that crystal. I was going to name it after you, but the sculpture speaks for itself. When I first saw you on the beach, I gave you that piece of kelp, but you gave me eternal inspiration. Ever since that day, I wanted to sculpt you, but I decided to wait until my skills improved. After I finished it, I glazed it in a shimmer gloss because you're a star. I like to think of it as my best attempt at a copy of the best sculpture there is. Chaos truly is the best sculptor of all. This painting is a reflection of how I feel when I look into those cosmic, chaotic eyes of yours. I hope you like my gifts."

Amethyst didn't know what to say. She was literally speechless. She was in tears, but she couldn't stop smiling. Then she hugged him and kissed him so passionately, even Aphrodite blushed and wiped a few tears. "Alright lovebirds. Time to break it up," Chance smiled.

I love you infinity.

It was now time for the performances to start. Iris started it off by playing a piece she wrote for her on her violin. Reign was next. She demonstrated her insurmountable strength by doing a series of tasks. Chance showed off his best magic tricks that made Hermes himself blink twice. Just as the squad predicted, Bella impressed Apollo with his mellifluous voice. Xenon was the last performer. Amethyst was captivated by his magnificent dancing.

You know I'm in love with you right, Moon Beam?

"I know we're running on CPT but ain't it time to eat?" asked Chance.

"We're just waiting for Blue to change his clothes," Iris laughed.

Lunch was served in the ballroom. Amethyst and Thetis were the last ones to walk in. She saw a watermelon cube and went for it. Thetis giggled and said, "We have to bless the food first."

"Oh shit. My bad," she finished the watermelon. "I mean oh snap. I said oh snap. My bad y'all." After they blessed the food, Amethyst went to go get in line.

The squad was dying laughing at their table. "Look at this hungry dumbass," said Chance.

"Maybe she forgot where we're sitting," said Reign. "Look how small she is compared to everyone else. You can barely see her."

"Is she in line?" asked Bella. "How cute." *FYI. He's in a pool next to their table.*

"People who didn't grow up as royalty make the best princesses," Iris smiled.

Xenon went to go get her. "They're going to bring the food to you, Little Scallop."

"Oh, my goddess. This potato salad is sooooo good. Who made this?" asked Amethyst.

"The Naiads," said Xenon. "I was going to have the sky nymphs make it because they had to make something, but nobody wants their bland ass potato salad."

"OMG. PAUSE. WHO? MADE. THIS." Amethyst closed her eyes as she savored the ooey gooey macaroni and cheese.

"I-I did," Xenon blushed.

"What the hell? No way. What the f***? You fosho getting in trouble later. Oh, f***! Ummm. F*** babe." As she continued tasting all the food, someone walked up to their table. "Huuuh! Are you Chiron? OMG! I'm a Sagittarius!" Amethyst said as she continued to chow down on her macaroni and cheese. "That constellation isn't you is it?"

"You are correct. The constellation is named after my sister. We're twins like you and Iris."

"How many sets of twins did Kronos have? Who are the other twins?"

"You ask really good questions," he smiled. "I'm afraid I don't know. Metis is the only one with the answer to that question. Anyway, your gifts are in the grotto. I had a few sapodilla trees planted."

She didn't know what kind of tree that was, but she said thank you anyway. The goddesses and gods came over to chat one by one. Then the moment the whole squad had been waiting for finally came. "Shhh! Here they come!" said Xenon. While Amphitrite was talking to Thetis, Poseidon jogged over to the squad's table and pulled up a chair right between Ame and Xe. They loved how he always smelled good and how he was always chewing gum.

"Wassup y'all. Is it me or is it hot in here? I wore extra layers because it's usually cold as hell here."

"You know... I think it's you," Amethyst smiled. Xenon covered his face.

"Did Christos come over here yet? Christos!"

"Heya there. I was too shy to talk you in front of all them people. You can call me Chris. I live in the northern part of the grotto. I'll make some bubblegum from the sapodilla trees. I can also move some of the honeybees near the orange tree, so you can have some orange blossom honey if you like. We can do the same thing with some of the lavender. I know I'm just the farm help, but you all can come and visit me."

"Awww, you're not just the farm help. We're cousins!" said Amethyst. "And yes! I would looove that!!! OMG!"

After he left, Poseidon whispered, "He got a crush on yo momma. Anyways, I came over here to tell you not to worry about the hyperbolt because we have a plan now. She'll tell you about it later. F*** Zeus," he smiled.

Once everyone finished saying their goodbyes, the squad went up to the grotto. "Hey, Kynthia. Where are the others?"

"Come here little tiny ponies." They were sleeping, so she used her fluke to splash water on them. "Get up sleepyheads!"

"Ahhh!" screamed the twins. "Oh, it's just Amethyst and her friends. We weren't scared. Just ready for battle…"

"What kind of name would you like?" Amethyst giggled. "Feminine, masculine, neither, both…"

"Both or neither," they said at the same time.

"Aren't you more male?" one of them asked. "I think you're more male."

"What are you talking about? We don't have any genitalia, dummy!"

"I know that! I meant more masculine. Wait. So how were we born? I think I zoned out when Dad was explaining that."

"Magic duh!"

"Oh, right. Anyways, Triton and Dad are masculine, and you three have similar vibes!"

"Whatever! I don't really care. Well… That does sound right. Why are you so smart? Wait. So, what are you then?"

"I think I'm more feminine than you are. Do you have our names yet, Amethyst?"

"You're Nightmare and you're Daydream. How's that sound?" Their names suited them. Nightmare had the deepest purple coat that was almost black, matching wings, and a silver horn to match their stormy grey eyes. Daydream also had a silver horn but didn't have wings. They had a pastel lavender coat, a mane of a slightly darker shade of lavender, and cloudy grey eyes.

"YAY!" they shouted. "You adopted us, right? You're our mom?" asked Nightmare.

"How do you know she's not our dad?" asked Daydream.

"I don't know. She's like Amphitrite, and Amphitrite prefers mom, so I just assumed!"

"I like mom," Amethyst giggled.

"What about her soulmate? What is he?"

"Huuummm... He's like Poseidon, and Poseidon says it doesn't matter so... How about mom?"

"Yeah! Let's have two moms!" said Kynthia. "We already have a dad, and Crissy's annoying tail acts like he's our dad so... Wait. We should ask first."

"Oh, right. Is it okay if we call you mom too?" asked Daydream.

"Sure," Xenon smiled.

"How are you going to differentiate between the two?" asked Reign.

"She's Mommy and he's Mom," said Nightmare.

"Awww," said Bella. "I adore them."

"I know right. They're adorable," said Iris.

"They're hella funny too," Chance added. "These my little n*****."

"The good news is that we have a plan," said Thetis. "The bad news is that it has to be done with perfect timing which leaves no room for any error."

"What has to be done?" asked Iris.

"Athena did the calculations," said Jeremy. "We know all 8 of the times Zeus might strike, but we don't know the direction."

"Poseidon, Hades, Demeter, and Hera are the four strongest Olympians," said Thetis. "They are each going to use both of their hands to create force fields in a circle around you. This will only help the water slow the hyperbolt down somewhat. Within this circle will be the four Olympians with the quickest reflexes. They are Artemis, Apollo, Ares and unfortunately Hermes. You two will be in the middle of them. Athena will be keeping track of time."

"Quick question. What is a hyperbolt made of because I know when lightning touches the ocean, it only spreads across," said Amethyst.

"Hyperbolts are not made of lightning. They are made from white light which is why they cannot be stopped, only absorbed. They are made of pure white energy, so only pure darkness can absorb them without risk."

"So, only a black hole can absorb this thing?" said Amethyst.

"Yes. And one more thing. I've been keeping something hidden because of what some of our people have become because of Zeus. I'm sorry I waited so long, but it was for the best. Follow me to my lair." They were all eager for their own reasons. "Tethys and Okeanos are the parents of the first Haliai. They gave birth to twins. My mother Doris and my aunt Metis... Doris and Nereus are the parents of the first Nereids which includes myself and Amphitrite. One of us was born with a fluke and the other with legs. I have a fluke."

"I knew it! Can I see it? What color is it? This is so cool!" said Amethyst.

"It isn't going to make you uncomfortable?"

"Ummm no. Why would it? Plus, I knew all along. I wouldn't care if you have octopus tentacles. I just care that you're my mom."

"Wait. We'll do it together," said Iris. Then they both revealed their true forms.

"I knew I wasn't crazy," Chance smiled.

"Ooooo! Mom your fluke is the perfect smoky grey color! I love the birthmark near the tip. It adds variation. I'm surprised your fluke is almost black Iris. I wasn't expecting that. Cool!"

"Bloody hell! Auntie, you grew hella! You gotta be like 8ft 6 and Iris what are you like 6ft 1? You're almost the same height as Reign!"

"So, why are we so short?" asked Amethyst.

"Because in his true form, Zeus is only like 40 meters tall. The average height for an Olympian is 45 meters," Jeremy laughed. "He gave you two the short gene."

"So, how big are Titans?" asked Amethyst.

"They start off at around 500 meters, but they can shift to any size they have the energy for," said Thetis.

"What about Mer?"

"The same height as Hailai on average."

"Amethyst can use her Titan power, so how big could she get once she masters the technique?" asked Xenon.

"I don't know. She's microscopic compared to them, but she's also an energetic. Before her, the only energetic was Hera and she's an Olympian."

"I heard you say that before," said Amethyst. "What does energetic mean? Is it because I can make myself purple? Is that what Titans do?"

"You and Hera have the ability to absorb energy which is why you both have the ability to become light energy. She can also use energy, but only as much as she can absorb. I believe you can too. Titans must consume energy by eating something of their element and can only use how much they can consume. There has never been an energetic Titan, but you seem to utilize both techniques. I don't quite understand that yet. That would imply you inherited two dominant Titan genes and studies show the dominant Titan gene can only be passed down to a child through twins."

"Which would mean Zeus has a twin," said Amethyst.

"Exactly but technically none of the original Olympians are related," said Thetis.

"Shouldn't Iris be able to use her Titan power since we're twins?"

"In theory yes, but I think the gene can only be passed down to one child. You two are helping me figure out the genetics behind all this. Currently, I'm thinking Titans cannot produce related offspring. Therefore, Olympian twins are children that were born at the same time but not related. In other words, they are born heterofraternal. Once I figure that out, I will be able to figure out your specific genetics. I have a feeling they are very unique due to the possible overlap. I wouldn't be surprised. Aside from the obvious, everything about you two is one of a kind. For example, Iris's heart points towards the left side, but Amethyst's points towards the right side. A surface doctor wouldn't have noticed. She's never had a surface X-ray. Would you two mind standing next to each other? Notice how whenever they stand next to each other, Iris is to the left of Amethyst. Iris is also left-handed. Amethyst is ambidextrous which is also very intriguing because why isn't she just right-handed. I think Amethyst is left and right brained whereas Iris is right brained. Look at their physical features. They're amazing. Anyway, my point is that I think they have more similar DNA than single siblings but less than identical twins. I think they missed being completely identical by a few genes. Their eye colors for example. Some things about their phenotypes are different. I think they have some different alleles. They could be monozygotic mirror twins that developed a little differently or semi-identical mirror twins. The term mixed twins could also be thrown in there since I'm a Nereid and Zeus is an Olympian. Sorry. That was a lot."

"Whoa!"

"It's cool how I have something to do with all these rare events, and Chance is my brother. LOL. Chance. But then again, how much of this is by chance?"

Chapter 25: Mirror Fission

DAY 28

"Iris."

"I'm okay, Xenon. Dead or alive, I will protect my sister."

"Amethyst."

"Yeah, Dad?"

"I don't know what's going to happen but—" He wrapped his arms around her as tightly as he could just in case this was the last hug he'd get. "I love you, Cupcake."

"Alright, everyone! Let's get moving! This has to be done perfectly! If you do as I say there shouldn't be any problems," said Athena. She swam around and double checked everyone's positioning. "Wonderful! Remember that there are 8 possible moments Zeus will strike, but each one is a possibility. There is no way to tell if it will be the first or the last, so treat each moment as THE moment. Do I make myself clear?"

Thetis, Jeremy, Amphitrite, and the squad were standing off to the side. Hermes was surprisingly not being pervy. The other Olympians were watching from Olympus. They had no idea where Zeus had been for the past 6 days, but he was just as anxious as they were. "Iris."

"Yes, Sister?"

"Promise you won't leave me."

"I promise." Iris and Amethyst held each other in their arms.

"First window approaching in 10… In 5… In 3…" There was no bolt. "8 minutes until the next window!" There was no bolt for the next 6 windows. "The 8th window approaching in 8 minutes. This is the last window. This is it. Chaos be with us."

8 seconds before the hyperbolt came, Iris had a vision. They weren't able to dodge the bolt in time. Hermes had missed it by a hair. Amethyst died. There was no way Iris was going to let that happen. During the last 3 seconds, Iris locked her fluke around Amethyst and used her strength to overpower her, so they'd switch spots. Iris held her sister, so she couldn't move. Amethyst was looking into Iris's eyes when the hyperbolt pierced her skull from behind. "Ahhh!" Amethyst screamed, and a pulse pushed all the goddesses and gods away from the center. "No. No. No. Iris!" Iris's body began to sink, so she did her best to lift her. Thetis was the first one to reach them. Amethyst was sick to her stomach. She had seen a lot of dead bodies before, but if you were her, you'd know it's not about how many. It's always about who. "Iris. Wake up. Now's not the time for a prank. Come on. Ha. Ha. You got me. Wake up." Everyone's heart shattered when they heard her say that. Even Athena was weeping.

"I-It's not a prank," said Hermes. "I-I missed."

"No, no you didn't. It's just a prank! IRIS! IT'S JUST A PRANK! WAKE UP! IRIS! PLEASE! DAD! MOM! IT'S JUST A PRANK RIGHT?" Iris's hair and eyes turned white, and she began to decay as light. Now Amethyst was shaking. "No. Iris. Don't go. You promised! Y-You promised you wouldn't leave me! It should have been me! Why Iris, why? It should have been me." When Iris's body was gone, Amethyst looked around and then into her mother's eyes. "Mom. Xenon. I'm so sorry. I'm so sorry, Mom." She felt like her body was being torn apart. She was numb. The only thing she could feel was her heart exploding.

"Oh, my goddess. Thetis. Thetis stand back," said Hera.

Amphitrite had to peel her away. "Sister. Who the hell did you give birth to?"

They all watched in awe and in horror as Amethyst shifted, and her body began to create two half-bodies. "What's happening now?!?!?" Xenon cried.

"She's splitting herself. I don't know what to call this," said Athena. "She's splitting herself. She's making two separate halves…"

"Energy is matter. She's using the energy from the universe to complete the two halves," said Hera. "This is…"

"She's making a copy of Iris's body. Iris is her inverse," said Thetis. "She's making an inverse copy of herself and a regular copy of herself by converting her body into light energy."

"I would call it bioengineering, but she isn't using artificial matter," said Hera.

"It's nuclear fission," said Athena.

"She's twinning herself again," said Thetis. "Just like in the womb."

"But how is this possible?" asked Hera.

"Because everything goes back to balance," said Athena. "Naturally, the universe is repairing the imbalance."

After the process was complete, Thetis held Iris's new body while Amphitrite held Amethyst up. "Oh, my goddess. I see something other than Amethyst's aura," said Bella. "There's another dot. It looks different."

Iris appeared as a light phantom. "Iris?" Amethyst said in a sleepy voice. She was exhausted.

"Chaos wouldn't let me return. She said it wasn't time to return." When Iris entered her new body, her hair turned silver and so did her fluke. Although the brown flecks remained, her eyes turned grey. Then her pearl reappeared. "Look, Sister. I can move it. I can use telekinesis now." After that, Amethyst closed her eyes and fell into a deep sleep.

"Wait! Everyone keep your eyes open!" said Athena. "With an influx of chaotic energy comes white energy. Leukos will come." Suddenly, Hermes pushed Amphitrite and grabbed Amethyst. Before anyone could do something, he teleported to Zeus's unknown location. *How? *sips tea** "Dammit! We can't let him kill her!"

"He won't. Amethyst is technically a prisoner of war since she was taken after the hyperbolt struck," said Hera. "If he kills her, he loses his throne on Olympus. He's in a dilemma. He will use her as a hostage during the war. That's when we get her back. We must return to Olympus." She opened the security camera app on her phone. "He's already at the sky kingdom thanking Leukos. Poseidon and Amphitrite are the only ones who can fight in this war."

"What's the plan, Sister?" asked Amphitrite.

"We can handle the Nereids, but not for very long. I am sure Zeus will equip them with special weapons. The main problem is that we have to fight on two fronts. Can you make an ice cap on the surface, so we can keep the fight with Nereids and floaters separate?"

"You got it, Sister. Just one thing. What can we do down here? Should Sei stay down here?"

"No. We need Sei up there with Zeus, and you up there maintaining the ice cap and protecting Amethyst. The Nereids will try to break the ice, and Zeus will try to melt it by warming the air. Speaking of that, we need you to keep the heat from impacting the Oceanids. We can only fight so many floaters at once, so you two will have to hold some of them back. Zeus will send thousands."

"I know some people who can help," said Reign.

"This is not the Mer's fight. I couldn't ask them to do that. They've purposely stayed out of this mess."

"We've tried to stay out of it, but regardless we are affected by this too," said Bella. "I'm proof."

"I'll go get them. We don't need weapons. We use our tails," said Reign as she revealed her golden yellow tail. She dove down at top speed as soon as Thetis gave the okay.

"The Nereids will come tonight or tomorrow morning. They will come from the North," said Thetis. "Oceanids will be lined up at all angles. There will be five groups. Leios will lead the front group. They will begin the fight on my signal. Then the left, right, and rear groups will close in. Iris will lead the left and right groups. I will lead the rear. Xenon, you will lead the group above. Your group will be fighting the floaters on the ice once they arrive with Zeus. Chance, we need you to keep watch just in case Zeus has something else up his sleeve. You will be in the Zeta Beta tower. By the time the tower is finished rising, the force fields will be up, and we will be lined up and ready to fight."

"What about me?" asked Bella.

"Maybe we can show them that they are being manipulated by Zeus. We have proof," said Iris. "I might not be able to convince people like Amethyst or persuade people like Peitho, but I know how to use evidence to prove a point."

"When are you going to do that?" asked Thetis. "We would need a loud, ear-splitting noise to get everyone's attention during the fight."

"I'm a mermaid. I can scream really, really loudly. So loud, everyone will need time to recalibrate. It will work better if they're tired. We're only supposed to do it when there's a threat, so I think this is appropriate."

"Do it after the Mer arrive and even the odds," said Thetis. "Chance, Bella, I have armor for you. Right now, we must initiate the final warning. Then we will take our positions and wait."

"Amethyst planted a stinger on Hermes yesterday. You can use this to listen to his conversations and track his location," said Xenon as he hooked the tracker up to Chance's phone. "I've been listening. Nothing has been said yet, but he's in the sky kingdom just like Hera said."

"Aristide will take you to your armor and then to the tower," said Thetis. "Silvercrest will be your messenger," she handed Chance an audio star. "It will translate for you. Everyone knows what they're doing?" They all said yes, and everyone rushed to their positions.

Chapter 26: She's Cranky in the Mourning

DAY 29

"Oh, my goddess. Amethyst. Did I bring you here? I'm so sorry. You have to wake up." Hermes tried to free her from the light chains Zeus put her in, but it was no use. He had his head in his hands when he noticed something on his arm. It was so tiny and translucent, he had trouble finding it again. "You beautiful genius! I love you! So dangerous yet so beautiful."

"HERMES!" Zeus boomed. "You will make sure she doesn't escape those chains. If she wakes up, let me know immediately."

"Yes, sir. Where should she be transported to?"

"Keep her here for now. We will bring her with us. They will never expect us to come at twilight."

"What of Poseidon and Amphitrite, sir?"

"Don't worry about them. Sure, I'm not as strong at the moment, but I'm sure they'll have their hands full. I have a few tricks up my sleeve."

"Hermes snapped out of it," said Chance. "He found the stinger and is using it to our advantage. Zeus is coming at twilight, and he said Poseidon and Amphitrite will have their hands full because he has a few tricks up his sleeve." Silvercrest delivered the message pronto.

Thetis was right. The Nereids did have special weapons. They had electric spears ready to pierce and electrocute Oceanids. The Oceanids the Nereids fought in the last war were not the Oceanids they were fighting now, but the Nereids still had the advantage. That advantage didn't last long though. "Aquaria! Aquaria! I'm so sorry to return like this, but there is a war happening right now," said Reign. "Thetis needs our help."

"A war?!?!? Thetis?!?!?" Aquaria summoned all the Mer. "Tell us what's going on!"

"There's this girl… Well, there's this person named Amethyst. She's the daughter of Thetis, and she's the chosen one of this prophecy that's connected to the ancient prophecy. I'm sure Thetis will explain later, but Zeus threw a hyperbolt and declared war on Oceanids. Are we not Oceanids? The Haliai have to fight on two fronts. Nereids and floaters. We think the Nereids are being brainwashed by Zeus like the floaters, but the point is that they need our help. We were forced into the depths because we chose not to fight. We wanted to protect ourselves, but look where hiding got us. There is no escaping reality. Did you know that Thetis takes in our own when they are rejected by us? How can we sit here and not fight? I know the difference between a peacemaker and a coward. I was a coward once, but not anymore. The Mer are not cowards. We are not cowards, and it's time we fight alongside the other Oceanids. We weren't there for the Haliai before, but that changes today." Everyone cheered.

"Reign speaks the truth. There's no time to talk. You heard her. Let's go. Reign, lead the way."

"With pleasure."

The Mer swam up from the depths right under them. They were so silent, so elegant, but so deadly. It was a terrifying sight to see. The Mer weren't as muscular or as large as the Nereids, but they were far more agile and most of their strength was in their tails. They wrapped their flexible tails around the Nereids' necks and dragged them downwards until they were no longer breathing. Some of the more hands-on Mer used their best hunting techniques that involved slamming their tails against their prey and crushing their bones by snaking around their bodies. Of course, Reign managed to take out an entire group by herself. "Thetis, I am so sorry. The

Mer should have stood with you all. We've gotten so comfortable in the depths, but Reign helped us see the light. From now on the Mer will be there."

"Oh, Aquaria. Thank you for coming. All that matters is that you're here now."

"Whenever you're ready, Bella," said Iris. Bella's scream sounded like a banshee skating on black ice.

"Oh, my goddess," said Aquaria. "Who was that? They're a yeller. All Mer scream, but that's a rare call. Huh! They're a..."

"A Mer. And a Nereid," Thetis smiled. "His name is Bella. He's my nephew."

"Listen!" said Iris. "Zeus has brainwashed you to think there is a reason to be against us. He's been trying to tear apart the strength of the ocean realm for centuries. Lower your weapons. Have we ever attacked you? No. You have been manipulated to attack us. Did you know that some of your people steal our teknon and rape our people? After all these years, have you forgotten who we are? Have you forgotten who you are? We are all Oceanids. We come from the same bloodline. I'm sure you all want proof, right?"

"If you couldn't tell, I'm Mer and Nereid. My mother was raped." All the Mer children in the bas swam up to the force fields to reveal themselves. Iris told him, and he was moved by their bravery. Little did he know, he inspired a whole generation.

"My mother is Thetis, daughter of Doris. This is our true form. Doris is a Haliai, and she is the mother of all Nereids. Mer are descendants of Nereids. My sister once told someone, 'We are not your enemy. The enemy is what is corrupting people throughout the realms.' This blood, all these bodies... This is what he wants. Zeus declared war on all Oceanids. We are all Oceanids, so we ought to act like it."

"What have we done to our own people..." said one of the group leaders. "We owe you our lives." All the Nereids wept and prepared to kill themselves.

"No," said Iris. "Use your lives to make a difference. You do not owe us your lives. You owe us respect, and you cannot give us that if you're dead. Zeus is the one in debt. He needs to be held accountable." Then the Nereids bowed to Iris. "M-Meter, what's this?"

"They want to be a part of the basileia," she smiled. "They want you to be their queen. I think you'd make a great queen."

"B-But…"

"Don't worry. I'll still be here. You'll be basilis of the basileia and queen of the Nereids."

"I, Iris, basilis of the basileia, and daughter of Thetis hereby accept the title of queen of the Nereids and celebrates the reunion of all Oceanids." Everyone cheered. The fight was far from over though.

Silvercrest came with a message. "Zeus has arrived. The floaters are here 8,000 strong. The fighting on the surface has begun. He has Amethyst in light chains. She's still asleep."

"Everyone! Listen up!" said Thetis. "Amphitrite is maintaining the ice cap we are using as a battleground. Floaters are not strong fighters, but they are very sneaky and agile. Zeus has an unknown secret weapon that will likely be enough to distract Poseidon and Amphitrite. We are going to reduce their numbers. Amphitrite will make holes in the ice, and we will swim up and grab as many floaters as we can. Remove their masks, and they won't be able to breathe underwater. We will swim down and then jump through the holes after the signal. Bella will stay closer to the surface and let us know when she opens the holes again. Bella, Chance will tell you when to yell. It doesn't need to be ear-splitting. Just loud. Everybody got that? Silvercrest, be sure to tell him to not wake Amethyst up. She's regaining her energy. Don't say her name."

Silvercrest informed Chance about the plan. "Aye! The tables have turned. The Mer and Nereids are with us now! They are going to jump through the holes in the ice! Amphitrite. Poseidon. Do not wake her up!"

"Alright," said Poseidon. "Ame, how's it going over there?"

"Holes in the ice?" said Amphitrite. "Sister, that's genius!!!" The plan worked. From an aerial view, it looked like a game of whack-a-mole except it would probably be called grab-a-floater. "Sei, go get em babe! I got it from here."

"Nope," said Zeus. "I don't think so." Suddenly a seven-headed hydra appeared.

"HYDRA!!!" Chance yelled.

"Shit! They're female! He must have their baby. They're going to destroy everyone trying to get to Zeus," said Poseidon. "I have to hold them back."

"SHE'S STILL NOT WAKING UP!" said Chance.

"Thetis! Show yourself!" When she came onto the ice, Zeus said, "I have your precious daughter. Give me Amethyst or Iris dies!"

Thetis snarled. "You can't have her! You wouldn't dare kill her. If you kill a prisoner of war, you lose your authority."

"Then I'll keep her as my prisoner!"

"Mother. I'll go. Just trust me," Iris whispered. She put on her best act. "Hey b****! Didn't I tell you not to f*** with my family? Your little hyperbolt might have turned my hair grey, but it's your tricks that are getting old! You want me? Fine! But you gotta release my sister. On god, bruh."

"Exactly as I thought. That's a good girl." Amethyst was almost done charging.

Hermes teleported into the Zeta Beta tower where Chance was. "Amethyst is the one in chains, right?"

"Yeah, bro. I'm still mad at you for taking my sister by the way. If I had powers, I'd beat your ass. Anyways, how come you ain't out there fighting?"

"I'm not the combat type."

"Weak ass n****. Get the f*** out my face. Lame ass perv god."

622

Iris could have changed into her phantom form and rose to where Amethyst was suspended in the air, but that probably would have ruined the plan. Instead, she allowed Zeus to carry her up on a light disc. He placed Iris right in front of her. Then he said, "HA. Did you really think I was that stupid? Now that you're up here, Amethyst, I can imprison both of you. The structure Amethyst was chained up in extended to make room for one more. Iris was now on the left side of her sister.

Iris saw how the outside energy was causing Amethyst's charm to crack. She targeted her hardest blow towards Amethyst's charm. With her strength added to the energy from the light chains, she released the energy Amethyst needed to wake up. "I'm here, Sister." When they locked hands, they seemed to start having some kind of metaphysical glitch-like seizure. With their eyes closed, they started doing a hypnotic mirror dance. When they opened their eyes, they had the same violet headlights. The fighting stopped. Everyone was watching. They both placed a hand out and immobilized Zeus.

"Yo, that shit looked demonic as f***," said Chance. "I ain't gon lie. I might have peed a little."

Something about that triggered Hermes. "So, you're Amethyst's brother?"

"Yeah. Why? Thanks for teaching me Greek and OSL by the way."

"Oh, you're very welcome. Anything for Amethyst's siblings. That's not the only thing I can teach you. Do you have a preference? I can shapeshift."

"Oh, hell no. I don't f*** with lame ass perv gods. Get the f*** out my tower."

The Alpha Iota duo spotted all their loved ones except for Jeremy. They were completely in sync. "Where's Daddy?"

The crowd split to reveal Jeremy. Jeremy waved. "I'm right here, Cupcake. Well... Cupcake and Iris."

Hand in hand, they moved as one unit and found the invisible box that held the baby hydra. They levitated over to the mother and said, "We're sorry about your baby. We know our father is cruel. Would you mind sticking around for a bit? I have something to show you." After they pet the hydra, they made their way over to the battlefield. They made thousands of violet energy rods and held them in the air. "We don't want to hurt you, but we will slaughter all of you if you don't return to the sky kingdom." That was all the floaters needed to hear.

"Iris. I'll take it from here." They let go of each other's hands, and Amethyst shifted. Iris stayed close behind Amethyst. When she approached Zeus, she said, "What. Did. I. F******. Tell. You." She freed him from immobilization. "I said I couldn't fight a god, but I didn't say anything about an energy drained god. This should be fun."

"Yaaasssss, Sister. Beat his ass. Do him like you did that one guy."

"Go best friend, that's my best friend!!!" Xenon chanted.

"Ayyye," Reign sang background.

"And she finna…" Bella kept it going.

"…f*** you up," said Chance.

In the sky, Amethyst made a thundercloud and drowned Zeus in it. Then she grabbed him and threw him to the surface effortlessly. His nails made a death trail as she dragged him by his hair along the ice. She put him on his knees and yanked his head up, forcing him to face all the Oceanids. "If you don't want to watch, close your eyes." She broke one of his arms and legs. "Run," she giggled. "The sky king everyone! Wow. Look at him go." Once he got far enough so people wouldn't be able to see the details, she chased after him and tackled him on the ice. The squad moved in as close as possible, so they could watch and hopefully participate. *Yes, Chance's asthmatic ass ran all the way from the top of the tower.*

"Come on, Red! Hurry up!" said Xenon.

"Ooo, shit." He had to catch his breath. "I'm… Coming…"

Amethyst flipped Zeus on his back and smiled in his face. She started an internal fire in his heart simply by making eye contact with him. Then she gave him the same lightning fast power combo she gave Angelica except this time with her new godly reflexes. Next, she slowly dismembered his hands by hand. Then his feet. She was only toying with him. After that, she turned to the squad. "You have 7 seconds." She let the squad get their hits in. "EYE CONTACT!" she told Zeus. Chance stomped on his head like a mad ass. Like a breaching cetus, Reign body slammed him elbow first. Then Bella crawled onto the ice like a swamp monster from a horror film and gently bit his ear off. Xenon got on top of him and brought down both of his fists onto his chest like a Man. Then he smashed eyes. Lastly, like the faerie she is, Iris ever so elegantly guided her pearl through his head as payback for what he was going to do to Amethyst. And to finish the task, Amethyst set violet flames to the ice, and warmed her hands over his misery. Literally. They all watched him burn in the name of Chaos. "See you soon," she giggled.

"OMG, Sister. You're a bad ass b****. What the f***? I love you. Yaaasssss b****."

Amphitrite recorded the whole thing, and Thetis was smiling and taking pictures of her badass kids. Hera showed up as everyone left and started chatting with the momma twins. "How you holding up, Jay?" asked Poseidon.

"I'm cool. You know how it is," he smiled. "Gotta keep the womxn happy."

"Yes, yes you do," Hera laughed.

"Yeah, man. Fosho, fosho. I'm still trying to figure out if the crazy gene comes from them or Zeus," Poseidon laughed. "Damn."

Amphitrite and Thetis put a piece of ice down their soulmates' backs. "We heard that," they giggled.

"You remember what we used to do back in the day?" asked Poseidon.

"Yeah. It's been a while," said Jeremy.

"Don't get yourselves into something you can't handle boys," said Hera.

"Shhh. Here come the kids," said Thetis. Amethyst and Iris were in the front holding hands. "Oh, my sweet little babies. Oh, I'm so glad you're all okay. I'm pretty sure I set the record for the number of heart attacks in a single month. Oh, I'm so proud you," she cried.

"So, what now?" asked Iris.

"I think they could use a vacation," said Amethyst. "Right y'all? I know this whole thing is far from over. The universe hasn't even gotten out of balance yet. LOL."

"For now, let's just go home," Thetis smiled.

"Honestly, I don't have a topic for today," said Iris. "Let's just debrief."

"Zeus deserved it, but I feel so guilty," Reign wept.

"Me too." Bella held his face in his palms.

"Maybe we over did it," said Iris.

"What the f***?" Amethyst laughed. "I don't regret shit. I could have done worse things to him. We barely did anything. Y'all need to grow some ovaries."

"Don't feel sorry for him. That's what the f*** his ass get," said Chance. "The n**** f***** with the wrong n*****. She tried to tell him. God knows what else his ass has done."

"Oh, my goddess. Suck that shit up," Xenon rolled his eyes. "It wasn't even that f****** bad. We were just having a little fun."

"Oh shit," Chance smiled. "That's the first time I've heard you talk like that, Blue. Oh yeah and I seen that shit you did to his eyes. You and her are perfect for each other."

"You three are right," said Iris. "Woo. Okay. I'm good."

"What did you do with Zeus's ear?" asked Reign.

"I don't know. It's gone," said Bella. The squad gave each other looks. "What?" he smiled. "I'm vegan."

"How the f*** did you do that nuclear fission shit?" asked Chance. "That was dope as hell."

"I don't even know," she laughed. "I'm just juiced because I wanted a Mer and a Nereid friend, and I got two of each. Chance, how you feel?" Amethyst teased.

"Hey! What I tell you about that?" he laughed. "There you go with yo bullshit."

"So, can you go ghost?" asked Bella.

"Yep. Well… I guess I'm more of a ghoul." Iris changed and grabbed his arm. "I can touch you, but you can't touch me. I can see you all, but the rest of you can't see me."

"LMAO. John Cena ass," said Chance. Reign laughed with him.

"By the way, I think I'm an Oracle now."

"Ayyye, *That's So Raven* got an upgrade!" Chance laughed.

"Red! Shut the f*** up before I beat your ass, feed you to my f****** sharks ALIVE, murder them, and then eat them raw."

"Jeez," Chance laughed. "Well that was dark."

"There's my grim twin," Amethyst giggled. "So ghastly. Woo hoohoo hoo hoo." Iris laughed with her.

"Oh okay! So, she can make jokes, but when I do it's a problem," Chance laughed.

"A silver fluke looks nice on you," said Reign. "Absolutely beautiful."

"And that hair and eye color is bomb as f***," said Amethyst. "You lookin' like a whole ass snack."

"Your tail is so, so, so pretty, Reign. Damn," Iris smiled. "You're golden."

"You really think so?" she smiled. "Thanks."

"Blue, why you so quiet?" Chance asked.

"I'm thinking. You can't talk, Tic Toc… You and your little counting sessions. What happened with you and Hermes in the tower?"

"F*** you, Blue," he laughed. "Ain't shit happened up there. The n**** was trying to molest me."

"And he says he's straight," said Iris. "I know we can't judge. I'm not judging. I'm just telling you what he told me."

"Sips tea," Amethyst giggled. "We don't wanna claim his ass anyway."

"Exactly. No pervs in the squad," said Chance.

"I love how we aren't talking about all that shit Amethyst did," Bella laughed. "Even I have never heard anyone scream like that before. And he's a grown ass male. Not a 12-year-old boy."

"Even I heard that shit," Iris smiled.

"Duuuuuh," said Reign.

"Let's not talk about what I did," Amethyst laughed.

"Can we talk about how fine Poseidon is?" said Reign.

"Oh, most definitely," said Amethyst. "After that, I need y'all to help me learn all these royal people names. I remember faces but not names."

"He is impressively ripped!" said Bella. "And his skin is incredibly soft. Oh, and his voice is so rich! I just want him to hold me."

"I love how his hair is so curly and how his eyes are such a deep blue!" said Reign. She laid on the floor. "Shiiit. He can f*** me uuuuup!"

"He is a very attractive person," said Iris. "Good thing we aren't related."

"WHAT? That's it? Nah. He gotta be the finest n**** in the damn world. And I know he rich as f*** too. My biromantic ass would bottom like dirt on the f****** ground for his aquatic ass. I don't give a f***," Chance smiled. "Oh yeah. By the way, I'm all the way bi. Honestly, I don't f****** know y'all. Shit. I like what I like. It depends. HA. My ass didn't know to use lube the first time. Ame enlightened me. Shit. For Poseidon, Ima have to invest in a whole bucket."

They all couldn't stop laughing. Xenon theatrically opened his legs and softly said, "I'd have his kids." Then he started rubbing his chest.

"All Ima say is that if he say 'come here', I'm cumming fast as f***," said Amethyst. "Oh shit," she checked herself. "I'm just kidding," she laughed.

"Ahhh! Sister, you are too much," Iris giggled.

"OMG! I cannnnn't! We all would," Xenon laughed. "He's daddy as f***."

"Agreed!" said Reign. "That he is!" she twirled.

"How come the underworld doesn't have royalty?" asked Amethyst.

"We don't know. We've never even been there," said Iris.

"Let's start with the land queendom. We'll just go in order, so you remember," said Reign. "Althea has olive skin, black eyes, and short wavy brown hair. Basil has dark brown skin, eyes the color of grass, and low cut kinky hair."

"Ooooo. Grass is similar to kelp, right? How's his voice?"

"His voice is pretty deep," said Reign. That made Bella do a twirl.

"Juniper is the one with the dark skin, brown eyes, and the super long wavy greenish black hair. She always has lots of flowers in her hair. Sage is the one with the light brown skin and eye color and the medium length sandy brown kinky hair," said Iris.

"Ebony has black eyes, dark skin, and curly jet-black hair. Ivory is albino and has short kinky hair," said Xenon.

"River has black eyes, dark reddish-brown and beige vitiligo, and short curly dark brown hair. Estuary has light skin, blue eyes, and short wavy blond hair," said Reign.

"Chauncey is the one with brown skin, long kinky red hair, freckles, and brown eyes. Sharun is the one with the white skin, pale blue eyes, and long straight blond hair."

"Two things. One, doesn't Chauncey look like Chance. Two, didn't something seem off about Sharun. He seems a little evil."

"OMG! She does!" said Reign. "And yeah. No one likes him. We don't even know how he became pharaoh."

What did you sense, Moon Jelly?

I don't know. It's probably nothing.

What are you doing later?

LMAO nothing… What's up?

You in the mood for HJ&O? I'll do that tongue thing you like.

In the physical?

Yep. In the physical.

Hell yeah. It's still bright out. Wanna go up to the grotto? I'm finna take yo chocolate, clit-eyed ass to the moon and back.

Oh shit. Okay. It's like that? In that case, let me get your rockets ready.

"Naseem has dark skin, grey eyes, and short kinky powder blue hair. Anemone has light brown skin, black eyes, and medium length curly bright pink hair."

"Eden has dark brown eyes, skin, and long curly hair. Dawn is your skin color and has long orangish-brown curly hair and eyes."

"Aster is the one with olive skin, short curly blue hair, and magenta eyes. Celestia is the one with brown skin, medium length kinky purple hair, and teal eyes."

"Okay, thanks. I need to add them on social media."

"They're probably waiting for you to add them back," Iris smiled.

"Who tryna take a nap?" asked Amethyst. Atoz's plan worked. After the squad feel asleep, they went up to the grotto. "Go head and do your thang, boo."

Chapter 27: What the Haven?

DAY 30

"I thought basilica was on the first of the month," said Amethyst.

"It is," said Jeremy. "But yesterday was the 1st."

"Ohhh! For real? I didn't even peep. 5... 4... 3... 2... 1... HAPPY BELATED NEW YEAR!!!!! What do y'all teach at church?"

"Love," Jeremy smiled.

"Ready, Sister? We have to get there early."

"Yeah. Bye, Dad. Bye, Mom. Oops. I mean see you later."

"Where's Blinky?" Thetis whispered. "Is he coming?

"He's in his lair. I don't know what that son of yours is doing."

"Wow. This is the first time I've walked into a church and not felt like everyone hated me," said Amethyst.

"Exactly. I love this church. I can't wait for the message. These stone benches lowkey comfortable AF too."

"Shut the f*** up, Chance," she whispered. "Yo ass probably gonna fall asleep. You know the music is the best part. Alright y'all... I gotta go get the youth choir ready."

Thetis, Jeremy, and the squad were all in the front row enjoying the music. Chance was mixing his shit up, so Reign popped him for dancing like that in the house of Chaos. "Behave," she whispered. "And stop looking at Thetis."

"Whatchu mean? How you gon tell me how to praise the lord. Nah. I'm just kidding. Ima chill out," he smiled.

After Bella finished singing his sermonic solo, the choir got ready to perform. Of course, Iris was the conductor. Xenon swam in when they were on their second song. Everyone clapped for him, and Thetis couldn't stop smiling. Iris knew he'd be coming, so she planned a special surprise. The choir played his favorite song and convinced him to sing the lead as he always did before he stopped coming. He asked them where Amethyst was, but they all shrugged even though they knew she was in the other room waiting for their cue. "I love how clapping sounds underwater. Wait! OMG! Is that Xenon? That's Xenon!"

"He's your soulmate, right?"

"I heard you two are soulmates!"

"Yeah! Is it true? Is it true?"

"Yes. They're my soulmate. We're soulmates," she giggled. "Alright. There's our cue. Come on."

Iris knew the song would put Xenon in his feelings especially since it had so much more meaning now. When he was starting to get into it, Amethyst and the youth choir swam out. Chance was proud because Amethyst taught them some borderline NSFC moves. *Not safe for church.* The kids were all her height or taller and mimicking her every move. Everyone thought they were adorable. They sang all the high notes. When Amethyst was close enough to Xenon, Iris gave the signal. Everyone started singing background, so the two lead singers' voices would be more prominent. Alpha and Zeta's duet warmed everyone's hearts. They were so passionate, so chaotic.

"Where do you want to go for our vacation?" Jeremy asked.

"You just came home," said Thetis. "We can stay here if you like and have someone watch the kids."

"Really? You're cool with that?" he smiled. "I'd like that. Who are we gonna have watch the kids though? Wait. Before you answer that, tell me who you were seeing since I've been gone."

"Who have you been seeing?"

"A few humans. They were eh. Tell me. Was it Hera?"

"No," she laughed. "Why are you always worried about her? Selene."

"I knew it! I'm glad the kids woke Endymion up," he smiled.

"Oh, hush. You know you're my soulmate, Jeremias."

"I know," he kissed her. "Okay, so about the kids… How about Ame and Sei?"

"Really?" she laughed. "Are you serious? That's going to be wild as f***."

"Ummm. How about Demeter?"

"She never stays in one place long enough."

"Dionysus?"

"Too irresponsible."

"Shit. You're right. Okay, what about Aph and Ares?"

"They're always having sex. How about the kids' god mom?"

"Nope. Absolutely not. Hera wants them to be her kids so bad. What about Hades?"

"Hades?!?!? You're hilarious. Look, Jeremy… Hera and I have been done for centuries."

"Yeah but she still loves you."

"Don't say that."

"She does T. I can see it in her eyes. Plus, they'll be closer to Zeus up there. And his power will be restored."

"You know it's not about how close they are to Zeus. It's about how far they are from Hera. It's the safest place for them, and you know she's lonely. Come on, Jeremias. We need some alone time. Please, Jear Bear."

"I know, I know. Huuuh. Let's call her."

"OMG! Hera's house is so awesome!" said Iris. "Wait until we get there!"

"It's so big! And she has a lot of gold!" said Reign. "There's literally gold everywhere!"

"It's sooooo nice," said Xenon. Then he looked at Jeremy. "Hera's our god mom, but she's more like our third parent."

Damn babe. Hella petty.

"No, she is not," said Jeremy.

"He's jealous of Hera," said Xenon.

"I'm not jealous. I'm just— Okay maybe I'm a little jealous. But then I shouldn't be because I got the girl! I got the girl dammit! She's my soulmate."

"Jeremias is worried for no reason," Thetis giggled. "Everyone packed? It's only for a week." Iris, Amethyst, and Xenon packed hella shit. I'm sorry. I don't know how else to put it. 'A lot of stuff' doesn't have the same effect. *LOL. When you have to be (somewhat) professional…?*

"Wait," said Bella. "I have a tail."

"Don't worry about that," said Hera. Jeremy flinched because he didn't notice Hera teleported. "I can give you the same ability as Reign. Hey, hun," Hera planted a kiss on Thetis's cheek. Jeremy gave her the eye. "Hey, Jay," she smiled and gave him a hug.

"Amethyst doesn't eat meat, but she might eat a little chicken," said Jeremy. "She's also lactose intolerant. Chance is allergic to nuts and has very bad asthma. Oh, and make sure he takes his medicine. Also, Bella is a strict vegan."

"I got it Jeremy or as the kids say... Don't trip," she smiled. Then she led the squad through her portal. "This is the light palace."

"Whoa! Reign, you weren't kidding," said Amethyst. "HUH! She has peacocks too!!!"

"The flowers are delightful!" said Bella. "So heavenly!" He did one of his signature twirls and almost fell. Reign caught him. "Legs are weird. I like them though!"

"Each of you has your own room here. You three just need to decorate. You can come here whenever you like. Do you all want to sleep in separate rooms, or do we want to do this sleepover style?"

"SLEEPOVER!"

"That's what I thought. You all can have your sleepover in here." She showed them a room that looked more like a daydream. "So, what are our pronouns right now?"

"They."

"They."

"Okay. Dinner will be ready soon. This is your other home. Make yourself comfortable. If you need anything, I'm in my room. Oh, and make sure you stay hydrated."

"Her aesthetic is a warm, golden, dreamy, tropical paradise," said Amethyst. "Yaaasssss!"

"Are y'all finna change? Ima just wear my robe. It's hot as f***," said Chance. *SMH. He's always looking for an excuse to get naked.*

"That's what we do," said Iris. "Just our underwear and silk robes."

"Blue, what the hell? What you doing with all them blue ass, fruity ass cherry blossoms?" Chance joked.

"Shut up, Red. Unlike you, I'm cute as f***. You look like the non-existent fifth member of The Cheetah Girls. Isn't pink considered a feminine color on the surface?"

"Oh, damn. Okay. I see how it is." Chance threw something at him.

"Don't throw shit at me while I'm doing my nails!" Xenon rolled his eyes. "I won't forget to f*** you up after they dry!" Xenon threw something back.

"Hey! Don't throw shit at me while I'm applying my face mask!"

"Iris, can you help me with something?" Amethyst needed assistance getting her sports bra off.

"Woo," she got it off. "Why do you wear that thing? Oh. Never mind."

"Yeeesssss girls! Weeeerk," Reign said when Amethyst and Iris walked out with their matching robes.

"Ooooo. Thiiiiick," Xenon added.

"Slay!" said Bella.

"Oh, no. Absolutely the f*** not. Please don't hype them up," said Chance.

"Don't hate," said Amethyst. Chance was so irritated when the twins both stuck their tongues out and did the eh-heh noise. "Twerk, twerk, twerk!"

"What's twerking?" asked Bella. Amethyst showed him a little something. "Ooooo! Let me try." He started twerking on Chance. Then they all felt like dancing. Reign was twerking on Iris, and Amethyst and Xenon kept switching.

Two of the girls tied their hair up with their silk scarves. The other two put on silk bonnets. That made Chance feel some type of way. "Oh, hell nah," he told Bella. "Uuuh. The girls think they hella cute and shit. That's okay. That's why I brought my durag. Here. I got one for you too, bro."

After Bella was done with his face mask, Amethyst asked him, "Do you want me to do your nails?"

"Yeah. I want something masculine. Can you make my middle fingers kelp green, and do grey for the other nails?"

"Of course. I got you."

"Hey! What about me?!?!? Why are y'all leaving a brotha out? F*** y'all too."

"We thought you and Reign just wanted to do face masks," said Xenon. "I'll do yours if you want, Reign."

"Iris, can you do mine? I want the soft pink. Wait. We have polish remover, right? I ain't really tryna wear the shit."

"No."

Chance was hurt. "Really? That's how it is? Fine. F*** you, Iris. I'll do them myself."

"I was just kidding, damn," she laughed. "Do you want me to just do a shimmer coat? Oh, look. I even have this crystal pink. It's basically clear with a slight pink tint. It looks a step up from natural."

"Oh shit. Fosho. Let's do that."

"I want you all to know that I'm proud of you," said Hera. "You're all gifted in your own ways and are capable of more than you know. I've been keeping an eye on you all over the years. Soon we'll learn what your capabilities are."

"So, you know about what we did?!?!?" Atoz asked.

"Yes, I know," she smiled.

"How come we can't know?" asked Chance. "We can handle it."

"Let's save it for one of our circles," said Amethyst.

DAY 31

"Good morning children!" Hera gleamed. "Would you like to come with me to Olympus? I also have to run a few errands."

Of course they did! "Isn't Zeus going to be there though?" asked Reign.

"Yes."

"Ooooo! Auntie Hera a savage," Chance laughed.

"Auntie Hera? I like that," she smiled. "Come on you all. Gather along."

"Whoa! The thrones are gigantic! Everything is gigantic!" said Amethyst. "Are you going to get bigger?"

"Yes." After she grew to her true size, she picked them up in her hand.

"HERA!!!!!" Zeus boomed. "HOW DARE YOU BRING THOSE PESTS TO OLYMPUS!"

"SILENCE!" said Hera. Then there was silence. It was so silent, you could hear the squad giggling. After Hera filled out the paperwork for possession of the sky kingdom, Zeus had no choice but to sign it. "Today, the sky kingdom has become the sky queendom!" Everyone there cheered.

"Where are the other Olympians?" asked Amethyst.

"They're rarely here. We only come here for meetings and whatnot. Now I have to go greet the sky nymphs." There were signs that said, 'There are only two genders: male or female', 'No queers!', 'No lassas!', 'No Oceanids!' and so much more. That made the squad sick to their stomachs. Hera destroyed everything that promoted hatred on sight. The sky queendom was so happy to have Hera as their queen. Those that had been brainwashed by Zeus had already moved out to join his cult. "Since he chose to continue living in the sky palace, he has to give me a copy of the key. He wants to do it in private, so I agreed to pick it up."

"So, you're his landlord?" Iris laughed.

"Yes." Everything was white and silver in the sky palace. It had a very high-tech I'm-wealthy-and-you're-not minimalist feel to it. Like the light palace, it wasn't supersized like Olympus, so Hera minimized her size. She knew Zeus was going to make things difficult. "I'm here."

"I'm in the bath! You'll just have to wait until I get out," said Zeus.

"Feel free to run around," Hera smiled. "I'm going to indulge myself in some reading."

"Y'all thinking what I'm thinking?" said Amethyst.

"I have some ideas," Iris smiled. The squad found the bathroom Zeus was in and his bedroom. Then they scavenged some things from his kitchen. They peeled back his bed cover, drizzled honey underneath it, and put holes in all his underwear.

"LOL. Do y'all hear him singing?" said Amethyst.

"I don't," Iris laughed. Amethyst placed Iris's hand on the door. "Ew. He's terrible."

"It's unlocked. I'm going in," Amethyst giggled. "Come on girls. His bathroom is huge. He won't know we're here."

"Let's cut a butt gap in his robe," said Chance. "That shit gonna be hella funny."

"We should put whipped cream in his slippers," Reign snickered.

"Look what I found," said Xenon. "I think he's using this to shave his private parts."

"Perfect. Let's put some cinnamon and stuff in it," Amethyst giggled.

"What does that do?" asked Bella.

"It makes it tingle," said Iris.

"Ooooo!" Bella clapped his hands. He liked the sound of that. Just as they finished setting up their prank, Zeus farted, and they all jumped. They all did their best not to laugh. It smelled awful.

Of course, Amethyst had to make a pun. "Holy shit." They all couldn't hold it in anymore. Iris counted down, and they all said, "F*** Zeus," and ran out giggling. They sprinted straight to Hera and hid behind her on the couch.

"What did you do?" she laughed.

"You'll see," Amethyst giggled.

"THESE RACCOONS PUT WHIPPED CREAM IN MY BRAND-NEW SLIPPERS! HOW DARE YOU COME INTO MY BATHROOM! THEY ALSO DROPPED AN F-BOMB! DAMN DEMONS! I OUGHT TO CRUSH YOU!" He had recently bought new slippers and posted them on Iros because everyone was roasting him for his dirty ones.

"Oh, relax. They're just kids," Hera smiled. "Besides, you're the one hunting them. What's a small prank?"

"Whatever!!! Here's the—" Zeus felt his private parts starting to burn. "Um... Here's the key. Take it and leave me be." The squad made fart noises as Zeus ran to his bathroom, revealing his exposed butt cheeks. Naturally, he flicked them off.

"You 6 are a mess," she laughed.

"We also put honey in his bed," said Iris.

"He doesn't know yet," Xenon smiled.

"He farted in the shower," Amethyst giggled. "He's the one who dropped a bomb."

"It was super loud," Bella laughed.

"It was like a rumble," said Chance. He made sure to roll the 'r'.

"It totally scared us," Reign giggled. "My heart was beating so fast."

Back at Hera's house, Amethyst said, "What'd you take, babe?"

"I scanned his key. When we get back home, I can make another one."

"I f****** love you."

"What are we? Ocean's 6?" Chance laughed.

"We're worse," said Iris. "We need a squad name."

"I have a meeting to go to and then we can get to know each other," said Hera.

"It's about us isn't it?" said Amethyst.

"They want us dead too now, don't they?" Xenon cried.

"Awww, come here kids. You'll be alright. You see, some of the Olympians still have some loyalty left for Zeus. Those particular gods also happen to be the ones worried because of the power you possess. They've seen what you can do to a weakened god and can only imagine what else you can do. The fact that you're an energetic titan-goddess makes some of them uncomfortable. The others know better."

"Amethyst is of good nature," said Demeter. "This is nonsense."

"How can we know her true nature?" asked Dionysus. "How can we know she's not evil? That's the only issue."

"I agree," said Apollo. "And not only does she have an active Titan gene. She's an energetic. We have to take precaution just in case."

"She is Skotos," said Athena. "That's not a problem for good people."

"What type of Skotos? Orderly, dynamic, or chaotic?" asked Dionysus.

"Chaotic. She's chaotic. Why does that matter? All that matters is that she isn't evil," said Athena.

"Sure, she is very dangerous. Potentially more dangerous than any Titan, but she is no threat to us," said Poseidon. "She is a gift from the universe."

"You should only feel uncomfortable if you are guilty of something or are planning to do something evil," said Hades. "The prophecy has already told us she is the solution, not the problem."

"I agree," said Hermes. "I see why she makes some of you nervous, but from what I know about you all, the fear you have for what she might do to you is illogical."

"And what about her friends?" said Ares. "They're dangerous too. This war that she started is much bigger than what happened the other day."

"She did not start this war, Ares. You know that," said Aphrodite. "But I guarantee you she will finish it. She has a strong will."

"We should be discussing ways to support them," said Artemis. "This is silly. We don't have time for this. Plus, you'd be celebrating if she was male. Something tells me this has more to do with pride. Does her being female make you uncomfortable?" she called them out. "You don't give her nearly as much praise as the males some of you labeled as all powerful heroes. Don't say it's because you feel threatened because some of those so-called heroes have killed many of you in worse ways many times before. Some of them have also temporarily withheld the power to return you to Chaos."

"I agree with you," said Athena. "Well said. Furthermore, she is a child. Thetis's child." They couldn't argue anymore.

"Very well then," said Hera. "There will be no precautions. If anyone of you feels the need to take matters into your own hands, you will receive maximum punishment."

Epilogue

"Success! My master plan is working accordingly!" Metis let out an evil cackle. "My little puppet has no idea he is doing exactly what I want him to do!"

"What now, Your Majesty?"

"We must expand our army ten-fold! The time has almost come!"

"What of the girl? Isn't she Skotos?"

"Don't worry about her," Metis giggled. "I have the perfect solution to that problem."

"What about her friends?"

"They won't be of much trouble. Those foolish twins awakened the crystals when they synchronized which means we should be able to detect those precious gems," she laughed. "Finally! Now we can narrow down the location of the crystals!!!!! How many Agathos are there?"

"There are 3 Agathos and 2 more Skotos."

"WHAT?!?!? You mean there's only a total of 5?!?!?"

"There are 6 in total, Your Majesty."

"No there aren't!!!!! She doesn't count!!!!!"

"Oh, right."

"Where are the other 2?!?!? There are supposed to be 7!!!!! Check the monitor!!!!! See if the other colors showed up!!!!!"

"There's no sign of the others."

"The last two crystals must not be detecting their hosts! Ugh! Where are they dammit?"

"Wait. It's beeping, Your Highness! Look! One of them just showed up! How was the monitor not picking them up? Can't it detect if they're on earth?"

"Yes, but that's not important right now. We must find their crystals before they do. We have a little extra time since they haven't all found each other yet, but it's not much. These 7 groups will search for the crystals. As for the rest of you, go recruit as many soldiers as possible. Humans in particular. Godspeed."

Hey Reader!

If you want to know about terms, the next book, and other cool stuff check out www.myreseajackson.xyz!!!

I made the website myself, so please go to it. Be sure to subscribe! I promise won't blow up your e-mail account. Ain't nobody got time for that. LOL. Make sure you log in too! :) <3

So, what's on my website?

- My blog!!!
- Character bios and Tumblrs
- Texting stories
- Discussion questions/forum
- Mental health resources
- Glossary
- …and more!

I'm always adding things, so make sure you visit it often.

Do me a favor and post a picture of my book on social media. Tag me and add #SiO4 #Myverse and #CosmicInkling.

About the Author

I'm am currently attending UCLA (class of 2021 yaaasssss…) as an English major with a minor in Gender Studies. Liiiiit! I have a whole YouTube video and bio on my website, so I'll use this page to talk about my blog.

On my blog, I analyze my own writing and highlight the things in between the lines. The discussion forum is a space where I post close-reading questions! Share one of my posts on social media with your response! Start a conversation!

Make sure you make a post about something that stood out to you, something you liked, something you go OMG, etc.

TAG ME!

Instagram - @myreseajacks

Twitter - @myreseajacks

Tumblr - myrese.tumblr.com

SnapChat - itsmymy67

E-mail - myreseajacks@gmail.com

And if you were wondering… The answer is yes. She's here and she's queer. ~~*drops mic*~~ *drops pen*

Thank you so much. Your support means the stars to me. I am so excited for you to watch me blossom.

Go to my website www.myreseajackson.xyz to learn more about me!!!

IDK what to call this. I'll call it a maieutic (even though that's not how you're supposed to use the word). Hehehe. Scholars don't come for me. I'm just playing around. Obviously, it's nowhere near being on that level, but you'll see what I mean. All I'm really doing is asking questions. I'm just trying to figure out what the f*** is going on.

One of my good friends from HS thought I didn't know the Atlantic Ocean is warmer than the Pacific Ocean and had our teacher tell me what I already knew. LMFAO. My anxiety has a good memory.

I was starting to space out. I had to bring myself back down to earth.

Weight? I'm over it.

I love the size of SiO4. I love how it fits in my hands. Such a nice girth and just the right length.

I never walked in on my parents because I was too busy making sure no one walked in on me, myself, and I. Oof.

- "Moon" by Turnstile
- "Can't Deny Me" by Pearl Jam
- "Domino" by Turbowolf (feat. Mike Kerr)
- "Separate Ways (Worlds Apart)" by Journey
- "Spray Paint Love" by Frank Carter & The Rattlesnakes
- "Jonah" by Kaya Stewart
- "Stoned, Alone" by Teenage Wrist
- "Somebody to Love" by Queen
- "Total Eclipse of the Heart" by Bonnie Tyler
- "Diamonds and Pearls" by Prince & The New Power Generation
- "Purple Rain" by Prince & The Revolution
- "All The Stars" by Kendrick Lamar, SZA
- "We Belong Together" by Mariah Carey
- "Neon Lights" by Demi Lavato

Go to www.myreseajackson.xyz to find the squad's playlists!!!

Made in the USA
San Bernardino, CA
04 December 2018